Before writing full-time, Michael Robotham was an investigative journalist in Britain, Australia and the US. He is the pseudonymous author of ten best-selling non-fiction titles, involving prominent figures in the military, the arts, sport and science. He lives in Sydney with his wife and daughters.

MICHAEL ROBOTHAM
OMNIBUS

The Drowning Man

Bombproof

SPHERE

This omnibus edition first published in Great Britain in 2011 by Sphere

Copyright © Bookwrite Pty 2010

Previously published separately:
The Drowning Man first published in Great Britain as *Lost* in 2005 by Time Warner
Books
Paperback edition published by Time Warner Paperbacks in 2006
Reissued by Sphere in 2010
Reprinted 2010 (twice)
Copyright © Michael Robotham 2004
Bombproof first published in Australia and New Zealand in 2008 by
Sphere/Hachette Australia for Books Alive
First published in Great Britain in 2009 by Sphere
Reprinted 2010
Copyright © Bookwrite Pty 2008

A CIP catalogue record for this book
is available from the British Library.

ISBN 978-0-7515-4746-7

Printed and bound in Great Britain by
Clays Ltd, St Ives plc

Sphere
An imprint of
Little, Brown Book Group
100 Victoria Embankment
London EC4Y 0DY

An Hachette UK Company
www.hachette.co.uk

www.littlebrown.co.uk

THE DROWNING MAN

For my mother and father

Acknowledgements

I wish to thank the usual suspects Ursula Mackenzie and Mark Lucas for helping me find the heart of *The Drowning Man*. They share my gratitude with the many others at Little, Brown and LAW who toil in the background bringing books to life.

Again I am indebted to Vivien, a passionate reader, stern critic, bedroom psychologist, gentle reviewer and mother to my children who has lived with my characters and my sleepless nights. Last time I said a lesser woman would have slept in the guest room. I was wrong. A lesser woman would have banished *me* to the guest room.

Wealth lost, something lost;
Honour lost, much lost;
Courage lost, all lost.

German proverb

1

The Thames, London

I remember someone once telling me that you know it's cold when you see a lawyer with his hands in his *own* pockets. It's colder than that now. My mouth is numb and every breath like slivers of ice in my lungs.

People are shouting and shining torches in my eyes. In the meantime, I'm hugging this big yellow-painted buoy like it's Marilyn Monroe. A very fat Marilyn Monroe, after she took all the pills and went to seed.

My favourite Monroe film is *Some Like It Hot* with Jack Lemmon and Tony Curtis. I don't know why I should think of that now, although how anyone could mistake Jack Lemmon for a woman is beyond me.

A guy with a really thick moustache and pizza breath is panting in my ear. He's wearing a life vest and trying to peel my fingers away from the buoy. I'm too cold to move. He wraps his arms around my chest and pulls me backwards through the water. More people, silhouetted against the lights, take hold of my arms, lifting me on to the deck.

'Jesus, look at his leg!' someone says.

'He's been shot!'

Who are they talking about?

People are shouting all over again, yelling for bandages and plasma. A black guy with a gold earring slides a needle into my arm and puts a bag over my face.

'Someone get some blankets. Let's keep this guy warm.'

'He's palping at one-twenty.'

'One-twenty?'

'Palping at one-twenty.'

'Any head injuries?'

'That's negative.'

The engine roars and we're moving. I can't feel my legs. I can't feel anything – not even the cold any more. The lights are also disappearing. Darkness has seeped into my eyes.

'Ready?'

'Yeah.'

'One, two, three.'

'Watch the IV lines. Watch the IV lines.'

'I got it.'

'Bag a couple of times.'

'OK.'

The guy with pizza breath is puffing really hard now, running alongside the gurney. His fist is in front of my face, pressing a bag to force air into my lungs. They lift again and square lights pass overhead. I can still see.

A siren wails in my head. Every time we slow down it gets louder and closer. Someone is talking on a radio. 'We've pumped two litres of fluid. He's on his fourth unit of blood. He's bleeding out. Systolic pressure dropping.'

'He needs volume.'

'Squeeze in another bag of fluid.'

'He's seizing!'

'He's seizing. See that?'

One of the machines has gone into a prolonged cry. Why don't they turn it off?

Pizza breath rips open my shirt and slaps two pads on my chest.

'CLEAR!' he yells.

The pain almost blows the top of my skull clean off.

He does that again and I'll break his arms.

'CLEAR!'

I swear to God I'm going to remember you, pizza breath. I'm going to remember exactly who you are. And when I get out of here I'm coming looking for you. I was happier in the river. Take me back to Marilyn Monroe.

I am awake now. My eyelids flutter as if fighting gravity. Squeezing them shut, I try again, blinking into the darkness.

Turning my head, I can make out orange dials on a machine near the bed and a green blip of light sliding across a liquid-crystal display window like one of those stereo systems with bouncing waves of coloured light.

Where am I?

Beside my head is a chrome stand that catches stars on its curves. Suspended from a hook is a plastic sachet bulging with a clear fluid. The liquid trails down a pliable plastic tube and disappears under a wide strip of surgical tape wrapped around my left forearm.

I'm in a hospital room. There is a pad on the bedside table. Reaching towards it, I suddenly notice my left hand – not so much my hand as a finger. It's missing. Instead of a digit and a wedding ring I have a lump of gauze dressing. I stare at it idiotically, as though this is some sort of magic trick.

When the twins were youngsters, we had a game where I pulled off my thumb and if they sneezed it would come back again. Michael used to laugh so hard he almost wet his pants.

Fumbling for the pad, I read the letterhead: 'St Mary's Hospital, Paddington, London.' There is nothing in the drawer except a Bible and a copy of the Koran.

I spy a clipboard hanging at the end of the bed. Reaching

down, I feel a sudden pain that explodes from my right leg and shoots out of the top of my head. Christ! Do not, under any circumstances, do that again.

Curled up in a ball, I wait for the pain to go away. Closing my eyes, I take a deep breath. If I concentrate very hard on a particular point just under my jawbone, I actually feel the blood sliding back and forth beneath my skin, squeezing into smaller and smaller channels, circulating oxygen.

My estranged wife Miranda was such a lousy sleeper she said my heart kept her awake because it beat too loudly. I didn't snore or wake with the night terrors, but my heart pumped up a riot. This has been listed among Miranda's grounds for divorce. I'm exaggerating, of course. She doesn't need extra justification.

I open my eyes again. The world is still here.

Taking a deep breath, I grip the bedclothes and raise them a few inches. I still have two legs. I count them. One. Two. The right leg is bandaged in layers of gauze taped down at the edges. Something has been written in a felt-tip pen down the side of my thigh but I can't read what it says.

Further down I can see my toes. They wave hello to me. 'Hello toes,' I whisper.

Tentatively, I reach down and cup my genitals, rolling my testicles between my fingers.

A nurse slips silently through the curtains. Her voice startles me. 'Is this a very private moment?'

'I was – I was – just checking.'

'Well, I think you should consider buying that thing dinner first.'

Her accent is Irish and her eyes are as green as mown grass. She presses the call button above my head. 'Thank goodness you're finally awake. We were very worried about you.' She taps the bag of fluid and checks the flow control. Then she straightens my pillows.

'What happened? How did I get here?'

'You were shot.'

'Who shot me?'

She laughs. 'Oh, don't ask me. Nobody ever tells me things like that.'

'But I can't remember anything. My leg . . . my finger . . .'

'The doctor should be here soon.'

She doesn't seem to be listening. I reach out and grab her arm. She tries to pull away, suddenly frightened of me.

'You don't understand – I *can't* remember! I don't know how I got here.'

She glances at the emergency button. 'They found you floating in the river. That's what I heard them say. The police have been waiting for you to wake up.'

'How long have I been here?'

'Eight days . . . you were in a coma. I thought you might be coming out yesterday. You were talking to yourself.'

'What did I say?'

'You kept asking about a girl – saying you had to find her.'

'Who?'

'You didn't say. Please let go of my arm. You're hurting me.'

My fingers open and she steps well away, rubbing her forearm. She won't come close again.

My heart won't slow down. It is pounding away, getting faster and faster, like Chinese drums. How can I have been here eight days?

'What day is it today?'

'October the third.'

'Did you give me drugs? What have you done to me?'

She stammers, 'You're on morphine for the pain.'

'What else? What else have you given me?'

'Nothing.' She glances again at the emergency button. 'The doctor is coming. Try to stay calm or he'll have to sedate you.'

She's out of the door and won't come back. As it swings closed I notice a uniformed policeman sitting on a chair outside the door, with his legs stretched out like he's been there for a while.

I slump back in bed, smelling bandages and dried blood. Holding up my hand I look at the gauze bandage, trying to wiggle the missing finger. How can I not remember?

For me there has never been such a thing as forgetting, nothing is hazy or vague or frayed at the edges. I hoard memories like a miser counts his gold. Every scrap of a moment is kept as long as it has some value.

I don't see things photographically. Instead I make connections, spinning them together like a spider weaving a web, threading one strand into the next. That's why I can reach back and pluck details of criminal cases from five, ten, fifteen years ago and remember them as if they happened only yesterday. Names, dates, places, witnesses, perpetrators, victims – I can conjure them up and walk through the same streets, have the same conversations, hear the same lies.

Now for the first time I've forgotten something truly important. I can't remember what happened and how I finished up here. There is a black hole in my mind like a dark shadow on a chest X-ray. I've seen those shadows. I lost my first wife to cancer. Black holes suck everything into them. Not even light can escape.

Twenty minutes go by and then Dr Bennett sweeps through the curtains. He's wearing jeans and a bow tie under his white coat.

'Detective Inspector Ruiz, welcome back to the land of the living and high taxation.' He sounds very public school and has one of those foppish Hugh Grant fringes that falls across his forehead like a serviette on a thigh.

Shining a pen torch in my eyes, he asks, 'Can you wiggle your toes?'

'Yes.'

'Any pins and needles?'

'No.'

He pulls back the bedclothes and scrapes a key along the sole of my right foot. 'Can you feel that?'

'Yes.'

'Excellent.'

Picking up the clipboard hanging at the end of my bed, he scrawls his initials with a flick of the wrist.

'I can't remember anything.'

'About the accident.'

'It was an accident?'

'I have no idea. You were shot.'

'Who shot me?'

'You don't remember?'

'No.'

This conversation is going around in circles.

Dr Bennett taps the pen against his teeth, contemplating this answer. Then he pulls up a chair and sits on it backwards, draping his arms over the backrest.

'You were shot. One bullet entered just above your gracilis muscle on your right leg leaving a quarter-inch hole. It went through the skin, then the fat layer, through the pectineus muscle, just medial to the femoral vessels and nerve, through the quadratus femoris muscle, through the head of the biceps femoris and through the gluteus maximus before exiting through the skin on the other side. The exit wound was far more impressive. It blew a hole four inches across. Gone. No flap. No pieces. Your skin just vaporised.'

He whistles impressively through his teeth. 'You had a pulse when they found you but you were bleeding out. Then you stopped breathing. You were dead but we brought you back.'

He holds up his thumb and forefinger. 'The bullet missed your femoral artery by this far.' I can barely see a gap between them. 'Otherwise you would have bled to death in three minutes. Apart from the bullet we had to deal with infection. Your clothes were filthy. God knows what was in that water.

We've been pumping you full of antibiotics. Bottom line, Inspector, you are one lucky puppy.'

Is he kidding? How much luck does it take to get shot?

I hold up my hand. 'What about my finger?'

'Gone, I'm afraid, just above the first knuckle.'

A skinny looking intern with a number two cut pokes his head through the curtains. Dr Bennett lets out a low-pitched growl that only underlings can hear. Rising from the chair, he buries his hands in the pockets of his white coat.

'Will that be all?'

'Why can't I remember?'

'I don't know. It's not really my field, I'm afraid. We can run some tests. You'll need a CT scan or an MRI to rule out a skull fracture or haemorrhage. I'll call neurology.'

'My leg hurts.'

'Good. It's getting better. You'll need a walking frame or crutches. A physiotherapist will come and talk to you about a programme to help you strengthen your leg.' He flips his fringe and turns to leave. 'I'm sorry about your memory, Inspector. Be thankful you're alive.'

He's gone, leaving a scent of aftershave and superiority. Why do surgeons cultivate this air of owning the world? I know I should be grateful. Maybe if I could remember what happened I could trust the explanations more.

So I should be dead. I always suspected that I would die suddenly. It's not that I'm particularly foolhardy but I have a knack of taking shortcuts. Most people die only the once. Now I've had two lives. Throw in three wives and I've had more than my fair share of living. (I'll definitely forgo the three wives, should someone want them back.)

My Irish nurse is back again. Her name is Maggie and she has one of those reassuring smiles they teach in nursing school. She has a bowl of warm water and a sponge.

'Are you feeling better?'

8

'I'm sorry I frightened you.'

'That's OK. Time for a bath.'

She pulls back the covers and I drag them up again.

'There's nothing under there I haven't seen,' she says.

'I beg to differ. I have a pretty fair recollection of how many women have danced with old Johnnie One-Eye and, unless you were that girl in the back row of the Shepherd's Bush Empire during a Yardbirds concert in 1961, I don't think you're one of them.'

'Johnnie One-Eye?'

'My oldest friend.'

She shakes her head and looks sorry for me.

A familiar figure appears from behind her – a short square man, with no neck and a five-o'clock shadow. Campbell Smith is a Chief Superintendent, with a crushing handshake and a no-brand smile. He's wearing his uniform, with polished silver buttons and a shirt collar so highly starched it threatens to decapitate him.

Everyone claims to like Campbell – even his enemies – but few people are ever happy to see him. Not me. Not today. I remember him! That's a good sign.

'Christ, Vincent, you gave us a scare!' he booms. 'It was touch and go for a while. We were all praying for you – everyone at the station. See all the cards and flowers?'

I turn my head and look at a table piled high with flowers and bowls of fruit.

'Someone shot me,' I say, incredulously.

'Yes,' he replies, pulling up a chair. 'We need to know what happened.'

'I don't remember.'

'You didn't see them?'

'Who?'

'The people on the boat.'

'What boat?' I look at him blankly.

His voice suddenly grows louder. 'You were found floating

in the Thames shot to shit and less than a mile away there was a boat that looked like a floating abattoir. What happened?'

'I don't remember.'

'You don't remember the massacre.'

'I don't remember the fucking boat.'

Campbell has dropped any pretence of affability. He paces the room, bunching his fists and trying to control himself.

'This isn't good, Vincent. This isn't pretty. Did you kill anyone?'

'Today?'

'Don't joke with me. Did you discharge your firearm? Your service pistol was signed out of the station armoury. Are we going to find bodies?'

Bodies? Is that what happened?

Campbell rubs his hands through his hair in frustration.

'I can't tell you the crap that's flying already. There's going to be a full inquiry. The Commissioner is demanding answers. The press will have a fucking field day. The blood of three people was found on that boat, including yours. Forensics says at least one of them must have died. They found brains and skull fragments.'

The walls seem to dip and sway. Maybe it's the morphine or the closeness of the air. How could I have forgotten something like that?

'What were you doing on that boat?'

'It must have been a police operation . . .'

'No,' he declares angrily, all pretence of friendship gone. 'You weren't working a case. This wasn't a police operation. You were on your own.'

We have an old-fashioned staring contest. I own this one. I might never blink again. Morphine is the answer. God, it feels good.

Finally Campbell slumps into a chair and plucks a handful of grapes from a brown paper bag beside the bed.

'What is the last thing you remember?'

We sit in silence as I try to recover shreds of a dream.

10

Pictures float in and out of my head, dim and then sharp: a yellow life buoy, Marilyn Monroe . . .

'I remember ordering a pizza.'

'Is that it?'

'Sorry.'

Staring at the gauze dressing on my hand, I marvel at how the missing finger feels itchy. 'What was I working on?'

Campbell shrugs. 'You were on leave.'

'Why?'

'You needed a rest.'

He's lying to me. Sometimes I think he forgets how far we go back. We did our training together at the Police Staff College, Bramshill. And I introduced him to his wife Maureen at a barbecue thirty-five years ago. She has never completely forgiven me. I don't know what upsets her most – my three marriages or the fact that I palmed her off on to someone else.

It's been a long while since Campbell called me buddy and we haven't shared a beer since he made Chief Superintendent. He's a different man. No better and no worse, just different.

He spits a grape seed into his hand. 'You always thought you were better than me, Vincent, but I got promoted ahead of you.'

You were a brown-noser.

'I know you think I'm a brown-noser. (*He's reading my mind.*) But I was just smarter. I made the right contacts and let the system work for me instead of fighting against it. You should have retired three years ago, when you had the chance. Nobody would have thought any less of you. We would have given you a big send-off. You could have settled down, played a bit of golf, maybe even saved your marriage.'

I wait for him to say something else but he just stares at me with his head cocked to one side.

'Vincent, would you mind if I made an observation?' He doesn't wait for my answer. 'You put a pretty good face on

11

things considering all that's happened but the feeling I get from you is . . . well . . . you're a sad man. But it's something more than that . . . you're angry.'

Embarrassment prickles like heat rash under my hospital gown.

'Some people find solace in religion and others have people they can talk to. I know that's not your style. Look at you! You hardly see your kids. You live alone . . . Now you've gone and fucked up your career. I can't help you any more. I told you to leave this alone.'

'What was I supposed to leave alone?'

He doesn't answer. Instead he picks up his hat and polishes the brim with his sleeve. Any moment now he's going to turn and tell me what he means. Only he doesn't; he keeps on walking out of the door and along the corridor.

My grapes have also gone. The stalks look like dead trees on a crumpled brown paper plain. Beside them a basket of flowers has started to wilt. The begonias and tulips are losing their petals like fat fan dancers and dusting the top of the table with pollen. A small white card embossed with a silver scroll is wedged between the stems. I can't read the message.

Some bastard shot me! It should be etched in my memory. I should be able to relive it over and over again like those whining victims on daytime talk shows who have personal injury lawyers on speed dial. Instead, I remember nothing. And no matter how many times I squeeze my eyes shut and bang my fists on my forehead it doesn't change.

The really strange thing is what I imagine I remember. For instance, I recall seeing silhouettes against bright lights; masked men wearing plastic shower caps and paper slippers, who were discussing cars, pension plans and football results. Of course this could have been a near-death experience. I was given a glimpse of Hell and it was full of surgeons.

Perhaps, if I start with the simple stuff, I may get to the point where I can remember what happened to me. Staring at the ceiling, I silently spell my name: Vincent Yanko Ruiz; born 11 December 1945. I am a Detective Inspector of the London Metropolitan Police and the head of the Serious Crime Group (Western Division). I live in Rainville Road, Fulham . . .

I used to say I would pay good money to forget most of my life. Now I want the memories back.

2

I know only two people who have been shot. One was a chap I went through police training college with. His name was Angus Lehmann and he wanted to be first at everything – first in his exams, first to the bar, first to get promoted . . .

A few years back he led a raid on a drugs factory in Brixton and was first through the door. An entire magazine from a semi-automatic took his head clean off. There's a lesson in that somewhere.

A farmer in our valley called Bruce Curley is the other one. He shot himself in the foot when he tried to chase his wife's lover out of the bedroom window. Bruce was fat with grey hair sprouting from his ears and Mrs Curley used to cower like a dog whenever he raised a hand. Shame he didn't shoot himself between the eyes.

During my police training we did a firearms course. The instructor was a Geordie with a head like a billiard ball and he took against me from the first day because I suggested the best way to keep a gun barrel clean was to cover it with a condom.

We were standing on the live firing range, freezing our bollocks off. He pointed out the cardboard cutout at the end of the range. It was a silhouette of a crouching gun-wielding villain with a painted white circle over his heart and another on his head.

Taking a service pistol the Geordie crouched down with his legs apart and squeezed off six shots – a heartbeat between each of them – every one grouped in the upper circle.

Flicking the smoking clip into his hand, he said, 'Now I don't expect any of you to do that but at least try to hit the fucking target. Who wants to go first?'

Nobody volunteered.

'How about you, condom boy?'

The class laughed.

I stepped forward and raised my revolver. I hated how good it felt in my hand. The instructor said, 'No, not like that, keep both eyes open. Crouch. Count and squeeze.'

Before he could finish the gun kicked in my hand, rattling the air and something deep inside me.

The cutout swayed from side to side as the pulley dragged it down the range towards us. Six shots, each so close together they formed a ragged hole through the cardboard.

'He shot out his arsehole,' someone muttered in astonishment.

'Right up the Khyber Pass.'

I didn't look at the instructor's face. I turned away, checked the chamber, put on the safety catch and removed my earplugs.

'You missed,' he said triumphantly.

'If you say so, sir.'

I wake with a sudden jolt and it takes a while for my heart to settle. I look at my watch – not so much at the time but the date. I want to make sure I haven't slept for too long or lost any more time.

It's been two days since I regained conciousness. A man is sitting by the bed.

'My name is Wickham,' he says, smiling. 'I'm a neurologist.'

He looks like one of those doctors you see on daytime chat shows.

'I once saw you play rugby for Harlequins against London Scottish,' he says. 'You would have made the England team that year if you hadn't been injured. I played a bit of rugby myself. Never higher than seconds . . .'

'Really, what position?'

'Outside centre.'

I figured as much – he probably touched the ball twice a game and is still talking about the tries he *could* have scored.

'I have the results of your MRI scan,' he says, opening a folder. 'There is no evidence of a skull fracture, aneurysms or a haemorrhage.' He glances up from his notes. 'I want to run some neurological tests to help establish what you've forgotten. It means answering some questions about the shooting.'

'I don't remember it.'

'Yes, but I want you to answer regardless – even if that means guessing. It's called a forced-choice recognition test. It forces you to make choices.'

I think I understand, although I don't see the point.

'How many people were on the boat?'

'I don't remember.'

Wickham reiterates, 'You have to make a choice.'

'Four.'

'Was there a full moon?'

'Yes.'

'Was the name of the boat the *Charmaine*?'

'No.'

'How many engines did it have?'

'One.'

'Was it a stolen boat?'

'Yes.'

'Was the engine running?'

'No.'

'Were you anchored or drifting?'

'Drifting.'

'Were you carrying a weapon?'

'Yes.'

'Did you fire your weapon?'

'No.'

This is ridiculous! What possible good does it do? I'm guessing the answers.

Suddenly, it dawns on me. They think I'm faking amnesia. This isn't a test to see how much I remember – they're testing the validity of my symptoms. They're forcing me to make choices so they can work out what percentage of questions I answer correctly. If I'm telling the truth, pure guesswork should mean half of my answers are correct. Anything significantly above or below 50 per cent could mean I'm trying to 'influence' the result by deliberately getting things right or wrong.

The chance of someone with memory loss answering only ten questions correctly out of fifty, for example, is smaller than 5 per cent. I know enough about statistics to see the objective.

Wickham has been taking notes. No doubt he's studying the distribution of my answers – looking for patterns that might indicate something other than random chance.

Stopping him, I ask, 'Who wrote these questions?'

'I don't know.'

'Guess.'

He blinks at me.

'Come on, Doc, true or false? I'll accept a guess. Is this a test to see if I'm faking memory loss?'

'I don't know what you mean,' he stammers.

'If I can guess the answer, so can you. Who put you up to this – Internal Affairs or Campbell Smith?'

Struggling to his feet, he tucks the clipboard under his arm and turns towards the door. I wish I'd met him on the rugby field. I'd have driven his head into a muddy hole.

* * *

Swinging my legs out of bed, I put one foot on the floor. The lino is cool and slightly sticky. Gulping hard on the pain, I slide my forearms into the plastic cuffs of the crutches.

I'm supposed to be using a support frame on wheels but I'm too vain. I'm not going to walk around in a chrome cage like some geriatric in a post office queue. I look in the cupboard for my clothes. Empty.

I know it sounds paranoid but they're not telling me every-thing. Someone *must* know what I was doing on the river. Someone will have heard the shots or seen something. Why haven't they found any bodies?

Halfway down the corridor I see Campbell talking to Wickham. Two detectives are with them. I recognise one of them: John Keebal. I used to work with him until he joined the Met's Anti-Corruption Group, otherwise known as the Ghost Squad.

Keebal is one of those coppers who call all gays 'fudge-packers' and Asians 'Pakis'. He is loud, bigoted and totally obsessed with the job. When the *Marchioness* riverboat sank in the Thames, he did thirteen death-knocks before lunchtime, telling people their kids had drowned. He knew exactly what to say and when to stop talking. A man like that can't be all bad.

'Where do you think you're going?' asks Campbell.

'I thought I might get some fresh air.'

Keebal interrupts, 'Yeah, just got a whiff of something myself.'

I push past them heading for the lift.

'You can't possibly leave,' says Wickham. 'Your dressing has to be changed every few days. You need painkillers.'

'Fill my pockets and I'll self-administer.'

Campbell grabs my arm. 'Don't be so bloody foolish.'

I realise I'm shaking.

'Have you found anyone? Any . . . any bodies.'

'No.'

'I'm not faking this, you know. I really can't remember.'

'I know.'

He steers me away from the others. 'But you know the drill. The IPCC has to investigate.'

'What's Keebal doing here?'

'He wants to talk to you.'

'Do I need a lawyer?'

Campbell laughs but it doesn't reassure me like it should. Before I can weigh up my options, Keebal leads me down the corridor to the hospital lounge – a stark, windowless place, with burnt orange sofas and posters of healthy people. He unbuttons his jacket and takes a seat, waiting for me to lever myself down from my crutches.

'I hear you nearly met the Grim Reaper.'

'He offered me a room with a view.'

'And you turned him down?'

'I'm not a good traveller.'

For the next ten minutes we shoot the breeze about mutual acquaintances and old times working in west London. He asks about my mother and I tell him she's in a retirement village.

'Some of those places can be pretty expensive.'

'Yep.'

'Where you living nowadays?'

'Right here.'

The coffee arrives and Keebal keeps talking. He gives me his opinion on the proliferation of firearms, random violence and senseless crimes. The police are becoming easy targets and scapegoats all at once. I know what he's trying to do. He wants to draw me in with a spiel about good guys having to stick together.

Keebal is one of those police officers who adopt a warrior ethic as though something separates them from normal society. They listen to politicians talk about the war on crime and the war on drugs and the war on terror and they start picturing themselves as soldiers fighting to keep the streets safe.

'How many times have you put your life on the line, Ruiz? You think any of the bastards care? The left call us pigs and the right call us Nazis. *Sieg, sieg*, oink! *Sieg, sieg*, oink!' he throws his right arm forward in a Nazi salute.

I stare at the signet ring on his pinkie and think of Orwell's *Animal Farm*.

Keebal is on a roll. 'We don't live in a perfect world and we don't have perfect police officers, eh? But what do they expect? We have no fucking resources and we're fighting a system that lets criminals out quicker than we can catch them. And all this new age touchy-feely waa waa bullshit they pass off as crime prevention has done nothing for you and me. And it's done nothing for the poor misguided kids who get caught up in crime.

'A while back I went to a conference and some lard-arse criminologist with an American accent told us that police officers had no enemies. "Criminals are not the enemy, crime is", he said. Jesus wept! Have you ever heard anything so stupid? I had to stop myself giving this guy a slap.'

Keebal leans in a little closer. I smell peanuts on his breath.

'I don't blame coppers for being pissed off. And I can understand when they pocket a little for themselves, as long as they're not dealing drugs or hurting children, eh?' He puts his hand on my shoulder. 'I can help you. Just tell me what happened that night.'

'I don't remember.'

'Am I correct in assuming therefore you cannot identify the person who shot you?'

'You would be correct in that assumption.'

My sarcasm seems to light a fire under Keebal. He knows I'm not buying his we're-all-alone-in-the-trenches bullshit.

'Where are the diamonds?'

'What diamonds?'

He tries to change the subject.

'No. No. Stop! What diamonds?'

He shouts over me. 'The decks of that boat were awash with blood. People died but we haven't found any bodies and nobody has been reported missing. What does that suggest to you?'

He makes me think. The victims probably had no close ties or they were engaged in something illegal. I want to go back to the diamonds, but Keebal has his own agenda.

'I read an interesting statistic the other day. Thirty-five per cent of offenders found guilty of homicide claim amnesia of the event.'

More bloody statistics. 'You think I'm lying.'

'I think you're bent.'

I reach for my crutches and swing on to my feet. 'Since you know all the answers, Keebal, you tell me what happened. Oh, that's right – you weren't there. Then again – you never are. When real coppers are out risking their lives, you're at home tucked up in bed watching reruns of *The Bill*. You risk nothing and you persecute honest coppers for standards that you couldn't piss over. Get out of here. And next time you want to talk to me you better come armed with an arrest warrant and a set of handcuffs.'

Keebal's face turns a slapped red colour. He does lots of preening and flexing as he walks away, yelling over his shoulder, 'The only person you got fooled is that neurologist. Nobody else believes you. You're gonna wish that bullet had done the job.'

I try to chase him down the corridor, hopping on one crutch and screaming my head off. Two black orderlies hold me back, pinning my arms behind my back.

Finally, I calm down and they take me back to my room. Maggie gives me a small plastic cup of syrupy liquid and soon I'm like Alice in Wonderland shrinking into the room. The white folds of the bedclothes are like an Arctic wasteland.

The dream has a whiff of strawberry lip gloss and spearmint breath – a missing girl in a pink and orange bikini. Her name is Mickey Carlyle and she's wedged in the rocks in my mind like a spar of driftwood, bleached white by the sun – as white as her skin and the fine hairs on her forearms. She is four feet high, tugging at my sleeve, saying, 'Why didn't you ever find me? You promised my friend Sarah that you'd find me.'

She even says it in the same voice that Sarah used when she asked me for an ice-cream cone. 'You promised me. You said I could have one if I told you what happened.'

Mickey disappeared not far from here. You might even be able to see Randolph Avenue from the window. It's a solid, red-brick canyon of mansion blocks built as cheap Victorian housing but now the flats cost hundreds of thousands of pounds. I could save for ten years or two hundred and never afford to buy one.

I can still picture the lift, an old-fashioned metal cage that rattled and twanged between the landings. The stairs wrapped around the lift shaft, turning back and forth as they rose. Mickey grew up playing on those stairs, holding impromptu concerts after school because the acoustics were so good. She sang with a lisp because of the gap in her front teeth.

Three years have passed since then. The world has tuned out of her story because there are other crimes to titillate and horrify – dead beauty queens, the war on terror, sportsmen behaving badly . . . Mickey hasn't gone away. She is still here. She is like the ghost who sits opposite me at every feast and the voice inside my head when I fall asleep. I know she's alive. I know it deep down inside, where my guts are tied in knots. I know it but I can't prove it.

It was the first week of the summer holidays, three years ago, when she entered my life. Eighty-five steps and then darkness; she vanished. How can a child disappear in a building with only five floors and eleven flats?

We searched every one of them – every room, cupboard and crawl space. I even checked the same places over and over again, somehow expecting her suddenly to be there, despite all the other searches.

Mickey was seven years old with blonde hair, blue eyes and a gap-toothed smile. She was last seen wearing a bikini, a white Alice band, red canvas shoes and carrying a striped beach towel.

Police cars had blocked the street outside and the neighbours were organising searches. Someone had set up a trestle table with jugs of iced water and bottles of cordial. The temperature reached 30°C at nine o'clock that morning and the air smelled of hot bitumen and exhaust fumes.

A fat guy in baggy green shorts was taking photographs. I didn't recognise him at first but I knew him from somewhere. Where?

Then it came back to me, like it always does. Cottesloe Park – an Anglican boarding school in Warrington. His name was Howard Wavell, a baffling, unfortunate figure, who was three years behind me. My memory triumphs again.

I knew Mickey hadn't left the building. I had a witness. Her name was Sarah Jordan and she was only nine but she knew what she knew. Sitting on the bottom stair, sipping a can of lemonade, she brushed mousy brown hair from her eyes. Tiny crosses clung to her earlobes like pieces of silver foil.

Sarah wore a blue and yellow swimsuit, with white shorts over the top, brown sandals and a baseball cap. Her legs were pale and spotted with insect bites pink from her scratching. Too young to be body conscious, she swung her knees open and closed, resting her cheek against the coolness of the banister.

'My name is Detective Inspector Ruiz,' I said, sitting next to her. 'Tell me what happened again.'

She sighed and straightened her legs. 'I pressed the buzzer, like I said.'

'Which buzzer?'

'Eleven. Where Mickey lives.'

'Show me which button you pressed.'

She sighed again and walked across the foyer through the

23

large front door. The intercom was just outside. She pointed to the top button. Pink nail varnish had been chipped off her fingernails.

'See! I know what number eleven is.'

'Of course you do. What happened then?'

'Mickey's mum said Mickey would be right down.'

'Is that exactly what she said? Word for word?'

Her brow furrowed in concentration. 'No. First she said hello and I said hello. And I asked if Mickey could come and play. We were going to sunbathe in the garden and play under the hose. Mr Murphy lets us use the sprinkler. He says we're helping him water the lawn at the same time.'

'And who is Mr Murphy?'

'Mickey says he owns the building, but I think he's just the caretaker.'

'Mickey didn't come down?'

'No.'

'How long did you wait?'

'Ages and ages.' She fans her face with her hand. 'Can I have an ice cream?'

'In a minute . . . Did anyone come past you while you were waiting?'

'No.'

'And you didn't leave these steps – not even to get a drink . . .'

She shook her head.

' . . . or to talk to a friend, or to pat a dog?'

'No.'

'What happened then?'

'Mickey's mum came down with the rubbish. Then she said, "What are you doing? Where's Mickey?" And I said, "I'm still waiting for her." Then she said she came down ages ago. Only she never did because I've been here the whole time . . .'

'What did you do then?'

'Mickey's mum told me to wait. She said not to move, so I sat on the stairs.'

24

'Did anyone come past you?'

'Only the neighbours who helped look for Mickey.'

'Do you know their names?'

'Some of them.' She counted quietly on her fingers and listed them. 'Is this a mystery?'

'I guess you could call it that.'

'Where did Mickey go?'

'I don't know, sweetheart, but we're going to find her.'

3

Professor Joseph O'Loughlin has arrived to see me. I can see him walking across the hospital car park with his left leg swinging as if bound in a splint. His mouth is moving – smiling, wishing people good morning and making jokes about how he likes his martinis shaken not stirred. Only the Professor could make fun of Parkinson's disease.

Joe is a clinical psychologist and looks exactly like you'd expect a shrink to look – tall and thin with a tangle of brown hair like some absent-minded academic escaped from a lecture theatre.

We met a few years back during a murder investigation when I had him pegged as a possible killer until it turned out to be one of his patients. I don't think he mentions that in his lectures.

Knocking gently on the door, he opens it and smiles awkwardly. He has one of those totally open faces with wet brown eyes like a baby seal just before it gets clubbed.

'I hear you're suffering memory problems.'

'Yeah, who the fuck are you?'

'Very good. Nice to see you haven't lost your sense of humour.'

He turns around several times trying to decide where to

put his briefcase. Then he takes a notepad and pulls up a chair, sitting with his knees touching the bed. Finally settled, he looks at me and says nothing – as though I've asked him to come because there's something on my mind.

This is what I hate about shrinks. The way they create silences and have you questioning your sanity. This wasn't my idea. I can remember my name. I know where I live. I know where I put the car keys and parked the car. I'm tickety-boo.

'How are you feeling?'

'Some bastard shot me.'

Without warning his left arm jerks and trembles. Self-consciously, he holds it down.

'How's the Parkinson's?'

'I've stopped ordering soup at restaurants.'

'Very wise.'

'Julianne?'

'She's great.'

'And the girls?'

'They're growing up.'

Swapping small talk and family stories has never been a feature of our relationship. Usually, I invite myself round to Joe's place for dinner, drink his wine, flirt with his wife and shamelessly milk him for ideas about unsolved cases. Joe knows this, of course – not because he's so bloody clever but because I'm so transparent.

I like him. He's a privately educated, middle-class pseud but that's OK. And I like Julianne, his wife, who for some reason thinks she can marry me off again because my track record shouldn't be held against me.

'I take it you met my boss.'

'The Chief Superintendent.'

'What did you make of him?'

Joe shrugs. 'He seems very professional.'

'Come on, Prof, you can do better than that. Tell me what you really think.'

Joe makes a little 'Tsh' sound, like a cymbal. He knows I'm challenging him.

Clearing his throat, he glances at his hands. 'The Chief Superintendent is a well-spoken career police officer, who is self-conscious about his double chins and colours his hair. He is asthmatic. He wears Calvin Klein aftershave. He is married with three daughters, who have him so tightly wrapped around their little fingers he should be dipped in silver and engraved. They are vegetarians and won't let him eat meat at home so he eats meals at the station canteen. He reads P. D. James novels and likes to think of himself as Adam Dalgleish, although he doesn't write poetry and he's not particularly perceptive. And he has a very irritating habit of lecturing rather than listening to people.'

I let out a low admiring whistle. 'Have you been stalking this guy?'

Joe suddenly looks embarrassed. Some people would make it sound like a party trick but he always seems genuinely surprised that he knows even half this stuff. And it's not like he plucks details out of the air. I could ask him to justify every statement and he'd rattle off the answers. He will have seen Campbell's asthma puffer, recognised his aftershave, watched him eat and seen the photographs of his children . . .

This is what frightens me about Joe. It's as if he can crack open someone's head and read the contents like tea leaves. You don't want to get too close to someone like that because one day they might hold up a mirror and let you see what the world sees.

Joe is thumbing through my medical notes, looking at the results of the CT and MRI scans. He closes the folder. 'So what happened?'

'A rifle, a bullet, usual story.'

'What's the first thing you do recall?'

'Waking up in here.'

'And the last thing?'

I don't answer him. I've been racking my brain for two days – ever since I woke up – and all I can come up with is pizza.

'How do you feel now?'

'Frustrated. Angry.'

'Because you can't remember?'

'Nobody knows what I was doing on the river. It wasn't a police operation. I acted alone. I'm not a maverick. I don't go off half-cocked like some punk kid with "Born to Lose" tattooed on my chest . . . They're treating me like some sort of criminal.'

'The doctors?'

'The police.'

'You could be reacting to not being able to remember. You feel excluded. You think everyone knows the secret except you.'

'You think I'm paranoid.'

'It's a common symptom of amnesia. You think people are holding out on you.'

Yeah, well that doesn't explain Keebal. He's visited me three times already, making false charges and outrageous claims. The more I refuse to talk, the harder he bullies.

Joe rolls his pen over his knuckles. 'I once had a patient, thirty-five years old, with no history of neurological or psychiatric disorders. He slipped on an icy footpath and hit his head. He didn't lose consciousness or anything like that. He bounced straight up on to his feet and kept walking . . .'

'Is there a point to this story?'

' . . . He didn't remember falling over. And he no longer knew where he was going. He had totally forgotten what had happened in the previous twelve hours, yet he knew his name and recognised his wife and kids. It's called Transient Global Amnesia. Minutes, hours or days disappear. Self-identification is still possible and sufferers behave otherwise normally but they can't remember a particular event or a missing period of time.'

'But the memories come back, right?'

'Not always.'

'What happened to your patient?'

'At first we thought he'd only forgotten the fall, but other memories had also gone missing. He didn't remember his earlier marriage; or a house he'd once built. And he had no knowledge of John Major ever being Prime Minister.'

'It wasn't all bad then.'

Joe smiles. 'It's too early to say if your memory loss is permanent. Head trauma is only one possibility. Most recorded cases have been preceded by physical and emotional stress. Getting shot would qualify. Sexual intercourse and diving into cold water have also triggered attacks . . .'

'I'll remember not to shag in the plunge pool.'

My sarcasm falls flat. Joe carries on. 'During traumatic events our brains radically alter the balance of our hormones and neuro-chemicals. This is like our survival mode – our fight or flight response. Sometimes when the threat ends, our brains stay in survival mode for a while – just in case. We have to convince your brain it can let go.'

'How do we do that?'

'We talk. We investigate. We use diaries and photographs to prompt recollections.'

'When did you last see me?' I ask him suddenly.

He thinks for a moment. 'We had dinner about four months ago. Julianne wanted you to meet one of her friends.'

'The publishing editor.'

'That's the one. Why do you ask?'

'I've been asking everyone. I call them up and say, *"Hey, what's new? That's great. Listen, when did you last see me? Yeah, it's been too long. We should get together . . . "*.'

'And what have you discovered?'

'I'm lousy at keeping in touch with people.'

'OK, but that's the right idea. We have to find the missing pieces.'

'Can't you just hypnotise me?'

'No. And a blow on the head doesn't help either.'

Reaching for his briefcase, his left arm trembles. He retrieves a folder and takes out a small square piece of cardboard, frayed at the edges.

'They found this in your pocket. It's water-damaged.'

He turns his hand. Saliva dries on my lips.

It's a photograph of Mickey Carlyle. She's wearing her school uniform and grinning at the camera with her gappy smile like she's laughing at something we can't see.

Instead of confusion I feel an overwhelming sense of relief. I'm not going mad. This *does* have something to do with Mickey.

'You're not surprised.'

'No.'

'Why?'

'You're going to think I'm crazy, but I've been having these dreams.'

Already I can see the psychologist in him turning my statements into symptoms.

'You remember the investigation and trial?'

'Yes.'

'Howard Wavell went to prison for her murder.'

'Yes.'

'You don't think he killed her?'

'I don't think she's dead.'

Now I get a reaction. He's not such a poker face after all.

'What about the evidence?'

I raise my hands. My bandaged hand could be a white flag. I know all the arguments. I helped put the case together. All of the evidence pointed to Howard, including the fibres, bloodstains and his lack of an alibi. The jury did its job and justice prevailed; justice polled on one day in the hearts of twelve people.

The law ruled a line through Mickey's name and put a full stop after Howard's. Logic agrees but my heart can't accept it. I simply cannot conceive of a world that Mickey isn't a part of.

Joe glances at the photograph again. 'Do you remember putting this in your wallet?'

'No.'

'Can you think why?'

I shake my head but in the back of my mind I wonder if perhaps I wanted to be able to recognise her. 'What else was I carrying?'

Joe reads from a list. 'A shoulder holster, a wallet, keys and a pocket knife . . . You used your belt as a tourniquet to slow the bleeding.'

'I don't remember.'

'Don't worry. We're going to go back. We're going to follow the clues you left behind – receipts, invoices, appointments, diaries . . . We'll retrace your steps.'

'And I'll remember.'

'Or learn to remember.'

He turns towards the window and glances at the sky as though planning a picnic. 'Do you fancy a day out?'

'I don't think I'm allowed.'

He takes a letter from his jacket pocket. 'Don't worry – I booked ahead.'

Joe waits while I dress, struggling with the buttons on my shirt because of my bandaged hand.

'Do you want some help?'

'No.' I say it too harshly. 'I have to learn.'

Keebal watches me as I cross the foyer, giving me a look like I'm dating his sister. I resist the urge to salute him.

Outside, I raise my face to the sunshine and take a deep breath. Planting the points of my crutches carefully, I move across the car park and see a familiar figure waiting in an unmarked police car. DC Alisha Kaur Barba (everyone calls her Ali) is studying a textbook for her sergeant's exam. Anybody who commits half that stuff to memory deserves to make Chief Constable.

Smiling at me nervously, she opens the car door. Indian

women have such wonderful skin and dark wet eyes. She's wearing tailored trousers and a white blouse that highlights the small gold medallion around her neck.

Ali used to be the youngest member of the Serious Crime Group and we worked on the Mickey Carlyle case together. She had the makings of a great detective but Campbell wouldn't recommend a promotion.

Nowadays she works with the DPG (Diplomatic Protection Group), looking after ambassadors, diplomats and protecting witnesses. Perhaps that's why she's here now – to protect me.

As we drive out of the car park, she glances at me in the mirror, waiting for some sign of recognition.

'So tell me about yourself, Detective Constable.'

A furrow forms just above her nose. 'My name is Alisha Barba. I'm in the Diplomatic Protection Group.'

'Have we met before?'

'Ah – well – yes, sir, you used to be my boss.'

'Fancy that! That's one of the three great things about having amnesia: apart from being able to hide my own Easter eggs, I get to meet new people every day.'

After a long pause, Ali asks, 'What's the third thing, sir?'

'I get to hide my own Easter eggs.'

She starts to laugh and I flick her on the ear. 'Of course I remember you. Ali Baba, the catcher of thieves.'

She grins at me sheepishly.

Beneath her short jacket I notice a shoulder holster. She's carrying a gun – an MP5 Carbine A2, with a solid stock. It's strange seeing her carrying a firearm because so few officers in the Met are authorised to have one.

Driving south-east past Victoria and Whitehall to the Thames Embankment, we skirt parks and gardens that are dotted with office workers eating lunch on the grass – healthy girls with skirts full of autumn sunshine and fresh air and men dozing with their jackets under their heads.

Turning along Victoria Embankment, I glimpse the

Thames, sliding between the smooth stone banks. Waxing and waning beneath lion-head gargoyles, it rolls under the bridges, past the Tower of London and on towards Canary Wharf and Rotherhithe.

Ali parks the car in a small lane alongside Cannon Street Station. There are seventeen stone steps leading down to a narrow gravel beach slowly being exposed by the tide. On closer inspection the beach is not gravel but broken pottery, bricks, rubble and shards of glass worn smooth by the water.

'This is where they found you,' Joe says, sliding his hand across the horizon until it rests on a yellow navigation buoy, streaked with rust.

'Marilyn Monroe.'

'I beg your pardon?'

'It's nothing.'

Above our heads the trains accelerate and brake as they leave and enter the station across a railway bridge.

'They say you lost about four pints of blood. The cold water slowed down your metabolism, which probably saved your life. You also had the presence of mind to use your belt as a tourniquet . . .'

'What about the boat?'

'That wasn't found until later that morning, drifting east of Tower Bridge. Any of this coming back?'

I shake my head.

'There was a tide running that night. The water level was about four feet higher than it is now. And the tide was running at about five knots an hour. Given your blood loss and body temperature that puts the shooting about three miles upstream . . .'

Give or take about a thousand different variables, I think to myself, but I see where he's coming from. He is trying to work backwards.

'You had blood on your trousers, along with a mixture of clay, sediment and traces of benzene and ammonia.'

'Was the boat engine running?'

'It had run out of fuel.'

'Did anyone report shots being fired on the river?'

'No.'

I stare across the shit-brown water, slick with leaves and debris. This was once the busiest thoroughfare in the city; a source of wealth, cliques, clubs, boundary disputes, ancient jealousies, salvage battles and folklore. Nowadays, three people can get shot within a few miles of Tower Bridge and nobody sees a thing.

A blue and white police launch pulls into view. The sergeant is wearing orange overalls and a baseball cap, along with a life vest that makes his chest look barrel-shaped. He offers his hand as I negotiate the gangway. Ali has donned a sunhat as though we're off for a spot of fishing.

A tourist boat cruises past, sending us rocking in its wake. Camcorders and digital cameras record the moment as though we're part of London's rich tapestry. The sergeant pushes back on the throttle and we turn against the current and head upstream beneath Southwark Bridge.

The river runs faster on the inside of each bend, rushing along smooth stone walls, pulling at boats on their moorings, creating pressure waves against the foundations of the bridge.

A young girl with long black hair rows in a single scull. Her back is curved and her forearms slick with perspiration. I follow her wake and then raise my eyes to the buildings and the sky above them. High white clouds are like chalk marks against the blue.

The Millennium Wheel looks like something that should be floating in space instead of scooping up tourists. Nearby a class of school children sit on benches, the girls dressed in tartan skirts and blue stockings. Joggers ghost past them along Albert Embankment.

I can't remember if it was a clear night. You don't often see stars in London because of light and air pollution. At most they appear as half a dozen faint dots overhead or sometimes you can see Mars in the south-east. On a cloudy night some stretches of the river, particularly opposite the parks, are almost in total darkness. The gates are locked at sunset.

A century ago people made a living out of pulling bodies from the Thames. They knew every little race and eddy where a floater might bob up. The mooring chains and ropes, the stationary boats and barges that split the current into arrow-heads.

When I first came down from Lancashire I was posted with the Thames Water Police. We used to pull two bodies a week out of the river, mostly suicides. You see the wannabes all the time, leaning from bridges, staring into the depths. That's the nature of the river – it can carry away all your hopes and ambitions or deliver them up unchanged.

The bullet that put a hole in my leg was travelling at high velocity: a sniper's bullet fired from long range. There must have been enough light for the shooter to see me. Either that or he used an infrared sight. He could have been anywhere within a thousand yards but probably only half that distance. At five hundred yards the angle of dispersion can be measured in single inches – enough to miss the heart or the head.

This was no ordinary contract killer. Few have this sort of skill. Most hitmen kill at close range, lying in wait or pulling alongside cars at traffic lights, pumping bullets through the window. This one was different. He lay prone, completely still, cradling the stock against his chin, caressing the trigger . . . A sniper is like a computer firing system, able to calculate distance, wind speed, direction and air temperature. Someone had to train him – probably the armed forces.

Scanning the broken skyline of factories, cranes and apart-ment blocks, I try to picture where the shooter was hiding. He must have been above me. It can't have been easy trying to hit targets on the water. The slightest breeze and movement of the boat would have caused him to miss. Each shot would have created a flash, giving away his position.

The tide is still going out and the river shrinks inwards exposing a slick of mud where seagulls fight for scraps in the slime and the remnants of ancient piles stick from the shallows like rotting teeth.

The Professor looks decidedly uncomfortable. I don't think speed or boats agree with him. 'Why were you on the river?'

'I don't know.'

'Speculate.'

'I was meeting someone or following someone . . .'

'With information about Mickey Carlyle?'

'Maybe.'

Why would someone meet on a boat? It seems an odd choice. Then again, the river at night is relatively deserted once the dinner party cruises have finished. It's a quick escape route.

'Why would someone shoot you?' asks Joe.

'Perhaps we had a falling out or . . .'

'Or what?'

'It was a mopping-up operation. We haven't found any bodies. Maybe we're not supposed to.'

Christ this is frustrating! I want to reach into my skull and press my fingers into the grey porridge until I feel the key that's hidden there.

'I want to see the boat.'

'It's at Wapping, sir,' replies the sergeant.

'Make it so.'

He spins the wheel casually and accelerates, creating a wave of spray as the outboard engine dips deep into the water and the bow lifts. Spray clings to Ali's eyelashes and she holds her flapping hat to her head.

Twenty minutes later, a mile downstream from Tower Bridge, we pull into the headquarters of the Marine Support Unit.

The motor cruiser *Charmaine* is in dry dock, propped upright on wooden beams and surrounded by scaffolding. At first glance the forty-foot inland cruiser looks immaculate, with a varnished wooden wheelhouse and brass fittings. A closer inspection reveals the shattered portholes and splintered decking. Blue and white police tape is threaded around the guardrails and small white evidence flags mark the various bullet holes and other points of interest.

Ali explains how the *Charmaine* had been reported stolen from Kew Pier in west London fourteen hours after I was found. She rattles off the engine size, range and top speed. She knows I appreciate facts.

A SOCO (scene-of-crime officer) in white overalls emerges from the wheelhouse and crouches near the stern. Running a tape measure across the deck, she makes a note of the measurement and adjusts a surveyor's theodolite mounted on a tripod beside her.

Turning, she shields her eyes from the sun behind us, recognising the sergeant.

'This is DC Kay Simpson,' he says, making the introductions.

Only in her thirties, she has short-cropped blonde hair and inquisitive eyes. She keeps staring at me like I'm a ghost.

'So what exactly are you doing now?' I ask, self-consciously.

'Trajectories, impact velocity, yaw angle, the point of aim, distances, margin for error and blood patterns . . .' She stops in mid-sentence when she realises that she has left us all behind. 'I'm trying to work out how far away the shooter must have been, as well as his elevation and how often he missed his target.'

'He hit me in the leg.'

'Yes, but he could have been aiming at your head.' She adds the word 'sir' as an afterthought, just in case I'm offended. 'The shooter used Boat Tail Hollow Point ammunition with a velocity of 2675 feet per second. They're not widely available commercially but nowadays you can source almost anything from Eastern Europe.'

A thought occurs to her. 'Would you mind helping me, sir?'

'How?'

'Can you lie on the deck just here?' She points to her feet. 'Half on your side, with your legs stretched out, one just crossing the other.' Letting go of my crutches I let her move me into position like an artist's model.

As she leans over me I get a sudden image of another woman bending to brush her lips against mine. The air twitches and the picture is gone.

DC Simpson takes the tripod and angles it down towards my legs. A bright red beam of light reflects on my trousers above my bandaged thigh.

Pure fear rushes through me and suddenly I'm screaming at her to get down. Everyone! Get down! I remember the red light, a dancing red beam that signalled death. I lay in darkness, doubled over in pain as the beam moved back and forth across the deck, searching for me.

Nobody seems to have noticed me screaming. The sound is inside my head. They're all listening to the DC.

'The bullet came down from here, entered your thigh here, exited and lodged in the deck. It nudged against your femur and tumbled end on end, which is why the exit wound was so large . . .'

She walks several paces away and uses a tape measure to measure the distance between the side rail and another bullet hole. 'For years people have debated whether momentum or kinetic energy is the best means of determining the striking power of a bullet. The answer is to merge the two parameters of bodies in motion. We have software programs that can tell us – based on measurements – the distance travelled by a particular bullet. In this case we're looking at 430 yards, with a 2 per cent margin for error. Once we know the location of the shooting we can reconstruct the trajectory and find out where the shooter was hiding.'

She looks down at me as though I should have an answer ready for her. I'm still trying to slow my heart rate.

'Are you OK, sir?'

'I'm fine.'

Joe is crouching next to me now. 'Maybe you should take it easy.'

'I'm not a fucking invalid!'

Instantly I want to take it back and apologise. Everyone is uncomfortable now.

DC Simpson helps me stand.

'How much more can you recreate of what happened?' I ask.

She seems quite pleased with the question.

'OK, this is where you were initially shot. Someone else got hit and fell on top of you. Traces of their bone and blood were found in your hair.'

She sits down and drags herself backwards until her back is braced against the side railing.

'One of the main clusters of bullets is this one.' She points to the deck near her legs. 'I believe you pulled yourself back here to get cover but more bullets went through the sides and hit the deck. You were too exposed, so . . .'

'I rolled across the deck and took cover behind the wheel-house.'

Joe looks at me. 'You remember?'

'No, but it makes sense.' Even as I answer I realise that part of it must be memory.

The DC scrambles across the deck to the far side of the wheelhouse. 'This is where you lost your finger. You wanted to look inside or to see where the shooting was coming from. You were badly wounded. You hooked your fingers over the ledge around the porthole and raised yourself up. A bullet came through the glass and your finger disappeared.'

Dried blood stains the outside of the wall, leaking around exit holes in the splintered wood.

'We found twenty-four bullet holes in the vessel. The sniper fired only eight of them. He was very controlled and precise.'

'What about the others?'

'The rest were 9mm rounds.'

My Glock 17 self-loading handgun was signed out of the station armoury on 22 September and still hasn't been found. Maybe Campbell is right and I shot someone.

DC Simpson continues with her hypothesis. 'I think you were dragged over the railing at the stern with the help of a boat hook which tore one of your belt loops. You vomited just here.'

'So I must have been in the water first – before I was shot?'

'Yes.'

I look at Joe and shake my head. I can't remember. Blood – that's all I can see. I can taste it in my mouth and feel it throbbing in my ears.

I look at the DC and my voice catches in my throat. 'You said someone died, right? You must have tested the blood. Was it . . . I mean . . . did it belong to . . . could it have been . . . ?' I can't get the words out.

Joe finishes the question and answers it all at once.

'It wasn't Mickey Carlyle.'

Back in the car, we edge through Tobacco Dock, past a grey square of water surrounded by warehouses. I can never tell if these new housing developments are gentrification or reclamation – most of them were derelict before the developers arrived. The dockside pubs have gone, replaced by fitness centres, cybercafés and juice bars selling shots of wheatgrass.

Further from the river, squeezed between the Victorian terraces, we find a more traditional café and take a table by the window. The walls are decorated with posters of South and Central America; and the air smells of boiled milk and porridge.

Two grey plump women run the dining room – one taking orders, the other cooking.

Fried eggs stare up from my plate like large jaundiced eyes, along with a blackened sausage and a twisted mouth of bacon. Ali has a salad sandwich and pours the tea from a stainless steel teapot. The brew is a dark shade of khaki, thick with floating leaves.

A local school has just broken for lunch and the street is full of black teenagers eating buckets of chips. Some of them smoke by the phone box while others swap headphones, listening to music.

Joe tries to stir his coffee with his left hand and stalls, switching to the right. His voice cuts through the sound of metal knives scraping on crockery. 'Why did you think Mickey might have been on the boat?'

Ali's ears prick up. She's been asking herself the same question.

'I don't know. I was thinking about the photograph. Why would I carry it – unless I wanted to recognise her? It's been three years. She won't look the same.'

Ali glances from me to the Professor and back to me again. 'You think she's *alive*?'

'I didn't imagine all this.' I motion to my leg. 'You saw the boat. People died. I know it has something to do with Mickey.'

I haven't touched my food. I don't feel hungry any more. Perhaps the Professor is right – I'm trying to right the wrongs of the past and ease my own conscience.

'We should get back to the hospital,' he says.

'No, not yet, I want to find Rachel Carlyle first. Maybe she knows something about Mickey.'

Joe nods in agreement. It's a good plan.

4

The autumn leaves swirl across Randolph Avenue, collecting against the steps of Dolphin Mansions. The place still looks the same, with a white trimmed arch over the entrance and bronze letters etched into the glass above the door.

Ali taps impatiently on the steering wheel with short manicured fingernails. The place unnerves her. We both remember a different time of year, the haste and noise and sullen heat, the shock and sadness. Joe doesn't understand but must sense something. Shuffling through leaves, we cross the road and climb the front steps. The bottom buzzer automatically opens the door between nine and four each day. Standing in the foyer, I glance up the central stairwell as though listening for a distant echo. Everything passes up and down these stairs – letters, furniture, food, newborn babies and missing children.

I can remember the names and faces of every resident. I can draw lines between them on a whiteboard showing relationships, contacts, employment history, movements and alibis for when Mickey disappeared. I remember it not like yesterday, but like I remember the meal I just failed to eat, the fried eggs and lean bacon.

Take Rachel Carlyle, for instance. The last time I saw her was at the memorial service for Mickey, a few months after the trial. I arrived late and sat at the back, feeling like I was intruding. Rachel's soft, drugged sobs filled the chapel and she looked devoid of hope and tired of living.

Some of the neighbours from Dolphin Mansions were there, including Mrs Swingler, the cat lady, whose hairdo resembled one of her tabbies curled on top of her head. Kirsten Fitzroy had her arm over Rachel's shoulders. Next to her was S. K. Dravid, the piano teacher. Ray Murphy, the caretaker, and his wife were a few seats back. Their son Ronnie sat between them, twitching and mumbling. Tourette's had hard-wired his movements to be quicker than a light switch.

I didn't stay for the whole service. I slipped outside, pausing to look at the plaque waiting to be blessed:

MICHAELA LOUISE CARLYLE
1994–2001
We didn't have time to say goodbye, my Angel, but
you're only a thought away

There were no lessons to be learned, no logic or plot to be raked over, no moral comfort to be gained. According to the trial judge, her death had been pointless, violent and put into context.

I interviewed Howard Wavell a dozen times after that, hoping he might give up Mickey's burial place, but he said nothing. Periodically, we investigated new leads, excavating a garden in Pimlico and dredging the pond in Ravenscourt Park.

I haven't talked to Rachel since then but sometimes, secretly, I have found myself parked outside Dolphin Mansions, staring out of the windscreen, wondering how a child disappears in five storeys and eleven flats.

* * *

The old-fashioned metal lift rattles and twangs between the landings as it rises to the top floor. I knock on the door of No. 11 but there's no answer.

Ali peers through the leadlight panels and then lowers herself on to one knee and pushes open the hinged mail flap.

'She hasn't been home for a while. There are letters piled up on the floor.'

'What else can you see?'

'The bedroom door is open. There is a dressing gown hanging on a hook.'

'Is it light blue?'

'Yes.'

I remember Rachel wearing the robe, sitting on the sofa, cradling the telephone.

Her forehead was pasty with perspiration and her eyes fogged. I had seen the signs before. She wanted a drink; she *needed* a drink; a steadier to get her through.

'Seven years old. That's a great age.'

She didn't respond.

'Did you and Mickey get on well?'

She blinked at me in bafflement.

'I mean, did you ever fight?'

'Sometimes. No more than normal.'

'How often do you think normal families fight?'

'I don't know, Inspector. I only see normal families in TV sitcoms.'

She looked at me steadily, not with defiance but with a sure knowledge that I was following the wrong line of questioning.

'Does Mickey hang out with anyone in particular in the building?'

'She knows everyone. Mr Wavell downstairs, Kirsten across the hall, Mrs Swingler, Mr Murphy, Dravid on the ground floor. He teaches the piano . . .'

'Is there any reason why Mickey might have wandered off?'

'No.' One bra strap slid down her shoulder and she tugged it back. It slid down again.

'Could someone have wanted to take her?'

She shook her head.

'What about her father?'

'No.'

'You're divorced?'

'Three years.'

'Does he see Mickey?'

She squeezed a ball of soggy tissues in her fist and again shook her head.

My marbled notebook rested open on my knee. 'I need a name.'

She didn't reply.

I waited for the silence to wear her down but it didn't seem to affect her. She had no nervous habits like touching her hair or biting her bottom lip. She was totally enclosed.

'He would never hurt her,' she pronounced suddenly. 'And he's not silly enough to take her.'

My pen was poised over the page.

'Aleksei Kuznet,' she whispered.

I thought she was joking. I almost laughed.

Here was a name to conjure with: a name to tighten the throat and loosen the bowels: a name to speak softly in quiet corners with fingers crossed and knuckles rapping on wood.

'When did you last see your ex-husband?'

'On the day we divorced.'

'And what makes you so sure he didn't take Mickey?'

She didn't miss a beat. 'My husband has a reputation as a violent and dangerous man, Inspector, but he is not stupid. He will never touch Mickey or me. He knows I can destroy him.'

'And how exactly can you do that?'

She didn't have to answer. I could see my reflection in her unblinking stare. She believed this. There was absolutely no doubt in her mind.

46

'There's something else you should know,' she said. 'Mickey has a panic disorder. She won't go outside by herself. Her psychologist says she is agoraphobic.'

'But she's only a . . .'

'Child? Yes. People don't expect it, but it happens. Even the thought of going to school used to make her sick. Chest pains, palpitations, nausea, shortness of breath . . . Most days I had to walk her right to the classroom and pick her up from the same place.'

The tears almost came again, but she found a place to put them. Women and tears – I'm no good with them. Some men can just wrap their arms around a woman and soak up some of the hurt, but that's not me. I wish it were different.

Rachel seemed too damaged to hold herself together but she wasn't going to break in front of me. She was going to show me how strong she could be. I didn't doubt it. Any woman who walked away from Aleksei Kuznet needed courage beyond words.

'Have you remembered something?' asks Joe, close to me now.

'No. I'm just daydreaming.'

Ali looks over the banister. 'Maybe one of the neighbours knows where Rachel is. What about the one with the cats?'

'Mrs Swingler.'

A lot of the neighbours have moved on since the tragedy. The Murphys were managing a pub in Esher and Kirsten Fitzroy, Rachel's best friend, had moved to Notting Hill. Perhaps tragedy permeates a place like a smell you can't get rid of.

Taking the lift to the first floor, I knock on Mrs Swingler's door. Resting on my crutches, I hear her coming down her hallway. Long strings of coloured beads threaded into her hair gently clack as she moves. The door opens a crack.

'Hello, Mrs Swingler, do you remember me?'

She peers at me aggressively. She thinks I'm a health

inspector from the local council, come to take away her cats.

'I was here a few years ago – when Mickey Carlyle disappeared. I'm looking for Rachel Carlyle. Have you seen her?'

The smell coming from inside is a fetid stench, part feline and part human. She finds her voice. 'No.'

'When did you last see her?'

She shrugs. 'Weeks back. She must have gone on holiday.'

'Did she tell you that?'

'No.'

'Have you seen her car parked outside?'

'What sort of car does she drive?'

I think hard. I don't know why I remember. 'A Renault Estate. It's black.'

Mrs Swingler shakes her head, making the beads clack.

The hallway behind her is crammed with boxes and chests. I notice a small movement, then another, as though the shadows are shifting. Cats. Everywhere. Crawling out of boxes and drawers, from under the bed and on top of wardrobes. Dark shapes leak across the floor, gathering around her, rubbing against her pale legs and nipping her ankles.

'When did you last see me?'

She looks at me oddly. 'Last month . . . you was in and out of here all the time.'

'Was I with anyone?'

She glances at the Professor suspiciously. 'Is your friend trying to be funny?'

'No. He has just forgotten a few things.'

'You were seeing her upstairs, I suppose.'

'Do you know why?'

Her laugh rasps like a violin. 'Do I look like your social secretary?'

She's about to shut the door but thinks of something else. 'I remember you now. You was always looking for that little girl got murdered. It's her fault, you know.'

'Whose fault?'

48

'People like her shouldn't have kids if they can't control them. I don't mind my taxes going to sick kiddies in hospitals and to fix the roads but why should I pay for single mothers, sponging off the social and spending their money on cigarettes and booze?'

'She didn't need handouts.'

Mrs Swingler hitches up her kaftan. 'Once an alky, always an alky.'

I step towards her. 'You think so?'

Suddenly she's less sure of her ground.

'I'll be sure to tell my mother. One day at a time, eh?'

The Professor pulls the cage door closed and the lift jerks into motion. When we reach the foyer, I turn back towards the stairs. I have searched this building dozens of times – in reality and in dreams – but I still want to search it again. I want to take it apart, brick by brick.

Rachel is missing. So are the people who left bloodstains on the boat. I don't know what any of it means but a twitch of the brain, a nervous shudder and something like instinct tells me to worry.

It's getting late. Streetlights are beginning to blink and tail-lights glow. We skirt along the side path and reach the rear garden – a narrow rectangle of grass surrounded by brick walls. A child's paddling pool lies upturned in the shadows and outdoor furniture has been stacked against a garden shed.

Beyond the rear fence is Paddington Recreation Ground where muddy puddles dot the turf. To the left is a lane with garages, while to the right, across a half-dozen walls, is the Macmillan Estate, a drab, post-war council estate. There are ninety-six flats, with laundry hanging from the balconies and satellite dishes bolted to the walls.

This is the spot where Mickey and Sarah used to sunbathe. Above is the window Howard watched them from. On the day Mickey disappeared I came to the garden to find some shade and quiet. I knew then that she hadn't just wandered off. And a child doesn't accidentally go missing in a five-storey mansion block. It felt like a kidnapping or something worse.

Missing children, you see: no good news can come of them. Dozens disappear every day, mostly runaways or throwaways. A seven-year-old is different because the only possibilities are the stuff of nightmares.

I crouch gingerly and stare into the pond where koi are lazily circling. I have never understood why people keep fish. They're indifferent, expensive, covered in scales and have such a fragile hold on their lives. My second wife, Jessie, was like that. We were married for six months and then I went out of fashion faster than male thongs.

As a kid I bred frogs. I used to collect the spawn from a pond on our farm and keep them in a forty-four-gallon drum cut down the middle. Baby frogs are cute but put a hundred of them in a bucket and you have a squirming, slippery mass. They finished up invading the house. My stepfather told me I was 'fantastic' at raising tadpoles. I'm assuming he didn't mean 'fantastic' in a good way.

Ali is standing next to me. She pushes hair behind her ears. 'You thought she might already be dead on that first day.'

'I know.'

'We hadn't done background checks and SOCO hadn't arrived. There were no bloodstains or suspects, but you still had a bad feeling.'

'Yes.'

'And right from the outset you noticed Howard Wavell. What was it about him?'

'He was taking photographs. Everyone else in the building was searching for Mickey but he went back to get his camera. He said he wanted to have a record.'

'A record?'

'Of all the excitement.'

'Why?'

'So he could remember it.'

5

By the time I get back to the hospital it's almost dark. The whole place has a sour smell like the dead air in closed-up rooms. I have missed a physiotherapy session and Maggie is waiting to change my bandages.

'Somebody took some pills from the pharmacy trolley yesterday,' she says, cutting the last of the bandages. 'It was a bottle of morphine capsules. My friend is in trouble. They think it's her fault.'

Maggie isn't accusing me but I know there's a subtext. 'We're hoping the capsules might turn up. Maybe they were misplaced.'

She withdraws, walking backwards, the tray with bandages and scissors held before her.

'I hope your friend doesn't get into too much trouble,' I say.

Maggie nods, turns and is gone without a sound.

Lying back, I listen to the trolleys rattling to distant rooms and someone waking from a nightmare with a scream. Four times during the evening I try to phone Rachel Carlyle. She's still not home. Ali has promised to run her name and vehicle through the Police National Computer.

There's nobody in the corridor outside my room. Maybe the weasels from the ACG have grown tired of watching me.

At 9.00 p.m. I call my mother at Villawood Lodge. She takes a long while to answer the phone.

'Were you sleeping?'

'I was watching TV.' I can hear it buzzing in the background. 'Why haven't you come to see me?'

'I'm in hospital.'

'What's wrong with you?'

'I hurt my leg, but I'm going to be fine.'

'Well, if it's not serious you should come to see me.'

'The doctors say I have to be here for another week or so.'

'Do the twins know?'

'I didn't want to bother them.'

'Claire sent me a postcard from New York. She went to Martha's Vineyard last weekend. And she said Michael might be doing a yacht transfer to Newport Rhode Island. They can catch up with each other.'

'That's nice.'

'You should call them.'

'Yes.'

I ask her a few more questions, trying to make conversation, but she isn't concentrating on anything except the TV. Suddenly, she starts sniffling. It feels like her nose is right in my ear.

'Goodnight, Daj.' That's what I call her.

'Wait!' She presses her mouth to the phone. 'Yanko, come and see me.'

'I will. Soon.'

I wait until she hangs up. Then I hold the receiver and contemplate calling the twins – just to make sure they're OK. It's the same call I always imagine making but never do.

I imagine Claire saying, 'Hi, Dad, how are you doing? Did you get that book I sent you? No, it's not a diet book; it's about lifestyle . . . cleansing your liver, purging toxins . . .'

Then she invites me round for a vegetarian dinner that will purge more toxins and clear entire rooms.

I also imagine calling Michael. We'll get together for a beer, swapping jokes and talking football like a normal father and son. Only there is nothing normal about any of this. I'm imagining someone else's life. Neither of my children would waste a phone conversation, let alone an evening, on their father.

I love my children fit to bust – I just don't understand them. As babies they were fine, but then they turned into teenagers who drove too fast, played music too loudly and treated me like some fascist conspirator because I worked for the Metropolitan Police. Loving children is easy. Keeping them is hard.

I fall asleep watching a holiday programme on TV. The last thing I remember is seeing a woman with a permanent smile drop her sarong and dive into a pool.

Some time later the pain wakes me. There's a lethal swiftness in the air, like the vortex left behind by a passenger jet. Someone is in the room with me. Only his hands are in the light. Draped over the knuckles are polished silver worry beads.

'How did you get in here?'

'Don't believe everything you read about hospital waiting lists.'

Aleksei Kuznet leans forward. He has dark eyes and even darker hair combed in rigid lines back from his forehead and kept there with hair gel and willpower. His other most notable feature is a puckered circle of scar tissue on his cheek, wrinkled and milky white. The watch on his wrist is worth more than I earn in a year.

'Forgive me, I didn't ask after your welfare. Are you well?'

'Fine.'

'That is very pleasing news. I am sure your mother will be relieved.'

He's sending me a message.

Tiny beads of perspiration gather on my fingertips. 'What are you doing here?'

'I have come to collect.'

'Collect?'

'I seem to remember we had an arrangement.' His accent is classic public school English – perfect yet cold.

I look at him blankly. His voice hardens. 'My daughter – you were to collect her.'

I feel as though some snippet of the conversation has passed me by.

'What do you mean? How could I collect Mickey?'

'Dear me, wrong answer.'

'No, listen! I can't remember. I don't know what happened.'

'Did you see my daughter?'

'I don't think so. I'm not sure.'

'My ex-wife is hiding her. Don't believe anything else.'

'Why would she do that?'

'Because she's a cruel heartless bitch, who enjoys turning the knife. It can feel like a jousting stick.'

The statement is delivered with a ferocity that lowers the temperature.

Regaining his calm, he tugs at the cuffs of his jacket. 'So I take it you didn't hand over the ransom.'

'What ransom? Who wanted the ransom?'

My hands are shaking. The uncertainty and frustration of the past few days condenses down to this moment. Aleksei *knows* what happened.

Tripping over the words, I plead with him to tell me. 'There was a shooting on the river. I can't remember what happened. I need you to help me understand.'

Aleksei smiles. I have seen the same indolent, foreknowing expression before. The silence grows too long. He doesn't believe me. Bringing a hand to his forehead, he grips the front of his skull as though trying to crush it. He's wearing a thumb ring – gold and very thick.

'Do you always forget your failures, Inspector?'

'On the contrary, they're normally the only ones I remember.'

'Somebody must take responsibility for this.'

'Yes, but first help me remember.'

He laughs wryly and points at me with his hand. His right index finger is aimed at my head and his gold thumb ring is like the hammer of a gun. Then he smoothly turns his hand and frames my face within a backwards L.

'I want my daughter or I want my diamonds. I hope that's clear. My father told me never to trust gypsies. Prove him wrong.'

Even after Aleksei has gone I can feel his presence. He's like a character from a Quentin Tarantino film with an aura of violence barely held in check. Although he hides behind his tailored suits and polished English accent, I know where he comes from. I knew kids just like him at school. I can even picture him in his cheap white shirt, clunking shoes and over-sized shorts, taking a beating at lunchtimes because of his strange name and his peasant-poor clothes and his strange accent.

I know this because I was just like him – an outsider – the son of a Romany, who went to school with *ankrusté* – small balls of dough flavoured with caraway and coriander – instead of sandwiches, wearing a painted badge on my blazer because we couldn't afford to buy a stitched one.

'Beauty cannot be eaten with a spoon,' my mother would tell me. I didn't understand what she meant then. It was just another one of her queer sayings like 'One behind cannot sit on two horses.'

I survived the beatings and the ridicule, just like Aleksei. Unlike him I didn't win a scholarship to Charterhouse, where he lost his Russian accent. None of his classmates were ever invited home and the food parcels his mother sent – with their chocolate dates, gingerbread and milk candy – were kept hidden. How do I know these things? I walked in his shoes.

Aleksei's father, Dmitri Kuznet, was a Russian émigré who started with a single flower barrow in Soho and cultivated a small empire of pitches around the West End. The turf war left three people dead and five unaccounted for.

On Valentine's Day in 1987 a flower seller in Covent Garden was nailed to his barrow, doused in petrol and set alight. We arrested Dmitri the following day. Aleksei watched from his upstairs bedroom as we led his father away. His mother wailed and screamed, waking half the neighbourhood.

Three weeks before the trial Aleksei left school and took over the family business alongside Sacha, his older brother. Within five years Kuznet Bros controlled every flower barrow in central London. Within a decade it held sway over the entire cut-flower industry in Britain with more influence over prices and availability than Mother Nature herself.

I don't believe the urban myths or bogeyman stories about Aleksei Kuznet but he still frightens me. His brutality and violence are by-products of his upbringing, an on-going act of defiance against the genetic hand that God dealt him.

We might have both started off the same, suffering the same taunts and humiliation, but I didn't let it lodge like a ball of phlegm in my throat and cut off oxygen to my brain.

Even his brother disappointed him. Perhaps Sacha was too Russian and not English enough. More likely Aleksei disapproved of his cocaine parties and glamour-model girlfriends. A teenage waitress was found floating face down in the swimming pool after one such party, with semen in her stomach and traces of heroin in her blood.

Sacha didn't face a jury of twelve. Only four men were needed. Dressed in balaclavas they broke into his house one night, smothered his wife and took Sacha away. Some say Aleksei had him strung up by his wrists and lowered into an acid bath. Others say he took off his head with a wood-splitting axe. For all anyone knows Sacha's still alive, living abroad under a different name.

For people like Aleksei there are only two proven categories of people in the world – not the rich and the poor or the good and the evil or the talkers and the doers. There are winners and losers. Heads or tails. His universal truth.

Under normal circumstances, better circumstances, I try not to dwell on the past. I don't want to envisage what might have happened to a child like Mickey Carlyle or to the other missing children in my life.

But ever since I woke up in hospital I can't stop myself going back there, filling in the missing hours with horrible scenarios. I see the Thames littered with corpses that bob along beneath the bridges and tumble in the wake of passing tourist boats. I see blood in the water and guns sinking into the silt.

I look at my watch. It's 5.00 a.m. That's when predators do their hunting and police come knocking. Human beings are more vulnerable at that hour. They wake and wonder, pulling the covers close around them.

Aleksei mentioned a ransom. Keebal mentioned diamonds. I must have been there – on the ransom drop. I wouldn't have gone ahead without proof of life. I must have been sure.

Against the quietness comes commotion – people running and shouting. I can hear a fire alarm.

Maggie appears in the door. 'There's been a gas leak. We're evacuating the hospital. I'll get a wheelchair – I don't know how many are left.'

'I can walk.'

She nods approval. 'We're taking the sickest patients first. Wait for me. I'll come back.'

In the same breath she has gone. Police and fire sirens wail against the glass. The sound is soon masked by gurneys rattling down the corridors and people shouting instructions.

After twenty minutes the noise level abates and the minutes stretch out. Maybe they've forgotten me. I once got left behind on a school field trip to Morecambe Bay. Someone decided to dare me to walk the eight miles across the mudflats from Arnside to Kents Bank. People drown out there all the time, getting lost in the fog and trapped by the incoming tides.

Of course, I wasn't foolish enough to take up the dare. I spent the afternoon in a café eating scones and clotted cream, while the rest of the class studied waders and wildfowl. I convinced everyone that I'd made it. I was fourteen at the time and it almost got me expelled from Cottesloe Park but for the rest of my schooldays I was famous.

My aluminium crutches are beside the door. Swinging my legs out of bed, I hop sideways until my fingers close around the handles and my upper arms slip into the plastic cuffs.

Leaving the room, I look down a long straight corridor to a set of doors and through the glass panels I see another corridor reaching deeper into the building. There is a faint smell of gas.

Following the exit signs I start walking towards the stairs, glancing into empty rooms with messed-up bedclothes. I pass an abandoned cleaner's trolley. Mops and brooms sprout from inside like seventies rock stars.

The stairs are in darkness. I look over the handrail, half expecting to see Maggie on her way up. Turning back I catch sight of something moving at the far end of the corridor, the way I've come. Maybe they're looking for me.

Retracing my steps, I push open closed doors with a raised crutch.

'Hello? Can you hear me?'

Behind green tinted Perspex I find an operating theatre with a blood-stained paper sheet crumpled on the operating table.

The nursing station is deserted. Files are open on the counter. A mug of coffee is growing cold.

I hear a low moan coming from behind a partition. Maggie is lying motionless on the floor with one leg twisted under her. Blood covers her mouth and nose, dripping on to the floor beneath her head.

I feel for a pulse. She's alive.

A muffled voice makes me turn. 'Hey, man, what you still doing here?'

A fireman in a full face mask appears in the doorway. The breathing apparatus makes him look almost alien but he's holding a spray can in his hand.

'She's hurt. Quick. Do something.'

He crouches next to Maggie, pressing his fingers against her neck. What did you do to her?'

'Nothing. I found her like this.'

I can just see his eyes behind the glass but he's looking at me warily. 'You shouldn't be here.'

'They left me behind.'

Glancing above my head, he stands suddenly and pushes past me. 'I'll get you a wheelchair.'

'I can walk.'

He doesn't seem to hear me. Less than a minute later he reappears through a set of swing doors.

'What about Maggie?'

'I'll come back for her.'

'But she's hurt . . .'

'She'll be fine.'

Nursing the aluminium crutch across my lap, I lower myself into the chair. He sets off at a jog down the corridor, turning right and then left towards the main lifts.

His overalls are freshly laundered and his heavy rubber boots slap on the hard polished floor. For some reason I can't hear the flow of oxygen into his mask.

'I can't smell gas any more,' I say.

He doesn't respond.

We turn into the main corridor. There are three lifts at the far end. The middle one is propped open by a yellow main-tenance sign. He picks up the pace and the wheelchair rattles and jumps over the linoleum.

'I didn't think it would be safe to use the lifts.'

He doesn't answer or slow down.

'Maybe we should take the stairs,' I repeat.

He accelerates, pushing me at sprinter's pace towards the open doors. The blackness of the shaft yawns like an open throat.

At the last possible moment I raise the aluminium crutches. They brace across the doors and I slam into them. Air is forced out of my lungs and I feel my ribs bend. Bouncing backwards, I twist sideways and roll away from the chair.

The fireman is doubled over where the handle of the wheel-chair has punched into his groin. I scramble up and pull his arm through the wheel of the chair. Spinning it a half-turn, I jam his wrist against the frame. Another quarter-turn will snap it like a pencil.

He is flailing now, trying to reach me with his other fist. I keep twisting away from him, with the chair between us.

'Who are you? Why are you doing this?'

Cursing and struggling, his mask is nearly off. Suddenly, he changes his point of attack and sinks his fist into my damaged leg, grinding his knuckles into the bandaged flesh. The pain is unbelievable and white spots dance in front of my eyes. I spin the wheelchair sideways, trying to escape. At that same moment I hear the crack of his wrist breaking. He groans.

Both of us are on the floor. He launches a kick at my chest, sending me backwards. My head slams against the wall. Up on his knees, he grips me by the back of my shirt with his good hand and tries to drag me towards the lift shaft. I kick at the floor with my one good leg and wrap my fingers around the harness on his jacket. I'm not letting go.

Exhaustion is slowing us down. He wants to kill me. I want to survive. He has strength and stamina. I have fear and bloody-mindedness.

'Listen, Tarzan, this isn't working,' I say, sucking in air between each word. 'The only way I'm going down that hole is if you go with me.'

'Go to hell! You broke my fucking wrist!'

'And someone shot me in the leg. You see me crying?'

Somewhere below us an engine grinds into motion. The lifts are moving. He glances up at the numbers above the door. Scrambling to his feet, he stumbles down the corridor, carrying his busted wrist as though it's already in a sling. He is going to escape down the stairs. There is nothing I can do.

Reaching for my shirt pocket I feel for the small yellow tablet. My fingers are too large for such a delicate task. I have it now, squeezed between my thumb and forefinger . . . now it's on my tongue.

The adrenalin leaks away and my eyelids flutter like moths' wings on wet glass. Someone wants me dead. Isn't that strange?

I listen to the lifts rise and the murmur of voices. Pointing down the corridor, I mumble, 'Help Maggie.'

6

There are police patrolling the corridors, interviewing staff and taking photographs. I can hear Campbell berating some poor doctor about hampering a police investigation. He makes it sound like a hanging offence.

The morphine is wearing off and I'm shaking. Why would someone want to kill me? Maybe I witnessed a murder on the river. Maybe I shot someone. I don't remember.

Campbell opens the door and I get a sense of *déjà vu* – not about the place but the conversation that's coming. He takes a seat and gives me one of his ultra-mild smiles. Before he can speak I ask about Maggie.

'She's in a room downstairs. Someone gave her a broken nose and two black eyes. Was it you?'

'No.'

He nods. 'Yeah, that's what she said. You want to tell me what happened?'

I go through the whole story – telling him about 'Fireman Sam' and the wheelchair sprint down the corridor. He seems happy enough with the details.

'What did the cameras pick up?'

'Sod all. He blacked out the lenses with spray paint. We got one image from the nursing station but no face behind the mask. You didn't recognise him?'

'No.'

He looks disgusted.

'I'm convinced this has something to do with Mickey Carlyle,' I tell him. 'Someone sent a ransom demand. I think that's why I was on the river . . .'

'Mickey Carlyle is dead.'

'But what if we got it wrong?'

'Bullshit! We got it right.'

'There must have been proof of life.'

Campbell knows about this. He's known all along.

'IT'S A HOAX!' he rasps. 'Nobody believed any of it except you and Mrs Carlyle. A grieving mother I can understand – but you!' His fingers curl and uncurl. 'You were the officer in charge of a successful murder prosecution yet you chose to believe a hoax that cast doubt on the outcome. First you ordered a DNA test, and then you went off half-cocked like some maverick Hollywood vigilante and got yourself shot.'

Campbell is close now. I can see the dandruff in his eyebrows. 'Howard Wavell murdered Mickey Carlyle. And if that sick, perverted, murdering son of a bitch walks free because of you, there won't be a police officer in the Met who will ever work with you again. You're finished.'

A deep continuous vibration has built up inside me, like the sound of a ship's engine deep within a hull.

'We *have* to investigate. People died on that boat.'

'Yeah! For all I know, you shot them!'

My resolve is disintegrating. I don't know enough details to argue with him. Whatever happened on the river was my fault. I stirred up something poisonous and nobody wants to help me.

Campbell is still talking. 'I don't know what you did, Vincent, but you made some serious enemies. Stay away from Rachel

Carlyle. Stay away from this. If you jeopardise Wavell's conviction – if I hear so much as a mouse fart from you – your career is finished. That's a cast-iron fucking guarantee.'

He's gone then, storming down the corridor. How long was I unconscious, eight days or eight years? Long enough for the world to change.

The Professor arrives, his cheeks red from the cold. He hovers in the doorway as though waiting for an invitation. Behind him I see Ali sitting on a chair. She is now officially my shadow.

There are metal detectors being installed in the lobby and my medical personnel are being screened. Maggie isn't among them. I am responsible.

Although I've been over it a dozen times with detectives, I don't mind talking to Joe about the attack because he asks different questions. He wants to know what I heard and smelled. Was the guy breathing heavily? Did he sound scared?

I take him on a guided tour, showing him where the fight took place. Ali stays two paces away from me, scanning the corridors and rooms.

Leaning on my crutches, I watch Joe do his mad professor routine, pacing out distances, crouching on the floor and studying angles.

'Tell me about the gas leak.'

'One of the delivery drivers noticed the smell first but they couldn't find the source. Someone opened up a valve on one of the feeder pipes from the gas tanks near the loading docks.'

Joe kicks at the ground as though trying to make it even. I can almost see his mind moving forwards and backwards as he tries to reconstruct what happened.

Out loud now, he says, 'He knew his way around the hospital but he didn't know which room you were in. Once he evacuated the floors there was nobody to ask.'

Joe turns and strides down the corridor. I struggle to keep up without overbalancing. He stops beneath a CCTV camera and reaches towards it as if holding a spray can. 'He must have been about six two.'

'Yeah.'

He continues to the nursing station, eyes darting over the long narrow counter and kitchenette. There are clipboards hanging on a wall. Each one corresponds to a patient.

'Where did you find Maggie?'

'On the floor.'

Joe drops to his knees and then lies down, with his head towards the sink.

'No, she was lying this way, with her head almost under the desk.'

Jumping to his feet, he stands facing the clipboards and half-closes his eyes. 'He was looking at the clipboards to find your room number.'

'How do you know?'

Joe crouches and I follow his outstretched finger. There are two black smudges on the skirting board made by the heels of the fireman's boots.

'Maggie came up the corridor. She was coming back to get you. He heard her coming and he stepped back to hide . . .'

I can picture Maggie bustling up the corridor, admonishing herself for being late.

' . . . As she passed the doorway, she turned her head. He struck her with his elbow across the bridge of her nose.' Joe tumbles to the floor and lies where she fell. 'Then he went to your room but you had already gone.'

All this sounds reasonable.

'There is something I don't understand. He could have killed me right away, here in the corridor, but he collected a wheel-chair and tried to push me down the lift shaft.'

Still lying on the floor, Joe points past my shoulder at the CCTV camera. 'It's the only one he didn't black out.'

'It didn't matter, he wore a mask.'

'Psychologically it made a big difference. Even with his face

65

hidden, he didn't want to star in a home movie. The footage was evidence against him.'

'So he took me out of view.'

'Yes.'

Joe is thinking out loud now, unaware of his twitches and trembles. I follow him down the corridor to the stairs. He pauses, puzzled by something.

'The gas leak was part of both plans,' he announces.

'Both plans?'

'One for outside and one for inside . . .'

I don't understand. Joe seems to have forgotten I'm even here. He climbs two flights of stairs until he reaches a heavy fire door. Pushing it open we emerge on to a barren rectangle of bitumen, the rooftop of the hospital. A gust of wind slaps me in the face and Joe grabs my shirt front to steady me. A big-bellied grey sky hangs overhead.

Circular ducts and metal air-conditioning plants punctuate the bitumen. A low brick wall with white capping stones marks the outside edge of the building. A wire security fence is attached, curling inwards before being topped with barbed wire.

Joe slowly walks the perimeter, occasionally glancing at surrounding buildings as though adjusting his internal compass. When he reaches the north-east corner of the building, he leans close to the fence. 'You see that park down there – the one with the fountain?' I follow his gaze. 'That's the evacuation meeting point. Everyone was supposed to meet there when they emptied the hospital. You were supposed to be with them. There is no way they could have known you were going to be left inside.'

We are both on the same page now. 'Perhaps he was supposed to hide in my room and kill me when I came back.'

'Or they were going to kill you outside.'

Joe drops on to his haunches, studying the thin layer of soot on the capping stones. It's the same black film that settles on everything in London until the next shower. Three penny-sized circles smudge the surface. Joe swings his eyes to the ground where two larger smudges appear beneath the wall.

Someone knelt here and rested a tripod on the wall – a lone sniper with a finger on the trigger and his eyelashes brushing the lens, studying the park below. The hair on my forearms is standing on end.

Fifteen minutes later the rooftop has been sealed off and a SOCO team is at work, searching for clues. Campbell is smarting about being shown up by a clinical psychologist.

Joe takes me downstairs to the canteen – one of those sterile food halls with tiles on the floor and stainless steel counters. Cedric, the guy in charge, is a Jamaican with impossibly tight curls and a laugh that sounds like someone cracking nuts with a brick.

He brings us coffee and pulls a half-bottle of Scotch from the pocket of his apron. He pours me a slug. Joe doesn't seem to notice. He's too busy trying to fill in the missing pieces.

'Snipers have very little emotional investment in their victims. It's like playing a computer game.'

'So he could be young?'

'And isolated.'

True to form, the Professor is more interested in why than who; he wants an explanation while I want a face for my empty picture frame, someone to catch and punish.

'Aleksei Kuznet visited me this morning. I think I know why I was in the river. I was following a ransom.'

Joe doesn't bat an eyelid.

'He wouldn't tell me the details, but there must have been proof of life. I must have believed Mickey was still alive.'

'Or wished it.'

I know what he's saying. He doesn't think I'm being rational.

'OK, let's ask ourselves some questions,' he says. 'If Mickey is alive, where has she been for the past three years?'

'I don't know.'

'And why would anyone wait three years to post a ransom demand?'

'Maybe they didn't kidnap her for ransom, not at first.'

'OK. If not for ransom, why?'

I'm struggling now. I don't know. 'Maybe they wanted to punish Aleksei.'

It doesn't sound convincing.

'It sounds like a hoax to me. Someone close to the family or to the original investigation knew enough to convince desperate people Mickey might still be alive.'

'And the shootings?'

'They had a falling out or someone got greedy.'

It sounds so much more rational than my theory.

Joe takes out his notebook and starts drawing lines on the page as if playing hangman.

'You grew up in Lancashire, didn't you?'

'What's that got to do with anything?'

'I'm just asking a question. Your stepfather was an RAF pilot in the war.'

'How do you know that?'

'I remember you telling me.'

'Bullshit!'

A ball of anger forms in my throat. 'You're just itching to get inside my head, aren't you? The Human Condition – isn't that what you call it? You got to watch out for that bastard.'

'Why do you keep dreaming about missing children?'

'Fuck you!'

'Maybe you feel guilty.'

I don't answer.

'Maybe you blocked it out.'

'I don't block things out.'

'Did you ever meet your real father?'

'You're going to have trouble asking questions with your jaw wired shut.'

68

'A lot of people don't know their fathers. You must wonder what he's like; whether you look like him or sound like him.'

'You're wrong. I don't care.'

'If you don't care, why won't you talk about it? You were probably a war baby – born just afterwards. A lot of fathers didn't come home. Others were stationed overseas. Children get lost . . .'

I hate that word 'lost'. My father didn't go missing. He isn't lying in some small part of France that will forever be England. I don't even know his name.

Joe is still waiting. He's sitting there, twirling his pen, waiting for Godot. I don't want to be psychoanalysed or have my past explored. I don't want to talk about my childhood.

I was fourteen years old the first time my mother sat down and told me about where I came from. She was drunk, of course, curled up on the end of my bed, wanting me to massage her feet. She told me the story of Germile Purrum, a gypsy girl, with a 'Z' tattooed on her left arm and a black triangle sewn into her rags.

'We looked like bowling balls with sticky-out ears and frightened eyes,' she said, nursing a drink between her breasts.

The prettiest and the strongest gypsy girls were sent to the homes of the officers in the SS. The next group were used in camp brothels, gang-raped to break them in and often sterilised because the Roma were considered unclean.

My mother was fifteen when she arrived at Ravensbrück, the largest concentration camp for women in the Reich. She was put to work in the camp brothel, working twelve hours a day.

She didn't go into details but I know she remembered every one of them.

'I think I'm pregnant,' she slurred.

'Are you sure?'

'I haven't had my monthly days.'

'Have you been to see the doctor?'

She looked at me crossly. 'Esther tried to make me bleed.'

'Who is Esther?'

'A Jewish angel . . . but you clung to my insides. You didn't want to leave. You wanted so much to live.'

Daj was talking about *me*. I knew this part of the story. She was three months pregnant when the war ended. She spent another two months looking for her family, but they were all gone – her twin brothers, her mother, her father, aunts, uncles, cousins . . .

At a displaced persons camp near Frankfurt, a young British immigration officer called Vincent Smith told her she should emigrate. The United States and England were taking refugees if they had identity papers and skills. Germile had neither.

Because nobody would take a gypsy she lied on the application form and said she was Jewish. So many had perished it was easy to get identity papers in someone else's name. Germile Purrum became Sofia Eisner, aged nineteen instead of sixteen, a seamstress from Frankfurt – a new person for a new life.

I was born in a rain-swept English town in a county hospital that still had blackout curtains on the windows. She didn't let me die. She didn't say, 'Who needs another white-haired German bastard with cold blue eyes?' and even when I rejected her milk, puking it down her open blouse (another sign perhaps that I was more of him than her), she forgave me.

I don't know what she saw when she looked in my eyes: the enemy, perhaps, or the soldiers who raped her. I looked as though I owned the world, she said. As though everything in creation would be recast or rearranged to suit me.

I don't know who I am now. I am either a miracle of survival or an abomination. I'm part German, part gypsy, part English, one-third evil, one-third victim and the other third angry. My mother used to say I was a gentleman. No other language has such a word to describe a man. It's a paradox. You can't claim to be such a thing but you hope others see you that way.

I look up at Joe and blink away the past. I've been talking all this time.

His voice is softer than mine. 'You're not responsible for your father's sins.'

Yeah, right! I'm angry now. Why did he start me out on this? I don't want any of his airy-fairy, touchy-feely, Pollyanna-pass-the-tissues psychological crap.

We sit in silence. I'm through with talking. My nightmares march in jackboots and are best left alone.

Joe stands suddenly and begins to pack his briefcase. I don't want him to go now.

'Aren't we going to talk about the ransom?'

'You're tired. I'll come and see you tomorrow.'

'But I remembered some of the details.'

'That's good.'

'Isn't there something you can tell me; something I should be doing?'

He looks at me quizzically. 'You want some advice?'

'Yes.'

'Never go to a doctor whose office plants have died.'

Then he's gone.

7

When Mickey disappeared I didn't sleep for the first forty-eight hours. If a missing child isn't found within the first two days the chances of her being found alive diminish by 40 per cent. Within two weeks it is down to less than 10 per cent.

I hate statistics. I read somewhere that the average person uses 5.9 sheets of toilet tissue when they wipe their arse. It proves nothing and helps no one.

Here are some more figures. There were six hundred volunteers scouring the streets and eighty officers going door to door. The sense of urgency bordered on violence. I wanted to kick open doors, shake trees and chase every child from the parks and pavements.

We checked alibis, stopped motorists, interviewed tradesmen and tracked down visitors to Dolphin Mansions in the previous month. Every resident was interviewed. I knew which of them beat his spouse, slept with prostitutes, lied about sickies, owed money to bookies and cultivated marijuana in a box under her bed.

There had been sixty-five unconfirmed sightings of Mickey and four confessions (including someone claiming to have sacrificed her to the pagan god of the forest). We had also been offered the services of twelve psychics, two palm readers and a guy calling himself the Wizard of Little Milton.

The closest we came to a confirmed sighting was by an elderly couple at Leicester Square tube station on Wednesday evening. Mrs Esmerelda Bird wasn't wearing her glasses and her husband Brian didn't get close enough to see the girl clearly. There were twelve CCTV cameras at the station but the angles were wrong and the footage such poor quality it resolved nothing and risked derailing the entire investigation if we made it public.

Already the search had become a media event. TV vans blocked Randolph Avenue, beaming pictures to boxes within boxes, so that people who had never met Mickey could look up from their breakfast cereal and fleetingly adopt her.

Purple ribbons were tied to the railings outside Dolphin Mansions. Some were threaded with flowers and photographs of Mickey. There were pictures of her displayed on building sites, lamp-posts and shop windows.

The sex offenders' register threw up 359 names for Greater London. Two dozen of them either lived in or had some link to the area. Every name was cross-checked; every detail compared and contrasted, looking for those ley lines of human connection that thread the world together.

Unfortunately, this took time and the tyranny of the clock was absolute. It ticked away with a mechanical heart. A minute doesn't become any longer just because a child is missing. It only feels that way.

After two days I went home for just long enough to shower and change my clothes. I found Daj snoring at the kitchen table with her head between her arms and a Siamese cat curled up on her lap. A glass of vodka was wedged between her fingers. Her first drink every day was always a revelation, she said, the juice of angels copulating in flight. Gin was too English and whisky too Scottish. Port made her teeth and gums go crimson. And when she vomited it looked like black-currants shat out by sparrows.

Daj had become more like a gypsy as she grew older (and drunker), reverting to type; wrapping herself in layers of the past like the layers of her petticoats. She drank to forget and to deaden the pain. She drank because her demons were thirsty.

I had to prise her fingers from the glass before I carried her to bed. The Siamese slid off her lap and settled like liquid filling a puddle. As I pulled the bedclothes over her, she opened her eyes.

'You'll find her won't you, Yanko?' she slurred. 'You'll find that little girl. I know what it's like to lose someone.'

'I'll do the best I can.'

'I can see *all* the lost children.'

'I can't bring them back, Daj.'

'Close your eyes and you'll see her.'

'Shush now. Go to sleep.'

'They never die,' she whispered, accepting my kiss on her cheek. A month later she went into the retirement home. She has never forgiven me for abandoning her but that's the least of my sins.

The hospital room is dark. The corridors are dark. The world outside is dark except for the streetlights, shining on parked cars that are covered in icy white fur.

Ali is asleep in a chair beside my bed. Her face is ashen with weariness and her body held stiffly. The only light is from the TV flickering in the corner.

Her eyes open.

'You should have gone home.'

She shrugs. 'They have cable here.'

I glance at the TV. They're showing an old black and white film – *Kind Hearts and Coronets* with Alec Guinness. The over-acting is more obvious with the sound turned down.

'I'm not obsessed, you know.'

'What do you mean, sir?'

'I'm not trying to bring Mickey Carlyle back from the dead.'

Ali brushes hair from her eyes. 'Why do you think she's alive?'

'I can't explain.'

She nods.

'You were sure about Howard once.'

'Never completely.' I wish I could explain but I know I'll sound paranoid. Sometimes I think there is only one person in the world I know didn't kidnap Mickey – and that's me. We conducted more than eight thousand interviews and took twelve hundred statements. It was one of the largest, most expensive abduction investigations in British policing history but still we couldn't find her.

Even now I still come across posters of Mickey stuck on lamp-posts and building sites. Nobody else seems to note her features or stare at her wistfully but I can't help it. Sometimes, in the dark hours, I even have conversations with her, which is strange because I never really talked to Claire, my own daughter, when she was Mickey's age. I had more in common with my son because we could talk about sport. What did I know about ballet and Barbie dolls?

I know more about Mickey than I did about Claire. I know she liked glitter nail polish, strawberry-flavoured lip gloss and MTV. She had a treasure box with polished pebbles, painted clay beads and a hair clip that she told everyone was decorated with diamonds rather than chips of glass.

She loved to sing and dance and her favourite driving song was 'Row, row, row your boat gently down the stream and if you see a crocodile don't forget to scream'. I used to sing the same song to Claire at bedtime and chase her giggling around the room until she dived under the covers.

Maybe this is guilt I'm feeling. It's something I know a lot about. I have lived with it, been married to it and watched it float beneath an ice-covered pond. Guilt I'm an expert at. There are other missing children in my life.

'Are you OK?' asks Ali, reaching over to rest her hand on the bed next to me.

'Just thinking.'

She puts an extra pillow behind my back and then turns away, bending over the sink and splashing water on her face. My eyes are now graded to the darkness.

'Are you happy?'

She casts her face back to me, surprised by the question.

'What do you mean?'

'Do you like working for the DPG? Is it what you wanted to do?'

'I wanted to be a detective. Now I chauffeur people around.'

'But you're going to sit your sergeant's exam.'

'They'll never put me in charge of an investigation.'

'Did you always want to be a police officer?'

She shakes her head. 'I wanted to be an athlete. I was going to be the first British-born Sikh sprinter to compete at the Olympics.'

'What happened?'

'I couldn't run fast enough.' She laughs and stretches her arms above her head until her joints crack. Then she looks at me sideways along her cheek. 'You're going to keep investigating this, aren't you, despite what the Chief Super says?'

'Yes.'

A streak of lightning breaks through the gloom outside the window. The flash is too far away for me to hear the thunder.

Ali clicks her tongue against the roof of her mouth. She's trying to make a decision. 'I'm owed a few weeks' long-service leave. Maybe I could help, sir.'

'No. Don't jeopardise your career.'

'What career?'

'Seriously, you don't owe me any favours.'

She glances at the TV. The grey square of light reflects in her eyes.

'You probably think this sounds pretty wet, sir, but I've always looked up to you. It's not easy being a woman in the Met but you never treated me any differently. You gave me a chance.'

'They should have promoted you.'

'That's not your fault. When you get out of here, maybe you should come and stay with me . . . in the spare room. I can keep you safe. I know you're going to say no, sir, because you think you don't need my help or you're worried about getting me in trouble, but don't just dismiss the idea. I think it's a good one.'

'Thank you,' I whisper.

'What did you say?'

'I said thank you.'

'Oh! Right. Jolly good.'

Ali wipes her hands on her jeans and looks relieved. Another streak of lightning paints the room white, taking a snapshot of the moment.

I tell her to go home and rest because in a few hours I'm leaving hospital. Despite Keebal's efforts, I'm not under arrest. The police are here to protect me, not hold me. I don't care what the doctors say or what Campbell Smith might do. I want to go home, collect my diary and find Rachel Carlyle.

From now on, I'm not going to rely on my memory coming back. It might never happen. Facts, not memories, solve cases. Facts not memories will tell me what happened to Mickey Carlyle. They say a bad cop can't sleep because his conscience won't let him and a good cop can't sleep because there's still a piece of the puzzle missing.

I don't think I'm a bad cop. Maybe I'll find that out too.

8

Dr Bennett is walking backwards down the corridor in his Cuban-heeled cowboy boots.

'You're not supposed to leave. This is madness. Think about your leg.'

'I feel fine.'

He puts his hand over the button for the lift. 'You're under police protection, you can't leave.'

I pretend to stumble and he reaches out to catch me. At the same moment I stab the walking stick against the down arrow. 'Sorry, Doc, but I've arranged my own protection.' I motion to Ali, who's carrying my belongings in a plastic bag. That's all I want to take out of here.

For the first time since the shooting I feel like my old self. I'm a detective not a victim. Members of staff begin appearing in the corridor. Word is spreading. They've come to say goodbye. I shake hands and mumble 'thank you' while I wait for the lift to arrive.

The doors open and Maggie emerges. She looks like a jovial panda with black eyes and a bandaged nose. I don't know what to say to her.

'Were you going to leave without saying goodbye?'

'No.'

Ali produces a bunch of flowers and Maggie beams, throwing her arms around me, crushing the blooms against my chest. I've been a pain in the arse and managed to put her in a hospital bed but she still wants to hug me. I'll never understand women.

Downstairs, rocking on a walking stick, I cross the foyer. My leg is getting stronger and if I concentrate really hard I look like someone with a pebble in his shoe rather than a bullet wound. More nurses and doctors wish me good luck. I'm a celebrity – the detective who survived an assassination attempt. I want my fifteen minutes of fame to be over.

The place is crawling with police officers, guarding the entrances and rooftops. They're wearing black body armour and carrying automatic weapons. None of them knows what to do. They're supposed to be guarding me but now I'm leaving.

Ali leads the way, taking me through an exit door and down concrete stairs to the car park. As I cross towards her car, I notice John Keebal leaning against a concrete pillar. He doesn't approach. Instead he cracks a peanut and drops the shells into a neat pile at his feet.

Briefly leaving Ali, I walk over to him.

'Are you visiting a sick granny or waiting for me?'

'Thought I'd give you a ride home but I guess you're covered,' he replies, giving Ali the once over. 'Bit young for you, isn't she?'

'That'd be none of your business.'

We look at each other for a few moments and Keebal grins. I'm getting too old for these swinging dick contests.

'What exactly do you want?'

'I thought you might invite me back to your place.'

'Couldn't you get a warrant?'

'Seems not.'

79

What a nerve! He can't convince a judge to let him search my house and then expects me to say yes anyway. It's all part of building a case. If I say no, Keebal will say I'm being unco-operative. Fuck him!

'Listen, under normal circumstances, you know I'd happily let you come over. If I'd known I'd have cleaned up the place and bought a teacake but I haven't been home in a few weeks. Maybe some other time.'

I pivot on the walking stick and rejoin Ali.

She raises an eyebrow. 'I didn't know he was a friend of yours.'

'You know how it is – everyone is worried about me.'

I slip into the back seat of a black Audi. Ali takes the wheel and the car swings through bends and beneath a raised barrier before emerging into the sunshine. She doesn't say a word on the drive. Instead her eyes flick between her mirrors and the road ahead. She purposely drops her speed and acceler-ates, weaving between traffic, checking to see if we're being followed.

Ali rummages on the seat next to her and tosses me a bullet-proof vest. We argue over whether I'm going to wear it or not. I can see her losing patience with me.

'Sir, with all due respect, you either wear this vest or I will put a bullet in your other leg and drive you back to hospital.'

Looking at her eyes in the mirror, I don't doubt her for a second. There are too many women in my life and none of the fringe benefits.

We drive south through Kensington and Earl's Court, past the tourist hotels and fast-food joints. The playgrounds are dotted with mothers and toddlers playing on brightly coloured swings and slides.

Rainville Road runs alongside the Thames, opposite the Barn Elms Wildfowl Reserve. I like living by the river. Of a morning I can look of out my bedroom window at the expanse of sky and pretend I don't live in a city of seven million.

Ali parks at the front of the house, scanning the riverside footpath and the houses on the opposite side of the street. Out of the car, she moves quickly up the stairs, using my key to unlock the front door. Having searched the rooms, she comes back to me.

With her arm around my waist, I hobble inside. A mound of unopened letters, bills and junk mail has collected on the front mat. Ali scoops it all up in her arms. I haven't time to sort them out now. We have to leave quickly. Dumping the letters in a shopping bag, I walk through the house, trying to resurrect my memories.

I know this place by heart but there is nothing reassuring in the familiar. The dimensions seem the same, the colours and the furniture. The kitchen benches are clear except for three coffee mugs in the sink. I must have had company.

The kitchen table is littered with scraps of orange plastic, masking tape and squares of polystyrene foam cut with a serrated knife. I must have been wrapping something. Foam dust looks like fake snow on the floor.

My diary is beside the telephone – open at the day before I was shot – Tuesday 25 September. Tucked into the spine is an invoice for a classified advertisement in the *Sunday Times*. The text is in my handwriting:

Tuscan villa wanted: to sleep 6. Pool preferable. Patio. Garden. Short drive from Florence. Sept/Oct. Two-month booking.

I paid for the advertisement by credit card four days before the shooting. Why would I want to rent a Tuscan villa?

I don't recognise the mobile phone number printed at the bottom. Picking up the receiver, I punch the numbers. A metallic voice tells me the number is unavailable. I can leave a message. It beeps. I don't know what to say and I don't want to leave my name. It might not be safe.

I hang up and flick backwards through the diary, skimming

over final reminders for unpaid bills and dental appointments. There must be other clues. One name stands out – Rachel Carlyle. I met her six times in the ten days prior to the shooting. Hope rises in me like a wave.

Going further back through the pages, I look at the previous month. On the second Thursday in August I wrote a name: Sarah Jordan – the girl who waited on the front steps for Mickey to arrive. I don't remember meeting Sarah. How old would she be now – twelve, maybe thirteen?

Ali is upstairs trying to pack some clothes for me. 'Do you have any spare sheets?' she calls.

'Yeah. I'll get them.'

The linen cupboard is in the hallway near the laundry. I lean my walking stick against the door and reach up with both hands.

A sports bag is jammed at the back of the shelf. I pull it out and drop it to the floor until I find the sheets. Only then does it dawn on me. I stare down at the bag. I know there's a lot I have forgotten but I can't recall owning such a bag.

Easing myself on to one knee, I peel back the zipper. Inside there are four bright orange packages. My hands are steady as I tear open the tape and peel back the plastic. A second layer is underneath and inside there is a black velvet pouch. Diamonds spill out on to my hand, tumbling into the crevices between my fingers.

Ali is coming down the stairs. 'Did you find those sheets?'

There's no time to react. I look up at her, unable to explain. My voice sounds hoarse.

'Diamonds! It must be the ransom!'

Ali's hands are steady as she breaks ice from the freezer and drops it into my glass of whisky. She makes herself a cup of coffee and slides on to the bench seat opposite me, waiting for an explanation.

I don't have one. I feel as if I'm lost in a strange place,

surrounded by countries on the map I can't even name.

'They must be worth a fortune.'

'Two million pounds,' I whisper.

'How do you know that?'

'I have no idea. They belong to Aleksei Kuznet.'

Fear clouds her eyes like the onset of fever. She knows the stories. I can imagine them being told after lights out at probationer training.

Again I notice the scraps of plastic on the floor and dusting of foam. I wrapped the packages here; four identical bundles, each lined with polystyrene and wrapped in fluorescent plastic. They were meant to float.

Diamonds are easy to smuggle and hard to trace. They can't be picked up by sniffer dogs or tracked with serial numbers. Selling them isn't a problem. There are plenty of buyers in Antwerp or New York who deal in 'blood' diamonds from dubious places like Angola, Sierra Leone and the Congo.

Ali leans forward, resting her forearms on the table. 'What's the ransom doing here?'

'I don't know.' What was it that Aleksei said to me at the hospital: 'I want my daughter or I want my diamonds.'

'We have to hand them in,' insists Ali.

The trailing silence goes on too long.

'You can't be serious! You're not going to keep them?'

'Of course not.'

Ali is staring at me. I hate the way I look in her eyes – diminished, undermined. She turns her head away, as though she doesn't want to see the mess I've made of my life. Is this why Keebal wanted a search warrant and the 'fireman' tried to kill me?

The doorbell rings. Both of us jump.

Ali is on her feet. 'Quick! Hide them! Hide them!'

'Calm down, you get the door.'

There are certain rules in policing that I learned very early on. The first is never to search a dark warehouse with an armed cop whose nickname is 'Boom-Boom'. And the second is to take your own pulse first.

Using my forearm I scoop the bundles into the bag and notice beads of moisture left on the smooth surface of the table. The packages have been in water.

I hear Keebal's voice! He's standing in the front hall, silhouetted against the light. Ali turns back towards me, her eyes wide with alarm.

'I bought a cake,' he announces, holding up a shopping bag.

'You better come in then.'

With her back to him, Ali looks at me incredulously.

'Will you put the kettle on please, Ali,' I say, putting my hand on the small of her back and guiding her across to the sink.

'What are you doing?' she whispers, but I'm already turning back to Keebal.

'How do you take your tea?'

'Just a splash of milk.'

'We have none, I'm afraid.'

He holds up a carton of Long Life milk. 'I think of everything.'

Ali sets out the cups, keeping out of the way because her hands are shaking. Keebal finds a sports bag sitting on a chair.

'Just toss it on the floor,' I say.

He picks up the handles and swings the bag beneath his feet. Ali's hands are suspended over the teacups, frozen there.

'So what do you think happened, Ruiz? Even if you're telling the truth and you can't remember, you must have a theory.'

'Nothing as concrete as a theory.'

Keebal glances at his shoes, which are resting on the sports bag. He leans down and brushes a speck of dirt from one polished toe.

'You want my theory,' I say, attracting his attention. 'I think this has something to do with Mickey Carlyle.'

'She died three years ago.'

'We didn't find her body.'

'A man went to prison for her murder. That makes her dead. Case closed. You resurrect her and you better be God Almighty because otherwise you're in big trouble.'

'But what if Howard Wavell is innocent?'

Keebal laughs at me. 'Is that your theory! What do you want to do – set a paedophile free from jail? You sound like his defence lawyer. Remember what you're paid to do – protect and serve. You're doing just the opposite if you let Howard Wavell walk out of jail.'

A few token rays of sunshine have settled on the paving in the garden. We sit in silence for a while, finishing our tea and leaving the cake uneaten. Eventually, Keebal rises to his feet and puts the sports bag on the chair where he found it. He glances around the kitchen and then at the ceiling as if trying to penetrate the wood and plaster with X-ray vision.

'You think your memory is going to come back?' he asks.

'I'll keep you posted.'

'Do that.'

After he's gone Ali lowers her head on to the table in a mixture of relief and despair. She's scared, but not in a cowardly way. She doesn't understand what's happening.

I take the bag and drop it beside the front door.

'What are you doing?' she asks.

'We can't leave it here.'

'But it almost got you killed,' she says without flinching.

Right now I can't think of a better plan. I have to keep going. My only way out is to gather the pieces.

'What if you don't remember?' she whispers.

I don't answer. When I contemplate failure every scenario finishes with the same unpalatable truth. I put men in prison. I don't go there.

9

My clothes are in a suitcase in the boot of Ali's car along with the shopping bag full of the unopened mail. The diamonds are there too. I have never had two million pounds. I've never had a Ferrari either or a wife who could tie knots in cherry stalks with her tongue. Maybe I should be more impressed.

The Professor is right: I have to follow the trail – the invoices, phone calls and diary appointments. I have to retrace my steps until I find the ransom letters and the proof of life. I wouldn't have delivered a single stone without them.

Sarah Jordan lives around the corner from Dolphin Mansions. Her mother answers the door and remembers me. Behind her Mr Jordan is double-parked on the sofa with the *Racing Post* on his stomach and the TV blaring.

'Sarah won't be long,' she says. 'She's just gone to pick up a few things from the supermarket. Is everything all right?'

'Fine.'

'But you talked to Sarah a few weeks ago.'

'It's just a follow-up.'

The supermarket is only around the corner. I leave Ali at the house and go looking for Sarah, happy to stretch my legs.

The brightly lit aisles are stacked with cartons and half-empty boxes, creating an obstacle course for shopping trolleys.

On my second circuit, I see a young girl in a long coat lurking at the far end of the aisle. She glances in both directions and then stuffs chocolate bars into her pockets. Her right arm is pressed against her side, holding something else beneath her coat.

I recognise Sarah. She's taller, of course, having lost her puppy fat. A light-brown fringe falls across her forehead and her fine straight nose is dusted with freckles.

I glance up at the surveillance camera bolted to the ceiling. It is pointing down the aisle away from her. Sarah knows the blind spots.

Wrapping the coat around her, she walks towards the checkout and puts a box of breakfast cereal and a bag of marshmallows on the conveyor belt. Then she picks up a magazine and flicks through the pages, looking uninterested as the cashier deals with the customer ahead of her.

A young mother and toddler join the queue. Sarah looks up and notices me staring at her. Immediately she looks away and counts the loose change in her hand.

The store security guard, a Sikh wearing a bright blue turban, has been watching her through the window, hiding behind the posters for 'red spot' specials. He marches through the automatic doors with one hand on his hip as though reaching for a non-existent gun. The light behind him creates a halo around his turbaned head: The Sikh Terminator.

Sarah doesn't realise until he grabs hold of her arm and bends it behind her back. Two magazines tumble from beneath her coat. She twists from side to side and screams. Everything stops – the cashier chewing her pink bubble gum, a shelf stacker on a stepladder, the butcher slicing ham . . .

A frozen chicken korma is burning my fingers. I can't remember picking it out of the freezer. I push past the queue and hand it to the cashier. 'Sarah, I told you to wait for me.'

The security guard hesitates.

'I'm sorry about this. We didn't have a basket.' I reach into Sarah's pockets and take out the chocolate bars, placing them on the conveyor belt. Then I pick up the magazines from the floor and find a packet of biscuits tucked into the waistband of her jeans.

'She was trying to steal those,' protests the guard.

'She was holding them. Take your hands off her.'

'And who the fuck are you?'

My badge flips open. 'I'm the guy who's going to charge you with assault if you don't let her go.'

Sarah reaches inside her coat and takes a box of teabags from an inner pocket. Then she waits while the cashier scans each item and packs them into a plastic bag.

I take hold of the shopping and she follows me through the automatic doors. The manager intercepts us. 'She's not welcome here. I don't want her coming back.'

'She pays, she comes,' I say, as I pass him and walk into the bright sunshine.

For a fleeting moment I think Sarah might run but instead she turns and holds out her hand for her groceries.

'Not so fast.'

She shrugs off her overcoat revealing khaki jeans and a T-shirt.

'It's a bit of a giveaway.' I motion to the coat.

'Thanks for the advice.' Her voice is full of fake toughness.

'You want a cold drink?'

She baulks. She's waiting for a lecture on the evils of shoplifting.

I hold up the shopping bag. 'You want this stuff, you have a cold drink.'

We go to a juice bar on the corner and take a table outside. Sarah orders a banana smoothie before eyeing up the muffins. I get hungry watching her eat.

'I saw you a few weeks ago.'

She nods.

'What did we talk about?'

She gives me an odd look.

'I had an accident. I've forgotten a few things. I was hoping you could help me remember them.'

Sarah glances at my leg. 'You mean like amnesia?'

'Something like that.'

She takes another mouthful of muffin.

'Why did I come and see you?'

'You wanted to know if I ever cut Mickey's hair or counted the coins in her moneybox.'

'Did I say why?'

'No.'

'What else did we talk about?'

'I dunno. Stuff, I guess.'

Sarah glances down at her shoes, stubbing the toes against the legs of the chair. The sun is pitched high and sharp, like the last hurrah before winter.

'Do you ever think about Mickey?' I ask.

'Sometimes.'

'So do I. I guess you have lots of new friends now.'

'Yeah, some, but Mickey was different. She was like an . . . a . . . a . . . appendix.'

'You mean appendage.'

'Yeah – like a heart.'

'That's not really an appendage.'

'OK, like an arm; real important.' She drains her smoothie. 'You ever see Mrs Carlyle?'

Sarah runs her fingers around the rim of her glass, collecting froth. 'She still lives in the same place. My mum says it'd give her the creeps living where someone got killed but I reckon Mrs Carlyle stays for a reason.'

'Why's that?'

'She's waiting for Mickey. I'm not saying that Mickey is gonna come home, you know. I just figure Mrs Carlyle wants to know where she is. That's why she goes to prison every month and visits him.'

'Visits who?'

'Mr Wavell.'

'She visits him!'

'Every month. My mum says there's something sick about that. Gives her the creeps.'

Sarah reaches across the table and turns my wrist so she can read the time. 'I'm in heaps of trouble. Can I have my stuff now?'

I hand her the plastic shopping bag and a ten quid note. 'If I catch you shoplifting again, I'll make you mop supermarket floors for a month.'

She rolls her eyes and is gone, pedalling furiously on her pushbike, carrying her coat, the bag of groceries and my frozen chicken korma.

The idea of Rachel Carlyle visiting Howard Wavell in prison sends chills through me. A grooming paedophile and a grieving parent – it's wrong, it's sick, but I know what she's doing. Rachel wants to find Mickey. She wants to bring her home.

I remember something she said to me a long while ago. Her fingers were tumbling over and over in her lap as she described a little routine she had with Mickey. 'Even to the post office,' they would say to each other, as they said goodbye and hugged.

'Sometimes people don't come back,' said Rachel. 'That's why you should always make your goodbyes count.'

She was trying to hold on to every detail of Mickey – the clothes she wore, the games she played, the songs she sang; the way she frowned when she talked about something serious, or a hiccupping laugh made milk spurt out of her nose at the dinner table. She wanted to remember the thousands of tiny details and trivia that give light and shade to every life – even one as short as Mickey's.

Ali meets me at the juice bar and I tell her what Sarah said.

'You're going to go and see Howard, aren't you, sir?'

'Yes.'

'Could he have sent the ransom demand?'

'Not without help.'

I know what she's thinking, although she won't say anything. She agrees with Campbell. Every likely explanation has the word 'hoax' attached, including the one where Howard uses a ransom demand to win an appeal.

On the drive to Wormwood Scrubs prison we cross under the Westway into Scrubs Lane. Teenage girls are playing hockey on the playing fields, while teenage boys sit and watch, captivated by the blue pleated skirts that swirl and dip against muddy knees and moss-smooth thighs.

Wormwood Scrubs looks like a film set for a 1950s musical, where the filth and grime have been scrubbed off for the cameras. The twin towers are four storeys high and in the centre is a huge arched door impregnated with iron bolts.

I try to picture Rachel Carlyle arriving here to visit Howard. In my mind I see a black cab pull up in the forecourt and Rachel sliding out, never letting her knees separate. She walks carefully over the cobblestones, wary of turning her ankle. Glamour hasn't been bred into her, despite her family's money.

The visitors' centre is located to the right of the main gate in a set of temporary buildings. Wives and girlfriends have already started to gather, some with children who fidget and fight.

Once inside they are searched and asked for proof of identity. Their belongings are stored in lockers and gifts are vetted in advance. Anyone wearing clothes that too closely match the prison uniform is asked to change.

Ali gazes up at the Victorian façade and shivers.

'You ever been inside?'

'Once or twice,' she replies. 'They should tear the place down.'

'It's called a deterrent.'

'Works on me.'

Leaving her for a moment, I open the boot and retrieve the diamonds. I can fit two packages in the inside pockets of my overcoat and two more in the outer pockets. I put the coat on the seat beside her.

'I want you to stay with the car and look after the diamonds.'

She nods. 'You want to wear the vest?'

'I think I'm safe enough in prison.'

Crossing the road, I show my badge at the visitors' centre. Ten minutes later I climb two flights of stairs and emerge into a large room with a long continuous table divided down the centre by a partition. Visitors stay on one side and prisoners on the other. Knees can't touch or lips meet. Physical contact is restricted to holding hands or lifting young children over the divide.

Heavy boots echo in the corridors as the cons are brought in. Each visitor hands over a docket and has to wait until the prisoner is in place before being admitted.

I watch a young prisoner greet his wife or girlfriend. He kisses her hand and doesn't want to let it go. They both lean forward as though trying to breathe the same air. His hand reaches under the table.

Suddenly, the screws seize her chair and wrench it backwards. Falling to the floor, she shields her swollen belly. She's pregnant for Christ's sake. He only wants to feel his baby, but there's no sign of empathy from the screws.

'DI Ruiz, you can't stay away.'

The Governor appears beside me. Barrel-chested and balding, he's in his late forties. Finishing a sandwich, he dabs at his lips with a paper napkin, missing egg on his chin.

'So what brings you back?'

'It must be the ambience.'

He laughs roughly and glances through the Perspex screen at the reunions.

'How long since I was here last?'

'Don't you remember?'

'Old age; I'm getting forgetful.'

'About four weeks ago; you were interested in that woman who comes to see Wavell.'

'Mrs Carlyle.'

'Yeah. She's not here today. She comes every month and tries to bring the same gifts: kiddie catalogues. That sick fuck better not get an appeal!'

I try to picture Howard sitting opposite Rachel. Did she reach across the partition and take his hand? I even feel a pang of jealousy and imagine his eyes travelling down the V-neck of her blouse. We live in a sick sick world.

'I need to talk to him.'

'He's in segregation.'

'Why?'

The Governor picks at his fingernails. 'Like I told you before, nobody expected him to live this long. He killed Aleksei Kuznet's little girl! That's a death sentence whichever way you look at it.'

'But you've managed to protect him.'

He laughs wryly. 'You could say that. He was only here four days before someóne ran a razor blade across his throat. He spent the next month in hospital. Nobody's touched him since then so I figure Aleksei must want him alive. Howard doesn't care.'

'What do you mean?'

'Like I told you before, he keeps refusing to take his insulin. Twice in the last six months he's lapsed into a diabetic coma. If he can't be bothered why should Her Majesty, eh? I'd let the bastard die.'

The Governor senses I don't agree with him.

'Contrary to popular opinion, Inspector, I'm not here to play nursemaid to prisoners. I don't hold their hands and say, "You poor things, you had a lousy childhood or a crap lawyer or a hanging judge." A dog on a leash could do what I do.'

(With a lot more compassion no doubt.)

'I still need to see him.'

'He wasn't listed for visitors today.'

'But you can bring him up.'

The Governor grunts softly to a senior guard, who picks up a phone, setting the chain of command into motion. Somewhere deep in the intestines of this place someone will fetch Howard. I can picture him lying in a narrow cot, smelling the sourness of the air. The future is a scary business when you're a paedophile in prison. It's not next summer's holiday or a long weekend in the Lake District. The future stretches from when you wake up until you go to sleep again. Sixteen hours can seem like a lifetime.

Visiting time has almost ended. Howard pushes against the tide, walking as though his legs are shackled. He gazes around the room, looking for his visitor, perhaps expecting Rachel.

More than forty years on I can still recognise him as the fat kid from school, who changed behind a towel and chain-smoked on an asthma puffer. He was almost a semi-tragic figure but not quite so tragic as Rory McIntyre, a sleepwalker who did a high dive off the third-floor balcony in the early hours of Foundation Day. They say that sleepwalkers wake up in midair but Rory didn't make a sound. Nor did he make a splash. He always was a good diver.

Howard takes a seat and doesn't seem surprised by the sound of my voice. Instead he stops, arches his neck and swivels his head like an old tortoise. I step in front of him. He blinks at me slowly.

'Hello, Howard, I want to talk to you about Rachel Carlyle.'

He smiles little by little but doesn't answer. A scar runs from one side of his throat to the other, just beneath his chins.

'She comes to see you. Why?'

'You should ask her.'

'What do you talk about?'

He glances at the screws. 'I don't have to tell you anything. My appeal application is in five days.'

'You're not getting out of here, Howard. Nobody wants to set you free.'

Again he smiles. Certain people don't seem to match their voices. Howard's is like that. It is pitched too high, as though laced with helium, and his pale face seems disconnected from his body like a white balloon moving gently in a breeze.

'We can't all be perfect, Mr Ruiz. We make mistakes and we deal with the consequences. The difference between you and me is that I have my God. He will judge me and get me out of here. Do you ever wonder who is judging you?'

He seems confident. Why? Maybe he knows about the ransom demand. Any suggestion Mickey might still be alive would automatically grant him a retrial.

'Why does Mrs Carlyle come here?'

He raises his hands in mock surrender and lowers them again. 'She wants to know what I did with Mickey. She's worried I might die before telling anyone.'

'You're messing up your insulin injections.'

'Do you know what happens when someone goes into a diabetic coma? First my breathing becomes laboured. My mouth and tongue are parched. My blood pressure falls and my pulse accelerates. I get blurred vision, then pain in my eyes. Finally, I slip into unconsciousness. If they don't reach me quickly enough, my kidneys will fail completely and my brain will be permanently damaged. Soon after that I will die.'

He seems to revel in these details, as if looking forward to it.

'Did you tell her what happened to Mickey?'

'I told her the truth.'

'Tell me.'

'I told her that I'm not an innocent man but I am innocent of this crime. I have sinned but not committed *this* sin. I believe in the sanctity of human life. I believe all children

95

are gifts from God, born pure and innocent. They only act with hate and violence because we teach them hate and violence. They are the only ones who can truly judge me.'

'And how are the children going to judge you?'

He goes silent.

Sweat rings beneath his arms have spread out and merged, plastering his shirt to his skin so that I can see every freckle and mole. There's something else on his back, beneath the fabric. Something has discoloured the material, turning it yellow.

Howard has to look over his right shoulder to see me. He grimaces slightly. At that same moment, I force him forwards across the table. Deaf to his squeals that are muffled against my forearm, I lift his shirt. His flesh is like pulped melon. Angry weeping wounds crisscross his back, weeping blood and yellow crystalline scum.

Prison guards are running towards us. One of them puts a handkerchief over his mouth.

'Get a doctor,' I yell. 'Move!'

Commands are shouted and phone calls are made. Howard is screaming and thrashing like he's on fire. Suddenly, he lies still, with his arms stretched across the table.

'Who did this to you?'

He doesn't answer.

'Talk to me. Who did this?'

He mumbles something. I can't quite hear him. Leaning closer, I pick up the words, 'Suffer the little children to come unto me and forbid them not . . . never yield to temptation . . .'

There is something tucked inside the sleeve of his shirt. He doesn't stop me pulling it free. It's the wooden handle of a skipping rope, threaded with a twelve-inch strand of fencing wire. Self-flagellation, self-mutilation, fasting and flogging – can someone please explain them to me?

Howard shrugs my hand away and gets to his feet. He won't wait for a doctor and he doesn't want to talk any more. He shuffles towards the door, with his flapping shoes, yellow skin and shallow breathing. At the last possible moment he turns and I'm expecting one of those pleading, kicked dog looks.

Instead I get something different. This man who I helped lock away for murder; who flays himself with fencing wire, who every day is spat upon, jeered, threatened and abused . . . this man looks sorry for *me*.

Eighty-five steps and ninety-four hours – that's how long Mickey had been missing when I served a search warrant on No. 9 Dolphin Mansions.

'Surprise, surprise,' I said as Howard opened the door. His large eyes bulged slightly and his mouth opened but no sound came out. He was wearing a pyjama top, long shorts with an elasticated waist and dark-brown loafers that accentuated the whiteness of his shins.

I started like I always did – telling Howard how much I knew about him. He was single, never married. He grew up in Warrington, the youngest of seven children in a big loud Protestant family. Both his parents were dead. He had twenty-eight nieces and nephews and was godfather to eleven of them. In 1962 he was hospitalised after a traffic accident. A year later he suffered a nervous breakdown and became a voluntary patient at an outpatients' clinic in north London. He had worked as a storeman, a labourer, a painter and decorator, a van driver and now a gardener. He went to church three times a week, sang in the choir, read biographies, was allergic to strawberries and took photographs in his spare time.

I wanted Howard to feel like he was fifteen and I had just caught him wanking in the showers at Cottesloe Park. And no matter what excuses he offered, I'd know he was lying. Fear and uncertainty – the most powerful weapons in the known world.

'You left something out,' Howard mumbled.

'What's that?'

'I'm a diabetic. Insulin shots, the whole business.'

'My uncle had that.'

'Don't tell me – he gave up chocolate bars and started jogging and his diabetes went away. I hear that all the time. That and "Christ, I would just die if I had to stick a needle in myself every day." Or this is a good one, "You get that from being fat, don't you?"'

People were trooping past us, wearing overalls and gloves. Some carried metal boxes with photographic equipment and lights. Duckboards had been laid like stepping stones down the hall.

'What are you looking for?' he asked softly.

'Evidence. That's what detectives do. It's what we use to support a case. It turns hypothesis into theories and theories into cases.'

'I'm a case.'

'A work in progress.'

That was the truth of it. I couldn't say what I was looking for until I found it – clothing, fingerprints, binding material, videos, photographs; a seven-year-old girl with a lisp . . . any of the above.

'I want a lawyer.'

'Good. You can use my phone. Afterwards we'll go outside and hold a joint press conference on the front steps.'

'You can't take me out there.' The television cameras were lined up along the footpath like metal Triffids, waiting to lash out at anyone who left the building.

Howard sat down on the staircase, holding on to the banister for support.

'I can smell bleach.'

'I was cleaning.'

'My eyes are watering, Howard. What were you cleaning?'

'I spilt some chemicals in my dark room.'

There were scratches on his wrists. I pointed to them. 'How did you get those?'

98

'Two of Mrs Swingler's cats got loose in the garden. One of your officers left the door open. I helped her get them back.'

He listened to the sound of drawers being opened and furniture moved.

'Do you know the story of Adam and Eve, Howard? It was the most important moment in human history, the telling of the first lie. That's what separates us from the other animals. It has nothing to do with humans thinking on a higher plane or having easily available credit. We lie to each other. We deliberately mislead. I think you're a truthful person, Howard, but you're providing me with false information. A liar has a choice.'

'I'm telling you the truth.'

'Do you have any secrets?'

'No.'

'Did you and Mickey have a secret?'

He shook his head. 'Am I under arrest?'

'No. You're helping us with our inquiries. You're a very helpful man. I noticed that right from the beginning when you were taking photographs and printing flyers.'

'I was showing people what Mickey looked like.'

'There you go. Helpful. That's what you are.'

The search took three hours. Surfaces were dusted, carpets vacuumed, clothes brushed and sinks dismantled. Overseeing the operation was George Noonan, a veteran scene-of-crime investigator who is almost albino with his completely white hair and pale skin. Noonan seems to resent searches where he doesn't have a body to work with. For him death is always a bonus.

'You might want to see this,' he said.

I followed him down the hallway to the lounge. He had sealed off all sources of light by blacking out windows and using masking tape around the edges of the doors. He positioned me in front of the fireplace, closed the door and turned off the light.

Darkness. I couldn't even see my feet. Then I noticed a

small pattern of droplets, glowing blue green, on the carpet.

'They could be low-velocity bloodstains,' explained Noonan. 'The haemoglobin in blood reacts with the luminol, a chemical that I sprayed on the floor. Substances like household bleach can trigger the same reaction but I think this is blood.'

'You said low-velocity?'

'A slow bleeder – probably not a stab wound.'

The droplets were no bigger than breadcrumbs and stopped abruptly in a straight line.

'There used to be something here – possibly a carpet or a rug,' he explains.

'With more blood on it?'

'He may have tried to get rid of the evidence.'

'Or wrapped up a body. Is there enough to get DNA?'

'I believe so.'

My knee joints creaked as I stood. Noonan turned on the light.

'We found something else.' He held up a pair of child's bikini briefs sealed in a plastic evidence bag. 'There don't appear to be traces of blood or semen. I won't be sure until I get it back to the lab.'

Howard had waited on the stairs. I didn't ask him about the bloodstains or the underwear. Nor did I query the eighty-six thousand images of children on his computer hard drive or the six boxes of clothing catalogues – all featuring children – beneath his bed. The time for that would come later.

Howard's world had been turned upside down and emptied like the contents of a drawer yet he didn't even raise his head as the last officer left.

Emerging on to the front steps, I blinked into the sunshine and turned to the cameras. 'We have served a search warrant at this address. A man is helping us with our inquiries. He is not under arrest. I want you to respect his privacy and leave the residents of this building alone. Do not jeopardise this investigation.'

A barrage of questions came from beyond the cameras.

'Is Mickey Carlyle still alive?'

'Are you close to making an arrest?'

'Is it true you found photographs?'

Pushing through the scrum I walked to my car, refusing to answer any questions. At the last moment, I turned back and glanced up at Dolphin Mansions. Howard peered from the window. He didn't look at me. Instead he stared at the TV cameras and realised, with a growing sense of horror, that they weren't going to leave. They were waiting for *him*.

10

Emerging from the prison, I get a sudden, stultifying sense of *déjà vu*. A black BMW pulls up suddenly, the door opens and Aleksei Kuznet steps on to the footpath. His hair is dark and wet, clinging to his scalp as though glued there.

How did he know I was here?

A bodyguard appears behind him, the sort of paid thug who bulks up in prison weight rooms and settles arguments with a tyre iron. He has Slavic features and walks with his left arm swinging less freely than his right because of the gun beneath his armpit.

'DI Ruiz, are you visiting a friend?'

'I could ask you the same question.'

Ali is out of the car and running towards me. The Russian reaches inside his coat and for a moment I have visions of all hell breaking loose. Aleksei flashes a look and the situation defuses. Hands are withdrawn and coats are buttoned.

Ali's aggressive demeanour amuses Aleksei and he spends a moment examining her face and figure. Then he tells her to 'run along' because he doesn't need cookies today.

Ali glances at me, waiting for a signal. 'Stretch your legs. I won't be long.'

She doesn't go far, just to the other side of the square, where she turns and watches.

'Forgive me,' Aleksei says, 'I didn't mean to insult your young friend.'

'She's a police officer.'

'Really! They take all colours nowadays. Has your memory returned?'

'No.'

'How unfortunate.'

His eyes rove over mine with an aloof curiosity. He doesn't believe me. He glances around the square.

'Do you know that nowadays there is a digital shotgun microphone that can pick up a conversation in a park or a restaurant more than a thousand feet away?'

'The Met isn't that sophisticated.'

'Maybe not.'

'I'm not trying to trap you, Aleksei. Nobody is listening. I honestly can't remember what happened.'

'It is very simple – I gave you 965 one-carat or above, superior quality diamonds. You promised to pick up my daughter. I made myself perfectly clear – I don't pay for things twice.'

His phone is ringing. Reaching into his jacket, he pulls out a sleek mobile, smaller than a cigarette packet, and reads the text message.

'I am a gadget geek, Inspector,' he explains. 'Someone stole my phone recently. Of course, I reported it to the police. I also called the thief and told him what I would do to him.'

'Did he return your property?'

'It makes no difference. He was very apologetic when I saw him last. He couldn't actually tell me this in his own words. His vocal cords had burnt off. People should mark acid bottles more carefully.'

103

Aleksei's eyes ghost across the cobblestones. 'You took my diamonds. You were going to keep my investment safe.'

I think of my overcoat on the seat of Ali's car. If only he knew!

'Is Mickey still alive?'

'You tell me.'

'If there was a ransom demand, there must have been proof of life.'

'They sent strands of hair. You organised the DNA tests. The hair belonged to Mickey.'

'That doesn't prove she's alive. The hair could have come from a hairbrush or a pillow; it could have been collected three years ago. It could have been a hoax.'

'Yes, Inspector, but you *were* sure. You staked your life on it.'

I don't like the way he says 'life'. He makes it sound like a worthless wager. Panic spikes in my chest.

'Why did you believe me?'

He blinks at me coldly. 'Tell me what choice I had?'

Suddenly, I recognise his dilemma. Whether Mickey was alive or dead made no difference – Aleksei *had* to provide the ransom. It was about saving face and grasping at straws. Imagine a one in a thousand chance of getting her back. He couldn't ignore it. How would it look? What would people say? A father is supposed to cling to impossible dreams. He must keep his children safe and bring them home.

Maybe it's this knowledge but I feel a sudden rush of tenderness towards Aleksei. Almost as quickly I remember the attack at the hospital.

'Somebody tried to kill me yesterday.'

'Well, well.' He makes a little church with his fingers. 'Perhaps you took something from them.'

It's not an admission.

'We can discuss this.'

'Like gentlemen?' He's teasing me now. 'You have an accent.'

'No, I was born here.'

'Maybe so, but you still have an accent.'

He takes a paper tube of sugar from his pocket, biting off the end.

'My mother is German.'

He nods and pours the sugar on his tongue. '*Zigeunerin?*' It's the German word for gypsy. 'My father used to say gypsies were the eighth plague of Egypt. Forget about locusts.'

The insult is delivered without any sense of malice.

'Do you have children, Detective?'

'Twins.'

'How old are they?'

'Twenty-six.'

'You see much of them?'

'Not any more.'

'Maybe you forget how it feels. I am thirty-six now. I have done things I am not particularly proud of but I can live with that. I sleep like a baby. But let me tell you – I don't care how much someone has in the bank – until they have a child they have nothing of value. Nothing!'

He scratches at the scar on his cheek. 'My wife turned against me a long time ago but Michaela was always going to be half mine . . . half of me. She was going to grow up and make up her own mind. She was going to forgive me.'

'You think she's dead?'

'I let you convince me otherwise.'

'I must have had a good reason.'

'I hope so.'

He turns to leave.

'I'm not your enemy, Aleksei. I just want to find out what happened. What do you know about the sniper? Does he work for you?'

'Me?' He laughs.

'Where were you on the night of 24 September?'

'Don't you remember? I have an alibi. I was with you.'

He swivels and signals to the Russian who's been waiting like a dog tied to a post. I can't let him leave. He *has* to tell me about Rachel and the ransom demand. I grab his arm and twist it outwards until his back arches and he drops to his knees. My walking stick clatters to the footpath.

Pedestrians and prison visitors turn to watch. It strikes me how vaguely ridiculous I must look – making an arrest with a walking stick. Vanity still matters.

'You're under arrest for withholding information from a police investigation.'

'You're making a big mistake,' he hisses.

'Stay down!'

A shape materialises behind me and the warm metal of a gun brushes the base of my skull. It's the Russian, massive, filling the space like a statue. Suddenly, his attention shifts. Ali is standing with her feet apart in a half-crouch and her gun pointed at his chest.

Still holding Aleksei's arm, I put my face close to his ear.

'Is this what you want? Are we all going to shoot each other?'

'*Nyet!*' he says. The Russian takes a step back and slips the gun into its holster. He looks closely at Ali, memorising her face.

I'm already steering Aleksei towards the car. Ali walks backwards behind me, watching the Russian.

'Call Carlucci,' Aleksei yells. Carlucci is his lawyer.

Pushing his head down, he sits in the back seat. I slide alongside him. My overcoat is hanging over the seat in front of us. Ali hasn't said a word but I know her mind is working faster than ever.

'You're going to be sorry,' mutters Aleksei, peering past me out of the window. 'You said no police. We had a deal.'

'Help me then! Tell me! What happened that night?'

His tongue rolls around his mouth like he's sucking on the idea.

'Someone shot me. I suffered something called Transient Global Amnesia. I can't remember what happened.'

'Go to hell!'

Frank Carlucci is already at the Harrow Road Police Station when we arrive. Small, tanned and very Italian, his face is wrinkled like a walnut except for around his eyes. A surgeon has been at work.

He scuttles up the stairs beside me, demanding to speak with his client.

'You can wait your turn. He has to be processed.'

Ali has stayed in the car. I turn back towards her. 'Look after my coat.'

'What do you want me to do?'

'Find the Professor. Tell him I need him. Then look for Rachel. She must be somewhere.'

Ali's face is full of questions. She's not sure if I know what I'm doing. I try to muster a confident smile and turn back to Aleksei.

As we enter the charge room the place falls silent. I swear I can actually hear the indoor plants growing and ink drying on paper. That's how quiet things get. These people are my friends and colleagues. Now they avoid my eyes or ignore me completely. Maybe I died on the river and just don't realise it yet.

I leave Aleksei in an interview room with Carlucci. My heart is pounding and I want to pull myself together. First up I call Campbell. He's in a meeting at Scotland Yard so I leave a message on his voice mail. Twenty minutes later he comes storming through the front door looking for a cat to kick.

He finds me in the corridor.

'ARE YOU COMPLETELY INSANE?'

I put this down as a rhetorical question. 'Would you mind keeping your voice down?'

'What?'

'Please keep your voice down. I have a suspect in the inter-view room.'

Calmer this time, 'You arrested Aleksei Kuznet.'

'He knows about the ransom demand. He's withholding information.'

'I told you to stay away from this.'

'People were shot. Mickey Carlyle might still be alive!'

'I've heard enough of this. I want you back in hospital.'

'No, sir!'

He lets out a deep growl like a bear coming out of a cave. 'Surrender your badge, Detective. You're suspended!'

Along the corridor a door opens and Frank Carlucci emerges followed by Aleksei. Carlucci yells and points a finger at me. 'I want that officer charged.'

'Fuck you! You want a piece of me? Outside!'

It's like someone hits a panic button inside me and I'm consumed by a blood-red rage. Campbell has to hold me back. I'm fighting at his arms.

Aleksei turns slowly and smiles. His physical smoothness is remarkable.

'You have something of mine. It's like I said, I don't pay for things twice.'

11

I have been sitting in silence in an interview room, having finished my tea and eaten the ginger nut biscuits. The room smells of fear and loathing. Maybe it's me.

Given a choice, Campbell would have had me arrested. Instead he wants me taken back to hospital because he can't guarantee my safety. In reality, he wants me out of the way.

Almost instinctively my fingers find the morphine capsules. My leg is hurting again but maybe it's my pride. I don't want to think about anything for a while. I want to forget and float away. Amnesia isn't such a bad thing.

This is where I interviewed Howard Wavell for the first time. He had been holed up in his flat for three days with people buzzing on the intercom and the media camped outside. Most people would have disappeared by then – gone to stay with friends or family – but Howard wouldn't risk bringing the circus with him.

I remember him standing at the front counter, arguing with the desk sergeant. He rocked from one foot to the other, glancing over his shoulder. The short sleeves of his shirt stretched tight over his biceps and the buttons pulled across his stomach.

'They put dog shit through my letterbox,' he said, incredulously. 'And someone threw eggs at my windows. You have to stop them.'

The desk sergeant regarded him with an exhausted authority. 'Are you reporting a crime, sir?'

'I'm being threatened.'

'And who exactly is threatening you?'

'Vigilantes! Vandals!'

The sergeant pulled an incident pad from beneath the counter and slid it across the bench top. Then he took a cheap pen and placed it on the pad. 'Write it down.'

Howard looked almost relieved when I made an appearance.

'They attacked my flat.'

'I'm sorry. I'll send someone over to stand guard. Why don't you come and sit down.'

He followed me along the corridor to the interview room and I pulled his chair nearer to the air-conditioning unit, offering him a bottle of water.

'I'm glad you're here. We haven't really had a chance to catch up. It's been a long time.'

'I guess,' he said, sipping at the water.

Acting like we were old friends I started reminiscing about school and some of the teachers. With a little prompting, Howard added his own stories. There is a theory about interrogations that once suspects begin talking easily about any particular topic it is harder for them to stop talking about other topics that you raise or for them to suddenly start lying.

'So tell me, Howard, what do you think happened to Mickey Carlyle? You must have given it some thought. Everyone else seems to be trying to figure it out. Do you think she just walked out of the front door without anyone seeing her or was she abducted? Maybe you think aliens whisked her away. I've heard every bizarre theory you can imagine over the past seven days.'

Howard frowned and moistened his lips with the tip of his tongue. A pigeon landed on the ledge outside, beside the air conditioner. Howard gazed at the bird as though it might have brought him a message.

'At first I thought she might just be hiding, you know. She used to like hiding under the stairs and playing in the boiler room. That's what I thought last week but well, now, I don't know. Maybe she went to sell cookies or something.'

'There's a possibility I hadn't considered.'

'I didn't mean to sound flippant,' he said clumsily. 'That's how I first met her. She knocked on my door selling Girl Guide cookies – only she wasn't wearing a uniform and the cookies were home-made.'

'Did you buy any?'

'Nobody else was going to – they were burnt to a crisp.'

'So why did you?'

He shrugged. 'She showed a bit of initiative. I got nieces and nephews . . .' The statement tailed off.

'I thought you might have a sweet tooth. Sugar and spice and all things nice, eh?'

A pale wave of pink shaded his cheeks and his neck muscles tightened. He couldn't tell if I was insinuating something.

Changing focus, I took him back to the beginning, asking him to explain his movements in the hours before and after Mickey disappeared. His blinds had been drawn that Monday morning. None of his workmates saw him mowing the covered reservoir at Primrose Hill. At one o'clock the police searched his flat. He didn't go back to work. Instead he spent the afternoon outside, taking photographs.

'You didn't go to work on Tuesday morning?'

'No. I wanted to do something to help. I printed up a photograph of Mickey to put on a flyer.'

'In your darkroom?'

'Yes.'

'What did you do after that?'

'I did some washing.'

'This is Tuesday morning, right? Everyone else is out searching and you're doing your laundry.'

He nodded uncertainly.

'There used to be a rug on the floor in your sitting room.' I showed him a photograph – one of his own. 'Where is this rug now?'

'I threw it away.'

'Why?'

'It was dirty. I couldn't get it clean.'

'Why was it dirty?'

'I spilt some potting compost on it. I was making hanging baskets.'

'When did you throw it away?'

'I don't remember.'

'Was it after Mickey disappeared?'

'I think so. Maybe.'

'Where did you throw it?'

'In a skip off the Edgware Road.'

'You couldn't find one closer?'

'Skips get filled up.'

'But you work for the council. There must have been dozens of bins you could have used.'

'I . . . I didn't think . . .'

'You see how it looks, Howard. You cleaned up your flat, you took out the rug, the place smelled of bleach – it looks like you might be hiding something.'

'No, I just cleaned up a bit. I wanted the flat to look nice.'

'Nice?'

'Yeah.'

'Have you ever seen these before, Howard?' I held up a pair of girl's panties enclosed in a plastic evidence bag. 'They were found in your laundry bag.'

His voice tightened. 'They belong to one of my nieces. They stay with me all the time – my nieces and nephews . . .'

112

'Do they sleep over?'

'In my spare room.'

'Has Mickey Carlyle ever been in your spare room?'

'Yes. No. Maybe.'

'Do you know Mrs Carlyle very well?'

'Only to say hello when I see her on the stairs.'

'She a good mother?'

'I guess.'

'A good-looking woman.'

'She's not really my type.'

'Why's that?'

'She's kind of abrupt, you know, not very friendly. Don't tell her I said that; I don't want to hurt her feelings.'

'And you prefer?'

'Um, you know, it's not a sexual thing. I don't know really. Hard to say.'

'You got a girlfriend, Howard?'

'Not just now.'

He made it sound like he had one for breakfast with his coffee.

'Tell me about Danielle.'

'I don't know any Danielle.'

'You have photographs of a girl called Danielle – on your computer. She's wearing bikini bottoms.'

He blinked once, twice, three times. 'She's the daughter of a former girlfriend.'

'She's not wearing a top. How old is she?'

'Eleven.'

'There's another girl pictured with a towel over her head, lying on a bed. She's only wearing a pair of shorts. Who is she?'

He hesitated. 'Mickey and Sarah were playing a game. They were putting on a play. It was just a bit of fun.'

'Yeah, that's what I figured,' I smiled reassuringly.

Howard's hair was plastered to his head and every so often a drop of perspiration leaked into his eyes, making him blink.

Opening a large yellow envelope, I pulled out a bundle of photographs and started laying them out side by side, row after row. They were all shots of Mickey – two hundred and seventy of them – pictures of her sunbathing in the garden with Sarah, others of them playing under a sprinkler, eating ice creams and wrestling on his couch.

'They're just photographs,' he said defensively. 'She was very photogenic.'

'You said "was", Howard. Like you don't think she's still alive.'

'I didn't mean . . . you're . . . you're trying to make out I'm . . . I'm . . . a . . .'

'You take pictures, Howard, it's obvious. Some of these are very good. You're also in the church choir and you're an altar boy.'

'An altar server.'

'*And* you teach Sunday school.'

'I help out.'

'By taking kids away on day trips – to the beach or to the zoo?'

'Yes.'

I made him look closely at a photograph. 'She doesn't look very comfortable posing in a bikini, does she?' I put another photograph in front of him . . . then another.

'It was just a bit of fun.'

'Where did she get changed?'

'In the spare room.'

'Did you take photographs of her getting changed?'

'No.'

'Did Mickey ever stay overnight with you?'

'No.'

'Did you ever leave her alone in your flat?'

'No.'

'And you wouldn't take her outside without permission.'

'No.'

114

'You didn't take her to the zoo or for any day trips?'

He shook his head.

'That's good. I mean, it would have been negligent, wouldn't it, to leave such a young child alone or to let her play with photographic chemicals or with sharp implements?'

He nodded.

'And if she cut herself you might have to explain this to her mother. I'm sure Mrs Carlyle would understand. Accidents happen. Then again, you wouldn't want her getting angry and stopping Mickey from seeing you. So maybe you wouldn't tell her. Maybe you'd keep it a secret.'

'No, I'd tell her.'

'Of course you would. If Mickey cut herself, you'd have to tell her mother.'

'Yes.'

I picked up a blue folder and slid a sheet into view, running my finger down several paragraphs and then tapping it thoughtfully with my index finger.

'That's very good, Howard, but I'm puzzled. You see, we found traces of Mickey's blood on your sitting-room floor as well as in the bathroom and on one of your towels.'

Howard's jaw flapped up and down and his voice grew strident. 'You think I did something – but I didn't.'

'So tell me about the blood.'

'She cut her finger. She and Sarah were making a tin-can phone but one of the cans had a sharp edge. I should have checked it first. It wasn't a deep cut. I put a plaster on it. She was very brave. She didn't cry . . .'

'And did you tell her mother?'

He looked down at his hands. 'I told Mickey not to. I was scared Mrs Carlyle might stop her coming over if she thought I was negligent.'

'There was too much blood for a cut finger. You tried to clean it all up but the rug was too stained. That's why you threw it away.'

'No, not blood. Soil from the hanging baskets – I spilt some.'

'Soil?'

He nodded enthusiastically.

'You said you never took Mickey on an excursion. We found fibres from her clothes in your van.'

'No. No.'

I let the silence stretch out. Howard's eyes were filled with a mixture of fear and regret. Suddenly, he surprised me by speaking first. 'You remember Mrs Castle . . . from school? She used to take us for ballroom dancing lessons.'

I remembered her. She looked like Julie Andrews in *The Sound of Music* (after she left the convent) and featured in every fifth form boy's wet dreams except perhaps for Nigel Bryant and Richard Coyle who batted for the other side.

'What about her?'

'I once saw her in the shower.'

'Getaway!'

'No, it's true. She was using the dean's shower and old Archie the sports master sent me to pick up a starter's pistol from the staff quarters. She came out of the shower drying her hair and didn't see me until it was too late. She let me look. She stood there and let me watch her drying her breasts and pulling on her tights. Afterwards she made me promise not to tell anyone. I would have been the most famous kid at school. All I had to do was tell that story. I could have saved myself a dozen beatings and all those taunts and jibes. I could have been a legend.'

'So why didn't you?'

He looked at me sadly. 'I was in love with her. And it didn't matter that she wasn't in love with me. I loved her. It was *my* love story. I don't expect you to understand that but it's true. You don't have to be loved back. You can love anyway.'

'What does this have to do with Mickey?'

'I loved Mickey too. I would never have hurt her . . . not on purpose.'

116

His pale green eyes were filled with tears. When he couldn't blink them away he wiped them away with his hands. I felt sorry for him. I always did.

'It's important that you listen to me right now, Howard. I'll let you talk later.' I pulled my chair closer so that we were sitting knee to knee. 'You're a middle-aged guy, never married, living alone, spending all his spare time with children, taking pictures of them, giving them ice creams, taking them on outings . . .'

His cheeks darkened but his lips stayed white and narrow. 'I have nieces and nephews. I take pictures of them, too. There's nothing wrong with that.'

'And you collect kiddie clothing catalogues and magazines?'

'It's not against the law. They're not pornographic. I want to be a photographer, a children's photographer . . .'

Getting to my feet I moved behind him. 'Here's the thing I can't understand, Howard. What do you see in little girls? No hips, no breasts, no experience. They're straight up and down. I can understand the sugar and spice and all things nice stuff – girls smell nicer than boys – but Mickey had no curves. The adolescent good fairy hadn't sprinkled that magic dust in her eyes that makes their eyelids flutter and her body develop. What do you see in little girls?'

'They're innocent.'

'And you want to take that away from them?'

'No. Never.'

'You want to hold them . . . to touch them.'

'Not like that. Not in a dirty way.'

'Mickey must have laughed at you. The creepy old guy across the hall.'

Louder this time: 'I never touched her!'

'Do you remember *To Kill a Mockingbird*?'

He paused, looking at me curiously.

'Boo Radley was the scary guy with a disfigured face who lived over the road. All the kids were frightened of him. They

117

threw stones on his roof and dared each other to go into his yard. But in the end it's Boo Radley who saves Scout and Jem from the real villain. He becomes the hero. Is that what you were waiting for, Howard – to rescue Mickey?'

'You don't know me. You don't know anything about me.'

'Oh, yes I do. I know exactly what you are. There's a name for people like you: grooming paedophiles. You pick out your victims. You isolate them. You befriend their parents. You slowly work your way into their lives until they trust you . . .'

'No.'

'What did you do with Mickey?'

'Nothing. I didn't touch her.'

'But you wanted to.'

'I just took pictures. I would never hurt her.'

He was about to say something else but I raised my hand and stopped him.

'I know you're not the sort of guy who would have planned to hurt her, Howard. You're not like that. But sometimes accidents happen. They aren't planned. They get out of hand . . . you saw her that day.'

'No. I didn't touch her.'

'We found her fingerprints and fibres from her clothes.'

He kept shaking his head.

'They were in your van, Howard. They were in your bedroom.'

Reaching over his shoulder, I jabbed my finger at each of the different girls in his photographs.

'We're going to find your "models", Howard, this one and this one and this one. And we're going to ask these girls what you did to them. We're going to find out if you touched them and if you took any other sorts of photographs . . .'

My voice had grown low and harsh. I leaned against him, shoulder to shoulder, forcing him sideways off his chair. 'I'm not leaving you alone, Howard. We're in this together – like

118

Siamese twins, joined at the hip, but not up here,' I tapped my head. 'Help me understand.'

He turned slowly towards me, searching my eyes for sympathy. Then suddenly, he toppled backwards, scurrying to the corner of the room where he crouched, covering his head with his arms.

'DON'T HIT ME! DON'T HIT ME!' he screamed. 'I'll tell you what you want . . .'

'What are you doing?' I hissed.

'NOT MY FACE, DON'T HURT MY FACE.'

'Stand up! Cut this out!'

'PLEASE . . . NOT AGAIN . . . AAAARGH!'

I opened the door and called for two uniforms. They were already coming down the corridor.

'Pick him up. Make him sit in his chair.'

Howard went limp. It was like trying to pick up spilled jelly. Each time they tried to lift him on to a chair he slid to the floor, quivering and moaning. The uniforms looked at each other and back to me. I knew what they were thinking.

Finally we left him there, lying beneath the table. I turned back in the doorway. I wanted to say something. I wanted to tell him that it was just the beginning.

'You can't bully me,' he said softly. 'I'm an expert. I've been bullied all my life.'

Sitting in the same interview room, three years on, it's still not over. My mobile is ringing.

The Professor sounds relieved. 'Are you OK?'

'Yeah, but I need you to come and get me. They want to send me back to hospital.'

'Maybe it's a good idea.'

'Are you going to help me or not?'

Shifts are changing at the station. The evening crews are coming on watch. Campbell is somewhere upstairs, shuffling paper or whatever else justifies his salary. Slipping along the

119

corridor past the charge room, I reach a door to the rear car park. A blast of cold wind ushers me outside.

Gears on the electric gate grind into motion. Hiding in the shadows, I watch an ambulance pull through the opening. It's coming to pick me up. The gates are shutting again. At the last possible moment I step through the closing gap. Turning right, I follow the footpath and turn right twice more until I'm back on the Harrow Road. Slow lines of traffic puncture the darkness.

There's a pub called the Greyhound on the Harrow Road – a smoky, nicotine-stained place with a jukebox and a resident drunk in the corner. I take a table and a morphine capsule. By the time the Professor arrives I'm floating on a chemical cloud. The Greeks had a god called Morpheus – the god of dreams. Who said studying the classics was a waste of time?

Joe pokes his head through the door and looks around nervously. Maybe he's forgotten how authentic pubs used to look before the continental café culture turned them into white-tiled waiting rooms serving overpriced cooking lager.

'Have you taken something?'

'My leg was hurting.'

'How much are you taking?'

'Not enough.'

He waits for a better explanation.

'I started on about two hundred milligrams but lately I've been popping them like tic tacs. The pain won't go away. I function better if I don't have to think about the pain.'

'The pain?' He doesn't believe me. 'You're a mess! You're jumpy and anxious. You're not eating or sleeping.'

'I'm fine.'

'You need help.'

'No! I need to find Rachel Carlyle.'

The statement is harsh and abrupt. Joe swallows some uneasy thoughts and drops the subject. Instead, I tell him about visiting Howard and arresting Aleksei Kuznet. He looks at me in disbelief.

'He wouldn't tell me about the ransom.'

'What ransom?'

Joe doesn't know about the diamonds and I'm not going to tell him. It won't add to his understanding and I've already put Ali in danger. Nothing has become any clearer in the past few hours but at least I have a goal – to find Rachel.

'How did Aleksei find you?'

'I don't know. He didn't follow me from the hospital and nobody knew I was going to Wormwood Scrubs. Maybe someone called him from the prison.'

I close my eyes and replay events. I'm totally flying but can still think straight. Snatches of conversation drift back to me.

'God is going to set me free.' That's what Howard said.

If Howard sent the ransom demand why did he wait so long? He could have set up a hoax during his trial or at any stage since then. He would have needed help from the outside. Who?

The Home Office keeps a record of all visitors to Her Majesty's prisons. Howard's eldest sister visits him every few months, travelling down from Warrington and staying overnight at a local B&B. Apart from her there's only been Rachel.

In the first few months after his conviction he received bundles of fan mail. Many of the letters were from women who fell in love with his lonely countenance and his crime. One of them, Bettina Gallagher, a legal secretary from Cardiff, is a notorious pin-up among the lifers. She sends pornographic photographs of herself and has twice been engaged to death-row inmates in Alabama and Oklahoma.

Howard is allowed one free postage-paid letter a week but can buy more stationery and stamps from the prison shop. Each prisoner is also given a unique PIN number he must use when using the telephone. Paedophiles and child molesters can dial only approved numbers. Letters and calls are monitored.

These details rattle in the emptiness. I can't see Howard arranging a ransom drop – not from inside a prison cell.

'Give your eyes a chance,' my stepfather used to say when we were looking for newborn lambs on frosty nights. White on white is difficult to see. Sometimes you have to look past things before you really see them.

There used to be a really good comedian who called himself Nosmo King. I watched this guy for years and didn't realise where the name came from. NO SMOKING. Nosmo King. That's why you have to keep your eyes open. The answer can be right in front of you.

The Professor has opened his briefcase and pulled out a photograph album. The cover is frayed and silverfish have given it a mottled finish along the spine. I recognise it from somewhere.

'I went to see your mother,' he says.

'You did what!'

'I went to see her.'

My teeth are clenched. 'You had no right.'

Ignoring me, he runs his fingers over the album cover. Here it comes – the search backwards, the probing of my childhood, my family and my relationships. What does it prove? Nothing. How can another human being have any appreciation of my life and the things that shaped me?

'You don't want to talk about this.'

'No.'

'Why?'

'Because you're poking your nose into my business – you're screwing with my head.'

It takes me a moment to realise that I'm shouting at him. Thankfully, there's nobody around except the barman and the sleeping drunk.

'She doesn't seem very happy in the nursing home.'

'It's a fucking retirement village.'

He opens the album. The first photograph is of my step-father, John Francis Ruiz. A farmer's son from Lancashire, he's dressed in his RAF uniform, standing on the wing of a Lancaster bomber. His hair already receding, his high forehead makes his eyes seem bigger and more alive.

I remember that photograph. For twenty years it stood on the mantelpiece beside a Silver Jubilee picture frame and one of those tacky snowballs of St Paul's Cathedral.

John Ruiz went missing over Belgium on 15 July 1943, while on his way to bomb a bridge in Ghent. The Lancaster was hit by German fighters and exploded in midair, dropping like a fiery comet.

'Missing in action. Presumed dead,' the telegram said. Only he wasn't dead. He survived a German POW camp and came home to discover that the 'future' he had fought so hard to protect had run off and married an American catering corps sergeant and moved to Texas. Nobody blamed her, least of all him.

And then he met Sofia Eisner (or Germile Purrum) a 'Jewish' seamstress, with a newborn son. She was striding down the hill from Golders Green, between two young friends, their arms locked together, laughing.

'Don't forget now,' shouted the eldest of them. 'We're going to meet the men we're going to marry tonight.'

At the cinema at the bottom of the hill they came across a group of young men waiting in the queue. One of them wore a single-breasted jacket with notched lapels and three buttons.

Germile whispered to her friends, 'Which one's mine?'

John Ruiz smiled at her. A year later they were married.

Joe turns another page of the album. The sepia images seem to have soaked into the paper. There is a photograph of the farm – a ploughman's cottage with small leadlight windows and doors so low my stepfather had to duck his head to get through them. My mother filled the rooms with bric-à-brac and souvenirs, managing to convince herself they were heirlooms of her vanished family.

Outside the ploughed fields were milk chocolate brown and smoke fluttered like a ragged white flag from the chimney. In late summer bales of hay were piled on the hillsides forming mini-castles.

I can still smell the mornings sometimes – the burnt toast, strong tea and the talcum powder my stepfather sprinkled between his toes before pulling on his socks. As he closed the door the dogs barking excitedly, dancing around his feet.

I learned all about life and death on the farm. I snipped the scrotums of newborn lambs and pulled out the testes with my teeth. I put my forearm deep in a mare, feeling for the dilation of the cervix. I killed calves for the butcher and buried dogs that were more like siblings than working animals.

There aren't any photographs of everyday workings on the farm. The album records only special occasions – weddings, births, christenings and anniversaries.

'Who's this?' Joe points to a picture of Luke, who is wearing a sailor's suit and sitting on the front stairs. His blond cowlick stands up like a flag fall on an old-fashioned taxicab meter.

The lump forming in my throat feels like a tumour. Covering my mouth with my fingers, I try to stop the alcohol and morphine from talking but words leak out through my open pores.

Luke was always small for his age but he compensated for it by being loud and annoying. Most of the time I was at boarding school so I only saw him during the holidays. Daj would tell me to keep an eye on him and at the same time she'd tell Luke to stop irritating me because he constantly wanted to play Old Maid and to look at my football cards.

In the depths of winter when it snowed I used to go tobogganing down the hill field, starting off near the front door and finishing at the pond. Luke was too young so he rode on a toboggan with me. Several hillocks along the way would throw us in the air and he squealed with laughter, clinging to my knees.

The track levelled off towards the end and a mesh fence sagged between posts, having been hit so many times by braced feet.

My stepfather had gone into town to get a thermostat for the boiler. Daj was trying to hand-dye my bedsheets a darker colour to hide the semen stains. I can't remember what I was doing. Isn't that strange? I can remember every other detail with the clarity of a home movie.

At bath time we noticed him missing. We used a spotlight, powered by the tractor engine, to search the pond but the hole in the ice had closed over.

I lay awake that night, trying to will Luke into being. I wanted him to be lying in his bed, snuffling in his sleep and twitching like a dog dreaming of fleas.

They found him in the morning beneath the ice. His face was blue, his lips bluer. He was wearing hand-me-down trousers and hand-me-down shoes.

I watched from my bedroom window as they laid him on a sheet and tucked another beneath his chin. The ambulance had mud-streaked arches and open doors. As they lifted the stretcher I went flying out of the front door, screaming at them to leave my brother alone. My stepfather caught me at the gate. He picked me up and hugged me so hard I could barely breathe. His face was grey and prickly. His eyes were blurred with tears.

'He's gone, Vince.'
'I want him back.'
'We've lost him.'
'Let me see.'
'Go back inside.'
'Let me see.'
His chin was pressing into my hair. Daj had fallen to her

knees beside Luke. She screamed and rocked back and forth, rubbing her fingers through his hair and kissing his closed lids.

She would hate me now. I knew that. She would hate me for ever. It was my fault. I should have been looking after him. I should have helped him count his football cards and played his childish games. Nobody ever blamed me; nobody except me. I knew the truth. It had been my fault. I was responsible.

'We lost him,' my stepfather had said.

Lost? You lose something down the back of the sofa or through a hole in your pocket; you lose your train of thought or you lose track of time. You don't lose a child.

I wipe the wetness from my eyes and look at the Professor. I've been talking all this time. Why did he start me on this? What does he know about guilt? He doesn't have to look at it every day in the mirror or scrape whiskers off its soapy skin or see it reflected in his mother's eyes. I turned Daj into an alcoholic. She drank with the ghosts of her dead family and her dead son. She drank until her hands shook and her world smeared like lipstick on the edge of a glass. Alcoholics don't have relationships – they take hostages.

'Please leave this alone,' I whisper, wanting him to stop.

Joe closes the photograph album. 'Your memory loss was the result of psychological trauma.'

'I was shot.'

'The scans showed no injuries or bruising or internal bleeding. You didn't get a bump on the head. You didn't lose particular memories; you blocked them out. I want to know why.'

'Luke died more than forty years ago.'

'But you think about him every day. You still wonder if you could have saved him just like you wonder if you could have saved Mickey.'

I don't answer. I want him to stop talking.

'It's like having a film inside your head, isn't it, eh? Playing on a continuous loop, over and over . . .'

'That's enough.'

'. . . You want to be riding down the icy hill with Luke sitting between your knees. You want to hold on tightly to him and drive your boots into the snow, making sure the toboggan stops in time . . .'

'Shut up! Just shut the fuck up!'

On my feet now, I'm standing over him. My finger is pointed between his eyes. The barman reaches behind the counter for a phone or a metal pipe.

Joe hasn't moved. Christ, he's cool. I can see my reflection – desolate and hollow – mirrored in his eyes. The anger leaks away. My mobile is rattling on the table.

'Are you OK?' asks Ali. 'I heard about what happened at the station.'

Bile blocks my throat. I finally get the words out. 'Have you found Rachel?'

'No, but I think I've found her car.'

'Where?'

'Someone reported it abandoned. It was towed away from Haverstock Hill about a fortnight ago. Now it's at a car pound in Regis Road. You want me to check it out?'

'No, I'll go.'

I look at my watch. It's nearly six. Car pounds stay open all night. It's not about the revenue, of course, it's about keeping the city moving. If you believe that I could sell you the Tower of London.

Finishing my beer, I grab my things. The Professor looks ready to wave me off.

'You're coming too,' I tell him. 'You can drive, just keep your mouth shut.'

12

Camden Car Pound looks like a World War II prison camp with razor wire on the fences and spotlights around the perimeter. It even has a wooden hut where a lone security guard has his polished boots propped on a desk with a small TV perched between his knees.

I hammer on the window and his head snaps around. Swinging his feet to the floor, he hoists his trousers. He has a baby face and spiked hair. A nightstick in a leather pouch sways on his belt.

'My name is Detective Inspector Ruiz. You have a vehicle here that was towed from a street on Haverstock Hill two weeks ago.'

His eyes flick up and down, sizing me up. 'You here to collect it?'

'No. I'm here to inspect it.'

He glances at the Professor, wondering why his left arm is trembling. What a pair we make – Hopalong Cassidy and Peg-Leg Pete.

'Nobody told me you was coming. I should have been told. You gonna pay the towing fee?'

'We're not taking the vehicle. We're just looking at it.'

Something stirs behind him. An Alsatian uncurls and seems to self-inflate until it stands as high as the desk. The dog growls and the guard hisses a command.

'Don't mind him. He won't hurt you.'

'You'll make sure of it.'

There must be a hundred cars on the lot, each with a number and grid reference. It takes the guard several minutes to find the details of Rachel's Renault Estate.

The reference says the car was found in Lyndhurst Road with the keys in the ignition and the doors unlocked. Someone had stolen the stereo and one of the seats.

He directs us across the pound, which is divided into painted squares.

Rachel's car is beaded with rain and the internal light doesn't work when I open the door. I reach inside and trigger it automatically.

There is no front passenger seat. The space is empty except for a dark blanket bundled on the floor. Carefully lifting the blanket I find a bottle of water, chocolate bars and a hand-held periscope.

'Someone was meant to lie on the floor, out of sight,' says Joe.

'Rachel must have delivered the ransom. Someone went with her.'

We're both thinking the same thing – was it me? Campbell called me a vigilante. Aleksei said no police, which means there were no surveillance teams in cars, on motorbikes or in the air.

'If I were delivering a ransom, what would I make sure of?'

'Proof of life!' says Joe.

'Yes, but apart from that – when I was physically carrying the ransom, what would I be sure of?'

Joe shrugs. I answer for him. 'Back up. I would have wanted someone following me, at least from a distance. And I would have made sure they didn't lose me.'

'How?'

'A tracking device.' I would have put one in the car and another with the ransom.

The universe suddenly shrinks to one thought. That's how Aleksei found me at the prison. And that's why Keebal wanted to search the house. The diamonds are a tracking device.

Ali!

One ring, two rings, three rings . . .

'Pick up the phone. Pick it up now!' I wait several seconds. She's not answering.

I try her home number. Pick up the phone, Ali. Please.

'Hello.' (Thank God.)

'What did you do with my coat?'

'It's here.'

'Stay right there! Lock the door. Stay away from the windows.'

'What's wrong?'

'Please, Ali, just do as I say. There's a tracking device with the diamonds. That's how Aleksei found me.'

The traffic suddenly melts away. Joe has his foot down, weaving through backstreets, taking shortcuts across garage forecourts and parking lots. God knows where he learned to drive like this. He's either an expert or a complete amateur who's going to put us through a plate-glass window.

'What diamonds? What are you talking about?' he yells.

'Just shut up and drive.'

Ali is still on the phone.

'I might be wrong about the transmitter,' I tell her. 'Just relax.'

She's already ahead of me – ripping open the packages. I can hear her breaking open the blocks of foam. I know what she's going to find. Radio transmitters can weigh less than eighty grams and have a battery life of three maybe four weeks. My kitchen floor was dusted with polystyrene foam and scraps of plastic. I hollowed out the foam with a knife.

'I found it.'

'Disconnect the battery.'

Joe is yelling at me. 'You have Aleksei Kuznet's diamonds! Are you crazy?'

The car swerves suddenly into Albany Street and he brakes hard, pulling us around a line of traffic. He accelerates hard again and we leap over a speed bump.

Ali lives in a run-down, crumbling neighbourhood in Hackney, in a narrow street of soot-blackened warehouses and barred shop windows. She's still on the phone.

'Where are you now?'

'Close. Are the lights turned off?'

'Yes.'

In the background I hear a doorbell ringing.

'Are you expecting anyone?'

'No.'

'Don't answer it.'

Ten . . . twenty . . . thirty seconds pass. Then comes the sound of breaking glass.

'Someone just smashed a door panel,' says Ali, her voice thick with fear. The burglar alarm is sounding.

'Are you armed?'

'Yes.'

'Just give them the diamonds, Ali. Don't take any risks.'

'Yes, sir. I can't talk any more. Hurry!'

The phone goes dead.

The next few minutes are the longest I can remember. Joe has his foot hard on the floor, braking hard around the corners and running red lights. Weaving on to the wrong side of the road, he accelerates past three buses and forces on-coming cars off the road.

Wrenching the wheel, he puts us into a half-spin, sliding around a tight bend. I'm thrown against the door and the phone smacks my ear. I'm calling the police, telling them there's an officer in trouble.

'It's the next on the left . . . about halfway down.'

There are terraced houses on either side of the road. The streetlights have turned everything yellow, including the pebbledash façades and net curtains.

Ali's place is ahead of us. The burglar alarm is still ringing. The car brakes and I'm out of the door hobbling in a half-run towards the house. Joe is yelling at me to slow down.

The front door gapes darkly. Pressing my back to the outside wall, I glance inside. I can see the hallway and the stairs to the upper floor. Sliding sideways, I move inside, letting my eyes get used to the darkness.

I have visited Ali's house once before. It was years ago. We sat outside on her roof garden, drinking beer and resting our feet on a skylight. Everything was painted gold by the sunset and I remember thinking that maybe London *was* the new Babylon after all. The thought disappeared in the darkness.

There's a living room just off to the left and a dining room further along the hall. The kitchen is at the rear. I can see moonlight coming through the window and no sign of a tell-tale silhouette.

The shrill alarm is shredding my senses. Running my fingers along the wall, I search for the control panel. The alarm will be linked to the mains supply and have a back-up twelve volt battery with an anti-tamper switch.

Joe puts his hand on my shoulder and nearly gets flattened with a walking stick. Shouting to be heard, I tell him to go back outside, find the alarm bell and pull it off the wall.

'With what?'

'Use your imagination.'

He disappears and I search the kitchen and lounge. A street-light is shining outside and I can see Joe crossing the road with a tyre iron. Hoisting himself on to a brick wall, he takes a swing at the alarm bell. Twice more he tries and suddenly the alarm falls silent. The change is so dramatic that it feels like the air pressure has dropped.

Climbing the stairs, I step quietly on to the next landing. For all my opposition to firearms, I wish I had one now. My gun is somewhere at the bottom of the river or fenced on the black market.

Reaching the first door I pause and listen. I can only hear my heartbeat. Then, in the stillness, I pick up another sound, someone breathing. Pressing my ear against the door, I wait, trying to hear the sound again.

Weighing my walking stick, I reach for the handle and push it open. The darkness is more intense than the dimness behind me.

Here, too, I wait.

I hear metal shaking . . . springs. It's a tremble born of dependency rather than fear. Reaching forward, I flick the light switch. Ali is perched on her bed, her MP5 Carbine A2 pointing directly at my chest.

We gaze into each other's eyes. She blinks at me slowly and lets out a long slow breath. 'You were lucky I didn't shoot you.'

'I had it covered.'

Pulling open my shirt, I show her the bullet-proof vest.

The Professor slumps in a chair, his arms gripping the armrests. The last few minutes have drained his reserves. Ali pours him a glass of water. He takes it with his right hand – the steady one.

'Where did you learn to drive like that?'

'At Silverstone,' he replies. 'I won an advanced driving course at a school quiz night.'

'Michael Schumacher eat your heart out.'

Ali has barricaded the front door and is moving through the rooms, checking to see if anything is missing. Whoever broke in triggered the alarm and then fled.

'Did you see anyone?'

'No.'

'Where are the diamonds?'

Ali opens a drawer. 'I put them where a girl puts anything personal – with her underwear.'

Four velvet pouches are tucked inside. She opens one of them and diamonds spill through her fingers on to the duvet. Sometimes when you see an excess of something rare and beautiful it begins to pale. Diamonds are different. They always take your breath away.

I can hear police sirens approaching. Ali goes downstairs to meet them. I don't expect there'll be fingerprints or physical evidence left behind but we'll go through the motions of making statements and dusting for prints.

Joe still doesn't understand how the ransom finished up with Ali. I relate the whole story about the linen cupboard and the scraps of plastic on my kitchen floor.

I have to admire his sense of priorities. Instead of being frightened or angry, he sits on Ali's bed and studies the remnants of the packages, the dull orange plastic, white foam and electrical tape. The transmitter is the size of a matchbox with twin wires separated from a smaller battery unit.

'Why are they packed like this?'

'I think they were meant to float.'

'So you took the diamonds to the river.'

'I don't know. This type of transmitter sends out a signal every ten seconds and is picked up by a receiver. Unlike a satellite tracking device the transmitter has a limited range – about three miles in the city and six miles in the countryside.'

'How accurate is it?'

'Down to within fifty yards.'

If Rachel acted as the ransom courier and I went with her, I would have arranged for someone to follow us, tracking the signals. Aleksei had most to gain. They were *his* diamonds and it was *his* daughter.

Joe weighs the transmitter in his hands. 'But how did the ransom finish up in your cupboard? Something must have gone wrong.'

'Tell me about it! I got shot.'

'No, but think about it. You were in hospital for ten days. If Aleksei knew you had the diamonds, he could have taken them back at any time. Instead he waited.'

'Perhaps he wanted someone else to find them first – like Keebal.'

Almost immediately, I try to push the thought away. I'm not a believer in conspiracy theories and I have nothing against Keebal except the job he does – spying on his colleagues – but someone tipped him off about the diamonds. It must have been Aleksei. Are they working together or feeding off each other?

The Professor is still studying the packaging as if trying to recreate the dimensions.

'What do we do now?' asks Ali, returning upstairs.

'We take advantage of this.' I toss her the transmitter.

She grins. We're both singing from the same song sheet. 'Are you thinking InterCity Express?'

'Nah, it's too fast.' I look at my watch. 'The printing presses are just starting to run at Wapping. Some of those newspaper trucks drive all the way to Cornwall.'

Bon voyage!

13

Condensation drips steadily down the dormer window creating rainbow patterns on the windowsill. What day is it? Thursday. No, it's Friday. Lying in bed, I listen to the delivery trucks, pneumatic drills and workmen shouting to each other. This is London's dawn chorus.

Against my better judgement I let Ali bring me here last night – to her parents' house in Millwall. We couldn't stay at her place – not after what happened.

Ali's parents were both asleep when we arrived and exhaustion drove me to bed soon afterwards. Ali showed me the spare room and left a fresh towel and cake of soap on the end of the bed like at some fancy B&B.

This must be Ali's old room. The shelves and tops of bookcases are crammed with elephants of all description ranging from tiny blown-glass figurines to a large furry mammoth guarding the wooden chest at the end of the bed.

There's a light knock on the door. 'I brought you a cup of tea,' says Ali, pushing it open with her hip. 'I also have to change the dressing on your leg.'

She's wearing a dressing gown with a frayed cord and an

elephant sewn into the pocket. Her bare feet are outturned slightly, which splays her knees and puts me in mind of a penguin, which is strange considering she moves so gracefully.

'How did you sleep?'

'Great.'

She knows I'm lying. Sitting next to me, she sets out scissors, bandages and surgical tape. For the next fifteen minutes I watch her unwrapping and rewrapping my thigh.

'These stitches are nearly ready to come out.'

'Where did you learn first aid?'

'I have four brothers.'

'I thought most Indian lads were pretty peaceful.'

'They don't start the fights.'

She cuts off the last strip of tape and wraps it around my leg. 'Does it hurt, today?'

'Not so much.'

She wants to ask about the morphine but changes her mind. As she leans forward to retrieve the scissors, her dressing gown falls open and I glimpse her breasts beneath a T-shirt. The nipples are dark, sharp peaks. Immediately, I feel guilty and look away.

'So what are you going to do with the diamonds?' she asks.

'Hide them somewhere safe.' I glance around the room. 'You seem to like elephants.'

She smiles self-consciously. 'They bring good luck. That's why their trunks are raised.'

'What about that one?' I point to the woolly mammoth, which has a lowered trunk.

'An ex-boyfriend gave that to me. He's also extinct.'

She picks up the scraps of bandages and straightens a lace doily on the bedside table. 'I had a call this morning about Rachel Carlyle.' She pauses and my hopes soar. 'She suffered some sort of nervous breakdown. A night watchman found her sitting in a stolen car on some wasteland in Kilburn.'

137

'When was this?'

'On the morning you were pulled from the river. The police took her to hospital – the Royal Free in Hampstead.'

Rather than joy I feel relief. Up until now I have tried not to think of who might have been on the boat. The longer Rachel remained missing, the harder this had become.

'Was she interviewed?'

'No. The police didn't talk to her at all.'

This is Campbell's doing. He won't investigate anything associated with Mickey Carlyle because he's frightened of where it might lead. It's not a cover-up if you don't lift the covers in the first place. Plausible deniability is a coward's defence.

'They searched Rachel's flat and found your messages on her answering machine. They also found a set of your clothes. They don't want you anywhere near her – not so close to Howard's appeal.'

'Where is Rachel now?'

'She checked out eight days ago.'

Someone close to Campbell must have told Ali these things, a detective who worked on the original investigation. It was probably 'New Boy' Dave King, who has always fancied her. We call him 'New Boy' because he was the newest member of the Serious Crime Group but that was eight years ago.

'How is your boyfriend?'

She screws up her face. 'That would be none of your business.'

'He's a good lad, Dave. Very fit looking. I think he must work out.'

She doesn't respond.

'He's not the sharpest quill on the porcupine but you could do a lot worse.'

'He's not really for me, sir.'

'Why's that?'

'Well, for one thing his legs are skinnier than mine. If he

can *fit* into my pants he can't *get* into my pants.'

She keeps a completely straight face for about fifteen seconds. Poor Dave. She's far too sharp for him.

Downstairs in the kitchen I meet Ali's mother. She's barely five foot tall, dressed in a bright green sari that makes her look like a bauble on a Christmas tree.

'Good morning, Inspector, welcome to our home; I trust you slept well.' Her dark eyes seem to be smiling at me and her accent is incredibly proper as though I'm someone important. She doesn't even know me.

'Fine, thank you.'

'I have prepared you breakfast.'

'I normally eat breakfast closer to lunch.'

Her fleeting look of disappointment makes me regret the statement but she is already clearing the table from an earlier sitting. Some of Ali's brothers still live at home. Two of them run a garage in Mile End, one is an accountant and the other is at university.

A toilet flushes at the rear of the house and Ali's father appears moments later dressed in a railway uniform. He has a salt and pepper beard and a bright blue turban. Shaking my hand, he bows his head slightly.

'You are welcome, Inspector.'

Ali appears, dressed in jeans and a sweatshirt. Her father swallows his disappointment.

'We're all British now, Babba,' she says, kissing him on the forehead.

'Outside these walls, yes,' he replies. 'In this house you are still *my* daughter. It's bad enough that you cut your hair.'

Ali is supposed to wear a sari when she visits her parents. I saw her once, looking self-consciously beautiful, wrapped in orange and green silk. She was on her way to a cousin's wedding. I felt strangely envious. Instead of being caught between two cultures she seemed to straddle them.

'Thank you for letting me stay like this,' I say, trying to change the subject.

Mr Barba shakes his head from side to side. 'That's quite all right, Inspector. My daughter has explained everything . . .'

Somehow I doubt that.

' . . . You are very welcome. Sit. Eat. I must apologise for leaving.'

He takes a lunchbox and thermos from the kitchen bench. Mrs Barba walks him to the front door and kisses his cheek. Whistling steam billows from the kettle and Ali begins making a fresh pot of tea.

'You'll have to forgive my parents,' she says. 'And I should warn you about the questions.'

'Questions?'

'My mother is very nosy.'

A voice answers from the hallway. 'I heard that.'

'She also has ears like a bat,' whispers Ali.

'I heard that too.' Mrs Barba appears again. 'I'm sure you don't talk to *your* mother like this, Inspector.'

I feel a stab of guilt. 'She's in a retirement home.'

'And I'm sure it's very nice.'

Does that mean expensive?

Mrs Barba puts her arms around Ali's waist. 'My daughter thinks I spy on her just because I come to clean her house once a week.'

'I don't need you to clean.'

'Oh, yes! And if you are Queen and I am Queen, who is to fetch the water?'

Ali rolls her eyes. Mrs Barba directs a question at me. 'Do you have any children, Inspector?'

'Two.'

'You're divorced, aren't you?'

'Twice. I'm trying for third time lucky.'

'That is sad for you. Do you miss your wife?'

'Yes, but my aim is improving.'

The joke doesn't make her smile. She puts a fresh cup of tea in front of me. 'Why didn't your marriages work out?'

Ali looks horrified, 'You don't ask questions like that, Mama!'

'That's all right,' I say. 'I don't really know the answer.'

'Why not? My daughter says you are very clever.'

'Not in matters of the heart.'

'It's not hard to love a wife.'

'I could love one, I just couldn't hold on to her.'

Without realising how it happens, I'm telling her how my first wife, Laura, died of breast cancer at thirty-eight and my second wife, Jessie, left me when she realised that marriage wasn't just for the weekend. Now she's in Argentina filming a documentary about polo players and most likely shagging one of them. And my current wife, Miranda, packed her bags because I spent more time in the office than I did at home. It sounds like a soap opera.

Mrs Barba picks up on the melancholy note in my voice when I talk about Laura who should have been my childhood sweetheart because then I would have known her longer than fifteen years. We deserved more. She deserved more.

One thing leads to another and soon I'm telling her about the twins – how Claire is dancing in New York and every time I see her disfigured toes I feel like arresting everyone at the New York City Ballet; and the last I heard from Michael he was crewing charter yachts in the Caribbean.

'You don't see much of them.'

'No.'

She shakes her head and I wait for a lecture on parental responsibility. Instead, she pours another cup of tea and begins talking about her children and her faith. She doesn't see any difference between races or genders or religions. Humanity is all the same except in some countries where life is held more lightly and hatred gets a hearing.

Ali apologises again for her mother when we get outside.

'I thought she was very nice.'

'She drives me crazy.'

'Wanna swap?'

We have changed vehicles since yesterday. Ali has borrowed a car from one of her brothers. I know it is part of her training – never using the same vehicle or driving the same route two days in a row. People spend years learning this stuff. I wonder what happens to them afterwards. Are they frightened of the world, just like Mickey Carlyle?

Edging through the traffic, north along the Edgware Road, I feel a sense of expectation. The uncertainty could end today. Once I find Rachel she'll tell me what happened. I might not *remember* but I'll know.

We cross a railway bridge and turn right into an industrial area, full of car repair shops, breaker yards, spray painters and engineering workshops. Pigeons pick at the bins behind a café.

The road runs out and we pull up on a patch of wasteland littered with rusting drums, broken chimney pots, fence posts and scaffolding. An abandoned freezer, pock-marked by stones, rises above the weeds.

'This is where they found Rachel. She was sitting in the passenger seat of a stolen car,' says Ali, studying an Ordnance Survey map on her lap. 'The car was reported missing the previous evening from a multi-storey in Soho.'

The skies have cleared and the sun is shining strongly, reflecting off the puddles. Climbing out of the car, I walk towards the freezer, moving gingerly across the broken ground. The nearest factory or warehouse is fifty yards away. London is littered with sites like this one. People imagine high-density living with every spare foot being utilised, but there are thousands of empty warehouses, vacant blocks and patches of waste ground.

I don't know what I expected to find. Answers. Witnesses.

Something familiar. Everybody leaves a trail. The ridiculous thing is, I can't look at a vacant lot without thinking what crops might grow there. I'm in the middle of a vast city and I'm thinking about barley and rape seed.

'Why can't I remember any of this?'

'You might never have been here,' says Ali. 'Rachel abandoned her car three miles from here.'

'I would have followed her.'

'How?'

'I don't know.'

Finding the smoothest path through the weeds and rubble, she moves ahead of me until we reach a wire fence. Beyond are railway tracks – the Bakerloo Line. The ground trembles as a train rattles past.

Turning left at the fence, we come to a pedestrian footbridge over the lines. The platforms of Kilburn Station are partially visible to the north. The dual tracks have weeds growing at the edges and rubbish has collected in the ditches.

This is a good location to drop a ransom. Quiet. The factories and warehouses would have been empty at night. There are major roads leading north and south. The railway line runs east–west. Ten minutes travelling in any direction would put someone miles away.

'I need you to get hold of the incident logs from the local police stations,' I tell Ali. 'I want to know everything that happened that night within a two-mile radius – burglaries, assaults, parking tickets, broken streetlights, whatever you can find.'

'What are you looking for?'

'I'll tell you when I find it.'

The Royal Free Hospital in Hampstead is less than half a mile from where Rachel's car was abandoned and three miles from where she was found. Ali waits outside while I go through the main doors.

The receptionist is in her fifties with reddish-brown hair, pinned tightly to her skull. She might be a nurse but it's hard to tell without a uniform.

'I'm Detective Inspector Ruiz. I need some information about a woman who was treated here a week or so ago.' I notice her nametag and add, 'Thank you very much, Joanne.'

She straightens and touches her hair.

'Her name is Rachel Carlyle. She was brought in by the police.'

Joanne is leaning on her elbows, looking at me.

'Perhaps you should check on the computer,' I suggest.

Blushing slightly, she turns to the keyboard. 'I'm afraid Miss Carlyle is no longer a patient.'

'Why was she admitted?'

'I'm afraid I can't give you that sort of information.'

'What day did she check out?'

'Let me see . . . 29 September.'

'Do you know where she went?'

'Well, there is an address . . . I'm not sure . . .'

I know what she's going to say. She's going to ask for some official identification or a letter of authority. I no longer have a badge.

Then I notice her staring at my hands, in particular my gypsy ring. It's fourteen-carat yellow gold, mounted with a champagne-coloured diamond. According to Daj it belonged to my grandfather, although I don't know how she knows this or how she managed to recover it from Auschwitz.

People are superstitious about gypsies. My mother used to play on it. At school fetes and local fairs she would set down her cloth-covered table and shuffle the tarot cards, telling fortunes at a few quid a time. Private readings were conducted in the cottage parlour, with the curtains drawn and incense stinking the air.

'The dead come back through children,' Daj would say. 'They steal their souls.'

None of this crap about gypsy curses and fortune-telling

144

impressed me but sometimes, when I interview a suspect, I notice them grow suddenly anxious when they see my ring. They look just like Joanne does now.

Her eyes move to my left hand – the one missing a finger. 'A bullet did that,' I say, holding it up for her. 'Sometimes I think the finger is still there. It itches. You were going to give me the address.'

She shudders slightly. 'I think her father might have signed her out. Sir Douglas Carlyle.'

'Don't bother about the address. I know where he lives.'

Sir Douglas Carlyle is a retired banker and a descendant of Robert the Bruce, King of Scotland. I interviewed him during the original investigation and he didn't seem to like me very much. Then again, he didn't have much time for Rachel either. The two of them hadn't spoken in eleven years – ever since she dropped out of university, embraced the politics of the left and disowned him for being rich and titled.

Rachel tried everything she could to provoke him, working part-time for homeless shelters, housing associations and environmental groups, saving the world one tree at a time. However, the real sword in her father's side was marrying Aleksei Kuznet, a foreigner and flower seller.

Yet the thing that struck me about Sir Douglas was his equanimity and patience. He remained convinced that one day Rachel would come back to him. Now it seems he may have been right.

Parking in front of the large house in Henley, I self-consciously check my appearance in the side mirror. I could never be a class warrior. Titled people make me feel uncomfortable. A large white fountain dominates the garden, surrounded by paths that radiate between flowerbeds and angular patches of lawn.

I can hear laughter coming from outside and the gentle *thwack* of ball on racquet. There are wild cries of exultation

145

and breathless moans of despair. Either someone is playing tennis or it's the soundtrack to a sixties blue movie.

The tennis court at the side of the house is hidden behind fences draped with ivy. We follow a path and emerge at a pagoda beside the court, where trays of cold drinks have been set out on the table. Two couples are on court. The men are my age, sporting expensive suntans and muscled forearms. The women are younger and prettier, wearing miniskirts and midriff tops that show off their flat stomachs.

Sir Douglas is about to serve. With his aggressive countenance and eagle nose, he makes a social game look serious.

'Can I help you?' he asks, irritated by the interruption. Then he recognises me.

'I am sorry to trouble you, Sir Douglas, I am looking for Rachel.'

Angrily, he slams the ball into the side fence. 'I really can't be dealing with this now.'

'It's important.'

He troops off the court with his playing partner, who brushes past me as she reaches for a zip-up jacket to stay warm. She towels her face and neck. It's a very long neck. I read about Sir Douglas's divorce from Rachel's mother.

'This is Charlotte,' he says.

She beams. 'You can call me Tottie. Everyone does. I've been Tottie for ever.'

I can see that.

Sir Douglas waves to the far end of the court. 'And those are friends of ours.' He shouts to them, 'Why don't you go and get ready for lunch? We'll meet you inside.'

The couple wave back.

Sir Douglas looks even fitter than I remember, with one of those deep suntans you see on sailing types and Australians. You could cut off his arm and it would go all the way through.

'Is Rachel here?'

'What makes you think that?' He's testing me.

'You collected her from hospital more than a week ago.'

He plays an imaginary backhand. 'I don't know if you recall, Inspector, but my daughter has never liked me very much. She thinks the Establishment is some sort of criminal society like the Mafia and that I am the Godfather. She doesn't believe in titles or privilege or the education that I paid for. She thinks there is only dignity in being poor and has swallowed the popular mythology of the working class being full of decent hard-working people possessed of piety and common sense. Breeding, however, is a curse.'

'Where is she?'

He drinks from a glass of lemonade and looks at Tottie. Why do I get the impression I'm about to be fed a plate of bullshit?

'Perhaps you should go inside, sweetheart,' he says. 'Tell Thomas he can clear these things away.'

Thomas is the butler.

Tottie stands and stretches her long legs. She pecks him on the cheek, 'Don't let it upset you, dear.'

Sir Douglas motions us to the chairs, holding one for Ali.

'Do you know the hardest thing about being a father, Inspector? Trying to help your children *not* make the same mistakes as we did. You want to guide them. You want them to make certain decisions, marry certain people, believe certain things, but you can't make them go that way. They make their own decisions. My daughter chose to marry a gangster and a psychopath. She did it partly to punish me, I know that. I knew what sort of man Aleksei Kuznet was. It was bred into him. Like father, like son.'

Sir Douglas slides his racquet into a sports bag. 'Oddly enough, I actually felt sorry for Aleksei. Only an innocent millionaire would have satisfied Rachel, and short of winning the lottery or finding buried treasure there's no such thing.'

I don't know where he's going with this but I try to keep the desperation out of my voice. 'Just tell me where Rachel is.'

He ignores the statement. 'I have always felt sorry for those

147

people who choose not to have children. They miss out on what it means to be human, to feel love in all its forms.' His eyes have misted over. 'I wasn't a very consistent father and I wasn't objective. I wanted Rachel to make me proud of her instead of realising that I should always be proud of her.'

'How is she?'

'Recovering.'

'I need to speak to her.'

'I'm afraid that won't be possible.'

'You don't understand . . . there was a ransom demand. Rachel believed that Mickey was still alive. We both did. I need to find out why.'

'Is this an official investigation, Detective?'

'There must have been proof. There must have been some evidence to convince us.'

'I had a phone call from Chief Superintendent Smith. I don't know him well but he seems quite an impressive man. He alerted me to the fact that you might try to contact Rachel.'

He is no longer looking at me. He could be talking to the trees for all I know. 'My daughter has suffered a breakdown. Some very callous and cruel people took advantage of her grief. She has barely said a word since the police found her.'

'I need her help . . .'

He raises his hand to stop me. 'We have medical advice. She can't be upset.'

'People have died. A serious crime has been committed . . .'

'Yes, it has. But now something good has happened. My daughter has come home and I'm going to protect her. I'm going to make sure nobody hurts her again.'

He's serious. His eyes have a gleam of pure, unadulterated, idiotic determination. The whole conversation has had a ritu-alistic quality. I even expect him to say 'Maybe next time', as though nothing would be simpler or more obvious than coming back another day.

Warm, melting undulations of fear ripple through me. I

can't leave without talking to Rachel; too much is at stake.

'Does Rachel know that before Mickey disappeared you applied for custody of your granddaughter?'

He flinches now. 'My daughter was an alcoholic, Inspector. We were concerned for Michaela. At one point Rachel fell in the bathroom and my granddaughter spent the night lying next to her on the floor.'

'How did you find out about that?'

He doesn't answer.

'You were spying on her.'

Again he doesn't respond. I've known about the custody application from the start. If Howard Wavell hadn't emerged as such a strong suspect I would have investigated it further and confronted Sir Douglas.

'How far would you have gone to protect Mickey?'

Angry now, he exclaims, 'I didn't kidnap my granddaughter, if that's what you're suggesting. I wish I had – maybe then she would still be alive. Whatever happened in the past has been forgiven. My daughter has come home.'

He stands now. The conversation is over.

On my feet, I swing towards the house. He tries to intercept me but I brush him aside and begin yelling.

'RACHEL!'

'You can't do this! I demand you leave!'

'RACHEL!'

'Leave my property this instant.'

Ali tries to stop me. 'Perhaps we should leave, sir.'

Sir Douglas tackles me in front of the conservatory. With his tanned forearms and sinewy legs, he's surprisingly strong.

'Let it go, sir,' says Ali, taking hold of my arms.

'I have to see Rachel.'

'Not this way.'

At that moment Thomas appears, wearing an apron over a pressed white shirt. He's carrying a silver candlestick like a club.

Suddenly, the whole scene registers as being vaguely ridiculous. In Cluedo there is a candlestick among the possible murder weapons but, surprisingly, not a butler among the suspects. Blaming the staff is just another lousy cliché.

Thomas is standing over me, while Sir Douglas brushes mud and grass clippings from his knees. Ali takes my arm and helps me up, steering me towards the path.

Sir Douglas is already on the phone, no doubt complaining to Campbell. Turning, I shout, 'What if you're making a mistake? What if Mickey is still alive?'

Only the birds answer back.

14

Fumbling in my pocket, I take out a morphine capsule and swallow it dry, feeling it catch in my throat. Opening my eyes twenty minutes later, I'm peering through pale translucent gauze. The car seems to float between the red lights and people drift along the pavements like leaves on a river.

A conga line of buses comes to a stuttering halt. My step-father died at a bus stop in Bradford in October 1995. He had a stroke on his way to see a heart specialist. See what happens when buses don't run on time? He looked very distinguished in his coffin, like a lawyer or a businessman rather than a farmer. His remaining hair was plastered across his scalp and parted exactly in a manner he never managed in life. I copied it for a while. I thought it made me look more English.

Daj came to live in London after the funeral. She moved in with me and Miranda. The two of them were like oil and vinegar. Daj was the vinegar, of course: balsamic – strong and dark. No matter how much they were mixed together they always separated and I found myself caught between them.

On the pavement, beneath a canvas awning, a young flower seller is enclosed by buckets of blooms. Tugging at the sleeves of her jumper, she covers her fists and hugs herself to keep warm. Aleksei employs a lot of refugees and immigrants on his flower stalls because they're cheap and grateful. I wonder what this girl dreams about when she goes to sleep at night in her bedsit hotel or shared house. Does she see herself as being blessed?

Tens of thousands of Eastern Europeans have washed up here from former Soviet satellite states that have declared themselves independent and then immediately begun to crumble. Sometimes it seems as if the whole of Europe is destined to tear itself apart, divided into smaller and smaller parcels until there isn't enough land left to sustain a language or a culture. Maybe we're all destined to become gypsies.

Fury and fear are driving me. Fury at being shot and fear of not finding out why. I want either to remember or forget. I can't live in the middle. Either give me back the missing days or erase them completely.

Ali senses my despair. 'Facts not memories solve cases. That's what you said. We just have to keep investigating.'

She doesn't understand. Rachel had the answers. She was going to tell me what happened.

'He was never going to let you see her. We have to find another way.'

'If I could get a message to her . . .'

Suddenly, the curious, chemical detachment lifts and a face floats into my thoughts – a woman with dark-brown hair and a birthmark that leaks across her throat like spilled caramel. Kirsten Fitzroy – Rachel's best friend and former neighbour.

Some women have a particular gaze from the day they are born. They look at you as though they know exactly what you're thinking and will always know. Kirsten was like that. In the days after Mickey disappeared she was the rock that Rachel clung to, shielding her from the media and making her meals.

Kirsten could get a message to her. She could find out what

happened. I know she lives somewhere in Notting Hill.

'I can get the address,' says Ali, pulling off the road. She punches speed dial on her mobile, no doubt calling 'New Boy' Dave.

Twenty minutes later we pull up outside a large whitewashed Georgian house in Ladbroke Square, overlooking the communal gardens. The surrounding streets are painted in candy colours and dotted with coffee shops and restaurants. Kirsten has moved up in the world.

Her flat is on the third floor, facing the street. I pause on the landing to get my breath back. That's when I notice the door is slightly ajar. Ali peers up and down the stairwell, automatically on edge.

Nudging the door open, I call Kirsten's name. No answer. The lock has almost been torn off and splinters of wood lie inside the door. Further along the hallway there are papers and clothes strewn haphazardly on the seagrass matting.

Ali unclips her holster and motions for me to stay put. I shake my head. It's easier if I cover her back. She spins through the door and crouches, peering down the hallway to the kitchen. I enter behind her, facing in the opposite direction into the lounge. Furniture is overturned and someone has filleted the sofa with a samurai sword. The stuffing spills out like the bloated intestines of a slain beast.

Rice-paper lampshades lie torn and crushed on the floor. Floating flowers are marooned in a dry bowl and a shoji screen is smashed into pieces.

Moving from room to room, we discover more wreckage. Foodstuffs, appliances and utensils litter the kitchen floor between upturned drawers and open cupboards. A chair lies broken. Someone has used it to search above the cabinets.

At first glance it looks more like an act of vandalism than a robbery. Then I notice several envelopes lying amidst the destruction. The return addresses have been carefully torn off. There is no diary or address book beside the telephone.

Someone has also cleared the corkboard of notes and photographs. Torn corners are all that remain, trapped beneath coloured pins.

The morphine has left me with a sense of depleted reality. I go into the bathroom and splash water on my face. A towel and chemise are folded over the towel rail and a lipstick has fallen into the bath. Retrieving it, I unscrew the lid and stare at the pointed nub, holding it like a crayon.

Above the washbasin, tilted slightly downwards, is a rectangular mirror with mother-of-pearl inlaid into the frame. I've lost weight. My cheeks are hollow and my eyes are deeply wrinkled at the edges. Or maybe it's someone else in the mirror. I have been replicated and imprisoned in a slightly different universe. The real world is on the other side of the glass. Already I can feel the opiate wearing off. I want to hold on to the unreality.

Returning the lipstick to a shelf, I marvel at the salves, pastes, powders and potpourri. From amongst them I can summon up Kirsten's fragrance and our first meeting at Dolphin Mansions the day after Mickey disappeared.

Tall and slim with tapered limbs, Kirsten's cream-coloured slacks hung so low on her hips I wondered what was holding them up. Her flat was full of antique armour and weaponry, including two samurai swords crossed on the wall and a Japanese warrior's helmet made from iron, leather and silk.

'They say it was worn by Toyotomi Hideyoshi,' Kirsten explained. 'He was the *daimyo* who unified Japan in the sixteenth century: The "Age of Battles". Are you interested in history, DI?'

'No.'

'So you don't believe we can learn from our mistakes?'

'We haven't so far.'

She acknowledged my opinion without agreeing with it. Ali was moving through the flat, admiring the artefacts.

'What did you say you did?' she asked Kirsten.

'I didn't.' Her eyes were smiling at the edges. 'I manage an employment agency in Soho. We provide cooks, waitresses, hostesses, that sort of thing.'

'Business must be good.'

'I work hard.'

Kirsten prepared us tea in a hand-painted Japanese teapot and ceramic bowls. We had to kneel at a table while she dipped a ladle into simmering water and beat the powdered tea like scrambled eggs. I didn't understand the elaborate ceremony. Ali seemed more in tune with the idea of meditation and 'the One Mind'.

Kirsten had lived at Dolphin Mansions for three years, moving in just a few weeks after Rachel and Mickey. She and Rachel became friends. Coffee buddies. They shopped together and borrowed each other's clothes. Yet apparently Rachel didn't confide in Kirsten about Aleksei or her famous family. It was one secret too far.

'Who would have thought . . . talk about Beauty and the Beast,' Kirsten told me, when she learned the news. 'All that money and she's living here.'

'What would you have done?'

'I would have taken my share and gone to live in Patagonia – as far away as possible – and slept with a gun under my pillow for the rest of my life.'

'You have a vivid imagination.'

'Like I said, I've heard the stories about Aleksei. Everyone's got one, right? It's like the one about him playing blackjack in Las Vegas and this Californian dot-com millionaire comes over and tells him that he's sitting in his chair. Aleksei ignores him, so the Californian says, "Listen, you limey faggot, I'm worth sixty million dollars and this is my goddamn chair". So Aleksei takes a coin out of his pocket and says, "Sixty million? I'll toss you for it".'

She didn't expect anyone to laugh. Instead she let the silence stretch out. I wish my legs could have done the same.

She had an alibi for when Mickey disappeared. The care-taker Ray Murphy was fixing her shower. It had only taken him three attempts, she said.

'What did you do afterwards?'

'I went back to sleep.'

She looked at me quizzically and then added the word 'alone'.

Twenty years ago I would have said she was flirting, but I knew she was making fun of me. Being older and wiser doesn't help the ego. Youth and beauty rule the world.

Returning to the lounge, I find Ali going through the contents of the toppled bookcase. Whoever did this opened every book, box file and photograph album. Diaries, address books, computer disks and photographs were taken. This wasn't a robbery, it was a search. They were looking for Kirsten. They wanted the names of friends and contacts – anyone who might know her.

'We should call this in, sir.'

'Yes.'

'What do you want me to say?'

'Tell them the truth. We found a break-in.'

We wait downstairs for the uniforms to arrive, sitting on the front steps and going over possible scenarios. Misty rain has started falling. It settles on Ali's hair and the weave of her coat.

Across the road a handful of muddy boys spill from a Range Rover with football boots hanging from laces and socks around their ankles.

Further along the street, someone is waiting in a car. I wouldn't have noticed except for the flare of a cigarette lighter. It crosses my mind that Keebal has had me followed but almost immediately I consider another explanation. Maybe someone is waiting for Kirsten to come home.

I step out on to the pavement and stretch. The sun is trying to break through but keeps getting swallowed by fat putty-grey clouds. I begin to walk around the square. At first I'm heading away from the suspicious car but at the corner I turn and cross the street. I pause to read the plaque beneath a statue of a bronze horseman.

I turn again and set off. A pigeon takes wing in an awkward flurry. I'm walking towards the car now. I can just make out the silhouette of someone at the wheel.

I stay close to the gutter, keeping the line of vehicles between us. At the last possible moment I step alongside the Audi. Resting on the passenger seat is a photograph of Kirsten Fitzroy.

A burly, grey-haired man gapes at me dumbfounded. I can see two bloated versions of myself in his sunglasses. I try to open the door. He reaches for the ignition and I yell at him to stop.

At that moment Ali arrives, slewing her car across the road to block his getaway. Finding reverse, he plants his foot and rubber shrieks on tarmac. He slams into the car behind and then lurches forward, pulling the cars apart. Tyres screech and smoke as he fires into reverse again.

Ali is out of the door with a hand on her holster. The driver sees her first. He raises a pistol, aiming at her chest.

Instinctively, I smash my walking stick across the windscreen, where it explodes into shards of lacquered wood. The sound is enough to make him hesitate. Ali drops and rolls into the gutter. I spin the other way, falling fast and nowhere near as gracefully.

In the adjacent house, barely eighteen feet away, the door opens. Two teenage girls appear, one of them pushing a bicycle. The pistol swings towards them.

I yell a warning, but they stop and stare. He won't miss from this range.

I glance across at Ali. She has her feet planted and arms

outstretched, with the Glock in her right hand and her left hand cupped underneath.

'I can take him, sir.'

'Let him go.'

She drops her arms between her thighs. The driver accelerates backwards along the road, doing a handbrake turn at the end of the square, before swinging north into Ladbroke Grove.

Ali sits next to me in the gutter. The air stinks of burning clutch and rubber. The teenage girls have gone but curtains have opened and anxious faces are pressed to windows.

Ali wipes a smudge of gun oil from her fingers. 'I could have taken him.'

'I know.'

'Why?'

'Because when they teach you how to shoot people, they don't teach you how to live with it.'

She nods and a flurry of breeze pushes her fringe across her eyes. She brushes it away.

'Did you recognise him?'

I shake my head. 'He was waiting for Kirsten. Someone wants her very badly.'

A police patrol car rounds the corner and cruises slowly up the street. Two kids in uniform peer from side to side, looking for house numbers. Five minutes earlier they would have shat themselves or been shot. Thank heavens for small mercies.

Interviews must be conducted and statements taken. Ali fields most of the questions, giving a description of the car and driver. According to the computer the number plates belong to a builder's van in Newcastle. Someone has either stolen or copied them.

Under normal circumstances, the local CID would label the whole incident as road rage or call it a fail-to-stop accident. By normal circumstances, I mean if ordinary members of the public were involved instead of two police officers.

The Detective Sergeant, Mike Drury, is one of the Young Turks from Paddington Green, who cut his teeth interviewing IRA and now al-Qaeda suspects. He looks up and down the street burying both hands in his pockets. His long nose sniffs the air as though he doesn't like the smell of it.

'So tell me again, why did you want to see Kirsten Fitzroy?'

'I'm trying to find a friend of hers – Rachel Carlyle.'

'And why do you want to see her?'

'To catch up on old times.'

He waits for something more. I'm not budging.

'Did you have a warrant?'

'I didn't need one. Her door was open when we arrived.'

'And you went inside?'

'To make sure there wasn't a crime in progress. Miss Fitzroy might have been hurt. There was probable cause.'

I don't like the tone of his questions. This is more like an interrogation than an interview.

Drury scribbles something in his notebook. 'So you reported the break-in and then noticed the guy in the car.'

'He seemed out of place.'

'Out of place?'

'Yes.'

'When you approached him, did you show him your badge?'

'No. I don't have my badge with me.'

'Did you announce yourself as a police officer?'

'No.'

'What *did* you do?'

'I tried to open the passenger door.'

'So this guy was just sitting in a car, minding his own business, and you appeared from nowhere and tried to break into his car?'

'It wasn't like that.'

Drury is playing devil's advocate. 'He didn't know you were police officers. You must have scared the shit out of him. No wonder he took off . . .'

'He had a gun. He pointed it at my partner.'

'Partner? I was under the impression that DC Barba worked for the Diplomatic Protection Group and is currently on holiday leave . . .' He consults his notebook. 'And according to my information, you were suspended from all duties yesterday and are now the subject of an investigation by the Independent Police Complaints Commission.'

I'm getting pretty pissed off with this guy. It's not just him – it's the whole attitude. Forty-three years in the force and I'm being treated as if I'm Charles Bronson making *Death Wish XV*.

In the old days there would have been sixty officers crawling all over this place – searching for the car, interviewing witnesses. Instead, I have to put up with this crap. Maybe Campbell's right and I should have retired three years ago. Everything I do nowadays is either against the rules or treading on someone's toes. Well, I haven't lost my edge and I'm still smarter than most scrotes and a damn sight cleverer than this prick.

'Ali can answer the rest of your questions. I have better things to do.'

'You'll have to wait. I haven't finished,' says Drury.

'Are you carrying a gun, DS?'

'No.'

'What about handcuffs?'

'No.'

'Well, if you can't shoot me and you can't shackle me – you can't keep me here.'

15

The Professor lives in Primrose Hill, at the poor end of a leafy street where every house is worth seven figures and every car is covered in bird shit. The perverse symmetry appeals to me.

Joe answers the door on the second ring, dressed in corduroy trousers and an open-neck shirt.

'You look awful.'

'Tell me about it! People keep wanting to shoot me.'

Julianne appears behind him, looking like a woman plucked off a film poster. High cheekbones, blue eyes, perfect skin . . . In a soft voice, she announces, 'You look terrible.'

'So everyone keeps telling me.'

She kisses me on the cheek and I follow her down the hall towards the kitchen. A toddler sits in a high chair, holding a spoon. Pureed apple is stuck to her cheeks and forehead. Charlie, aged ten, is home from school and in charge of feeding.

'I'm sorry,' I whisper to Julianne, suddenly embarrassed to barge in. 'I didn't realise . . . you're all here.'

'Yes, we have children, remember?'

Joe wants to ask me what happened but he holds off for the sake of Charlie, who has a fascination with police stories – the more gruesome the better.

'Have you arrested anyone today?' she asks me.

'Why? Have you done something wrong?'

She looks horrified. '*No!*'

'Keep it that way.'

Julianne hands me coffee. She notices my missing finger. 'I guess it's official then – you're not the marrying kind.'

Charlie is equally fascinated, leaning closer to examine the blunt stump where pink skin has puckered at the join.

'What happened?'

'I ate a hamburger too quickly.'

'That's gross.'

'I didn't taste a thing.'

Julianne admonishes me. 'Shush, you'll give her nightmares. Come on, Charlie, you have homework.'

'But it's Friday. You said you'd take me shopping for new boots.'

'We'll go tomorrow.'

Her spirits soar. 'Can I get heels?'

'Only if they're this high.' She holds her thumb and forefinger an inch apart.

'Sick.'

Charlie lifts the baby on to her hip, dips her head and tosses the fringe out of her eyes. Christ, she looks like her mother!

Joe suggests we go to his study. I follow him up the stairs into a small room, overlooking the garden. A desk takes up most of the available space, squeezed between bookshelves and a filing cabinet. To the right on the wall is a corkboard, covered in notes, postcards and family photographs.

This is Joe's bolthole. If I lived with three women I'd want one too, although mine would come with a bar fridge and a TV.

Joe scoops files off a chair and tidies his desk. I get the

impression he's not so organised any more. Maybe it's the Parkinson's.

'You've stopped using the walking stick,' he observes.

'I broke it.'

'I can lend you another one.'

'That's OK. My leg is getting stronger.'

For the next hour we pick over the wreckage of my day. I tell him about Sir Douglas and the attack outside Kirsten's flat. His face gives nothing away. It's like a blank page on one of his notepads. He once told me about something called a Parkinson's mask. Maybe this is it.

Joe begins drawing lines on the pad. 'I've been thinking about the ransom.'

'And what did you come up with?'

'There must have been an initial letter or an e-mail or a phone call. You mentioned DNA tests.'

'On strands of hair.'

'That first contact must have come as a tremendous shock. We have a dead girl, a man in prison for her murder, then suddenly a ransom demand arrives. What did you think?'

'I can't remember.'

'But you can imagine. You can put yourself in the same position. What are you going to think when the ransom letter arrives?'

'It's a hoax.'

'You've *never* been convinced of Howard's guilt.'

'It still smells like a hoax.'

'What would change your mind?'

'Proof of life.'

'The letter contains strands of hair.'

'I have it tested.'

'What else?'

'I have everything analysed – the ink, the handwriting, the paper . . .'

'Who does that?'

'The Forensic Science Service.'

'But your boss refuses to believe you. He tells you to leave the case alone.'

'He's wrong!'

'Nobody believes the letter except you and the girl's mother. Why do you believe?'

'It can't just be the hair. I need more proof.'

'Like what?'

'A photograph or, better still, a video. And it has to include something time-sensitive like the front page of a newspaper.'

'Anything else?'

'Blood or skin tissue – something that can't be three years old.'

'If there's no such proof – do you still go ahead with the ransom drop?'

'I don't know. It could be a hoax.'

'Maybe you want to catch the hoaxers.'

'I wouldn't put Rachel in danger for that.'

'So you must believe it.'

'Yes.'

'None of your colleagues agree with you. Why?'

'Perhaps the proof of life isn't conclusive.'

Joe has turned his chair slightly away from me, so his gaze fixes me off-centre. Whenever I pause or falter, he finds a new question. It's like painting by numbers, working inwards from the edges.

'Why would someone wait three years to post a ransom demand?'

'Maybe they didn't kidnap her for ransom – not at first.'

'Why kidnap her then?'

I'm struggling now. According to Rachel, nobody in England knew that Aleksei was Mickey's father. Sir Douglas Carlyle obviously did, but if he kidnapped Mickey he's hardly likely to send a ransom demand.

'So someone else took Mickey and we go back to the same questions: why wait three years?' says Joe.

Again, I don't know the answer. I'm guessing. 'Either they didn't have her or they wanted to keep her.'

'Why give her up now?'

I see where he's going now. The ransom makes no sense. What do I really imagine: that Mickey has been chained to a radiator for the past three years? It's not credible. She isn't sitting in a waiting room, rocking her legs beneath a chair, waiting to be rescued.

Joe is still talking. 'There's another issue. If Mickey is still alive, we have to consider whether she wants to come home. Three years is a long time at the age of seven. She could have formed attachments; found a new family.'

'But she wrote a letter!'

'What letter?'

The realisation is like a sharp gust of wind. I remember this! A postcard in a child's hand – written in capital letters! I can recite the text:

DEAR MUMMY,
I MISS YOU VERY MUCH AND I WANT TO COME HOME. I SAY MY PRAYERS EVERY NIGHT AND ASK FOR THE SAME THING. THEY SAY THEY WILL LET ME GO IF YOU SEND THEM SOME-THING. I THINK THEY WANT MONEY. I HAVE £25 AND SOME GOLD COINS IN MY MONEY BOX UNDER MY BED. PLEASE HURRY. I CAN SEE YOU AGAIN SOON BUT ONLY IF YOU DON'T CALL THE POLICE.
    LOVE
    MICKEY.
PS. I HAVE BOTH MY FRONT TEETH NOW.

For a moment I feel like I might hug Joe. God, it's good to remember. It's better than morphine.

'What did you do with the postcard?' he asks.

'I had it analysed.'

'Where?'

'A private lab.'

I can picture the postcard flattened under glass, being scanned by some sort of machine – a video spectral comparator. It can tell if any letters have been altered and what inks have been used.

'It looked like a child's handwriting.'

'You don't sound certain.'

'I'm not.'

I remember a handwriting expert explaining to me how most children tend to write 'R's with the extender coming down from the intersection of the vertical line and the loop. This didn't happen on the postcard. And children also draw the capital 'E' with a centre line the same length as the upper and lower lines. And they cross their capital 'J's, whereas adults drop the line.

But the main clue came from the lines. Children have difficulty writing on blank paper. They tend to slew their writing down to the lower right corner. And they have trouble judging how much space words will use so they run out of room on the right-hand margin.

The ransom letter was perfectly straight.

'So it wasn't written by a child?' asks Joe.

'No.'

My heart suddenly aches.

Joe tries to keep me focused. 'What about the strands of hair?'

'There were six of them.'

'Any instructions for the ransom?'

'No.'

'So there must have been more letters . . . or phone calls.'

'That makes sense.'

Joe is still drawing on his pad, creating a spiral with a dark centre. 'The ransom packages were waterproof and designed to float. The orange plastic made them easier to see in the dark. Why were there four identical bundles?'

'I don't know. Maybe there were four kidnappers.'

'They could have divided the diamonds themselves.'

'You have a theory.'

'I think the packages had to fit into something . . . or float through something.'

'Like a drain.'

'Yes.'

I'm exhausted but exhilarated. It feels like my eyes have been partially opened and light is filtering inside.

'You can relax now,' he says. 'You did very well.'

'I remembered the postcard.'

'Yes.'

'It mentioned Mickey's money box. It even gave a specific amount. Only someone very close to Mickey and Rachel would know something like that.'

'A verifiable detail.'

'It's not enough.'

'Give it time.'

16

London has three private laboratories that do genetic testing. The biggest is Genetech Corporation in Harley Street. The reception area has a granite counter, leather chairs and a framed poster that reads, 'Peace of Mind Paternity Kits'. Isn't that an oxymoron?

The receptionist is a tall pale girl with straggly hair and a vacant face. She's wearing pearl earrings and has a plastic cigarette lighter tucked under her bra strap.

'Welcome to Genetech, how can I help you?'

'Do you remember me?'

She blinks slowly. 'Um, well, I don't think so. Have you been here before?'

'I was hoping you might be able to tell me. I might have been here about a month ago.'

'Did you order a test?'

'I believe so.'

She doesn't bat an eyelid. I could be asking for a paternity test on Prince William and she'd act like it happens every day. She takes my name and flicks at the keys of a computer. 'Was it a police matter?'

'A private test.'

She flicks at a few more keys.

'Here it is – a DNA test. You wanted a comparison done on an earlier sample . . .' She pauses and gives a puzzled hum.

'What is it?'

'You also wanted us to analyse an envelope and a letter. You paid cash. Almost £450.'

'How long did the tests take?'

'These were done in five days. It can sometimes take six weeks. You must have been in a hurry. Is there a problem?'

'I need to see the test results again. They didn't arrive.'

'But you collected them personally. It says so right here.' She taps the computer screen.

'You must be mistaken.'

Her eyes fill with doubt. 'So you want copies?'

'No. I want to speak to whoever conducted the tests.'

For the next twenty minutes I wait on a black leather sofa, reading a brochure on genetic testing. We live in suspicious times. Wives check on husbands; husbands check on wives and parents discover if their teenage children are taking drugs or sleeping around. Some things are safer left alone.

Eventually, I'm escorted upstairs, along sterile corridors and into a white room with benches lined with microscopes and machines that hum and blink. A young woman in a white coat peels off her rubber gloves before shaking hands. Her name is Bernadette Foster and she doesn't look old enough to have done her A levels let alone mastered these surroundings.

'You wanted to ask about some tests,' she says.

'Yes, I need a fuller explanation.'

Sliding off a high stool, she opens a filing cabinet and produces a bright green folder.

'From memory the results were self-explanatory. I extracted DNA from strands of hair and compared this with earlier tests done by the Forensic Science Service, which I assume you provided.'

'Yes.'

'Both samples – new and old – belonged to a girl called Michaela Carlyle.'

'Could the test be wrong?'

'Thirteen markers were the same. You're looking at one chance in ten billion.'

Even though I'm expecting the news, I suddenly feel unsteady on my feet. Both samples were the same. This doesn't breathe air into Mickey's lungs or pump blood through her veins but it *does* prove that at some point, however long ago, the hair fell across her shoulders or brushed against her forehead.

Miss Foster looks up from her notes. 'If you don't mind me asking, why did you ask us to do the test? We don't usually do police work.'

'It was a private request from the girl's mother.'

'But you're a detective.'

'Yes.'

She looks at me expectantly but then realises I'm not going to explain. Referring back to the folder, she takes out several photographs. 'Head hairs are usually the longest and have a uniform diameter. Uncut hair appears tapered but in this case you can see the cut tip from a hairdresser's scissors or clippers.'

She points to a photograph. 'This hair hadn't been dyed or permed.'

'Are you sure?'

'Positive.'

'Can you tell her age?'

'No.'

'Could she be alive?'

The question sounds too hopeful but she doesn't appear to notice. Instead she points to another highly magnified image. 'When hair originates from a body in a state of decomposition a dark ring can sometimes appear near the root. It's called a post-mortem root band.'

'I can't see it.'

'That makes two of us.'

A second set of photographs show the postcard. The wording is just as I remember, with large block letters and completely straight lines.

'The envelope and card didn't tell us much. Whoever sent this didn't lick the flap and we didn't find any fingerprints.' She shuffles through the photographs. 'Why is everyone so interested in this case all of a sudden?'

'What do you mean?'

'We had a lawyer phone last week. He asked about forensic tests relating to Michaela Carlyle.'

'Did he give his name?'

'No.'

'What did you say?'

'I told him we couldn't comment. Our tests are confidential.'

It may have been Howard's lawyer, which begs the question, how did he know? Miss Foster returns the file to the cabinet. I seem to have exhausted my questions.

'Don't you want to know about the other package?' she asks.

My confusion lasts a fraction of a second – long enough to give myself away.

'You don't remember, do you?'

I feel a wave of heat down my neck.

'I'm sorry. I had an accident. I was shot.' I motion to my leg. 'I have no memory of what happened.'

'Transient Global Amnesia.'

'Yes. That's why I'm here – putting the pieces together. You have to help me. What was in the package?'

Opening a cupboard beneath the bench, she takes out a hard plastic box. Reaching inside she produces a transparent Ziploc bag. It holds several triangles of pink and orange polyester. A bikini!

She turns it around in her fingers. 'I did a little research.

Michaela Carlyle was wearing a bikini like this when she disappeared, which I assume is why you asked us to analyse this.'

'I assume so, too.' My mouth is suddenly dry.

'Where did you get this?'

'I don't remember.'

She hums knowingly. 'So you can't tell me what's going on?'

'I can't, I'm sorry.'

Reading something in my eyes, she accepts this.

'Is it Mickey's bikini?'

'We couldn't extract any DNA materials but we did find slight traces of urine and faeces. Unfortunately, there isn't enough to analyse. I did, however, discover that it was part of a batch manufactured in Tunisia and sold through shops and catalogues in the spring of 2001. Three thousand units were imported and sold in the UK; five hundred were size seven.'

Rapidly I try to process the information. A few triangles of polyester weave, size seven, don't constitute proof of life. Howard could have kept the swimsuit as a souvenir or someone else could have found one similar. The details were widely publicised. There was even a photograph of Mickey wearing the bikini.

Would this be enough to convince me that Mickey was still alive? I don't know. Would it convince Rachel? Absolutely.

Stifling a groan, I try to make my brain function. My leg has started to hurt again. It doesn't feel like part of me any more. It's like I'm dragging around someone else's limb after a failed transplant.

Miss Foster takes me downstairs.

'You should still be in hospital,' she warns.

'I'm fine. Listen. Are there any more tests you can do . . . on the bikini?'

'What do you want to know?'

'I don't know – traces of hair dye, fibres, chemicals . . .'

'I can have another look.'

'Thank you.'

Every criminal investigation has loose ends. Most of them don't matter if you get a confession or a conviction; they're just white noise or static in the background. Now I keep going back to the original investigation looking for something we missed.

We interviewed every resident of Dolphin Mansions. They all had an alibi except for Howard. He couldn't have known the exact contents of Mickey's money box – not unless she told him. Sarah told me she didn't know. Kirsten might have learned such a detail.

I need to see Joe again. He has the sort of brain that might be able to make sense of this. Somehow he can join random, unconnected details and make it look like dot-to-dot drawings that even a child could do.

I don't like calling him on a Saturday. For most people it's a family day. He picks up before the answering machine. I can hear Charlie laughing in the background.

'You had lunch?' I ask.

'Yeah.'

'Already?'

'We have a baby, remember – it's strained food and nursing home hours.'

'Do you mind watching *me* eat?'

'No.'

We arrange to meet at Peregrini's, an Italian in Camden Town where the chianti is drinkable and the chef could have come straight from central casting with his walrus moustache and a booming tenor voice.

I pour Joe a glass of wine and hand him a menu. He soaks up his surroundings, collecting information without even trying.

'So what made you choose this place?' he asks.

'Don't you like it?'

'No, it's fine.'

'Well, the food is good, it reminds me of Tuscany and I know the family. Alberto has been here since the sixties. That's him in the kitchen. You sure you won't eat something?'

'I'll have pudding.'

While we wait to order, I tell him about the DNA tests and the bikini. The likelihood of other letters is now obvious.

'What would you have done with them?'

'Had them analysed.'

'And then what?'

'Put them somewhere safe . . . in case something happened to me.'

Joe nods and stares into his wine glass. 'OK, show me your wallet.' He reaches across the table.

'I'm not worth robbing.'

'Just give it to me.'

He thumbs through the various pockets and pouches, pulling out receipts, business cards and the plastic that pays for my life. 'OK, imagine for a moment that you don't know this person but you find his wallet on the ground. What does it tell you about him?'

'He doesn't carry much cash around.'

'What else?'

This is one of Joe's psychological games. He wants me to play along. I pick up the receipts, which have dried into a clumped ball. The wallet was in the river with me. I peel them apart. Some are impossible to read but I notice half a dozen receipts for takeaway food. I bought a pizza on 24 September – the night I was shot. When Joe came to see me in hospital he asked me the last thing I remembered. I told him it was pizza.

Glancing at the table, I feel depressed. My life is piled in front of me. There are business cards from rugby mates; a discount voucher from some random shop; a reminder note from British Gas that my central heating needs servicing; a Royal Mail receipt for registered mail; my driver's licence; a photograph of Luke . . .

It's a snapshot taken on the seafront at Blackpool. We were on a day trip and Daj is wearing a dozen petticoats and lace-up shoes. Her hair is hidden beneath a scarf and she is scowling at the photographer because my stepfather has asked her to smile. Luke is swinging from her hand and laughing. I'm in the background, staring at the bottom of one of my sandals as if I had just stepped in something.

'You were always looking at the ground,' Daj used to tell me. 'And you still managed to fall over your own feet.'

I remember that day. There was a talent competition on the pier. Hundreds of people were sitting in the sun listening to amateur Joe Bloggs singing songs and telling jokes. Luke kept tugging on Daj's hand, saying he wanted to sing. He was only four. She told him to be quiet.

Next thing we were watching this guy in a checked jacket and slicked-down hair, pulling faces and telling jokes. He suddenly stopped because a little kid had walked right on to the stage. It was Luke with a blond cowlick and ice-cream-stained shorts. This comedian made a big fuss about lowering the microphone so he could ask Luke a question.

'Well, now, little boy, what's your name?'

'Luke.'

'Are you here on a holiday, Luke?'

'No, I'm here with my mum.'

Everyone laughed and Luke frowned. He couldn't work out why they were laughing.

'Why are you up here, Luke?'

'I wanna sing a song.'

'What are you gonna sing?'

'I don't know.'

They laughed again and I could have died, but Luke just stood there and stared, mesmerised by the crowd. Even when

175

Daj dragged him off the stage and they all clapped, Luke didn't wave or acknowledge them. He just stared.

Joe is still sifting through the contents of my wallet. 'Everyone leaves a trail,' he says. 'It isn't just scraps of paper and photographs. It's the impression we make on other people and how we confront the world.'

He glances to his right. 'You take that couple over there.'

A man and a woman are ordering lunch. He's wearing a casual jacket and she's dressed in a classic A-line skirt and cashmere sweater.

'Notice how he doesn't look at the waiter when he's being told the specials. Instead he looks down as though reading from the menu. Now, his companion is different. She's leaning forward, with her elbows on the table and her hands framing her face. She's interested in everything the waiter says.'

'She's flirting with him.'

'You think so? Look at her legs.'

A shoeless stockinged foot is raised and resting on her partner's calf. She's teasing him. She wants him to loosen up.

'You have to look at the whole picture,' says Joe. 'I know you can't remember things – not yet, anyway. So you have to write things down or make mental notes. Flashes, images, words, faces, whatever comes to you. They don't make sense right now but one day they might.'

A waitress arrives at the table with a plate of sardines.

'Compliments of the chef,' she says.

I raise my glass to Alberto who is standing in the kitchen door. He thumps his chest like a gladiator.

Sucking fish oil from his fingers, Joe begins to focus on the bikini and who might have had it. Mickey was wearing very little when she disappeared and her beach towel became the most important piece of evidence against Howard.

All investigations need a breakthrough – a witness or a piece of evidence that turns theory into fact. In Mickey's case it had been her striped beach towel. A woman walking her dog had found it at East Finchley Cemetery. It was heavily stained with blood, vomit and traces of hair dye. Howard had no alibi for when Mickey disappeared and had been working at the cemetery in the days that followed.

A precipitin test confirmed the blood on the towel to be human – A negative, Mickey's group (along with 7 per cent of the population). The DNA tests were conclusive.

Without hesitation, I ordered a search of the flowerbeds and recently dug graves. We used ground-penetrating radar and caterpillar diggers, as well as SOCO teams with hand spades and sieves.

Campbell went ballistic, of course. 'You're digging up a fucking cemetery!' he yelled. I had to hold the phone six inches from my ear.

I took a deep breath. 'I'm conducting a limited search, sir. We have the cemetery records showing all the recently dug graves. Anything that doesn't match is worth investigating.'

'What about the headstones?'

'We'll try not to touch them.'

Campbell began listing all the people who had to sanction an exhumation, including a County Court judge, the Administrator of Cemeteries and the Chief Medical Officer of Westminster Council.

'We're not snatching bodies or robbing graves,' I reassured him.

Eighty feet of lawn and flowerbed had been dug up by then. Paving stones were propped against walls and turf rolled into muddy faggots. Howard had helped plant the garden two months earlier for Westminster in Bloom, a flower competition.

Twenty-two other sites were also excavated within the cemetery. Although it sounds like a clever hiding place, it's not an easy thing to conceal a body in a graveyard. First you have to bury it without anyone noticing, most probably at night. And it doesn't matter if you believe in ghosts or not, very few people are comfortable in cemeteries after dark.

A media blackout covered the dig, but I knew it couldn't hold. Someone must have phoned Rachel and she turned up that first afternoon. Two police officers had to hold her back behind the police tape. She fought against their arms, pleading with them to let her go.

'Is it Mickey?' she yelled at me.

I pulled her to one side, trying to calm her down. 'We don't know yet.'

'You found something?'

'A towel.'

'Mickey's towel?'

'We won't know until . . .'

'Is it Mickey's towel?'

She read the answer in my eyes and suddenly broke free, running towards the trench. I pulled her back before she reached the edge, wrapping my arms around her waist. She was crying then, with her arms outstretched, trying to throw herself into the hole.

There was nothing I could say to comfort her – nothing that would *ever* be able to comfort her.

Afterwards, I walked her up to the chapel, waiting for a police car to take her home. We sat outside on a stone bench beneath a poster on the noticeboard, which said, 'Children are the Hope of the World'.

Where! Show me! You can want them, worry about them, love them with all your being, but you can't keep them safe. Time and accidents and evil will defeat you.

Somewhere in the restaurant kitchen a tray of glasses shatters on the floor. Diners pause momentarily, perhaps in sympathy, and then conversations begin again. Joe looks across the table, inscrutable as ever. He'll say it's the Parkinson's mask but I think he enjoys being impenetrable.

'Why the hair dye?' he asks.

'What do you mean?'

'You said there were traces of hair dye on the towel. If Howard snatched Mickey off the stairs and killed her in his flat, why bother dyeing her hair?'

He's right. But the towel might have been stained earlier. Rachel could have coloured her hair. I didn't ask her. I can see Joe filing the information away for future reference.

My main course has arrived but I'm no longer hungry. The morphine is doing this to me – ruining my appetite. I roll the spaghetti around a fork and leave it resting on the plate.

Joe pours another glass of wine. 'You said you had doubts about Howard. Why?'

'Oddly enough, it's because of something *you* once said to me. When we first met and I was investigating the murder of Catherine McBride, you gave me a profile of her killer.'

'What did I say?'

'You said that sadists and paedophiles and sexual psychopaths aren't born whole. They're made.'

Joe nods, either impressed by my memory or the quality of his advice.

I try to explain. 'Until we found Mickey's towel, the case against Howard was more wishful thinking than hard evidence. Not a single complaint had ever been made against him by a parent or a child in his care. Nobody had ever called him creepy or suggested he be kept away from children. There were thousands of images on his computer, but only a handful of them could be classed as questionable and none of them proved he was a paedophile. He had no history of sexual offences, yet suddenly he appeared, a fully fledged child killer.'

Joe peers at the wine bottle wrapped in raffia. 'Someone can fantasise about children but never act. Their fantasy life can be rich enough to satisfy them.'

'Exactly, but I couldn't see the progression. You told me that deviant behaviour could be almost plotted on the axis of a graph. Someone begins by collecting pornography and progresses up the scale. Abduction and murder are at the very end.'

'Did you find any pornography?'

'Howard owned a caravan that he claimed to have sold. We traced the location using petrol receipts and a dry-cleaning docket. It was at a camping ground on the south coast. He paid the fees annually in advance. Inside there were boxes of magazines mostly from Eastern Europe and Asia. Child pornography.'

Joe leans forward. His little grey cells are humming like a hard drive.

'You're describing a classic grooming paedophile. He recognised Mickey's vulnerability. He became her friend and showered her with praise and presents, buying her toys and clothes. He took her photograph and told her how pretty she looked. Eventually, the sexual part of the "dance" begins, the sly touches and play wrestling. Non-sadistic paedophiles sometimes spend months and even years getting to know a child, conditioning them.'

'Exactly, they're extremely patient. So why would Howard invest all that time and effort into grooming Mickey and then suddenly snatch her off the stairs?'

Joe's arm trembles as if released from a catch. 'You're right. A grooming paedophile uses slow seduction not violent abduction.'

I feel relieved. It's nice to have someone agree with me.

Joe adds a note of caution. 'Psychology isn't an exact science. And even if Howard is innocent – it doesn't bring Mickey to life. One fact doesn't automatically change the other. What happened when you told Campbell Smith about your doubts?'

'He told me to put my badge down and act like a real person. Did I think Mickey was dead? I thought about the blood on the towel and I said yes. Everything pointed to Howard.'

'You didn't convict him – a jury did.'

Joe doesn't mean to sound patronising but I hate people making excuses for me. He drains his glass. 'This case really got to you, didn't it?'

'Yeah, maybe.'

'I think I know why.'

'Leave it alone, Professor.'

He pushes our wine glasses to one side and plants his elbow in the centre of the table. He wants to arm wrestle me.

'You don't stand a chance.'

'I know.'

'So why bother?'

'It'll make you feel better.'

'How?'

'Right now you keep acting as though I'm beating up on you. Well, here's your chance to get even. Maybe you'll realise that this isn't a contest. I'm trying to help you.'

Almost immediately my heart feels stung. I notice the bitter yeasty odour of his medication and my throat constricts. Joe's hand is still waiting. He grins at me. 'Shall we call it a draw?'

As much as I hate admitting it, Joe and I have a sort of kinship – a connection. Both of us are fighting against the 'bastard time'. My career is coming to a close and his disease will rob him of old age. I think he also understands how it feels to be responsible, by accident or omission, for the death of another human being. This could be my last chance to make amends; to prove I'm worth something; to square up the Great Ledger.

17

It's dark by the time a black cab drops me at Ali's parents' place. She opens the door quickly and closes it again. A dustpan and brush rest on the floor amid broken pieces of pottery.

'I had a visitor,' she explains.

'Keebal.'

'How did you know?'

'I can smell his aftershave – Eau de Clan. Where are your parents?'

'At my Aunt Meena's house – they'll be home soon.'

Ali gets the vacuum cleaner, while I dump the broken pottery in the dustbin. She's wearing a sari, which seems to own her as much as she owns it. Scents of cumin, sandalwood and jasmine escape from the folds.

'What did Keebal want?'

'I'm being charged with breaching protocols. Police officers on leave are not allowed to undertake private investigations or carry a firearm. There's going to be a hearing.'

'I'm sorry.'

'Don't worry about it.'

'No, this is my fault. I should never have asked you.'

She reacts angrily. 'Listen. I'm a big girl now. I make my own decisions.'

'I think I should leave.'

'No! This is not some glorious career I'm risking. I take care of ambassadors and diplomats, driving their spoiled children to school and their wives on shopping trips to Harrods. There's more to life.'

'What else would you do?'

'I could do lots of things. I could set up a business. Maybe I'll get married . . .'

'To "New Boy" Dave?'

She ignores me. 'It's the politics that piss me off most – and guys like Keebal who should have been weeded out years ago but instead they get promoted. He's a racist, chauvinistic prick!'

I look at the broken vase. 'Did you hit him?'

'I missed.'

'Shame.'

She laughs and I want to hug her. The moment passes.

Ali puts the kettle on and opens a packet of chocolate biscuits.

'I found out some interesting stuff today,' she says, dipping a biscuit into her coffee and licking her fingers. 'Aleksei Kuznet has a motor cruiser. He keeps it moored at Chelsea Harbour and uses it mainly for corporate hospitality. The skipper is Serbian. He lives on board. I could ask him some questions but I thought maybe we should tread softly.'

'Good idea.'

'There's something else. Aleksei has been selling a lot of stocks and shares in his companies. His house in Hampstead is also on the market.'

'Why?'

'A friend of mine works for the *Financial Times*. She says Aleksei is liquidating assets but nobody knows exactly why. He's rumoured to be highly leveraged and might need to pay off debts; or he could be getting ready to take over something big.'

'Selling his house.'

'It's been listed for the past month. Maybe we can dig up the basement and see where he buried his brother.'

'I heard Sacha got disembowelled.'

'That must have been before he went in the acid bath.'

We laugh wryly, each aware of how apocryphal stories have just enough truth to keep them alive.

Ali has something else but she pauses, holding me in suspense. 'I did some checking on Kirsten Fitzroy. Remember she told us she ran an employment agency in the West End? It operated from a building in Mayfair, leased by a company registered in Bermuda. The lease expired eight months ago and all the bills were paid. Since then any correspondence has been directed to a serviced office in Soho and then redirected to a Swiss law firm, which represents the beneficial owners, a Nevada-based company.'

Corporate structures like this stand out like a punk's haircut to everyone except DTI watchdogs. The only reason for them is to hide something or avoid paying taxes or escape liability.

'According to the neighbours the agency sometimes hosted private functions but mostly they hired staff out to short-term positions. The time sheets refer to cocktail waitresses, hostesses and waiters but there are no security numbers or tax records. Most were women and most had foreign-sounding names. Could be illegals.'

It smells like something else to me – cleft cheeks, dewy thighs and hollows between elastic and skin. Sex and money! No wonder Kirsten could afford the antique armour and medieval swords.

Ali retrieves her notes and sits on the sofa, massaging her feet as she reads. 'I did a property search on Kirsten's flat. She bought that place for only £500,000 – half the market value – from a private company called Dalmatian Investments.

The major shareholder of Dalmatian Investments is Sir Douglas Carlyle.'

A *frisson* runs through me. 'How do Kirsten and Sir Douglas know each other? And why was he so generous to her?'

'Maybe he was using her *services*,' suggests Ali.

'Or she did him some other favour.'

I might have misjudged Kirsten. It always struck me as odd her friendship with Rachel. They had very little in common. Rachel seemed determined to escape from her family's money and her privileged childhood, while Kirsten was equally devoted to moving up in the world and mixing in the right circles. She moved into Dolphin Mansions only weeks after Rachel did and the two became friends. They lived in each other's pockets, shopping, socialising and swapping clothes.

Sir Douglas knew about Rachel collapsing drunk on the bathroom floor and Mickey spending the night lying next to her. He had a spy, a rat in the ranks – Kirsten. Half a million pounds is a lot of money for simply keeping watch on a neighbour. It's enough to make kidnapping a possibility and could also explain why someone wants to find Kirsten.

Ali collects my coffee cup. 'I know you don't agree, sir, but I still think it's a hoax.'

'Motive?'

'Greed, revenge, getting Howard out of jail – could be any of them.'

'Where does Kirsten come into it?'

'You said yourself she had the opportunity. She knew enough about the case and was close enough to Rachel to set up a hoax.'

'But would she do it to her friend?'

'You mean the one she was spying on?'

We could argue all night and still not find an answer that fits all the known facts.

'There's one more thing,' says Ali, handing me a bundle of papers. 'I managed to get hold of the incident logs for the night you were shot. It can be your bedtime reading.'

The photocopied pages cover four square miles of north London between the hours of 10.00 p.m. and 3.00 a.m.

'I can tell you now there were five drug overdoses, three stolen cars, six burglaries, a carjacking, five hoax calls, a brawl at a buck's night, a house fire, eleven complaints about ringing burglar alarms, a burst water main, minor flooding, a nurse attacked on her way home from work and an unexploded tear gas shell found in a rubbish bin.'

'*How* many burglar alarms?'

'Eleven.'

'In the one street?'

'Yes. Priory Road.'

'Where was the burst water main?'

She consults the map and narrows her eyes. 'In Priory Road. A row of shops got flooded.'

'Can you find me the crew who repaired the water main?'

'You want to tell me why?'

'A man's allowed to have his secrets. What if I'm wrong? I don't want to destroy your delusions of my grandeur.'

She doesn't even bother rolling her eyes. Instead she reaches past me and takes the phone.

'Who are you calling?'

'My boyfriend.'

18

I dream of drowning – sucking watery mud into my lungs. There's a bright light and a chaos of voices against the darkness. My chest heaves vomit and brown water that runs from my nose, mouth and ears.

A woman appears, hovering over me. Her hips rest on mine and her hands press against my chest. She bends again and her lips touch mine. A pale birthmark leaks across her throat, spilling into the hollow between her breasts.

It takes me a long while to wake. I don't want to leave the dream. Opening my eyes, I get a sense of something that hasn't happened for a long while – not like this. I raise the covers a few inches to make sure I'm not mistaken. I should be embarrassed but feel somewhat elated. Any time I manage the one-gun salute these days is cause for celebration.

My euphoria doesn't last. Instead I think of Mickey and the ransom and the shootings on the river. There are too many missing pieces. There must have been other letters. What did I do with them? I put them somewhere safe. If something happened to me on the ransom drop, I would have wanted someone to know the truth.

There was a Royal Mail receipt in my wallet when Joe looked through it yesterday. I sent a registered letter to someone. Dragging my trousers off the chair, I tip the receipts on to the bed. The ink has almost washed away and I can only make out the postcode but it's enough.

Daj answers on the first ring and yells down the phone. I don't think she understands wireless technology and imagines I'm talking into a tin can.

'It's been three weeks. You don't love me.'

'I've been in hospital.'

'You never call.'

'I called you twice last week. You hung up on me.'

'Piffle!'

'I was shot.'

'Are you dying?'

'No.'

'See! You're such a drama queen. Your friend came to see me – that psychologist chap, Professor O'Loughlin. He was very sweet. He stayed for tea . . .'

Throughout this guilt trip, she carries on a second conversation with someone in the background. '*My other son, Luke, is a god. A beautiful boy, blond hair . . . eyes like stars. This one breaks my heart.*'

'Listen, Daj, I need to ask you a question. Did I post you something?'

'You never send me anything. *My Luke is such a sweet soul . . . Maybe you could knit him something. A vest to keep him warm.*'

'Come on, Daj. I want you to think really hard.'

Something resonates in her. 'You sent me a letter. You told me to look after it.'

'I'm coming to see you now. Keep the letter safe.'

'Bring me some dates.'

The main building of Villawood Lodge looks like an old school, with gable roofs and gargoyles above the downpipes.

The sandstone is just a façade and behind it is a seventies red-brick building, with aluminium window frames and cement roofing tiles.

Daj is waiting for me on the enclosed veranda. She accepts two kisses on each cheek and looks disappointed with only one box of dates. Her hands and fingers are moving constantly, brushing her arms as though something is crawling on her skin.

Ali tries to stay in the background but Daj looks at her suspiciously. 'Who are you?'

'This is Ali,' I say, making the introductions.

'She's very dark.'

'My parents were born in India,' explains Ali.

'Hmmmphf!'

I don't know why parents must embarrass their children. Maybe it's punishment for the mewling and puking and nights of broken sleep.

'Where is the envelope, Daj?'

'No, you talk to me first. You're going to take it and run away – just like last time.' She turns to a group of elderly residents. 'This is my son, Yanko! Yes, he's the policeman. The one who never comes to see me.'

I feel my cheeks redden. Daj didn't just steal a Jewish woman's name – she adopted a whole demeanour.

'What do you mean, I ran away last time?'

She turns to Ali. 'You see, he never listens. Not even as a baby. Head full of fluff.'

'When was I here last?'

'See! You've forgotten. It's been so long. Luke doesn't forget. Luke looks after me.'

'Luke is dead, Daj. What day did I come?'

'Hmmphf! Sunday. You had the newspapers and you were waiting for a call.'

'How do you know?'

'The mother of that missing girl called you. She must have

189

been very upset. You were telling her to be patient and wait for the call.'

She returns to brushing her arms with her hands.

'I need to see that envelope.'

'You won't find it unless I tell you where it is.'

'I don't have time for this.'

'You never have time. I want you to take me for a walk.'

She's wearing her walking shoes and a warm coat. I take her arm and we shuffle along the white gravel path, moving in slow motion as her feet struggle to keep up with mine. A handful of residents are doing t'ai chi on the lawn. Elsewhere the gardeners are planting bulbs for the spring.

'How is the food?'

'They're trying to poison me.'

'Have you been playing bridge?'

'Some of them cheat.'

Even the half-deaf can hear her.

'You really should make an effort, Daj.'

'Why? We're all just waiting to die.'

'It's not like that.'

I stop and button up the top of her coat. Spidery wrinkles radiate from her lips but her eyes haven't aged. From a distance we are mother and son sharing an intimate moment. Up close we are a stuttering monosyllabic tragi-comedy played out over fifty years.

'Can I have the envelope now?'

'After morning tea.'

Inside we sit in the dining room and go through the ritual of stilted conversation served with jam and cream. The manager is wandering between the tables.

'Hello there! How lovely to see you. Isn't it nice to have your son here, Mrs Ruiz? Maybe he'd like to come and hear Mr Wilson's lecture on trekking in the Andes.'

I'd rather be strung up and dunked head first into a vat of cold porridge.

Daj announces in a loud voice, 'Yanko was always the

strongest baby. I needed both hands to pull him away from the bottle. He didn't want the breast. '

'Nobody wants to know that, Daj.'

Louder this time, 'His father was a Nazi, you know. Like Arnold Schwarzenegger's father.' I feel my cheeks redden. She's on a roll. 'I don't know if he looks like his father. There were so many of them. Maybe all their sperm got mixed up inside me.'

The manager almost chokes and quickly makes her excuses before escaping. Her parting look reminds me of those my teachers used to give me when Daj came to Open Day at my school.

With the tea grown cold and a token scone left on the plate, I go back to Daj's room and collect the envelope. On my way out I drop into the manager's office and write a cheque.

'You must love your mother very much,' the secretary says.

I look at her impassively. 'No. She's my mother.'

Back in the car I open the large padded envelope. Inside are copies of the original postcard and envelope, along with the DNA tests and analysis of the ink, stationery and hair samples.

There is another letter in a plain plastic sleeve. Slipping my hand inside, I withdraw the note, blowing it open with my breath.

Dear Mrs Carlyle,

Your daughter is alive. She will remain so if you cooperate. Any mistakes and she will die. Her life is in your hands.

We require two million pounds' worth of superior quality cut diamonds, with no stone smaller than a carat. You will separate these stones into four velvet pouches. Each pouch must be taped to a square of quarter-inch-thick polystyrene foam and then double sealed in fluorescent plastic. Each package must be no more than six inches long, $2^1/_2$ inches wide and $^3/_4$ inches deep. They are to be placed inside a twenty-inch pizza box.

Three days from now you will place an advertisement in the Sunday Times travel classifieds seeking to rent a Tuscan cottage. This will contain a mobile phone number for further communications.

You must always answer the phone, Mrs Carlyle. Only you. Anyone else picks up and Michaela dies.

No negotiation will be possible. No excuses are acceptable. If the police are involved, you know the outcome. YOU HAVE ONE CHANCE.

The letter is neatly typed and appears to have been laser-printed. Although there is no attempt at childish handwriting this time, the emotional blackmail is just as great.

I placed the advertisement. I obtained the mobile phone. I must have believed Mickey was still alive. Maybe it was the weight of evidence rather than conclusive proof that convinced me. We convicted Howard on circumstantial evidence and perhaps I resurrected Mickey on anecdotes and inferences.

'At least it's confirmation,' says Ali, reading the DNA report.

'But it doesn't change the story. Chief Superintendent Smith won't reopen the investigation or admit mistakes were made. The forensic experts, lawyers, police witnesses and politicians aren't going to backtrack on Howard's conviction.'

'Do you blame them? Do you really want to set him free?'

'No.'

'Well, why are we doing this, sir?'

'Because I don't believe the ransom was a hoax. I think she's alive! Why else would I have risked everything?'

I stare across the road at a bus shelter where a young girl, barely twelve, looks longingly down the street for the 11.15 that won't arrive until 11.35.

This isn't about Howard. I don't care about reasonable doubt or innocence or guilt. I just want to find Mickey.

A storm is coming. The static electricity in the air lifts strands of hair on Ali's head and suspends them like invisible wires.

Within minutes raindrops are bouncing off the windscreen like marbles and the gutters are choked with leaves. Put it down to global warming or climate change, but I don't remember storms like this when I was younger.

The tyres of the Vauxhall swish through the wet. Ali has a way of concentrating when she drives that brings to mind an arcade game. It's as though she expects someone to jump a red light or step out from the pavement.

We cross Tower Bridge and turn east along the A2, passing through Blackheath and Shooters Hill before reaching Dartford. The storm has passed and the sky is low and grey. A cold wind picks up scraps of paper that swirl and dip along the pavements.

This is real English suburbia, with privet hedges and puddle-sized birdbaths. I can even smell the lawn fertiliser and watch television three houses away through the picture windows.

The White Horse pub advertises all-day breakfasts but doesn't open until midday. Peering through the windows I see an empty bar, chairs stacked on tables, a vacuum cleaner squatting on claret carpet, a dartboard and a brass foot-rail along the base of the bar.

I circle around the back, Ali never more than a few feet away. The large wooden gate is shut but not locked. It leads to a brick courtyard, full of silver kegs, with a motorbike and two cars, one of them marooned on bricks and painted camouflage green.

Just outside the door, a teenage boy, perhaps fifteen, is sitting on the bonnet, cleaning a carburettor with an oily rag. His worn sneakers swing back and forth and his jaw moves constantly – biting off words, chewing them up and spitting them out.

Spying me, his head jerks. 'FUKLEMICK!'

'Hello, Stevie.'

Sliding off the car he grasps my hand, pressing his ear to my wristwatch. 'Tickatock, tickatock.'

Tourette's syndrome has turned him into a riot of twitches, cusses and screeches – 'a human freak show', according to his father, Ray Murphy, the former caretaker at Dolphin Mansions.

I turn to Ali. 'This is Stevie Murphy.'

'S. Murphy. Smurfy. Smurf. Smurf.' He barks the words like a seal.

Ali runs her fingers through his short-cropped hair and he looks ready to purr like a kitten.

'Is your dad inside?'

His head jerks. 'FUKLEOFF! GONE!'

'Where's he gone?'

He shrugs.

Ray Murphy provided Kirsten with her alibi on the morning Mickey disappeared. According to both their statements, he was fixing her shower. A small man, slung low to the ground like a dachshund; I remember seeing Murphy fight at Wembley – top of the bill for the British bantam weight title. That must have been the early eighties.

I interviewed him twice during the original investigation. I thought he might have some ideas on how Mickey got out of the building.

'Same way as everyone else,' he told me. 'Through the front door.'

'You think maybe her friend Sarah missed her.'

'Kids don't always do what you want.'

He was speaking from experience. His eldest boy, Tony, was in Brixton nick, doing five years for armed robbery.

Turning away from Stevie, I knock three times on the pub door. A chair scrapes and the door opens a few inches. A large women with nicotine-coloured hair, lacquered to concrete, regards me suspiciously. She is wearing a furry yellow pullover and black leggings that make her look like an oversized duckling.

'Mrs Murphy?'

'You found him yet?'

'Excuse me?'

'You found my Ray? What slut is he shagging?'

194

Ali tries to sort out the confusion. 'Are you saying that you haven't seen your husband?'

'No shit, Miss Marple!'

She turns away from the door and waddles to her chair. The remains of breakfast cover the table and a TV perched on the counter is broadcasting images of a couple on a sofa, looking cheery and bright.

'I remember you,' she says, not looking away from the screen. 'You're that copper who looked for that little girl.'

'Mickey Carlyle.'

She gestures with her hand. 'Stevie remembers. He doesn't forget things.'

'Mickey ficky sticky licky,' says Stevie, playing with the rhyme.

'Don't you be disgusting,' scolds Mrs Murphy. Stevie flinches and avoids her slap. He steps back and swivels his hips in an oddly adult dance.

The kitchen is small and cluttered. A strange collection of souvenirs and bric-à-brac decorates the mantelpiece, including a Mickey Mouse salt and pepper set, a boxing trophy and a signed photograph of Henry Cooper.

Stevie is still dancing while Mrs Murphy has her eyes glued to the TV. I could be eighty before I get her undivided attention. I hit the standby button on the TV remote and Mrs Murphy looks at me as if I've turned off her life support.

'When did you last see Ray?'

'It's like I told them – 24 September.'

'Who did you tell?'

'The police! Twice I been down to see them, but they never believed me. They figured Ray had just taken off like before.'

'Before?'

She wipes her eyes and glances at Stevie. Ali picks up on the signal.

'Perhaps we should go outside,' she suggests. Stevie grins and hugs her around the waist.

'Just make sure he keeps his hands off you,' says his mother, glancing forlornly at the blank TV.

When the door closes, Mrs Murphy continues. 'Ray could never keep his trousers buttoned. But ever since we got the pub he stayed home. He loved the White Horse . . .' The statement trails off.

'Being a caretaker must have paid pretty well to afford this place.'

She bristles. 'We bought it fair and square. An uncle left Ray some money.'

'You ever meet this uncle?'

'He worked in Saudi Arabia. You don't pay taxes in Saudi Arabia. And Ray deserved it. He worked down them sewers for twenty years as a flusher. You know what that means? He shovelled shit. He worked knee deep in the stuff, in the dark, with the rats. He used to come across huge nests of them, writhing like worms in a bucket.'

'I thought he used to work on flood management.'

'Yeah, later, but that's only after his back gave out. He helped Thames Water Board draw up plans in case a surge tide flooded London. People forget the Thames is a tidal river. Always was, always will be.'

Her voice takes on a bitter tone. 'When they built the Thames Barrier they said surge tides weren't a problem no more. They got rid of Ray. He said they were idiots! Sea levels are rising and the south-east of England is sinking. You work it out.'

'What made him choose a pub?'

'You show me a man who doesn't want to own one.'

'Most of them drink away the profits.'

'Not my Ray – he hasn't touched a drop in sixteen years. He loved this place. Things were going OK, you know, until that bleedin' theme pub opened up the street. The Frog & Lettuce. What sort of name is that for a pub, eh? We were gonna do this place up and put on darts tournaments. Our Tony was going to arrange it. He knows lots of them professional players.'

'How is Tony?'

She goes quiet.

'I was hoping to have a word with him.'

'He's not here.'

The answer is too abrupt. I glance towards the ceiling. The woman is like a fortune-telling ball – shake her up and the answer is written all over her face.

'He's done nothing wrong, my Tony. He's been a good boy.'

'When did he get out?'

'Six months ago.'

'You ever hear Ray mention Kirsten Fitzroy.'

The name slowly rings a bell.

'She was that uppity bird who lived in Dolphin Mansions. Had that scar on her neck . . .'

'A birthmark.'

'Whatever,' she says dismissively.

'She ever visit or telephone?'

'Ray wouldn't be shagging her. She's too skinny. He likes his women with some meat on their bones. That's where he'll be now – screwing some tart. He'll come home soon enough. Always does.'

A car engine splutters and snarls outside. Stevie is peering under the bonnet while Ali sits behind the wheel, working the throttle. Somewhere on the floor above me a sash window opens and a string of invective fills the air, telling them to be quiet.

'Now that Tony is awake . . .' I say, maximising her discomfort.

She plants both hands flat on the table, rises to her feet and clumps wearily up the stairs.

A few minutes later Tony emerges, wiry and loose-limbed in a dressing gown. He has shaved his head until only one tuft of hair remains, cut into a circle above the nape of his neck. With the tattoos on his forearms and ears that stick out like satellite dishes, he looks like an extra from an episode of *Star Trek*.

Like his father, Tony had been a promising fighter until he

197

tried to apply some elements of the World Wrestling Federation to his boxing. The pageantry and phoney feuds might have been OK but when he started fixing fights he got into trouble. He came unstuck again when he tried to fix a darts tournament. He broke the fingers of a player who miscounted and won a game he was supposed to lose.

Tony opens the fridge and drinks from a carton of orange juice. Wiping his lips, he sits down. 'I don't have to answer nothing. I don't even have to get out of bed for you.'

'I appreciate you making the effort.' The sarcasm is lost on him. 'When did you last see your father?'

'Do I look like I keep a fucking diary?'

Reaching quickly across the table, avoiding the soggy cereal, I pin his forearm in my fist. 'Listen, you vicious little scumbag! You're still on parole. You want to go back inside? Fine. I'll make sure you're sharing a cell with the biggest, meanest faggot in the place. You won't have to get out of bed at all, Tony. He'll let you stay there all day.'

I can see him eyeing a butter knife on the table but it's only a fleeting thought.

'It was about three weeks ago. I gave him a lift into south London and picked him up that afternoon.'

'What was he doing?

'I dunno. He wouldn't talk about it.' Tony's voice rises. 'None of this involves me, you know. Not a fucking thing.'

'So you think he was up to something?'

'I don't know.'

'But you know something, don't you? You got suspicions.'

He chases spit around his mouth with his tongue, trying to decide what to tell me. 'There's a guy I used to share a cell with at Brixton nick. Gerry Brandt. We called him Grub.'

There's a name I haven't heard for a while.

Tony is still talking. 'Never seen anyone sleep like Grub. Never. You'd swear he was dead half the time except his chest was moving up and down. Guys would be kicking off in their cells or getting beat up by screws but Grub would sleep through it all, drooling all over himself like a baby. I'm telling you, that guy could *sleep*.'

Tony takes another swig of orange juice. 'Grub was only in for a few months. I hadn't seen him in years, you know, but about three months ago he turned up here looking like a playboy with a suntan and a suit.'

'He had money?'

'Maybe on his back, but he was driving a heap of shit. Not worth stealing, not worth burning.'

'What did he want?'

'I dunno. He didn't come to see me. He wanted to talk to the old man. I didn't hear what they were saying but they argued about something. My old man was spitting chips. Later he said Grub was looking for a job, but I know that's bullshit. Gerry Brandt don't wash glasses. He thinks he's a player.'

'They were doing business.'

Tony shrugs. 'Fuck knows. I didn't even know they knew each other.'

'When you shared a cell with this Gerry Brandt, did you ever mention your old man to him?'

'Might have said something. Cell talk, you know.'

'And when your dad went up to London, what makes you think he was going to see Gerry?'

'I dropped him outside a boozer in Pentonville Road. I remember Grub talking 'bout the place. It was his local.'

I take a photograph of Kirsten from my jacket pocket and slide it across the table. 'Do you recognise her?'

Tony studies it for a moment. Lying comes easier than telling the truth, which is why he takes so long. He shakes his head. I believe him.

Back in the car I go over the details with Ali, letting her bounce questions off me. She is one of those people who reasons out loud whereas I work things out in my head.

'Do you remember someone called Gerry Brandt?'

She shrugs. 'Who is he?'

'A nasty toerag with a toilet mouth and a taste for pimping.'

'Charming.'

'His name came up in the original investigation. When Howard was taking photographs outside Dolphin Mansions on the day Mickey disappeared, Gerry Brandt turned up in one of the shots – a face in the crowd. Later his name popped up again, this time on the sex offenders' register. He had an early conviction for sex with a minor. Nobody read much into the sex charge. He was seventeen at the time and the girl was fourteen. They knew each other. We wanted to interview Gerry but we couldn't find him. He just seemed to vanish. Now he's turned up again. According to Tony, he came to see Ray Murphy three months back.'

'It could be just a coincidence.'

'Maybe.'

Kirsten and Ray Murphy are both missing. Three years ago they provided each other with alibis when Mickey disappeared. She must have walked straight past Kirsten's door on her way downstairs to meet Sarah. Meanwhile, Sir Douglas Carlyle was paying Kirsten to keep watch on Rachel and gather evidence for a custody application. Perhaps he decided to go one step further and have his granddaughter kidnapped. It doesn't explain where she's been or why a ransom demand has arrived three years later.

Maybe Ali is right and it's all a hoax. Kirsten could have collected Mickey's hair from a pillow or a brush. She might have known about the money box. She could have concocted a plan to take advantage of the situation.

A chill wades through my skin like it's five o'clock in the morning. The Professor says coincidences are just two things happening simultaneously, but I don't believe that. Nothing twists a knife quicker than fate.

19

The Thames Water truck is parked halfway down Priory Road, facing south into the low sun. A foreman is standing beside it, sucking on a cigarette. He straightens up and adjusts his crotch. 'This is my day off; it had better be important.'

Not surprisingly, he looks like a man with nothing more important to do than play snooker with his mates at the pub.

Ali makes the introductions and the foreman grows more circumspect.

'Mr Donovan, on 25 September you repaired a burst water main in this street.'

'Why? Is someone complaining? We did nothing wrong.'

Interrupting his protestations, I tell him I just want to know what happened.

Crushing the cigarette under his heel, he nods towards a dark stain of fresh bitumen covering thirty feet of road. 'Looked like the Grand fucking Canyon, it did. Half this road got washed away. I ain't never seen a water main rupture like that one.'

'How do you mean?'

He hitches up his trousers. 'Well, you see, some of these

pipes have been around for a hundred years and they're wearing out. Fix one and another one goes. Bang! It's like trying to plug a dozen holes when you only got ten fingers.'

'But this one was different?'

'Yeah. Mostly they break on a join – the weakest point. This one just sort of blew apart.' He presses his hands together and springs them open. 'We couldn't reseal it. We had to replace twenty feet of pipe.'

'Any idea what would have caused a break like that?' asks Ali.

He shakes his head and adjusts his crotch again. 'Lew – a guy on our crew – used to be a sapper in the army. He reckoned it was some sort of explosion because of the way the metal got bent out of shape. He figured maybe a pocket of methane ignited in the sewers.'

'Does that happen often?'

'Nope. Used to happen a lot. Nowadays they vent the sewers better. I heard about something similar to this a few years back. Flooded six streets in Bayswater.'

Ali has been walking up and down the road, peering between her feet. 'How do you know where the pipes are?' she asks.

'That depends,' says Donovan. 'A magnetometer can pick up iron and sometimes we need ground-probing radar, but in most cases you don't need any gizmos. The mains are built alongside the sewers.'

'And how do you find those?'

'You walk downhill. The whole system is gravity fed.'

Crouching down I run my fingers over a metal grate covering a drain. The bars are about three-quarters of an inch apart. The ransom had been wrapped very carefully. Each package was waterproof and designed to float. They were six inches long, $2\frac{1}{2}$ inches wide and $\frac{3}{4}$ inches deep . . . just the right size.

Whoever sent the demand must have expected a tracking device. And the one place a transmitter or a global positioning system can't operate is below ground.

'Can you get me down in the drains, Mr Donovan?'

'You're joking, right?'

'Humour me.'

He rocks his hand back and forth. 'Since 9/11 they been right edgy about the sewers. You take the Tyburn Sewer – it runs right under the US ambassador's residence and Buckingham Palace. The Tachbrook goes under Pimlico. You won't find 'em on maps – least, not the maps they publish nowadays. And you won't even find the records in public libraries. They took 'em away.'

'But it still must be possible. I can make an application.'

'Yeah, I guess so. Might take a while.'

'How long?'

He rubs his chin. 'Few weeks, I guess.'

I can see where this is going. The vast, moribund wheels of British bureaucracy will take my request and pass it between committees, sub-committees and working groups where it will be debated, deliberated upon, knocked about and run up the flagpole – and that's just to decide a form of words for the rejection.

Well, there is more than one way to skin a cat. There are three according to the Professor and he should know – he's been to medical school.

Nearly a decade ago in the battle over the Newbury bypass a man lived in a hole no wider than his shoulders for sixteen days. Police had to dig him out but he could tunnel faster with his bare hands than a dozen men with picks and shovels.

Back then he called himself an eco-warrior, fighting the 'earth rapists'. The tabloids nicknamed him 'Moley'.

It takes Ali three hours and fifty quid in bribes to find his last known address – an abandoned warehouse in Hackney in one of those run-down areas that are hard to find unless you have a can of spray paint or need a fix.

Driving slowly between soot-blackened factories and

boarded-up shops, we pull up opposite wasteland where kids are playing football between goals marked out by their puffa jackets. Our arrival is noted. The message will be telegraphed through the neighbourhood on whatever grapevine reaches under rocks and into holes.

'Maybe I should stay with the car,' suggests Ali, 'while it still has four wheels.'

Ahead of us, a disused factory has soaked up layers of graffiti until one forms an undercoat for the next. At one end is a raised loading dock and large shutters. To one side a regulation doorway has been covered with a sheet of corrugated iron. Levering it open, I step inside. Shafts of light slant through windows high up on the walls, turning floating cobwebs into silver threads.

The ground floor is mostly empty, apart from discarded crates and boxes. Climbing to the second floor, I find a series of former offices, with broken plasterboard panels and exposed wires. One particular room, barely six feet square, has a narrow shelf with a blanket and a mattress stuffed with clothes. A pair of trousers hangs from a nail and cans of food are lined up on one of the beams. Resting on a box in the centre of the room is a tin plate and a mug with a Batman logo.

I trip over an oil lamp on the floor and catch it before it breaks. The glass is warm. He must have heard me coming.

Around me the walls are plastered with sheets of newspaper and old election posters, forming a collage of faces from the news – Saddam Hussein, Tony Blair, Yasser Arafat and David Beckham. George Bush jnr is dressed in desert fatigues holding a Thanksgiving turkey.

Another page has a picture of Art Carney along with an obituary. I didn't know Art Carney had died. I always remember him in *The Honeymooners* with Jackie Gleason. He was the neighbour upstairs. In this one episode he and Jackie are trying to learn golf from a book and Jackie says to him,

'First you must address the ball.' So Art gives it a wave and says, 'Helloooo ball!'

At precisely that moment my fist punches through the newspaper and closes around a clump of filthy, matted hair. As I drag my arm forward, the paper shreds and a squealing, feral creature squirms at my feet.

'I didn't do it! It wasn't me!' cries Moley, as he rolls into a ball. 'Don't hurt me! Don't hurt me!'

'Nobody is going to hurt you. I'm the police.'

'Trespassing. You're trespassing. You got no right! You can't just come in here – you can't.'

'You're squatting illegally, Moley, I don't think you have many rights.'

He looks up at me with pale eyes in a paler face. Hair twisted into dreadlocks hangs down his neck like rats' tails. He's wearing cargo pants and a camouflage jacket, with metal buckles and handles that look like ripcords for a non-existent parachute.

Having been coaxed to sit on a packing case, he watches me suspiciously. I marvel at his makeshift furniture.

'I like your place.'

'Keeps the rain off,' he says, with no hint of sarcasm. His sideburns make him look like a badger. He scratches his neck and under his arms. Christ, I hope it's not contagious.

'I need to go into the sewers.'

'Not allowed.'

'But you can show me.'

He shakes his head and nods at the same time. 'No. No. No. Not allowed.'

'I told you, Moley, I'm a police officer.'

I light the oil lamp and set it on a box. Then I spread a map on the floor, smoothing the creases. 'Do you know this place?'

I point to Priory Road but Moley stares at it blankly.

'It's near the corner of Abbot's Place,' I explain. 'I'm looking for a storm-water drain or a sewer.'

Moley scratches his neck.

Suddenly, it dawns on me – he can't read a map. All his points of reference are below ground and he can't equate them to crossroads or landmarks above ground.

I take an orange from my pocket and put it on the map. It rolls several times and rocks to a stop. 'You can show me.'

Moley watches it intensely. 'Follow the fall. Water finds the way.'

'Yes, exactly, but I need your help.'

Moley is still fixated by the orange. I hand it to him and he puts it into his pocket, zipping it closed. 'You want to see where the devil lives.'

'Yes.'

'Just you.'

'Just me.'

'Tomorrow.'

'Why not today?'

'I need to see Weatherman Pete. Pete will give us the forecast.'

'What difference does it make in a sewer?'

Moley makes a whooshing sound like an express train. 'You don't want to be down there when it rains. It's like God himself pulled the chain.'

20

'Why are you so interested in the drains?' asks Joe. He motions me to sit with a mannered, almost mechanical movement, as though he's been practising.

It's Monday morning and we're in his office, a private practice just off Harley Street. It's a Georgian house with black painted downpipes and white painted windowsills. The plaque on the door has a string of initials after his name, including a small round smiley face designed to make patients feel less intimidated.

'It's just a theory. The ransom was supposed to float.'

'Is that all?'

'Ray Murphy used to work in the sewers. Now he's missing.'

Joe's left arm jerks in his lap. There's a book lying open on his desk: *Reversing Memory Loss*.

'How's the leg?'

'Getting stronger.'

He wants to ask me about the morphine but changes his mind. For a few seconds the silence spreads out like thick oil. Joe stands and sways for a moment, fighting for balance. Then he begins a slow, deliberate walk around the room, each step containing a struggle. Occasionally, he drifts to the right and has to straighten.

Glancing around his office, I notice that things are slightly skew-whiff – the books on the shelves and files on the filing cabinet. He must be finding it harder to keep things tidy.

'Do you remember Jessica Lynch?' he asks.

'The US soldier captured in Iraq.'

'When they rescued her she had no recollection of any events from the time of the ambush until she awoke in an Iraqi hospital. Even months afterwards, despite all the debriefings and mental evaluations, she still couldn't remember. The doctors called it a memory trace, which is completely different from amnesia. Amnesia means you have a memory but something traumatic happens and you suddenly forget. In Jessica's case her brain never allowed her to collect memories. It was like she was sleepwalking.'

'So you're saying I might never remember everything that happened?'

'You might *never have* remembered.'

He lets the news sink in while I try desperately to push it away. I don't want to accept an outcome like that. I *am* going to remember.

'Have you ever been involved in a ransom drop?' he asks.

'About fifteen years ago I helped run an operation to catch an extortionist. He threatened to contaminate baby food.'

'So what do you plan for?'

'There are two types of drop – the long haul or the quick intervention. The long haul involves a complex set of instructions, making the courier jump through hoops, moving him around from A to B to C, stretching the resources of the police.'

'And the alternative?'

'Well, it starts off the same way, sending the courier back and forth between public phone boxes, on or off buses, swapping directions . . . then suddenly, somewhere along the way, something happens. They strike hard and fast, radically changing the plan.'

'For example?'

'Back in the eighties a fellow called Michael Sams kidnapped a young estate agent, Stephanie Slater, and demanded a ransom. Stephanie's boss was the courier. It was a dark, foggy night in an isolated part of South Yorkshire. Sams left messages on lamp-posts and in public phone boxes. He moved the courier around like a chess piece through narrow country lanes until suddenly he stopped the car with a roadblock. The courier had to leave the money on a wooden tray on the edge of a bridge. Sams was down below. He pulled a rope, the tray fell down and he escaped on a motor scooter along a muddy track.'

'He got away?'

'With £175,000.'

The Professor's eyes betray a glimmer of admiration. Like a lot of people he appreciates ingenuity but this wasn't a game. Michael Sams had already killed a girl.

'Would you have chosen Rachel to be the courier?'

'No.'

'Why?'

'You can't expect to make rational decisions when it's your own child involved. They must have nominated Rachel. It's what I would have done in their shoes.'

'OK, what else would you have done?'

'I would have prepared her. I would have gone over the different scenarios and tried to get her ready.'

'How?' Joe points to an empty chair. 'Imagine Rachel is sitting here now. How would you prepare her?'

I stare at the empty chair and try to picture Rachel. There were three coffee cups in my kitchen sink. Rachel was with me. Who else? Aleksei perhaps. They were *his* diamonds.

Closing my eyes I can see Rachel in black jeans and a grey pullover. Until now her appearance has melted into vagueness because of her pain but she's an attractive woman, rather bookish and sad. I can see why Aleksei was drawn to her.

She has her legs together and a soft leather satchel on her lap. Scraps of plastic and confetti-like foam are scattered on the kitchen floor.

'Remember, this is not a done deal,' I say. 'This is a negotiation.'

She nods at me.

'They want you to follow blindly but we cannot let them dictate terms,' I tell her. 'You have to keep insisting on assurances that Mickey is alive. Keep asking for proof. Say you want to see her and speak to her.'

'But they'll say we have the hair and bikini to prove it.'

'And you'll say they prove nothing. You just want to be sure.'

'What if they want me to drop the ransom somewhere?'

'Don't do it. Demand a straight exchange – Mickey for the diamonds.'

'And if they don't agree?'

'It's no deal.'

Her voice is as fragile as spun glass. 'What if they don't bring Mickey? What if they want the diamonds first?'

'You say no.'

'They'll kill her.'

'No! They'll claim that she's alone or hungry or running out of air or water. They'll try to frighten and bully you . . .'

'But what if . . . ,' her voice catches, ' . . . what if they hurt her?'

I can almost see the penny dropping.

'They're going to kill her, aren't they? They'll never let her go because she can identify them . . .'

I cover her hands with mine and make her look at me. 'Stop! Pull yourself together. Right now Mickey is their most valuable asset.'

'And afterwards?'

'That's why we have to dictate the terms and you have to be ready.'

On my feet now, I stand behind her. 'OK, let's practise what you're going to say.' I pull out my mobile and dial. The phone in front of her begins to ring. I nod towards it.

Uneasily she flips open the receiver. 'Hello?'

'DITCH THE FUCKING WIRE!'

She looks up at me and stutters. 'What do you mean?'

'NOW, BITCH! DITCH THE WIRE OR I KILL MICKEY. RIGHT NOW.'

'I'm not . . . I'm not wearing a wire.'

'DON'T LIE TO ME. Dump it out the window.'

'No.'

'SHE'S DEAD. YOU HAD YOUR CHANCE.'

'I'll do whatever you say. Anything. Please. I'm doing it . . .'

Rachel is shaking. I take the phone from her hands and terminate the call.

'OK, he didn't know you had a wire. He bluffed you. You should have called his bluff.'

Rachel nods and takes a deep breath.

We go through the rehearsal again. I want her to be polite and forceful without being confrontational. Disagree but don't challenge. Delay.

'Tell them you're scared. You're new to this. You're nervous. They want control so let them think you're vulnerable.'

For the next two hours we practise, going through the various scenarios. Realistically, I can only instil a handful of ideas. Over and over I repeat the same question. 'What are you going to ask?'

'To *see* Mickey.'

'When are you going to hand over the ransom?'

'When I *have* Mickey.'

'That's right. When you're holding her by the hand.'

I look into her eyes, hoping to see the same resolve that I witnessed at the first press conference after Mickey had gone missing when Rachel refused to break down or cry. I saw the same determination on the courthouse steps after the verdict when she read from a prepared statement.

'You don't have to go through with this,' I remind her. Rachel doesn't blink or even breathe. Her fingers flutter against the buckles of the satchel.

On the edge of consciousness I hear a phone ringing. Joe leans across his desk and diverts the call. He looks at me expectantly, his left arm jerking like a broken fire hose.

'You remembered something.'

I feel my stomach heave and settle again. 'Not enough.'

His arm has stopped shaking. His face assumes a pale blankness except for the brightness in his eyes. Life is one big mystery to him, an ever-shifting puzzle. Most people don't stop to think. Joe can't stop himself thinking.

21

Ali has had her phone turned off all evening. Finally she calls me.

'Where have you been?'

'Working. I'm coming home now.'

'Not on my account.'

'I've been *working*.'

Twenty minutes later she comes through the door looking different. They say you can tell when a woman has had sex. Maybe I never did it well enough.

Ali has something for me. The Police National Computer confirmed that Gerry Brandt shared a prison cell with Tony Murphy four years ago. Brandt was released on parole two months before Mickey disappeared.

'And how's this for another coincidence?' she says. 'Tony Murphy got paroled six months ago – just in time to be involved in all this.'

'How is "New Boy" Dave?'

With just a hint of a smile, 'He's a very happy bunny.'

Although tired, she sits and goes through her notes. Gerry Brandt disappeared off radar screens in the same month that

Mickey went missing. Since then there have been no tax returns, social security payments, traffic fines, police cautions or overdue library books . . . He popped up again three months ago when he applied for the dole.

'So tell me, my clever young thing, does Mr Brandt have a current location?'

'As a matter of fact he does,' she says, holding up her hand. Between her fingers is a small piece of folded paper – an address in south London.

Bermondsey is one of those areas that has been raped twice – once by the Luftwaffe and then by architects in the seventies who put up Stalinesque tower blocks and concrete council estates. It's like seeing a set of healthy teeth riddled with fillings.

We pull up outside a big old white place, veiled in foliage. Beneath a pelmet of ivy, I see a small balcony supported by ornate brackets and above a steep slate roof as dark and wet as a washed blackboard.

I look at my watch. It's just gone seven in the morning.

'Rise and shine, Princess.'

A girl of about nineteen with tousled hair peers from the partially opened door. She's wearing a rugby jumper and a pair of cotton briefs. A tattoo peeps from beneath the waistband.

She looks at Ali's badge and unlocks the chain. Then we follow her down the hallway to the living room. Ali admonishes me silently for checking out the swaying arse.

Two more girls are asleep on the floor wrapped in each other's arms. Someone else of indeterminate sex is cocooned in a bedspread on the sofa. The air stinks of hash and stale cigarette smoke.

'Heavy night?'

'Not me, I don't drink,' she says.

'We're looking for Gerry Brandt.'

'He's upstairs.'

She sits on a dining chair and rests her bare foot on the table to pick at a scab on her knee.

'Well, maybe you'd like to go and tell him that we'd like a word,' Ali replies.

The girl ponders this and then slides her foot off the table. She makes the stairs seem very steep. The dining room is plastered with cheap flyers for pub bands and there is a padded bench in the corner beneath a bar and weights. Through the door into the kitchen I see last night's takeaway curry spilling out of the pedal bin.

The girl has returned. 'Grub says he'll be a minute.'

She goes into the bathroom and, without bothering fully to close the door, sits on the toilet and urinates. After finishing, she cleans her teeth, watching me in the mirror. Another toilet flushes upstairs, followed by the sound of a window opening. A few seconds later a figure drops past the kitchen window and lands in the yard.

I get a glimpse of his face and see pure unadulterated fear in his eyes.

By the time I reach the back door he has vaulted the fence and is sprinting up the rear lane. He is barefoot, wearing a cotton vest and faded tracksuit bottoms.

I do a stomach roll over the fence and land heavily on cobblestones. He's thirty yards in front of me, heading for a gate. I figure Ali has gone out the front, trying to cut him off.

The bastard leaps the gate almost without breaking his stride. My approach is to demolish it because it's slippery underfoot and I can't stop in time. He turns left, dodges an overflowing skip and crosses the road, leaping a hedge as he cuts the corner into an adjoining road.

Give me twenty years and two good legs and I still couldn't catch this guy. I'm dropping further behind, coughing up phlegm and seeing dots dance in front of my eyes.

A British Gas crew is digging a trench down one side of

the street. The red clay is piled up next to the open pit. I make the jump easily enough, but I haven't looked for traffic. The silence of the electric motor is what deceives me. The milk float has pulled out of a parking space and is only travelling a few miles per hour, but I'm in full flight and still in midair. I clip the front corner nearside mudguard and it feels like the entire All Black front row had driven me into the tarmac.

Rolling half a dozen times, I collide with the gutter and know my thigh is corked. What is it about my legs? People are just picking on me now!

Gerry is at the end of the road. He turns his head to look over his shoulder and at that moment is up-ended. Ali has driven her shoulder into his stomach, wrapped her arms around his waist and used his momentum to lift him up and throw him down. She drops her knees into his back and I can almost feel the air leaving his lungs.

She is sitting on him, trying to drag his arms behind his back to handcuff them. As she reaches to her belt for the cuffs, Gerry snaps his head back, slamming into her chin. She almost loses her balance but she keeps her knees locked to his sides, trying to hold him down.

I'm on my feet, limping towards them. My leg is numb and next to useless.

Ahead of me Gerry has dragged himself up on all fours. Ali has her thighs locked around his waist and is riding him like a kid playing 'horsies' with her father. She wraps her forearm around his neck, trying to compress his windpipe. Gerry is on his haunches, trying to stand. Now he's up. He's six one and over sixteen stone.

I can see what's going to happen. I can hear myself screaming at Ali to let go, but she's clinging tight. There is a low brick wall fronting the yard. It's only a foot high, with a straight edge.

He lines Ali up, holding her legs now. Then he looks directly

216

at me. A strange noise, an animal sound comes from inside him. Then he falls backwards. Every bit of their combined weight comes to bear across Ali's spine and the edge of the wall. She bends and she breaks.

No sound reaches me. I hear my own voice calling her name. The gas board workers are transfixed, standing in their cement-coloured overalls as if suddenly turned to stone. I focus on one of them, yelling at him until his eyes shift from Ali and lock on to mine.

'Get an ambulance. Now!'

The pain in my leg is forgotten. Ali's body is draped over the wall. She hasn't moved. Fragments of light leap from the chrome on the parked cars and the tears in her eyes.

Kneeling beside her, I can see myself reflected in her corneas as she stares upwards.

'I can't feel my legs,' she whispers.

'Just stay where you are. Help is coming.'

'I guess I fucked up pretty good.'

'That was some tackle. Where did you learn to tackle like that?'

'Four brothers.'

'Whatever happened to Home Economics?'

She takes a ragged breath. God knows what's broken. I want to reach inside her body and hold her together.

'I wouldn't ask you normally, sir, but can you brush the hair out of my eyes?'

I push the fringe across her forehead and tuck it behind her ears.

'Maybe I'll take tomorrow off,' she says. 'I could catch the Eurostar and go shopping in Paris.'

'Maybe I'll come with you.'

'You hate shopping and you hate Paris.'

'I know, but it's good to get away sometimes.'

'What about Mickey?'

'We'll have found her by then.'

There are no soft blankets to tuck under her chin or canteens of water she can sip. She isn't crying any more. Her eyes are as serene as a deer's. I can hear the ambulance siren.

Gerry Brandt has long gone. He has left behind a trampled flowerbed and a torn scrap of his T-shirt trapped in Ali's fingers.

22

I hate hospitals. They're full of horrible diseases that end with 'ia' and 'oma'. I know what I'm talking about. My first wife died in one of them, eaten away by cancer. Sometimes I wonder if the hospital didn't make her sicker than the disease.

It took two years for her to die but it seemed longer. Laura celebrated every day as a bonus but I couldn't do the same. It was like a slow torture, the endless, repetitive round of doctors' appointments, scans, drugs, bad news and cheerful smiles to hide the truth.

Claire and Michael were only thirteen but they handled it well enough. It was me who went off the rails. I disappeared and spent eighteen months driving aid trucks into Bosnia-Herzegovina during the war. I should have been at home looking after my children instead of sending postcards. Maybe that's why they've never forgiven me.

They won't let me see Ali. The doctors and nurses move past me as if I'm a plastic chair in the waiting room. The triage nurse, Amanda, is plump and composed. When she speaks the words tumble out like paratroopers.

'You'll have to wait for the spinal surgeon. He won't be long. There are hot drinks and snacks in the machines. Sorry, I can't provide change.'

'We've been waiting for four hours.'

'Won't be long now,' she says, counting rolls of bandages in a box.

Ali's family is listening to the conversation. Her father leans forward until his head rests on his folded arms. A gentle, respectful man, he's like a torpedoed ship sinking beneath the waves.

Her mother is holding a paper cup of water, occasionally dipping her finger into the liquid and painting it across her eyelids. Three of her brothers are also in the waiting room and watch me with cold stares.

The stench of my own body odour rises from my shirt. It's the same smell that fills airline cabins when businessmen take off their jackets. Turning away from the nurse, I walk slowly back to my seat. As I pass Ali's father, I pause and wait for him to look up.

'I'm sorry this happened.'

Out of politeness he shakes my hand.

'You were with her, Detective Inspector?'

'Yes.'

He nods and looks past me. 'What is a woman doing catching miscreants and criminals? That is men's work.'

'She is a very fine police officer.'

He doesn't reply. 'My daughter was a very good athlete as a teenager. A sprinter. I once asked her why she wanted to run so fast. She said she was trying to catch up with the future – to see what sort of woman she was going to become.' He smiles.

'You should be proud of her,' I say.

He nods and shakes his head at the same time.

Moving past him, I slip into the toilet and douse my face with cold water. Taking off my shirt, I rub water under my arms, feeling it leak down to the belt of my trousers. Shutting the cubicle door, I lower the toilet lid and sit down.

This is my fault. I should have gone upstairs to find Gerry Brandt. I should have caught him before he escaped over the back fence. I can still see the look on his face as he held Ali's legs and fell backwards, breaking her body against the wall. He knew what he was doing. Now I'm going to find him. I'm going to bring him in. And maybe, if I'm lucky, he might resist arrest.

The next moment my body jerks awake. I have fallen asleep in a toilet cubicle with my head against the wall. The knots in my neck feel like fists as I drag myself upwards.

What day is it – Monday, no Tuesday morning? It must be morning but it's dark. I don't even look at my watch.

My head starts to clear as I make it outside to the waiting room. My hair is matted on my forehead and my nose is crusted and dry.

The consultant is talking to Ali's family. Sick with fear I cross the room, zigzagging through rows of plastic chairs. Gloom seems to grow under the harsh strip lighting.

I hesitate for a moment, unsure whether to intrude, but the need to know is too great. As I reach the cluster of people, nobody looks up. The consultant is still talking.

'She has fractured two vertebrae and dislocated them, squeezing her spine like toothpaste in a tube. Until the bruising goes down we won't know for certain the extent of the paralysis or whether it's permanent. I have another patient, a jockey, who has similar injuries. He was thrown off a horse and landed on the running rail. He's doing very well and should walk again.'

Sweat chills on my skin and the long empty corridors drop away in every direction.

'She's zonked out on painkillers but you can see her,' he says, scratching his unshaven chin. 'Try not to upset her.' At that same moment his bleeper sounds and concusses in my ears. He looks at Ali's parents apologetically and leaves in a clatter of shoes along the corridor.

I wait my turn outside Ali's room. I can't look at her parents' faces as they leave. Her mother has been crying and her brothers want someone to blame. There's nowhere to hide.

A wave of nausea ebbs inside me as I push open the door, taking several steps into the semi-darkness. Ali is lying flat on her back, staring upwards. A skeletal steel frame holds her neck and head in place, preventing her from turning.

I don't get too close, hoping to spare her my stench and ugliness. It's too late. She sees me in the mirror above her head and says, 'Morning.'

'Morning.'

I glance about the room and take a chair. Gold bars of light leak through the curtains, falling across her bed.

'How are you feeling?' I ask.

'Right now I'm flying with Lucy and her diamonds. I don't feel a thing.' She takes a breath, which is half a groan, and manages a smile. Tear trails have dried on either side of her eyes. 'They say I need an operation on my spine. I'm going to get them to add a few inches. I've always wanted to be six feet tall.'

She wants me to laugh but I can't manage more than a smile. Ali has gone quiet. Her eyes are closed. Quietly, I stand to leave, but her hand reaches out and grabs my wrist.

'What did the doctor tell you?'

'They won't know for a few days.'

Choking on the words. 'Will I be able to walk?'

'They think so.'

Her eyes squeeze shut and tears form in the delta of wrinkles.

'You'll be fine,' I say, trying to sound convincing. 'You'll be back at work in no time – all six feet of you.'

Ali wants me to stay. I watch her sleeping until a nurse

shoos me outside. It's almost midday. A dozen calls are waiting in my message bank – most of them from Campbell Smith.

Calling the operations room, I try to get the latest on Gerry Brandt, who is still missing. Nobody will talk to me. Finally I get through to the SIO, who takes pity on me. There were three hundred Ecstasy tablets beneath the floorboards in Gerry Brandt's bedroom, as well as traces of speed in the S-bend of the upstairs toilet. Is that why he ran?

I arrive at the Harrow Road Police Station just before two and pass through a crowded front office where two motorists with bloodstained shirts are yelling about a traffic accident.

Campbell shuts the office door behind me. He looks every inch a Chief Constable-in-waiting, with his arms behind him and a face stiffer than shirt cardboard.

'Jesus Christ, Ruiz! Two fractured vertebrae, broken ribs and a ruptured spleen – she could finish in a wheelchair. And where were you? Being run over by a fucking milk float . . .'

I can still hear them laughing down the hall. The jokes haven't started yet but that's only because Ali is so sick.

Campbell opens his top drawer and produces a sheet of typed paper. 'I warned you. I told you to stay out of this.'

He hands me a resignation letter. Mine. I am to retire immediately on health grounds.

'Sign this.'

'What are you doing to find Gerry Brandt?'

'That's not your concern. Sign the letter.'

'I want to help you find him. I'll sign the letter if you let me help find him.'

Campbell grows indignant, huffing and puffing like a pantomime wolf. I can't see his eyes. They are hidden beneath eyebrows that crawl across his forehead, fleeing towards his ears.

I tell him about the ransom letters and the DNA tests, recounting what I've managed to piece together about the ransom drop. I know it sounds far-fetched but I'm getting closer. I just need help to follow the trail. Gerry Brandt had something to do with it.

'What?'

'I don't know yet.'

Campbell shakes his head in disbelief. 'You should hear yourself. You're obsessed.'

'You're not listening. Someone kidnapped Mickey. I don't think Howard killed her. She's still alive.'

'No! You listen to me. This is bullshit. Mickey Carlyle died three years ago. Answer me something – if someone kidnapped her, why did they wait three years before sending a ransom demand? It doesn't make sense because it isn't true.'

He pushes my resignation letter back at me. 'You should have retired when I gave you the chance. You're divorced. You hardly see your kids. You live alone. Look at you! Christ, you're a mess! I used to tell young detectives to model themselves on you, but now you're an embarrassment. You stayed on too long, Vincent . . .'

'No, don't ask me.'

'You're over the hill.'

'What hill? I didn't see any hill!'

'Sign the letter.'

Turning my face away, I squeeze my eyes shut, blinking away the bitterness. The more I think about it, the angrier it makes me. I can feel it stirring in my guts, churning around like the pistons of a steam engine.

Campbell withdraws the fountain pen and returns it to his drawer. 'You give me no option. I regret to inform you that your commission with the London Metropolitan Police has been withdrawn. The Commissioner has decided you are a liability. He won't let you give evidence under the label of a serving officer.'

'What do you mean, give evidence?'

Campbell takes another letter from his desk drawer. This one is a subpoena.

'At ten o'clock this morning lawyers for Howard Wavell subpoenaed you to give evidence at his appeal hearing at midday tomorrow. They know about the ransom demand and the DNA test. They're going to argue that if a senior serving police officer approved the payment of a ransom for Michaela Carlyle we must believe she's still alive.'

'How did they find out?'

'You tell me. They're also applying for bail. Howard Wavell could be out of prison by tomorrow afternoon.'

Suddenly, I understand. My sacking will be part of the damage limitation. I'll be a maverick cop instead of a serving officer.

Breathing dies in the room. Campbell is still talking but I don't hear the words. I'm living ten seconds ahead of time or ten seconds behind. Meanwhile, a phone is ringing somewhere that nobody wants to answer.

23

Sitting low on worn springs in the front seat of the van, I peer through the windscreen at the growing darkness. An Elvis doll on a suction cup dances to and fro on the dashboard.

Weatherman Pete is driving, with his woollen hat and walrus moustache. His jaw moves constantly on a wad of chewing gum that he retrieved from behind his ear.

In the back of the van are his four companions, who refer to themselves as 'urban explorers'. Barry, a cockney, has only two front teeth and a complete absence of hair. He is arguing with Angus, a retired coal miner, about which heavyweight champion had the weakest jaw. Opposite them, Phil tries to join in the conversation but his stutter gives the others too much time to interrupt. The only quiet member of the crew is Moley, who sits on the floor of the van checking ropes and lamps.

'It's the last frontier,' says Pete, talking to me. 'Forty thousand miles of sewers, some of them hundreds of years old – it's a feat of engineering to rival the Suez Canal, but nobody gives your sewers a second thought. They just purge their poisons and flush them away . . .'

'But why explore them?'

He gives me a disappointed look. 'Did they ask Hillary why he climbed Everest?'

'Yeah, they did.'

'OK. OK. Well these sewers are like Everest. They're the last frontier. You'll see. It's another world. Go down thirty feet and it's so quiet you can hear your pores opening and closing. And the darkness – it's unnatural. It's not like outside where, if you wait, your pupils dilate so that you can start making out shapes. Down there it's blacker than black.'

Barry leans through from the back of the van. 'It's like a lost city. You got streams, culverts, shelters, basements, grottos, graves, crypts, catacombs, secret places that the Government don't want nobody to know about. It's a different world. One layer burying the next, just like rock sediments. Whenever the great civilisations crumble – Egyptian, Hittite, Roman – the one thing they always leave behind is their sewers and latrines. A million years from now archaeologists are going to be digging up our fossilised turds, take my word for it.'

'And a lot more besides,' adds Angus. 'We find all sorts of stuff – jewellery, false teeth, spectacles, torches, gold coins, hearing aids, harmonicas, shoes . . .'

'I once saw a full-grown p-p-p-p-pig,' interrupts Phil. 'Biggest p-p-p-porker you ever saw.'

'Happy as a pig in shit, was he?' cackles Angus. Barry joins in until Weatherman Pete tries to raise the tone.

'You know what a tosher is?'

'No.'

'Back in the eighteenth century they used to scour the sewers, panning the muck like you'd pan for gold. Imagine that! Then you had your gongfermers and rakers, who cleaned the sewers and repaired them. Nowadays they call them flushers. You might even hear some of 'em working tonight.'

'Why do they work at night?'

'There's less shit flowing.'

I wish I hadn't asked. Ray Murphy's wife had talked about him working as a flusher. Pete explains how teams of six men, with a ganger in charge, clear blockages by hauling silt out through the manholes.

'I know it sounds pretty antiquated but there's some high-tech stuff too. They got these little boats – more like hover-crafts, really – with cameras on 'em that film the inside of the sewers, looking for problems. You got to watch out for 'em. You don't want to get caught down there.'

The van skids to a halt on loose gravel in a deserted car park. As the rear doors open, Moley climbs out first and hands me a pair of overalls and waist-high waders. Next comes a safety harness and Sellafield gloves. Meanwhile, Weatherman Pete opens a yellow plastic suitcase and unfurls a retractable aluminium pole with a tripod and wind cups on the top.

'It's a portable weather station,' he explains. 'It gives me wind speed, wind direction, temperature, relative humidity, barometric pressure, solar radiation and precipitation. Every-thing gets fed into a computer.' He opens a laptop and taps the keyboard. 'Right now, you have a window of four hours.'

Moley adds a safety helmet and an emergency breathing apparatus to his outfit. He scratches his armpits one last time before he shimmies into his waders.

'Any cuts? Cover them up with waterproof plasters,' says Barry, tossing a box towards me. 'Weil's disease – you get that from rat's urine. It gets into a cut and ends up in your brain.'

He checks my harness. 'Let me tell you what can go wrong down there: fire, explosions, asphyxiation, poisoning, infection and rats that can strip the flesh off your bones. Nobody knows we're down there, so we can't guarantee the sewers are vented. There could be pockets of methane, ammonia, hydrogen sulphide, benzene, CO_2 and gases I swear don't even have names yet. Don't touch your eyes or mouth with your gloves. Stick close to Moley. Nobody knows his way around like he does.'

He clips a gas monitor on to my harness.

Weatherman Pete gives a thumbs up and Moley levers open a manhole cover, rolling it to one side. Then he lowers a safety lamp down the small circular shaft. Angus and Phil descend first, climbing down the iron rings. I'm squeezed between Barry and Moley.

The sewer is less than five feet high, forcing me to bend, and the air smells of faeces and a putrid dampness. The brick walls curve at the sides and disappear into a shallow stream running down the centre. Our shadows are distorted against the brickwork.

'Don't forget to put the seat down,' says Angus, urinating against a wall.

Moley looks at me, the whiteness of his eyes glowing in the lamplight. He doesn't say anything but I know he's giving me one last chance to go back.

Weatherman Pete rolls the manhole cover back into place, sealing us inside.

I suddenly feel nervous.

'How is he going to contact us if it rains?'

'The old-fashioned way,' replies Barry. 'He's going to pick up a manhole cover and drop it six inches. We'll hear it miles away.'

Angus claps me on the shoulder. 'So what do you think?'

'It doesn't smell so bad.'

He laughs. 'Come down here on Saturday morning. Friday is curry night.'

Moley has moved off, wading along the stream. Barry falls in behind me, crouching more than most, as his ample frame is buttressed on all sides by the harness. Water swirls around my knees and the sweating bricks look almost silver in the torchlight.

'We call these snotsicles,' says Barry, pointing out the stalactites brushing against our helmets.

Despite the cold I'm already starting to perspire. A hundred yards and a permanent shiver sets in. Every sound is magnified and it makes me edgy. I have been trying to weave Mickey into the various scenarios but it's getting harder.

Another part of me thinks of Ali in hospital, staring at her crippled self in the mirror, wondering if she's ever going to walk again. I started this. I let her come along when she had far more to lose than I did. Now I'm wading in filth and shit and it seems appropriate. When you consider the state of my life, my career and my relationships, I belong down here.

'The place you showed us on the map. We're under it now,' says Barry, his head torch momentarily blinding me.

I glance up at a large opening and a side tunnel. The broken water main on the night of the ransom drop sent a thousand gallons a minute flooding through the streets and into the drains – enough to carry a ransom; maybe even enough to carry me.

'If something got washed down here, where would it finish up?'

'It's a top-down system. Operates on gravity,' says Angus.

Moley nods in agreement.

'Go-go-go-got flushed away,' stutters Phil.

Barry begins to explain. 'These small local sewers feed into main sewers and the waste is then drawn off into one of five interceptory sewers that run west to east – all fed by gravity. The high-level sewer begins at Hampstead Hill and crosses Highgate Road near Kentish Town. Further south you got two middle-level sewers. One begins close to Kilburn and runs under the Edgware Road to Euston Road, past King's Cross. The second runs from Kentish Town under Bayswater and along Oxford Street. Then you got two low-level sewers, one under Kensington, Piccadilly and the City; and the other right under the Thames Embankment, following the northern bank of the river.'

'Where do they all go?'

'To the sewage treatment works at Beckton.'

'And the system gets flushed out by rainfall?'

He shakes his head. 'The main sewers are built alongside old rivers that provide the water.'

The only river I know that enters the Thames Estuary from the north is the River Lea, which is a long way east of here.

'There are heaps of them,' scoffs Angus. 'You can't just wish a river away. You can cover 'em over or divert 'em into pipes but they'll keep flowing just the same as always.'

'Where are they?'

'Well, you got the Westbourne, the Walbrook, the Tyburn, Stamford Brook, Counter's Creek and the Fleet . . .'

Each of these names is familiar. There are dozens of streets, parks and estates named after them, but I had never equated them with ancient rivers. The fine hairs on my neck are standing on end. You hear stories about secret cities beneath cities; tunnels that took prime ministers to War Cabinet rooms and passageways that carried mistresses for rendezvous with kings, but I had never imagined a world of water, unseen blind rivers, coursing beneath the streets. No wonder the walls are crying.

Moley wants us to keep moving. The tunnel goes straight on with occasional vertical shafts emptying into it from above, creating mini waterfalls. Keeping to the centre of the stream, our boots slosh through the sediment and cold greyish water. Slowly the passages grow wider and taller and our shadows no longer stoop against the walls.

Tethered together we descend a shaft and wade silently along a larger sewer. Occasionally we slide down cement slopes, splashing through several inches of stinking water. At other times we near the surface and faint beams of light angle through iron grates.

I try to imagine the ransom, divided and sealed in plastic, being carried through these tunnels, dropping over waterfalls, floating through crypts.

For another hour we walk, crawl and slide. Eventually, we emerge into a cavernous Victorian brick chamber supported by pillars and arches. It must be thirty feet high, although it's hard to tell in the darkness. White-green water seems to boil at my feet, plunging over a waterfall.

Everywhere there are rusty iron gratings and long chains hanging from the roof. A concrete weir, made up of two large spillways, divides the room. Foaming gouts of waste are swept away by a great culvert that intercepts the flow above the spillway.

Below it, down the sliding concrete weir, is a large empty concrete pool featuring huge hinged steel gates with counter-weights on the top end to act like levers and seal the doors closed.

Angus sits on the edge of the spillway and takes a sandwich from his pocket, unwrapping the plastic film.

He motions with his sandwich. 'That over there is the low-level interceptory sewer. It starts at Chiswick and runs east beneath the Thames Embankment to the Abbey Mills pumping station in east London. Everything gets diverted from here to the treatment works.'

'Why the spillway?'

'Storms. You get a decent downpour in London and there's nowhere for the rain to go except into the drains. Thousands of miles of small local lines feed into the main sewers. First you get a gust of wind and then the whoosh!'

'Whoosh!' echoes Moley.

Angus picks a crumb off his chest. 'The system can only accommodate a certain level of water. You don't want it backing up or the politicians would be knee-deep in shit in Westminster. I'm talking literally. So when the water reaches a certain level it spills over the weir and gets diverted through those gates.' He points at the huge iron doors, which must each weigh about three tons. 'They open like a valve when flood waters come roaring over the weir.'

'Where does it go?'

'Straight into the Thames at a good ten knots.'

Suddenly, another scenario emerges, swirling around me like the smell of almonds. The Thames Water foreman described the water main having 'blown apart', creating a tremendous flood. This would have discouraged anyone from following the ransom and could also have served another purpose – to carry the packages over the weir.

'I need to get through those gates.'

'You can't,' says Moley. 'They only open during floods.'

'But you can get me there. You know where it comes out?'

Moley scratches his armpits and rocks his head from side to side. My whole body has started to itch.

24

Weatherman Pete produces a high-pressure hose and hooks it up to a tap. The blast of water knocks me back a step. I turn round and round, getting pummelled by the spray.

The van is parked almost directly above an open manhole in Ranelagh Gardens in the grounds of the Royal Hospital, Chelsea. The grand hospital buildings, painted by the rising sun, are just visible through the trees. Nearby, at Chelsea Barracks, I can hear the strains of a military band practising.

These gardens are normally closed until 10 a.m. and I don't know how Weatherman Pete managed to get through the gates. Then I notice magnetic mats on the side of his van advertising the 'City of Westminster'.

'I got dozens of them,' he explains, rather sheepishly. 'Come on, I'll show you what you want to see.'

Shedding the overalls and waders, we seal them into plastic sacks and load up the van. Moley has changed into his camouflage uniform and blinks into the sunlight as though frightened it might do him permanent damage. The others are drinking tea from a flask and recounting the night's journey.

Piling into the van, I lean over the seat as Weatherman Pete drives along the narrow tarmac paths and waves at a trio of Chelsea Pensioners on their morning walk. Pulling through the front gate, we circle the outer walls of the gardens until we reach the Thames.

From where he parks in the Embankment Gardens, I cross the road to Riverside Walk. The Thames, caught between tides, smells like perfume after where I've been.

Pete joins me and glances towards the water. Clambering on to the wall, he hooks his arm around an iron lamp-post and leans out over the muddy bank.

'There it is.'

I follow his outstretched arm and notice a depression in the stone bank. A round metal door seals the entrance of a pipe that disappears underground. Water dribbles from the edge, forming a puddle in the mud.

'That's the Ranelagh storm relief sewer. The door opens when it floods and closes again to stop the tide washing back into the sewer.'

He turns and points past the hospital. 'You were directly north of here. You followed the fall of the Westbourne River.'

'Where does it come from?'

'It rises in West Hampstead and gets fed by five streams that join near Kilburn. Then it crosses Maida Vale and Paddington before flowing into Hyde Park where it fills the Serpentine. After that it disappears underground again, down William Street, under Cadogan Lane and the King's Road, past Sloane Square and finally beneath Chelsea Barracks.'

'I can't see any water flowing.'

'Most of it gets used by the sewer. You won't see this gate open unless they get surplus water in the system.'

I don't hear the rest of his explanation. Instead I think of a story my stepfather told me about the old blind horse that falls into a dried-up well and the farmer decides he isn't worth saving. Killing two birds with one stone, he begins shovelling earth into the well to bury the horse, but the horse just shakes off the dirt and stamps it down. As more earth falls the old horse keeps stamping, until slowly he begins rising out of the darkness.

People have been trying to bury me but I keep stamping it down. Now I'm close to climbing out and, I promise you this, anyone holding a shovel will get a kick in the head.

I think I know what happened that night. We built a valuable boat and it floated away, sealed in plastic and buoyed by foam. The diamonds washed through Ranelagh sewer, pushed along by water from a burst main. Someone was waiting for the ransom; someone who knew his or her way around the sewers; someone like Ray Murphy.

Only now am I beginning to realise how angry I've been ever since I woke in hospital with a gunshot wound, dreaming of Mickey Carlyle. This is far bigger than the sum of its parts. Clever, driven, cunning people have manipulated the emotions of a desperate mother and taken advantage of my own blinkered desire. Where has Mickey been all this time? I know she's alive. I can't explain why or point to the proof; I just know she belongs in the world on a morning like this.

Weatherman Pete is packing the van, while Moley takes batteries from the gas monitors. Angus and Barry have already gone – walking to the Underground station. It is almost eight in the morning.

'Can I drop you somewhere, DI?'

I think for a moment. I'm due in court at midday. I also want to visit Ali in hospital. At the same time, having come this far, I don't want to stop searching. Facts, not memories, solve cases. I have to keep going.

'Maida Vale.'

'Sure. Jump in.'

The traffic seems to grow lighter as I get closer to Dolphin Mansions. My shoulders still ache from my journey in the sewers and I can smell the foulness in my nostrils.

Weatherman Pete drops me on the corner opposite the delicatessen and I walk the final seventy yards. Nestled in the lint of my trouser pocket are my last two morphine capsules. Every so often I reach inside and feel their smoothness with my fingertips.

The façade of Dolphin Mansions is in full sunshine. Stopping periodically, I study the gutters, looking for the openings and metal grates. I notice the camber of the road and where down-pipes enter the ground.

Some of the mansion blocks have basement flats that are below street level. They have drains to take rainwater away and stop them flooding.

The bottom buzzer automatically opens the door and I glance up the central stairwell of Dolphin Mansions. Skirting the lift well, I discover the door leading to the basement. A low-wattage naked bulb suspended from the ceiling transforms the darkness. The stairs are narrow and steep and the walls are a mottled grey where patches of damp have broken through the plaster.

Reaching the bottom of the stairs I try to put myself back in this place, three years ago. I remember searching the base-ment. Like every other room it was turned upside down. Along one wall, cut into an alcove, is a large disused boiler. It must be fifteen feet round, with meters, valves and pipes of every calibre. The square copper nameplate bears the inscription 'Fergus & Tate'. The floor is covered with half-bags of plaster, tins of paint, off-cuts of carpet and a Victorian gas lamp encased in bubble wrap.

Moving materials aside, I begin searching the floor.

A noise makes me turn. A young boy sits on the top step holding a plastic robot on his lap. His khaki trousers are stained with paint and his dark eyes peer at me suspiciously.

'Are you a stranger?' he asks.

'Yes, I suppose I am.'

'My mum says I shouldn't talk to strangers.'

'That's very good advice.'

'She says I could get kidnapped. A girl got kidnapped from

here – from right off the stairs. I used to know her name but I forgot. She's dead, you know. Do you think it hurts when you die? My friend Sam broke his arm when he fell out of a tree and he said it really hurt . . .'

'I don't know.'

'What are you looking for?'

'I don't know that either.'

'You'll never find my hiding place. She used to hide there too.'

'Who?'

'The girl who got kidnapped.'

'Michaela Carlyle.'

'You know her name! Do you still want to see it? You have to promise not to tell anyone.'

'I promise.'

'Cross your heart and hope to die, stick a needle in your eye.'

I cross my heart.

Tucking his robot into his belt, the boy slides on his backside down the remaining stairs and steps past me towards the boiler. He disappears through a gap no wider than his shoulders where the curved side of the boiler doesn't quite touch the brickwork.

'Are you all right in there?'

'Yes,' he replies, emerging again. He's holding a book in his hand. 'That's my cubbyhole. Do you want to come in?'

'I don't think I'll fit. What have you got there?'

'A book. It used to be hers but it's mine now.'

'Can I have a look?'

He hands it to me reluctantly. The front cover is tattered and chewed at the edges but I can still make out the illustration of a mother duck and ducklings. On the inside cover there is a large label with a scrolled border. Written on it is: 'Michaela Carlyle, 4½.'

The story is about the five little ducks that go out one day, over the hills and far away. The mother duck says 'Quack,

238

quack, quack, quack' but only four little ducks come back. The ducklings disappear one by one but on the final page they all return.

Handing the book back to him, I slide to my knees and put my head on the floor, peering into the gap between the boiler and the brickwork.

'It's dark in there.'

'I have a torch.'

'Is that running water I can hear?'

'My dad says there's a river down there.'

'Where?'

He gives me a thumbs down and I look at his feet. A sudden chill rushes through me, like ice at the roots of my hair.

Dragging aside half-bags of plaster and cement, I find a frayed square of carpet, folded twice. Pulling it back I reveal a metal grate with perpendicular bars embedded into the stone floor. Pressing my face close, I try to peer between them. My eyes follow the bricks downwards, along walls that seem to be weeping black tears. I can hear water gurgling below as if filling a giant cistern.

The boy is still talking but I'm no longer listening. We should have found this three years ago. We weren't looking for tunnels and the noise of the search would have drowned out the sound of water.

'What's your name?'

'Timothy.'

'Can I borrow your torch, Timothy?'

'Sure.'

Although not powerful, it illuminates an extra six feet of the shaft. I can't see the bottom.

Hooking my fingers between the bars, I try to lift the grate. It's wedged into place. Looking around for a lever, I find an old blunt chisel with a broken handle. Sliding it into the gap between metal and stone, I work it from side to side, pushing it deeper. Then I force the chisel sideways, leaning my weight against it. The grate lifts just enough for me to squeeze my fingers beneath one edge. Christ, it's heavy!

Timothy gives me a hand as we push it past vertical and let it drop with a clatter. He leans over and peers into the square black pit.

'Wow! Are you gonna go down there?'

I shine the torch into the hole. Instead of penetrating the darkness the light seems to bounce back at me. There are U-shaped handholds down one side.

'I'm a police officer,' I tell the boy, taking my wallet from my pocket and giving him a business card. 'Have you a watch, Timothy?'

'No.'

'OK, do you know how long an hour is?'

'Yeah.'

'If I haven't come to find you within an hour, I want you to give this card to your mum and ask her to call this number.' I write down the Professor's details. 'Tell him where I went. Do you understand?'

He nods.

Tucking the torch into my belt, I lower myself into the hole. Within a few feet I am soaking wet and the sound of running water is constant. The boy is still there. I can see his head silhouetted against the square of light.

'Go upstairs now, Timothy. Don't come down here again.'

Fifteen feet down, I pause, holding on to a metal rung with one hand and aiming the torch below me. Nothing.

I descend further, feeling the air grow colder, until my foot strikes something flat and hard. The torch picks up a river rushing through a tunnel. A ledge seems to run along the edge, about ten inches above the water, in both directions before the torch beam disappears into the darkness. This is not a sewer. Large beams support the ceiling and the walls are worn smooth by the current.

I feel my way along the ledge by sliding each foot a few

inches, expecting the stonework to collapse at any second and pitch me into the stream. I can pick up only small sections of the tunnel. Tiny yellow lights reflect back at me – the eyes of rats escaping along the ledge.

The moss on the walls is like slick black fur. Pressing my ear against the bricks I feel a slight vibration. Somewhere above my head is a road and traffic. The sound makes the tunnel seem alive, like some ancient, consumptive beast. Breathing. Digesting me.

Time and distance seem longer underground. I feel like I've been down here for hours yet I've probably only travelled a hundred yards. I don't know what I expected to find. Any evidence could never survive – not this long. The tunnel has been swept clean by seasonal downpours and storms.

I try to imagine someone taking Mickey through here. Unconscious, she could have been lowered down the shaft and then carried. Conscious, she would have been terrified and too hard to control. Another possibility catches in my throat. What better way to dispose of a body? The river would sweep it away and the rats would pick it clean.

Shuddering, I push the thought aside.

Any kidnapping would have needed at least two people and remarkable preparation. Someone had to replace the grate and cover it with bags of plaster and cement.

My clothes cling to me and my teeth are chattering. Unlike the expedition with Moley, I'm not prepared for this. It was a stupid idea. I should go back.

Ahead of me the ledge suddenly stops and starts again. There is a four-foot gap where it has collapsed into the stream. I could try to jump it but even with two good legs I couldn't guarantee landing safely.

I kneel down and feel ahead with my fingers. There's a gap in the wall just above the level of the water. Rolling up my sleeve, I reach down, feeling for the bottom. The opening is two feet high and a similar width, channelling water away from the river. This could be one of the conduits that feed the sewers.

Lowering myself into the channel, water soaks my trousers and fills my shoes. My chest is submerged and my back scrapes against the roof. Holding the torch in my mouth, I crawl forwards. The darkness pushes back at me.

Mud sticks to my knees and shoes, three or four inches deep; I feel as though I'm wiggling through it like an earthworm. The grunts and groans belong to me but echo back as though there's someone ahead of me . . . waiting.

After fifteen feet the channel begins to slope downwards, getting gradually steeper. My hands slip and I fall on my face into the water. The torch is submerged. Thank God it still works.

The steeper gradient and the force of the water behind me push me forwards. If the tunnel gets any narrower I'll be wedged inside, trapped. My back scrapes against the ceiling. The water seems to be rising. Perhaps I'm being paranoid.

I slip again and shoot forwards, pushing mud, gravel and water ahead of me. Convulsing and trying to retreat, I can't stop. My legs are useless. I rise over a hump and then feel myself in midair, falling. I land with a splash in water and muck. The smell is unmistakably a sewer. My first impulse is to vomit.

A poultice of dark mud covers my eyes. I scrape it off, trying to see, but the darkness is absolute. The torch has gone, either washed away or water-damaged.

Sitting up, I check that nothing is broken. My hands are shaking from the cold and I can't feel my fingers. Water cascades from the opening above my head. I have to get out of here.

Taking stock, I try to plot where I might be in relation to Dolphin Mansions. I can't read my watch so I don't know how long I've been down here. The ledge was narrow and my progress slow. I might only have travelled a few hundred yards. I heard traffic. I must have passed under a road. I listen again. Instead of a distant rumbling I feel a faint breeze against one cheek.

Standing too quickly, I smack my head against the roof. Don't do that again. Crouching, I spread my palms against the curved brick wall and feel my way forwards like a blind man in a maze. Occasionally, I pause and try to feel the breeze again. My mind wants to play tricks on me. Either the breeze disappears or seems to be coming from the opposite direction.

I can feel the desperation rising in me, scalding my oesophagus. Maybe I should turn back. In the darkness I could plunge into a shaft and never get out.

Suddenly, a faint glow appears ahead of me. The shaft of light looks like a ghostly hologram in the centre of the tunnel. I step inside and raise my face. I can see the sky through a rectangular grate. The edges are softened by turf spilling over the sides. I see football boots, shin guards and muddy knees. A handful of schoolboys and teachers are watching the game. Someone shouts, 'Press forward.' Someone else bellows, 'Offside!'

Nearest to me a lone teenager appears to be reading a book.

'Help me!'

He looks around.

'I'm down here!'

He peers at the grate.

'Help me get out!'

Dropping to his knees, he puts an eye against the bars.

'Hey! What are you doing?'

'I'm a police officer.'

I know it doesn't answer the question but it seems to be enough. He goes to fetch a teacher. I can hear him.

'Sir, there's someone in a hole over there. I think he might be stuck.'

A new face appears at the grate, older and in charge.

'What are you doing down there?'

'Trying to get out.'

More faces arrive and cluster around the drain. The football game appears to have been forgotten. Most of the players are now scrabbling to get a look at 'this guy stuck down a hole'.

A crowbar is summoned from a car boot. Turf is kicked away from the edges.

The grate is pulled aside and strong hands reach inside. I emerge on to a patch of English autumn, blinking into the sunlight and wiping the remains of the sewer from my face.

Reaching into my sodden pocket I retrieve the last of the morphine capsules. Magically, the pain lifts and a wave of emotion passes over me. I don't normally like emotion. It's a wishy-washy, moist-eyed, soft-in-the-head state, good for post-coital bliss and rugby reunions, but, you know something, I love these lads. Look at them, all dressed up in their school scarves, kicking a ball around the place. They look so cute. They even let me shower in the pavilion and someone lends me a shirt, tracksuit bottoms and a pair of trainers. I look like a senior citizen on a power walk.

The Professor is summoned and finds me in the pavilion. Straight off he treats me like a patient, taking my face in his hands and holding my eyelids open.

'How many did you take?'

'The last two.'

'Jesus!'

'I'm fine, really. Listen to me. I've been down there . . . in the river. We should have seen it years ago.'

'What are you talking about?'

'I know how they got her out of Dolphin Mansions. She went down the hole – just like Alice in Wonderland.'

I know I'm not making sense but Joe perseveres. Finally, I tell him the story but instead of getting excited he gets angry. He calls me stupid, foolhardy, rash and impulsive, but each of the criticisms is prefaced by the term 'with all due respect'. I've never been so politely told off.

I look at my watch. It's almost eleven o'clock. I'm due in court at midday.

'We can still make it.'

'I have to stop off somewhere first.'

'To change your clothes.'

'To see a boy about a torch.'

25

The Royal Courts of Justice in the Strand are composed of a thousand rooms and three miles of hallways, most of them lined with dark wooden panels that soak up the light and add to the gloom. The architecture is Victorian gothic because the courts are meant to intimidate the crap out of people, which they do.

For Eddie Barrett, however, it's just another stage. Striding along corridors, he pushes through doors and scatters the clusters of whispering lawyers. For a man with short legs and a bulldog swagger, he moves surprisingly quickly.

Barrett is to the legal profession what hyenas are to the African plains – a bully and a scavenger. He takes cases according to how much publicity they generate rather than the fees and he uses every legal loophole and ambiguity while grandly extolling the British judicial system as 'the finest and fairest in the world'.

In Eddie's mind the law is a flexible concept. It can be bent, twisted, flattened and stretched until it becomes whatever you want it to be. He can even make it disappear when turned sideways.

A dozen steps behind him comes Charles Raynor QC, known as 'The Rook' because of his black hair and beaked nose. He once made a former cabinet minister cry under cross-examination about his taste in women's underwear.

Eddie spies me and swaggers over. 'Well, lookie see who's here – Inspector Roooeeeez. I hear all sorts of stories about you. I hear your wife is banging someone else – his dick, her pussy, making whoopee. I'd be pretty pissed if I caught my missus shagging her boss. For richer, for poorer, in sickness and in health, isn't that what they say? No mention there of giving it up for the firm's accountant.'

My jaw clenches and I feel the red mist descending.

Eddie takes a step back. 'Yeah, that's the temper I heard so much about. Have fun in court.'

I know he's winding me up. That's what Eddie does – gets under people's skin, looking for the softest flesh.

Spectators are crammed into the public gallery and there are three full rows of press, including four sketch artists. The furnishings and fittings pre-date microphones and recording equipment so cables snake across the floor, pinned beneath masking tape.

I look around for Rachel, hoping she might be here. Instead I see Aleksei, who is watching me as though waiting for me instantly to disintegrate. To his left is the Russian and to the right a young black man with loose limbs and liquid eyes.

The Rook adjusts his horsehair wig and glances across at his adversary, Fiona Hanley QC, a handsome woman who reminds me of my second wife, Jessie, who has the same cool detachment and honey-coloured eyes. Miss Hanley is busy shuffling papers and rearranging box files as though creating a mini-fortress around her. She turns and gives me an uncertain smile as though we might have met somewhere before (only about a dozen times).

'All rise.'

Lord Connelly, the Chief Justice, enters and pauses, surveying the courtroom as though keeping watch over the Pearly Gates. He sits. Everybody sits.

Howard appears next, climbing the stairs into the dock. Gape-mouthed and grey, with his hair hanging limply across his forehead, he has a vague, forgetful frown as though he's lost his bearings. Eddie whispers something to him and they laugh. I'm seeing conspiracies everywhere.

Campbell thinks this has been Howard's plan all along. The ransom demand, the lock of Mickey's hair, her bikini, were all part of an elaborate hoax designed to cast doubt on his conviction and set him free.

I don't buy it because it begs the same question that Joe keeps asking me – why wait three years?

Lord Connelly adjusts a lumbar cushion behind his back and clears his throat. He spends a moment studying the court-room ceiling and begins.

'I have studied the defence submissions regarding the orig-inal trial of Mr Wavell. While I am willing to agree with several of the points raised about the trial judge's summing up, on balance I don't feel they altered the outcome of the jury's deliberations. However, I am willing to hear oral arguments. Are you ready to proceed, Mr Raynor?'

The Rook is on his feet, pushing his black gown along his forearms. 'Yes, Your Honour, I will be seeking to introduce fresh evidence.'

'Does this evidence address the grounds for appeal or the original offence?'

'The original offence.'

Miss Hanley objects. 'Your Honour, my learned friend seems intent on rerunning this trial even before being granted leave to appeal. We have been given a witness list with two dozen names. Surely he doesn't intend calling them all?'

Lord Connelly looks at the list.

The Rook clarifies the situation. 'It may be that we call only one witness, Your Honour. It very much depends upon what he has to say.'

'I hope you're not embarking on a fishing expedition, Mr Raynor.'

'No, Your Honour, I can assure you that's not the case. I wish to call the Detective Inspector who was in charge of the original investigation into the disappearance of Michaela Carlyle.'

Lord Connelly underlines my name on the list. 'Miss Hanley, the overriding purpose of the Criminal Appeal Act is to further the interests of justice. It allows fresh evidence to be admitted by the prosecution and the defence. However, I warn you, Mr Raynor, that I'm not going to allow you to rerun this trial.'

Miss Hanley immediately makes an application for the proceedings to be heard in a closed court.

'Your Honour, there are issues involved that go beyond the immediate fate of Mr Wavell. An important criminal investigation could be jeopardised if certain information is made public.'

What investigation? Campbell is only interested in nailing me.

'Does this investigation involve Mr Wavell?' asks Lord Connelly.

'Indirectly, it may do. I'm aware of the nature of the investigation but not the precise details. There is a media blackout in place.'

The Rook puts his oar in, more out of habit than desire. 'Justice must be seen to be done, Your Honour.'

Lord Connelly rules in favour of the Crown, and the public gallery and press benches are cleared. This is when the real arguments begin, full of phrases like 'with all due respect' and 'my learned friend' (legal shorthand for 'you complete moron'). Then again, what do I know? The Rook and Miss Hanley could be the best of friends. They could be shagging each other's wigs off in chambers.

My name is called. I button my jacket on the walk to the witness box and unbutton it as I sit down.

The Rook looks up from his notes as if surprised that I've bothered turning up. He rises slowly to his feet, drops his chin and tries to look at me through the top of his head. The first few questions are the easy ones – name, rank, years of experience as a police officer.

Miss Hanley is on her feet. 'My learned friend seems to be placing great faith in the credibility of this witness. However, he has failed to mention that DI Ruiz was suspended as head of the Serious Crime Group several days ago and yesterday afternoon, following an internal disciplinary hearing, he was sacked. He is no longer a serving member of the London Metropolitan Police and is the subject of a criminal investigation . . .'

Lord Connelly motions her to sit down. 'You'll get your opportunity to question the witness.'

The Rook consults his notepad and then does something I don't expect. He takes me through the original investigation, getting me to restate the evidence against Howard. I talk about the photographs, the bloodstains, the missing carpet and Mickey's beach towel. He had the opportunity, the motive and the corrupted sexuality.

'At what point did Howard Wavell become a suspect in the original investigation?'

'Everyone who lived in Dolphin Mansions was immediately a suspect.'

'Yes, but at what point did you focus your attentions upon Mr Wavell?'

'He became of particular interest when he was seen acting suspiciously on the day Michaela disappeared. He also failed to provide an alibi.'

'He failed to provide one or didn't have one?'

'He didn't have one.'

'In what way was he acting suspiciously?'

'He was taking photographs of the search parties and

people who had gathered outside Dolphin Mansions.'

'Was there anyone else taking photographs?'

'There were several press photographers.'

The Rook gives a wry smile. 'So having a camera didn't automatically make someone a suspect?'

'A young girl was missing. Most of the other neighbours were helping to look for her. Mr Wavell seemed more interested in recording the event for posterity.'

The Rook waits. He's letting everyone know that he expects a better answer.

'Prior to your seeing Howard Wavell at Dolphin Mansions that day, had you ever come across him before?'

'We went to the same boarding school back in the sixties. He was a few years behind me.'

'Did you know each other well?'

'No.'

'As the officer in charge of the investigation, did you think about either stepping down or absenting yourself from interviews because of your past association?'

'No.'

'Did you know Mr Wavell's family?'

'I may have met one or two of them.'

'So you don't remember going out with his sister?'

I pause, racking my brains.

The Rook smiles. 'Perhaps you went out with too many girls to remember.'

Everyone cracks up. Howard laughs as hard as anyone.

The Rook waits for the laughter to subside. Almost in passing, he remarks, 'Four weeks ago you took an envelope containing six hairs to a private laboratory in central London and asked for a DNA test to be carried out.'

'Yes.'

'Is that normal police procedure – using a private facility to conduct DNA tests?'

'No.'

'I think I'm right in saying that the Forensic Science Service do DNA tests for the police.'

'It was a private request not a police one.'

He raises his eyebrows. 'Unofficial? How did you pay?'

'Cash.'

'Why?'

'I don't see how that's relevant . . .'

'You paid in cash because you didn't want a record of the transaction, isn't that the case? You didn't leave your address or phone number with the laboratory.'

He doesn't give me a chance to answer, which is probably for the best. I'm dying here. Perspiration is leaking down my chest and settling in a pool at my navel.

'What exactly did you ask the technicians at Genetech to do for you?'

'I wanted them to extract DNA from the hair strands and compare it with the DNA of Michaela Carlyle.'

'A girl who is supposed to be dead.'

'Someone had sent a ransom demand to Rachel Carlyle alleging that her daughter was still alive.'

'And you believed this letter?'

'I agreed to have the hair tested.'

The Rook is more insistent. 'You still haven't explained why you asked a private laboratory to conduct the test?'

'It was a favour for Mrs Carlyle. I didn't believe the hair would be a match for her daughter.'

'You wanted to keep it a secret?'

'No. I was concerned that any official request would be misconstrued. I didn't want it perceived that I had doubts about the original investigation.'

'You wanted to deny Mr Wavell his right to natural justice?'

'I wanted to be sure.'

The Rook walks back to the table and picks up a second sheet of paper, snapping it with his fingers as though calling the edges to attention.

Why doesn't he ask me the result of the DNA test? Perhaps he doesn't know the answer. If the hair didn't match Mickey's DNA profile, the ransom demand was more likely to be a hoax, weakening Howard's case.

The Rook begins again. 'Subsequently, a second package was posted to Mrs Carlyle. What did it contain?'

'A child's swimsuit.'

'What can you tell us about this swimsuit?'

'It was a pink and orange bikini, similar to the one worn by Michaela Carlyle on the day she disappeared.'

'Similar or the same one?'

'Forensic analysis couldn't produce a definitive answer.'

The Rook is circling now. He has the face of a bird and the soul of a crocodile. 'How many murders have you investigated, Detective Inspector?'

I shrug. 'Upwards of twenty.'

'And how many missing children cases?'

'Too many.'

'Too many to remember?'

'No, sir.' My eyes are locked on his. 'I remember every last one of them.'

The power of the statement throws him slightly. He turns back to the bar table, consulting his notepad.

'There must be a degree of pressure on the officer in charge of a high-profile investigation. A young girl is missing. Parents are scared. People want to be reassured.'

'It was a thorough investigation. We didn't cut corners.'

'No, quite right.' He reads from a list. 'Eight thousand interviews, twelve hundred statements, more than a million man-hours . . . many of them focused on my client.'

'We followed every important lead.'

The Rook is leading me somewhere. 'Were there any suspects you didn't pursue?'

'Not if they were important.'

'What about Gerry Brandt?'

I can feel myself hesitate. 'He was a person of interest for a short time.'

'And why did you discount him?'

'We made extensive inquiries . . .'

'You couldn't find him, isn't that the case?'

'Gerry Brandt was a known drug dealer and burglar. He had contacts within the criminal underworld who, I believe, helped hide him.'

'This is the same man who was photographed outside Dolphin Mansions on the day Michaela disappeared?'

'That's correct, sir.'

He turns away from me now, addressing a wider audience. 'A man with a previous conviction for sexually assaulting a minor?'

'His girlfriend.'

'A sex offender who was seen outside Dolphin Mansions but you didn't regard him as being an important enough suspect to bother finding. Instead you focused your investigation exclusively on my client, a committed Christian, who had never been in trouble with the law. And when you obtained evidence that could suggest Michaela Carlyle might still be alive you sought to hide it.'

'I made the results available to my superiors.'

'But not to his defence.'

'With all due respect, sir, it's not my job to help defence lawyers.'

'You're absolutely right, Mr Ruiz. Your job is to establish the truth. And in this case you sought to hide the truth. You sought to ignore evidence or at worst conceal it, just as you ignored Gerry Brandt as a suspect.'

'No.'

The Rook sways back and forth on his heels. 'Was the ransom demand a hoax, Detective Inspector?'

'I don't know.'

'And are you willing to stake your career . . .' – he corrects himself – '... your reputation and, more importantly, my client's freedom on the absolute conviction that Michaela Carlyle was murdered three years ago?'

There's a long pause. 'No.'

Even The Rook is taken by surprise. He pauses to compose himself. 'So you believe she may still be alive?'

'When you don't find a body there is always a chance.'

'And has that possibility become greater as a result of this ransom demand?'

'Yes.'

'No further questions.'

I don't look at Campbell or Eddie Barrett or Howard Wavell. I keep my eyes straight ahead as I walk out of the courtroom. Inside my jacket, pressed against my heart, a mobile phone is vibrating.

Fumbling for the button, I take the call.

'I've just heard the news on the radio,' says Joe. 'They've found a body in the river.'

'Where?'

'Somewhere near the Isle of Dogs.'

This is how it looks: a bleak Wednesday afternoon, a strong wind and water slapping against the weathered piles of Trinity Pier. A dredger squats low in the water, with skeletal arms held aloft and black pipes snaking across the decks. Spotlights have turned brown water into a murky white. Two water police Zodiacs made of rubberised canvas with wooden bottoms fight the outgoing tide, dropping floating plastic pontoons in their wake.

The Professor parks on a slip road that comes to a dead end where the River Lea enters the Thames Estuary. The river is two hundred yards wide at this point, with the Millennium Dome silhouetted against the porridge-like sky on the distant bank.

Halfway down the sloping metal ramp 'New Boy' Dave

steps away from a huddle of detectives. His shoulders are shaking and he's caught between wanting to spit in my face or smash it with his fists. Bubbles of saliva gather above his bottom lip.

'Fuck off! Just fuck off!' It's almost a wail. This is about Ali.

I look over his shoulder at the police divers preparing their tanks and equipment. 'Who did they find?'

Dave sucks the saliva into his mouth and pushes me in the chest. I want to say I'm sorry but the lump in my throat won't move. The other detectives have circled like spectators at a playground fight. None of them want me here. I'm an outsider, a maverick, worse still a traitor. Joe tries to intervene. 'Ali wouldn't want this. Just tell us who you found?'

'Fuck you!'

As I try to push past, Dave grabs me by the arm, swinging me hard into the brick-and-wire retaining wall. A kidney punch sends me down. Dave is standing over me looking wasted and wild. There's a trickle of blood down his chin where he's bitten his lip.

What happens next lacks a certain degree of elegance. I sink my fist into his groin and take hold. Dave groans in a high reedy voice and drops to his knees. I don't let go.

He raises his fists, wanting to pound me into the ground, but I squeeze even harder. He curls up in pain, unable to lift his head. My breath is hot on his cheek.

'Don't go bad on me, Dave,' I whisper. 'You're one of the good ones.'

Letting him go, I ease myself up until I'm sitting against the wall, staring at the smooth darkness of the water. Dave drags himself up next to me, trying to get his breath back. I look up at the other detectives and tell them to leave us alone.

'Who did they find?'

'We don't know,' Dave says, grimacing slightly. 'The dredger sliced the body in half.'

'Let me see it.'

'Unless you can recognise this poor bastard from below the waist you're no use to anyone, especially me.'

'How did he die?'

He pauses too long before he answers. 'There is evidence of a gunshot wound.' In the same breath, he arches his neck and looks past me. A coroner's van has pulled alongside the wharf. The back doors open. A stretcher slides from within.

'I didn't mean for Ali to get hurt – you know that.'

He looks at his fists. 'I'm sorry I hit you, sir.'

'That's OK.'

'The Chief Super will go apeshit if he knows you're here.'

'So don't tell him. I'll stay out of the way.'

As the last rays of token sunlight strike the towers of Canary Wharf, four divers tumble backwards from the Zodiacs. Slick as seals, they disappear beneath the surface leaving barely a trace behind.

The officer in charge is short and barrel-chested, clad in a wetsuit that makes him look as if he's carved from ebony. He swings an air tank into a boat and wipes both hands before offering one to me. 'Sergeant Chris Kirkwood.'

'Ruiz.'

'Yeah, I know who you are.'

'You got a problem talking to me?'

'Nah.' He shakes his head. 'I got other problems. Visibility is down to three feet and the current is running at four knots. Someone chained this bastard to a barrel of concrete. We're gonna need cutting gear.' He swings another air tank into the boat.

'How long has he been in the water?'

'Most bodies eventually come up. Takes about five days at this time of year, but this guy was meant to stay down there. Usually a body stays together pretty good in the Thames. None of the marine life can chew through ligaments. I reckon chummy has been down there about three weeks . . .'

I can picture what he's saying – a body swaying beneath the water, white and wax-like, moving back and forth with the tide. At the same time I feel for a morphine capsule. There are none left.

The closer of the Zodiacs rocks in the wake of a passing water taxi. I notice bubbles on the surface and a masked face emerges, with an upraised fist. A police-issue handgun is clenched in his gloved fingers.

The water ripples and sways. Something else is coming up. A rope appears in a second diver's hand and is hooked on to a winch. Suddenly, it feels like a cold grasping hand has taken hold of my heart. The air has condensed into water and the current is sucking me down.

Sergeant Kirkwood catches me as I fall. He has his arms under mine, pulling me back from the edge of the wharf. A box is found and I sit down. Joe is beside me, shouting at someone to get me a glass of water. I try to turn away but he holds my face.

My vision clears and I watch the first of the Zodiacs. The divers have hauled something from the water. The outboard engine rumbles and the Zodiac swings towards the wharf. A rope is thrown into willing hands and is looped around a cleat on the pier. The Zodiac is pulled closer.

Lying on the wooden base is a bloated, discoloured torso hung with fronds of weed and wrack. It is barely recognisable as being human, yet I do recognise him; I recognise his name and his face and boxer's hands. And then I remember . . .

26

Deep inside my head doors and windows suddenly open. Files blow off desks, lights go on, photocopiers hum and phones ring. A closed office has suddenly come to life and the man hunched over his desk looks up from his hands and yells, Eureka!

Single frames and snapshot memories are put in order like a film being spliced together. I can picture scenes and hear dialogue. A phone is ringing. Rachel picks it up. The pre-recorded message is a single question. One sentence: 'Is my pizza ready?'

The phone goes dead. Rachel stares at me in disbelief.

'Don't worry – they'll call back.'

We're sitting in my kitchen. Rachel is dressed in black jeans and a grey pullover. She has the dazed disbelieving air of a refugee who no more than an hour ago escaped over the border.

For the next three hours she doesn't move. She barely dares to breathe. Her hands are locked in a battle, each finger wrestling the others. I try to make her relax. I want her to conserve her energy.

Aleksei is nearby, waiting and watching with an animal quickness. Sometimes he wanders into my lounge to make a call on his mobile then he drifts back, regarding Rachel with a strange mixture of longing and disgust. The diamonds are packed and ready. They were delivered in a velvet-lined brief-case – 965 stones, one carat or above, superior quality.

Aleksei is going to follow us – tracking the signals from the transmitter and a GPS beacon in Rachel's car.

'Nobody is going to know we're being followed,' I reassure her. 'Aleksei has promised to stay well away unless he gets a signal. I'm going to be with you. Just relax.'

'How can I relax?'

'I know it's hard but it could be a long night.'

Outside on the street, her Renault Estate is fresh from a local garage workshop. The front passenger seat has been removed and the doors reinforced. A hands-free phone will let me hear both sides of any conversation.

'Whatever happens, you must try to stay with the car. Don't let them draw you away unless you have absolutely no choice. Don't look down at me. Don't talk to me. They might be watching. If I ask you a question and the answer is yes, I want you to tap the top of the steering wheel once. If the answer is no I want you to tap it twice. Do you understand?'

She nods.

Again, I deliver the most important message. 'What are you going to ask?'

'To *see* Mickey.'

'When are you going to hand over the ransom?'

'When I *have* Mickey.'

'That's right. They want you to follow blindly but you have to keep insisting on assurances that Mickey is alive. Keep asking for proof . . .'

'They'll say the hair and bikini prove it.'

'And you'll say they prove nothing. You just want to be sure.'

'What if they want me to drop the ransom somewhere?'

'Don't do it. Demand a straight exchange – Mickey for the diamonds.'

'And if they don't agree?'
'It's no deal.'

At 11.37 p.m. the phone rings again. The caller is male but a voice-changing device has digitally altered his vowels and flattened the pitch. He instructs Rachel to drive to the Hanger Lane roundabout on the A40. She holds the mobile in both hands, nodding rather than answering. She doesn't hesitate. She picks up the pizza box and walks to the door.

Aleksei follows, looking suddenly concerned. I don't know whether he wants to wish her luck or take her place. Maybe he's just worried about his diamonds. Further down the street he opens a car door and I see the Russian behind the wheel.

Lying on the floor of Rachel's car, my shoulders are braced against the dashboard panel and my legs concertinaed towards the back seat. I can only see one side of her face. She looks straight ahead, with both hands on the wheel, as though retaking her driving test.

The caller has hung up.

'Just relax. We could put on some music.'

She taps the steering wheel once.

I flip open the vinyl case of her CD collection. 'I'm fairly easy to please – anything except Neil Diamond or Barry Manilow. I have a theory that 90 per cent of deaths in nursing homes are caused by Neil Diamond and Barry Manilow.'

She smiles.

I have a walkie-talkie clipped to my top pocket and a Glock 17 self-loading pistol in a holster under my left arm. The radio receiver tucked into my right ear is tuned to the same frequency as a handset in Aleksei's car.

I also have a dark blanket I can pull across myself at traffic lights or when vehicles pull alongside us.

'Remember not to look at me. If you have to park some-where, try to avoid streetlights. Choose somewhere darker.'

She taps the steering wheel once.

The mobile rings again. She reaches down and presses the speaker button.

In the background a girl is crying. The male voice, still heavily distorted, screams at her to be quiet. Rachel flinches.

'You called the police, Mrs Carlyle.'

'No.'

'Don't lie to me. Never lie to me. A detective visited you at work five days ago.'

'Yes, but I didn't invite him. I told him to leave.'

'What else did you tell him?'

'Nothing.'

'Don't insult my intelligence.'

'I'm telling the truth. I swear. I have the ransom.' Rachel's voice is shaking but she doesn't waver.

If this were a police operation we would be tracing the call, narrowing down the signal to the nearest transmitting tower. Then again, he's probably moving and he won't stay on the line for more than a few minutes at a time.

'I just need some assurance. I want to see Mickey,' says Rachel. 'I need to know she's OK, otherwise I don't think I can get through this . . .'

'SHUT THE FUCK UP! Don't try to bargain, Mrs Carlyle.'

'I'm not trying to be unreasonable. I just need to know she's . . .'

'Alive? Can't you hear her?'

'Yes, but . . . how do I know . . . ?'

'Well, let me see, I could cut out one of her big brown eyes and post it to you. Then again, maybe I should just run a knife across her pale pretty throat and send her head in a box. Then you can put it on the mantelpiece as a reminder of what a STUPID COW YOU ARE!'

Everything reels. I can see Rachel's chest heaving. For a long while she can't speak.

'Mrs Carlyle?'

'I'm here.'

'Are we clear?'

'Yes. Just don't hurt her.'

'Listen very carefully. You get one chance at this. Disobey my instructions and I hang up. Argue with me and I hang up. You mess up and you won't hear from me again. You know what that means?'

'Yes.'

'OK, let's do this one more time.'

What does he mean by 'one more time'? Has he done this before? Everything about his vocal tone and pace of his speech suggests he's not a first-timer. A cold draught of fear settles over me. Mickey's not coming home tonight. She's never coming home. And these people won't baulk at killing Rachel. What was I thinking? It's too dangerous!

'Where are you now?'

'Ah, um, I'm getting close to the roundabout. It's just ahead of me.'

'Circle the roundabout three times and then go back the way you came.'

'Where to?'

'Prince Albert Road roundabout near Regent's Park.'

Roundabouts are open and hard to police. They're making her circle so they can check she's not being followed. Hopefully, Aleksei will realise and hang back.

We're travelling back towards the West End now. From my hiding place, below the level of the windscreen, I can see only the upper floors of buildings and the globes of streetlights. Ahead of us, above the Post Office Tower, a blinking red light moves across the sky; a helicopter, perhaps, or a plane.

The phone line is still open. I raise my hand and make a talking motion. Rachel taps once on the steering wheel.

'Is Mickey OK?' she asks tentatively.

'For now.'

'Can I speak to her?'

'No.'

'Why did you wait so long?'

He doesn't answer. Then, 'Where are you now?'

'Just passing the London Mosque.'

'Turn right into Prince Albert Road. Follow it around Regent's Park.'

There is something about the voice. Even with the distortion I detect a slight accent, possibly south London or further east. Beads of perspiration shine on Rachel's top lip. She licks them away and keeps her eyes fixed on the road.

'Get to Chalk Farm Road. Follow it north.'

Through the windows I see the faintest wisps of clouds, engraved against the night sky by a half-moon. We must be climbing Haverstock Hill towards Hampstead Heath.

The caller begins naming crossroads and counting them down. 'Belsize Avenue . . . Ornan Road . . . Wedderburn Road . . .' And then suddenly, 'Turn left now. Now!'

My knees bang against the gear stick. Fifty yards further, he yells, 'STOP! Get out of the car. Bring the pizza.'

'But where . . . ?' pleads Rachel.

'Walk along the street and find the car that isn't locked. The keys are in the ignition. Leave the phone. There's another waiting for you.'

'No. I can't . . .'

'DO AS YOU'RE TOLD OR SHE DIES!'

The phone goes dead. Rachel seems to be frozen in place, both hands still locked on the wheel.

'You OK?'

She taps the steering wheel once.

'You see anyone?'

She taps it twice.

'What about behind us?'

Two taps.

I ease myself upwards, fighting the cramp in my legs. We're in a tree-lined street, with major intersections at each end. Branches shield the parked cars from above.

Rachel reaches for the door handle.

'Wait!'

'I have to go. You heard him.'

He knew the crossroads. He was rattling off the distances. Either he's nearby or everything has been planned in advance. Can I take the risk of going with her?

'OK, I want you to take the ransom and walk along the street. When you find the car unlock the boot.'

She reaches on to the back seat and retrieves the pizza box. The door opens. The interior light has been disconnected. Using a hand-held periscope with a zoom lens, I watch her walk away from me, at the same time scanning the street for any movement. I punch the button on the two-way.

'Oscar Sierra this is Ruiz. Rachel is on foot. The target vehicle is changing. Be vigilant.'

Rachel tries each car door and then moves on. She's getting further and further away from me. Far off I see the interior of a car light up. Rachel slips inside and picks up another mobile phone. The door closes and the brake lights flare. It's now or never.

I'm out of the car. Running. My legs are so stiff and cramped that they work only from memory. The pavement is uneven and broken by tree roots, which are hard to see in the deeper shadows of the trees.

A Vauxhall Vectra is pulling out ahead of me. Rachel spies me at the last minute in her rear mirror and slows down. I open the boot and tumble heavily inside, pulling the lid closed until it jams hard on my fingers but doesn't lock shut.

We're moving again. I'm curled up in a ball, with my cheek pressed against the nylon floor mat and my heart pounding. The wheel arches amplify the sound of the tyres on the road and I can hear nothing else.

I feel for the earpiece. It's fallen out and is dangling down on my chest. Putting it back into my ear, I hear Aleksei yelling in Russian. They don't know which car to follow. There are two vehicles leaving the street – a BMW turning south down Fitzjohn's Avenue and the Vectra turning north.

They're trying to contact me. The walkie-talkie is digging into my chest. I lever myself upwards and pull it free. There's no response when I depress the talk button. I must have broken the two-way when I rolled into the car.

Aleksei won't know which vehicle to follow until the cars are far enough apart for the transmitter to identify which one is carrying the ransom. By then he risks losing us completely.

I can't help. Instead I concentrate on creating a mental map of north London in my head, trying to calculate which turns we make and the direction we're heading. The minutes and miles tick by.

The weight of the boot lid is keeping it closed until we hit a pothole, when it tries to jump open. I raise my head and try to peer through the narrow gap. The only thing visible is the light grey tarmac of the road and occasional flashes of headlights.

Through the earpiece I can monitor Aleksei and the Russian. The BMW has been discounted. Now they're heading towards Kilburn, relying solely on the signal from the diamonds.

Rolling on to my back, I keep one hand on the lid of the boot and feel along the inside walls until I locate the internal light. The bulb feels smooth in my fingertips and I twist it free from the socket.

Several times the car stops and does a U-turn. Either Rachel is lost or they're still making her jump through hoops. She's driving faster now. The streets are emptier.

The car crosses a speed hump and suddenly stops. Is this it? I slide my gun from its holster and cradle it on my chest.

'Hey, lady, you want to slow down. I almost took you for a joyrider.' It is a man's voice. He might be a security guard with too much time on his hands. 'Are you lost?'

'No. I'm looking for a . . . for a friend's house.'

'I wouldn't recommend you hang around here, lady. Best you head back the way you came.'

'You don't understand. I have to keep going.'

I can almost hear him chewing this over as if he wants to phone a friend before making a decision. 'Maybe I didn't make myself clear,' he drawls.

'But I have to . . .'

'Keep your hands where I can see them,' he says. He's walking around the car, kicking at the tyres.

'Please let me go.'

'And what's the big hurry? You in some sort of trouble?'

A wind has come up. Corrugated iron sheets flap on the ground and I can hear a dog barking. When the man reaches the rear of the car he notices the boot popped off its latch. His fingers hook under the lid.

As it opens, I slide my gun through the opening and press it into his groin. His jaw drops open and helps him take a deep breath.

'You are jeopardising a police undercover operation,' I hiss. 'Back away from the car and let the lady go.'

He blinks several times and nods, before slowly lowering the boot. As the car pulls away I see his hand raised as if holding a salute.

Moving quickly again, we appear to be circling an industrial estate. Rachel is looking for something. She pulls off the road on to rough ground and stops, killing the engine.

In the sudden silence I can hear her voice but only one side of the conversation.

'I can't see any traffic cone,' she says. 'No, I can't see it.' She's growing desperate. 'It's just a vacant lot . . . Wait! I see it now.'

The door opens. I feel the car gently rock. I don't want her leaving. She has to stay close to me. There is no time to weigh up my options. Hopefully, Aleksei and the Russian will have caught up with us and are holding their position.

Easing open the boot, I roll over the lip and land heavily on the ground, using the momentum to spin away from the light. Then I lie dead still with my face pressed against loose gravel and mud.

Lifting my head I spy Rachel in the beam of the headlights. Ahead of her is a discarded industrial freezer standing upright in the middle of an empty lot. The stainless steel door is pitted and dented by stones, but still reflects the light. Sitting on top of it is an orange traffic cone.

Rachel walks towards it, stumbling over the broken bricks and rubble. Her jeans snag on a coil of barbed wire, half-buried in the ground. She twists her leg free.

She's there now, standing in front of the freezer. It's almost as tall as she is. Reaching forwards, she grips the handle and pulls open the door. A child's body tumbles forwards. Small. Almost liquid. Rachel's arms instinctively reach out and her mouth opens in a silent scream.

I'm on my feet and running towards her. It's the longest forty yards – a horizontal Everest – crossed with my arms pumping and my stomach in my boots. Rachel is on her knees cradling the body. I grab her around her waist and lift her. She's adrenalin light. There's nothing of her. A cloth head lolls backwards from her arms, with crosses for eyes and tufts of wool for hair. It's a child-size rag doll with a beige torso and beige limbs and a knobbly bald face, all swollen and worn.

'Listen to me, Rachel. It's not Mickey. It's just a doll. Look! See!'

She has a strange, almost serene look on her face. Only her eyelids are moving of their own accord. Slowly, I pry her fingers loose from the doll and lean her head against my chest.

A note is tied around the doll's neck, threaded with the same blue wool as the hair. Each letter is smeared dark red. I pray to God that it's paint.

Four words – written in capitals: *THIS COULD BE HER!*

Wrapping my jacket around Rachel, I lead her slowly back

to the car and sit her inside. She hasn't uttered a sound. Nor does she respond to my voice. Instead she stares straight ahead at a point in the distance or in the future, a hundred yards or a hundred years from here and now.

I pick up the mobile on the front seat. Silence. Inside my head I scream in frustration.

'They'll call back,' I tell myself. 'Sit tight. Wait.'

Sliding on to the seat beside Rachel, I take her pulse and tug my jacket tighter around her shoulders. She needs a doctor. I should call this off now.

'What happened?' she asks, regaining some hold on reality.

'They hung up.'

'But they'll call back?'

I don't know how to answer her. 'I'm calling an ambulance.'

'No!'

It's amazing! Although deep in shock there is still one, pure, undamaged, functioning brain cell working inside her. It's like the queen bee of brain cells, being guarded by the hive . . . and it's buzzing now.

'If they have Mickey they'll call back,' she says. The statement is so forceful and clear that I can't help doing as she says.

'OK. We wait.'

She nods and wipes her nose with my sleeve. The headlights still pour white light in a path across the weeds and debris. I can just make out a line of trees, bruised purple against the ambient light.

We messed up. What else could we have done? I glance across at Rachel. Her lips are blue and trembling. With her arms hanging loosely by her sides, it seems only her skeleton is keeping her upright.

The silence amplifies the distant traffic noise . . . and then the phone!

Rachel doesn't flinch. Her mind has gone somewhere safer. I glance at the square glowing screen and take the call.

'Mrs Carlyle?'

'She's not available.'

I could finish a book in the pause.

'Where is she?' The voice is still distorted.

'Mrs Carlyle is in no condition to talk. You'll have to talk to me.'

'You're a policeman.'

'It doesn't matter who I am. We can end this now. A straight exchange – the diamonds for the girl.'

There is another long pause.

'I have the ransom. It's right here. Either you deal with me or you walk away.'

'The girl dies.'

'Fine! I think she's dead already. Prove me wrong.'

The screen goes blank. He's hung up.

27

The door in my mind is suddenly sucked closed. A feeling of desperation replaces it, along with the sound of the wind. Joe is kneeling over me. We gaze at each other.

'I remember.'

'Just lie still.'

'But I remember.'

'There's an ambulance coming. Stay calm. I think you just fainted.'

Around us the police divers are dragging air tanks from the Zodiacs and dropping them on the dock. The sound reverberates through my spine. Navigation lights have appeared on the water and the towers of Canary Wharf look like vertical cities.

Joe was right all along. If I kept gathering details and following the trail, something would eventually trigger my memories and the trickle would become a torrent.

I take a sip of water from a plastic bottle and try to sit up. He lets me lean on his shoulder. Somewhere overhead I see a passenger airliner on its final approach to Heathrow.

An ambulance officer kneels next to me.

'Any chest pains?'

'No.'

'Shortness of breath?'

'No.'

The guy has a really thick moustache and pizza breath. I recognise him from somewhere. His fingers are undoing the buttons of my shirt.

'I'm just going to check your heart rate,' he says.

My hands shoot out and grip him by the wrist. His eyes widen and he gets a strange look on his face. Slowly, he shifts his gaze to my leg and then to the river.

'I remember you,' I tell him.

'That's impossible. You were unconscious.'

I'm still holding his wrist, squeezing it hard. 'You saved my life.'

'I didn't think you'd make it.'

'Put paddles on my chest and I'll rip your heart out.'

He nods and laughs nervously.

I take a belt of oxygen from a mask, while he takes my blood pressure. The clatter and crash of remembering has stopped for a moment. It's like a held breath. I know it's going to come again.

In the spotlights I can see the swell sliding across the rocks like a black tide. 'New Boy' Dave has sealed off the dock with crime-scene tape. The divers are coming back in the morning to continue searching. How many more secrets lie in the silt?

'Let's go home,' says Joe.

I don't answer him but I can feel my head shaking from side to side. I'm so close to remembering. I have to keep going. It can't wait for another day or be slept on overnight.

Joe calls Julianne and tells her he'll be late home. Her second-hand voice sounds tinny through the mobile. It's a voice from the kitchen. She has children to feed. We have a child to find.

On the drive away from the Thames, I tell Joe about what

I've remembered – describing the phone calls, the rag doll and the cold finality of the last phone call. Everything had a meaning, a function, a place in the pattern: the diamonds, the tracking devices, the pizza box . . .

We park on the same plot of waste ground, opposite the abandoned industrial freezer. Headlights reflect from the pitted silver door. The rag doll has gone but the witch's hat traffic cone lies amid the weeds.

I get out of the car and move gingerly towards the freezer. Joe does his royal consort trick of walking four paces behind me. He's wearing a crumpled-looking linen jacket as if he's going on safari.

'Where was Rachel?'

'She stayed with the car. She couldn't go on.'

'What happened next?'

I rack my brains, trying to trigger the memories again.

'He must have called back. The man who hung up the phone – he called again.'

'What did he say?'

'I don't know. I can't remember. Wait!'

I look down at my clothes. 'He wanted me to take my shoes off, but I didn't do it. I figured he couldn't be watching me – not all this time. He told me to walk straight ahead, past the freezer.'

I'm moving as I talk. Ahead of us is a wire fence and beyond that the Bakerloo Line. 'I heard a young girl crying on the phone.'

'Are you sure?'

'Yes, in the background.'

The glow of the headlights is fainter now as we move further from Joe's car. My eyes grow accustomed to the dark but my mind plays tricks. I keep seeing figures in the shadows, crouching in hollows and hiding behind trees.

The purple sky has no stars. That's one of the things I miss about living in the country – the stars and the silence and the frost on winter mornings that covers the earth like a freshly laundered sheet.

'There is a chain-link fence up ahead. I turned left and followed it until I reached the footbridge. He was giving me instructions on the phone.'

'Did you recognise his voice?'

'No.'

The fence appears, dividing the darkness into black diamonds with silver frames. We turn and follow it to an arched footbridge above the railway line. A generator rumbles and repair crews are working beneath spotlights.

In the middle of the footbridge, I peer over the side at the silver ribbons curving to the north. 'I can't remember what happened next.'

'Did you drop the ransom off the bridge?'

'No. This is where the phone rang again. I was travelling too slowly. They were tracking me. The mobile phone must have had a GPS device. Someone was sitting in front of a computer screen plotting my exact position.'

We both peer down at the tracks as though looking for the answer. The breeze carries the smell of burning coal and detergent. I can't hear the voice in my head any more.

'Give it time,' says Joe.

'No. I can't give it any more. I *have* to remember.'

He takes out his mobile and punches a number. My pocket vibrates. I flip it open and he turns away from me.

'Why have you stopped? KEEP MOVING! I told you where to go.'

The knowledge rises up and breaks soundlessly through the surface. Joe has done it again – helped me to go back.

'Will Mickey be there?' I yell down the phone.

'Shut up and keep moving!'

Where? It's close by. The car park on the far side of the station! Move!

Running now, I quickly descend the stairs. Joe has trouble

273

keeping up. I can barely see where I'm going but I remember the path. It curves alongside the railway line, above the cutting. Rigid steel gantries flank the tracks carrying the overhead wires.

A wind has sprung up, rattling fences and sending rubbish swirling past my legs. There are lights along the path, making it easier to see. Abruptly, the footpath opens into a deserted car park. A solitary lamp-post at the centre paints a dome of yellow on the tarmac. I remember a traffic cone sitting under the light. I ran towards it, holding the pizza box under one arm. It seemed an odd place to bring me. It was too open.

Joe has caught up with me. We're standing beneath the lamp-post. At my feet is a barred metal grate.

'He wanted me to push the packages into the drain.'

'What did you do?'

'I told him I wanted to see Mickey. He threatened to hang up again. His voice was very calm. He said she was close.'

'Where?'

I turn my head. Thirty yards away is the dark outline of a storm-water drain. 'He said she was waiting for me . . . down there.'

Walking to the edge, we peer over the side. The steep concrete walls are sprayed with graffiti.

'I couldn't see her. It was too dark. I shouted her name. "*Mickey! Can you hear me?*" I was yelling into the phone. "I can't see her. Where is she?" "She's in the pipe," he said. "*Where?*" I shouted: "*Mickey. Are you in there?*"'

Joe has hold of me now. He's frightened I might fall over the edge. At the same time he wants me to go on. 'Show me,' he says.

Set into the wall of the drain is a steel ladder. The rungs feel cold against my fingers. Joe is following me down. I couldn't hold the Glock and carry the pizza box at the same time. I left the gun in its holster and tucked the pizza box under my arm.

'Mickey! Can you hear me?'

My feet touch the bottom. Against the nearside wall I can just make out the deeper shadow of an access pipe.

She must have been in the pipe. It was the only place to hide.

'Michaela?'

There was a muffled rumble, like distant thunder. I could feel it through my shoes. I reached for my gun but left it there.

'Mickey?'

Wind ruffled my hair and I heard a rushing sound, like a train in a tunnel or the thunder of hooves on a loading ramp. My head jerked left and right, looking for her. The sound grew louder. It was coming towards me, coming out of the darkness . . . a wave.

Again the door opens and the world dissolves into noise and movement. Gravity is no more. I am flying, tumbling over and over, as an ocean roars past my ears. Head up, half a breath and I'm underwater, plunging into blackness.

Totally disorientated, I can't find the surface. I'm dragged sideways by the current and carried down a pipe or tunnel. My fingernails are torn and broken as they claw at the slick sides.

Seconds later I tumble into another vertical shaft. Snatching a half-breath, I suck in silt and shit and detritus. I'm in a flooded sewer, full of reeking gases and decomposing turds. I'm going to die down here.

There are flashes of light above me. Iron grates. I reach out and my fingers close around the metal bars. The pressure of the water surges against my chest and neck, filling my mouth with foulness.

Holding my mouth and nose above the water, I try to push the grate upwards. It won't budge. The force of the water pulls me horizontally.

Through the grate I see lights. Moving shapes. Pedestrians. Traffic. I try to scream something. They can't hear me.

Someone steps off the pavement and tosses a cigarette into the gutter. Red sparks shower into my eyes.

'Help me! Help me!'

Something is crawling on my shoulder. A rat digs its claws into my shirt, dragging its sodden body from the current. I can smell wet fur and see sharp teeth, reflected in the square of light. My whole body shudders. Rats are all around me, clinging to crevices.

Finger by finger my hands surrender. I can't hold on much longer. The current is too strong. I think of Luke. He had such great lungs; air-sucking bags. He could hold his breath for much longer than I could, but not beneath the ice.

He was a stubborn little tyke. I used to give him Chinese burns. 'Give up?' I'd say.

Tears would be welling in his eyes. 'Never!'

'You just have to give up and I won't hurt you any more.'

'No.'

In awe of him I'd offer a truce, but he refused.

'OK, OK, you win,' I'd say, sick of the game and embarrassed at hurting him.

My last finger surrenders. I roll face up in the current and take a deep sulphurous breath. Washed into darkness, I tumble over a waterfall and get dragged into a larger pipe.

I don't know where the ransom has gone. Washed away, along with my shoes. And what of Mickey – is she drowning somewhere ahead of me or behind me? I heard a soft cry when I peered into the pipe. Perhaps it was the wind or the rats.

So this is how it ends! I am going to drown in stinking slime water, which is pretty much how I've lived – in a putrid soup of thieves, liars, murderers and victims. I'm a rat catcher and a sewer hunter, a bone grubber and a muck dredger. Poverty, ignorance and inequality create criminals and I lock them away so that polite society doesn't have to smell them or fear them.

My shoulder strikes something hard and the pressure of the water rolls me over. Gulping a mouthful of air, I flail from side to side, trying to find a handhold as I tumble down a sloping ramp or weir.

Blindly, I plunge into a deep pool. I don't know which way is up. I could be swimming away from safety. My hand breaks the surface but the current won't let me go. A whirlpool drags me round and round, sucking me under. I want the air but the water wins.

The end is close now. I'm inside a narrow pipe, barely wide enough for my shoulders. There is no air pocket. My chest feels as if it is wrapped in cables pulled tight with a ratchet.

I need to breathe. Carbon dioxide is building up in my blood. I'm being poisoned from within. The instinct not to breathe is being overcome by the agony of airlessness. My mouth opens. The first involuntary breath fills my windpipe with water. My throat contracts but can't stop water flooding into my lungs. I'm as helpless as the day I was born.

My shoulders are no longer scraping along the walls. A different, slower current has picked me up, turning me over and over like a leaf caught in a gust of wind.

I'm dying but I can't accept it. Above me – or maybe it's below – there is a solid grey light. I feel myself rising, fighting for the surface; climbing one hand at a time as if trying to pull the light towards me like it's a candelabrum at the end of a long table. The last few strokes are impossibly hard.

Breaking free, I vomit water and phlegm, making room for that first breath. A floodlight is blinding me. Something hard hooks my belt from behind and hauls me upwards, dragging me on to a wooden deck. My lungs are heaving in their cage like bloated battery hens. Strong hands pump my stomach. Someone leans over me and wipes my chin and neck. It's Kirsten Fitzroy!

I loll back against her arm. She strokes my head, pushing wet hair across my forehead.

'Jesus, you're a crazy bastard!' she mutters, wiping my mouth again.

My stomach is still contracting and I can't speak.

The boat engine is idling in neutral. I can smell the fumes and see a dull light shining in the cockpit. Taking ragged, greedy gulps of air I turn my head and recognise Ray Murphy kneeling next to me, dressed all in black. 'We should have let him drown,' he says.

'Nobody is supposed to get hurt,' replies Kirsten.

They argue with each other but Kirsten refuses to listen.

'Where's Mickey?' I whisper.

'Sshhh, just relax,' she says.

'Is she OK?'

'Don't tell him a fucking thing!' threatens Murphy.

A tiny red dot is dancing on his forehead as though bouncing over the lyrics of a song. A fraction of a second later he makes a noise like a popped water balloon and half his head disappears in a spray of fine red mist and shattered bone. One eye, one cheek, half a jaw are suddenly erased from his face.

The sound of the bullet comes a heartbeat later. *Zip!*

Kirsten screams. Her eyes are as wide as a child's. Blood has splattered her cheeks.

Murphy's body is lying across me with his head on my chest. I roll him off me, kicking my legs to get away, sliding on the wet and bloody deck.

Kirsten still hasn't moved, immobilised by the shock. I turn and crawl back towards her.

A bullet enters my thigh. It's only a small hole, no bigger than my little finger, but as it exits it vaporises skin, muscle and flesh, leaving a wound the size of a pie tin. Part of me is impressed. It's like watching a building getting blown up, or a car crash.

Another bullet passes close to my ear and hits the deck near my right knee. Whoever is shooting is above us. I roll sideways, sliding through blood, until I reach Kirsten and pull her below the level of the wooden railings.

A section of the polished wood above our heads disintegrates and a splinter slices into her neck. She screams again.

Unbuckling my belt I lever myself upwards and pull it around my upper thigh. I hold one end of the belt between my teeth and pull it tightly, trying to stem the flow of blood. I tie it off with sticky fingers.

Beside me, Ray Murphy's body flinches as a bullet tears through his thigh and enters the deck beneath him. On the far side, almost touching his leg, is a fisherman's net on a long pole. Lodged within the mesh are a handful of plastic packages. The ransom.

Someone is in the wheelhouse trying desperately to engage the throttle but the mooring rope is still looped through a large silver cleat on the stern. Reaching under my armpit I feel for the Glock and pull it out of the holster. I look at Kirsten. She's deep in shock but listening.

'We can't stay here! You have to get to the wheelhouse. Quickly! Now!'

Kirsten nods.

I push her across the deck, watching her slip and slide through the blood. At the same time I spin around and aim the Glock blindly into the night sky. Nothing happens when I pull the trigger.

Kirsten's body spins and she clutches her side. A fraction of a second later I hear the bullet. Blood flows over her fingers but she keeps moving.

The choice of two targets has distracted the shooter but I have to do something about the floodlight. It's made of brass and chrome and fixed to a pillar in the centre of the deck.

I spin the Glock until I'm holding it like a hammer. Using Ray Murphy's body as a shield, I slide across the deck until I'm beneath the light. Reaching up I smash the glass. The bulb flares and dies.

A shadow passes in front of me, tripping over my feet and sprawling on the deck. Gerry Brandt scrambles to his feet and tries to reach the diamonds. Launching a kick at his groin, I send him in the opposite direction. A bullet detonates in the space he left behind. He yowls and gives me a murderous look. I save the arsehole's life and this is the thanks I get.

His face is a pale blankness of shock. A red dot appears in the centre of his chest. Even without the spotlight the sniper can still see us. He must have an infrared scope.

Gerry looks at his chest and then at me. He's about to die.

He rolls and the deck splinters beneath him. Over and over he tumbles, past the netting and the packages. He disappears off the stern but the splash is muffled by the sound of the engine revving at full throttle. I have visions of him falling directly on to the spinning propeller.

Kirsten is in the wheelhouse, opening the throttle. A mooring rope is still looped through a cleat on the stern. The boat dips and sways, going nowhere. The dual engines are pulling us under. Rolling across the deck, I reach up and uncoil the last loop of rope from the cleat, feeling it whip through my fingers. The boat pitches forwards but instead of turning away from the bank we steer towards it, colliding heavily against the stonework.

For fuck's sake, what's she doing!

The boat collides with a sunken pile or another boat, before spinning into open water. There's nobody at the wheel. Where's she gone?

The boat is going round in circles. The shooter is waiting to get another clean shot at me.

Half-crawling and half-dragging myself across the deck towards the wheelhouse, I brace my back against the outside wall. Reaching up, I hook my fingers over the edge of the porthole, pulling myself upwards until my eyes reach the glass window.

There's nobody there. In that same instant a dark stain fills my vision, a spray of blood. My finger disappears along with my wedding ring. It's a neat, clean amputation by a high-velocity bullet. I slide backwards, landing heavily on the deck.

The shooter is somewhere high up on a bridge or a building.

Now he's aiming at the engines or the fuel tanks. The current is turning the rudder and we're drifting on the tide. Soon we'll be out of range.

I suck the stump of my missing finger. There's surprisingly little blood. Where's Mickey? Was she in the pipe? Is she down below? I can't leave her behind.

I hear another sound – a different engine. With my back against the wall, I lever myself upwards again, peering through the shattered porthole. I can't see any navigation lights. Instead I make out the silhouette of a boat. There is someone standing on the bow holding a gun.

I can either stay here or take my chances in the river. It takes less than a fraction of a second to decide.

Then I see Kirsten lying under a tarpaulin against the bow. I don't see her face, just her outline as she tries to stand and falls. She tries again and rolls over the side. I hear the splash followed by the sound of men yelling and bullets hitting the water.

The boat is getting closer. I have one good leg and one leaking. Pushing off the wall, I take two stumbling steps and roll over the railing. The cold comes as a shock. I don't know why. I'm still wet from before.

Kicking with one good leg and whipping my arms across my body, I swim down into the darkness where I'm going to drown or bleed to death. I'll let the river decide.

28

Joe is holding on to me. I'm growing accustomed to his face. He lays my arm over his shoulders and braces his body against mine.

'C'mon, let's get you out of here.'

'I remembered.'

'Yes, you did.'

'What about Mickey?'

'She's not here. We'll find her.'

I climb out of the drain and we limp across the car park. A pair of teenagers, a boy and a girl, have parked their car away from the light. I wonder what they make of two middle-aged men arm in arm. Are we drunks or lovers? I'm way past caring.

I have remembered. I have waited and hoped for this to happen. I have feared it. What if I shot someone? What if I had Mickey in my arms and lost her to the river? I dreamed the nightmare because I didn't have the truth.

It's almost ten o'clock when we reach Primrose Hill. Yellow light paints the edges of the curtains and a coal fire warms the sitting room.

'You'll stay here tonight,' says Joe, opening the door.

I want to say no, but I'm too tired to argue. I can't go home or to Ali's parents' place. I'm like an infectious disease – poisoning those around me. I won't stay long. Just tonight.

I keep getting flashbacks of being underwater, unable to breathe. I smell the foulness of the sewers and see the white-green water boiling at my feet. Each time it happens I take a ragged urgent breath. Joe looks at me. He thinks I'm having a heart attack.

'I should take you to hospital. They could run some tests.'

'No. I need to talk.' I have to tell him what I remember in case I forget again.

Joe pours me a drink and then moves to sit down. He suddenly freezes. For a split second he looks like a statue, trapped between sitting and standing. Just as suddenly, he moves again as the signals reach his limbs. He smiles at me apologetically.

The mantelpiece is decorated with photographs of his family. The new baby has a moon face and a tangle of blonde hair. She looks more like Joe than Julianne.

'Where is your lovely wife?'

'Tucked up in bed. She's an early riser.'

Joe rocks forward with his hands between his thighs. I tell him about being washed through the sewers and what happened on the boat. I remember Kirsten Fitzroy wiping vomit from my lips and feeling the dead weight of Ray Murphy slumped across me. His blood leaked down my neck, pooling in the depression beneath my Adam's apple. I remember the sound of high-velocity bullets and seeing Kirsten spinning across the deck, clutching her side.

Memories carry more memories – fleeting images captured before they fade. Gerry Brandt going over the stern, the silhouette of a gunman, my finger disappearing . . . These things have all become substance now and nothing else is real except what happened that night. Even as I try to explain this to Joe I have the horrors of hindsight and regret to contend with. If only I could change what happened. If only I could go back.

Ray Murphy worked for Thames Water. He knew his way through the storm-water drains and sewers because he used to be a flusher and a flood planner. He knew what water main to sabotage to create a flood. The explosion would be blamed on methane or a gas leak and nobody would bother investigating further.

Radio transmitters and satellite tracking devices are useless underground and nobody was likely to make such a journey. Ray Murphy would also have known about the underground river beneath Dolphin Mansions. He and Kirsten provided each other with an alibi on the morning Mickey disappeared. But where did Gerry Brandt come into the operation? Perhaps they needed a third person for the plan.

'You still can't be sure they kidnapped Mickey,' says Joe. 'There's no direct evidence.' A sudden spastic movement of his arm flicks up at my face. 'It could still be a hoax. Kirsten had access to Rachel's flat. She could have taken strands of Mickey's hair and counted the money in her money box. If they kidnapped her three years ago, why wait until now to send a ransom demand?'

'Perhaps it was never about a ransom – not at first. Sir Douglas Carlyle said he would do almost anything to safeguard his grand-daughter. We know he hired Kirsten to spy on Rachel. He was gathering evidence for a custody battle, but his lawyers told him he couldn't succeed. He might have taken the law into his own hands.'

'What about Mickey's towel – how did it get to the ceme-tery?'

My brain is caught in a vague, desperate pause. Maybe they framed Howard. They put Mickey's blood on a towel and planted it in the cemetery. The police and the courts did the rest.

'You still have no proof that Mickey is alive.'

'I know.'

Bending towards the fire, Joe asks a question of the flames instead of me. 'Why send the ransom demand now?'

'Greed.'

At least it's a motive I understand. Joe can have his psychopaths and sadists but give me an old-fashioned everyday motive I can identify with.

'Who did the shooting? Who wanted them dead?'

'Someone who wanted to silence them or punish them,' I whisper, rocking forward in the armchair. 'It could have been Sir Douglas. If he arranged Mickey's kidnapping he may have been threatened with blackmail.'

'Or what else? I know you don't think it's him.'

'Aleksei.'

'You said he was following you and Rachel that night.'

'Following the diamonds.'

Joe waits for my explanation. I know he's already there but he wants to hear me lay out the arguments. 'Aleksei was never going to stand back and let anyone walk away with two million pounds. Whether they had kidnapped Mickey or not; whether she was dead or alive; somebody was going to pay. Look what he did to his own brother.'

'Did that include killing you?'

'No. I wasn't supposed to be on the boat. Nobody expected anyone to follow the ransom through the sewers.'

'And the attack in the hospital?'

The memory climbs up my throat and hangs there. 'I don't know. I haven't worked that out yet. Maybe he was frightened that I'd work out what happened or perhaps he thinks I saw something that night . . .'

I still can't explain how the diamonds finished up in my linen cupboard. I know they were in the pizza box and I saw the packages on the deck of the *Charmaine*. Most of the facts fit but not all of them.

I have to convince the Met to reopen the investigation. This isn't about Howard Wavell any more. Yes, he belongs in prison but not for this crime. Aleksei is the true monster.

*　　*　　*

I shudder awake and feel like weeping with tiredness. The day is just beginning but I can't tell where the last one ended. All night I have drowned in sewers and watched red dots dancing across the walls.

Julianne gives me a cheery smile in the kitchen. 'How are you feeling?'

Five seconds of my life evaporate considering this and I decide not to answer. Instead I gratefully accept a cup of coffee.

'Where are the girls?'

'Joe is dropping Charlie at school. He took Emma along for the ride.'

Her pale-blue eyes stare at me with the vague, almost accusatory air of someone who has discovered the one true path to happiness – married life. Wrapped in a crimson skirt and light jumper, she looks beautiful, as always. I can imagine her walking barefoot along a beach in some warm country, supporting a child on her slender hip. The Professor is a lucky man.

The front door opens. Joe is carrying Emma in one arm and the morning papers under the other. Julianne takes the toddler and kisses her nose, running her fingers through her curls.

Joe opens a paper on the table. 'There's a very small piece – just a couple of paragraphs about a body found in the Thames.'

'It's too early. They won't do a post-mortem until today.'

'What are you going to do?'

'I have to convince them to investigate the shootings. Will you come with me? I need someone to back me up.'

'I don't think they'll listen to me.'

'We have to try.'

On the drive to New Scotland Yard my hands begin to shake. Maybe it's obvious to Joe what I'm going through – the headaches, stomach cramps, the constant churning in my guts. If he *does* recognise the withdrawal symptoms he doesn't say anything.

At the Yard we are made to wait like any other members of the public. My request to see the Commissioner is sent via the public affairs department through various branches of bureaucracy, only to be rejected. I ask to see the Assistant Commissioner. Again the request goes upstairs and is passed around like a problem that nobody wants. Eventually, I'm directed back to Campbell Smith.

We cross the city and spend another hour downstairs at the Harrow Road Police Station. Joe spends his time studying the 'Missing Persons' posters as if he's at the National Portrait Gallery. Receptionists, secretaries and uniforms ignore us. A month ago I used to run this place. I gave it my life.

Eventually, Campbell agrees to see us. Joe limps along the corridor alongside me, our footsteps echoing on the shiny floor. At the far end of the incident room civilian operators sit at a bank of computer screens. The flurry of their keystrokes sounds like rain falling on plastic. Some wear ear microphones, talking to officers in the field, running checks on names, addresses and number plates.

There's a new head of the Serious Crime Group – DI John Meldrum. He spies me. 'Hey, we once had a guy who looked just like you working here. I think he might be dead.'

'But not buried,' I yell back. 'Congratulations on the promotion.'

I try to sound genuine but it doesn't work. Instead I feel a juvenile rush of anger and jealousy. Meldrum is in *my* office. His jacket is hanging over *my* chair.

Campbell makes us wait again outside his office. Joe doesn't understand the politics involved. It's not actually politics – it's spite.

Finally we are summoned. I let the Professor walk ahead of me. Campbell shakes his hand and gives him the no-brand smile. Then he studies me for a moment and motions to a chair. Meldrum slides his chair back a few inches, taking himself outside the circle. He's here to watch and witness.

I should be addressing a task force. There should be detectives sitting on chairs and corners of desks – men in grey suits with Father's Day ties and women with sensible hairstyles and minimal make-up. Instead I have to argue my case in front of a Chief Superintendent who thinks I betrayed my fellow officers and jeopardised a murder conviction.

Using a whiteboard, I explain what happened on the river. I write four names across the top: Ray Murphy, Kirsten Fitzroy, Gerry Brandt and Aleksei Kuznet. Ray Murphy is dead. Kirsten and Gerry Brandt are missing.

Taking out the brown envelope, I show him the ransom letters and the DNA reports, before describing the ransom drop and my trip through the sewers.

'I know it sounds far-fetched but I've been down there. I've followed the trail. They were waiting at the other end. Ray Murphy was the caretaker at Dolphin Mansions when Mickey Carlyle disappeared. I saw him shot and killed on the *Charmaine*. They'll match the blood and the bullets to the boat.'

'Who killed him?'

'A sniper.'

Meldrum leans closer. 'And this is the same sniper who tried to kill you?'

'I got in the way.'

Campbell hasn't said a word but I know he's struggling to remain composed.

'Kirsten Fitzroy lived at Dolphin Mansions when Mickey disappeared. She was Rachel Carlyle's best friend. I saw her shot on the *Charmaine*. She suffered a stomach wound and went over the side. I don't know if she survived.'

'Her flat was burgled,' says Meldrum.

'Not burgled. It was searched. I think Aleksei Kuznet is looking for Kirsten. He wants to punish the people who sent the ransom demand. I believe they're the same people who kidnapped his daughter.'

Campbell scoffs angrily. 'Howard Wavell killed Mickey Carlyle.'

'Even if you believe that – you have to accept that someone

else sent the ransom demand. They included a lock of Mickey's hair and the bikini.'

'Neither of which prove she's alive.'

'No. But Ray Murphy is dead and Kirsten is in danger. Aleksei Kuznet was never going to let anyone steal two million pounds from him. He organised an execution. Now he's looking for Kirsten and Gerry Brandt – to finish the job.'

I make a decision not to mention Sir Douglas Carlyle. Campbell is already on the edge. My only chance of persuading him to investigate is to let him believe the ransom was a hoax. I still can't prove otherwise.

'What does Gerry Brandt have to do with this?'

'He was on the *Charmaine*. I saw him go over the side.'

I wait. I don't know if I've done enough.

Campbell has assumed a perfect proprietary air. 'So let me get this straight. So far you have mentioned a kidnapping, a revenge killing, a shooting and a ransom demand. I'll add a few to the list: dereliction of duty, crippling a fellow police officer, withholding information and disobeying orders . . .'

A sense of alarm spreads through me. He doesn't understand. He can't see past Howard Wavell.

'We have to find Kirsten before Aleksei does. If she survived she would have needed medical help. We have to search local hospitals and ask doctors to go back through their files. We have to check her bank, telephone and travel records. We need to know her last known movements, possible associations and favourite haunts.'

Campbell's look is piercing. 'You're using the word "we" a lot. For some reason you seem to be under the misapprehension that you're still a serving member of the Metropolitan Police.'

I'm so angry my vision blurs.

Joe tries to calm things down. 'It seems to me, gentlemen, that we're all seeking the truth. DI Meldrum here is investigating the shootings on the river. DI Ruiz is a witness. He's offering to make a statement. He won't interfere with the investigation.'

Meldrum nods. Satisfied.

Campbell points his finger at me. 'I want you to know one thing, Ruiz. I know the truth.'

'Sure you do,' I say.

Campbell gives me a triumphant smile. 'You're right about Aleksei Kuznet. He's not the sort of man who lets someone take two million pounds from him. He claims *you* stole his diamonds and he's made an official complaint. We're drawing up a warrant for your arrest. If I were you I'd get myself a lawyer.'

Rage quickens my footsteps. Joe struggles to keep up with me as I stride down the corridor and punch through the swing glass doors.

On the pavement a voice hits me like a cold wind. 'Did you shoot him?'

Tony Murphy is asking the question with his entire body. 'You ever seen a body like that . . . in pieces? I had to go to the morgue to identify him. He was bloated and white like a candle melted into a puddle. The police say someone shot him. They got a witness. Was it you?'

'Yes.'

He chews the inside of his cheek. 'Did you shoot him?'

'No.'

'Do you know who did?'

'I don't know who pulled the trigger but I saw him go down. I couldn't help him.'

He swallows a lump in his throat. 'So I'm looking after Mum and Stevie now. The pub is all we got left.'

'I'm sorry.'

He wants to do something more but can only stand there, a prisoner of his own misery, caught in the guard tower spotlights.

'Go home, Tony. I'll sort this out.'

29

Joe is waiting for me to say something. His dark-brown eyes are staring at me with a vague sadness and certainty that he can't help me. Meanwhile, I keep considering what should have happened. Campbell should have set up a task force. There should be two dozen detectives looking for Kirsten and Gerry Brandt. We should have Aleksei under surveillance and be searching his boat.

For one cool precise hour I want to know what to do. I want every decision to be the right one.

We're driving along Euston Road, past Regent's Park.

'So what are you going to do?' he asks.

'Find them.'

'You can't do it alone.'

'I have no choice.'

Joe looks like a man with a plan. 'What if we got some volunteers? We could call friends and family. How many people do you need?'

'I don't know. We need to contact the hospitals and doctors' surgeries and clinics. One of them must have treated Kirsten.'

'We can use my office,' says Joe. 'It's not very big but

291

there's the waiting room and the storeroom and a kitchen. There are six phone lines and a fax. We could get some more handsets. I'll get my secretary Philippa to start calling people.'

We pull up outside his office. 'What are you going to do?'

There's a small invisible shock in the air. A decision is made.

'One way or another, I'm going to see Rachel Carlyle.'

There will be no tennis today. Puddles cover the court and fat drops hang on the net like glass beads. It must be autumn – the rain is colder.

Parked in front of the Carlyle house, I watch the driveway and listen to the radio. Ray Murphy's name has been released but there's no mention of Kirsten. Campbell won't allow it.

Glancing up at the house, I watch a dark Mercedes glide through the front gates and pause before turning left. Sir Douglas and Tottie are going out.

I give them a few minutes and then approach the house. Soggy mounds of leaves have gathered along the drive, trapped by the hedges. Some have clogged the fountain and the water spills over the side, flooding the footings.

Avoiding the front door, I skirt the building and use a set of stone steps at the right-hand side of the house. I knock four times before it opens. Thomas stands there.

'I need to speak to Rachel.'

'Miss Rachel isn't here, sir.'

He's lying.

'You don't have to protect her. I don't want to cause any trouble. If she doesn't want to speak to me I'll leave.'

He looks past me into the garden. 'I don't think Sir Douglas would approve.'

'Just ask her.'

He contemplates this and agrees, leaving me waiting on the steps. A fire is smouldering somewhere, turning the air the colour of dirty water.

Thomas appears again. 'Miss Carlyle will see you in the kitchen.'

He leads the way. We pass along hallways lined with paintings of foxhounds, horses and pheasants. The frames are so dark they blend into the walls and the animals appear to be suspended, set in aspic. Above the stairs there are English landscapes of lakes and rivers.

At first I don't realise that Rachel is already in the kitchen. She stands with the stillness of a photograph, tall and dark, with her hair drawn back.

'Your father said I couldn't see you,' I say.

'He didn't ask me.'

She is wearing jeans and a raw silk shirt. Her wedge-shaped face is softened by the cut of her hair, which is shorter than I remember, loosely brushing her shoulders.

'I hear you couldn't remember what happened that night.'

'Yes, for a while.'

She bites her bottom lip and weighs up whether to believe me. 'You didn't forget about me.'

'No. I didn't know what happened to you. I only discovered a few days ago.'

Urgency fills her eyes. 'Did you see Mickey? Was she there?'

'No, I'm sorry.'

She purses her lips and turns her face away. 'Losing your memory, forgetting everything, must be nice. All the terrible things in your life, the guilt, the regret, gone, washed away. Sometimes I wish . . .' She doesn't finish. Leaning over the sink, she fills a glass of water from the tap and empties it into a row of African violets on the windowsill. 'You never asked me why I married Aleksei.'

'It's none of my business.'

'I met my ex-husband at a fundraising dinner for Bosnian orphans. He wrote a very large cheque. He wrote a lot of very large cheques in those days. Whenever I took him to lectures and documentaries about deforestation or animal cruelty or

293

the plight of the homeless – he pulled out his chequebook.'

'He was buying your affection.'

'I thought he believed in the same things.'

'Your parents didn't like him?'

'They were horrified. Aleksei had no equal – anybody would have been better than a Russian émigré with a murdering father.'

'Did you love him?'

She ponders this. 'Yes. I think so.'

'What happened?'

She shrugs. 'We got married. For the first three years we lived in Holland. Mickey was born in Amsterdam: Aleksei was building up the business.'

Rachel's voice is low and introspective. 'In spite of what my father says, I'm not a foolish person. I knew something was going on. Mostly it was just rumours and nervous glances in restaurants. I used to ask Aleksei but he told me people were jealous of him. I knew he was involved in something illegal. I kept asking questions and he grew irritated. He told me that a wife should not question her husband. She must obey.

'Then one day the wife of a Dutch flower grower visited me at home. I don't know how she found my address. She showed me a photograph of her husband. His face was so scarred by acid that his skin looked like melted wax.

'"Tell me why a woman would stay with a man who looks like this?" she asked me. I shook my head. Then she said, "Because it cannot be as bad as staying with the man who would do such a thing."

'From then on I began to discover things. I eavesdropped on conversations, read e-mails and kept copies of letters. I learned things . . .'

'Enough to get you killed.'

'Enough to keep me safe,' she corrects. 'I learned how Aleksei does business. It is simple and brutal. First he offers to buy a business. If a price cannot be agreed he burns it down. If they set up again he burns their houses down. And if the message still fails to be heard, he burns down the houses of their relatives and the schools of their children.'

'What did Aleksei do when you left him?'

'First he begged me to come back. Then he tried to bribe me with grand gestures. Finally he tried to bully me.'

'You didn't go back to your family.'

Pushing hair behind her ears with both hands, she shakes her head. 'I've been running away from them my whole life.'

We sit in silence. The warm air rising from the Aga lifts loose strands from her fringe, suspending them in midair.

'When did you last see Kirsten Fitzroy?'

'About two months ago; she said she was going abroad.'

'Did she say where?'

'America or South America; she had some brochures. It might have been Argentina. She was going to send me post-cards but I didn't receive a thing. What's happened? Is she in trouble?'

'You met at Dolphin Mansions.'

'Yes.'

'Did Kirsten ever meet your father?'

'No, I don't think so.'

'Are you sure?'

'Please tell me what she's supposed to have done?'

'Sir Douglas paid her rent at Dolphin Mansions. Later he helped her buy her flat in Notting Hill.'

Rachel doesn't react. I can't tell if she's shocked or if she suspected it all along.

'She was keeping watch on you. Your father wanted custody of Mickey. He had his lawyers preparing an application. They were going to argue you were unfit to care for a child because of your drinking. The application was withdrawn after you joined AA.'

'I can't believe any of this,' she whispers.

There's more. I don't know how much to tell her.

'On the night of the ransom drop, I followed the diamonds through the sewers. I washed up in the Thames. Kirsten saved my life.'

'What was she doing there?'

'She and Ray Murphy were waiting for the diamonds. They organised the whole thing – the ransom demand, the locks of hair, the bikini. Kirsten knew everything about you and Mickey. She counted the money in Mickey's money box. She knew exactly what buttons to press.'

Rachel shakes her head. 'But the bikini . . . it belonged to Mickey.'

'And they took it from her.'

Suddenly, she realises what I'm saying. The sense of alarm spreads through her before the instant of comprehension.

At that moment a door swings open somewhere in the house and the air pressure changes. Sir Douglas comes storming through the main hall, yelling at Thomas to call the police. The butler must have phoned him the moment I arrived.

I lose sight of him for a moment and then he appears in the doorway of the kitchen. He's carrying a shotgun. His face is like a warning light.

'You stay here! Don't go anywhere. You're under arrest.'

'Calm down.'

'You're trespassing on my property.'

'Put the gun down, Daddy.'

He waves the gun at me. 'Stay away from him.'

'Please put that down.'

Rachel is watching him with a 'you-must-be-crazy' look. She takes a step towards him, distracting him for a moment. He doesn't see me close the final two paces. I seize the gun, twisting it out of his hands and drop him with a punch just below his ribs. I look at Rachel apologetically. I didn't want to hit him.

Sir Douglas takes a long staggering breath. He tries to talk, telling me to get out. I'm already leaving. Rachel follows, pleading with me to explain.

'Why would they do that? Why would they take Mickey?'

Turning back, I blink at her sadly. 'I don't know. Ask your father.'

I don't want to give her false hopes. I'm not even sure if I'm talking sense. I've been wrong so often lately.

Out of the front door and down the steps, I crunch along the gravel drive. Rachel watches from the steps.

'What about Mickey?' she yells.

'I don't think Howard killed her.'

At first she doesn't react. Maybe she's given up hope or she's shackled to the past. This is only for a moment and then she's running towards me. I have given her a choice between hating, forgiving and believing. She wants to believe.

30

'Where are we going?' asks Rachel.

'You'll see. It's right up here.'

We pull up before a cottage in Hampstead; there is an arbour over the front gate and neatly pruned rose bushes along the path. Making a dash through the light rain, we squeeze beneath the overhang until the doorbell is answered.

Esmerelda Bird, a matronly woman in a skirt and cardigan, leaves us waiting in the sitting room while she gets her husband. We perch on the edge of sofas looking at a room full of crocheted cushion covers, lace doilies and photographs of overweight grandchildren. This is how sitting rooms used to look before people started buying up warehouses full of lacquered pine from Scandinavia.

I met the Birds three years ago, during the original investigation. Retired and pensioners, they're the sort of couple who clip their vowels when addressing a police officer and have special voices for the telephone.

Mrs Bird returns. She's done something to her hair, tied it back or perhaps just brushed it a different way. And she's changed into a different cardigan and put on her pearl earrings.

'I'm just making a pot of tea.'

'That really won't be necessary.'

She doesn't hear me. 'I have a cake.'

Brian Bird hobbles into view, a slow-motion cadaver who has a completely bald head and a face as wrinkled as crushed Cellophane. He rocks forward on a walking stick and takes what seems like an hour to lower himself into a chair.

Nothing is said as the tea is brewed, poured, strained and sweetened. Slices of fruitcake are offered around.

'Do you remember when I last came to see you?'

'Yes. It was about that missing girl – the one we saw on the station platform.'

Rachel looks from Mrs Bird's face to mine and back again.

'That's right. You thought you saw Michaela Carlyle. This is her mother, Rachel.'

The couple give her sad smiles.

'I want you to tell Mrs Carlyle what you saw that night.'

'Yes, of course,' says Mrs Bird, 'but I think we must have been mistaken. That dreadful man went to prison. I can't think of his name.' She looks to her husband who stares at her blankly.

Rachel finds her voice. 'Please tell me what you saw.'

'On the platform, yes . . . let me see. It was . . . a Wednesday evening. We'd been to see *Les Misérables* at the Queen's Theatre. I've been to see *Les Mis* over thirty times. Brian missed out on some shows because of his heart bypass operation. Isn't that right, Brian?'

Brian nods.

'What made you think it was Mickey?' I ask.

'Her picture had been in all the papers. We were just going down the escalator. She was loitering at the bottom.'

'Loitering?'

'Yes. She seemed a little lost.'

'What was she wearing?'

'Well, let me think. It's so long ago now, dear. What did I tell you then?'

'Trousers and a jacket,' I prompt.

'Oh, yes, although Brian thought she was wearing a pair of those trousers that zip up at the bottom. And she definitely had a hood.'

'And this hood was up?'

'Up.'

'So you didn't see her hair – if it was long or short?'

'Just the fringe.'

'What colour was her hair?'

'Light brown.'

'How close did you get to her?'

'Brian couldn't move very quickly because of his legs. I was ahead of him. We were maybe ten feet away. I didn't recognise her at first. I said to her, "Can I help you, dear? Are you lost?" but she just ran off.'

'Where?'

'Along the platform.' Her hand points the way, past Rachel's shoulder, and she nods resolutely. Then she leans forward with her teacup, using her other hand to find the saucer and bring both together.

'I think I talked to you back then about your glasses, do you remember?'

She touches the bridge of her nose self-consciously. 'Yes.'

'You weren't wearing them?'

'No. I normally don't forget.'

'Did she have pierced ears?'

'I can't remember. She ran off too quickly.'

'But you did say she had a gap in her teeth and freckles. She was also carrying something. Could it have been a towel?'

'Oh dear, I don't know. I didn't look that closely. There were other people on the platform. They must have seen her.'

'We looked for them. Nobody came forward.'

'Oh dear.'

300

A teacup rattles against a saucer. Rachel's hands are shaking. 'Do you have grandchildren, Mrs Bird?'

'Oh, yes, dear. Six of them.'

'How old are they?'

'They're aged between eight and eighteen.'

'And the girl you saw on the platform, she was about the same age as your youngest grandchild is now.'

'Yes.'

'Did she seem frightened?'

'Lost. She seemed lost.'

Rachel's eyes are fixed with an almost ecstatic intensity.

'I'm sorry I can't remember any more. It's so long ago.' Mrs Bird glances at her hands. 'It did look like her but when the police arrested that chap . . . well . . . I thought we must have been mistaken. When you get old your eyes play tricks. I'm very sorry for your loss. Another cup of tea?'

Back in the car Rachel is full of questions, most of which I can't answer. There were dozens of reported sightings of Mickey in the weeks after she disappeared. Without any independent corroboration, and given that Mrs Bird wasn't wearing her glasses, I couldn't rely on her account.

'There must have been cameras at the station,' says Rachel.

'The footage is useless. We couldn't even tell if it was a child.'

Rachel is adamant. 'I want to see it.'

'Good. That's where we're going now.'

The headquarters of London Underground is on Broadway, around the corner from New Scotland Yard. The Area Commander of the Transport Police, Chief Superintendent Paul Magee, is an old friend. I've known him for thirty years. Back in those days the IRA kept him awake at night. Now it's a different type of terrorist.

His face is thin and shaven. He looks almost youthful, despite his grey hair, which seems whiter every time I see him. Soon he'll pass for blond.

'You look like shit, Vince.'

'People keep telling me that.'

'I hear you're getting divorced again. What happened?'

'I forgot to put sugar in her tea.'

He laughs. Paul is married to a girl he met in grammar school. Shirley is a real keeper, who thinks I'm a bad influence but still asked me to be godfather to her eldest boy.

We're sitting in Paul's office, which has a view over Wellington Barracks. He can watch the 'new guard' leave every morning and parade down Birdcage Walk to Buckingham Palace. Rachel is hanging back, waiting for an introduction. He doesn't recognise her name. I tell him we need to see a CCTV tape from three years ago.

'We don't keep them that long.'

'This one you kept. I asked you to.'

He suddenly puts two and two together and glances back at Rachel. Without another word, he takes us out of his office and down the corridor, tapping security codes into consoles and leading us deeper into the building.

Eventually, we're sitting in a small room, waiting for a video player to rewind a tape. Rachel watches motionless; even her breathing seems suspended. Grainy black and white images appear on the screen. They show a figure at the bottom of the escalators at Leicester Square Underground. Assuming it's a girl, she is wearing a dark-blue tracksuit and carrying something in her arms. It might be a beach towel. It could be anything.

There were twelve security cameras at the station, each mounted above platforms and escalators. The angles were wrong because they didn't pick up faces. No amount of computer enhancement could make someone look up into the lens.

Paul Magee has left us alone. I rewind the security video and play it again. Leaning closer, we watch the girl descend, almost willing her to glance up at the camera. She pauses at the bottom of the escalator, as though momentarily unsure of where to go. Mrs Bird comes into view and then Mr Bird a few moments later, planting his walking frame and shuffling behind her. Mrs Bird can be seen saying something to the girl, who turns away, disappearing through an arch on to the south-bound platform.

The time and date are displayed in the bottom right-hand corner of the screen. 22:14 July 25. Wednesday evening.

A second camera on the platform picked up the girl again, but from much further away. She appeared to be alone. A plump, dark-haired woman dressed in a nurse's uniform walked past her.

'So what do you think?' I ask Rachel.

She doesn't answer. I turn to face her and see tears welling up in her eyes. She blinks and they fall.

'Are you sure?'

She nods, still silent.

'But she could be seven or seventeen. You can't even see her face.'

'It's her. I know my daughter. I know how she walks and holds her head.'

Nine times out of ten I would not believe it was anything more than a mother's desperate desire to believe her daughter is alive. That's why I didn't show Rachel the tape three years ago. It risked derailing the entire investigation and sending dozens of officers off on a tangent and diverting public attention instead of focusing it.

Now I believe Rachel. I know there isn't a judge or a jury in the land who would accept beyond doubt that Mickey is the person on the tape but that doesn't matter. The person who knows her best is sure. On Wednesday 25 July – two days after she disappeared – Mickey was still alive.

31

The only other person in Joe's waiting room is a middle-aged man in a cheap suit that bunches at his shoulders when he folds his arms. He picks at his teeth with a matchstick and watches me take a seat.

'The secretary went to get coffee,' he says. 'The Professor has a patient.'

I nod and notice him watching me. Finally, he asks, 'Do we know each other?'

'I don't think so. Are you a copper?'

'Yeah. DS Roger Casey. They call me The Dodger.' He moves a few seats closer and thrusts out his hand, at the same time eyeing up Rachel.

'So where are you working, Roger?'

'Vice, from Holborn.'

He's sitting close, feeling a sense of camaraderie. I should probably remember his face but a lot of guys his age have left the service in the past ten years.

'You heard this one,' he asks. 'How many coppers does it take to throw a man down the stairs?'

'I don't know. How many?'

'None. He fell.'

Roger laughs and I offer him a chiselled smile. He lifts an eyebrow and goes quiet.

The Professor's secretary arrives back, carrying takeaway coffee and a brown-paper bag stained by a pastry. She looks barely out of high school and blinks through wire-frame glasses as though she should have known we were coming.

'I'm DI Ruiz. Could you tell the Professor that we're here?'

She sighs. 'Join the queue.'

At that moment the inner door opens and a young woman emerges with red-rimmed eyes.

Joe is behind her.

'So I'll see you next week, Christine. Remember, it's not immodest to wear culottes and it doesn't make you less feminine.'

She nods and keeps her eyes down. Everyone in the room does the same apart from Roger who starts giggling. The poor woman flees down the corridor.

Joe gives him an angry stare that softens when he sees me and he recognises Rachel. 'Come inside, you two.'

'The Detective Sergeant was here first,' I suggest.

Joe shakes his head and sighs. 'Oh dear . . . and you were doing so well Roger.' He turns to his secretary. 'For future reference, Philippa, DI Ruiz is a *real* police officer. Not everyone who comes in here claiming to be a detective is a fantasist.'

Philippa's cheeks redden and Rachel starts to giggle. I can feel myself blushing.

'I'm sorry about Roger,' says Joe, as we're ushered into his office. 'He pretends to be a police officer and tricks prostitutes into giving him free sex.'

'Does it work?'

'Apparently.'

'He's a freak!'

Joe looks at me awkwardly. 'Well, he's part of our team.'

There's a promising start!

Joe has spent the morning calling in favours. So far we have thirteen volunteers including two of my old rugby mates and a snout called 'Dicko' who has a nose for trouble and no sense of smell at all, which unfortunately means his personal hygiene leaves a lot to be desired.

Over the next hour the rest of the 'team' arrives. Joe has managed to recruit his brother-in-law, Eric, and his younger sister, Rebecca, who works for the United Nations. Julianne is coming after she picks up Charlie from school. There are also several patients, including Margaret, who is nursing a torpedo-shaped life buoy and another woman, Jean, who keeps disinfecting the phones with wet wipes.

Margaret sidles up to me. 'I hear you almost drowned. Don't trust bridges.' She taps her orange torpedo reassuringly.

When the last of the stragglers arrive, I gather them together in the waiting room. It is the strangest collection of 'detectives' I have ever commanded.

Pinning two photographs to a corkboard, I clear my throat and introduce myself – not as a detective inspector but as a member of the public.

'The two people in these photographs are missing. Their names are Kirsten Fitzroy and Gerry Brandt. We hope to find them.'

'What did they do?' asks Margaret.

'I believe they kidnapped a young girl.'

A murmur goes around the room.

'We need to discover how they're linked – when they met, where they talked, what they have in common – but most importantly we have to locate them. Each of you will be given a task. You won't be asked to do anything illegal, but this is detective work and has to remain confidential.'

'Why don't we just ask the police to find them?' asks Eric, perched on the edge of the desk.

'The police aren't looking hard enough.'

'But you're a policeman!'

'Not any more.'

Moving on, I explain that Kirsten was last seen going over the side of the *Charmaine*. 'She suffered a stomach wound and may not have survived her injuries or the river but we're going to assume she's still alive. Gerry Brandt is a known drug dealer, pimp and armed robber. Nobody is to approach him.'

I glance at Dicko. The flesh around his mouth seems to be moving but no sound comes out.

Addressing him directly I say, 'I want you to talk to anyone who knows him – suppliers, junkies, mules, friends . . . He used to hang out in a pub on Pentonville Road. See if anyone remembers him.'

After a few seconds of clicking his teeth, he says, 'Might need some readies.'

'If I catch you drinking I'll drill a hole in your head.'

The women peel their eyebrows off their hairlines.

'Maybe I should go with him,' suggests Roger.

'Fine. Remember what I said. Under no circumstances do you approach Gerry Brandt.'

Roger gives me a casual salute.

'Philippa, Margaret and Jean, I want you to ring the hospitals, clinics and doctors' surgeries. Make up a story. Say you're looking for a missing friend. Rachel and the Professor will contact Kirsten's family and any former employees. She grew up in the West Country.'

'What are you going to do?' asks Joe.

'Gerry Brandt had a former girlfriend, a skinny thing with bleeding gums and blonde streaks. I'm hoping she might know where he's hiding.'

Hell's Half-Mile is a road behind King's Cross Station where the kerbs get crawled and prostitutes hunt in packs. Some of these girls are barely sixteen but there's no way of telling.

Even without the scars and bruises, a year on the streets adds five years to their faces.

Very few prostitutes work the streets any more because the police have chased them indoors. Now they work for escort agencies and massage parlours; or they move around following the political conferences, trade shows and exhibitions. Become a prostitute and see the world!

The walk-up places are open doorways leading to upstairs flats with signs in the windows announcing 'Busty Young Model' or something similar. Most have a maid, usually an older woman, who takes the money and a small tip.

Apart from passing trade, they advertise with cards in phone boxes or rely on that patron saint of the horny – the London cabbie.

Cruising the street slowly I try to recognise any of the girls. A pixie with a pageboy cut and a padded bra saunters over.

'You want to ask me something?'

'Yeah, what was on *Sesame Street* this morning?'

Her face flushes. 'Piss off!'

'I'm looking for a particular girl. Her name is Theresa. She's about five foot six. Blonde. Comes from Harrogate. And she has a tattoo on her shoulder, of a butterfly.'

'What's this girl got that I ain't?'

'Boobs. Cut the crap. Have you seen her?'

'Nah.'

'OK, here's the deal. I got a fifty here. You walk down the street, knock on the doors and ask if any of the girls know this Theresa. You get me the right answer and you get the fifty.'

'Are you a copper?'

'No.' For once I'm telling the truth.

'Why you want her?'

'She won the bloody lottery. What does it matter to you?'

'I'll do it for a ton.'

'You get fifty. It's the easiest money you ever made.'

'You reckon! Some of these guys blow just looking at me.'

'Sure.'

I watch her leave. She doesn't even know how to walk like a woman yet. Maybe it's an occupational trait.

The streetlights are beginning to glow and blink. I take a table at a delicatessen on the corner which is doing a roaring trade in takeaway coffee and homemade soup served by Czech girls with heavy accents and tight tops. I'm old enough to be their grandfather but that doesn't make me feel as guilty as it should. One of them brings me coffee and a muffin that looks half-cooked inside.

The place is full of pimps and working girls, counting the wages of sin. A couple of them regard me suspiciously, sitting still and very straight like a pair of magistrates.

Pimps don't look the same in real life as they do in films. They're not snappy dressers in long leather coats and lots of gold jewellery. Mostly they're dealers and boyfriends who'd spread their own legs if anyone would pay for the privilege.

The pixie with the pageboy cut has come back. She eyes the large pot of soup steaming on a burner. I buy her a bowl. An older black girl is looking at us nervously through the window. She's dressed in a microskirt and lace-up boots. Her hair is twisted into bangs that run back from her forehead between paler strips of scalp.

'She says she knows Theresa.'

'What's her name?'

'Brittany.'

'Why won't she come inside?'

'Her pimp might be watching. He don't like her slacking. Where's my fifty?'

She reaches to snatch it out of my fingers. I pin her wrist to the table and turn it over, pulling her sleeve up her arm. Her skin is pale and unblemished.

'I'm not using,' she sniffles.

'Good. Go home.'

'Yeah, sure – you should see where I live.'

Brittany talks to me outside. She has ants in her pants about something and can't stand still. Her jaw works constantly on gum, punctuating sentences with a sucking noise.

'What's Theresa done?'

'Nothing, I just want to talk to her.'

Brittany glances down the street, trying to decide if she believes me. Eventually, she surrenders to apathy and a twenty quid note.

'She lives in a tower block in Finsbury Park. She's got a kid now.'

'Is she still on the game?'

'Only a few regulars.'

Fifteen minutes later I'm climbing to the fourteenth floor of a tower block because the lift is out of order. Various cooking smells mingle in the stairwell, along with the noise from duelling TVs and domestic disputes.

Theresa must be expecting someone else because she opens the door with a flourish, wearing only a black teddy and bunny ears.

'Shit! Who are you?'

'The Big Bad Wolf.'

She looks past me into the hallway and then back at me. The penny drops. 'Oh, no!'

Turning away from the door she wraps a dressing gown around her shoulders and I follow her inside. There are toys scattered on the living-room floor and a baby monitor hums on top of the TV. The bedroom door is closed.

'You remember me?'

'Yeah.' She flicks her hair over her shoulder and lights a cigarette.

'I'm looking for Gerry.'

'You were looking for him three years ago.'

'I'm very patient.'

She glances at a pineapple-shaped clock on the wall. 'Hey, I got someone coming. He's my best customer. If he finds you here he'll never come back.'

'Married is he?'

'The best customers are.'

I push aside a baby gym and take a seat on the sofa bed. 'About Gerry.'

'I ain't seen him.'

'Maybe he's hiding in the bedroom.'

'Please don't wake the baby.'

She's quite a pretty looking thing, except for her crooked nose and the junkie hollows beneath her eyes.

'Gerry ran out on me three years ago. I thought he was probably dead until he turned up again during the summer with a suntan and lots of big-shot stories about owning a bar in Thailand.'

'A bar?'

'Yeah. He had a passport and a driving licence in the name of some other geezer. He must have pinched it.'

'You remember the name?'

'Peter Brannigan.'

'Why did he come back?'

'Dunno. He said he had a big payday coming.'

'When did you last see him?'

'Three days ago – it was late Monday night.' She stubs out her cigarette and lights another. 'He came busting in here, sweating and yelling. He was scared. I ain't never seen anybody that scared. He looked like the devil himself was chasing him.'

That must have been after he crippled Ali. I remember how terrified he looked when he took off. He thought Aleksei had sent us to kill him.

Theresa dabs at the lipstick in the corners of her mouth. 'He wanted money. Said he had to get out of the country. He was crazy, I tell you. I let him stay but as soon as he fell asleep I got a knife. I put it right under here.' She points to her septum, pushing up her nostrils. 'I told him to get out. If he comes back I'll kill him.'

'And that was Tuesday morning.'

'Yeah.'

'Do you know where he went?'

'Nope. And I don't care. He's a bloody nutcase.'

The packet of cigarettes is crushed in her hand. Glossy eyes slide over the sofa and the toys before resting on me. 'I got something good going here. I don't need Grub or Peter Brannigan, or whoever else he calls himself, to mess it up.'

Three hours ago it was midnight. The desk lamp in Joe's office casts a circular glow, harsh in the centre and soft at the edges. My eyes are so full of grit I can only look at the shadows.

I bought pizzas at nine and the coffee ran out at eleven. The rest of the volunteers have gone home except for Joe and Rachel, who are still hard at work. A large corkboard in the waiting room is plastered with phone messages and notes. Nearby there are box files stacked five abreast beneath the window forming a makeshift shelf for leftover pizza and bottles of water.

Rachel is still on the phone.

'Hello, is that St Catherine's? I'm sorry to call so late. I'm looking for a friend of mine who has gone missing. Her name is Kirsten Fitzroy. She's thirty-two, with brown hair, green eyes and a birthmark on her neck.'

Rachel waits. 'OK, she's not there now but she may have needed medical help in the past few weeks. You have a clinic. Is it possible you could check your files? Yes, I know it's late but it's very important.' She refuses to lose this battle. 'She's actually my sister. My parents are worried sick about her. We think she might have hurt herself . . .'

Again she waits. 'No record. OK. Thank you so much. I'm sorry to have troubled you.'

They have all worked so hard. Roger and Dicko took a magical mystery tour of London's underbelly, visiting pubs, illegal casinos and strip joints looking for Gerry. Meanwhile, Margaret proved to be a genius at getting passenger manifests out of airlines, ferry and train operators. So far we've established that Kirsten hasn't left the country on any regular transport service.

London's major hospitals and twenty-four-hour clinics have no record of a female victim of a shooting in the week after the ransom drop. Now we're ringing individual doctors and hospices.

We know more about Kirsten than we did six hours ago. She was born in Exeter in 1972, the daughter of a postman and a teaching assistant. Her two brothers still live in Devon. In 1984 she won a scholarship to Sherborne School for Girls in Dorset. She excelled in art and history. One of her sculptures was exhibited in the Summer Exhibition at the Royal Academy in London. In her final year she left school under a cloud, along with two other pupils. Drugs were mentioned but nothing went on her file.

A year later Kirsten sat A levels and won a place to read art and history at Bristol University. After several false starts she graduated with a first in 1995. That same year she was photographed at a polo match in Windsor by *Tatler* with the son of a Saudi minister. Then she seemed to disappear, surfacing again six years later as the manager of the employment agency.

'I spoke to a few people at Sotheby's,' says Rachel. 'Kirsten was well known among the dealers and salesroom staff. She always wore black to auctions and talked constantly on a mobile.'

'She was bidding for someone else?'

'Four months ago she bid £170,000 for a Turner watercolour.'

'Who was the *real* buyer?'

'Sotheby's wouldn't say, but they faxed me a photograph of the painting. I've seen it hanging in my father's study.'

Her eyes, unnaturally wide, flick back and forth between Joe and me. Her thoughts are moving at a terrible speed – making her whole body vibrate.

'I still can't believe she could have done this. She loved Mickey.'

'What are you going to do?'

'Ask my father?'

'Will he tell you the truth?'

'There's always a first time.'

Joe's arm twitches as he reaches for a bottle of water. 'We're a long way behind. Kirsten's family and friends have been contacted. Some have been threatened. One of Kirsten's brothers was beaten senseless only an hour after he slammed the door on a man claiming to be a debt collector.'

'Do you think her family know where she is?'

'No.'

Rachel nods. 'Kirsten wouldn't put them in danger.'

Why is Aleksei going to so much trouble? If he sat back he knows that Kirsten will turn up eventually. They always do; look at Gerry Brandt. This isn't just about the diamonds. It's more personal that that. According to the stories, Aleksei had his own brother killed for dishonouring the family. What would he do to someone who kidnapped his daughter?

Joe is sitting opposite me, making notes. He reminds me of my first primary school teacher, who knew exactly how many pencils, books and paintbrushes were in the storeroom, yet would arrive at school with shaving foam on his neck; or wearing different-coloured socks.

Julianne called me. She made me promise not to let him drive home. His Parkinson's gets worse when he's tired. She also talked to Joe and told him to look after me.

Rachel begins picking up cups and carrying them into the kitchenette. There isn't much to wash. Jean has been manically cleaning all afternoon.

Reaching into his pocket, Joe takes out a crumpled page of notes and smooths it on his thigh. 'I've been thinking.'

'Good.'

'I want to forget about the kidnapping question and concentrate on the ransom demand. If you look at the letters there's no indication of psychological looseness or obsession. They asked for a huge ransom but it was a feasible amount for someone like Aleksei to pay or even Sir Douglas. Enough to be worth the risk.'

'We know there were at least three people involved. Kirsten was the likely planner. Ray Murphy did the logistics. Intellectually Kirsten is above average. Everything about her typifies carefulness and preplanning. She must have experimented with the packages, getting the right dimensions. She was aware of tracking devices and forensic tests . . .'

The Professor is on a roll. I've seen him do this before — crawl inside someone's head until he knows what they know and feels what they feel. 'The ransom plot was clever but over-complicated. When people are faced with a complex problem they often only consider a certain number of options or scenarios. If there are too many unknowns, they get confused. That's why people plan up to a point or in sections. Sometimes they leave out the exit strategies because they don't consider failure as a possibility.

'Whoever conceived the plan worked everything out but they made it too complicated. Look at all the things that had to go right. The packaging of the ransom had to be perfect, the control of the courier, getting the diamonds to the storm-water drain, detonating the explosives, creating the flood . . . If any one of these things had gone wrong, the plan would have failed.'

'Maybe they tested the system first. The voice on the phone to Rachel said, "Let's do this one more time".'

Joe isn't convinced. 'This is the sort of operation you only mess up once. Given a second chance, you'd want to simplify things.'

He begins pacing, flourishing his hands. 'Let's assume just for a moment that they did kidnap her. They took her underground, which is also how they chose to collect the ransom. They needed somewhere to hold her. Somewhere that Ray

Murphy was most likely to have chosen.'

'Not in the sewers – it's too dangerous.'

'And taking her above ground meant risking recognition. Her photograph was everywhere.'

'You think they held her underground?'

'It's worth considering.'

There's someone I can ask – Weatherman Pete. I look at my watch. I'll call him in a few hours.

'What about Gerry Brandt?' asks Joe.

'He had a passport in the name of Peter Brannigan as well as a driver's licence. It costs a lot of money to get a new identity and to disappear – even to a place like Thailand. You need connections.'

'You thinking drugs?'

'Maybe. According to international directory inquiries there's a beach bar called Brannigan's in Phuket.'

'Fancy that. What's the time in Thailand?'

'Time to wake them up.'

Rachel has fallen asleep on the sofa in the waiting room. I gently shake her awake. 'Come on, I'll take you home.'

'But what about Mickey?'

'Get some sleep. We'll find her in the morning.'

Joe is still on the phone to Phuket talking to a waitress who doesn't understand English. He's trying to get a description of Peter Brannigan to confirm that he and Gerry Brandt are the same person.

Outside the streets are empty except for a council sweeping machine with twirling brushes and jets of water. I open the car door and she slips inside. The interior smells of pine air freshener and ancient tobacco.

Rachel has borrowed an overcoat and lays it like a blanket over her knees. I know she has questions. She wants reassurance. Maybe we're both deluding ourselves.

Headlights sweep across the interior of the car as we drive

towards Maida Vale. She rests her head against the seat, watching me.

'Do you have children, Inspector?'

'I'm not a policeman any more. Please call me Vincent.'

She waits for an answer.

'Twins. They're grown up now.'

'Do you see much of them?'

'No.'

'Why?'

'It's a long story.'

'How long can it be? They're your children.'

I'm caught now. No matter what I say to her she won't understand. She desperately wants to find her child and I don't even talk to mine. Where's the fairness in that?

She tucks her hair behind her ears. 'Do you know that sometimes I think I made Mickey frightened of the world.'

'Why do you say that?'

'I kept telling her to be careful.'

'All parents do that.'

'Yes, but it wasn't just the normal stuff like not patting stray dogs or talking to strangers. I made her frightened of what can happen if you love something too much and it disappoints you or gets taken away. She wasn't always scared to go outside. It only started when she was about four.'

'What happened?'

In a forlorn voice, tinged with regret, she describes a Saturday afternoon at a local park, where she and Mickey would often go to feed the ducks. This one particular Saturday there was an old fashioned fair, with a steam-powered carousel, candyfloss and whirligigs on sticks. Mickey rode all by herself on a gaily painted horse, proud of the fact that she didn't need her mother to sit behind her. When the ride finished, she was on the far side of the carousel. Rachel had been drawn into conversation with a woman from her mothers' group and didn't notice the ride ending.

Mickey stepped off. Instead of circling, she wandered through the forest of legs thinking that surely one of the hands belonged to her mother.

She walked back towards the pond where the ducks had gathered in the skirts of a willow tree. Peering over the low railing fence she watched two boys, no older than eleven, throwing stones. The ducks huddled together. Mickey wondered why they didn't fly away. Then she noticed the ducklings, sheltering beneath a feathered breast and muddy tail feathers.

One duckling – a dark ball of down against the darkness of the shade – separated from the others. It took the full force of a stone and disappeared beneath the surface. Seconds later it reappeared, floating lifelessly on the green scum in that corner of the pond.

Mickey burst into hysterical wailing. Tears streamed down her cheeks into the wide corners of her mouth. Her crying made the boys drop their stones and edge away, not wanting to be blamed for whatever had made her cry.

The howls from the edge of the pond created a strange dichotomy of reactions. Some people almost fell over each other to ignore them. Others watched and waited for someone else to intervene.

The pigeon man was nearest. Grizzled and yellow-toothed, he raised himself up from his bench, brushing pigeons off his lap as though they were spilt crumbs. Shuffling across to Mickey, he hitched up his trousers so that he could kneel beside her.

'You got a problem, missy?'

'Make them stop,' she wailed, with her hands clamped over her ears.

He didn't seem to hear her. 'You want to feed the birds?'

'The ducks,' she sobbed.

'You want to feed the ducks?'

Mickey howled again and the pigeon man raised his

eyebrows. He could never understand children. Taking her hand, he went in search of a park attendant or the girl's mother.

A policeman was already approaching. He pushed through the crowd and took in the scene. 'I want you to let her go,' he demanded.

'I'm looking for her mother,' explained the pigeon man. Spittle clung to his tangled beard.

'Just let the girl go and step away.'

By then Rachel had arrived. She swept Mickey up, held her tightly and the two of them tried to outhug each other. Meanwhile, the pigeon man had his arms stretched wide on the back of a park bench, while the policeman patted him down and searched his pockets, spilling birdseed on to the grass.

Mickey didn't ask to feed the ducks again. She didn't go to the park and soon she stopped going outside Dolphin Mansions. A year later she saw her first therapist.

The children's book that Timothy found in Mickey's cubbyhole in the basement was about five little ducks who go out in the world and return home again. Mickey knew from experience that not all little ducks come back.

32

Weatherman Pete brushes milk foam from his moustache and motions towards the river with his paper cup. 'Sewers are no place for little girls.'

His van is parked up on a slipway in the shadow of Putney Bridge where eight-oared shells skim the surface of the river like gigantic water beetles. Moley is asleep in the back of the van, curled up like a dog with one eye open.

'Where could they have kept her?'

Pete exhales slowly, making his lips vibrate. 'There are hundreds of places – disused tube stations, service tunnels, air raid shelters, aqueducts, drains . . . What makes you think he's hiding down there?'

'He's scared. People are looking for him.'

Pete hums. 'Takes a unique sort of individual to live down there.'

'He *is* unique.'

'No, you don't get me. You take Moley. If he disappeared down there you wouldn't find him in a hundred years. You see, he likes the dark, just like some people prefer the cold. You know what I mean?'

'This guy isn't like that.'

'So how does he know his way down there?'

'He's going from memory. Someone showed him where to hide and how to move around. A former flusher called Ray Murphy.'

'Saccharine Ray! The boxer.'

'You know him?'

'Yeah, I know him. Ray was never really the genuine article as a boxer. He took more dives than Ruud van Nistelrooy. I don't remember him working down the sewers.'

'It was a long time ago. After that he worked as a flood planner.'

A slow sweet smile spreads across Pete's face like jam on toast. 'The old HQ of London Flood Management is underground – in the Kingsway Tram Underpass.'

'But there haven't been trams in central London for more than fifty years.'

'Precisely. The tunnel was abandoned. If you ask me it was a bloody silly place to have a flood emergency centre. It would have been the first place underwater if the Thames broke its banks. Stupid!'

The Underpass is one of those strange, almost secret landmarks you find in cities. Tens of thousands of people walk past it and drive over it every day with no idea it's there. All you can see is a railing fence and a cobblestone approach road before it disappears underground. It runs beneath Kingsway – one of the busiest streets in the West End – down to the Aldwych, where it turns right and comes out directly beneath Waterloo Bridge.

Weatherman Pete parks his van on the approach road, ignoring the red painted lines and 'no waiting' signs. He hands me a hard hat and pulls out a construction sign. 'If anyone asks, we work for the council.'

The remnants of the tram tracks are embedded in the stones and a large gate guards the entrance to the tunnel.

'Can we get inside?'

'That'd be illegal,' he says, producing the biggest set of bolt cutters I've ever seen. Moley moans and pulls a blanket over his head.

Trying to curb Pete's enthusiasm I explain that Gerry Brandt is dangerous. He's already put Ali in hospital and I don't want anyone else getting hurt. Once we know he's in there, I'll call the police.

'We could send a mole down the hole.' Pete nudges the bundle of blankets. Moley's head appears. 'You're up.'

Trooping down the ramp we look like a trio of engineers on our way to survey something on a typical Friday morning. The padlock on the gate looks secure enough but the bolt cutters snap it like balsawood. We slide inside.

Although I can see only about twenty feet of tunnel it appears to open out and grow wider before the darkness becomes absolute. The most obvious feature is a pile of road signs stacked against the walls – street names, traffic controls, bollards and paving slabs. The council must use the tunnel for storage.

'We should wait here,' whispers Pete. 'No use us blundering around in the dark.' He hands Moley what looks like an emergency flare. 'Just in case.'

Moley presses his ear to the wall of the tunnel and listens for about fifteen seconds. Then he jogs forward silently and listens again. Within seconds he is out of sight. The only sounds are my heartbeat and the throb of traffic forty feet above our heads.

Fifteen minutes later Moley returns.

'There's someone there. About a hundred yards further on there are two Portakabins. He's in the first one. I can smell an oil lamp.'

'What's he doing?'

'Sleeping.'

I know I have to call it in. I can talk directly to 'New Boy'

Dave and hopefully bypass Meldrum and Campbell. Dave hates Gerry Brandt as much as I do. We look after our own.

But another part of me has a different desire. I can't rid myself of the memory of Gerry Brandt holding Ali against his back, looking directly at me, as he fell backwards, crushing her spine. This is just the sort of place I wanted to find him – a dark place, with nobody around.

The police will come charging in here, armed to the teeth. That's when people get hurt or get killed. I'm not talking conspiracies here, I just know the reality – people fuck up. I can't afford to lose Gerry Brandt. He's a violent impulsive thug who peddles misery in tiny packets of foil but I need him for Ali's sake and for Mickey. He knows what happened to her.

'So what do you want to do?' whispers Pete.

'I'm going to call the police but I also want to talk to this guy. I don't want him getting away or getting hurt.'

The light from the entrance forms a halo around Moley's head. He cocks his face to one side and looks at me with a mixture of apprehension and expectancy. 'He did a bad thing, this guy?'

'Yes, he did.'

'You want me to take you in there?'

'Yes.'

Pete gives it five seconds of contemplation and nods his head. It's like he does this every day of the week. Back at the van I call 'New Boy' Dave. Glancing at my watch, I realise that Ali will be in surgery by now. I don't know the exact details but they're going to insert pins into her spine and fuse several vertebrae.

Weatherman Pete has collected some gear from the van – extra flares and his 'secret weapon'. He shows me two ping-pong balls. 'I make these myself. Black powder, flash powder, magnesium ribbon and a drop of candle wax.'

'What do they do?'

'Kerboom!' He grins at me. 'Nothing but sound and fury. You should hear one of them go off in a sewer.'

The plan is simple enough. Moley is going to make sure there are no other exits. Once he's in place, he'll set off the flash bangs and flares.

'We're going to scare the son of a bitch half to death,' he says excitedly.

Pete looks at me. 'You got sunglasses – wear them. And don't look at the light. You only have a few seconds to grab him while he's disorientated.'

We give Moley ten minutes' head start. Weatherman Pete and I keep on opposite sides of the tunnel, feeling our way blindly along the walls and stepping in oily puddles and nests of leaves.

Slowly the tunnel begins to change in character. The roof slopes down where the roadway above has been cut into the old ceiling. The Portakabins are just ahead of me. I can see the faint yellow glow of the lantern, leaking around the edges of a window that has been covered up or taped over.

Crouching, I wait for Moley. He could be right next to me and I wouldn't know it. My mouth is dry. For two days I've been popping codeine forte and craving morphine, telling myself my leg doesn't hurt and it's just my imagination.

What happens next wouldn't find a place in many training manuals. The explosion of noise is so sudden and ferocious it feels like I've been shot from a cannon. Darkness turns to light, as a flare of brilliant white arcs overhead and lands nearby.

Squinting into the dazzling ivory, my eyes sting. I see nothing but white. Turning my face away, I begin to move, crossing the last ten feet to the door of the first Portakabin. The second flash bang explodes and a shape comes bursting out of the entrance, with legs pumping in midair as though trying to gain traction. Blinded by the light, he runs smack bang into the far wall and almost knocks himself unconscious.

I grab him from behind, locking my arms around his waist.

He pitches to the left, arms flailing. Both of us crash into a puddle. I don't let go. Pulling his arm behind his back, I try to put on the cuffs. He snaps his head back but I'm ready.

He's fighting blindly. I'm still behind him, straddling his torso and twisting his arm until he roars. He arches his spine, trying to reach me, and I wrap my forearm around his throat, cutting off his windpipe. With my arm still across his throat, I add more weight, pushing his face into the floor. He can't breathe. His legs are twitching as if he's made of rubber.

I could kill him now, so easily. I could either hold on until he suffocates or snap his neck. So what if he dies? It's no great loss to humanity. There won't be any grand achievements left unfulfilled or prizes unclaimed. The only mark Gerry Brandt was ever likely to leave on the world was a bloodstain.

My forearm loosens and I let his head drop. It makes a dull noise against the concrete. He's gasping for breath.

Dragging his other arm behind his back, I snap on the handcuffs and roll away. Stumbling to my feet I look down at him for a moment. Dark hair spikes from his head and pieces of crushed glass are stuck to his cheekbone. A thin line of blood trickles past his ear as the burning flares begin to die out.

There are police sirens in the distance. 'Come on, let's get him out of here.'

'Are we going to get in trouble?' asks Moley, falling into step beside Weatherman Pete.

'You'll be fine. Get to the van and let me do the talking.'

We're almost at the end of the tunnel. The gate gives off a hollow clang as it opens. Two armed response vehicles have pulled on to the ramp beside the van. The officers are armed with MP5 carbines. An unmarked police car pulls up along-side them. 'New Boy' Dave gets out, along with Campbell who walks like he's got bowling balls down his Y-fronts.

'Arrest him,' he yells, pointing at me. Gerry Brandt raises his head. 'I didn't mean to do it. I let her go.'

'Where is she?'

He shakes his head. 'I let her go.'

'What did you do with Mickey?'

'You got to tell Mr Kuznet, I let her go.'

A red dot appears on his cheek, just above where he's bleeding. For a moment it catches in his eye, making him blink, and then rises to his forehead. Recognition jars inside me but it's too late. In a fleeting puff of blood and vapour, he spins and falls.

The bullet, fired from somewhere above, has passed through his cheek, down his neck and exited below his collarbone. I can't hold him. He's six one and over sixteen stone. He carries me down. I roll away, letting gravity take over, bouncing my head against the cobblestones until I strike the wall.

The ramp is empty. People have scattered like cockroaches. Only Gerry Brandt is unmoved by it all, lying with his jacket half-covering his head, slowly soaking up the blood.

There are no more shots. One was enough.

33

According to the experts the world is going to end in five thousand million years, when the sun swells up and engulfs the innermost planets and turns the rest of them into charcoal. I've always imagined it more like a dual second coming, where Jesus and Charlton Heston compete to see who gets the final word. I don't suppose I'll be around.

This is what I think about as I sit in the back seat of a police car, watching them photograph Gerry Brandt's body. Teams of armed officers are going door to door, searching shops, offices and flats. They won't find anything. The sniper is long gone.

Campbell has also slipped away, escaping from me. I followed him all the way to his car, yelling: 'Who did you tell? Who knew?'

The moment I phoned for backup, somebody put in a separate call, tipping off Aleksei. How else did the sniper know where to find Brandt? It's the only logical explanation.

A dozen police officers walk in single file down the ramp, peering between their polished boots at the cobblestones and sodden leaves. A handful of Camden Council workers watch proceedings as though they're going to be tested on it later.

This whole business reeks of a setup. The guilty are gunned down and innocent people get caught in the crossfire. Howard might be one of them. I still can't work out where he fits into all this, but I can picture him, lying on his prison bunk, planning his first days of freedom.

Child molesters sleep the sleep of the damned in prison. They listen to their names being whispered from cell to cell, turning to a chant as the noise rises and becomes a frightening symphony that must open and close their sphincters like the wings of a butterfly.

The SOCO team, dressed in white overalls, has set up arc lights on mobile gantries, casting grotesque shadows against the walls. Noonan is in charge, shouting into a tape recorder: 'I'm looking at a well-developed, well-nourished white male. A light-purple contusion is visible on the left forehead and another over the bridge of the nose. He may have fallen after the shooting or someone hit him in the face prior to the shooting . . .'

'New Boy' Dave brings me a coffee. It tastes like tar and brings back memories of surveillance operations and endless predawn shifts.

Noonan rolls the body over and checks the pockets and lining. His hand emerges with a small foil packet wedged between his fingertips.

Dave screws up his face, 'Well, I'm glad he's dead.'

I guess that's understandable given what happened to Ali. He doesn't understand why I needed Gerry alive. Dave loosens his tie and undoes the top button of his shirt.

'They say you're trying to destroy the Howard Wavell conviction.'

'No.'

'They also say you stole diamonds from Aleksei Kuznet. They say you're bent.'

'What do you think?'

'Ali doesn't think so.'

A double-decker bus rumbles by, glowing red and yellow.

Bored faces peer out from the bright interior, heads resting against the glass. London doesn't seem so exciting from this angle. The landmarks are rendered featureless by the gloom and there is no magic in the Monopoly board names.

I am under arrest. Campbell insisted on it. At least Dave hasn't bothered with handcuffs so my past must count for something. I could even handle the police officers staring at me, if one of them was Ali and she'd never been involved in this.

After SOCO has finished at the crime scene, I'm driven to the Harrow Road Police Station and taken through a back door into the charge room. I know the drill. Strands of hair are sealed in plastic. Saliva and skin cells dampen a cotton swab. My fingers are pressed in ink. Afterwards I am taken to an interview room rather than a police cell.

They make me wait. I lean forward, with my elbows braced on my knees, counting the pop rivets on the side of the table. This is all part of any interrogation. Silence can be more important than the questions.

When Keebal finally arrives, he carries a large bundle of files and proceeds to shuffle through the papers. Most of them probably have nothing to do with me but he wants me to think evidence is stacking up against me. Everybody is having fun today.

Keebal likes to pretend he's a patient man but it's bullshit. Maybe it's the Rom blood in me but I can sit opposite someone all day and not say a thing. Gypsies are like Sicilians. We can share a drink and be smiling our heads off while out of sight a knife or a shotgun is pointed directly at the other guy's stomach.

Finally he turns on the tape recorder, giving the time, date and names of everybody present.

He pats at his coiffed hair. 'I hear you got your memory back.'

'Can we do this later? You obviously have an appointment at a beauty salon.'

He stops touching himself and glares at me.

'At approximately 1600 hours on 24 September, you were given a briefcase containing 965 one-carat and above superior quality diamonds. Is that correct?'

'Yes.'

'When did you last see these diamonds?'

I feel my stomach lurch as if an internal gear has suddenly engaged. I can still picture the packages spilling from the sports bag beneath my linen cupboard. A dry thunder is pounding in my head – the beginnings of a migraine. 'I don't know.'

'Did you give them to someone?'

'No.'

'What were these diamonds for?'

'You know the answer to that question.'

'For the benefit of the tape, please answer the question.'

'A ransom.'

He stares blankly at me, not batting an eyelid. I'm doing just what he wants – digging myself deeper into a hole. Taking a deep breath I begin going through the story. I have nothing left to lose, but at least I'm getting it down. There'll be a record somewhere if something happens to me.

'Someone sent a ransom demand for Mickey Carlyle. They provided strands of her hair, a bikini like the one she wore and information that only someone very close to the family could possibly have known.'

'A ransom for a girl who died three years ago.'

'I don't believe she's dead.'

He makes a note. This is a game. I'm playing black. For the next ninety minutes I relate the details. Hundreds of cumulative hours are condensed and laid out like stepping stones for him to follow. Even so, it sounds more like a confessional than an interrogation.

Keebal looks like he should be selling used cars or life insurance. 'You admit you were present on the boat when Ray Murphy died?'

330

'Yes.'

'And you say the diamonds were in packages on the deck?'

'Yes.'

'Was there a tracking device with the diamonds?'

'Yes.'

'When you went overboard did you take the diamonds?'

'No.'

'Where are they now?'

'What makes you think I know?'

'So they could be tucked under your mattress at home?'

'Could be.'

He studies my face, looking for the lie. It's there. He just can't see it.

'Let me help you out,' he says. 'Next time you try to steal a ransom, remember to take the tracking device out. Otherwise someone might follow you and realise what you're doing.'

'How is Aleksei? How much is he paying you to recover his diamonds?'

Keebal tightens his lips and sighs through his nose like I've disappointed him.

'Tell me this,' I ask him. 'A sniper put a bullet in my leg and I nearly bled to death. Eight days I lay in a coma. You think I took the diamonds. How? When?'

A sense of triumph is stencilled on his face. 'I'll tell you how – they never left your house. You helped set this whole thing up – the ransom letters, the DNA tests . . . you fooled everyone. And the people who know the truth keep dying when you're around. First it was Ray Murphy and then Gerry Brandt . . .'

Keebal can't really believe any of this. It's crazy. I always had him pegged as a fanatic but the man has squirrels juggling knives in his head.

'I got shot.'

'Maybe because you tried to double-cross them.'

I'm shouting at him now. 'You called Aleksei. You told him

where he could find Gerry Brandt. All these years you've been persecuting honest cops and now we see your true colours – yellow right through.'

In the silence I can hear my clothes creasing. Keebal thinks he knows. He knows nothing.

The Professor collects me just after five.

'How are you?'

'I still have my health.'

'That's good.'

I savour the sound of my shoes on the tarmac, pleased to be free. Keebal didn't have enough to hold me and there isn't a magistrate in the land who would deny me bail with my record of service.

Joe's office is still full of our ragtag task force, manning telephones and tapping at keyboards. They're searching electoral rolls and reverse phone directories. Someone has pinned a photograph of Mickey by the window – to remind everyone of why we're here.

The familiar faces acknowledge me – Roger, Margaret, Jean, Eric and Rebecca – along with a few new ones, two of Ali's brothers.

'How long have they been here?'

'Since lunchtime,' says Joe.

Ali must have called them. She must be out of surgery. I wonder if she's heard the news about Gerry Brandt.

Rachel spies me from across the room. She looks at me hopefully, her hands fidgeting with her collar.

'Did you talk to him? I mean . . . did he say anything?'

'He said he let Mickey go.'

A breath snags in her throat. 'What happened to her?'

'I don't know. He didn't get to tell me.' I turn to the others and let them all hear. 'It's now even more imperative that we find Kirsten Fitzroy. She may be the only one left who knows what happened to Mickey.'

Gathering the chairs in a circle, we hold a 'kitchen cabinet' meeting.

Margaret and Jean have managed to find a dozen of Kirsten's ex-employees. All are women aged between twenty-two and thirty-four, many of them with foreign-sounding names. They were nervous about talking – sex work isn't something you advertise. None of them has seen Kirsten since the agency closed down.

Meanwhile, Roger visited the old offices. The managing agent had kept two boxes of files that had been left behind when the agency vacated the premises. Among the documents were invoices from a pathology lab. The girls were being tested for STDs.

Another file contained encoded credit card details and initials. Kirsten probably had a diary with names matching the initials. I run my finger down the page searching for Sir Douglas's initials. Nothing.

'So far we've called over four hundred clinics and surgeries,' says Rachel. 'Nobody has reported treating a gunshot victim but a pharmacy in Southwark had a break-in on 25 September. Someone stole bandages and painkillers.'

'Call the pharmacist back. Ask him if the police pulled any fingerprints.'

Margaret hands me a coffee. Jean takes it away and washes the cup before I can take a sip. Someone gets sandwiches and soft drinks. I feel like something a lot stronger, something warm and yeasty and golden.

Joe finds me sitting alone on the stairs and takes a seat beside me. 'You haven't mentioned the diamonds. What did you do with them?'

'Put them somewhere safe.'

I can picture the velvet pouches stitched inside a woolly mammoth in Ali's old room. I should probably tell Joe. If something happens to me, nobody will know where to find them. Then again, I don't want to put anyone else in danger.

'Did you know that elephants with their trunks raised are meant to symbolise good luck?'

'No.'

'Ali told me. She's got a thing about elephants. I don't know how much good luck it's brought her.'

My mouth has gone dry. I stand and slip my arms through my jacket sleeves.

'You're going to see Aleksei, aren't you?' asks Joe. I swear to God he can read minds.

My silence responds eloquently.

'You know that's crazy,' he says.

'I have to stop this.'

I know it sounds foolishly old-fashioned but I'm stuck with this idea that there is something dignified and noble about facing your enemy and looking him squarely in the eye – before you thrust a sabre in his heart.

'You can't go alone.'

'He won't see me otherwise. I'll make an appointment. People don't get killed when they make an appointment.'

Joe considers this. 'I'll come with you.'

'No, but thanks for the offer.'

I don't know why people keep offering to help me like this. They should be running a mile. Ali says I inspire loyalty but I seem to be taking kindnesses that I can never hope to repay. I am not a perfect human being. I'm a cynic and a pessimist and sometimes I feel as though I'm locked into this life by an accident of birth. But at times like this, a random act of kindness or the touch of another human being makes me believe I can be different, better, redeemed. Joe has that effect on me. A poor man shouldn't borrow so much.

The phone call to Aleksei is diverted through several numbers before he answers. I can hear water in the background. The river.

'I want to talk. No lawyers or police or third parties.'

I can hear him thinking. 'Where did you have in mind?'

'Neutral ground.'

'No. If you want a meeting you come to me. Chelsea Harbour. You'll find me.'

A black cab drops me at the entrance to the marina shortly before ten. I lift my watch and count the final minutes. It's no use being early for your own funeral.

Spotlights reflect from the whiteness of the motor yachts and cruisers, creating pools like spilt paint. By comparison, the interlocking docks are weathered and grey, with life buoys hanging from piles driven deep in the mud.

Aleksei's boat, draped in fairy lights, takes up two moorings and has three decks with sleek lines that angle like an arrowhead from bow to stern. The upper deck bristles with radio antennae and satellite tracking devices.

I spent five years mucking about on boats. I know they float and soak up money. People with a highly defined sense of balance are more likely to get seasick, they say. I can vouch for my equilibrium but an hour in rough weather on a cross-Channel ferry can still feel like a year.

The gangway has a thick rubber mat and railings with brass pillars. As I step on board the vessel shifts slightly. Through an open doorway I see a stateroom and a large mahogany dining table with seating for eight. To one side is a bar area and several sofas arranged in front of a flat-screen TV.

Descending the steps I duck my head, which isn't necessary. Aleksei Kuznet is sitting behind a desk, his head lowered, reading the screen of a laptop computer. He raises his hand, making me wait. It remains there, suspended. Slowly the hand turns and his fingers wave me forwards.

When he raises his eyes he looks past me as though I might have forgotten something. The ransom. He wants his diamonds.

'Nice boat.'

'It's a motor yacht.'

'An expensive toy.'

'On the contrary – it is my office. I had her built to an American design at a boatyard on the Black Sea near Odessa. You see, I take the best from different cultures – American design, German engineering, Italian craftsmen, Brazilian teak and Slav labourers. People often criticise Eastern European nations and say they don't do capitalism well. But the truth is that they operate the purest form of capitalism. If I had wanted to build this boat in Britain I would have had to pay standard wages, workers' compensation, national insurance, design fees and bribes to keep the unions happy. It's the same when you put up a building. At any stage someone can stop you. In Russia or Latvia or Georgia none of this matters if you have enough money. That's what I call *pure* capitalism.'

'Is that why you're selling up? Are you going home?'

He laughs mordantly. 'Inspector, you mistake me for a patriot. I will employ Russians, I will fund their schools and hospitals and prop up their corrupt politicians but do not expect me to live with them.'

He has moved across to the bar. My eyes flick around the stateroom, almost waiting for the trap to snap shut.

'So why *are* you selling up?'

'Greener pastures. Fresh challenges. Maybe I'll buy a football club. That seems very popular nowadays. Or I could just go somewhere warm for the winter.'

'I have never understood what people see in hot climates.'

He glances into the darkness of the starboard window. 'Each man makes his own paradise, DI, but it's hard to love London.'

He hands me a glass of Scotch and slides the ice bucket towards me.

'Are you a sailor?'

'Not really.'

'Shame. With me it's flying. You ever see that episode of *The Twilight Zone* where William Shatner looks out of the window of a plane at twenty thousand feet and sees a gremlin tearing off pieces of the wing? They made it into a movie, which was nowhere near as good. That's how I feel when I step on a plane. I'm the only person who *knows* it's going to crash.'

'So you never fly?'

He turns over both his palms, as if revealing the obvious. 'I have a motor yacht.'

The Scotch burns pleasantly as I swallow but the aftertaste is not like it used to be. All that morphine has deadened my tastebuds.

Aleksei is a businessman, accustomed to cutting deals. He knows how to read a balance sheet, to manage risk and maximise profit.

'I might have something to trade,' I announce.

He raises his hand again, this time pressing a finger to his lips. The Russian steps from the companionway looking as if he's been trapped in an ill-fitting suit.

'I'm sure you understand,' says Aleksei apologetically as the bodyguard sweeps a metal detector over me. Meanwhile, he issues instructions via a radio. The engines of the boat rumble and the ice shudders in my glass.

He motions me to follow him along the companionway to the galley where a narrow ladder descends to the lower deck. We reach a heavily insulated door that opens into the engine room. Noise fills my head.

The engine block is six feet high with valves, fuel cocks, radiator pipes, springs and polished steel. Two chairs have been arranged on the metal walkways that run down each side of the room. Aleksei takes a seat as if attending a recital and waits until I join him. Still nursing his drink, he looks at me with an aloof curiosity.

Shouting to be heard above the engines, I ask him how he found Gerry Brandt. He smiles. It is the same indolent fore-knowing expression he gave me when I saw him outside Wormwood Scrubs. 'I hope you're not accusing me of any wrongdoing, Inspector.'

'Then you know who I'm talking about?'

'No. Who is he?'

This is like a game to him – a trifling annoyance compared to other more important matters. I risk boring him unless I get to the point.

'Is Kirsten Fitzroy still alive?'

He doesn't answer.

'I'm not here to accuse you, Aleksei. I have a hypothetical deal to offer.'

'A hypothetical one?' Now he laughs out loud and I feel my resolve draining away.

'I will trade you the diamonds for Kirsten's life. Leave her alone and you get them back.'

Aleksei runs his finger though his hair, leaving a trail in the gel. 'You have my diamonds?'

'Hypothetically.'

'Then hypothetically you are obliged to give them back to me. Why should I have to trade?'

'Because right now this is only hypothetical; I can make it real. I know you planted the diamonds in my house to frame me. Keebal was supposed to get a warrant but I found them first. You think I saw something that night. You think I can hurt you somehow. You have my word. Nobody else has to get hurt.'

'Really?' he asks sarcastically. 'Do not attempt a career as a salesman.'

'It's a genuine offer.'

'A hypothetical one.' Aleksei looks at me, pursing his lips. 'Let me get this straight. My daughter is kidnapped and you fail to find her. She is murdered and you do not recover her body. Then people try to extort two million pounds from me and you fail to catch them. Then you steal my diamonds and accuse me of planting them on you. And on top of it all, you want me to forgive and forget. You people are scum. You have preyed on my ex-wife's grief. You have taken advantage of my good nature and my desire to make things right. I didn't start this . . .'

'You have a chance to end it.'

'You mistake me for someone who desires peace and harmony. On the contrary, what I desire is revenge.'

He moves to stand. The negotiation is over.

I feel my temper rising. 'For Christ's sake, Aleksei, I'm trying to find Mickey. She's your family. Don't you want to know what happened?'

'I know what happened, Inspector. She's dead. She died three years ago. And let me tell you something about families – they're overrated. They're a weakness. They leave you or get taken from you or they disappoint you. Families are a liability.'

'Is that why you got rid of Sacha?'

He ignores me, pushing open the heavy door. We're outside now. I can hear myself think. Aleksei is still talking.

'You say to trust you. You say trust the deal. You have no idea, do you? Not a clue. You're like the three wise monkeys all rolled into one. Now let me make a deal with you – hypothetically speaking, of course. You return the diamonds to me and then step back. Let people work things out for themselves. Market forces, you see, capitalism, supply and demand, these are the things I understand. People reap what they sow.'

'People like Gerry Brandt?' With a flick of my wrist, I grip his forearm. He doesn't flinch. 'Leave Kirsten alone.'

His eyes are narrow and dark, with something toxic behind them. He thinks I'm some dumb plod, barely off the beat, whose idea of subtle interrogation is a nightstick and a strong right arm. That's how I'm acting.

'You know what a Heffalump is?' I ask.

'Winnie-the-Pooh's friend.'

'No, you're thinking of Piglet. Heffalumps and Woozels are the nightmare creatures that Pooh Bear dreams about. He's afraid they're going to steal his honey. Nobody can see them except Pooh. That's who you remind me of . . .'

'A Heffalump?'

'No. Pooh Bear. You think the world is full of people who want to steal from you.'

The sky is grey and the evening air damp and heavy. Away from the throb of the engines my headache finds its own rhythm. Aleksei walks me to the gangway. The Russian is close behind him, swinging his left arm a little wider because of his holster.

'Have you ever thought of getting a normal job?' I ask.

Aleksei contemplates this. 'Maybe we should both do something new.'

Then it dawns on me that he's right – we're not so different. We both screwed up our relationships and lost our children. And we're too old to do anything else. I have spent two thirds of my life putting criminals away, most of them small-timers and low life. Aleksei was what I was working towards. My ambition. He's the reason I did the job.

As I step on to the gangway the Russian follows, two paces behind. The rope handrails are looped between brass posts. He closes the last step and I feel the warm metal of the gun brush the short hairs at the base of my skull.

Aleksei explains. 'My employee will go with you and collect the diamonds.'

In the same instant I fall over the side, plunging towards the water. Reaching up in midair, I grab on to the rope railing and hang on as my body swings through an arc, tipping the gangway on its side. The Russian plunges past me.

Swinging my good leg on to the dock, I climb to my feet. Aleksei is watching the Russian flailing his arms as he tries to stay afloat.

'I don't think he can swim,' I point out.

'Some people never learn,' says Aleksei, unconcerned.

I take a life buoy from its bracket and toss it into the water. The Russian hugs it to his chest.

'One last question: how did you know where the ransom was going to surface? Somebody must have told you.'

Aleksei pulls back his lips in a grimace but his eyes are empty. 'You have until tomorrow morning to return my diamonds.'

34

Ali is asleep. Tubes flow into her carrying painkillers and out of her carrying waste. Every few hours they add another bag of liquid morphine. Time is measured by the gaps between them.

'You really can't stay,' says the nursing sister. 'Come back in the morning and she'll be awake.'

The corridors of the hospital are almost deserted. I walk to the visitors' lounge and take a seat, closing my eyes. I wish I could have made Aleksei understand but his hatred has blinded him. He doesn't believe Mickey is still alive. Instead, he thinks people have taken advantage of him because of his weakness – his family.

I think of Luke and wonder if maybe he's right. Daj is still grieving about her lost family. I'm still fretting about Claire and Michael, wondering what went wrong. Not caring would be so much easier.

My muscles ache and my whole body seems to be fighting against itself. Dreamlike images fill my head: bodies lowered into rivers or washed down sewers. Kirsten's turn is coming.

Darkness presses against the window. I gaze at the street

below and feel nostalgic for the countryside. The rhythms of a city are set by pneumatic drills, traffic lights and train time-tables. I barely notice the seasons.

A reflection appears in the window beside me.

'I thought I might find you here,' says Joe, taking a seat and propping his legs on the low table. 'How did it go with Aleksei?'

'He wouldn't listen.'

Joe nods. 'You should get some sleep.'

'So should you.'

'You're long enough dead.'

'My stepfather used to say that. He's getting plenty of sleep now.'

Joe motions to the sofa opposite. 'I've been thinking.'

'Yeah.'

'I figure maybe I know why this means so much to you. When you told me what happened to Luke you didn't tell me the whole story.'

I feel a lump forming in my throat. I couldn't talk if I wanted to.

'You said he was riding the toboggan on his own. Your step-father had gone to town, your mother was dyeing the bedsheets. You said you couldn't remember what you were doing but that's not true. You didn't forget. You were with Luke . . .'

I can see the day. Snow lay thick on the ground. From the top of the hill field you could see the entire farm, all the way to the Telegraph Point on the river and the windsocks on the aerodrome.

' . . . You were looking after him . . .'

He had biscuit on his breath. He sat between my knees, rugged up in one of my hand-me-down jackets. He was so small my chin rested on his head. He wore an old flying cap, lined with wool that flapped from his ears and made him look like a Labrador puppy.

Joe explains. 'When we were in the pub, before we found

Rachel's car, I started describing a dream to you. It was *your* dream. I said you fantasised about saving Luke; you imagined being there, riding the toboggan down the hill, driving your boots into the snow to stop him before he reached the pond. That's when I should have realised. It wasn't a dream – it was the truth.'

The bumps threw the toboggan in the air and Luke squealed with laughter. 'Faster, Yanko! Faster!' He hugged my knees, leaning back against my chest. The track levelled off towards the end where the mesh fence sagged between posts. We were travelling faster than normal because of the extra weight. I put my boots down to stop but we hit the fence too fast. One moment he was in my arms and the next I clutched at air.

The ice broke beneath him. It split into diamonds and triangles; shapes without curves. I waded in, screaming for him. I went under and under. If I could just feel his hair; if I could just grab his collar; he'd be OK. I could save him. But it was too cold and the pond was too deep.

My stepfather came. He used a spotlight powered by the tractor engine and laid planks across the pond to crawl out. He hammered on the ice with an axe and reached down with his hands, feeling for the bottom. I watched from the bedroom window, praying that somehow Luke would all right. Nobody said anything. They didn't have to. It was my fault. I killed him.

'You were twelve years old. It was an accident.'

'I lost him.'

Wiping wetness from my cheeks, I shake my head and curse him. What do other people know of guilt?

Joe is standing, offering his hand. 'Come on, let's go.'

I don't look diminished in his eyes but it will never be the same between us. I wish he could have left Luke alone.

On the drive to his office nothing is said. Rachel greets us at the door. She's been working all night.

'I might have found something,' she explains as we climb

the stairs. 'I remember something Kirsten told me during Howard's trial. We were talking about giving evidence in court and she said that she once got called as a character witness for a friend who was facing charges.'

'Do you know what sort of charges?'

'No. And she didn't mention a name.'

I pick up the phone. I'm not owed any favours but maybe 'New Boy' Dave will grant me one for Ali's sake.

'Sorry to wake you.'

I hear him groan.

'I need your help. I want to cross-reference police and court records for Kirsten Fitzroy.'

'It's been done.'

'Yes, but you've been treating her as the subject. She might have been a witness.'

He doesn't reply. I know he's debating whether to hang up on me. There is no reason to help and a dozen reasons to say no.

'Can it wait till *proper* morning?'

'No.'

There's another long pause. 'Meet me at Otto's at six.'

Otto's is a café between a betting shop and a launderette at the western end of Elgin Avenue. The Saturday morning clientele are mainly cabbies and delivery drivers, priming themselves with coffee and carbohydrates for the day ahead.

I wait by the window. 'New Boy' Dave is on time, dodging the dog shit and puddles before ducking inside. His shirt is creased and hair uncombed.

He orders coffee and pulls a scrap of paper out of his pocket, holding it out of reach. 'First, you can answer some questions for me. Gerry Brandt had a fake passport and driver's licence in the name of Peter Brannigan. For the last three years he's been running a bar in Thailand. The guy's a scrote – where did he get that sort of money?'

'Drugs.'

'That's what I thought, but the DEA and Interpol have nothing on him. He came back into the country two months ago. According to his uncle he was looking for investors.'

'That could explain the ransom demand. Ray Murphy's pub was also struggling.'

'Well, it got them killed. Ballistics has matched the bullet from Brandt with the one found in Ray Murphy's body. Same rifle.'

Dave looks at his watch. 'I got to get to the hospital. I want to be there when Ali wakes up.'

He hands over the scrap of paper. 'Six years ago Kirsten Fitzroy gave evidence at a soliciting trial at Southwark Crown Court. She was a character witness for a Heather Wilde, who was convicted of running a brothel and living off immoral earnings.'

I remember that case. Heather ran a swinging club from a house in Brixton. She had a website, Wilde Times, but claimed that no money changed hands so it wasn't prostitution.

Where in Brixton? Dumbarton Road.

My memory triumphs again. It's a curse.

35

The single door is set in a whitewashed brick wall with no number or letter box. Rising three floors, the façade has maybe a dozen windows, each divided by vertical bars and grey with dirt.

I don't know if Kirsten is inside. The place looks empty. I want to be sure but this time I won't be calling the police – not after what happened to Gerry Brandt.

Rain has beaded the bonnets of cars parked down either side of the street. Walking along the front path, I pass bicycles chained to the railing fence and dustbins waiting for collection.

I knock and wait. Bolts slide and a barrel lock turns, before the door opens no more than a crack. An unsmiling, fifty-plus face appears, looking me up and down.

'Mrs Wilde?'

'Do you know what time it is?'

'I'm looking for Kirsten Fitzroy.'

'Never heard of her.'

Looking past her I see a narrow entrance hall and dimly lit sitting room. She tries to shut the door but my shoulder strikes it first, forcing her backwards into a phone table that topples over.

'I don't want to cause any trouble. Just hear me out.' I help her right the table and pick up the phone books.

A greasy stain of lipstick smears her mouth and she reeks of damp ash and perfume. Her breasts are squeezed into a satin dressing gown, creating a cleavage that brings to mind honeydew melons. Daj always told me that you could tell a honeydew melon was ripe if it was whitish in colour. See how my memory works?

In the sitting room almost every piece of furniture is covered in a sheet except for a wicker chair by the fireplace and an ornate lamp on a trestle table. The table also carries an open book, a cigarette box, a full ashtray and a lighter in the shape of the Venus de Milo.

'Have you heard from Kirsten?'

'I told you, I never heard of her.'

'Tell her I have her diamonds.'

'What diamonds?'

I've sparked her curiosity. 'The ones she almost died for.'

Mrs Wilde hasn't offered me a seat but I take one anyway, pulling the cover from an armchair. Her skin is taut and almost translucent except for her neck and the backs of her hands. She reaches for a cigarette and watches me through the flame of the lighter.

'Kirsten is in a lot of trouble,' I explain. 'I'm trying to help her. I know she's a friend of yours. I thought she might come looking for you if she needed somewhere to hole up for a while.'

Smoke curls in ribbons from her lips. 'I don't know what you're talking about.'

I glance around the room at the deep velvet wallpaper and baroque furnishings. If there's one place more depressing than a brothel it's a former brothel. It's like they soak up the loathing and disappointment until they feel as tired and worn out as the sexual organs of the employees.

'A long while ago Kirsten told me that she would never cross Aleksei Kuznet or if she did she'd be catching the first plane to Patagonia. She missed her flight.'

Aleksei's name has shaken her calmness.

'Didn't Kirsten tell you? She tried to rip him off. You must realise how much danger she's in . . .' I pause – ' . . . how much danger you're both in.'

'I haven't done anything.'

'I'm sure Aleksei will understand. He's a reasonable man. I saw him only yesterday. I offered him a deal – two million pounds' worth of diamonds if he left Kirsten alone. He didn't take it. He sees himself as a man of honour. Money doesn't matter and neither do excuses. But if you haven't seen Kirsten, that's fine. I'll let him know.'

Ash falls from her cigarette and smudges her dress. 'I might be able to ask around. You mentioned money.'

'I mentioned diamonds.'

'It might help me find her.'

'And I had you down as a humanitarian.'

Her top lip curls. 'You see a limousine parked outside?'

Her eyelids seem to work on wires attached to the top of her forehead. I've heard it called a Croydon facelift – pulling back your hair so tightly that everything else lifts.

Drawing out my wallet, I peel off three twenties. She counts with her eyes.

'There's a clinic in Tottenham. It patched her up. Expensive. But discreet.'

I put another two twenties on the stack. She has the money in her hand and it vanishes down her cleavage as if part of a conjuring trick. She tilts her head as though listening to the rain.

'I know all about you. You're a gypsy.' My surprise pleases her. 'They used to say your mother had a gift.'

'How do you know her?'

'Don't you recognise a kindred spirit?' She cackles hoarsely, claiming to be a gypsy. 'Your mother told my fortune once. She said I would always be a great beauty and could have any man I wanted.'

(Somehow I don't think she was talking quantity.)

Daj had a gift all right – a gift for doing cold readings and predicting the bleeding obvious. She took people's money and tapped their spring of eternal hope. And afterwards, having ushered them out of the door, she ran to the off-licence and bought her vodka.

There's a sound from upstairs: something falling. Mrs Wilde looks up quickly.

'It's just one of my old girls. She stays sometimes.'

Her milky blue eyes betray her and her hand shoots out to stop me rising. 'Let me tell you the address of the clinic. They might know where she is.'

I brush her hand aside and move up the stairs, leaning out to peer between the banisters above me. On the first landing there are three doors, two open and one closed. I knock gently and turn the handle. Locked.

'Don't touch me! Leave me alone!'

It sounds like the voice of a child – the same one I heard on the phone during the ransom drop. I step away, bracing my back against the wall, with only my hand protruding past the doorframe.

The first bullet hits six inches to the right of the handle at stomach height. I sit heavily, letting my feet hit the opposite wall, letting out a low groan.

Mrs Wilde yells up the stairs. 'Is that my door? If that's my bloody door you'll be paying for it.'

A second bullet rips through the wood a foot above the floor.

Mrs Wilde again: 'Right, that's it! From now on I'm taking a fucking deposit.'

I sit quietly, listening to my own breathing.

'Hey, you out there,' says the voice, just above a whisper. 'Are you dead?'

'No.'

'Are you wounded?'

'No.'

She curses.

'It's me, Vincent Ruiz. I'm here to help you.'

A long silence follows.

'Please let me come in. I'm here alone.'

'Stay away. Please go.' I recognise Kirsten's voice, thick with phlegm and fear.

'I can't do that.'

After another long pause, 'How's your leg?'

'Half an inch shorter.'

Mrs Wilde calls up the stairs. 'I'm calling the police unless someone pays for my door!'

Sighing heavily, I tell Kirsten, 'You can keep the gun if you shoot your landlady.'

Her laugh is cut short by a hacking cough.

'I'm coming in.'

'Then I'll have to shoot you.'

'No you won't.'

I ease myself up and face the door. 'Are you going to unlock it for me?'

After a long wait there are two metallic clicks. Turning the handle, I push the door open.

Heavy curtains are drawn and the bedroom is in semi-darkness. The room has high ceilings and mirrors on two walls. A large iron bed occupies the centre and Kirsten is marooned amid the covers, with her legs drawn up and the gun resting on her knees. She has cut her hair and dyed it blonde. It falls in sweaty ringlets down her forehead.

'I thought you were dead,' she says.

'I could say the same about you.'

She lowers her chin on to the barrel of the gun, staring forlornly into the shadows. The cheap chandelier above her head catches the light leaking from the curtains and the mirrors reflect the same scene, each from a slightly different angle.

I lean against the windowsill letting the curtains sag against my back. I can hear the raindrops hitting the panes of glass.

Kirsten shifts slightly and grimaces in pain. Boxes of painkillers and torn silver foil litter the floor around her bed.

'Can I have a look?'

Without acknowledging me, she raises her shirt high enough to show me the yellowing bandage, crusty with blood and sweat.

'You need to get to hospital.'

She lowers the shirt but doesn't answer.

'A lot of people are looking for you.'

'And you get the prize.'

'Can I call an ambulance?'

'No.'

'OK, we'll just talk for a while. You want to tell me what happened.'

Kirsten shrugs and lowers the gun, resting it between her thighs. 'I saw an opportunity.'

'To play with fire.'

'To make a new life.' She doesn't finish the sentence. Licking her lips, she makes a silent decision and starts again. 'It was almost a joke at first; one of those "what if" ideas that you toss around amongst yourselves and laugh about. Ray was good at the technical side. He used to work in the sewers. I kept an eye on the little details. At first I thought Rachel might even play along. We could set the whole thing up and she'd finally get what she deserved from her family or her ex-husband. She was owed.'

'She wouldn't play along?'

'I didn't ask. I knew the answer.'

I look around the room. The wallpaper has a honeycomb

design and within each octagon is the outline of a naked woman in a different sexual pose. 'What happened to Mickey?'

Kirsten doesn't seem to hear me. She's telling the story in her own time.

'We would have been fine, you know, if it hadn't been for Gerry Brandt. Mickey would have made it home. Ray would still be alive. Gerry should never have let her go . . . not alone. He was supposed to take her home.'

'I don't understand. What are you talking about?'

A painful smile steals across her face but doesn't part her lips. 'Poor Inspector: you haven't worked it out yet, have you?'

The truth grows in me like a tumour with the cells doubling and dividing, invading the empty spaces and the gaps in my memory. Gerry Brandt said he let her go. They were his last words.

'We only had her for a few days,' says Kirsten, gnawing at a fingernail. 'Then he paid the ransom.'

'What ransom?'

'The first one.'

'What do you mean, a first ransom?

'We were never going to hurt her. Once we got the ransom, we told Gerry to take her home. He was supposed to drop her at the end of her street but he panicked and left her at an Underground station. The fucking idiot! He was always a loose cannon. Right from the first day he jeopardised everything. He was supposed to be looking after Mickey but he couldn't resist going back to Randolph Avenue to see the TV crews and police.

'We would never have included him except we needed someone to look after Mickey who she couldn't identify. Like I said, we were always going to let her go. She told Gerry she knew the way home. She said she'd change trains at Piccadilly Circus and catch the Bakerloo Line.'

This information seeps into my stomach and joins forces with the tepid nausea. My mind is tallying the details. Mr and Mrs Bird saw Mickey at Leicester Square. It's one stop from Piccadilly Circus.

'But if you let her go, what happened?'

Her misery is complete. 'Wavell!'

I don't understand.

'Howard Wavell happened,' she says again. 'Mickey made it home but she ran into Howard.'

God, no! Surely not! It was a Wednesday night. Rachel wasn't home. She was on *News at Ten* making another appeal. I remember watching her on TV at the station. They used footage of the press conference earlier in the day.

'I tell you we didn't mean to hurt her. We let her go. Then you found her bloodstained towel and arrested Howard. I wanted to die.'

An image presents itself. I picture a small, terrified child with a fear of being outside, crossing a city alone. She almost made it. Only steps away – not even eighty-five of them. Howard found her on the stairs.

My legs go weak and I struggle to stand. It's as though my insides have become liquid and want to flood out, throbbing and glistening on the floor. My God, what have I done? I couldn't have been more wrong. Ali, Rachel, Mickey – I let them all down.

'You don't know how many times I have wanted to change things,' says Kirsten. 'I would have brought Mickey home myself. I would have walked her right to her door. Believe me!'

'You were *friends* with Rachel. How could you do that to her?'

For a fleeting moment her sadness turns to anger, but takes too much energy to sustain. She whispers, 'I never meant to hurt them . . . not Mickey or Rachel.'

'Why then?'

'We were stealing from the ultimate thief – taking money

from Aleksei Kuznet, a monster. He murdered his own brother, for God's sake.'

'You wanted to take on the biggest bully in the playground.'

'We live in a new feudal age, Inspector. We fight wars over oil and we hand out reconstruction contracts in return for political donations. We have more parking wardens than we do police officers . . .'

'Oh for pity's sake, spare me the speeches!'

'We didn't want to hurt anyone.'

'Rachel was always going to be hurt.'

She looks at me with wet eyes. I can almost taste the salt in them.

'I didn't mean . . . we let Mickey go. I would never have . . .' She lowers the gun between her knees and her head follows, rocking back and forth. 'I'm sorry . . . I'm so sorry . . .'

Her self-pity irritates me. I keep pressing for the rest of the story. Kirsten doesn't look at me as she describes the cesspit in the basement and the underground river. Ray Murphy inflated a boat below ground and drew a map for Gerry to follow. He only had to travel a few hundred feet before bringing Mickey up through a storm-water drain.

'Ray knew a place to keep her. I never went there. My job was to send the ransom letter.'

'Where did you send it?'

'Directly to Aleksei.'

'What about the bikini?'

'Gerry held on to it.'

'What was she wearing when he let her go?'

'I don't know exactly.'

'Did she have her beach towel?'

'Gerry said it was like her security blanket. She wouldn't let it go.'

I'm struggling now. Of all the scenarios to contemplate I had left Howard out, convinced of his innocence. I had weighed up the evidence and the odds and decided he had been wrongly accused and convicted. Campbell said I was blind to the obvious. I thought he couldn't see anything except his own prejudices.

'Why in God's name did you try for a second ransom? How could you put Rachel through it again? You convinced her Mickey was still alive.'

Her face creases as she sucks back the pain. 'I didn't want to. You don't understand.'

'Then explain it to me.'

'When you arrested Howard for Mickey's murder Gerry went off his head. He kept saying we helped kill her. He said he couldn't go back inside – not for killing a child. He knew what they did to child murderers in prison. Right away I knew we had a problem. We either had to silence Gerry or help him disappear.'

'So you got him out of the country.'

'We gave him double what he deserved – four hundred grand. He was supposed to stay away but he poured his money down slot machines or shot it up his arm.'

'He bought a bar in Thailand.'

'Whatever.'

'And then he came back.'

'The first I knew about the second ransom was when Rachel received the postcard. Gerry came up with the idea all by himself. Mickey's body had never been found. He still had her swimsuit and strands of her hair. I went ballistic. His greed and stupidity threatened us all. Ray said he was going to stop Gerry before he gave us all away . . .'

'You could have walked away then. Nobody would have known.'

'I wanted to kill him – I really did.'

'What changed your mind?'

'None of us thought Aleksei would say yes – not after paying one ransom – but then straight off he agreed. I almost felt sorry for him then. He must have really wanted to believe Mickey was still alive.'

'He didn't have a choice. Fathers are meant to believe.'

'No, he wanted revenge. He didn't care what it cost. He didn't care about Mickey or Rachel. He wanted us dead – that's the only reason.'

Maybe she's right. Aleksei has always preferred to dispense his own brand of justice.

Outside Wormwood Scrubs prison and again at the police station, Aleksei had said, 'I don't pay for things twice.' This is what he meant. He had already paid a ransom for Mickey and wouldn't easily surrender another one.

'Why did you use the same drop procedure?'

'We didn't have time to come up with a new one. Aleksei must have figured it out. It's like I said, we didn't expect him to go through with it. We had to scramble to get everything ready. I didn't want to go ahead but Ray needed the money and he said it would be easier second time around.'

'You knew I was in the car with Rachel.'

'No. Not after we made her change vehicles. And we didn't expect anyone to be foolish enough to follow the ransom through the sewers.'

'During the ransom drop, I heard the sound of a child's voice. It was you, wasn't it?'

'Yes.'

The room has grown darker and she seems to be turning to shadow. The distance between us has grown wide and cold.

'When the shooting started, I thought it must be the police. Then they just kept firing.'

'Did you see the sniper?'

'No.'

'Did you see anyone?'

She shakes her head.

Although exhausted she looks almost relieved to be talking. She can't remember how long she spent in the water. The tide carried her east past Westminster. Eventually she crawled on to the steps at Bankside Jetty near the Globe Theatre. She broke into a pharmacy and stole bandages and painkillers. She slept in a shop that was being refurbished, lying beneath painters' sheets.

She couldn't run and she couldn't go to hospital. Aleksei would have found her. Once he knew who had kidnapped Mickey he was never going to stop looking.

'And since then you've been hiding?'

'Waiting to die.' Her voice is so soft it might be coming from another room.

The cloying smell of sweat and infection thickens the air. Either everything Kirsten has told me is the truth or an extra-ordinarily elaborate lie.

'Please move away from the window,' she says.

'Why?'

'I keep seeing red dots. They're burned into my eyelids.'

I know what she means.

Taking a chair beside the bed, I pour her a glass of water. Her finger is no longer curled around the trigger of the gun.

'What were you going to do with the ransom?'

'I had plans.' She describes a new life in America, making it sound almost irresistible, the idea of walking away and never looking back – the romance of the clean slate.

I have thoughts like that sometimes – wanting to be someone else or to start afresh – but then I realise I have no desire to see most of the world and I have enough trouble keeping old friends without meeting new ones. What would I be running from? I'd be another dog chasing its tail.

'We were foolish. We should have walked away and counted our blessings that nobody knew the truth about Mickey. Now it's too late.'

'I can protect you,' I say.

'Nobody can.'

'I can talk to the Crown Prosecution Service. If you give evidence against Aleksei they can put you . . .'

'What evidence?' she says harshly. 'I didn't see him shoot anyone. I can't point to a mug shot or pick someone out of a police line-up. So what if he paid two ransoms – it's not against the law.'

She is right. The most Aleksei is guilty of is withholding information from the police about the first ransom demand.

Surely there *must* be something more. A man organises to have people executed and nobody can touch him.

For the first time in a long while, I have no idea of what to do next. I know I have to call the police. I also have to keep her safe. There are witness protection programmes for IRA informers and organised crime witnesses but what can they offer Kirsten? She can't give them Aleksei. She can't link him to the executions or any of his many crimes.

'What if we arrange a meeting?'

'What?'

'Contact Aleksei – organise to see him.'

She puts her hands over her ears, not wanting to hear. Her skin is like metal, shining at angles in the light from the bedside lamp.

She's right. Aleksei would never agree.

'You can't save me. If I were you, I'd phone him now and tell him where I am. You might win a reprieve.'

'I'm going to call an ambulance.'

'No.'

'You can't stay here. How long before your landlady gives you up?'

'We're old friends.'

'I can see that! How much has it cost you to still be here.'

She holds up her fingers. Her jewellery has gone.

We sit in silence and after a while I hear her breathing find a steady rhythm. She's asleep. Moving to her side, I gently take the revolver from her lap before covering her with a blanket. Then I move to the landing and call 'New Boy' Dave. My hands are shaking.

'I've found Kirsten Fitzroy. I need an ambulance and a police escort. Don't tell Meldrum or Campbell Smith.'

'OK.'

Back in the room Kirsten's eyes are open.

'Are they coming?'

'Yes.'

'The cavalry or a hearse?'

'An ambulance.'

Gritting her teeth against the pain, she swings her legs off the bed and sits facing away from me. Her black shirt is stuck perfectly to her body with sweat and it looks as though someone has poured oil over her.

'You might be able to protect me today but it is just *one* day,' she says, managing to stand and shuffle towards the bathroom. Sensing I'm about to follow, she stops me. 'I have to go potty.'

I'm expected to wait on the landing, which I do – pleased to escape from the sick-room smell and the hypocrisy. The sheer number of lies and depth of betrayal is staggering. Mickey is dead! I failed. I want to crawl back into the sewer where I belong.

There's a knock on the door downstairs. Mrs Wilde answers. I look over the banister half-expecting to see 'New Boy' Dave. It's a courier. I can't make out what he's saying.

Mrs Wilde turns away from the door holding a bunch of flowers. In that same instant I hear a blunt sound, metal on bone. She topples forwards, crushing the flowers beneath her. A motorcycle courier in leathers and a gleaming black helmet steps over her body.

I hit the redial button on the mobile. Dave's number is engaged. He must be calling the ambulance or organising an escort.

The courier is moving. I can imagine him crouching and swinging the gun in a wide arc. He's a professional. Ex-military.

Kirsten flushes the toilet and walks from the bathroom. I signal for her to get down and she drops to her knees with a groan. She sees something in my eyes that wasn't there before.

'Don't leave me,' she mouths. I hold my finger to my lips and point above my head.

The courier has heard the toilet flushing and the cistern filling. Now he's at the bottom of the stairs. Turning away from Kirsten I climb to the next landing. Again I hit the speed dial. Engaged.

A floorboard depresses and releases. The noise vibrates through me. Kirsten fired two shots. Assuming the gun is fully loaded, I have four bullets left.

I should be scared but maybe I'm beyond that. Instead I think of the past six weeks and all those times that Aleksei has toyed with me. I'm not angry or bitter. This is like one of those children's stories, *Goldilocks and the Three Bears*, where Goldilocks gets chased out of the house for eating porridge and breaking a chair. Only in my new version she comes back with a gun and she's going to make sure she aims not too high and not too low but just right.

'New Boy' Dave answers his phone.

'Code One. Officer in trouble. Help!'

The courier is on the stairs, staying close to the wall to shield himself from above. When he turns on to the landing I should get a clean shot. I wait in darkness, trying to make myself small. A river leaks down my back.

Another step. His shadow appears. He's carrying a fully automatic machine pistol that sweeps from side to side. My finger pulls gently on the trigger, pushing the hammer backwards and compressing a metal spring in the handle. A ratchet rotates the cylinder, putting a bullet in the breech chamber in line with the barrel.

He's fully in view – about to turn into the bedroom. I can't see his face behind the visor.

'Police! Put the gun down!'

He drops and rolls, firing blindly up the stairs. Bullets punch tattered holes in the wallpaper beside my head and shatter the banister. A splinter of wood slices into my neck.

The moment I shoot he'll see the muzzle flash and know where I am. I pull the trigger lever all the way back, releasing the hammer.

The bullet enters through his shoulder, angling down into his chest. His head hits the wall. The wide dark visor is staring at me. His finger closes on the trigger again. We fire together and he tumbles backwards.

I can taste blood in my mouth where I've bitten my tongue and my lungs hurt like a bastard. Where has all the oxygen gone? I don't know how long I sit on the stairs. There are sirens and screeching tyres in the street. 'New Boy' Dave comes through the door so fast he almost trips over Mrs Wilde.

Kneeling on the landing, I put the gun at my side and stare down at my chest. Dave is climbing the stairs, yelling my name. Ripping open the buttons, I press my fingers to my chest bone. A neat depression, still warm from the bullet, lies at the centre of the vest.

Well I'll be damned! Ali saved my life.

Looking through the railings I see the courier's body crumpled at the foot of the stairs. Forty-three years in the police force, thirty-five of them as a detective, and I managed not to kill anyone. Another unwanted milestone reached.

36

Four hours ago a warrant was issued for Aleksei's arrest but it hasn't been served. His motor launch left Chelsea Harbour at midnight on Friday, only an hour after our meeting. The skipper claimed to be doing a transfer to Moody's boatyard in Hamble on the south coast but failed to arrive by midday on Saturday.

Coast-guards and lifeboat stations have been alerted and all vessels within a five-hundred-nautical-mile range have been told to report any sightings. Descriptions of the vessel are also being sent to harbour masters in France, Belgium, Holland, Denmark, Portugal and Spain.

I didn't expect Aleksei to run. A part of me still thinks he's going to waltz into a police station with a team of lawyers looking smug and ready to rumble. He knows there is nothing but circumstantial evidence. Nobody can put him at the scene of the murders. If Kirsten dies I can't even prove he paid the first ransom.

Of course, it's not my job to prove anything, as Campbell keeps telling me as he storms around the hospital, dressed in an overcoat of angry tweed. Every time his eyes reach me he looks away. He was right and I couldn't have been more wrong. Despite all the bloody mayhem of the past few weeks, the facts have remained unchanged – Mickey died three years ago and Howard Wavell killed her.

According to the X-rays my ribs are only bruised and the cut on my neck doesn't need stitches. Kirsten is under guard upstairs. Not even the paramedics knew her name when they delivered her into intensive care.

On Monday morning Eddie Barrett and The Rook will argue that Howard Wavell should be released from prison. They will claim that Mickey Carlyle was taken for a ransom and killed by her abductors. The CCTV footage from Leicester Square Underground could be of anyone. The towel found at East Finchley Cemetery was planted there to frame Howard for a murder he didn't commit.

It's a version of events that is far easier to argue than the truth. The police case against Howard was always circumstantial. Evidence had to be laid out piece by piece, showing the jury how it all fitted together. Now it seems more like a house of cards.

Howard will get his retrial and our only hope of maintaining his conviction is if a jury believes Kirsten's story. Defence barristers will be queueing up to dismantle her credibility as a confessed kidnapper, extortionist and manager of an escort agency.

I was wrong about Howard, wrong about Mickey, wrong about almost everything. A child-killer is going to walk free. I am responsible.

Things get messy when police shoot people. They get even messier when it's an ex-policeman. There will be an inquest and an investigation by the Police Complaints Commission. There will also be drug tests and psych reports. I don't know enough about morphine to say if the opiates are still in my system. If I test positive I'll be swimming in shit.

The man I killed hasn't been identified. He rode a stolen

motorbike and carried no papers. His dental work was Eastern European and he carried a fully automatic machine pistol stolen from a Belfast police station four years ago. His only other distinguishing feature was a small silver cross around his neck inlaid with a purple gemstone, chariote, a rare silicate found only in the Bratsk region of Siberia. Perhaps Interpol will have more luck.

Visiting hours are over but the nursing sister has let me in. Although flat on her back, staring at a mirror above her head, Ali gives me a bigger smile than I deserve. She turns her head, making it only part way before the pain catches in her throat.

'I brought you chocolates,' I tell her.

'You want me to get fat.'

'You haven't been fat since you were hanging off the tit.'

It hurts when she laughs.

'How is it going?' I ask.

'OK. I had pins and needles in my legs this afternoon.'

'That's a good sign. So when can we go dancing?'

'You hate dancing.'

'I'll dance with *you*.'

It sounds too maudlin and I wish I could take it back. Ali seems to appreciate the sentiment.

She explains that she has to wear a full body cast for the next three months and then a canvas brace with shoulder bands for another three months after that.

'With any luck I'll be walking by then.'

I hate the expression 'with any luck'. It's not a resounding affirmative but a fingers crossed, if-all-goes-well sort of statement. What sort of luck has Ali had so far?

I pull a bottle of whisky from a brown-paper bag and wave it in front of her eyes. She grins. Two glasses are next, pulled from the bag like a rabbit from a hat.

I pour her a glass and add water from a tap in the sink.

'I can't really handle a glass,' she says apologetically.

Reaching into the bag again, I produce a crazy drinking straw with spirals and loops. I rest the glass on her chest and put the straw in her mouth. She takes a sip and gasps slightly. It's the first time I have ever seen her drink.

Our eyes meet in the mirror. 'A Home Office lawyer came to see me today,' she says. 'They're offering a compensation deal with a full disability pension if I want to leave the job.'

'What did you tell them?'

'I want to stay.'

'They're worried you might sue them.'

'Why would I do that? It's nobody's fault.'

We look at each other and I feel grateful and undeserving all at once.

'I heard about Gerry Brandt.'

'Yeah.'

I watch the subtle change in her, a little shrinking created by a single affirmation. Something shifts inside me as well and I get a sense of how much pain she's endured already and the months of operation and physiotherapy still to come.

A swatch of her hair, shiny black, has come loose from a bobby pin. She drops her gaze and sets her mouth defiantly. 'And you found Kirsten. We should drink to that.'

She takes a sip and notices I haven't joined her. 'What's wrong?'

'I'm so sorry. It was a stupid, foolish quest. I just wanted . . . I just hoped Mickey might be alive, you know. And now look! You're here and people are dead and Rachel is grieving all over again. And tomorrow Howard is going to get his retrial. It's my fault. What I've done is unforgivable.'

Ali doesn't answer. Outside the sky is tinged with pink and the streetlights are blinking on. I rock forward and stare into the glass. She reaches out and puts her hand on my shoulder to stop it shaking.

'It hurts all over,' I moan. 'Why put a child on this earth

and give her seven years if you're going to allow her to be kidnapped, raped, tortured, terrified or whatever else happened?'

'There's no answer to that.'

'I don't believe in God. I don't believe in eternal life or Heaven or reincarnation. Will you ask your God for me? Ask him why.'

Ali looks at me sadly. 'He doesn't work like that.'

'Well, ask him for his grand plan. While he concentrates on the big picture, who looks after kids like Mickey? One child might seem petty and trivial among a few billion but he could start by saving one at a time.'

I down the rest of the whisky, feeling the alcohol burn my throat. I'm already drunk, but not drunk enough.

A black cab drops me home. Fumbling for the keys, I stagger inside and up the stairs, where I lean over the toilet and vomit. Afterwards I splash water on my face, letting it leak down my neck and chest.

Staring back from the mirror is a pallid, leering stranger. In his eyes I see Mickey standing at the bottom of the escalator and Daj behind the razor wire and Luke lying beneath the ice.

I seem to have no other memories. Missing children, abused children and dead children fill my thoughts. Babies drowned in bathtubs, toddlers shaken into comas, children sent to gas chambers or snatched from playgrounds or suffocated beneath pillows. How can I blame God when I couldn't save one little girl?

37

Opposite the Royal Courts of Justice a deliveryman is unloading naked mannequins from a truck. Male and female dummies are frozen in an orgy of plaster, some with wigs and others bare. The driver carries them two at a time, balanced across his shoulders, with his hands between each pair of buttocks to stop them falling. I can see him laughing as cab drivers toot their horns and office workers lean out of windows.

I stand and watch. It's good to smile.

The feeling doesn't last. Rachel Carlyle looks up as I approach along the corridor. Her gaze is not quite focused and her smile vague as though she doesn't immediately recognise me. Light coming through high windows is broken and refracted, dissipating before it reaches the depths of the marble entrance hall.

I take her off to one side, finding an empty conference room. Making her sit down I tell her the same story that Kirsten told me, trying to leave nothing out. When I reach the point about Mickey crossing London alone, late at night, she squeezes her eyes shut, endeavouring to rid herself of the image.

'Where is Kirsten now?'

'She's battling an infection. The next forty-eight hours will be crucial.'

Rachel's face is etched with concern. Her capacity for forgiveness is beyond mine. I can imagine her saying a prayer for Kirsten or lighting a candle. She should be railing against her and against me. I raised her hopes and look at us now.

Instead she blames herself. 'If I hadn't asked Aleksei for the ransom none of this would have happened.'

'No. He was punishing them for what happened to Mickey, not for anything you did.'

Her voice drops. 'I just wanted her back.'

'I know.'

I look at my watch. We're due in court. Rachel pauses for a moment, drawing strength, before leaving the room. The corridors and public areas have emptied slightly. The Rook is on the stairs. Eddie Barrett is three steps above him, putting their eyes on a level. The Rook looks invigorated while Eddie growls and gesticulates, almost eating the air.

Rachel takes my arm to steady herself. 'If Aleksei received an original ransom demand why didn't he say anything?'

'I guess he didn't want the police involved.'

'Yes, but afterwards, when Mickey didn't come home, he could have said something then.'

I don't know the answer. I suspect he didn't want to advertise his mistake. He is also conceited enough to believe he could find Mickey before the police. He must have known how close she came to making it home – less than eighty-five steps. How that must have torn him apart.

Lord Connelly keeps everyone waiting. He enters the courtroom at ten minutes past ten and the room rises. Then he carefully places his walnut gavel to his right and his glass of water to his left.

Howard emerges from below. He is clutching a Bible with red ribbons marking the pages. His eyes look bruised but defiant. Eddie Barrett shakes his hand and Howard gives him a weary smile.

Fiona Hanley QC is already on her feet. 'Perhaps I can expedite these proceedings a little, Your Honour. Due to information that has come to light over the weekend, the Crown does not oppose the defence application and is content for this case to be retried at the court's earliest convenience.'

There is an audible gasp. Blood surges in the air and eyes shift to Howard. I don't think he understands. Even Eddie Barrett looks amazed.

'My chambers,' Lord Connelly says. He exits stage right like a black-caped crusader.

Four of us wait in the outer office. Eddie Barrett and The Rook are whispering in one corner. The Rook is actually smiling, an expression that doesn't come naturally to him. Meanwhile, Fiona Hanley avoids my gaze, wrapping her robe around herself.

Lord Connelly's assistant, a large-breasted black woman, has a brilliant smile reserved only for His Honour. She has been with him fifteen years and we've all heard the rumours.

'He'll see you now,' she says, pointing to the door.

Eddie takes a step back and lets Miss Hanley go first, bowing slightly and showing his monk-like dome.

There are only three chairs in front of the judge's desk. I stand with my back to the bookshelves that line the walls. Lord Connelly has removed his wig. His *own* hair is similarly white, trimmed neatly above his ears. His voice takes on a kind of exalted public school inflection.

'I spent four days writing up this judgement and now you spring this.' His gaze settles on Fiona.

'I apologise, Your Honour, I only learned of this late yesterday.'

'And whose bright idea was it?'

'Further information has come to light . . .'

'Which casts doubt on Mr Wavell's guilt?'

She hesitates. 'It creates complications.'

'I hope you're not telling me one thing and meaning something else.'

Eddie is beside himself with glee. The judge fixes him with a glare. 'And you can keep your thoughts to yourself, Mr Barrett. I have had a bellyful of you in my courtrooms and I won't put up with it in here.'

Eddie's smile is erased.

Getting to his feet, Lord Connelly walks behind his chair and braces his hand on the backrest. His eyes settle on me. 'I understand that I shouldn't refer to your rank any more, DI Ruiz, but perhaps you can enlighten me on what is happening here.'

'The police have a new witness.'

'A witness or a suspect?'

'Both.'

'In your evidence several days ago you expressed an opinion that Michaela Carlyle might be alive. Is that still the case?'

'No, Your Honour.'

Sadness flickers in his eyes. 'And this new witness has led you to question what happened?'

'She has confessed to the kidnapping of Michaela Carlyle and sending a subsequent ransom demand. She will testify that Mickey was released unharmed after three days.'

'And then what?'

'We believe she made it as far as Dolphin Mansions.'

The judge can see where I'm going now. He grinds his teeth as though trying to wear them down. 'This is ridiculous!'

Eddie interrupts, 'We *will* be applying for bail, Your Honour.'

'*You* keep your mouth shut.'

I raise my voice above both of them. 'Howard Wavell is a child-killer. He should stay in prison.'

'Bullshit,' mutters Eddie. 'He's ugly and he's weird but last time I looked that still wasn't a crime. We can both be grateful for that.'

'You can both be quiet,' says Lord Connelly, wanting to tear strips off someone. 'Next person to utter a sound gets locked up for contempt.'

He addresses me. 'DI Ruiz, I hope you're going to explain to that poor girl's family what's happening.'

'Yes, Your Honour.'

He turns to the others. 'I am going to grant the defence leave to appeal. I am also going to make sure they have plenty of opportunity to examine this new evidence. I want a level playing field. You can make your case for bail, Mr Raynor, but I remind you that your client has been convicted of murder and the presumption of guilt must remain . . .'

'Your Honour, my client is gravely ill and requires medical attention he is not receiving in prison. The humanitarian considerations outweigh . . .'

Lord Connelly wags his finger. 'Now is not the time or the place. Make your case in court.'

The rest of the hearing passes in a blur of legal argument and ill temper. Leave to appeal is granted and Lord Connelly orders a retrial but refuses to release Howard from prison. Instead he orders that he be transferred to a civilian hospital under armed guard.

There is pandemonium outside the courtroom. Reporters yell into phones and jostle to get close to Rachel, shouting questions and answers, as though wanting her to agree.

Her arms are locked around my waist, her breasts against my back. It's like a rugby maul without the ball as we try to cross the gain line. Eddie Barrett, an unlikely saviour, takes his briefcase and swings it from side to side like a scythe, clearing a path.

'It might be time to consider an alternative exit,' he shouts, pointing to a door marked 'officials only'.

Eddie is an old hand at exiting courthouses through basements and back doors. He leads us down corridors, past offices and holding cells, getting deeper into the building. Eventually, we emerge into a cobblestoned courtyard where industrial bins await collection and wire netting is stretched above our heads to stop the pigeons landing.

The gates slide open electronically and an ambulance pulls through them. Howard is waiting on the stone steps, head in hands, staring sullenly at the tips of his scuffed shoes. Police officers and prison guards stand on either side of him.

Eddie lights a cigarette in the hollow of his hand, inclining his head as he does so. The smoke floats past his eyes and scatters as he exhales. He offers me one and I feel an impulse towards comradeship; the solidarity of lost soldiers on a battlefield.

'You know he did it.'

'That's not what he says.'

'But what do *you* think?'

Eddie chuckles. 'You want true confessions, talk to Oprah.'

Rachel is nearby, gazing towards Howard. The paramedics have opened the rear doors and are pulling out a stretcher.

'Can I talk to him?' she asks.

Eddie doesn't think it is appropriate.

'I just want to ask how he is.'

Eddie looks at me. I shrug my shoulders.

She crosses the courtyard. The police officers step aside and she stands beside the stretcher. I can't hear what they're saying. She reaches out and puts her hand on his shoulder.

Eddie raises his face to the square of sky above. 'What are you trying to do, Inspector?'

'I'm trying to get to the truth.'

He inclines his head, respectful but stubborn. 'In my experience almost all truths are lies.' His features have softened and his face looks unexpectedly gentle. 'You said Mickey was set free by her kidnappers. When was that?'

'Wednesday night.'

He nods.

I remember that night. I watched Rachel being interviewed on *News at Ten*. That's why she wasn't at home when Mickey pressed on the buzzer. I was working in the office, reading statements. My mind puts everyone where they should have been. Mentally I lift off the roof of Dolphin Mansions and put people inside or take them out. It's like playing with dolls in a doll's house. Mrs Swingler, Kirsten, Ray Murphy . . . I put Mickey outside, ringing the bell, but nobody was home.

A piece is missing. Turning away from Eddie I walk across the courtyard towards Howard. The paramedics have strapped him to a gurney and are lifting him into the ambulance.

'What did you do on Wednesday evenings, Howard?'

He looks at me blankly.

'Before you went to prison. What did you do?'

He clears his throat. 'Choir practice. I never missed a choir practice – not in seven years.'

There is a pause for the information to sink in – barely a heartbeat, even less, the pause between heartbeats. I have been a fool. I have spent so much time concentrating on finding Kirsten that I didn't see the other possibilities.

Moving away from them, I can see myself running into the street, whistling at cabs to stop. At the same time I yell down the mobile, making no sense at all. I don't have all the facts. But I have enough. I know what happened.

The traces of hair dye on Mickey's towel have bothered me all along. Gerry Brandt didn't dye her hair and why would Howard bother with a detail like that?

'I don't pay for things twice,' Aleksei said. I know what that means now. He didn't organise Mickey's kidnapping but, like Kirsten and Ray Murphy, he saw an opportunity. He wanted his daughter back – the only truly perfect thing he had ever created. So he paid the ransom in secret. No police and no publicity. And when Mickey arrived home that night it was Aleksei who found her. He was waiting.

Then he hatched his plan – one that hinged on convincing the world that Mickey was dead. At first he imagined he could blame the kidnappers. He would take some of Mickey's blood or make her vomit, plant the evidence and encourage everyone to think that she had died at the hands of her abductors. Unfortunately, he didn't know who they were. Then something serendipitous happened – a made-to-measure suspect, with a corrupt sexuality and no alibi. Howard Wavell. The opportunity was almost too perfect.

And what of Mickey? He spirited her away – smuggling her out of the country, most likely on board his boat. He changed her appearance and changed her name.

I don't know what Aleksei thought would happen then. Maybe one day, after enough years had passed, he planned to bring Mickey back to Britain with a new identity or perhaps he always intended to join her overseas.

The plan might have been flawless but for Gerry Brandt, a washed-up, drug-addled chancer, who thought he could steal apples from the same tree all over again. Having squandered the first ransom, he came back to Britain with a plan to do it all again. Mickey's body had never been found and he still had a lock of her hair and her swimsuit. Kirsten knew immediately that Gerry was back in the country. She talked to Ray Murphy. Gerry's greed and stupidity threatened to expose them.

Unbeknownst to them, he also threatened to destroy Aleksei's grand design. The world believed Mickey was dead. A second ransom demand called this into question. It must also have created a separate, more dangerous doubt in Aleksei's mind. Did these people *know*?

The only way to safeguard his secret completely was to silence them. He would pay the ransom, follow the trail and have everyone killed. I gave him the perfect alibi; he was following me.

These thoughts are coming almost too quickly to put in any

order or chronology, but like Sarah, Mickey's friend, on that first morning at Dolphin Mansions – 'I know what I know'.

'New Boy' Dave is on the end of the phone.

'Have you found Aleksei?'

'His motor yacht arrived in Ostend in Belgium at eleven o'clock on Saturday morning.'

'Who was on board?'

'Still no word.'

I can hear the rasp of my own breathing. 'You have to listen to me! I know I've made a lot of mistakes but this time I'm right. You have to find Aleksei. You can't let him disappear.'

I pause. He's still on the phone. The only thing we have in common now is Ali. Maybe that's enough. 'You have to check the passenger manifests of every ferry and hovercraft and the Eurostar train services out of Waterloo. You can forget about the airlines. Aleksei doesn't fly. You'll need warrants for his house, office, cars, lockups, boatsheds . . . And you'll want his phone records and details of bank transactions going back three years.'

Dave is starting to lose patience with me. He doesn't have the authority to do half of these things and Campbell and Meldrum won't listen to anything I say.

Leaning back, I stare out of the window of the cab not actually seeing anything but I'm turning pages in my head full of notes, diagrams and figures; searching through the past for a clue.

When I did my detective training a guy called Donald Kinsella took me under his wing. He'd spent a few years working undercover and wore his hair long, tied back in a ponytail, and he had a bushy moustache, which was a trademark for coppers in the seventies until the Village People made it a different sort of trademark.

'Keep it simple' was his motto. 'Don't believe in conspiracy theories. Listen to them, work out the odds, and then file them in the same drawer as you put stuff you read in the *Socialist*

Worker or on the *Daily Telegraph* editorial pages.'

Donald believed the truth lay somewhere in the middle. He was a pragmatist. When Diana, Princess of Wales, died in Paris he rang me. He'd retired by then.

'A year from now there will be a dozen books about this,' he said. 'People will be blaming the CIA, MI5, the PLO, the Mafia, Osama bin Laden, another shooter in the grassy knoll – you name it. There will be secret witnesses, missing evidence, mystery vehicles, stolen reports, tyre marks, poisonings and pregnancies . . . Let me tell you the one thing I can guarantee won't be in any of these books – the most likely answer. People *want* to believe in conspiracies. They eat them up and say, "Please can I have some more?" They don't want to think that someone close to them or someone famous could die a mundane, ordinary, kitchen-sink sort of death.'

What Donald was trying to say is that lives are complicated but most deaths aren't. People are complicated but not their crimes. Prosecutors and psychologists care about motives. I care about facts – the how, where, what and when, rather than the why. My favourite is 'who', the perpetrator – the face that fills my empty picture frame.

Eddie Barrett is wrong. All truth isn't a lie. I'm not naive enough to believe the opposite but facts I can hold on to. Facts I can write up in a report. Facts are more reliable than memories.

The cab driver is staring at me in his mirror. I'm talking to myself.

'The second sign of madness,' I explain.

'What's the first one?'

'Killing lots of people and eating their genitals.'

He laughs and sneaks another look at me.

38

Three hours ago I learned that Mickey Carlyle might still be alive. Forty-eight hours ago Aleksei's boat arrived in Ostend. He has a head start but will only travel overland. He might already be there. Where?

The Netherlands is a possibility. He and Rachel lived there and Mickey was born in Amsterdam. Eastern Europe is more likely. He has connections and maybe even family.

I glance around the Professor's office at the dozen people who are manning phones and staring at screens. They have all answered the call again – leaving work or taking time off. It almost feels like a proper incident room, full of energy and expectation.

Roger is talking to the harbour master at Ostend. There were six adults on board the motor launch, including Aleksei, but no sign of a child. The launch is now moored at the Royal Yacht Club, the largest marina in Ostend, in the heart of the city. We have a list of names for the crew. Margaret and Jean are ringing the local hotels. Others are calling hire car companies, travel agents and ticket offices for rail and ferry services. Unfortunately, the possibilities appear endless.

Aleksei could already have disappeared into Europe.

Without a warrant or a court order, we can't access his bank accounts, post boxes or telephone records. There is no way of tracing regular overseas payments and I doubt if the money would lead us to Mickey. Aleksei is too clever for that. His fortune will be spread around the world in offshore tax havens like the Caymans, Bermuda and Gibraltar. Experts could spend the next twenty years following that paper trail.

I look at my watch. Every minute puts him further away.

Grabbing my coat, I give Joe a nod. 'Come on, let's go.'

'Where to?'

'We're going to look at a house.'

Contrary to popular belief, the most powerful man in the cut-flower industry doesn't possess a green finger or even a greenhouse. The gardens surrounding Aleksei's mansion are rather rustic and overgrown with cedar trees and an orchard.

The electronic gates are open and we pull directly into the driveway, gravel snapping under the tyres. The house looks closed up. Turrets of dark slate stand out solidly against the sky as though turning their backs on the city and choosing to gaze instead across Hampstead Heath.

Stepping out of the car, I try to take in the building, swivelling my head upwards through the floors.

'OK, we're not doing anything illegal, are we?' asks Joe.

'Not yet.'

'I'm serious.'

'So am I.'

Walking slowly around the house, I marvel at the security. There are bars on the windows, security lights and sensor alarms attached to the exterior walls. A large converted stable block is garage to a dozen cars covered by cloth sheets.

At the back of the house, I notice smoke rising from an incinerator. A gardener with a solid build and a moustache like a hula skirt above his top lip looks up as we approach. He's wearing a tweed coat and trousers tucked into wellingtons.

'Good afternoon.'

He takes off his cap. 'Good afternoon to you.'

'You work here?'

'I do, sir.'

'Where is everyone?'

'Gone. The place is up for sale. I'm just keeping the gardens tidy.'

I notice boxes of leaves and grass clippings.

'What's your name?'

'Harold.'

'Did you ever meet the owner, Mr Kuznet?'

'Oh, yes, sir. I used to clean his motors. He was very particular about what wax and polish I used, with no abrasives. He knows the difference between a wax and a polish – not many people do.'

'Was he a good boss?'

'Better'n most, I reckon.'

'A lot of people were scared of him.'

'Yeah, but I can't see why. You hear stories, don't you? 'Bout him killing his brother, burying bodies in the basement and doing them other terrible things. But I say it like I see it. He was always good to me.'

'Did you ever see a young girl around here?'

Harold scratches his chin. 'Can't say I remember any children. Good house for a kiddie – look at them grounds – my grandkids would love this place.'

Joe has wandered off, staring upwards at the eaves, as though looking for nesting pigeons. He drifts sideways and almost falls over a sprinkler head.

'What's wrong with your mate – he got the shakes?'

'Parkinson's.'

Harold nods. 'My uncle had that.'

He sweeps more leaves into a mound.

'If you're thinking of buying the place you missed the agent.

She was here earlier showing the police around. I thought you were another copper.'

'Not any more. Do you think we could have a look inside?'

'I'm not allowed.'

'But you have a key?'

'Yeah, well, I know where she keeps them.'

I take a tin of boiled sweets from my pocket and remove the lid, offering him one.

'Listen, Harold, I don't have much time. There's a little girl who we're trying to find. She went missing a long time ago. It's important I look inside. Nobody is going to know.'

'A little girl, you say.'

'Yes.'

He contemplates this for a moment while sucking on a boiled sweet. Having made a decision, he puts down the rake and starts walking up the gentle slope towards the house. The ground levels out on a boggy croquet lawn in front of the conservatory. Joe catches up with us, trying not to wet his shoes.

The side door of the house opens into a small entrance hall with a stone floor and room to hang coats and deposit boots and umbrellas. The laundry must be close by. I can smell detergent and spray starch.

Harold unlocks the next door and we emerge into a large kitchen, with a central bench and brushed-steel appliances. It opens out through an arch into the conservatory, where the breakfast table could seat a dozen people.

Joe has wandered away from us again. This time he's peering beneath chairs and the table, following the edge of the skirting boards. 'Have you noticed anything unusual about this place?' he asks.

'Like what?'

'There are no telephone lines. The house isn't even hooked up.'

'Maybe they're underground.'

'Yes, that's what I thought, but I can't even see sockets in the walls.'

I turn to Harold. 'Are there any telephones?'

He grins. 'He's sharp, your mate. Mr Kuznet didn't believe in normal phones. I don't think he trusted 'em. We all got one of these.' Reaching into his jacket he pulls out a mobile.

'Everyone?'

'Yep. The cook, the driver, the cleaners, even me – s'pose I'll have to give mine back now.'

'How long have you had this one?'

'Not long. He made us swap numbers all the time. I never had the same number more than a month before he changed it.'

Aleksei was obviously paranoid about his telephones being tapped or monitored. He must have leased hundreds of mobile phones, doling them out to his employees at work and at home, rotating them, swapping his own number among them, making it almost impossible for anybody to keep track of his calls or fix on a particular phone number and trace it back to him. The list of numbers must read like lottery results – all put through the one account.

My mind clings to this idea as if for some reason I know it's important. They say elephants never forget. They remember watering holes hundreds of miles away that they haven't visited in twenty years. My memory is a bit like that. It throws away some things like people's birthdays, anniversaries and song lyrics, but give me eighty witness statements and I can remember every detail.

Here's what I remember now. Aleksei had a phone stolen. He told me about it when we were outside Wormwood Scrubs. It was a new model. He loves his gadgets.

Turning suddenly, I head for the door, leaving Joe scrambling to keep up. He chases me across the gravel trying to hear what I'm saying on the phone.

'New Boy' Dave answers but I don't give him a chance to

speak. 'Aleksei had a phone stolen a few months ago. He said he reported it to the police so there should be a record.'

I pause. Dave is still on the line. I can hear him tapping at a keyboard. The only other sound I hear is the soft stirring of every wet thing inside me.

Pacing across the driveway I wander along a path of crushed marble that circles the rose garden. At the far end, beyond an arbour, is a sandstone column supporting a sundial. It has a small plaque at the base. The inscription reads, 'Families Are Forever'.

Dave comes back to me. 'He reported a phone stolen on 28 August.'

'OK, listen carefully. You need to pull up the phone records for *that* number. Look for any international calls made on 14 August. It's important!'

'Why?'

Dave doesn't have children. He doesn't understand. 'Because a parent never forgets a birthday.'

39

Birch and elm trees are etched on the ridges like charcoal drawings and the clouds are white breath against a blue sky. The black Gallant rattles and bumps over the pitted tarmac, sliding through patches of black ice in the shadows.

Our driver wrestles with the wheel, seemingly oblivious to the deep ditches on either side of the road. Two identical black Gallants are following us, being sprayed with mud.

The surrounding marshland has iced over at the edges, forming a fragile layer that creeps towards the centre of pools and ponds. A refinery with a flaming orange tower reflects from the oily surface.

On one side of the road, separated by a ditch, is a railway track. A clutch of wooden shacks huddle alongside it, more like woodpiles than dwellings. Icicles hang from wet gutters and mounds of dirty snow are piled next to the walls. The only signs of life are thin wisps of smoke from the chimneys and the emaciated dogs picking through the rubbish bins.

The metalled road ends suddenly and we plunge into a monochrome forest on a track that snakes between the trees. There are tyre marks in the mud. One set. There are no return tracks and no roads other than this one. Aleksei's car is some-where up ahead.

Rachel has barely said a word since we arrived in Moscow. Sitting beside me in the back seat, her hands are at her sides as though bracing herself for the potholes.

Our driver looks more like a military cadet than a policeman. What looks like mildew sprouts from his top lip and his cheekbones are so sharp they could have been carved with a scalpel. Beside him is Major Dmitri Menshikov, a senior investigator with the Moscow Police. The major met us at Domodedovo Airport and ever since has provided a running commentary as though we're here on a guided tour.

For the past twenty-four hours we have tracked Aleksei Kuznet across Western Europe. After reaching Ostend, he stayed overnight and then caught a train from Brussels to Berlin on Sunday. He then transferred on to an overnight train to Warsaw, crossing into Poland in the early hours of Monday morning.

That's where we almost lost him. If Aleksei had continued by rail the most direct route to Moscow was via Brest in Belarus and Minsk, but, according to border guards who stopped the train in Belarus, he wasn't on board. He might have bought a car in Warsaw, but Russian authorities make it difficult to bring vehicles into the country, forcing delays of up to two days. Aleksei couldn't afford to wait. His other options were either to take a bus or a different train, through Lithuania and Latvia.

'New Boy' Dave came through for me. He found the mobile phone records for the stolen handset. Aleksei made dozens of international calls that month but on 14 August – Mickey's birthday – he telephoned a dacha south-west of Moscow and talked for over an hour.

Dmitri turns in his seat. 'And you have no idea who is living in this house?' He speaks English with an American accent.

'Nothing firm.'

'Are you even sure this girl is in Russia?'

'No.'

'So this is a theory.' He nods apologetically to Rachel.

Turning back to the track, he holds on to his hat as we hit another bump. The shadows are impenetrable spaces between the trees.

'And you think you will recognise this girl if she is your daughter?'

Rachel nods.

'After more than three years! Children forget. Maybe she is happy here. Maybe you should leave her alone.'

The forest relents for a moment, opening out into a clearing dotted with prefabricated houses, rusting cars and power cables slung from poles. Crows lift off from the ground like scraps of ash swirling from a fire.

Soon the trees blur the side of the track again and the car slides in and out of the ruts. Crossing a narrow bridge over a murky tributary, we come to an open gate across the road. A lake emerges on our left, the dark water broken by a makeshift pier that leans at an angle. Tied along each side there are inner tubes, marooned in thickening ice.

Overnight snow has settled on the newly formed crust, so thin I can see the darkness of the lake beneath it, thick like blood. A shiver runs through me and I imagine Luke's face, pressing up against the ice from below.

The house, screened by ash trees, emerges at the end of a driveway paved with loose gravel. Most of the windows are shuttered and outdoor tables and chairs rest upside down on a paved area within a rose garden.

The driveway runs out at a large rectangular courtyard. A silver Mercedes, streaked with mud, is parked near the doors to a stable. The driver's door is open and Aleksei is sitting on the ground, propped against the wheel. A fine rain is falling, collecting on the shoulders of his overcoat and clinging to his hair. His face is completely white except for a neat black hole in his forehead. He looks surprised, as though he slipped on the ice and is gathering his thoughts before he gets up again.

The black Gallants pull up on the far side of the courtyard. The doors open and guns are pointed across hoods or bonnets or whatever the Russians call them.

A man steps from the door of the house carrying a rifle in the crook of his arm. He is younger than Aleksei but has the same narrow nose and high forehead. His heavy trousers are tucked into lace-up boots and a knife hangs from a sheath on his belt.

Stepping out from behind the car, I walk towards him. He raises the rifle and rests it across his shoulder like a boy soldier.

'Hello, Sacha.'

He nods and doesn't answer. Glancing at Aleksei he shows a flicker of remorse in the lowering of his eyelids.

'Everyone thinks you're dead.'

'The old Sacha *is* dead. You von't find him here.'

He has lost almost all trace of his English accent. Unlike Aleksei, Sacha didn't ever try to hide his Russian accent or his roots.

Rachel steps out of the car. She hasn't taken her eyes off Aleksei. It is as if she imagines he is going to wipe the blood from his forehead and stand up, having rested long enough.

The rain has turned to sleet.

'You want to tell me what happened?'

He glances at his boots. 'Things have gone too far. He should never have come. He took her away from one home and now he wanted to take her away again. He has caused enough trouble.'

A woman appears in the doorway behind him. A young girl is pressed against her.

'This is my wife Elena,' says Sacha.

Her arm is wrapped around the girl's shoulders, shielding her from the sight of Aleksei's body.

'We have taken good care of her. She has never wanted for

anything.' Sacha searches for the words. 'She has been like a daughter . . .'

Rachel's hand flutters to her mouth as if trying to stop her breath escaping. She moves forwards, past my shoulder, crossing the distance between them.

Mickey is wearing jodhpurs and a riding jacket. Her hair is plaited and rests across her shoulder. Elena has an identical plait.

Edging closer, Rachel drops to her knees. The toes of her boots barely move the frozen gravel.

Mickey says something to Elena in Russian.

'English now,' says Sacha. 'You're going home.'

'But this is home.'

He smiles at her gently. 'Not any more. You are an English girl.'

'No!' She shakes her head angrily, beginning to cry.

'Listen to me.' Sacha rests the rifle against the wall of the house and crouches beside her. 'Don't cry. I have taught you to be strong. Remember when we went ice fishing last winter? How cold it was? You never once complained. *Nyet.*'

She throws her arms around him, sobbing into his neck.

Rachel has watched with a mixture of trepidation and expectation. She takes a deep breath. 'I've missed you, Mickey.'

Mickey lifts her face and smears a tear across her cheek with the palm of her hand.

'I've been waiting for you a long time. I stayed in the one place – hoping I might find you. I still have your room and all your toys.'

'I can ride a horse now,' announces Mickey.

'Really!'

'And I can ice-skate. I'm not scared of going outside any more.'

'I can see that. You've grown so tall. I bet you can reach the top cupboard in the kitchen, near the window.'

'Where you keep the treats.'

'You remember.' Rachel's eyes are shining. She holds out her fingers. Mickey looks at her tentatively and stretches out her own hand. Rachel draws her close and breathes in the smell of her hair.

'I'm OK now,' says Mickey. 'You don't have to cry.'

'I know.'

Rachel looks up at me and then at Sacha, who thumps his chest trying to clear his throat. The young Russian policemen have gathered around Aleksei's body, running fingers over the collar of his handmade shirt and feeling the softness of his cashmere overcoat. Dmitri has unclipped the wristwatch and compares it to his own.

Meanwhile, the snow whispers down, swirling in eddies and whirlpools, turning shades of grey into black and white.

Another country. Another mother and child.

Daj is in a wheelchair with me alongside, enduring one of those long silences that other people find awkward. She is wrapped in a white shawl that she holds together with her curling hands as she stares motionless out of the window like an ancient malevolent bird of prey.

Behind us a flower-arranging class is setting up on the tables. Blue rinses and grey heads hum, coo and twitter to each other, as they sort through greenery and blooms of different colours.

I show Daj the front page of a newspaper. The photograph is of Mickey and Rachel, embracing for the cameras in the arrivals hall at Heathrow Airport. You can just see me in the background, pushing the luggage trolley. Perched on the top suitcase is a hand-painted babushka doll.

Joe is in the photograph too. Standing next to him is Ali, leaning on his shoulder for support. She's holding a poster saying, 'Welcome home, Mickey!'

'Remember that missing girl, Daj – the one I tried to find all those years ago? Well, I found her. I brought her home.'

For a brief moment Daj looks at me proudly, curling her long fingers through mine. Then I realise that she doesn't understand. Her mind is answering a different statement.

'Make sure Luke doesn't go outside without his scarf.'

'OK.'

'And if he rides his bike make sure he tucks his trouser bottoms into his socks so he doesn't get grease on them.'

I nod. She lets go of my hand and brushes a non-existent crumb from her lap.

From now on I will visit her more often – not just at weekends but in the evening too. I know that most of the time she forgets I am here. She labours to remember but it's beyond her powers and fading strength.

Villawood Lodge is expensive and most of my savings are gone. For the briefest of moments I contemplated keeping a handful of the diamonds or perhaps giving some of them to Ali as compensation for what she's been through. She wouldn't have taken them, of course, and I can understand why. They're covered in blood.

Harold, the gardener at Aleksei's house in Hampstead, found the stones and gratefully accepted a reward. He was even photographed by the newspapers, leaning on a sundial and pointing to where he found the four velvet bags.

Daj turns her head and listens. Someone is playing the piano in the music room. Outside an exercise class power walks through the garden, a platoon of swinging arms and swaying buttocks. The leader lifts her knees and glances over her shoulder to make sure she hasn't left any stragglers behind.

'I can see all the lost children,' Daj whispers. 'You have to find them.'

'I can't bring them all back.'

'You haven't tried.'

She is looking at me now – recognising me. I want to hold on to the moment because I know it won't last. Something will stir the breeze and her mind will scatter like dandelion seeds.

I am not a believer in fate or destiny or karma. I don't think everything happens for a reason and that luck evens itself out over a lifetime. The law and order of the universe is breathtaking – the rising and setting of the sun, the seasons, the positioning of the stars. Without such certainties the heavens will fall on our heads. Society has laws too. My job was always to keep them. I know that's not much of a philosophy of life but so far it has been enough for me.

Kissing Daj on the forehead, I take my coat and walk down the hard smooth corridor towards the entrance of Villawood Lodge. Reaching into my pocket I take out my mobile and flip it open. Committed to memory I have the numbers for Claire and Michael. Some things you never forget.

The phone feels warm from my body as I punch the buttons and listen to the ringing. There have been many lost children in my life. I may not be able to bring them all back but I have to try.

BOMBPROOF

This one is for my dad

A Very Bad Day

Some days are diamonds. Some days are stones. John Denver used to sing that before he crashed a plane into Monterey Bay. It wasn't a diamond day for him.

Sami Macbeth's day has been nothing but stones. Emerging from Oxford Circus Underground, he blinks into the sunlight and coughs so hard it feels as if his sphincter is coming up through his lungs looking for clean air. His clothes are torn and bloody. His face streaked with sweat. His skin coated in dust.

Sami ducks beneath a makeshift barricade of crime-scene tape hanging from plastic bollards. People step aside and stare at him like he's some sort of ghost.

Six and a half pounds of TATP – the Mother of Satan – just blew a gaping hole in a packed carriage on the Central Line, peeling off the roof like a giant opening a big can of peaches.

It was horrible down there. Mayhem. One moment

Sami was standing near the train doors and the next he was lying on his back, flapping his arms and legs like an upturned beetle. Papers were blown through the air, glass showered down on him and the train shuddered to a halt. Things went quiet for a moment and completely dark. Then the screaming started.

People were hurt. Dying. God knows how many. Who was sitting in the other carriage next to Dessie? A guy in a Jesus T-shirt with his eyes closed, doing the nodding dog. Next to him was a suit with a briefcase. There was also a girl standing near the doors, wearing a short jacket. She had white headphones trailing from under her long hair.

Sami looks up and down Oxford Street. Traffic is at a standstill. Buses, vans, cars and cabs – nothing is moving. Someone hands him a bottle of water. He pours it over his head. Soot runs into his mouth and crunches between his teeth.

Crossing the road between two trucks, he forgets to lift his feet and trips over the gutter. A driver calls out. Sami doesn't answer. He turns down Argyll Street and crosses Great Marlborough, stepping round pedestrians. Moving quickly.

People are staring at each other. Shocked. Clueless. Sami hears snippets of their conversation: '. . . terrorists . . .' '. . . a bomb . . .' '. . . underground . . .'

They're frightened. Sami is frightened. Dessie just blew himself to Kingdom fucking Come. He'll need a very short coffin – Y-shaped to fit his legs and his bollocks.

The rucksack slaps against Sami's back. He should ditch it and run. Take his chances. But what would Murphy do to Nadia?

It's like the platform announcer said: 'Please keep your bags with you at all times and report any unattended items or suspicious behaviour to a member of staff.'

Sami should call Murphy. Explain. What would he say? 'Hey, Mr Murphy, a funny thing happened on the way home. We accidentally blew up a train and Dessie lost his head and a little bit more . . .'

Sami doesn't have a mobile. Dessie wouldn't let him carry one. Now he notices a guy sending a text message. He's unshaven, wearing Levi's, slung slow, showing his arse-crack.

Sami asks if he can borrow the phone. The guy stares at him. 'Were you down there, man? Respect.' He hands Sami the phone. 'Take it. I can't get a signal.'

Sami punches in a number. Nothing happens.

'Too many people trying to make calls,' says the arse-crack guy. 'The network is overloaded.'

Sami hands him back the phone and keeps walking, crossing at the next intersection. He notices a black cab. Opens the door. Slips onto the back seat. Dumps the rucksack on the floor between his knees.

'You're joking, aren't you, mate?' says the driver. He motions to the road ahead. 'I haven't moved in forty fuckin' minutes.'

Sami catches sight of himself in the rear mirror. His

3

face is caked in dark soot except for two streaks of white, one on the tip of his nose and the other a line of perspiration running over his cheekbone and down his neck. It could be war paint. He's been into battle.

The driver is listening to the radio.

'Bomb went off,' he explains. 'There could be more of them.'

'More what?'

'Suicide bombers.' The driver looks at him. 'You must have been down there. You look like Al fuckin' Jolson.'

'Who's he?'

'You never heard of Al fuckin' Jolson?'

'No.'

'He was a white guy used to black up his face and sing like a nigger.'

'Why?'

'Fuck knows.'

The driver has his door propped open. He lights a cigarette and the roll of smoke seems to evaporate on the breeze.

'You got a phone?' asks Sami.

'Yeah.'

'Can I borrow it?'

'Won't do you any good. They shut down the network, or the whole thing has crashed. Every man and his dog is trying to call home.'

'Why would they shut down the network?'

'Stop them setting off any more bombs. That's how

4

the ragheads do it – use mobile phones. Call the number and boom. Makes no sense to me. Live and let live, I say. We should make a deal with the terrorists – we won't invade their fucked-up countries if they stop blowing us up.'

'Maybe it wasn't terrorists,' suggests Sami.

'Of course it was fuckin' terrorists,' replies the driver. 'You're not bleeding, are you? I don't want friggin' blood on the seats.'

'I don't think so.'

'You're covered in that black shit. Maybe you should just get out.'

'Couldn't I just sit here?'

'Does this cab look like a fuckin' backpacker's?'

Sami gets out. Swings the rucksack over one shoulder. Drops his head and keeps moving.

Turning out of Rupert Street into Shaftesbury Avenue, he almost runs into a big black rozzer standing on the corner, directing traffic. Really big, two-fifty pounds at least, made even larger by his vest, which is bristling with Old Bill gadgets.

Sami apologises. The rozzer tells him to slow down and watch where he's going. Then he clocks Sami's clothes and the rucksack.

'What you carrying, lad?'

'Nothing.'

'Looks pretty heavy to be nothing.'

'Dirty laundry.'

5

'Show me.'

'It's locked.'

'You always lock up your dirty laundry?'

'There's loads of perverts about,' says Sami. 'You can't be too careful.'

The rozzer is already reaching for the radio on his arm. He tells Sami to put the rucksack down and slowly step back.

Sami's insides are betraying him now. His hair is full of broken glass. His clothes are covered in shit. He doesn't need this. Not today. Not after what he's been through. At that moment, somewhere in Sami's subconscious, a camera shutter blinks and he can see a dozen years in prison. The shutter blinks again and this time he pictures his sister Nadia lying on a bed, her dress plastered to her body, a crack whore for Tony Murphy.

The black constable grabs hold of Sami's arm. Instinct kicks in. Sami drops his head into the rozzer's stomach, hearing the wind whistle out of his mouth and nose. He's running now, dodging pedestrians, leaping over a dog on a lead, bursting through a queue, knocking over a man carrying a sandwich board.

The Underground is closed. The steps deserted. There are transport police at the stairs. Across the street, between ambulances and fire engines, there are proper police officers keeping the crowds back. Sightseers. Rubbernecks.

Sami crashes into an outdoor table, spilling a bottle of

wine and upending a woman in mid-meal. A waiter gives him a gobful. He keeps running. The bag over one shoulder. Slapping against his back. He should stop and tighten the straps, clip the belt around his waist, redistribute the weight, but he's too scared to stop.

Run. That's what every sense tells him to do. Just run. Get away. Find somewhere quiet. Hide the rucksack. Steal a moment to think.

He ducks into an alley, leans his back against a wall. The rucksack props him up. He listens. Sirens. Stuck in traffic. Trying to outrun them on foot is a loser's game. They'll corner him and wait for reinforcements.

Sami has to go off the radar. Disappear. He has money now – the stash from the safe. But first he has to get out of the West End . . . out of London.

There's a church across the square. He can hide inside. Stash the rucksack in a dark corner. Say a prayer. It's a good plan.

He comes out of the alley and finds three policemen in front of him. One of them has a gun and is crouching, holding it in two hands, like he knows how to use it.

'Don't move,' he yells. 'Put the bag down.'

Sami looks behind him . . . looks ahead. Holds his fist in the air; his thumb cocked. Empty, but they don't know that.

'I got a fucking bomb,' he yells, not recognising his own voice. 'Get back or I'll flatten this place.'

The rozzers melt away. Sami runs past them. The one

with the gun is lying on the ground, on his elbows, trying to get a shot. Sami keeps moving, stepping from side to side.

A bomb. He told them he had a bomb. What a prize fuck-up. What a joke! Sami isn't just unlucky; he's a walking jinx, a Jonah, a one-man wrecking crew. He's trouble with a capital 'T' and that rhymes with 'D' and that stands for dead.

Three days ago he walked out of prison and swore he'd never go back. Thirty-six hours ago he was shagging Kate Tierney, the woman of his wet dreams, in a suite at the Savoy thinking life was looking up. Now he's carrying a rucksack that could send him to prison for the rest of his life through the West End of London and he's turned himself into the most wanted man in Britain.

This is how it happened.

Three Days Ago

1

On his last morning in prison Sami Macbeth woke early, brushed his teeth, folded his blankets in a neat pile and sat on the bed, waiting.

He told himself that everything he did was for the last time. It was the last time he would piss into a steel bowl; the last time he was strip-searched, or deloused, or would wake to the dawn chorus of farting, belching, swearing and coughing.

Unable to keep still, he rests his feet on his bunk and counts down through a hundred push-ups, breathing through his nose. He stands and looks into a shaving mirror, no longer surprised at seeing himself with short hair, although it's growing out quickly. He's put on weight. Most of it is probably muscle but he's not like those cons who spend every waking moment pumping weights and flexing in front of the mirror. Who are they trying to impress?

With two short fast steps, Sami leaps at the wall, planting his foot at chest height and spinning in a complete somersault before landing on his feet. He does it again . . . and again.

A voice from below interrupts.

'Cut it out, cocksucker, I'm trying to sleep.'

'Almost done,' says Sami.

'Do it again and I'll kill your entire family.'

Sami's cell is on the first floor. No. 47. D-wing. It is eight feet wide and ten feet long, with brick walls and a cement floor. The only window, high on the wall, has tiny glass squares, some of them missing or broken. When he first arrived, in the middle of February, wind used to whistle through the gaps and the cell was freezing. Eventually, he filled the gaps with toilet paper, chewed into a pulp and wedged like putty into the holes.

He won't have to worry about another winter. By midday he's out of here. Not completely free, but as good as. Parole is a wonderful thing.

Sami yawns and rubs his eyes. He didn't sleep well. A fresh fish arrived yesterday and they put him in the cell next door. The kid tried to look relaxed and act tough but his eyes were big as saucers and he kept looking at people sideways like a bird in a cage.

The cons called him Baby Ray and he spent all night talking to Sami – too scared to go to sleep. First night jitters. Everyone has them. He told Sami he wouldn't be staying long, a short season, for one night only. He had a bail hearing the next day and his old man was going to pay whatever it took to get him out.

'Your old man must have deep pockets,' Sami said.

'I'm his only son.'

Baby Ray had a silver tongue, a sharp tongue, a tongue for every groove. He talked about the girls he'd shagged, the fights he'd won, the deals he'd done. Sami wasn't bothered. He was never going to sleep on his last night. He was going to count down the hours.

Baby Ray must have gone to breakfast or still be asleep. Sami's stomach rumbles. Normally, this is the only meal of the day he doesn't miss. You can't fuck up breakfast. You scramble eggs, you grill sausage, you heat up beans; nobody can fuck up breakfast.

Today he's not going. He doesn't want anything to go wrong. No shoving in the food queue, no fights, no bullying, nothing that could see him brought up on charges or see his parole revoked. Instead he sits on his bed, stares at the concrete wall and thinks of Nadia.

Nadia is his sister. She's nineteen. Beautiful.

They don't look like brother and sister. Nadia has long dark hair, brown eyes and golden brown skin. She's part Algerian. So is Sami, but he inherited his father's blue eyes and dirty blond hair.

Nadia was only seventeen when Sami was sent down. She was still at school. Now she's working as a secretary and going to college two nights a week. She's renting a flat and driving her own car – one of those Smart cars that look like it comes with a Happy Meal.

Sami hasn't seen her since Christmas. He only transferred back to the Scrubs a fortnight ago from Leicester nick, which was a long way for Nadia to travel, even with a rail warrant.

Someone drove her to see him. Waited outside. Her boyfriend. She wouldn't tell Sami his name. He had a sports car and drove with the top down, mussing up her hair.

When everyone has gone to breakfast, Sami leaves his cell to use his last phone card. He calls Nadia. No answer. It's been three days. She knows he's getting out today.

He goes back to his cell. Sits. Waits. Watches the clock.

Time has special meaning to him now. He has studied it closely and mastered the art of imagining it passing. For two years, eight months and twenty-three days he has become an expert in how much a minute takes out of an hour and how much an hour takes out of a day. How fast a fingernail grows. How long it takes for his fringe to cover his eyes.

He has missed two birthdays, two Christmases, two New Years and countless opportunities for meaningless one-night stands with single London girls who have a thing for guitar players. He'll have to play catch-up.

At 11.30 Mr Dean, the senior screw on D-wing delivers Sami's belongings in a pillowcase.

Mr Dean waits for him to get changed into a pair of jeans, a shirt, a leather bomber jacket and trainers. Sami has to hand back his prison kit which Mr Dean checks off on a list. Afterwards he walks in front of the warder to the reception centre, carrying his personal effects in his arms. They don't consist of much: a wristwatch, a transistor radio, three photographs – two of Nadia – a bundle of letters, a mobile phone with a flat battery and a plastic bag containing thirty-two pounds and seventy-five pence. Sami has to count the money and sign for it in three places.

As he walks along the landing and down the metal stairs, some of the other cons are calling out to him.

'Hey, Sparkles, when you get out get yourself laid for me.'

'Get shit-faced,' someone else yells.

At three minutes past noon, Sami walks out of the small, hinged door in the much larger gates of Wormwood Scrubs Prison. It's been raining, but the shower has passed. Puddles fill the depressions, reflecting blue sky. Bluer now he's outside. He raises his face and blinks at the sky. Takes a deep breath. He knows it's a cliché about freedom smelling sweeter, but it's a cliché for a reason.

He keeps walking across the cobblestones, away from the gates. There's no sign of Nadia. She could be running late. London traffic. There's a car parked opposite in a bus zone, a big black four-wheel drive Lexus with the darkest legal tint.

As Sami walks past a window glides down.

'Are you Sami Macbeth?' asks a squeaky voice coming

from a head so round and smooth it looks like it should be bobbing on the end of a string. Maybe that explains his voice, thinks Sami.

There are three other guys in the car all wearing dark suits like they're auditioning for a Guy Ritchie film. They're not friends of Nadia's and they're not from the local mini-cab firm.

'Are you fucking deaf?' asks the guy with the balloon-shaped head.

Sami scratches his cheek. Tries to stay calm. 'Why do you want Macbeth?'

'You him or not?'

'No, mate,' says Sami, swinging his bag over his shoulder. 'Macbeth kicked off at breakfast this morning. Got into a row with some bloke and threw a mug of tea in his face. They're keeping him in.'

'For how long?'

Sami motions over his shoulder. 'Knock on the door. Maybe they'll tell you.'

Then he gives a little skip as he walks away, telling himself not to look back. What do these guys want with him? Where's Nadia?

Down the street he finds a bus stop. Sits down. Waits some more.

A bus pulls up. The poster on the side shows a woman in a bikini lying on a pool chair. Golden skin. Clear eyes. Sami is so busy looking at the girl he forgets to get on the bus. The doors close. The bus pulls away.

He waits. Another bus comes. The driver doesn't look at him.

'Where you going?'

'Station.'

'Which one?'

'Nearest.'

'Two quid.'

Sami takes a window seat. Looks at the playing fields. Nadia must have had to work. She'll have left a note at the flat. They'll celebrate later. Order a curry. Watch a DVD.

Ever since their mum died, Sami and Nadia have looked after each other. And even before then, he'd kept Nadia out of harm's way when any of their father's lecherous friends took a liking to her.

She wanted to leave school at sixteen. Sami made her stay. He did courier jobs, drove a van. At night he played gigs. He wasn't cock deep in cash but he had enough to keep the wolf from the door.

Sami had often wondered what that saying meant. What sort of wolf – the fairytale kind, like in Little Red Riding Hood or the Three Little Pigs, or the human kind?

It wasn't always happy families. Sami and Nadia's fights were legendary. That's the thing about Nadia. She's not some sort of innocent butter-wouldn't-melt-in-her-mouth angel. She's had her moments. Skipping school. Underage drinking. Sneaking into nightclubs when she was only fifteen.

Nadia also had some black days. It was a family disease. A school counsellor wanted to send her to a psycho-whatsit, but Sami wouldn't let them. He also had to fight Social over letting her live with him. He went to court. Won. Didn't rub it in. You don't give them any excuses.

For a long time Nadia had no idea she was beautiful. Blokes would have licked shit off a stick for her, but she didn't care. After a while she began to realise.

She had a few modelling shots taken when she was sixteen, glossy professional ones, soft focus around the edges. She touted her portfolio around some of the modelling agencies but they said she didn't have the look they were after, you know, the anorexic don't-let-me-near-the-fridge heroin chic look.

She did have something going for her. The photographers knew it. One of the agents knew it. Nadia had that vulnerable, big eyes, full lips, just-been-shagged look that directors love. Porn directors.

Sweet but not so innocent Nadia.

Sami saved her from the wolves.

That's what big brothers are for.

2

Vincent Ruiz's worst dream has always included an orange sledge and an ice-covered pond with a hole at its centre. A child is pulled from within, blue lips, blue skin. He is to blame.

His second worst dream features a man called Ray Garza, who is like the ghost of Christmas past showing Ruiz his past failings. Garza's face has sharp features, bone beneath skin, with a scar across his neck where someone once tried to slice open his throat but didn't cut deep enough. Hopefully they were more successful at cutting their own throat because you'd want to die quickly if you crossed Ray Garza.

Garza is now a pillar of society, a member of the establishment, rich beyond counting. He is invited to dine at Downing Street, given gongs by Her Maj and gets mentioned in newspaper diaries as a philanthropist and patron of the arts.

Yet every time Ruiz sees a photograph of him at some charity function, or film premiere, he remembers Jane

Lanfranchi. It was twenty-two years ago. She was only sixteen. A wannabe beauty queen.

Garza was going to make her a page-three sizzler, the next Sam Fox. That's before he sodomized her and chewed her cheek open to the bone.

Such a beautiful face, destroyed. Such a sweet girl, traumatised. Ruiz promised Jane that he'd protect her. He promised that if she were brave enough to take the stand and tell the truth, he'd put Garza in prison. It was a promise he couldn't keep.

Jane Lanfranchi committed suicide two days before the trial, unable to look at her face in the mirror. The charges were dismissed. Garza went free. He smiled at Ruiz on the steps of the court. His crooked mouth lined up when he grinned and his acne-scarred cheeks looked like lunar craters.

Ruiz has always been a pragmatist. There are bad people in the world – rapists, murderers, psychopaths – many of them nameless, faceless men, who are never caught. The difference this time was that he knew Ray Garza's name, knew where he lived, knew what he'd done, but could never prove it.

One of Ruiz's mates, a psychologist called Joe O'Loughlin, once told him that some dreams solve problems while others reflect our emotions. Carl Jung believed that 'big dreams' were so powerful they helped shape our lives.

Ruiz thought this was bollocks, but didn't say so.

History showed that whenever he disagreed with Joe O'Loughlin, he ended up looking stupid. Ruiz knows why he had the dream. It happens every year. Just before his birthday. He's sixty-two today. In a couple of hours the first post will arrive. There'll be a birthday card from his son Michael and daughter Claire. Twins. His ex-wife Miranda will send him something funny about him being only as old as the woman he's feeling.

There'll be another card, one from Ray Garza. He sends one every year – a goading, vindictive, poisonous reminder of Jane Lanfranchi, of broken promises, of failure.

Ruiz looks at the clock beside his bed. It's gone six. He doesn't feel rested or rejuvenated. One of the annoying legacies of old age is the copious passing of water and learning the odours of various vegetables and beverages.

Pain is the other legacy, a permanent ache in his left leg, which is shorter than his right and heavily scarred. A bullet did the damage. High velocity. Hollow pointed. Painkillers were harder to recover from. Even now, as he lies in bed, it feels as though ants are eating away at his scarred flesh.

The pain always wakes him slowly. He has to lie very still, feeling his heart racing and sweat pooling in his navel. The hangover is entirely expected and nothing to do with pain management. Ruiz drank half a bottle of Scotch last night and almost fell asleep on the sofa, too cold to get comfortable and too drunk to go to bed.

Now it's morning. His birthday. He wants it to be over.

Ruiz gets out of bed at seven. Runs a cold tap in the bathroom. Fills his cupped hands. Buries his face in the water. He dresses slowly, methodically, as though working to a plan. Socks, trousers, shirt, shoes. There is order in his life. He might be retired but he has his routines. He goes downstairs and puts on a pot of coffee.

Sixty-two. When you reach such an age, you don't so much stop counting birthdays as *lose* count of them. Does that make him old or is he still middle-aged?

Most people can remember their childhoods with great clarity and later in life entire decades disappear into the ether. Ruiz is different. For him there has never been such a thing as forgetting. Nothing is hazy or vague or frayed at the edges. He hoards memories like a miser counts gold – names, dates, places, witnesses, suspects and victims.

He doesn't see things photographically. Instead he makes connections, spinning them together like a spider weaving a web, threading one strand into the next. That's why he can reach back and pluck details of criminal cases from five, ten, fifteen years ago and remember them as if they happened only yesterday. He can conjure up crime scenes, recreate conversations and hear the same lies.

He looks out the window. It's raining. Water ripples across the Thames, which is slick with leaves and debris.

He has lived by the river for twenty-five years and it's still a mystery to him.

Maybe the post won't arrive if it's raining. The post-man will stay at the sorting office. Keep dry. In which case the card from Ray Garza will come tomorrow. He'll have another night of waiting. Dreaming.

Darcy comes downstairs when the coffee is done. She must be able to smell it. She's dressed for college, in dance trousers, trainers, a sweater and sleeveless ski jacket.

'Happy birthday, old man.'

'Piss off.'

'Don't you like birthdays?'

'I don't like teenagers.'

'But we're the future.'

'God help us.'

Darcy isn't his daughter or his granddaughter. She's a lodger. It's a long story. Her mother is dead and her father has known her for less time than Ruiz. She's eighteen and studying at the Royal Ballet School.

She sits on a chair, crosses her legs and holds her coffee with both hands on the mug. She can bend like a reed and move without making a sound.

'I'm going to bake you a cake,' she announces.

'You don't have to do that.'

'What sort do you want? Do you like chocolate? Everyone likes chocolate. How old are you?'

'Sixty-two.'

'That's old.'

23

'You don't count the years, you count the mileage.'

'What does that mean?'

'It doesn't matter.'

She has found a piece of fruit. Breakfast. There's nothing of her.

'Are you ever going to get married again?' she asks.

'Never.'

'Why not?'

'It's an expensive way to get my laundry done.'

Darcy doesn't find him funny.

'How many times have you been married?'

'Haven't you got classes to go to, stretches to do, pirouettes?'

'You're embarrassed?'

'No.'

'Well, tell me. I'm interested.'

'My first wife died of cancer and my second wife left me for an Argentine polo player.'

'There were more?'

'My third wife doesn't seem to remember that we're divorced.'

'You mean she's a friend with benefits.'

'A what?'

'A friend who lets you sleep with her.'

'Christ! How old are you?'

Darcy doesn't answer. She sips her coffee. Ruiz starts thinking about sleeping with Miranda. It's a nice idea. She's still a fine looking woman and if memory serves they used to tear up the sheets. The sex was so good even the neighbours had a cigarette afterwards.

They divorced five years ago but stay in touch. And the intervening period hasn't been benefit-free. They had a steamy weekend in Scotland when one of her nephews got married, and had another brief fling when Ruiz got stabbed in Amsterdam and Miranda looked after him for a couple of days.

Friends with benefits – the idea could grow on him.

'What are you smiling about?' asks Darcy.

'Nothing.'

A metal clang echoes from the front hall. The post. Ruiz feels hollow inside. Darcy springs up and fetches the envelopes, counting out the birthday cards and putting them on the table.

'Aren't you going to open them?'

'Later.'

'Oh, come on.'

Michael has sent a postcard from Bermuda. He's sailing charter yachts. Claire's card has a portrait of a bulldog, all jowls and slobber. She's going to call and arrange lunch. She has a boyfriend now – a barrister, who knows all the scurrilous gossip and rumour. Ruiz suspects he's a Tory.

Miranda's card has a cartoon of a naked woman wearing an astronaut's helmet. The pay-off line is: 'Very funny, Scotty, now beam down my clothes.'

There is another envelope. Square. White.

'This one now,' says Darcy, handing it to him.

Ruiz slides his thumb under the flap. Tears it open. The front has a photograph of a kitten playing with a ball of wool.

'Many happy returns,' it says. Ray Garza has signed his initials and written a postscript.

She's still the best fuck I ever had.

Ruiz closes the card. His hands are shaking.

'Who is it from?' asks Darcy.

'Moriarty.'

3

Sami Macbeth got sent down for the Hampstead jewellery robbery, which isn't the whole story. He got sent down because a mate with a van ran across six lanes of motorway and got cleaned up by a German lorry carrying eighteen tons of pig iron.

Andy Palmer wasn't even a proper mate. He was a man with a van who used to take their gear to gigs; the amps, leads, mikes and drums. He was a roadie. A muppet. A hanger-on. Andy couldn't play an instrument, he could barely drive, but he loved bands and he loved live music.

This particular Saturday afternoon he and Sami were heading to Oxford to set up for a gig. They stopped at a motorway service area because Andy had turned one on the night before and needed one of those high-energy caffeine drinks and Tic Tacs. Sami waited in the van, listening to Nirvana and doing his Kurt Cobain impersonation.

A police car pulled up alongside the van. One of the officers nodded to Sami. Sami's eyes were closed, but his head was rocking back and forth.

Just then Andy came out of the automatic doors, sucking on a can of Red Bull. He spied the police car next to the van and took off, legging it past the pumps and sliding down the embankment. He sprinted across three lanes of westbound motorway and barely broke stride as he hurtled the crash barrier.

By then the rozzers were chasing him but Andy didn't stop. He sidestepped a BMW, dodged a caravan, slid between a transit van and an Audi station wagon and just beat a dual rig with a soft top that swerved to avoid him.

The rozzers were still stuck on the central reserve, trying to make the traffic slow down. Andy thought he was away. Six lanes. He'd crossed them all. Sad fucker didn't bank on the motorway exit, which is why a German truck driver turned him into a speed bump six times over. Bump. Bump. Bump. Bump. Bump. Bump.

Sami watched it happen. Nirvana was still playing. The guitars were screaming just like the truck tyres.

What Sami didn't know was that Andy Palmer had a bit of extra kit in the van. Tucked into one of the amplifiers was a diamond the size of a quail's egg and a dozen emeralds, all of them linked together.

The necklace belonged to a rich widow in Hampstead whose hubby used to be a diamond dealer in Antwerp. She wasn't some doddery old dear who put baubles in a pillowcase. She had a state-of-the-art, dog's-bollocks safe, imported from America, with motion sensors and alarms.

It was fireproof, earthquake proof, bomb proof, but for some reason it wasn't Andy Palmer proof.

Sami found this hard to believe. The same Andy Palmer who couldn't find his arse with both hands, had broken into the most sophisticated safe in the world. It was beyond comprehension – a mystery for the ages.

Sami's lawyer could see the funny side of it. His client was sitting in a van playing air guitar when he got nicked for the biggest jewellery robbery of the decade. Meanwhile Andy Palmer – the world's most unlikely safebreaker – became a skid-mark on a motorway off-ramp.

The trial was a farce. The arresting officer testified that Sami had been pursued on foot for a quarter of a mile before being crash tackled and apprehended. The fat fucker must have weighed two-fifty pounds. He couldn't have run down a traffic cone.

The CPS offered Sami a deal. If he pleaded guilty to possession they'd drop the robbery charge. Sami's lawyer thought it was a good offer. Sami's lawyer had a villa in Tuscany and plans for the long weekend.

'You do believe I'm innocent, don't you?' Sami asked him.

'Mr Macbeth, I'd still believe in Santa Claus if he hadn't stopped leaving me presents.'

'Can't you plead it down?'

'What would you like – pissing in a phone box?'

'Can you do that?'

'I'm being sarcastic, Mr Macbeth. Take the deal.'

'I didn't steal anything.'

'Possessing stolen property is a serious offence.'

'I didn't possess the stuff. I didn't even know it was in the van.'

'Then it's another shining example of you being in the wrong place at the wrong time. Take the deal.'

The courtroom was Victorian, huge, high-ceilinged and panelled with wood. The wigged judge told Sami to stand. Then he started talking about how society had to be protected from miscreants like the accused.

He can't mean me, thought Sami.

Nadia was crying in the public gallery.

Five years. Sami felt numb. They led him downstairs, handcuffed to a policeman. Outside there was a coach waiting to take him to jail. He had a number. He was in the computer. He was part of the vast human cargo system, silent and unseen, shuffling men around Britain, from one prison to the next. First it was Wormwood Scrubs, then Parklea, then Leicester before going back to the Scrubs.

Sami was scared that first night. He knew all the stories about prison bullying and the gangs; the prison sisters, the bikers, the sadistic screws.

But a funny thing happened on the way to the exercise yard. Sami was minding his own business, trying not to make eye contact with anyone, when a big fucker approached and offered him a cigarette.

The guy called him 'Sparkles'. It became Sami's nickname.

Sami had a rep. The cons thought he was a jewel thief. Not just any jewel thief, but the man who had broken into the biggest, baddest safe in the world. He had peeled it like a banana, stripped it like an engine, opened it like a tin of sardines.

And that's how Sami managed nearly three years inside without getting any aggro or becoming someone's bitch. Other newbies were worried about lights out or bending over for the soap, but not Sami; he was treated as an equal by geezers who would normally have kicked his body around the yard for the fun of it.

In spite of his newfound reputation, Sami learned there was nothing fraternal about the criminal fraternity. The only thing that mattered was the fear you engendered or the respect you were given. Either you were a ruthless fucker or you had a skill.

Sami unwittingly, accidentally, fraudulently, had a skill. He was a cat burglar, a safe breaker, a master craftsman, one of the elite.

Even so, he made sure he played down this talent. He did his time as quiet as possible. Kept away from the sex cases and nonces. Didn't associate with any of the serious heavies or complete nutjobs. Ninety five per cent of all cons are complete morons with IQs that match their shoe sizes, which is why they're always getting caught.

Now Sami is a free man. He's going home. 'Sparkles' is

deader than Andy Palmer. And no matter what else happens in his life, he's never going back inside. You can bank on it.

A bus ride. Two trains. Even the Tube smells good after the Scrubs. Sami walks out of the Underground and looks for the familiar. Nothing much has changed about Brixton, as far as Sami can tell. It's still full of two-up two-down terraces, in narrow streets that are grim and grey and devoid of colour. The corner shops are bolted with steel shutters, padlocked and alarmed, with razor wire on the rooftops.

Middle-class mortgage slaves who couldn't afford Balham and Clapham have tarted up some streets, planting flower boxes and painting terraces in pastel colours so that local teenagers with spray cans have a better canvas.

Ton-of-Brix is not a place you fall in love with, it's a place you survive. That's what his father used to say, which is ironic since he's dead now.

When he gets to Nadia's flat, Sami checks his reflection in a neighbour's window, wishing he could have cut his hair. A woman answers when he knocks. She is midthirties with a pie-plate face. Sami looks past her, expecting to see Nadia.

'Who are you?'

'I live here,' she says. 'Who are you?'

Sami looks at the number on the door.

'Where's Nadia?'

'Who?'

'My sister.'

32

'How would I know?' She tries to close the door. Sami spots cardboard packing crates and bulging plastic bags in the hallway behind her. She's just moved in.

'The woman who was here – did she leave a forwarding address?'

'No.'

'Did she say where she was going?'

She tries to stop Sami looking past her.

'I had some stuff here,' he says. 'Clothes, CDs, a TV.'

'Place was empty.'

'I had a guitar.'

'Ain't seen no guitar.'

'A Gibson Fender.'

'Who's he?'

Sami can hear Oprah in the background. He pushes past the woman into the living room. She's not happy. Screaming. Hurling abuse. Says she's going to call the police, the landlord, the social . . .

'That's my TV,' says Sami.

'Prove it!'

'How do I do that?'

'I bought it off the landlord,' she says, defensively. 'It was confiscated. Unpaid rent.'

Sami looks at her hands, which are twisted with arthritis. He's on shaky ground. Two hours out of prison and he's already breached parole.

Nadia has lost the flat. She wouldn't move without telling him. She'd leave word.

4

Ruiz settles onto a tube from Baron's Court. He never drives into Central London these days – not since the congestion charge. He's not opposed to road tolls or traffic fines as long as someone else is paying them.

The train moves through tunnels that pop his ears, before emerging into the light and disappearing again.

Peak-hour is over. The men in suits are in their offices. Not all wear suits these days. Some wear jeans and chinos. What do they do, wonders Ruiz? Sit in front of screens. It seems a poor substitute for hunting and gathering.

There's no romance in office work. No thrill of the chase. Ruiz was at a rugby dinner a few weeks back, sitting at a table with fifteen men. Successful professionals. A newcomer among them was asked what he did for a living. He said he made concrete blocks.

The conversation petered out. Nobody knew what to say. Then Ruiz pointed out that this guy was the only person at the table who actually *made* something. The rest of them shuffled paper, traded futures, negotiated deals, added value and took their margins. They didn't build anything, or save anyone, or make a mark on the world other than on a balance sheet.

Ruiz felt guilty about being too critical. There was no romance in police work either. That's why he retired – jumped before he was pushed or became an exhibit in the Black Museum.

At Regent's Park he emerges from below ground and walks to Harley Street. Today is his annual medical. It normally falls on either side of his birthday, but this year the dates have aligned.

He sits in the waiting room. Picks up a magazine. It's one of those celebrity rags full of paparazzi photographs and 'at-home-with' specials where TV stars announce how happy they are together and you know they'll be divorced within six months.

Ruiz is about to toss it back onto the coffee table when he notices a shot of Ray Garza, smiling at the cameras from the red carpet at Covent Garden. He is hosting a charity performance by the National Opera in aid of spina bifida. There are more shots over the page. Garza is mingling with the great and the good. The cast. The artistic director. The Arts Minister. Celebrities.

The media nicknamed him 'the Chairman' years ago and the name has stuck. It's almost like Garza plays up to it, dressing in charcoal grey suits, bright ties, and never being photographed without a cigar in his fist, unlit.

Three years after Jane Lanfranchi died, Garza married a society girl with a double-barrelled surname whose father had inherited a pile in Wiltshire but had to sell it to the Government in lieu of death duties. Garza rescued the old man when the only thing he had left was a few hereditary peerages that he was trying to flog off to rich Americans. Garza took over one of the titles: the Earl of Ipswich. It must look impressive on a business card.

Garza wasn't always a wealthy man. He started out as a soldier – an officer, who specialised in logistics and transport. As such, he understood supply and demand and the importance of being able to move quickly.

A lot of legends have grown up around the Chairman. Not all of them are true – but what's not in dispute is how he made his first million. Garza helped liberate Kuwait in the first Gulf War and was on hand when the Iraqis were pushed back across the border.

The world saw smoking convoys of vehicles, charred wreckage of luxury cars that had been looted from Kuwait and bombed by Allied planes as they fled across the desert. But that was only some of the stuff. Hundreds of luxury cars were abandoned. Untouched. Mercedes, BMWs, Jaguars and Bentleys were left sitting in the desert, the keys still in them.

There was more. Convoys of trucks full of computers, washing machines, air conditioning units and Mont Blanc pens. The Iraqis looted everything that wasn't bolted down and the Kuwaitis didn't want the stuff back. Oil drilling

equipment, earthmovers, yachts, helicopters, private jets –
Garza found a way of shipping them out of Kuwait.

He finished the job the Iraqis started. He looted
Kuwait, stealing from rich oil sheiks, who were so relieved
to have their country back they didn't give a shit about a
few missing cars or boats or planes.

Nobody raised an eyebrow. Nobody turned a hair.
The only hint of scandal came when a UK Sunday
paper did an exposé about an armour-plated Mercedes,
specially built for the Kuwaiti Minister for Trade, which
somehow finished up under the hammer at a car auction
in Croydon.

For Ray Garza it was just the beginning. He left the
army and soon he was moving massive shipments of
hardware out of countries in the midst of war, famine or
caught up in Africa's perverse interpretation of 'democ-
racy'.

Questions were asked in Parliament. MI6 took an
interest. Nothing stuck. Whenever Garza looked shaky he
managed to walk away. Witnesses disappeared. Cast iron
cases crumbled. One Spanish middleman jumped off
Waterloo Bridge with bricks in his pockets. A junior
accountant changed his testimony, spent six months
inside and that same year bought a sixty foot yacht.

Meanwhile, Garza launched himself on society. He
transformed himself into a patron of the arts, a media
darling, the orchestrator of a thousand publicity stunts
involving pretty girls in short skirts.

Garza suddenly had a finger in every pie. They were La Maison pies. River Café Pies. Savoy Grill pies. They were the dog's bollocks and the bee's knees of pies. He was dining at the head table, supping with the great and the good and the morally bankrupt.

His chequered past, the question marks over his business dealings, nothing seemed to matter. Not even the distant scandal of a rape allegation and a troubled teenager who threw herself off a tower block in Hackney.

A receptionist interrupts. Ruiz looks up from the magazine. Dr Reines will see him now. He tosses the rag aside and stares at the newsprint on his fingers, wanting to wash it off.

The doctor asks him to sit on the examination table. Takes him through the normal checks. Blood pressure, cholesterol, finger up the bum . . . Having his prostate checked always reminds Ruiz of a joke about knowing you're in trouble if your doctor checks your prostate and has both his hands on your shoulders.

Doctor Reines is telling him horror stories about fat-choked arteries and how people his age are dropping like flies. Then comes the lecture about him exercising more: walking or swimming – six laps of a pool or two miles on foot.

He listens to Ruiz's heart. It's strong. A champion's heart. A thoroughbred. Everything else about his body is turning to shit, but his heart is going strong.

Dr Reines asks after Ruiz's mother.

'How is her Alzheimer's?'

'She has good days and bad.'

'Does she still think I'm Josef Mengele?'

'She thinks all doctors are Josef Mengele.'

Ruiz's mother, Daj, doesn't live in the present any more. Most of the time she's reliving the war, escaping from the Gestapo and SS, surviving the concentration camps.

Daj met Mengele once. He was standing on a ramp in dress uniform and polished black boots. He wore white cotton gloves and held a cane, directing a sea of exhausted and starving women and children either left or right.

A handsome man, Daj said. Cold. He looked like a gypsy with dark hair, dark eyes and tawny skin. 'Perhaps that's why he hated us so much,' she said. 'He was purging the world of the things he hated about himself.'

Ruiz leaves the doctor's surgery and takes a bus to Victoria, before walking along Vauxhall Bridge Road. He has another appointment, another annual check-up.

Every year on his birthday, he has a beer with an old mate from the Met, his former second-in-command at the Serious Crime Group, Colin 'Bones' McGee.

McGee was a rising star when Ruiz first met him – one of the university graduates they fast-tracked through training and nudged upstairs after the Flying Squad got disbanded. He topped his class at Hendon, made

Detective Sergeant at thirty and Detective Inspector at thirty-five. Then his wings fell off.

It was 2002 – a sting operation involving twelve million quids worth of cocaine found in a shipping container in Rotterdam. McGee took the decision to leave the container on board and let the ship sail for Felixstowe. He ran the surveillance operation.

Can you see what's coming? The drugs vanished. Not a trace. Maybe the haul got tossed into the North Sea. Maybe it was never on board. It was all supposition and it didn't wash with McGee's bosses. That's when he got the nickname Bones because his career was dead and buried.

Since then Bones has been treading water with the Specialist Crime Directorate, tracking assets and chasing paper trails. It's a dead end job because no serious player will ever hold assets in their own names. They hide behind shelf companies and dodgy corporations based in the Bahamas and the Caymans.

Ruiz doesn't particularly like Bones. Never has. He was always a little too ambitious. Too grasping. But when he left the job, Ruiz handed over his old files – including the Lanfranchi case. He asked Bones to keep an eye on it . . . just in case.

They meet at a pub on Vauxhall Bridge Road. Union Jacks hang from the rafters.

Bones is at a table drinking single malt. He's lost his boyish innocence, thinks Ruiz – a receding hairline will do it every time – but he still dresses sharply in grey trousers, Italian loafers and a jacket. His copper-coloured hair – dyed most likely – is combed straight back on his scalp.

'How's it hanging, Vincent?'

'I'm good, Colin.'

They swap small talk. Retirements. Promotions. Prostate cancer. There's twenty years between them – almost a generation – but the job doesn't change, only the rules.

Eventually the talk gets around to Ray Garza. It's been years since there was any news on the Lanfranchi case. At past meetings, Bones has made shit up to keep Ruiz happy and Ruiz knew it, but this year he has something fresh, something new, something hot off the press.

'Ray Garza's boy got busted two nights ago after a high speed pursuit. They found eight kilos of cocaine in the boot of his Porsche and a semi-automatic, which he waved around at the coppers. Took a shot.'

Ruiz ponders the information. Garza's son – Ray Jnr – how old is he now? Out of school. Nineteen. Twenty tops.

'It's a commercial quantity,' says Bones. 'The kid's going down.'

'Where is he now?'

'Spent last night in the Scrubs. He's in court today.'

Bones continues talking, spinning a story about the Specialist Crime Directorate offering Ray Jnr a deal if he turns on the old man. It's not going to happen, thinks Ruiz. Junior won't bite the hand that feeds him – not unless he has bigger ambitions. But it still warms his heart to think of Ray Garza losing sleep over his precious boy.

Ray Jnr wasn't even born when his father raped Jane Lanfranchi and chewed open her cheek. Ruiz always thought Garza should have had a daughter. That way he could have worried when she turned sixteen and went out at night. Wondered about where she was and whom she was with. Hopefully, he's worried sick now.

'What about the Lanfranchi case?' he asks.

Bones shrugs.

'Any similar rapes?'

'Nope.'

'Any missing women with links to Garza?'

'Can't you forget the fucking Lanfranchi case for once?' says Bones. 'It's old news. Ancient bloody history.'

Ruiz ignores him. 'Garza likes the wholesome girl-next-door types. Suburban princesses. He thinks they're hiding their true natures.'

Bones shakes his head. 'You're fucking obsessed. I'd get more sense talking to the wall.'

'And less whisky,' says Ruiz swallowing the last of his Guinness.

There's a moment of friction. Bones wants to tell him to fuck off, but something about Ruiz's silences has always unnerved him.

'I'm just giving my opinion, Vince. You don't have to

take it,' he mutters, speaking slowly like he's talking to a child. 'There's a bail hearing today. Police are going to oppose because Ray Jnr took a shot at a copper.'

'He'll walk.'

'Yeah. Maybe. But it's going cost Daddy big time.'

'Where's Garza now?'

'He flew in from Geneva this morning. Smart money says he's going to be in court. Media haven't got wind of this yet, but the storm's coming.'

Ruiz takes another sip of beer. Maybe today won't be such an anticlimax after all.

5

Sami has called Nadia's friends, her workmates, and talked to her old neighbours. Nobody has seen her. She hasn't been at work for three days. Didn't call in sick. Didn't hand in her notice.

Next Sami calls the local hospitals and drops in to Brixton police station to lodge a missing persons report.

The desk sergeant is a doughnut short of being fat and has a torn piece of tissue paper, encrusted with blood, stuck to his neck.

'How long has she been missing?' he asks.

'Since the weekend.'

'Did you fight with her?'

'No.'

'Who was the last person to see her?'

'I don't know.'

'What was she wearing?'

'I don't know.'

'Do you have realistic fears for her safety?'

'I don't know. Yeah. Maybe.'

The sergeant presses his right hand into his lower back and grimaces as if relieving himself of lower back pain. 'Are you sure you even have a sister?'

Sami has to fill in a form. Tick boxes. Old Bill isn't going to raise a sweat looking for Nadia. He needs another plan.

Uncle Harry will know where she is. He promised to keep an eye on Nadia when Sami got put away. He's not really Sami's uncle: more of a family friend from the days when Sami's old man was still alive and running a bookmaking operation out of an upstairs room in Harry's boozer.

Going even further back, Harry used to be a professional boxer, whose fighting nickname was 'Homicide' on account of him killing a guy in one of his early fights. Sami has never met anyone who'd seen one of Harry's fights, but in his heyday he fought at Crystal Palace on the same card as Henry Cooper.

The White Swan is tucked behind Waterloo Station not far from the Old Vic Theatre. Sami pushes open the pub door and peers into the gloom. There are punters inside who act as though someone has opened the lid of their coffin.

Same faces. Same smells.

'You been away?' one of them asks.

'Something like that,' says Sami.

'It's your shout.'

'I'll buy you a pint if you can remember my name.'

The drunk looks at him hard. Looks at his empty glass. 'Rumpelstiltskin.'

'Close.'

Harry Galanto turns the corner and lets out a bellow. 'My boy! My boy!'

He squeezes through a gap in the bar and throws his arms around Sami in a bear hug, a beer hug, a cross between the two.

Harry has gone up a few weight divisions since he hung up the gloves. His stomach is like a different person, but he refuses to wear trousers any bigger than a forty-four waist. This has the effect of squeezing everything upwards until his gut spills over his belt in a doughy tsunami.

Harry dusts off a stool. Goes back behind the bar. Pours Sami a pint. It's his first alcohol in two years. He upends the glass. It's good.

'Have you seen Nadia?' he asks.

Harry grimaces slightly. 'She dropped by Tuesday.'

It's not the whole story.

'She was supposed to do a shift,' says Harry. 'She's been working behind the bar a few nights.'

'Yeah, she told me. What happened?'

'I told her not to bother.'

'Why?'

Harry eyes him sorrowfully. 'I didn't like some of the clientele she was attracting.'

'Like who?'

'Toby Streak.'

Sami feels his face twitch. 'What was the Streak doing here?'

'Sniffing round Nadia like she was on heat.'

'They were together?'

Harry nods and pours another pint. The beer has reached Sami's bloodstream. He wants more. Needs it badly. Suddenly, he wants to be one of the boozed up shit-kickers in the bar, living the simple life, drunk by midday and a kebab at closing time. Instead he has to deal with the implications and possible consequences of Nadia being hooked up with Toby Streak.

Sami doesn't know Streak well but he's aware of his reputation. He's a pimp and a small-time coke dealer, but these are just sidelines. His main action is running a lover-boy scam out of nightclubs and bars, picking up girls and showing them a good time.

Flash car, flash clothes, just the right patter. He wines them and dines them; buys them baubles, takes them to stay at expensive hotels. He treats them like film stars or supermodels and then introduces them to the snorting stuff.

And once he's swept them off their pretty little size-seven feet, he says, 'Do you love me?' And they say, 'Yeah.' And he says, 'How much do you love me.' And they say, 'Completely.'

'Would you do anything for me?'

'Anything,' they say.

And that's when he opens the door and invites another man or another girl into the room.

They do it for Toby. They do it for the cocaine. And soon they do it for the camera. Girl on girl. Threesomes. Straight sex and then more.

'If you love me you'll do it,' he tells them. 'If you love me you'll have your nipples pierced. If you love me you'll have a boob job. If you love me you'll have a "tramp stamp" tattooed on your back. If you love me you'll let these three men fuck you every which way . . .'

That's what Toby Streak does. That's how he operates. He finds girls, grooms them and sells them on.

Sami feels the vomit rise. He swallows hard. It's not the alcohol rushing around his bloodstream. It's the image of Nadia and Toby Streak. The foul taste in his mouth won't go away.

6

Ray Garza Jnr doesn't look much like his old man, thinks Ruiz, as he watches him being led into the dock. He looks more like a foppish public schoolboy, who can't flick the fringe out of his eyes because each of his hands is cuffed to a policeman.

Maybe he has the makings of a moustache on his top lip. Maybe he's been playing with a black crayon downstairs. Only his eyes betray his breeding. He's got that Garza don't-fuck-with-me glare.

Ruiz takes a seat in the public gallery. The cold wooden benches are designed to give you piles.

The prosecutor opposes bail, claiming that Ray Jnr is a flight risk. He talks about the seriousness of the charges, the discharging of a firearm and a high-speed pursuit that put lives at risk.

Meanwhile Ray Junior's silk is acting like he's heard it all before. He's bored. When are they going to get some new material or change the record? He's not saying any of this, but you can see it in his body language. Then it's his turn. He takes to his feet. Shoulders back. Launches into a booming defence of his young client, who is going to vigorously defend the charges and who disputes completely the police account of what happened.

It's a bravura performance, including a description of how earlier on in the evening in question, young Ray had been confronted by hooligans who had taken offence at the vehicle he was driving and made threats against 'his person'.

'When later that evening a vehicle came up behind Mr Garza at such speed on the motorway, he thought he was being chased and feared for his life.'

'The vehicle in question had a flashing light,' points out the judge.

'Absolutely, your honour,' replies the silk. 'And very similar lights are available at pound shops and only a month ago one was used by bogus policemen to hijack a high-performance vehicle in Manchester.'

The judge doesn't respond. The silk is in full flow.

'It will be our submission, your honour, that the police illegally searched my client's vehicle. Anything recovered is inadmissible in criminal proceedings.'

The judge has heard enough.

'This is a bail hearing, Mr Cleary. Save your argument for the trial.'

'Of course, your honour, I just wanted it clearly noted that my client will be pleading not guilty.'

'It's duly noted.'

Mr Cleary's next speech is almost as florid as the first one. Ray Jnr is portrayed as a model citizen, a promising young businessman and a credit to his schooling and his family.

'My client's father is a well-respected business figure and a patron of the arts. He is prepared to put up a substantial surety and to personally guarantee his son's appearance at any future court proceedings.

'The only witnesses in this case are the police officers involved so it's not a question of protecting their interests . . .'

Ruiz is watching the door as Garza Snr enters. He comes alone, wearing an expensive suit and a cashmere overcoat draped over his forearm.

Ruiz watches him descend three steps. Turn right. Find a seat. He glances into the body of the court, at the judge, the bench, the dock – surveying everything as if he's putting a value on it.

Finally his eyes rest on Ruiz. They don't change. Nothing about him suggests that he's surprised or anxious. This is what people mean when they talk about the stillness on the surface of the pond.

The judge is making his decision. A lot of words say very little.

Ray Jnr is granted bail: two million pounds and conditions. He has to surrender his passport and to report every day to Bow Street Police Station.

Ray Jnr hasn't said a word. Hasn't looked at his father.

There are problems, thinks Ruiz. Maybe Bones was right. The boy might be Ray Garza's blind spot.

Outside the Old Bailey, Ruiz waits under the arches. How does someone pay two million pounds in bail, he wonders. Do they write a cheque? Organise a bank transfer? Maybe Garza is so well respected now, they'll accept an IOU.

A black Mercedes is parked outside, the driver waiting. An hour passes. Garza emerges. Garza Jnr is behind him. They're still not talking.

'The wrong Garza was in the dock today,' says Ruiz, stepping from the shadows.

Ray Snr stops and turns. 'Many happy returns, Vincent. Did you get my card?'

'I haven't opened it.'

'I'm sure you have dozens waiting. How is retirement treating you?'

'Fine.'

'You were never really cut out to be a detective, were you? It must have been like climbing to the top of the ladder and finding it leaning against the wrong window.'

'The view doesn't change.'

Ray Snr smiles. 'That's where you're wrong. It's much better from where I am.'

Ray Jnr has gone to the car. He leaves the door open.

'I admire you, Vincent.'

'How so?'

'Most people choose the path that gains them the

52

greatest reward for the least amount of effort. It's a law of nature. You defied it. You could have made decent money. You could have had a reasonable life. Instead you chose to make a difference. You have issues, Vincent, an obsessive nature. Maybe your old man was a violent fucker, smacked you round; bruised you on the inside. Now you're damaged goods.'

'That's a fascinating story,' says Ruiz. 'Ever think about adapting it for the stage?'

Ray Jnr leans out the car door. 'Come on. Ditch the drunk. I'm hungry.'

His father laughs. 'He thinks you're a tramp, Vincent.'

'Is that right. Talking out of your arse must be hereditary.' Ruiz glances at the car. 'I'm sure they'll find a way of stopping that in prison.'

Garza slides his overcoat onto his shoulders, wearing it like a cape. He smiles, showing his incisors.

'Voltaire said that madness was thinking of too many things in succession too quickly or to think of one thing obsessively. Get a life, Vincent. Before it's too late.'

'Yeah, well, a philosopher called Jagger once said, "Anything worth doing is worth overdoing".'

'You're a Stones fan. I should have known.'

7

Sami has been sitting on the same beer for nearly an hour. It feels like it cost him his left testicle. Five quid. It's fucking outrageous!

The place is called the Rockpool, which is pretty apt considering they let slime like Toby Streak hang out here. He's not around yet, it's early days, but he's expected, according to the bartender. It took another fiver for the information. Extortion.

The dance floor is starting to fill. It's all yuppie music and rag trade types, wannabe models, wannabe wannabes and mega-rich girls with shit-paying jobs on *Tatler* and *Vogue*.

Sami knew the bouncer on the door, a Neanderthal called Albert, who used to do security at some of Sami's gigs. The queue stretched down the alley, most of them men. The good-looking birds were ushered inside.

It's a numbers game. Women won't go to a club where drunk blokes on the pull outnumber them and drunk blokes won't go to a club where there are no women.

Sami keeps scanning the room, looking for Nadia. He should never have left her. Never have allowed an incompetent lawyer to talk him into pleading guilty.

He keeps glancing at the door every time it opens, waiting for Streak to arrive. He knows what he looks like. They've met once before but he doubts if Streak will remember. It was at a party in Notting Hill full of music producers, sound engineers and managers. Sami had been invited to meet a top manager, one of those guys who turns run-of-the-mill pub singers into the next Robbie Williams.

Streak was there. He came in the back door, grabbed a Bollinger and acted like he was a proper guest, the life and soul, and everyone's best friend just because he was bringing their toot. But once they had their stuff they wanted him to fuck off – use the tradesman's entrance please.

That's the thing with pimps and coke dealers. They hang out at celebrity parties and backstage at rock concerts, thinking they're bosom buddies with celebrities but they're nothing but delivery boys.

Sami didn't sign with the manager or get a recording deal that night, but he did shag a cute-looking waitress from Rotherhithe who had a thing for doing it in the shower.

The club is heaving. Young babes and blokes with city jobs are bouncing up and down on the dance floor. Streak should be here by now.

There he is – on the stairs. He's wearing a Paul Smith suit and drinking a cocktail. He's with a girl. It's not Nadia. She's blonde, young, with an innocent face and an athletic body. She presses it against Streak, rubbing her tits against his chest.

Streak is treating her like she doesn't exist – gazing over the top of her head – perhaps looking for someone prettier.

Sami watches him for a while. Every so often someone approaches. A nod, a wink, a palm against palm, and then they wander off. A few minutes later, Streak sends the girl after them. She must be carrying the stuff. Where? There's no room in that dress for anything else but her tits.

She comes back again. Steak gives her a little something as a reward. She queues for a cubicle – the lines are longer outside than inside – and she comes back all dreamy and grateful, nibbling on his earlobe.

Sami waits for a while. Gets the lay of the land. A black girl in a short denim skirt sits on a stool next to him. Her handbag swings against her rump and her braided hair click-clacks like marbles in a sack.

'You look lonely,' she says.

'You look expensive,' replies Sami.

She gets the hump and walks off, swinging her hips.

Finally, Sami approaches Streak. Says hello. Watches his reaction. He doesn't remember him. Sami wants to reach out and squeeze his throat until his eyes pop out.

Instead he negotiates a score. He glances at the girl. She throws her shoulders back so her tits lift higher. So does the hem of her dress. My God, those legs! She's seventeen if she's a day.

'Outside in the alley,' says Streak, yelling over the music. 'Zoe will meet you there.'

Sami turns away and pushes through bodies on the dance floor. The music seems to die suddenly as the fire door closes. He can hear himself think.

A few minutes later, Zoe joins him. Her eyes check him out as if she's trying to decide if he's a player. Suddenly, she puts her arms around his neck and kisses him. The small silver foil wrap slides between his lips. Her tongue caresses his. His hard-on is instantaneous. He's been inside for nearly three years. It's criminal to press a body like that against him.

'You know someone called Nadia?' he asks.

Zoe frowns. 'Nah.'

She's lying.

'She used to hang out with Streak.'

Zoe glances toward the fire door.

'Nadia is my sister. I'm looking for her.'

Zoe steps back. She's wearing a handbag the size of a cigarette packet. She pulls a lipstick from inside.

'She used to hang out with Toby. He dumped her.'

'When?'

She shrugs. 'I have to get back inside. He's waiting.'

'Don't go. Stay here.'

'Hey, you're sweet and you're horny, but Toby is going to look after me.'

'Toby is going to pimp you the first chance he gets.'

Zoe doesn't believe him. She turns to go. Sami grabs her arm.

'Ow! You're hurting me.'

'I don't want to. Just stay here.'

'Toby's going to miss me.'

'That's the idea.'

Zoe doesn't say a dicky bird, but Sami knows she's worried. She's rocking from foot to foot like she's got to pee.

Sami doesn't regard himself as a violent type but sometimes the shortest answer to the hardest question is a smack in the head. He reaches into his pocket. Fingers a roll of ten pence pieces wrapped in brown paper.

He watches the door. Waits.

Sure enough, Toby comes looking. He peers out the door. Clocks Zoe. Sees Sami. He has this quizzical look on his face but it doesn't last. Sami sinks a fist into his stomach and then bounces his face off the doorjamb at a hundred miles an hour. Wrenches it back. Does it again.

Cartilage crunches. It's a gusher. Blood all over his nice suit.

Streak falls backwards. Zoe has her hand over her mouth. Her pretty legs are shaking.

Sami steps back. Breathing hard. Trembling.

'I'm looking for my sister.'

Toby spits blood onto the cobblestones. 'Nothing to do with me.'

'I haven't told you her name.'

'Yeah, well, I got a lot of jealous boyfriends looking for me. It's a nervous reaction.'

'What have you got to be nervous about?'

He raises his eyes to look at Sami for the first time.

'What's her name?'

'Nadia.'

'I'll have to check my phone.' He reaches into his jacket pocket. A flash of brightness. A blade opens.

Sami launches a kick before Streak can straighten his arm. The sprung steel blade spins out of his fingers and bounces off the wall.

A second kick connects with his stomach. Sami takes a four step run up and kicks him again.

Zoe lets out a sob. Sami tells her to go home. Watch *Sesame Street*. Learn something.

'Give him back his gear.'

She pulls a dozen small packets of silver foil from her handbag and another half dozen from her knickers. Tosses them at Streak. Some of them float in a puddle, silver on black, catching the light.

Zoe disappears through the fire door. Sami jams a rubbish bin across the frame to stop them being disturbed.

'Now it's just you and me, Toby. Your nose is broken. Maybe they can set it straight again. I could try. I could

59

mess it up a bit more. They say every beautiful face needs a blemish. Where's Nadia?'

Toby is sitting in a puddle. 'I don't fucking know,' he sniffles. 'I ain't seen her.'

'Since when?'

'Days.'

'What did you do?'

'Nothing.'

'Did you give her drugs?'

'She's a consenting adult.'

Louder this time: 'Did you give her drugs?'

'Nothing serious,' whines Toby. 'She wanted to party.'

'What did you give her?'

'She's eighteen.'

'Where is she?'

'Like I said, I ain't seen her.'

Sami takes off his jacket, rolls up his sleeve. Picks up the knife, cleans the blade on the front of his jeans.

'What are you doing?' asks Toby.

'Take off your pants.'

'Why?'

'I've been nearly three years in prison Toby. You get a taste for certain things.'

'You're kidding me, right.'

Sami unbuckles his belt. Toby's eyes pop. Suddenly, he's scuffling backwards through a puddle like a crab on polished marble. Sami steps past him, wraps a forearm around his neck.

Toby sobs, 'No fucking way, man. No way.'

'Where is she?'

'I swear I don't know.'

'You're lying.'

'OK. OK.'

'What did you do?'

'I just passed her on.'

'What do you mean?'

'Tony Murphy wanted her.'

Sami tries to get his head around this. Tony Murphy doesn't know Nadia. What's he got to do with any of this?

'We came to an arrangement,' sniffles Toby.

'What sort of arrangement.'

'I sold her to him.'

8

Sami jogs out of the alley and back onto the street. He walks fast, trying to be inconspicuous. He can hear sirens starting to wail. Zoe must have called the police.

Sami curses himself. He wasn't exactly subtle. If Toby Streak lodges a complaint, he's screwed. Parole revoked. Go straight to jail. Do not pass go . . .

He comes out of St Martins Lane into Charing Cross Road. Buys a copy of *The Times* from a news stand and hails a cab, keeping his face covered. The cab drops him at Waterloo Station. He walks towards Elephant and Castle and into Camberwell Road.

Toby Streak sits in a police car, holding a towel over his face. Two uniforms are interviewing Zoe, quizzing her about a fake ID. Neither of them seems too broken up about Toby.

'What took you so fucking long?' he complains.

'Just you mind your language, sir.'

They finish talking to Zoe. Tell her to go home. Toby's next.

'Do you want to file a complaint, sir?'

'Will it do any good?' he asks. His nose is blocked completely.

'That depends on the quality of your information and if we feel it warrants further investigation.'

Toby knows what that means. They're going to write this one off as a small time drug deal gone sour. He's not going to report Sami.

As soon as the uniforms leave, he opens his mobile. Punches in a number.

'Is that Mr Murphy?'

'This better be important, son.'

'That person you wanted to meet. He might be calling on you.'

Sami stands across the road from the bail hostel on Camberwell Road. There is a sign on the door: rules for residents. One of them is not to break the curfew.

It's 3.00 a.m. There is a light on. He presses a buzzer. A large woman swings open the door, black as paint with a square, hard-boned face. She stands in the doorway, unsmiling, as though waiting for his excuse.

'I've been looking for my sister. She's missing.'

'Not good enough.'

'I'm worried about her.'

'I don't want to hear your lies, honey. You break the rules, you go back to prison.'

'I'm not lying. It's my first day out.'

She steps back, opens the door wider. Sami has to detour to get around her hips. She's wearing a uniform – a light blue shirt with double pockets and dark blue trousers that stretch so tightly across her rump he can see the outline of her knickers. My God, she's wearing a G-string. A nightstick and a can of mace swing from her belt.

Sami follows her to the office. She turns down the TV. Moves a jumbo packet of crisps. Signs him in. Next she hands him two stiff bed sheets, a grey blanket, a towel and a bar of soap.

'The laundry is in the basement. Detergent is extra. Don't go leaving shit in your pockets when you use the machines. Two been fixed in the last month.'

She takes a swig of soft drink and wipes her hand across her mouth. 'You been doing something you ain't supposed to?'

'Nope.'

'Don't believe you.' Her hand shoots out and grabs Sami's wrist. Turns it over. His knuckles are torn and bleeding. She shakes her head. 'You're just aching to get back inside, ain't you, honey? Maybe you like the sex in there.'

She hoists herself out of her chair and gives him a tour, keeping her voice down because other 'residents' are sleeping.

'No eating in the common room. No smoking in the common room. No drinking. No drugs. No women . . .'

'And they leave you here to tempt us,' says Sami.

'You trying to be funny, skinny boy?'

'No, I'm just saying you're a fit-looking woman.'

'You trying to tell me you're not gay, honey? Well you don't have the hammer and you don't have the nail to impress me.'

She turns off the lights as she leaves each room. They climb the stairs to the first floor.

'No damaging property, no touching the CCTV cameras, no loud music – you wearing an electronic tag?'

'No.'

'Don't let anyone talk you into wearing theirs.'

'I won't. How many people are here?'

'Thirty.' They stop outside a door. 'This is your room. Don't lose the key.'

She waddles away, almost brushing each side of the hall with her hips. Sami closes the door. Locks it. Walks to the window. It overlooks a walled courtyard with empty flowerbeds that look silver under the security lights.

The room has a single bed, a lone chair, a wardrobe and a bedside table with a lamp, an ashtray and a Bible. A laminated copy of the House Rules is pinned to the back of the door.

Sami lies on the bed and feels himself slipping into a dark envelope of depression. He thinks about Nadia and about Tony Murphy and about the four guys who came looking for him earlier outside the Scrubs. Freedom wasn't supposed to be like this.

9

Under normal circumstances – better circumstances – Sami Macbeth might never have heard of a gangster like Tony Murphy, but there are two things you have in abundance when you're pacing an exercise yard: time and prison gossip.

Most of the stories are bullshit. Every con will tell that you he's innocent of the crime he was convicted of and then brag about the ones he got away with.

According to the skinny on Tony Murphy, he came from one of those big Irish families (seven brothers and sisters – the girls as mad as the boys) who seem to live everywhere except Ireland. Murphy grew up in Kilburn, North London, and began stealing cars to order when he was barely old enough to see over the steering wheel.

From car rackets he branched out to running escort agencies, nightclubs and casinos (illegal and otherwise), including a floating Chinese junk in Manchester that he shipped from Hong Kong. His latest passion was a restaurant on the river near the Millennium Bridge –

one of those up-market nosheries where the chef is a daytime TV star who can make a four course meal out of a bag of spuds and a Bisto cube.

The place has booths along the walls and linen table-cloths. The maître d' gives Sami the hairy eyeball.

'Do you have a reservation, sir?'

'I'm here to see Mr Murphy.'

'Do you have an appointment?'

'No.'

'Mr Murphy doesn't like being disturbed while he's dining.'

'Maybe you could pass him a note,' says Sami. He borrows a piece of paper and writes Nadia's name, draws a sad face on it, folding it twice before handing it to the maître d'. Then he watches him weave between the tables, up three stairs, pausing at a table overlooking the main seating area.

He hands the note to a fat man whose head seems to be stitched onto an oversized tweed jacket. A hard man turned to lard.

Murphy reads the note and sways back, sucking down an oyster from the shell. Juice dribbles over his chins. He wipes it away with a napkin. Waves Sami over.

Sami tells himself to relax. It's a busy restaurant. Nothing's going to happen.

Murphy's luncheon companion is a head taller, with ruddy cheeks discoloured by broken veins beneath his skin. This guy is walking proof of man's simian ancestry – flared nostrils, torso like a wardrobe, arms reaching his knees. He doesn't say a word.

Murphy and Sami make the introductions.

'What can I do for you, son?' asks the fat man, edging the blade of a knife beneath the flesh of another oyster.

Sami has to be careful here. It's a balancing act. Tony Murphy is not the sort of man you threaten or yank about. It's also not a good idea to crawl up his rectum and set up house. He has to be respectful. Considered. Polite.

'Toby Streak says you might know where my sister is.'

'What's your sister's name?'

'Nadia Macbeth.'

'What makes you think I know where she is?'

'Toby said he sold her to you.'

Murphy puts down his fork. Wipes his mouth. Folds his napkin. Places it on his side plate.

'Slavery was abolished in 1841, son. People don't get bought and sold any more. Didn't they teach you that at school?'

'Toby Streak seemed pretty confident, Mr Murphy.'

'What makes you think that?'

'I had my boot on his balls, sir. Figuratively speaking.'

'Well, if we're speaking figuratively, in my experience drugsters like Toby Streak can be coerced into saying almost anything.'

'Toby still seemed pretty sure.'

Murphy's voice drops an octave.

'Let me give you a piece of advice, Mr Macbeth. You don't want to be making unsupported allegations against people. There are laws about that sort of thing. Defamation. Slander.'

'I'm not here to cause any trouble,' says Sami. 'I just want my sister.'

'How old is she?'

'Eighteen.'

'Old enough to make up her own mind.' Murphy summons the waiter. Asks for another glass. Pours a wine for Sami.

'I appreciate your candour, Mr Macbeth. I can also see you got courage. You got balls as big as the Ritz to waltz in here and accuse me of wrongdoing. This makes me think that either you're a very loving brother or you're so dumb you couldn't piss straight with a hard-on.'

'I'm a loving brother.'

'That's good. Now let's talk about you.'

Murphy sucks down another oyster. He offers one to Sami, who'd rather eat cold snot.

'I heard about you, Mr Macbeth. I hear you're a talent.'

'Me? No.'

Murphy drizzles lemon juice on an oyster and gives the pepper mill a twist. 'Dessie has given me the skinny on the Hampstead job. Very impressive.'

Dessie must be the other guy at the table. Dessie Fraser. 'The Dobermann'. Sami remembers a story about Dessie, who used to be in the army, stationed in Northern Ireland. He was there when the IRA killed Earl Mountbatten by planting a bomb on his boat in County Sligo. Two more bombs went off that day, but nobody remembers them because old man Mountbatten made all the headlines.

One of them was detonated beside a road in County Down just as a Bedford drove by with Dessie Fraser and a load of Paras in back. A second bomb was timed to go off as people tried to help the wounded. A dozen soldiers died. Dessie survived.

A week later, dressed in uniform, Dessie walked into a notorious IRA bar in the Newry and ordered a beer. Waited. Not for long. He left three people near death, tore the place up and the COs needed teargas to get him out. Dessie was dishonourably discharged. Prematurely ejected. Returned to civilian life even less civilised than before he signed up.

Clearly he doesn't bear a grudge against Paddies, thinks Sami, glancing at Murphy.

'Don't believe everything you've heard about me, Mr Murphy. If I was so talented, I wouldn't have got caught.'

'You were unlucky,' says Murphy.

Tell me about it, thinks Sami.

'Modest, too, I like that in a young man, Mr Macbeth. You're not some cocky little gobshite who thinks he's seen it all. And you're not a flash prick like Toby Streak, who buys himself a sports car and rubs the law's nose in his success. You're old school. A

70

skilled technician. An artist. I like surrounding myself with talented people; people who use their god-given skills. You know what I'm saying, son?'

The answer is no, but Sami doesn't utter it out loud.

'You're a quiet achiever. That's why none of us had ever heard of you until the Hampstead job. You kept a low profile. Used your discretion.'

What the fuck is he talking about, thinks Sami.

'I could use someone gifted like you,' says Murphy. 'Someone who thinks on his feet, someone flexible, someone who can open things.'

'You got the wrong guy,' says Sami, feeling the conversation has taken a wrong turn. 'I just want to find my sister and get my shit together in one pile.'

Murphy slathers butter on one half of a torn bread roll.

'You work alone, I understand that, but I could open up whole new horizons.'

'It's not that,' says Sami. 'I'm going to concentrate on my music.'

'Come again?'

'I play guitar. I'm a musician.'

Murphy has stopped chewing. 'You taking the piss, son?'

Sami realises his mistake. 'No, no, I'm just thinking, given what's happened, that it might be best to change my career. I thought I might concentrate on my music, you know.'

Murphy gives him the pointy finger. 'You're planning something, aren't you? The big score.'

'No, sir.'

'Nobody fucking retires in this business unless they're planning a see-you-later job.'

'It's not about money.'

'It's always about fucking money. You want to contemplate retirement – you do it while you're tossing champagne bottles off the back of your yacht or sipping sangria in a Spanish villa.'

'I'm not planning anything,' says Sami.

Murphy looks at him dubiously, wondering if he's lost his bottle, or worse, gone over to the other side.

'How old are you, son?'

'Twenty-seven.'

'How much have you got in your pocket?'

Sami shrugs.

'You're potless, aren't you?' Murphy pushes back his chair. 'Poverty isn't freedom. Look at the poor fuckers out there.' He points to a bus queue over the road. People are shivering in the rain. 'Most of 'em ain't got a pot to piss in. They're shell-shocked, exhausted, they're tired of scraping away week after week, year after year, making the giro stretch till next pension day, living on overdrafts and plastic. Meanwhile, the politicians keep telling them they've never had it so good and they're too stupid to know they're being lied to. Only scraps ever fall from the top table, son. Toast crumbs and bacon rind. So when you hear a politician start talking about trickle down economics and how everyone benefits from the good times, that's because they're pissing on you from a great height.'

Dessie chuckles.

'Do you ever think about the future, Sami?' Murphy asks.

All the time, thinks Sami.

'What are you gonna do?'

'Start a band. Get some gigs. Look after Nadia.'

'Work with me, son. And I'll make sure you've got a tidy little stack before you walk away. I'll even throw you a farewell party.'

'What about Nadia?'

'I'll see what I can do to find her. I got contacts. I'll lean a little on Toby Streak. Get the real story.'

This is crazy, thinks Sami. He's two days out of prison – innocent as the day he was born – and Tony Murphy wants him to join the firm. His guts are churning.

'I just want to find Nadia,' he says.

'Like I said, I'll help you find her.'

'Do you know where she is?'

'Not without asking.'

Sami looks hard at Murphy's face, searching for a clue that he knows more. Out of the corner of his eyes he sees Dessie's right eyebrow go up a quarter of an inch. He doesn't understand what it means but he knows enough to sense trouble.

'It's nothing personal, Tony. I'm not interested.'

There's a moment. A heartbeat. Murphy's face has turned to stone. 'Don't fucking call me Tony, you little prick.'

'I apologise. No offence meant, Mr Murphy.'

'Listen, you dainty little poof, you come in here, interrupt my meal, make outrageous allegations and then piss on my offer to help like I'm some up-his-own-arse charity worker.'

'No, sir.'

'You consider what I have to say, son. And don't leave it too long.'

Somehow Sami finds his feet, makes it through the restaurant, down the stairs, outside. He walks along the river past a group of Japanese tourists who are following a yellow umbrella like it's a religious artefact.

10

Tony Murphy belches quietly, getting a second taste of his rabbit poached in red wine with mashed potato and truffle oil. His gout is acting up – his right toe swollen – but the pain is preferable to the controlled diet his doctor recommended. No pâté. No port. Bollocks to that!

Murphy sighs and lets out a stream of urine into the porcelain. Sami Macbeth is exercising his mind. The kid didn't come round. That's the problem with the new breed. Most of them are soft pricks and idiots, who grow up thinking they're entitled. Gimme a freebie; gimme a discount; gimme a spot of unsecured credit – they're a gimme fucking army who don't know the meaning of good honest criminal graft.

Life would be a lot simpler without families. Sami Macbeth wouldn't have to worry about his sister and Ray Garza wouldn't have to worry about his idiot offspring.

Ray Jnr started all this. The kid took liberties. Took something that didn't belong to him.

Murphy should have known better than to help the

boy out but he thought it might be useful having the Chairman's son in his debt. Big mistake. Huge fucking mistake. Next thing the kid is riding round town like some outlaw baddie, dealing cocaine and drag-racing rozzers.

He was always a fuck-up. That's why Ray Snr packed him off to boarding school at twelve. Thought it might improve his prospects mixing with a lot of chinless trout in straw boaters and blazers.

Education is never wasted on the young they say and Ray Jnr didn't waste his. By his second year he was running an SP operation out of the junior common room and selling contraband – cigarettes, dope, girlie magazines, you name it. In year ten he smuggled two hookers into the senior dorm as part of a 'use it or lose it' weekend for spotty virgins.

The Eton version of a court martial followed. It wasn't the last time. Ray Jnr went to three more posh schools in the next two years and was asked to leave each of them. His old man paid the damages, apologised to the parents and made donations to the building funds.

At one point he employed a brace of security specialists, ex-Paras, to keep an eye on Ray Jnr and make sure he didn't dig a tunnel under the fence. Made no difference. The kid was a chip off the old block, an entrepreneur, a mover and a shaker without the brains or the guile of his father.

Eventually, Garza's missus suggested he let Ray Jnr

leave school and bring him into the business where Daddy could keep an eye on him. They gave him a junior management position. Put him on a salary. Began showing him the ropes.

Unfortunately, the only ropes Ray Jnr was interested in were wrapped around a young lovely's wrist and knotted to the bedpost while he snorted cocaine off her gym-sculptured stomach.

Ray Jnr didn't have an A-level to his name but he wasn't a complete moron. He knew Daddy was worth millions and the trust fund kicked in when he turned twenty-five. All he had to do was wait.

Consequently, he stopped showing up for work and hung out with his hooray buddies, partying hard. He liked the ladies. He liked the clothes. He liked the flash sports car Daddy bought him for his eighteenth.

The Chairman must have been tearing his hair out, so he tried something different. Tough love. He cut the kid's allowance. Figured he'd bring Ray Jnr to heel. It didn't quite work out that way.

Ray Jnr went into business for himself, dealing coke and Gary Abletts to his trust fund buddies and posh mates. He had all the right connections and enough chutzpah to think he was a class act, when in reality he had about as much sophistication as a coat-hanger abortion.

Ray Jnr was dealing to the top end of the market, the quality street gang, the crème de la crème and didn't notice he was treading on some big hairy fucking toes. The Albanians and the Turks didn't give a shit if he was Ray Garza's boy. To them he was simply a young punk muscling in on their primo uno turf.

That's when Ray Jnr came to Murphy. Couldn't go to his old man. There was too much yuppie Mafioso shit going down and he wanted protection. Security.

Murphy offered him advice. Said he'd make some calls.

Ray Jnr was scared. He wanted a piece for his personal protection. Murphy promised to sort him out in a few days, but the kid took something from him. Something he shouldn't have. Something nobody could know about.

Maybe things would have worked out if Ray Jnr had kept his head down and let things cool off with the Albanians and the Turks. Instead he got clocked doing over a ton on the M40. The rozzers gave chase. Ray Jnr burned them off. An hour later they found his Porsche parked up outside a pub in Hammersmith. They wanted to search inside. Ray Jnr told them to fuck off. Rozzers just love it when you talk dirty to them. Their eyes must have lit up when they found eight kilos of cocaine under the spare wheel.

Ray Jnr went off his head. Pulled the semi-automatic out of his belt. According to Ray the shooter went off accidentally. According to the charge sheet it was attempted murder.

The rest is history, as they say, except Ray Garza wants

to rewrite the whole episode and get his boy off. Only this is a rap he can't bribe or beg or blag his way out of. And history is going to get rewritten a dozen different ways when the boffins in the ballistics lab test the gun Ray Jnr was waving around. It's all about scratch markings on the chamber of the gun. Telltale signs. Damning evidence.

The kid got bail yesterday. Daddy forked out two mill and Ray Jnr was probably straight down to his clubster mates, bragging about how he toughed out his first night in the Scrubs. How he ran the joint like King Rat.

The cack-handed moron has no idea of the chain of events he's set in motion or how much shit is gathering on the fan. It's a mess and Murphy has to clean it up before someone hits the switch.

He shakes. Shakes again. Zips his fly. Washes his hands.

Dessie is waiting outside the door, standing guard like a loyal Labrador with less intelligence.

Murphy has a plan, but he needs Macbeth.

'What do you want me to do?' asks Dessie.

'Persuade him.'

'And if he does the job?'

'Get rid of him.'

Murphy goes back to the table and orders a crème caramel for dessert, which isn't on the menu, but the chef will do it by special request. So he should, thinks Murphy. 'I own the poncy arsehole.'

11

Sami has an appointment. It's part of the deal with his early release – a once-a-month pow wow with a probation service supervisor.

He's late. Missed his turn. He sits on a plastic chair in the waiting room, staring at a potted plant that seems to be surviving without light or leaves.

'Hello, Mr Macbeth,' she says. 'Can I call you Sami?'

It's a woman, Miranda Wallace. Well-preserved. Mid-forties. Dressed in a grey suit with a pink ribbon pinned to her lapel. She calls herself Ms, which makes Sami think she could be gay but she's too hot for that.

They sit in her office with the door open. Paperwork comes first. Twenty questions. Notes. Finally, she leans back and pushes her fringe from over her left eye.

'How do you feel about being out?'

'Good.'

'Have you had any trouble adjusting?'

'No.'

'What plans do you have?'

'I want to be a rock god.'

'That's an ambition rather than a plan. Perhaps you should find a more realistic goal.'

'I play guitar.'

'That's a good life skill.'

She makes it sound like needlework.

Sami starts telling her how he used to be in a band, playing gigs and occasionally supporting indie bands from the States who have one hit song and think they're going to fill Wembley Arena.

'What sort of music?' she asks.

'Rock infused with blues,' says Sami. 'Solid wall of sound stuff full of attitude.'

'Live fast, die young.'

'Leave a pretty corpse.'

'Sounds great,' she says.

Sami's surprised. Maybe she's an old rock chick. 'When was the last time you went to see a band?' he asks.

'I saw REM at Wembley Stadium in the summer.'

He's impressed.

They talk music a bit more and then she steers him on to his future plans. She wants to know about his accommodation arrangements and his employment prospects.

One of the conditions of Sami's probation is that he looks for work.

'That's what I'm going to do,' he explains. 'Once I find Nadia, I'll get my Fender, call up the old band, rustle up a gig or two and get some money in the jam jar.'

'It's not exactly steady work,' says Ms Wallace. 'Who's Nadia?'

'My sister.'

Sami starts telling her about going to Nadia's gaff and finding someone else living there. She hasn't been to work. Isn't answering her mobile. He doesn't know how much he should tell her about what happened last night with Toby Streak or about his meeting with Tony Murphy. He could be back inside before his feet touch the ground.

Ms Wallace asks the questions. She wants to know if Nadia is the sort to go missing or take off without leaving a note.

'Never,' says Sami. 'We're tight, you know. We look after each other.'

Next thing Sami is telling her about their mother dying and how he won custody of Nadia. One thing leads to another and soon he's recounting the whole sorry saga of Andy Palmer becoming a speed bump and Sami pleading guilty to possession.

She doesn't say much. Sits. Listens. Maybe she hears stories like this all the time, thinks Sami, but it doesn't stop him spilling his guts. His whole life story comes tumbling out – how his father was a Scottish merchant seaman and his mother a French Algerian refugee when they met in Montpellier and eloped.

She was a Moslem but didn't wear the veil. She never mentioned her family. Didn't call them. Didn't write. It was as though when she married she ceased to have a history or a bloodline.

Sami's father quit the boats and worked in an abattoir in Glasgow, while running an SP operation on the side. He did everything at a hundred miles an hour, full bore – drinking, singing, fighting and fucking. Women loved him.

Sami's mother could tolerate his drinking and turn a blind eye to the bookmaking, but she hated the 'whores', as she called them.

'What happened to your father?' asks Ms Wallace.

'He drowned.'

'I'm sorry.'

'He was drunk.'

The parole officer is watching him intently, but whatever she's really thinking is hovering around the edges of her sentences.

'I'm not going back inside,' Sami tells her, his voice shaking. 'I just want to find Nadia. Make sure she's OK. I'll get a job, I promise. I'll pay the rent. It's not the whole future but it's a plan.'

'Who was the last person to see Nadia?' she asks.

'A tossbag called Toby Streak.'

'You've talked to him?'

Sami grimaces slightly. 'Yeah.'

'Did he know anything?'

'He mentioned an arrangement with Tony Murphy.'

'Do you know this Murphy?'

'I never met him until today.'

'What does he do?'

'He owns a restaurant, clubs . . . stuff like that.'

'Nightclubs.'

'Strip clubs.'

'Under the terms of your parole I'm sure you are aware that you're not supposed to be mixing with criminals or their associates.'

'I know, I know, but it's about Nadia.'

'If you have concerns for her safety you should take them to the police.'

'I've been to the police. They don't care.'

Ms Wallace seems conflicted. She's caught between her professional duty and her innate sense of concern.

'What did this Mr Murphy have to say?' she asks.

'He said he didn't know where Nadia was.'

'But you don't believe him.'

Sami shrugs. He's not going to tell her about Murphy's offer. He's said too much already.

Ms Wallace lets her gaze shift over Sami and her fingertips drum on the blotter. Sami can see in her eyes that she's already made assumptions about him. He's just another low-life fuck-up, who'll be back inside within a year.

Sami stands to leave. 'Will that be all?'

'Do you have somewhere else to be?' she asks.

'I have to find my sister.'

'Do you have a photograph of her?'

'Why?'

'I might know someone who could help you.'

Sami reaches into his pocket and pulls out a weathered Polaroid taken at Nadia's sixteenth birthday party. She's wearing a party hat and is draping streamers over Sami's head.

Ms Wallace studies the image and then writes a phone number on a piece of paper.

'If you don't hear from your sister you should give this man a call. His name is Vincent Ruiz and he owes me a big favour.'

'Why?'

'I was married to him for three years.'

12

Friday afternoon. Quarter to six. Ruiz presses the doorbell. Watches Miranda appear behind the frosted glass.

The door opens. She smiles. Kisses both his cheeks.

'I brought flowers,' he says.

'So I can see. Are the neighbours missing any?'

'That's cruel.'

Miranda leads him down the hall to the kitchen. Ruiz walks four paces behind. She looks great. She always does. Not just for a woman of her age but for any woman. Any age.

She fills a vase and arranges the flowers. Her cargo pants hang loose on her hips and her blouse is cut just low enough to show him what he used to have access to and is now off-limits. Another downside of divorce.

Miranda is a probation officer. That's how they met. Ruiz was working a case involving a boatload of stolen Levi's back in the late-eighties when 901s were the hottest ticket on the high street. Ruiz was married. Happily so, except for the cancer that was eating away at Laura from the inside.

He flirted a little with Miranda, became friends and then lost touch with her for a decade. By then Laura was dead and Jessie, his second wife, a suppressed memory.

He and Miranda were married for three years. They've been divorced for two. She's the sort of ex-wife blokes dream about. Low maintenance. Friendly. She's even tried to set him up on dates. Unmitigated disasters.

When they were married, Ruiz could never fully reconcile himself to the fact that Miranda worked as a parole officer. He didn't like the idea that low-life scrotes and toerags were sitting in her office wondering what underwear she was wearing. He half suspected – but never told Miranda – that half the reason she had such a good retention rate was because her parolees lusted after her.

Miranda was always careful. She dressed down. Minimal make-up. Nothing provocative.

'You want tea or coffee?' she asks.

'Got anything stronger?'

'Nope.'

'Is it proper tea?'

'Camomile.'

'Tastes of nothing, smells like potpourri.'

'It's very good for you.'

Ruiz produces a bottle of red wine from behind his back. 'So is this. It's full of antioxidants. Good for the heart. Ask the French. Sarkozy lives on this stuff and bags himself a pop star and a supermodel. What do we get? Gordon Brown. I rest my case.'

Ruiz finds a corkscrew and Miranda gets two glasses. The garden flat is nice. Homely. Ruiz likes the way it smells. He also likes the fact it's full of reminders and souvenirs of their marriage. The rug in front of the fireplace is from a holiday they took in Cornwall and the painting above the dining table was bought from a sidewalk artist in Florence.

Miranda sets out two balloon glasses and fills a bowl with roasted cashews. She's self-sufficient. Classy. Never asked him for a thing when they divorced except for the souvenirs. And all she asks of him now is that he returns her phone calls and lets her stay involved with Michael and Claire – the twins. Laura's kids, not hers. They still need a mother, she says, and she's happy to fill the role.

She sits down on the far end of the sofa. Curls her legs. Ruiz stares at her earlobes. He could nuzzle them for a few hundred years and never get bored.

'You called,' he says, trying to change the subject.

'What did the doctor say?' she asks.

'Is that why you asked me round?'

'Not entirely.' She sips her wine. 'But since you're here.'

'He said nothing.'

'What did you say?'

'Nothing.'

'It must have been very quiet.' Her eyes are dancing. 'Did he tell you to exercise?'

'I told him I was going to exercise by being a pallbearer for all my friends who exercise.'

'What about your weight?'

'What about it?'

'You've put on a few pounds.'

'No I haven't.'

'Stop trying to hold your stomach in.'

Ruiz relaxes. 'It looks good on me. You're too skinny.'

'I'm the same size as when you married me.'

'That's why I divorced you.'

Miranda gives him a hurt look. Ruiz wants to take the comment back. She has this way of acting that makes him believe that several women are living inside her and only one of them divorced him. The rest are still undecided.

Ruiz takes a sip of wine and a handful of cashews. Miranda has stopped talking and grown pensive, one tooth biting into her bottom lip.

'You all right?'

She nods and starts telling him about her new parolee, Sami Macbeth, released after nearly three years in prison. Tells him the story of his sister going missing.

Ruiz is thinking runaway. This Nadia is probably having the time of her life. She's found herself a boyfriend, doesn't want to associate with a jailbird brother.

Miranda hands him a photograph – a prison mugshot that must have come from Macbeth's file.

'What was this guy in for?'

'Possession of stolen goods.'

'First timer.'

She nods.

'What makes him think his sister is in trouble?'

Miranda tells him how Nadia abandoned her flat. She hasn't turned up for work or at college. Isn't answering her phone.

'When was the last time he heard from her?'

'A week ago.'

'This Nadia have a boyfriend?'

'According to Sami she had started seeing a guy called Toby Streak.'

Ruiz doesn't know the name. 'What does Streak have to say?'

'Says that he and Nadia parted company. Last time he saw her she was with Tony Murphy.'

Now there's a name that does ring a bell. Dozens of them, pealing from the rooftops.

Miranda senses as much.

'It's not good news, is it?'

Nothing about Murphy is good news, thinks Ruiz. 'What do you want me to do?'

'I thought you might ask around – make a few calls, you're good at that sort of thing.'

'What sort of thing?'

'Finding girls.'

'I'm a bit long in the tooth.'

'As a favour,' she says, rubbing her stockinged foot against his ankle. 'I feel good about this guy. I don't think he's a bad egg. He wants to straighten himself out.'

Ruiz has to fight the urge not to run his hand up her leg to her thigh. After another glass of wine he's beginning to settle in for the evening – something Miranda recognises.

'Off you go, big man,' she says.

'Why?'

'It's Friday night. I'm going out,' she says.

'Who with?'

'None of your business.'

She gives him a hug. Ruiz runs his hands down the small of her back and squeezes her backside.

'What was that for?' she purrs into his mouth.

'Old time's sake.'

'Stop calling yourself old,' she says.

'It's all right for you. You still look great.'

'It just takes me twice as long to look half as good.'

Ruiz smells her hair and turns away, walking up the stairs, onto the street. How is it, he wonders, that something so soft can make him so hard.

13

When Sami was in Wormwood Scrubs he received a letter from a girl called Kate Tierney. Kate used to hang around the band – not like a groupie, but as part of the entourage.

She was dating the drummer, Shortie, a good-looking bastard who treated her like shit. What is it about drummers? Ringo Starr falls out of the ugly tree, hits every branch, yet still manages to pull birds like Patti Boyd and Barbara Bach, a Bond girl for fuck's sake.

Sami used to lust after Kate from afar, or at least from the front of the stage. She was always upfront, in the mosh-pit, eyes closed, swaying to the music.

She was only eighteen when he first met her. When that particular band broke up, she drifted away. Over the next few years he bumped into her once or twice before losing touch.

Then Sami got sent down for a stretch. Three months in, he gets a letter from Kate Tierney. Perfumed. Little blue flowers around the border. Sami lay back in his cell and imagined the same little blue flowers on the edges of her knickers.

After that she wrote to him twice a week. Told him about her life. Her folks had been rich until her old man invested in junk bonds and blew the lot. Kate went from a private school in Surrey to a comprehensive in Hackney.

Sami had no idea why Kate decided to write to him. Maybe she felt sorry for him. Maybe she'd secretly fancied him for years. Maybe the reason was more fundamental and deep seated.

He asked her to send him a photograph. She sent one of her wearing a silk teddy, sitting astride a rocking horse. That's when he realised it was about lust. He was now a bad boy. An outlaw. Some girls think they deserve guys like that.

Kate Tierney studied hotel management and got a job working at the Savoy. She started in reception and worked her way up to night manager.

Sami calls her at work. Tells her he needs somewhere to stay. He's spent all afternoon and evening looking for Nadia. Visiting her friends, talking to her workmates. He's not going back to the bail hostel.

Kate thinks about it. Puts him on hold. Sami can hear her talking in a posh voice to one of the guests, telling Mr Somersby to have a nice evening and enjoy the opera.

Then she's back on the phone, whispering about the

tradesman's entrance in a side street near Embankment Gardens. He has to wait till ten. Call her when he's outside.

Sami does as she says.

The fire door opens. Kate looks great. She's dressed like an airline stewardess only sexier, in a black pencil skirt and a fitted black blazer. Armani. Her eyes are made up to look huge and her hair is piled up on her head, making her neck look even longer.

'You can stay, but you have to be out by six,' she whispers, waving him inside. The door shuts.

She takes him upstairs in a service lift. Unlocks a suite with a master key. The place is bigger than most of the houses Sami has lived in.

'Don't take anything from the mini-bar. I have to go. I'll come see you later.'

Sami has a shower. He's so whacked out he almost falls asleep under the water, which is spilling out of this big silver head the size of a dinner plate.

Afterwards, he puts on one of those soft white robes and crawls onto the bed. He needs to think. Needs to sleep. His eyes close. He dreams.

It's about Kate Tierney and it's not unlike a lot of the dreams he's had about her in the past two and a bit years. She's cupping his balls in her right hand and taking him in her mouth. She looks up his chest, into his eyes, and then rubs her tongue along the length of him, popping him into her mouth, sucking hard enough to almost bring him off. Just when he's about to blow, she pinches him hard just below the head of his penis.

That's when he wakes up and looks down. Sees her tousled blonde hair. She crawls up the bed, straddling his chest, rocking her hips back and forth.

She eases back, squats over him, takes him inside. He can see their reflection in the mirror. Sami looks twice to make sure it's him. Surely he must be in heaven. He's lying on Egyptian cotton sheets in one of the most expensive hotel suites in London, being screwed by a girl he's fantasised about for more nights than he can remember. Kate Tierney. No longer a wet dream. A reality.

Later, as they're lying in bed, they talk about old times, about the past couple of years. She wants to know all about prison, the nitty gritty, the violence, the gangs. Kate seems to get off on all those men being in the one place. Sexually frustrated men. Unfulfilled. Violent.

Sami doesn't need much time to recover. Kate gets on all fours and says, 'Show me how they do it in prison.'

Prison sex normally involves a left hand and a bartered copy of Big Jugs magazine but Sami thinks her version is a lot more interesting.

They cuddle afterwards. It's nice. They know stuff about each other. Sami remembers the details of her letters. He knows about her brothers and her father losing his job and how they always spend Christmas in Scotland with relatives. She wrote about ordinary run-of-the-mill stuff, but Sami loved reading about it. It made him feel normal or at least that one day his life could be normal.

At six the next morning he's out of the Savoy the way he came in, smelling of sex and tasting Kate on his lips. Sami buys a coffee from a kiosk near Embankment Tube. Sits on a bench in Victoria Gardens. Makes his plans for the day. The wind comes off the river and tugs at the coats of commuters leaving the station.

Tony Murphy denied any knowledge of Nadia, but he could have been lying. Toby Streak was too frightened to be telling lies. So what does he do next?

He takes a crumpled piece of paper from his pocket and smooths it on his knee. The name and number are written in pencil. Vincent Ruiz. Sounds foreign.

Sami looks at his watch. It's gone seven. He flips open his phone and punches the number. Gets an answering machine.

'Hello, ah, this is Sami Macbeth. You don't know me. I'm, ah, looking for my sister, Nadia. Ms Wallace, my probation officer, said you might be able to help me. You can call me on this number . . . if you're interested.'

Sami can't think of anything else to say. He hangs up and buys another coffee. Contemplates a doughnut. Suddenly, his mobile beeps and he glances at the screen. It's Nadia's number. His heart flip-flops in his chest like a landed fish. Hot coffee spills over his fingertips. He opens the handset.

Two words and an address, that's all she sends him.

Meet me, is the message. It's not an explanation. Not an apology.

The address is in the East End. Sami hits redial. Waits. The number rings out. Why is she playing games with him?

14

Sami emerges from Whitechapel Underground and studies a map on the wall beside the ticket office. He played his first pub gig not far from here – in the basement of the White Hart, with a band called Raw Liver.

The venue was so small and PA so large, it was noisier than the Blitz according to the locals, who called the police and tried to have the gig stopped. That's what young bands do – make bold statements, argued Sami. Raw Liver seemed to be saying, 'We might not be as good as the Stones, but we're louder.'

He walks the last half-mile to the address. The place looks like a fortress with barbed wire on the rooftops, metal shutters, broken windows and a graffiti paintjob.

Sami is feeling double uneasy. This reeks of a set-up. Why is Nadia's mobile still turned off? He looks at the message again . . . tries to read between the words.

Most of the flats don't have numbers. Some of them don't have doors. Sami finds the right one by a process of elimination. Second floor, third one along, with a patched plywood door and 'Fuck off' scrawled across it.

Sami knocks. Nobody answers. He tries again and then calls through the remnants of the mailbox.

Someone is coming.

A black rasta opens the door, with beads clacking. Levi's sit low on his hips and his tight-fitting red T-shirt has a picture of Bob Marley in full voice.

'What's up, mon?' he asks.

'I'm looking for Nadia.'

'What took you so long? She been waiting,' he says in a singsong voice.

'Who are you?'

'Puffa.'

Sami walks through the kitchen. The sink is overflowing with takeaway tins and garbage. No way Nadia is living in a place like this. There's a chicken sticking out of the plughole. Why in fuck's name did someone try to shove a chicken down the drain?

Next comes the lounge or maybe it's a bedroom. The floor is littered with punctured cans, pipes, cones, tin foil, burnt spoons, needles, tourniquets, half-filled bottles of water and wedges of lemon. It's a drug den, a crack house.

The room is dark. There are two bodies sleeping on beanbags and two more curled up on a mattress. Sami listens to make sure they're breathing. You got to be careful around junkies. They get paranoid. Psychotic.

Puffa has disappeared. He was here a moment ago. Sami moves along a corridor past another filthy room. Empty. Reeking. He opens the next door with his elbow. The smell hits him first. It's like something died weeks ago and nobody bothered giving it a decent burial.

Puffa is near the window.

The curtains open. The brightness is like an explosion.

Sami spots the baseball bat but sees it too late. He tries to duck and the bat bounces off the top of his head. Pain explodes and his brain washes from one side of his skull to the other.

The next blow almost breaks across his back. He drops to his knees in a world of hurt and tries to crawl away but the bat keeps hitting him, bouncing off his neck, his shoulders, his lower back . . .

Sami is doubled over and vomiting. Fingers lace in his hair and slam his head forward onto a raised knee. His bottom lip bursts against his teeth. Blood leaks into his mouth.

He doesn't want to fight. He doesn't want to get up. He just wants the beating to stop.

Someone drags him up. Sits him in a chair. Hits him again. Sami's head flies off at a different angle. The room goes dark. Drops away. Disappears.

Sometime later he sees a blurred light and the air swims for a moment before things come into focus. Nadia is curled at his feet, resting her head on his lap. She's wearing only jeans and a bra.

Sami wants to stroke her hair but his arms are tied behind his back. Bound to a chair. Blood and saliva stain his shirt.

Nadia turns her head. 'I'm so sorry, baby,' she whispers, stroking his cheek. Weightless and brittle, her eyes are black rimmed and cavernous.

Sami's mouth is taped. He can't answer.

He scans the room, looking for a way out. It has a wardrobe, a soiled mattress and two armchairs worn thin by squirming arses. A dirty brown blanket lies curled on the floor. Everything is brown – brown walls, brown carpet, brown furniture.

The door opens. Nadia stands. She smiles at Puffa, who sways into the room like he's on a catwalk. No way this emaciated crackhead beat Sami up. He must have had help.

Nadia becomes someone different. She wraps her arms around Puffa's neck. Squeezes her thighs around his leg.

'Have you got something for baby?' she purrs. 'Baby needs her medicine.'

Puffa grins with a gob full of gold.

'First you got to dance for me, princess. Show me how much you want it.'

Nadia hesitates. 'Don't make me do it now.'

'What's wrong?'

'Not in front of my brother.'

Puffa shakes his head. His dreadlocks swing. 'How bad you want to ride the dragon?'

'Please.'

'Come on, princess, just one dance. Show Sami how much you love the dragon.'

Nadia is about to cry. She pleads with him again.

'First you dance,' he says.

And she does, holding her arms above her head, rolling her hips in long slow circles. Her eyes are closed. Tears of shame glisten on her cheeks.

Puffa isn't watching her. He's looking at Sami. He pushes his face close.

'Do you know what crack is, mon?' He holds up a small yellow stone between his thumb and forefinger. 'It's the devil's sputum.'

Sami can feel his face burning and his skin crawling. He wants to cry. He wants to go home. He doesn't want to play any more. Puffa sits cross-legged in front of Sami, so he can watch what he's doing. Nadia is watching too, as she dances. Pale. Beautiful. Ugly.

Puffa burns a cigarette and collects the ash, putting it in a makeshift pipe fashioned from a mini whisky bottle, chewing gum, a rubber band and foil. He flattens the ash in the pipe and nestles the crack on top.

He signals Nadia. She drops to her knees like a dog begging for food or waiting for a scrap to fall from the table. She's hooked. Taken. Spoken for.

Sami wants to yell at her. He raises his feet a few inches from the floor and stamps them down, making the chair jump.

Nadia turns. Sami pleads with his eyes.

'I need to do this,' she says.

Sami stamps his feet again.

Puffa laughs. 'She doesn't love you any more, mon. She loves the rock. She loves the rockman.'

Sami tries to launch himself out of the chair. The bindings hold him back.

'Cool it bro, you got to chill,' says Puffa, as he holds the pipe towards Nadia and turns the lighter upside down. A bubbling crackling sound fills the room and smoke as white as cotton wool is trapped in the glass.

Nadia inhales. Her cheeks puff out. Her eyes shut. Her head lolls back. She tries to hold the smoke in her mouth and then swallow it bit by bit, holding it in her lungs for a minute or more until it seems as though she might pass out if she doesn't exhale.

Nadia looks at Sami and smiles. It's not her normal, beautiful, radiant smile. It's a chemical reaction. Opiate-induced. Her pupils are dilated. Her hands are twitching. She's blissful. Ecstatic. She's gone now. In another place.

Puffa chuckles. 'Don't she just love the dragon.'

Sami's head is spinning. The pain makes it hard to frame questions, let alone answers. He can see the pulse beating in Nadia's neck and the flaring of her nostrils.

She's started to come down. It's not like falling off a cliff. It's like the walls of paradise are nothing but stucco façades and behind them lie ugliness, anxiety, despair . . .

'The devil does it every time,' says Puffa. 'He tricks

you. Makes you believe you're in heaven, but when you've signed up, when you've taken the pledge, when you've hocked your soul, he shows you the gates of hell and says, "Don't believe the brochures, mon".'

Nadia is clawing at the skin on her forearms and whimpering like a frightened child in the biggest, darkest haunted house imaginable.

Sami looks at Puffa. Pleads with his eyes. He has to give her something. Make her better.

Puffa takes a tablet from his pocket. 'It's Valium,' he explains. 'It will help her come down.'

Puffa peels the wrapper off a chocolate bar and takes a bite. His eyes have a liquid sheen as he looks at Nadia proudly, as though his work here is done.

After ten minutes, she's calm.

'I need another pipe,' she says.

'Ain't got no more rock.'

'But I need some, baby.'

'Maybe I dropped some on the floor.'

Nadia doesn't hesitate. She's on all fours, looking for crumbs of crack on the stained rug or between the floorboards, trying to force the wooden planks apart with her fingernails. She's not Sami's sister any more. Not the one he remembers. She's a ghost. She's a crack whore.

The air pressure changes slightly. A door has opened and someone is standing behind Sami. Puffa isn't smiling any more. He opens his mouth to say something, but no words come out because a fist is squeezing his throat trying to narrow his neck size.

Puffa is scrabbling on his toes, but he can't get traction. Whoever has hold of his throat is 'walking' him outside. Meanwhile, Nadia has stopped looking for crack and is curled up in the corner, rocking gently, trying to make herself small.

Sami calls out but the gag muffles his voice. He wants Nadia to untie him. They can get away. He bounces on the chair and almost topples backwards.

Someone moves behind him and a voice whispers, pronouncing every syllable in a Scottish accent.

'You're taking a wee trip, Mr Macbeth. It's not the same sort of trip as your sister. Don't resist and you won't get hurt.'

Sami catches a whiff of the cologne and remembers smelling it before at Tony Murphy's restaurant. Dessie Fraser was wearing aftershave. Maybe he was the one who bounced the bat off Sami's head.

Oddly enough Sami feels relieved. Safer. Drugsters like Puffa see monsters in their Rice Krispies. At least Dessie is a professional. If he'd wanted to kill Sami he'd be dead already, despatched, gonski.

Sami takes a journey in a car boot. The darkness is oddly reassuring. He can feel the sides of the boot and smell the nylon carpet and spare wheel.

Nadia would have hated a ride like this. She would have panicked at the darkness and the enclosed space.

Even after thirteen years she still has nightmares. She hates wet nights. Swollen rivers. Drunk drivers. Narrow bridges. Nadia was in the front seat of the car. Sami in the back – just turned fifteen. Their father had been drinking at a casino in Brighton and had left them sleeping in the car. He woke them at 2.00 a.m., drunk, but determined to drive back to a cottage they were renting for the holidays.

The car demolished a crash barrier on the approach to a bridge, landing upside down in the water. The windows were open. It sank within seconds.

Douglas Macbeth was pinned by one leg behind the steering wheel, but he twisted his body so he could hold Nadia, pushing her face into the shrinking bubble of air. Sami tried to open the rear doors, but they were locked. Finally, he pulled one open. Grabbed Nadia. Scissored his legs to the surface.

They fought the current as it dragged them away, unable to go back. Swallowing water. Spluttering. Sucking air.

Sami no longer has nightmares about it; no longer has phantom phone calls from his father at three in the morning.

Douglas Macbeth was a coward and Sami feared him the way children fear all cowards, because they prey on the weak and make excuses about why they do it.

Some nights Douglas Macbeth would get so drunk that Sami would try to avoid him or give him one-word answers but his father would pull Sami onto his lap and tickle him mercilessly; tickle him until tears ran down his cheeks. Not tears of laughter. Douglas would use Sami's giggles to mask the moment that he drove his thumbs deep beneath his son's armpits, leaving bruises so deep they took a week to show and would always be hidden beneath his school uniform.

When the current dragged Sami and Nadia away that night, sweeping them down the swollen river, Sami didn't want to go back. He wanted to keep floating away. He wanted to forget he had a father.

Nadia couldn't forget. She clung to Sami for six hours before they were rescued. Clung to him on the way to the hospital. Wouldn't let him leave her side, even when they cut off her clothes and stitched the gash on her hip.

And for years after that she would crawl onto Sami's bed at night and curl asleep at his feet like a tabby cat, with one hand reaching across the bedclothes, making sure that he was still there.

The car stops. A roller door opens. Sami waits, listening. He doesn't want the boot to open. He wants to stay in the dark.

15

Saturday morning, Ruiz gets out of the shower, turns on his mobile and listens to his messages. The last one is from Sami Macbeth, who sounds tired and worried. He's still looking for his sister.

Ruiz makes himself breakfast. Looks at the headlines. Listens to the message again. Nadia is eighteen – old enough to disappear, old enough to find herself. Maybe he should flick past this one and find something better to do.

Only he can't think of anything better. That's one of the problems with being retired – he doesn't get any holidays. Every day is the same. Leisure. Leisure. Leisure. All play and no work.

He puts in a call to a prison psychologist and gets the skinny on Macbeth, who boasted a clean rap sheet until he got picked up for possession of stolen jewellery. He has a 150-point IQ, three A-levels and about as much common sense as a pork chop.

Next Ruiz calls Fiona Taylor, an old pal from his days

on vice. She began her career as a parking warden, putting tickets under wiper blades, and then spent ten years in uniform before they gave her sergeant's stripes. Now she's a Chief Inspector, which isn't surprising given her talent, but a minor miracle in the Metropolitan Police Service where the glass ceiling is bulletproof.

Blonde, muscular and unmarried, Fiona has the sort of aggressive posture that leads some men to think she's gay. In reality she's a challenge and well worth the effort, thinks Ruiz, who had a brief fling with her a decade ago before he hooked up with Miranda.

'I thought you were dead,' she says warmly.

'Not even in the departure lounge.'

'I'm glad to hear it.'

They swap small talk about family and mutual friends. He asks about work. The less said the better.

'What do you need?' she asks, knowing he's called for a reason.

'I want to bounce a name off you. Toby Streak.'

'I remember him. Why are you interested?'

'A favour for a friend.'

Fiona is typing on a keyboard. 'He's a pimp and dealer. I busted him ten years ago for statutory rape and he did a deal with the girl's father.'

'Paid him off?'

'You might very well think that; I couldn't possibly comment.' She's doing her Francis Urquhart impersonation.

109

Ruiz plays along. 'What *can* you comment upon?'

'Streak's main angle is a lover-boy scam, finding fresh meat for the pornsters.'

'Does he work for anyone in particular?'

'Freelance mainly. He started as a DJ working raves in the mid-nineties. He used to pick out the prettiest girls dancing around the cowpats and invite them to Ibiza for the summer. They'd begin by wearing bikinis and dancing in cages at the clubs. Then came the modelling shots, the promises of recording deals, the screen auditions . . . you know the rest.'

Ruiz asks about a last known address. Fiona checks the computer. Gives him the details of a flat off Abbey Road in St John's Wood.

Fiona is busy. She has to go.

'One more thing,' says Ruiz. 'Tony Murphy – is he still in the market for girls?'

'He still has a couple of clubs, but he doesn't have to recruit. The girls come to him.'

'Why's that?'

'His clientele are known to shower occasionally.'

'He's gone upmarket?'

'Right to the top.'

It's midday Saturday. The sun is shining. Toby Streak will still be asleep. Ruiz quite fancies a trip to Abbey Road. He might walk the famous crossing and relive a Beatles moment; even go barefoot like Paul.

Streak lives in a luxury block of flats with an intercom and security cameras. Business must be good. Ruiz tries the neighbours on the intercom and one of them buzzes him through the main door. He catches the lift to the fourth floor and hammers on the door until Toby stumbles from a bedroom and peers through a security peephole.

Ruiz gives him a spiel about reading the gas meter. Flashes a library card. Works every time.

'It's Saturday,' says the voice behind the door.

'I could come back Monday, but you won't have any gas by then. They'll have turned it off. Your meter hasn't been read for six months. Won't take a second.'

A deadbolt slides back. In the same instant Ruiz kicks the door open, hitting Streak in the head. Toby lets out a cry and falls to his knees, clutching his already bandaged nose. As he tries to scramble away on his hands and knees, Ruiz follows him down the hallway. Flicks a boot into his elbows. Toby falls on his face and Ruiz pins him to the floor, massaging his ear with his right heel.

A girl peers from the bedroom. She's young – maybe too young – wrapped in a sheet.

'You Nadia Macbeth?'

She shakes her head.

'Put your clothes on. I'll give you the cab fare home.'

She looks at Toby. Ruiz leans a little harder on his head.

'Go home, babe,' he says, trying to act cool with his face pressed into the hall runner.

The girl slips on a dress, wads up her underwear and shoes and steps over Streak, almost flying down the stairs.

'I'm looking for Nadia Macbeth,' says Ruiz.

'You and everyone else,' Toby sniffles. 'Can I get up now?' The plaster across his nose makes him sound like a cartoon character.

Ruiz lifts his foot. Toby climbs to his feet and slumps into a chair, tentatively touching his nose.

'If you've broken it again . . .' He doesn't finish the statement.

'Who broke it the first time?'

'That cunt Macbeth.'

Ruiz glances around the flat. The décor is a cross between bachelor chic and a seventies brothel.

'Let's start at the beginning,' he says, pulling up a chair.

It's not difficult to get the story out of Toby. He's an expert at telling it now. Tony Murphy paid him a thousand quid to hook Nadia Macbeth in a lover-boy scam.

'It wasn't worth the fucking aggravation,' says Toby, acting like a victim in all this.

'Why did Murphy want her?'

'Fuck knows.'

'But it had to be this particular girl?'

'Yeah.'

'You ever provided girls for Murphy before?'

'No.'

'Why this time?'

He shrugs. 'He said it had to be done quick – in three days. Sweep her off her feet. Deliver her.'

'Where?'

'Place off the Whitechapel Road.' He tilts his head back, trying to stop his nose bleeding. 'You won't tell Murphy I told you, will ya?'

'That's the least of your problems, Toby.'

16

'Sorry about the transport, son,' says Tony Murphy, brushing dust off Sami's shoulders. 'It's the best Dessie could come up with at short notice.'

They're standing in a concrete car park with numbered bays and reserved signs. Sami can hear a crowd cheering from somewhere outside. Maybe it's a football match.

Murphy's face is full of chubby bonhomie. He's playing the jolly fat man, dressed in a lightweight woollen suit with his pork pie hat at a jaunty angle.

'You remember Dessie.'

'He bounced a few things off me earlier,' replies Sami, flexing his left shoulder, which still aches. The swelling above his eye feels like a golf ball beneath his skin and he can taste blood in his mouth. He fingers his front teeth, counting them.

'He's a very capable individual, Dessie. He managed to find your sister.'

'He beat the crap out of me.'

'On the contrary, he saved your life. Those drugsters can be very fucking dangerous. You were lucky Dessie was there.'

Sami shakes his head in wonder. What sort of parallel universe has he been transported to?

'Where's Nadia?'

'In safe hands.'

Mr Murphy leads the way. Sami is to follow. A lift opens. It takes them upwards and they emerge into a carpeted room furnished with comfortable chairs facing a large picture window. A corporate box, but it's not a football match. They're at the dogs.

A moment later a bell sounds and gates open. Half a dozen loose-limbed greyhounds scramble into full stride and hurtle around the first bend, chasing a fake rabbit. Accelerating down the straight, the dogs fight to stay upright on the corners as the crowd roars. Sami watches, mesmerised. This isn't sport – it's an arcane spectacle, like seeing lions fight elephants at the Colosseum.

Murphy isn't taking any notice. He's on the phone arguing with his wife about where they should put the marquee. She must be throwing a party.

Sami smells the food. Curries. Two tables on either side of the viewing window are lined with stainless steel tureens. Samosas, onion bhajis, chicken korma, beef vindaloo, butter chicken, pilau rice, chapatis and naan bread.

Dessie is already tucking in. He must have worked up an appetite swinging that bat.

The race has finished. The rabbit won. A dog came second. Extra Chum for him tonight.

'Terrible thing crack,' says Tony Murphy, offering Sami a plate. 'It's a cocaine derivative. Not physically addictive like heroin. Psychologically addictive. Once your mind has been there it wants to go back again and again.'

Sami watches him spoon korma onto rice. 'People get all paranoid when they come down. Twitchy. Scared. It's so bad that some of them start taking heroin, which is the beginning of the end. Know what I'm saying? Once you're needled up and rattling, you're truly fucked.'

He takes a mouthful of naan bread and takes a seat. Sami stares at his plate of food, no longer hungry.

'I've never punted the stuff,' says Murphy. 'It's not a moral thing with me, just too much aggravation getting webbed up in shit like that. I did try it once though and I can understand the attraction. Do a pipe and get a blowjob at the same time. You'll believe you're in heaven.'

Sami weighs the fork in his hand. He wants to drive it through Murphy's throat.

'Are you a drug taker, son?'

Sami shakes his head.

'Very wise decision. It gives you an advantage. Power. You take your sister, Nadia. From what I hear that little moppet would suck off an Alsatian to get her next fix. It's a shame.'

Sami sees the red mist. He launches himself across the

116

room but seems to stop in mid-air and crash to the floor. On his knees, Sami takes a boot in the stomach and a punch to the kidneys. A socket of pain races up his spine and explodes like fireworks in his head.

Dessie grabs his collar. Sits him in a chair. Murphy takes another mouthful of chicken korma as though nothing has happened.

'You're not the complete package, son,' he says, picking a grain of rice from his shirt. 'Some parts are still missing.'

Sami's mouth is opening and closing like a guppy.

'This plan of yours to retire, I don't think it's a good one. You can't just walk away from the life you chose; the life that chose you. You're too good at what you do, son.'

Murphy loads his fork with Indian pickle and rice.

'Young bloke like you should use his talent wisely. Make a decent score. Know what I'm saying?'

Sami can breathe again. The pain is easing.

'You got savvy, son. You know what savvy means?'

'I'm not sure.'

'You're bright. You learn fast. You know your way around. Am I right?'

Sami feels like he's being led by the dick and there's nothing he can do about it.

'Let's face it, son, you're too young to retire. You're in your prime. You've come of age. You got that hungry look in your eyes.'

'That's cause I haven't eaten,' explains Sami.

'I'm speaking metaphorically, son. Work with me here.'

Sami sucks on a wobbly tooth and feels perspiration prickle along the skin beneath his hairline. Mr Murphy is getting to the point.

'That's why you're going to do this small favour for me. A single job and then you can walk away. And I promise you nobody is gonna give you any grief. You'll be out.'

'What about Nadia?'

'I'm going to look after your little sis. Get her straightened out. Clean.'

'Can I see her?'

'When the job is done.'

'What do I have to do?'

'I want you to open a safe for me. It's more of a strong room than a safe. Locks and metal bars. No funny combination whats-its. Someone of your experience will do it in his sleep. Blindfolded. One hand tied behind his back.'

'I can't do it,' says Sami.

Murphy stops chewing.

'You saying you can't open the safe?'

'Yes.'

'Why not?'

At this point Sami knows he's on shaky ground. He doesn't have the first fucking clue how to open a strong room. He's not a safecracker or a safe blower. 'Sparkles' is a figment of the imagination, an invention, a lie.

'What if I told you that I didn't do the Hampstead job?' he says.

'I don't understand.'

'I wasn't there. It was a guy called Andy Palmer. Or maybe it was someone else. I was just sitting in a van.'

Murphy laughs. 'Pull the other leg, son, it plays "Land of Hope and Glory".' Then his face grows hard. He gives Sami the pointy finger. 'Enough pissing about, son. You do this job and you have a future, simple as that.'

'I'm out of practice.'

'Nonsense. It's like riding a bike.'

'No offence, Mr Murphy, but it's nothing like riding a bike.'

'I'm speaking figuratively, son.'

'Yes, sir.'

Sami looks at Dessie and back to Murphy. He can't see a way out of this. He needs time to think. Time to come up with a plan.

'What sort of strong room?' he asks.

'Big fucker.'

'I need the make and model, the specs. I don't try to open a safe unless I know everything about it – the type, location, tensile strength of the steel. Manufacturer. How old it is?'

'I can get you that.'

'I don't have any tools.'

'What do you need?'

Sami is winging it now. 'It's very technical equipment.'

'Just tell me what you need.'

'Depends on the job.'

Sami starts talking about diamond tipped drills, fibre-optic cameras and stethoscopes. He doesn't know about half the stuff he's asking for, but hopefully neither does Murphy.

'I'm going to need explosives,' he says.

'Why?'

'A failsafe, just in case the door won't open.'

Murphy clips the end from a cigar and draws on a flame, puffing out clouds of smoke.

'Give Dessie a list.'

'What's in this strong room?' asks Sami.

'That ain't none of your business, son.'

'If I'm going to open it, I should know what's inside. Safety reasons, you know.'

'I am looking after your safety,' says Murphy. 'I'm giving you deniability.'

'Deniability?'

'Yeah. It's like the old song goes, "You don't put your dick in the blender if you're running short on swizzle sticks".'

'I don't know that one,' says Sami.

'I could get Dessie here to sing it for you, but he's not a fan of karaoke.' Murphy spits a fleck of tobacco leaf onto the floor. 'He's also not partial to smart-mouth sarky toerags who ask too many questions.'

Sami keeps his mouth shut.

'Right, that's decided,' says Murphy. 'We'll get you the specs. Dessie, here, will get you the equipment. You do the job tomorrow.'

120

'What do you mean tomorrow?' says Sami. 'I need more time to prepare . . . to practise.'

'Got no time.'

A bell clangs. The dogs are off again. Murphy turns to the window to watch. 'Another thing, son, I don't want you even thinking you might tip off Old Bill about these discussions. That's why you're going to stay with Dessie until tomorrow, understand?

'And if you did go shooting off your mouth at some later date, I got a dozen people, including a member of parliament, who'll put me three hundred miles from here, watching Man City play Everton.

'The CCTV cameras will tell 'em the same thing. Ever heard of body doubles, son? Saddam had used dozens of 'em – fat fuckers with moustaches who strutted around firing shots in the air. So did Adolf. Now I don't like the Krauts as a rule but they've had some pretty good ideas, Mercedes, BMWs. Gassing them Jews was right out of order, mind you, but some of the kikes I know wouldn't give you the steam off their piss unless they were charging usage. I shit you not.

'So don't you go blabbing about our little enterprise, before or afterwards. Understand? Or I'll have Dessie here hold open your smart mouth with a spout while I piss down your throat.'

17

The address is off Whitechapel Road – three streets back from the river. Jack the Ripper territory but nowadays it could be in Bangladesh or Mogadishu or Mecca. There are headscarves and Halal butchers, Halal bakers and Halal greengrocers. How do you get Halal fruit and veg, wonders Ruiz, as he parks the car on vacant ground beside a mosque.

A gaggle of teenagers in hoodies and low-slung jeans slink out of the shadows – every one of them a genetic time bomb. They begin checking out the Merc and regarding Ruiz with hate and envy.

The ringleader looks no older than twelve. Fearless. Freckled. Hostile.

'This is our fucking turf. You can't park here without our say so.'

'Is that right? I didn't see any signs. Must be getting old.'

'It's gonna cost you.'

'How much?'

The kid looks at his gang. 'A fiver.' And then adds, 'for a half hour.'

Ruiz takes out a tenner. 'You got change?'

The kid looks at it greedily. 'You can stay an hour.'

Ruiz balls up the ten quid note and looks at the gang. One of them is a mixed race kid, small and whippet thin. Built to run. Ruiz points to him. Motions him forward. Gives him the tenner.

'Whoever catches you, gets the money. Otherwise, you get to keep it.'

The kid takes off, darting across the allotment, leaping a fence, dodging rubbish bins and parked cars. He's flying down the street with the others in pursuit, screaming abuse.

Ruiz's mobile vibrates against his heart. Fiona Taylor sounds concerned.

'Funny thing happened after I talked to you. I typed Tony Murphy's name into the PNC and pulled up his file.'

'How many pages did it come to?'

'Oh, it's long, but I'm more interested in the pages I'm *not* allowed to see.'

'What do you mean?'

'There's a lock on some of the information. I don't have the security clearance to access it.'

Ruiz can hear her tapping a pencil on the edge of her desk. She's thinking. 'It could be special ops.'

'A surveillance operation?'

'MI5 or maybe MI6.'

'Murphy isn't in that league.'

'Maybe not, but it might be worth treading softly on this one,' she warns.

'I'm very light on my feet. You should see me dance.'

'A ballroom king – now I've heard everything.'

She hangs up and Ruiz contemplates why a club owner like Tony Murphy would warrant so much secrecy. There were rumours years ago that he laundered money for the IRA, but not even Murphy would be crazy enough to swim with those sharks.

Ruiz starts looking for the block of flats where Toby Streak said he dropped Nadia Macbeth. What he finds is a graffiti-stained pile of shit with scorch marks around the balconies and plywood nailed over most of the windows. A black guy with dreadlocks opens the door and blinks at the brightness, whacked out on something.

'You know what time it is, mon?'

'Four o'clock.'

'People are sleeping.'

'It's the afternoon.'

'Time is relative. That's what Mr Einstein say.'

'He also said only two things are infinite – the universe and human stupidity – and he wasn't completely sure about the universe.'

The rasta scratches his arse. Ruiz looks past him. The hallway is littered with junk mail, bills and final demands.

'I'm looking for someone.'

'You a copper?'

'Do I look like one?'

'You fat enough.'

'I'll polish my boot on your arse.'

'That would be police brutality, mon.'

'Not if my foot slipped. I'm looking for someone. Her name's Nadia Macbeth.'

'You want a girl. Why didn't you say so? Follow Puffa.'

He motions Ruiz inside and down the hall. The carpet sticks to his feet. Puffa leads him into a semi-dark room strewn with burnt spoons, bent cans, water bottles and foil wrappers. He kicks a mound of blankets. A white face emerges, with sunken cheeks and chemical green eyes. He calls her Treka.

'So what do you think? Talk to Puffa. We can negotiate.'

'I'm only interested in Nadia Macbeth.'

'Nobody here called Nadia.'

Treka crawls back under the blanket.

Ruiz brushes past Puffa and begins searching the flat. He talks to a kid who looks about twenty, but is probably younger. He's eating cereal straight from the box and staring at a corner where the TV used to be.

'You ever heard of Nadia Macbeth?' he asks.

'I heard of Macbeth. Studied it at school. It's one of them Shakespeare plays about three witches and a dude who wants to be king.'

'You must have been listening.'

Ruiz takes out his mobile and looks at the list of recent messages, before hitting a button to return a call. The sound of a phone ringing fills the room. Puffa looks at the ceiling pretending he can't hear it. The handset is vibrating in his pocket.

'Aren't you going to answer that?' asks Ruiz.

'Not just now,' says Puffa.'

'I think you should.'

Puffa pulls out the handset. Flips it open. 'Hello?' he asks nervously.

'Hello,' answers Ruiz.

'Can I help you?'

'Yes you can. Every time you open your mouth it's like a fart in a colander. From now on you're going to answer my questions honestly or I'm going to set fire to your dreads.'

Puffa's eyes go wide and he puts both hands on his head.

'How did you get this mobile?'

'Dude left it here.'

'What was his name?'

Puffa shrugs.

Ruiz points to the kid with the cereal box. 'What was the name of that play you studied?'

'Macbeth.'

He looks at Puffa. 'That's a clue.'

Puffa starts bleating about having memory problems. 'I smoke too much grass, mon. I forget things, you know.'

126

Ruiz gathers the occupants of the flat into one room. There are six of them – junkies, hookers and runaways, all of them whacked out on something, sweating or ill. He takes Puffa through the story again, marvelling at how he can tie himself into knots and harangue himself for telling lies, before starting a completely new explanation about how he came by Sami Macbeth's mobile.

Eventually, Puffa gets so tangled up in his lies that he starts telling bits of the truth. Someone paid him five hundred quid to get a girl hooked on crack. He had to start her on the brown, he explains, because she wouldn't co-operate but soon she rode the dragon and didn't want to stop.

'Who gave you the money?'

'Big white dude. Smelled like he fell in a tub of after-shave.'

'Give you a name?'

'Nope.'

'You didn't ask or you didn't care?'

'He wasn't a great talker.'

'How did you get the mobile?'

Puffa starts telling a lie. Stops. Starts again.

'Guy left it behind. He come looking for his sister. The big mon gave him a hiding and took him away.'

'What about Nadia.'

'Her too.'

'Are you sure that's how it happened?'

Puffa nods. 'If you want me to say it didn't happen, that's OK. Tell me what you want to hear.'

'The truth.'

'The truth is relative, mon.'

Ruiz slaps him around the head.

'Ow, that hurt!'

'Pain is relative, too.'

Ruiz keeps quizzing him, but the story doesn't change. The others are next to clueless. 'Anyone got anything to add?'

They shake their heads.

Ruiz puts a fatherly arm around Puffa's shoulders, flicking his beaded dreadlocks with his thumb.

'You got a passport, Puffa?'

'No, mon.'

'I'd get one if I were you. Maybe consider relocating. See the islands. Meet the distant cousins.'

Puffa frowns. 'Why's that, mon?'

'After I find the girl you got hooked on crack, I'm going to come back and turn your balls into worry beads.'

18

Tony Murphy has four mobiles on the table in front of him. He chooses one. Punches in a number.

'I thought we were going to talk tonight,' says a voice on the other end.

'I'm calling now. Is this line OK?'

'Yeah.'

'Where's the stuff now?'

'Same as before, but only till Monday. Should have gone to the lab yesterday.'

'Tell me about this strong room.'

'It's not really a room. It's more like an industrial wardrobe.'

'What's an industrial wardrobe?'

'It's like an ordinary wardrobe only it's made of steel.'

'Any locks?'

'Three of them: one internal and two padlocks.'

'Motion sensors or alarms?'

'It's the Old Bailey, not the Bank of England.'

Murphy doesn't appreciate his sarcasm. 'I need the make and a serial number.'

'You want fries with that?'

'Don't be a comedian. Brummies aren't funny.'

'What about Jasper Carrott?'

'My armpit is funnier than Jasper Carrott.'

They discuss the details. Decide the timetable. Murphy can get a floor plan and the location of the security cameras.

'What about our cover story?'

'I'm working on it. You just have to worry about the strong room.'

'It's under control.'

'I don't want a mess.'

'In. Out. I got an expert who's slicker than a butcher's prick.'

19

Sami spends the night on a bunk bed in a warehouse just off the south circular. The place is full of air-conditioning units, still in boxes. Some bright spark entrepreneur bought up four thousand of the systems from Taiwan figuring global warming was a sales opportunity. That was before the wettest, coldest summer in a century.

Bankruptcy resulted, allowing Tony Murphy to snap up the entire stock for a tenner each. It was the perfect example of stupidity and capitalism working in perfect harmony.

Sami didn't sleep. He spent the night thinking about Nadia and feeling sorry for himself. Bad luck is supposed to float around and fall randomly on people – a little here, a little there. It's been raining on Sami his whole life. Dumping on him. Now he's swimming in an ocean of shit (front crawl, not backstroke) and he doesn't know which shore to head for.

He still can't rid himself of the images of Nadia dancing for crack and crawling on her hands and knees, trying to prise apart the floorboards. His last glimpse of her was crouching in a corner, shivering, terrified, humiliated, unable to speak.

When Sami rescued her from the sunken car she was like that, struck dumb. For months Nadia didn't say a word. The psychologist said it was post-traumatic stress. Sami imagined the screams were trapped inside his sister's head, echoing so loudly that Nadia couldn't hear the sound of her own voice.

Sami took her to a place he knew – an underpass near Clapham Junction where the express trains roared overhead and created a wall of sound that nobody could shout over. He hired a portable generator and set up a microphone and the band's biggest PA amp beneath the underpass. They waited for the next train and he told Nadia she had to open her mouth and let the scream out. The train was roaring over their heads in a thunderous roll.

It took five more trains before it happened. Nadia squeaked, then she cried, then she screamed into the microphone, throwing back her head and howling as tears squeezed from her eyes. Sami always wondered what the passengers on the train must have made of the voice they heard booming from the underpass, drowning out the drumming wheels and rushing wind. Nadia had rediscovered her voice; heard it over the screams in her head; let it come pouring out in a rage of tears, snot and regret.

Sami pauses and listens. A vehicle has pulled up outside. The roller door opens and a white van pulls inside. Dessie is sitting up front next to a driver who's wearing dark sunglasses and looks like a hod carrier. Certain details about him seem familiar – the pallid skin and balloon-shaped head.

Then Sami remembers. It's the same geezer who spoke to him outside Wormwood Scrubs on the day he was released.

Sami imagines he's going to be huge, but when he steps out of the van he only comes up to Sami's chest. He calls himself Sinbad and doesn't bother shaking hands. Instead he cracks his knuckles and flexes tattooed forearms which are thicker than his legs.

The van has ladders on top and a logo on the side: *Elevation Solutions: Lift Repairs and Maintenance.*

Dessie tosses Sami a peaked cap, work boots and a blue boilersuit, nothing too new or clean. They're supposed to be repairmen. Professionals.

Inside the van there are ropes, pulleys and tools. Underneath a tarp is some extra gear: a fuck-off drill on a frame, a stethoscope and a fibre-optic camera still in the box.

Dessie hands Sami a brown manila A4 envelope. Sami has a feeling it isn't a permission slip. Opening the flap, he pulls out the specs for a strong room along with floor plans of a building showing the lift shafts, security doors and CCTV cameras.

Sami takes a seat and begins studying them, trying to look like he knows what he's doing, which couldn't be further from the truth.

'Got to get moving. Job's been called in,' says Sinbad.

'What job?'

'Broken lift.'

'I need longer.'

'No time.'

Sami dresses in the boilersuit and work boots that are a size and a half too big.

'I don't think I can go. These don't fit,' he tells Dessie.

'They're not supposed to, dickweed. We don't want you leaving any wee footprints that match your shoe size.'

'Good thinking,' says Sami, marvelling at the logic.

Sinbad hands him a canister.

'What's this?'

'Mate of mine knocked it up. It's called TATP.'

'What's that mean?'

'Triacetone tri-oxymoron,' says Sinbad, 'or something like that. You got to treat it real gentle or, you know what . . .'

'What?'

'It goes off.'

'You mean it goes bad?'

'No, it blows up, moron. The ragheads call it the Mother of Satan.'

'I said I wanted plastic explosives.'

'Tescos was fresh out.'

Sami takes the container from Sinbad. Holds it at arm's length. Sweat prickles on his forehead. This is crazy. He could get a twenty-year sentence for possessing even half this shit and now he's nursing a homemade bomb.

'Check the gear,' says Dessie. 'Make sure we got everything.'

Sami makes a show of flicking switches and holding up the fibre-optic camera, blowing on the lens. One half of his brain says, 'How hard can it be to open a strong room? Andy Palmer managed it.' The other half of his brain says, 'Who am I kidding?'

Dessie is counting out the latex gloves and balaclavas. He loads the gear into a zip-up holdall and tosses an empty rucksack in the back of the van.

'If anything goes wrong; if we get separated, call this number,' he tells Sami.

'I don't have a phone.'

'Use a call box.'

Dessie turns off his own phone. Mobiles can be traced.

He gives Sinbad the nod. They're ready. The roller door opens and the van pulls out into bright daylight.

Sami sits in the middle, next to Sinbad, whose feet barely reach the pedals. Nobody is saying much. There's not a lot to say. Sami decides to read the instructions for the fibre-optic camera.

'I thought you knew how to use this shit,' says Dessie.

'Different brand,' explains Sami. 'This one's Japanese.'

He shows him the box. Dessie blinks at the writing. It says *Made in Germany*. He can't read.

Sami met guys doing bird who were illiterate. Some of them used to bring their letters to him to read or ask him to write back to their wives and girlfriends. It could be heartbreaking because the news from home wasn't always positive.

A con called Phil Bucket (everyone called him Lunchbucket) got a letter from his missus one day and as Sami read the first line to himself he realised it was a Dear John letter. She was giving Phil the flick. Filing for divorce.

Sami looked at the expectation on Phil's face and couldn't do it. Phil had six years to go. If he took the news badly he might shoot the messenger and break a few of Sami's bones. So Sami made up a different letter – one that said everything was great at home and the kids were missing him.

Then he sat Phil down and they wrote a letter back. 'Tell me how you feel about Nancy,' he asked him.

'She's a good bird.'

'What's she like?'

'Well she's let herself go a bit, I guess, put on a few pounds.'

'But you love her, right?'

'You trying to be funny?'

'No.'

'You think I'm a soft prick?'

'No, Phil, not at all,' Sami stammered. 'I just think you

136

should tell Nancy how you feel about her. Let her know how much she means to you.'

'Why?'

'She deserves it, doesn't she? She's raising your kids on her own. You're not round to help.'

Phil thought about this. Mulled it over. 'She makes a cracking sherry trifle with those little sponge squares and custard.'

'I was thinking of something a little more romantic.'

'Like what?'

'How about we say this, "Dear Nancy, I think about you all the time. At night when I lie in bed I remember how nice it is to just hold you and hear you sleeping. A man like me doesn't deserve a woman like you".'

'You can't say that – she might leave me.'

'Trust me, Phil. She'll love it. Then you'll say, "I know you're paying for my mistakes, Nancy, but one day I'll make it up to you and the kids. I'm gonna show you how much you mean to me. How much I miss you. Don't give up on me, Nancy. Keep a candle burning for me in the window and I'll keep one burning in my heart."'

The letter did the trick. Nancy wrote back saying she'd changed her mind about the divorce. Mission accomplished. Body intact.

They're in central London. It's Sunday morning. The streets are full of tourists and tour buses. Rubbernecks. Sightseers. The city never sleeps.

They cross Blackfriars Bridge and turn right up

Ludgate Hill towards St Paul's Cathedral and left into Ave Maria Lane. They must be close to the Old Bailey, thinks Sami. The last time he was in this part of London he was being sentenced for the Hampstead job but he couldn't see much from the back of a prison van.

Sinbad pulls up at a large set of security gates flanked by spiked fences. A yellow sign declares: *Warning: No Unauthorised Admittance.* Beneath it are symbols for security cameras, dogs and armed guards.

'Why are we stopping?' asks Sami.

'We're here,' replies Dessie.

Sinbad is talking to a uniformed guard behind a grille. Hands him paperwork. A motor whirs and the metal gate slides open. The van swings into a parking area below the building and pulls up at a fire door. Dessie jumps out and begins unloading the tools and ropes onto a trolley. He's wearing surgical gloves beneath heavy-duty cloth gloves. Sami has trouble getting his fingers into the latex because one rogue finger always gets caught on the outside.

'Come on, dickweed.'

'Don't wait for me.'

Dessie gives him a clip behind the head. A security guard is watching him from a control booth that looks like a bomb shelter. Dessie gives him a wave, indicating everything is fine.

'Keep your head down. Don't look at the ready-eyes.'

Sami has to fight the urge to look up and wave at the

CCTV cameras, which are aimed at the doors and stair-wells. What would happen if the rozzers caught them now, he wonders. He could explain about Nadia, say he was acting under duress.

Dessie props open the fire door and they wheel the stuff inside. Meanwhile, Sinbad climbs behind the wheel of the van and spins back up the ramp.

'Where's he going?' asks Sami, feeling twitchy.

'Relax. He's going to wait for us outside.'

'But what if . . .'

'We don't want the van trapped down here.'

Wheeling the trolley along a basement corridor, they reach three lifts, including the broken one. Dessie sets up a red and yellow safety triangle and prises the doors open, peering up the darkened shaft.

'What are we supposed to be doing?'

'Fixing it.'

'Do you know how to fix a lift?'

'Does it fucking matter?'

Dessie separates the gear and wheels the trolley into the adjacent lift. He presses 5. The doors close. Sami watches the numbers light up as they rise between the floors. He can see himself reflected in a mirror. It's like he's going to a fancy dress party.

The doors slide open. Dessie straightens and pushes the trolley into a large open-plan office with smaller private offices and conference rooms running down both sides.

As they wheel the trolley along a corridor, Dessie pushes each door open, making sure they're empty. Most of the desks face away from the windows and the office walls are lined with shelves full of box files and bound volumes. Sami can see manila folders with red ribbons looped around cardboard wheels, like they're legal files.

The last office has an annexe. Half of it is filled with files. The other half has a metal door. It's the strong room.

'You get started. I'll be back,' says Dessie.

'Where are you going?'

'I'm going to lay down some tarps and bang a few cables, just in case they come looking.'

Suddenly Sami is alone. He looks at the strong room. Taps the door. Tries the handle, just in case someone forgot to lock it. No, he couldn't be that lucky. Not Sami Macbeth.

Then he glances over his shoulder at the nearest office. There's one of those really smart phones with a command unit sitting on a desk. It's most likely '9' to get an outside line.

He should call the police.

And say what?

The truth.

Yeah, like that worked last time.

What would Tony Murphy do if Sami grassed him up? Kill Nadia. Then he'd find a way of killing Sami. Slowly. Painfully. Sami considers his other options but whichever way he looks at the problem he's fucked seven different ways and it isn't even lunchtime.

Putting the stethoscope in his ears, he places the end against the metal door. Listens. Nothing.

'I'm sorry, sir, but we did all we could. In the end, we just couldn't save her.'

Dessie reappears. 'Who are you talking to?'

'Nobody.'

'So what do you think?'

Sami scratches his chin and tries to look crestfallen. 'Can't open this fucker.'

'Why not?'

'Too hard.'

'Tony said you opened a safe that was ten times harder. This should be a piece of cake.'

Sami tries to be decisive. 'They call it a strong room for a reason – 'cause it's strong. If they called it a weak room anyone could open it.'

Dessie isn't in the mood for sarcasm. He puts his face up close. Nose to nose. Bacon breath on the exhale. In the same instant he wraps the stethoscope around Sami's neck and pulls it tight. Lifts him off the floor. Watches his eyes bulge.

'You taking the piss? You taking the mickey?'

Sami doesn't have the oxygen to answer.

This is Dessie Fraser in full Dobermann mode. He slams Sami's head against the door, punctuating each of his statements with violent compelling exclamation marks.

'It's got locks! It's got a handle! Open the fucking door.'

Dessie lets him go. Straightens his cap.

'How long will it take?'

Sami rubs his neck. 'Give me fifteen.'

'You got ten.'

'Just tell me one thing,' he risks. 'What's inside?'

'Exhibits.'

He makes it sound like a science project.

'What sort of exhibits?'

'Courtroom exhibits. Exhibit A, exhibit B, that sort of shit.'

Oh, this is priceless, thinks Sami. They're inside the Old Bailey. The Central Criminal Court. The last time he was here he was wrongly convicted of carrying tools to commit a felony and being in possession of stolen goods. Now he's carrying almost identical tools and is supposed to rob the place.

Dessie has gone back to his pretend lift repairs. Sami looks at the drill and considers how long it would take to get through the door. If this were a movie, it would take about four minutes. You can multiply that by about a hundred in real life.

Then his eyes rest on the canister Sinbad gave him. Maybe he could wedge a little of the stuff near the hinges and set off a small explosion, just enough to lift the door off its frame.

That's one possibility. He considers the others. It's a short consultation.

Sami looks through the nearby offices, searching wastepaper bins and mini-fridges until he finds two plastic water bottles. Emptying them, he unscrews the metal container. Inside is a white powder, granulated like sugar. He gently pours a small amount into each bottle. It doesn't look like enough. He adds some more.

He puts one bottle at the base of the strong room door, beneath the lower hinge, and the second bottle balancing on top. Taking a length of electrical cord, he strips away the plastic coating from each end.

Among the gear that Sinbad had provided him are two small light bulbs. Sami shatters the glass and gently places the filaments into the powder in each bottle. He attaches a wire to the base of the bulbs and re-screws the bottle lids, before trailing the electric cord across the floor – ten, twenty, thirty feet . . . he should have asked for something longer. If he had a long enough wire he could be on a different floor or in another building or out of the county.

Dessie has come back.

'You want to do the honours?' Sami asks him.

'Why?'

'No reason.'

'Why are we standing way back here?'

'This is a job you can only fuck up once.'

Sami shoves two bare wires into a power socket and flicks the switch. He's hoping for a dull *kerplunk* as the hinges pop off. Instead he blows the door through the next wall, bringing half the ceiling down.

Brick and plaster dust fill the air. Every window in the vicinity has been blown out and the sprinklers have triggered. They'd be getting wet if the pipes weren't so twisted by the force of the blast that instead of spraying downwards the water is jetting off at crazy angles.

Dessie pushes a lump of plasterboard off himself. He looks like someone has painted his face white.

'Where's the safe?' he asks.

'It was here a minute ago,' says Sami.

They pull aside a desk and broken ceiling panels, looking for the strong room. Dessie wraps his arms around a buckled filing cabinet and tosses it to one side.

Sami's ears are ringing from the blast.

'Maybe we should get out of here,' he suggests.

Dessie doesn't answer.

'Well, if you don't need me, I'll catch up with you later.'

Dessie smacks him in the side of the head. 'Shut the fuck up and keep looking.'

20

For a moment Sami considers whether he could have blown the strong room through the floor. Instead he finds a cistern and a sink from the bathroom above.

Dessie tosses them aside like he's moving empty boxes. He discovers the strong room door behind a collapsed wall, which is still smoking from the blast.

Kicking away the last of the debris, he finds the room and starts going through drawers, pulling out exhibits and evidence bags, looking at the labels. There are guns, bags of drugs, knives and artefacts.

He picks up a semi-automatic – checks the label. Puts it in a rucksack. Then he grabs bags of white powder. Cocaine. Sami gets a look at one of the labels. *Court 4. Exhibit 1a. Raymond Peter Garza.*

One moment his heart is racing, the next it stops completely. It's a mistake. Insanity. No way they're doing a job for Ray Garza.

A sprinkler has been spraying down Sami's back, soaking his overalls. His face is coated in brick dust and the ringing in his ears turns out to be the fire alarms.

Dessie screams at him above the noise. 'Pack up the gear. Leave nothing behind.'

Sami tosses the drill, the camera and the canister of TATP into the holdall. He has to drag a shelf to one side to lift the bag. Suddenly he spies a lump of cash the size of a house-brick, wrapped in plastic cling film.

It has to be fifty grand. Maybe more.

Dessie looks at him. Looks at the cash. Grins. In a heartbeat Sami has gone from being a fuck-up to having golden bollocks. Dessie takes the money and tucks it into the rucksack.

Sami is still trying to get his head around the Garza connection. If he weren't so scared already, even the mention of Garza's name would make his throat close and scrotum tighten. Some criminals get their reputations for being violent bastards, but Ray Garza is notorious for being a completely ruthless fucker. The Keyser Söze of the British underworld.

Tony Murphy might rip off mug punters, horny businessman and foreign tourists, but Ray Garza ransacks entire countries. Diamond mines in Angola, nickel mines in Botswana, platinum mines in Zimbabwe. According to the press reports he's Mugabe's favourite Englishman – a pretty elite club.

Occasionally in prison Sami heard blokes brag about having worked for Garza. They said he was a genius, a visionary, top of the food chain, but most wouldn't talk about him or even mention his name.

Then some dumb moke would shoot his mouth off, saying Garza was a pussy or a wanker. From that moment you knew the poor bastard would spend the rest of his life looking over his shoulder, paranoid that Garza would find out. Every car backfiring, every set of headlights in the rear mirror, every bit of bad luck, every fuck-up and he'd be wondering if it was Garza. He might as well have bought a shovel and started digging his own grave.

Dessie is still stuffing evidence bags into the rucksack. The sirens are getting closer.

'We should go,' says Sami.

'Wait. I'm not finished.'

'No time. Let's split.'

'I said wait.'

Next minute they're legging it down the corridor. Dessie has the rucksack. Sami is trying to carry the holdall, which is bashing against his knees.

The lifts aren't working. They've managed to break all three of them. Either that or the fire alarms have cut the power. They head for the stairwell. A security guy comes charging out the door, puffing hard, hand on a nightstick.

'Thank God you're here,' says Dessie, pointing down the hall.

'What happened?'

'Some sort of explosion.'

He looks at their bags. 'What were you doing?'

'Fixing the lift,' answers Dessie. 'We smelled a bit of gas earlier. Must have been a leak. Blast brought the roof down.'

The guard looks at Sami for verification.

'Anyone hurt?'

Sami shakes his head.

'We could have been killed,' says Dessie. 'Health and Safety are gonna hear about this.'

The guard tells them to evacuate. They're supposed to wait for him on the ground floor. Next minute they're alone, swinging down the stairwell between the landings. Lugging the bags.

They reach the ground floor fire exit. Dessie pushes open the door, looks both ways. A fire engine is blocking the alley. Firemen are jogging towards them.

Dessie and Sami stroll past them, heads down, avoiding the ready-eyes. They turn left and left again, crossing a parking area. Following a railing fence they reach a gate leading up to a set of stairs. The gate is locked. They climb over, tossing the bags to each other.

There are more fire engines and police cars in Newgate Street. Dessie holds Sami back. Their blue boilersuits are streaked with plaster and soaked through. Dessie's hair looks like he's gone prematurely grey.

Waiting for another police car to pass, they leg it down Newgate Street and duck into Bishops Court and Fleet Passage, avoiding the major roads. Dessie seems to know where he's going.

'We got to get out of these clothes,' he says, peeling off his gloves. He spies a narrow alley with industrial bins on wheels. *Commercial waste only*. Crouching between two bins, Dessie begins unbuttoning his sodden boilersuit. He opens his rucksack. Shoves the overalls inside.

'Why not just ditch it?' asks Sami.

'Yeah, and let forensics have a field day.'

Sami copies Dessie. His jeans and shirt are wet, but they're clean. The boilersuit is packed away. He keeps the cap on his head.

Dessie hoists the rucksack onto his back. Checks the lane. Makes a decision. He jogs round the corner and down some stairs to Old Seacoal Lane and slows to a brisk walk, heading towards Farringdon Street.

Pedestrians give way to traffic. Buses, black cabs, cars and vans are banked up in every direction. Gridlock has choked Fleet Street, Ludgate Hill and Holborn Circus.

Dessie peers left and right, looking for something.

'What's wrong?'

'Sinbad isn't here.'

'Maybe this is the wrong corner.'

'I know the fucking corner.'

'He could be lost.'

'He's not lost.'

Dessie turns on his mobile. Calls Sinbad. Sami can only hear one side of their conversation, which mostly consists of cursing and Dessie calling Sinbad a yellow mongrel and a gutless prick.

The gist of their exchange is that a policeman moved Sinbad on, so he drove the van around the block, but each time he came back the rozzer was still standing there. It smelt like fish. Then he heard the explosion and got spooked.

'Where are you now?' asks Dessie. 'What do you mean you've gone home? We're fucking waiting.'

Dessie hurls the mobile onto the concrete shattering it into a dozen pieces.

'Is he coming?' asks Sami.

'No he's not fucking coming.'

Sami ponders this for a moment. Clearly the criminal code doesn't have the same 'never leave a man behind' philosophy as the SAS.

'So what do we do?' he asks.

'We leg it.'

Two police cars are heading down Farringdon Street towards them, negotiating the traffic by nudging other vehicles aside with duelling sirens. Sami and Dessie are too exposed. They have to stay off the main thorough-fares. Find somewhere to hide. Lie low.

'We could catch the tube,' suggests Sami.

'I don't catch trains,' replies Dessie.

'Why not?'

'I just don't.'

'We're running a bit low on choices for you to be taking a personal stand.'

Dessie grunts. Sami takes it as a yes.

They cross the road, walking between cars, not making eye contact with the drivers. They duck down St Bride Street and meet Shoe Lane. Dodging puddles and recycling bins, they weave left and right in narrow lanes, not talking, not looking back.

Sami could pass as a backpacker but Dessie looks like a German hiker with his trousers tucked into his boots. He keeps muttering under his breath about Sinbad.

He stops. 'Will you fucking keep up for fuck's sake.'

'This bag is heavy.'

'Don't be such a faggot.'

'I'm carrying the stuff that goes boom. I don't fancy being pavement art.'

Dessie takes the holdall and slings it over his shoulder. He gives Sami the rucksack with the drugs, the money and the semi-automatic. Happy days.

Sami makes another suggestion. 'We should think about splitting up. They'll be looking for two of us. We'll be less conspicuous if we travel alone.'

Dessie looks at him dubiously. 'I'm not taking my eyes off you, dickweed.'

'At least let's walk on opposite sides of the street.'

Dessie agrees. Sami crosses over and jogs past an Oxfam shop, a wine warehouse and a travel agency with billboards propped on the pavement. For thirty-eight quid he could fly to Milan. Five hundred gets him a week in Barbados. That's where he wants to be now – sipping pina coladas in the Caribbean while some island lovely who looks like Beyoncé rubs coconut oil into his chest with her breasts.

Moving at a half-jog, Sami weaves through Plough Place, Fetter Lane, and Norwich Street. Dessie is close. Puffing hard. His head looks like a turtle's popping out of its shell.

Many of the buildings have brass plaques announcing law offices and legal chambers. Sami's brief had a place around here. He was a QC. Mr Quick Cash.

The red, blue and white Underground sign is ahead, just visible above the roof of a flower barrow. Chancery Lane Station. They disappear down the stairs into the cool and dark. It's a hole to hide in. It's a way out.

21

Bones McGee is staring at the debris. The exhibits room at the Old Bailey has been demolished. The roof has partially collapsed and a sink from the bathroom above is lying in the middle of sodden plasterboard and broken ceiling panels.

Water has done most of the damage. It's still leaking down the walls and dripping from twisted pipes.

His stomach is churning. He let Tony Murphy call in one favour and look at the result. Murphy promised him a surgical strike. Quick. Clean. Nothing left behind. Instead some moron blew out every window on the fifth floor and brought down half the ceiling.

CID is calling it a terrorist bombing. Al Qaeda has been mentioned. Three Pakistani brothers are due to go on trial next week for plotting to bring down a British Airways flight out of Qatar. All the evidence was in the strong room.

Bones picks his way through the wreckage and finds a quiet corner. He calls Tony Murphy.

'What the fuck did you do?'

'Calm down, Bones, what's wrong?'

'You said you had an expert.'

'I did.'

'Well, I'm looking at a fucking bomb site.'

'You know what they say about making an omelette, Bones.'

'Yeah, well your boy just blew up the egg factory.'

Sami and Dessie are standing on the westbound platform of the Central line. The next train to Ealing Broadway is four minutes away. Commuters are milling at the edge of the platform, glancing at the electronic display.

'What's Ray Garza got to do with this?' Sami asks.

Dessie talks out the side of his mouth like he's in a prison yard. 'His boy got picked up with a shooter and eight kilos of charlie. He took a pot shot at one of the rozzers. They charged him with possession and attempted murder.'

Sami pauses to let the information sink in. The entire robbery was about perverting the course of justice. How many years do you get for that, he wonders.

Dessie is looking up and down the platform. His wet hair is stuck to his scalp like duck feathers.

'Hey, how's this for an idea?' asks Sami. 'Since I did my bit – opening the strong room and stuff – how about I split and you can deliver the gear to Mr Murphy.'

'Job's not over.'

'Yeah, but a deal's a deal. You got your stuff. Mission accomplished. Now Murphy can let Nadia go.'

'We started together, we finish together.'

Two transport policemen wander onto the platform, glancing up and down, trying to look like real bobbies instead of rejects from the Met. They're heading towards Dessie and Sami, who move further along, trying to be inconspicuous.

A train comes roaring through the tunnel, pushing air and rubbish ahead of it. The doors open. Dessie tells Sami to take a different carriage.

'If the transport cops get on, keep moving toward the back. And don't talk to a fucking soul.'

This is the Underground, thinks Sami. Nobody talks to anyone unless they're deranged or like talking to themselves. If he did strike up a conversation, what would he say?

'I'm the unwitting pawn in an evil conspiracy, which is why I have eight kilos of cocaine and a semi-automatic in my rucksack, along with a house-brick of money. And you see that guy in the next carriage? He's a complete psycho and he's carrying a can of explosives in his bag.'

That should liven up their Sunday afternoon in London.

The doors have closed. The train moves off. Sami can see Dessie take a seat and drop the holdall at his feet. Looking in the opposite direction, through the windows, he spies the transport cops, talking to passengers.

He takes a deep breath. Closes his eyes. Wishes he were somewhere else.

That's when it happens. Not right then. Three stops on, just outside Oxford Circus station. One moment Sami is standing near the door and the next he's upside down, in a dark world, full of smoke and shattered glass.

Something soft breaks his fall. A woman. He can't see her face in the dark but he hears her crying above the screams. Smoke pours through the air vents, making it hard to breathe. He can't see flames but it smells like the wiring is burning.

People are crawling on the floor, bumping into each other. Squares of light appear in the darkness. Mobile phones. Sami can see the faces of the people holding them. Fear. Disbelief. At the same time he begins hearing the dull thud of train windows being hit by dozens of fists.

The emergency lights flicker on, yellow and faint. A man staggers past him holding his head. A woman with her clothes blown into shreds has snot and tears leaking down her cheeks. Others are caked in dust and soot – a pregnant woman, her dress glued to her skin; a fat man with a mangled leg, leaking blood into his boot.

The woman Sami fell upon is holding her arm.

'What's your name?' he asks her.

'Stephanie.'

'Are you OK, Stephanie?'

'I think my arm is broken.' Her tears are black.

156

'Here, let me see.'

Sami squeezes her arm with his thumb and forefinger, feeling for a fracture.

'It's only sprained,' he tells her.

'What about the fire?'

'I don't think it's a fire.'

The man in a tweed jacket and matching tweed hat is staring at his leg as though it belongs to someone else. Blood is pouring across his ankle from a gaping wound.

'You should sit down,' Sami tells him. 'I'll put a tourniquet on that.'

The man looks at Sami and back at his leg. Still in shock, he follows orders, unsure of what else to do.

The smoke has cleared a little and it's easier to breathe. Most of the screams are coming from the other carriage – the one in front. That's where Dessie had been sitting.

Sami steps over people and peers through the shattered window. The roof of the carriage has been peeled open by the force of the blast. One wall is blackened and shredded and some seats have been torn from their mountings.

A man's face appears. His skin is splattered with blood. Wild-eyed, he pulls desperately at the door, which has been buckled by the blast and won't open more than a few inches. Sami can't see Dessie, which is strange because he's a big man – hard to lose. He was there only a minute ago.

Suddenly, he recognises Dessie's trousers and his over-sized work-boots. They're lying on the floor between two bench seats. The top half of Dessie seems to have disappeared. It must have been blown out the window by the force of the blast.

Sami wants to feel sorry for him, but can't muster any sympathy. Instead he turns away, walks back down the carriage, collecting warm coats, ties for tourniquets, anything to help.

Fifteen minutes is a long time when you're underground in a blown-up train with frightened and injured people. You keep saying things like, 'They'll be here soon', and then wondering quietly why it's taking so long. Where are the paramedics? The police? The driver must be still be alive – he should tell us what to do.

Waiting isn't the worst thing. It's listening to people pleading for help in the next carriage. He asks if anyone has any water and passes bottles through the shattered window. He wants to cry every time he looks at the carriage.

After a long time word filters through that people are leaving through a rear carriage and walking back along the tunnel to Oxford Circus. People are calm. Patient. There's no pushing or running.

Sami helps Stephanie and the man in a tweed hat get through the carriages. He has to lift them down the final step. The same two transport policemen are standing on the tracks. One of them has a torch and is telling people to start walking.

Sami asks about the live rail. It's been turned off. He hopes it stays that way.

Taking Stephanie's hand and hooking his other arm around the man in tweed, he leads them along the tunnel towards the station. Twisted metal, glass and plastic are scattered along the tracks. Sami half expects to see Dessie's torso propped against the wall.

Torches wave them forward.

Paramedics are waiting on the platform, giving oxygen, bandaging wounds; lifting people onto stretchers. Sami stands for a while, watching someone treating the man in tweed. Stephanie is talking to an Underground employee.

Without saying goodbye, Sami walks up the stairs, past the ticket barriers, across the concourse, into the daylight. It's a surreal experience to see how normal the world still looks. He moves past the waiting ambulances and fire engines, which are blocking Oxford Street. People are staring at him wordlessly, their eyes asking the questions: 'What was it like down there? What did you see?'

More sirens are coming. Sami tightens the straps on the rucksack and turns down Argyll Street, his head lowered, avoiding the stares.

He hears snatches of conversation. People are talking about a bomb, terrorists, a carriage destroyed . . . Someone says there are more bombs. One went off at the Old Bailey.

Pedestrians are holding mobile phones, raising them in the air, shaking them or pressing buttons, hoping for a signal or expecting them to ring.

Sami passes the London Palladium and heads towards Carnaby Street.

Dessie is dead. What's he supposed to do now? Call Murphy. He doesn't have a mobile. He has to find a phone.

Right now he's in Carnaby Street. He once had a girl-friend who worked in a clothing shop on the corner. She gave him Union Jack underwear for his birthday and said she wanted to lower the flag. What was her name? Stacy.

He turns into Broadwick Street. Remembers his mother bringing him here to get orthotics fitted. Then he jumps to a different memory. Her funeral. The December skies like darkness exhaled from the grave. The mourners in overcoats, black suits, dark stockings, holding black umbrellas: his mother's friends surrounding Nadia.

Scaffolding covered the crematorium, which looked as though it was being dismantled rather than renovated. Sami wondered why it was so cold inside. Surely they'd heat the place.

The priest said a few words, making out that he knew Sami's mother, which was unlikely, because to the best of Sami's recollection, his mother had never set foot in a church.

When the coffin disappeared, Nadia broke down and sobbed. Sami wanted to pick her up. Carry her away. Wipe away the hurt. Instead he held her and said nothing. The silence was so fragile he felt it could shatter.

Sami didn't cry. Crying was something he stopped doing years ago. He had to be strong for Nadia. It wasn't his turn to surrender to sorrow.

He's in Berwick Street and then Peter Street, where the sex shops masquerade as bookstores and the strip clubs masquerade as nightclubs. There are 'Live Nude Shows', peep shows, tattoo parlours and basement cinemas screening delights such as *Further Confessions of a Sixth Form Girl*.

Prostitutes have plastered phone boxes with glossy business cards. Wearing scanty lingerie and come-hither smiles, they have as much sex appeal as blow up mattresses.

Maybe Sami should get a girl and hide out for a few hours. She'd want to be paid by the quarter hour. How much would it cost?

He's puffing now. Lactic acid is building in his legs and the rucksack feels heavier. He's carrying eight kilos of cocaine and a semi-automatic pistol. That's worth about twelve years or ten grand a kilo, depending upon whether you're a glass half-full or glass half-empty kind of person. The explosion on the Underground is something different; a whole new ball game, a different league. Life imprisonment. Throw away the key.

He's in Leicester Square, opposite the Odeon. A busker is dancing on stilts, wearing a clown outfit. Another is dressed up as a cowboy, painted bronze, posing like a gunslinger ready to draw.

There are four cops standing near a statue. Two of them are talking to tourists, but the others seem to be looking for someone. Sami joins a queue waiting for discount theatre tickets. Head down. Trying to become invisible.

Then he remembers a pub in Lisle Street, the Crooked Surgeon. It's less than a hundred yards away. There'll be a phone. He can call Murphy.

Stepping out of the queue, he ducks down Leicester Place and pushes open the pub door. A dozen people are standing at the bar with their faces raised to a television set. Maybe there's a game on. Sami drops the rucksack at his feet. He's sweating. Out of breath. Then he glances up at the screen and sees fire engines, ambulances, paramedics and people on stretchers.

Nobody notices Sami. They're too interested in the bombing.

'You got a payphone?' he asks the barman.

'Take a number,' he replies, without taking his eyes off the screen.

He points. Three people are waiting to use the payphone, which is wedged under the stairs next to a slot machine. The woman at the back of the queue smiles at Sami. She has sticking plasters on her heels and is pulling one of those trolley bags that airline hostesses use.

'You want a drink?' the barman asks him.

Sami orders a beer. Upends the glass, his throat working rhythmically. Lowering the pint glass, he spies himself in the mirror behind the bar. Most of the soot on his face has rubbed off but he still has plasterboard and glass in his hair.

'Get caught in the bombings?' asks the barman.

Sami nods.

'This one's on me.' The barman pushes another pint into his hands. Then he motions to the TV. 'You were lucky. They're telling everyone to sit tight. Not much else we can do. Trains and buses aren't running.'

Sami glances at the payphone. It's almost his turn. The woman ahead of him fumbles for change. 'You can go first,' she says. 'I've talked to my husband already.'

Sami nods in thanks. Turns his back. Punches the number Dessie gave him. The call gets diverted. Someone picks up. Doesn't talk.

'Is that Mr Murphy?'

'He's busy.'

'Tell him this is Sami Macbeth and there's been a problem.'

'What sort of problem?'

'Dessie didn't make it.'

'He got caught?'

'He got blown up.'

Silence. Sami waits.

163

Murphy answers. 'Is this a secure line?'

'Yeah.'

'What happened?'

'Dessie blew himself up on the Tube.'

'How?'

'He must have dropped the bag or kicked it.'

'Where are you now?'

'A pub in Soho, the Crooked Surgeon.' Sami looks over his shoulder. 'The streets are crawling with cops.'

'Get out of there.'

'I can't. I think they're looking for me.'

Sami races through the story in an urgent whisper. When he finishes there's a long pause. Murphy is trying to think.

'I'm sorry about Dessie,' says Sami. 'He was very loyal to you.'

'Yes he was,' says Murphy. 'Loyalty is an admirable quality, but it doesn't help me now.'

How can he be so blasé and cold, thinks Sami.

'What about the stuff?'

'I got it.'

'The shooter?'

'Yeah.'

Murphy begins asking questions, talking very slowly and seriously like every answer is for a million quid, only Sami doesn't have any friends to phone.

'Get rid of the shooter.'

'What do you mean?'

164

'Get rid of the fucking thing. Make sure it's never found.'

'How?'

'Dump it in the river . . . down a drain. Better still, take it apart and ditch the pieces separately.'

'It's a courtroom exhibit.'

'So what?'

'You didn't say anything about Ray Garza being involved.'

'Forget about Garza. Just get rid of the shooter.'

'Then what do I do? You got to help me.'

Murphy ponders this for a moment.

'All right. All right. Keep your head down. I'm sending Sinbad.'

Yeah, right, thinks Sami, the same bastard that abandoned us in the first place. He doesn't say it out loud.

Murphy hangs up.

I got to sit tight, thinks Sami. Take my pulse. Take a deep breath. Help is on the way.

22

The head of Scotland Yard's Counter Terrorism Command, Commander Bob Piper, has always been self-conscious about his height. Five foot five simply isn't tall enough for a man of his achievements and ambition. He deserves another seven inches, maybe more.

Opening his locker, he pauses for a moment to appreciate its neatness and order. His eyes rest on his boots, which have been buffed and polished to a black sheen that catches light on the curves. The toes are steel reinforced, the soles fire-retardant rubber. They are tough boots. Working boots.

Carefully, Piper lifts his overalls from the top shelf and places them on a bench seat near his knees. Next comes his belt and toiletry bag. The boots are left till last. Once they're laced – pulled tight with a double knot – he rocks over the balls of his feet testing the snugness of the fit.

Two bombs have exploded in the West End – one at the Old Bailey and another on the Central Line near

Oxford Circus. The second was almost certainly triggered by a suicide bomber.

Although Bob Piper doesn't wish for terrorist acts (not like some firemen he knows who get a hard-on when they see a blazing building), he is a man who rises to an occasion; cometh the hour, cometh the man. A full-scale terror alert has been called in London. Code Red.

This is what he's trained for – in the field, on the firing range, in dress rehearsals and simulations. He spent four months at Quantico, the FBI headquarters in Virginia. Another two months with Mossad in Israel.

Bob Piper winks at himself in the mirror and plants a peaked cap firmly on his head, smoothing the brim in a boyish salute to his reflection. He closes the locker and turns for the door. He's ready.

23

Bones McGee has a bad feeling in his guts, which started in his stomach and seems to have shifted lower to his colon and his bowels. Now he feels as though his insides will flood unless he keeps clamping down on his sphincter.

Events have taken on a surreal, almost comic book sensibility. They're being played out on TV. Reported live from the scene. A banner rolls across the bottom of the screen declaring: LONDON UNDER ATTACK.

Another bomb has gone off – this time on the Underground. One person is dead and scores are injured. What are the chances of a bomb going off so close to the first explosion? Remote. Infinitesimal.

Forensics teams are vacuuming, dusting and bagging debris on the records floor of the Central Criminal Court. They're putting together a jigsaw or at least collecting the pieces in the hope they fit together. Meanwhile, detectives are interviewing the security guards and studying footage from the CCTV cameras.

Already a picture is emerging. The bombers had inside information and assistance. They knew the location of the security cameras. They had a cover story. The 'out-of-order' lift must have been sabotaged some time on Saturday evening. The building manager called the regular lift repair company, which promised to send a repair crew on Monday morning. That call was intercepted and a repair van stolen from outside a house in Ealing some time on Saturday night.

Bones calls Murphy. He can hear laughter and music. London is under attack and Murphy is throwing a party.

'Tony, mate, what are you doing to me? I'm feeling pretty vulnerable here.'

'You worry too much. It's under control.'

'Is that what you call it?'

'It's not your concern, Bones.'

'But I am concerned, Tony. I got MI5, Special Branch and the Counter-Terrorism boys rattling cages and putting a bug up people's arses. Your boys fucked up big-time.'

'My boys aren't your concern. This is just a squall. It's going to blow over.'

'A squall? This is a force ten gale, Tony, and we just hit the sodding iceberg.'

'Relax. Come over? Have a drink. I got a band.'

'Yeah, I can hear it. They had a band on the Titanic, which kept playing all the way down.'

Murphy loses his temper. 'You got a smart mouth,

Bones. You think you're funny. You think you can ring me and tell me what to do. You've taken my readies. You've eaten free at my restaurants. You've grown rich on my fucking largesse. So don't you start talking to me about icebergs or start eyeing the life-boats. I own you, Bones. I've owned you ever since you took that first free fuck at my club. I could have saved myself a lot of money and blackmailed you after that, but I kept being generous.'

'I don't think you should talk to me like that, Tony.'

'I'll fucking talk to you any way I please. Everything you have is down to me. The Italian kitchen, the season tickets to Stamford Bridge, that state-of-the-art, whatsit plasma TV you got in your front room.'

'You've never been to my house.'

'I know all about you and your little peccadillos, Bones, like that bird next door you're banging behind her husband's back and your bit of property speculation in Ibiza – the apartment in your brother's name. I funded that fucking thing as well.'

Bones has stopped trying to interrupt.

'. . . so don't talk to me about icebergs and force ten gales. This is a squall. They happen. That's why I take out insurance. You're my insurance policy, Bones. I paid my premium. I got you. That's why you're going to keep your mouth shut, your head down and your ear to the ground. You're my man on the inside. You can dictate events.'

Yeah, right, thinks Bones. Just like a fish in a whale.

24

Sami has washed his face, shaken the glass from his hair and tried to scrub the bloodstains from his shirt. Back in the bar he takes a seat and rests the rucksack between his knees, looping the strap around his left hand.

Sinbad is going to be here soon. That's got to be a good thing.

He glances at the TV. Footage from the Underground shows a twisted metal carriage and passengers emerging with blackened faces, covering their mouths with handkerchiefs and pieces of cloth.

Some survivors took mobile phone images in the seconds after the explosion. Sami spies himself in the background putting a tourniquet around a man's leg.

A blonde reporter appears on screen, nodding at the camera knowingly, as though she has seen it all before.

Someone turns up the volume.

'. . . television pictures don't really give a sense of what it's like to be standing here, Dean, knowing that less than forty feet below me a train carriage has been destroyed by a terrorist bomb causing death and destruction.'

The camera cuts to Dean in the studio: 'Have the police been able to confirm or deny if these were suicide attacks?'

The camera cuts back to Trisha: 'At this stage police are refusing to confirm or deny the nature of the attacks, Dean, but with multiple bombsites, one underground and the other at the Central Criminal Court, this will obviously be a very complex and difficult investigation. Forensic teams are sifting through the wreckage at each scene and detectives are examining thousands of hours of CCTV footage in a bid to identify the bombers.'

Cut to Dean: 'Have the police indicated who might be behind these attacks?'

Trisha nods. 'Not at this stage, Dean, but there is speculation that the Old Bailey blast could have been aimed at disrupting the trial of Pakistani-born brothers, Hammed and Mani Yousef, who face charges of plotting to blow up a British Airways flight from Qatar during the summer. That trial was due to begin on Tuesday.'

Dean nods: 'Some news outlets are reporting the possibility of more devices.'

Trisha nods: 'Yes, Dean, this is a major concern for police. Central London has been effectively locked down. All buses and trains have been stopped and are being searched. Police are also manning checkpoints on roads in and out of the West End. I have never seen such a large police presence on the streets of London.'

Dean seems to have run out of questions. Trisha doesn't want to go.

'There is a real sense of defiance among survivors and rescuers,' she says. 'Sadly, all too often, Londoners have experienced events like this before and refuse to be cowed or to submit.'

Dean adds, 'I guess the best description of it would be bloody but unbowed.'

'Absolutely, Dean,' says Trisha.

Who are these people, thinks Sami.

Back in the studio a professor of Middle Eastern Studies says the bombings are most likely the work of home-grown Islamic extremists. His Adam's apple is bobbing up and down beneath his skin as if trying to break out.

Sami has heard enough. He turns away from the screen. Orders another beer. Sami has fourteen pounds and fifty-five pence left – not counting the brick of money in the rucksack, which is not really his. Possession is nine-tenths. If he gets out of this, he'll give nine-tenths of the money to the victims of the bombing and the other tenth can go back.

If he gets out? Sinbad isn't coming. They've blocked the roads. They're going to search vehicles.

'Hey, listen to this,' says a guy at the bar, pointing to the TV.

A different reporter is standing outside New Scotland Yard. Wind rattles his microphone and his tie keeps blowing up into his face.

'. . . police have in the past few minutes released security camera footage of a suspected bomber seen fleeing the scene of the Underground blast.'

Video images replace the reporter – a street scene, shot from above in grainy colour. The flashing blue lights of a police car draw Sami's gaze and then something else – a figure moving towards the camera. Someone familiar.

It's a surreal experience to see himself depicted on TV running down Oxford Street. Only it it's not a depiction. Sami is playing himself. See Sami run. See Sami jump. See Sami knock over pedestrians.

There is a new banner rolling along the bottom of the screen: BOMB SUSPECT EVADES POLICE

The reporter is still talking: 'The suspect is described as being of medium height, slim build, wearing jeans, a sweatshirt and carrying a black rucksack . . .' At that moment the footage freezes and zooms in on Sami's face. Is he really that pale? It's the prison suntan.

Nervously, he glances around the bar. Everyone is still watching the TV. Staring at it. Contemplating the man. The mind. What possesses somebody to set off a bomb?

Another banner is running along the bottom of the screen: BUSES AND TRAINS SUSPENDED UNTIL FURTHER NOTICE.

A man next to Sami groans. 'I was supposed to be at Heathrow an hour ago. I got caught on the Piccadilly line.' He has a New Zealand accent. That must be his luggage near the door.

Sami nudges the rucksack further under his feet, but the Kiwi spies it anyway.

'Same boat, eh? Where were you heading?'

'Nowhere,' says Sami.

'On your way home, eh? Where you been?'

'Here and there.'

Suddenly, a woman's voice cuts across the conversation.

'He's got a rucksack!'

Sami's head jerks around as though tied to a string. The woman is wearing a business suit and pointing at him accusingly, her mouth preparing to scream. Her eyes meet Sami's. There is a tingling in his throat, like a taut wire vibrating against his neck.

Everyone in the bar has turned to stare. Even the reporter on screen appears captivated by the moment.

Sami straightens his legs and plants them on the floor. His hand is still wrapped around the strap on the rucksack.

'What you got in the bag?' asks the barman.

'Clothes and stuff.'

'Show us,' says the Kiwi.

'Why?'

''Cause you're making everyone nervous.'

Sami glances from face to face.

'I'm not the guy they're looking for.'

'That's cool.'

'I'm not dangerous.'

'Nobody is saying you are.'

A door behind Sami opens and closes. Someone has

175

slipped out. They'll probably stop the first policeman they see.

Sami slings the rucksack onto his back. A dozen people collectively crouch and swallow wetly.

Sami is at the door. Outside. Turning right. Right again. Where is he going? There are two police officers on the corner. He turns back heading down Whitcomb Street towards Trafalgar Square. A police van is on a slow circuit of Leicester Fields. He ducks into a laneway. Leans his back against a wall. Trying to outrun them on foot is a loser's game. They'll corner him and wait for reinforcements.

Sami has to go off the radar. Disappear. He has money now – the stash from the safe – but first he has to get out of the West End; out of London.

There's a church across the square. He can hide inside. Stash the rucksack in a dark corner. Say a prayer. It's a good plan.

He comes out of the alley and finds three policemen in front of him. One of them has a gun and is crouching, holding it in two hands, like he knows how to use it.

'Don't move,' he yells at Sami. 'Put the bag down.'

Sami looks behind him . . . looks ahead. Holds his fist in the air. His thumb cocked. Empty, but they don't know that.

'I got a fucking bomb,' he yells, not recognising his own voice. 'Get back or I'll flatten this place.'

The rozzers melt away. Sami runs past them. The one

with the gun is lying on the ground, on his elbows, trying to get a shot. Sami keeps moving, zigzagging from side to side like he's seen in the war movies.

A bomb! He told them he had a bomb. What a joke! What a prize fuck-up. Sami isn't just unlucky, he's a walking jinx, a Jonah; he's the one-legged man in an arse-kicking competition; he's the Irishman who burnt his lips trying to blow up a bus. Forget master criminal – Sami isn't even a minor one. He doesn't open safes. He doesn't threaten police. He doesn't blow up trains. He plays guitar and wants to be a rock god.

Fifty-four hours ago he got out of prison. Thirty-six hours ago he bedded Kate Tierney on Egyptian cotton sheets at the Savoy. Life was good. Life had promise. Now he's the most wanted terrorist in London.

25

Mid-morning. Bright and clear. Ruiz heads out of London towards Blackheath, staying south of the river and avoiding the congestion charge. His Mercedes 280E is forty years old but lovingly restored with two-tone wheels and a racing green paint job.

People look twice at a car like that. They wonder who's driving it. They envy him. They want to trade places.

Just after midday he pulls up at a house on Shooter's Hill Road, overlooking the heath. Tony Murphy has come a long way from a two-up, two-down in Kilburn. Now he lives in a mansion with columned porticos and oak trees shedding leaves into his swimming pool.

There's some sort of party in progress and cars are parked along the driveway and in front of the garages. A marquee has been set up on the lawn attached to the conservatory via a white tunnel of canvas. A buffet is laid out on long tables and waitresses in short black skirts and white blouses are carrying silver trays with champagne flutes.

Ruiz recognises some of the guests, but can't put names to their faces. Murphy's friends are a mix of bar-owners, licensing lawyers, union officials, bookmakers, porn stars and celebrity chefs.

A valet offers to park Ruiz's Merc. He tosses him the keys and walks across the grass.

Dressed in a beige suit and a cream turtleneck sweater, Murphy is holding court, telling a joke about three nuns and a blind man. Ruiz fills a plate with roast pork, venison, salad and a bread roll. Picks up a Corona, wanders over and joins the group.

' . . . So the air conditioning at the convent isn't working and the nuns are sweltering. They take off their clothes to cool down, but there's a knock on the door. The youngest nun yells from inside, "Who is it?" And a voice replies, "It's the blind man."

'The nuns look at each other, relieved, and let him in. This big burly fucker in overalls comes through the door and says, "Holy shit, sisters, great tits. Where do you want me to hang the blinds?"'

Laughs all round, too loud and too long.

Ruiz takes a mouthful of potato salad. 'You can't beat an old joke, can you, Tony?'

The gangster turns slowly with a fixed smile that might break into pieces if he moved too quickly. Violence flashes momentarily in his eyes. He touches his upper lip and examines his finger as if looking for blood.

'We haven't met.'

'Vincent Ruiz. Great party.'

The name means nothing to Murphy. He transfers his champagne glass to his left hand and raises a cigar to his lips.

'I know most people here, Mr Ruiz, since I invited them. I don't recall your name being on the guest list.'

Ruiz nods and rolls a strip of venison into a bread roll, making a sandwich. 'Nadia invited me.'

Murphy doesn't react. 'I don't know anyone called Nadia.'

'Sure you do. Nadia Macbeth. You paid a thousand quid for her. Toby Streak told me. Then you had her delivered to an address in Whitechapel where a sociopath called Puffa shot her full of brown and got her hooked on crack.' Ruiz takes a sip of his beer. 'Ring any bells yet?'

Murphy's nostrils dilate and his eyes are suddenly glazed. The guests are almost imperceptibly edging away from him in a slow motion social version of moonwalking, without the Michael Jackson music.

'You must have me confused with someone else, Mr Ruiz.'

'I'm just telling you what people told me.'

'They were lying.'

Ruiz plucks at a morsel of torn venison hanging from his lips and pops it inside his mouth. 'People tend not to lie to me.'

'Why's that?'

'They respect me too much.' His eyes are dancing.

'Are you a police officer, Mr Ruiz?'

'Used to be.'

'What's your interest in Nadia Macbeth?'

'I'm doing a favour for a friend.'

'Your friend's name?'

'She doesn't like the limelight. Shy, you know. Not like me. I love a good party.' Ruiz smiles at a waitress. 'Can you get me another beer, please, love?'

He turns back to Murphy. 'Hey, I just realised, we have a mutual acquaintance.'

'Who might that be?'

'Sami Macbeth.'

Murphy raises his meaty hand and sucks on the cigar. 'I don't think I know him.'

'That's strange. One of your waiters remembers him dining with you on Thursday. You had oysters to start and a crème brûlée to finish. Ordered specially.'

Murphy is looking over Ruiz's shoulder as if exchanging glances with someone. 'You're quite the detective.'

Murphy's gaze now drifts across his party, watching his guests enjoy themselves, but all traces of avuncular warmth have gone. It's almost as though he despises them as freeloaders and hangers-on, scoffing his food, drinking his booze.

'Maybe we can discuss this another time, Mr Ruiz – as you can see I'm rather busy.'

A bouncer has arrived, a body builder in Nike running

shoes and a dinner jacket with the sleeves pushed up over his gym-thickened arms.

'Gabriel, here, will make sure you find your way out.'

The bouncer grabs Ruiz by the arm, digging his fingers into his shoulder. Ruiz doesn't flinch. Instead, he leans down as though he's dropped something. He straightens suddenly, catching the bouncer under the chin with the back of his head.

Gabriel goes down like a two hundred pound bag of spuds on legs of jelly.

Ruiz looks at Murphy. 'Give me the girl, Tony. I'll owe you one.'

Murphy smiles at him, his teeth like yellowing tombstones. 'You got no juice any more, Mr Ruiz. There's nothing you can give me. Nothing I need.'

Gabriel is getting up. Holding his jaw. Tasting the blood. Someone crashes into Ruiz from behind and drives a fist into his back. A second fist hooks him across the jaw and strong hands wrestle him down. He can taste the vomit and beer rising from his stomach and settling again.

They haul him upright. Pin his arms.

'You're trespassing, Mr Ruiz. You have damaged my property and upset my guests. I don't know who your friend is, but she's sent you on a fool's errand. Sami Macbeth came to see me looking for a job. Offered his services. I told him I am a legitimate businessman. I don't associate with criminals and ex-cons. Now if you'll excuse me . . .'

Ruiz is marched across the lawn. His Mercedes is waiting. A side mirror has been torn off and the aerial is twisted into a modern sculpture. He looks at the damage and glances back towards Murphy, who is lighting another cigar, clicking his lighter shut.

OK, pal, now it's personal.

Ruiz gets behind the wheel. Heads down the drive. As he reaches the road he has to brake hard to avoid a Porsche 911 that cuts the corner and tries to spear through the gates before him. The plates say: RAY JNR.

The cars are nose to nose.

The Porsche driver leans on his horn. Ruiz doesn't move. A window glides down and Ray Garza's boy pops his head out.

'Move your fucking heap.'

Ruiz takes his foot off the clutch. Jerks forward. Nudges the Porsche.

The kid's eyes go wide. 'Are you fucking crazy?'

He's starting to get out. Ruiz nudges the Porsche again, pushing it towards the road. A car has to swerve.

Ray Jnr retreats. Reversing. The gates are clear. Ruiz gives him a wave as he passes. What is Ray Garza's boy doing at a Tony Murphy party?

Across the road he notices a van parked on the footpath. A plastic tent has been placed over missing pavestones and a workman in a hard hat is perched on the edge of the hole. Something strikes Ruiz as odd about the scene. It's not just the newness of his overalls or the paleness of the man's skin. They're working on a Sunday and the van has silver windows at the back. It's just the sort of vehicle used in surveillance operations.

Reaching the intersection, Ruiz turns south towards the city and ponders whether anything has been achieved by confronting Murphy. Not a lot, he suspects, but subtlety was never one of his strengths as a detective. Subtlety can serve a purpose, but sometimes you have to rattle a cage to wake a Norwegian Blue.

26

The Red Emperor Restaurant has ducks the colour of dog turds hanging in the window alongside some weird-looking sea creature that might be inside out or might be entrails.

The restaurant fronts Macclesfield Street on the corner of Horse and Dolphin Yard, near the pagoda-style gates of Chinatown. The front window is partly covered by the menu and sign advertising a hot buffet for £4.95, all you can eat.

A white Mercedes delivery van is parked at the entrance to the yard with a foot or so spare on either side. Sami tries the back door. Locked. He moves along the side and tries the driver's door. It opens. A real criminal would know how to hotwire a car. That's what he should have been learning in the Scrubs. Something useful. A life skill.

Maybe the van driver is inside the restaurant, thinks Sami.

A bell jangles above the door as he pushes it open. The

place is almost empty. The lunchtime rush is over. A couple are paying their bill at the cash register. A girl in a wheelchair is sitting with her mother. The van driver is at a table alone, hunched so low over a bowl of wonton soup that the spoon barely has to leave his lips.

He looks like a skinhead with close-cropped hair and scabby knuckles. Maybe he drives a van during the day and spends his nights kicking the shit out of gays, Pakis and Man United fans.

Sami takes a seat at a table nearby. The waitress is Chinese and barely out of her teens, with shiny black hair cut straight across her forehead. Everything about her is small except her almond shaped eyes, which are the colour of burnt toast.

Her nametag says *Lucy*. That's probably her mother at the front counter – an older version, shorter, plainer, with an unapologetic face and tiny rimless glasses. And that could be her father dressed in chef's whites, holding open the swinging half doors of the kitchen. His head is shaved and his legs are bowed.

Sami remembers his grandfather, who survived a Japanese POW camp in Burma, getting the cold sweats whenever he saw an Asian face. More than once he'd look at Japanese tourists and react as though he'd come face to face with Emperor Tojo himself.

Lucy brings the van driver a pot of green tea.

'I didn't order that,' he says.

'It's complimentary.'

'What else is complimentary?' His hand brushes her knee and slides up her leg until it touches the hem of her skirt.

Lucy steps back.

The driver winks at Sami. 'I just love chink women. They're like chink food – you fill up and an hour later you're hungry again.'

The nasal accent says he's a northerner.

'Ever been to Thailand?' he asks.

'No.'

'They got bar girls there who can fire ping pong balls out of their poongtangs.' He provides the sound effects. 'And I'll tell you something else for nothing. They might have slanty eyes but their pussies are straight up and down, know what I'm saying? Tight and sweet.'

He's not even bothering to whisper. That's the thing about a lot of northerners. They think they're droll but mostly they're gobby and annoying.

The keys to the van are clipped to his belt. Maybe Sami should just deck the guy and take the keys. How far would he get?

'The thing about Bangkok girls is this, right?' The van driver is leaning across the table. 'They might look like virgins but they fuck like demons, know what I'm saying? And if you like 'em young, Thailand's the place. I'm not talking about jailbait. I'm no ped. But the chinks just look younger, you know.'

At some point Sami finds himself switching off. Maybe it's the smell of the food or the less than riveting conversation. He hasn't eaten since yesterday.

The van driver has switched to a new subject. 'We should kick all the fuckers out, either that or hang them on the wall, know what I'm saying?'

Lucy brings him a plate of spare ribs and another of fried rice. He picks up a rib and chews it to the bone, sucking the sauce off his fingers.

'Is that your van parked in the lane?' asks Sami.

'Yeah.'

'You on a delivery run?'

'I was until them bombs went off.'

'Where you heading?'

'Shoreditch and then home.'

'Could you give me a lift?'

'Yeah, sure, where you heading?'

'Anywhere away from here.'

The driver attacks another rib. 'Might take a while.'

Lucy has come back with an order book. Sami asks for the soft shell crab and fried rice.

'You want anything to drink?'

'Just water, thank you.'

'Still or sparkling.'

'Still, please.'

'OK.'

The van driver watches her leave. 'Great little arse.'

Sami leans back in his chair. Takes a deep breath. His

heart has stopped racing. If he can stay off the street, he can give himself time to think.

He looks up and notices the girl in the wheelchair is staring at him. She must be going for the Goth look – blue lipstick, blue eye shadow and dyed black hair cut straight around her head like someone put a pudding bowl on her head and traced the edges.

Sami nods. She looks away.

Sami glances out the front windows. Between the hanging ducks he can see a police car pull up outside. They're stopping people and talking to them.

An old guy in six different layers of clothes is wandering back and forth along the footpath carrying a sandwich board that says, *Judgement Day is coming*. On the back it says, *Be ready to burn*.

People step off the pavement to avoid him.

Suddenly, he stops and peers at Sami through the window. Sami tries to look away but it's too late. The old guy bends his knees and sets down his sandwich board. He pushes open the restaurant door, walks past the cash register.

'You need saving,' he yells in a battered voice. 'You're a sinner, but there's still time.'

Sami has a helpless hollow feeling. Everyone in the restaurant is staring at him. The sandwich board guy leans over him with his hands outstretched, palms upward, like some American evangelist drawing out the evil spirits.

'This is a city of sin and sodomy. That's why God is punishing it today. This man has been down to the gates of hell. He has looked in Satan's eyes.'

'No, I haven't,' says Sami. 'You got it wrong. I'm just here for lunch.'

The sandwich board guy's voice grows louder. 'This man is a sinner, but he wants to repent.'

The doorbell jangles. A young bobby steps inside and stands at the front counter, holding a peaked hat in his hands.

'What does he have to repent for?' he asks the old guy.

'Nothing,' blurts Sami, squeezing his knees into the rucksack.

The bobby looks at him apologetically. 'Is this gentleman bothering you, sir?'

'A little.'

'I'll move him on directly.' He unfolds a piece of paper. 'I just wanted to ask if any of you have seen a man carrying a dark coloured rucksack? He's aged from 25 to 35, slim build, light brown hair, wearing jeans and a sweatshirt. If you do see someone matching this description, notify the police immediately. Please don't approach him.'

He folds the paper and puts it into his pocket.

The van driver looks at Sami. 'The guy sounds just like you.'

'Think so?'

'Yeah.'

Sami tries to laugh.

'Do you have a rucksack, sir?' asks the constable.

'It's a different colour.'

'Can I see it?'

Sami's hand is beneath the table, edging between his thighs, feeling for the rucksack. The zipper.

'What's this guy supposed to have done?' he asks, trying to sound relaxed.

'He's wanted in connection with a police investigation.'

'So he's not dangerous.'

'We're asking people not to approach him.'

Sami's right hand has found the main pocket of the rucksack. His fingers close around the semi-automatic, which is still in a plastic evidence bag. Labelled. Catalogued. Exhibit A.

The constable hasn't moved. He's looking for something in Sami's eyes. Guilt. Fear. Madness. At the same time he's edging towards the door, reaching for the handle.

He knows, he knows, thinks Sami. The only sound in his head is a dull rumbling like a bowling ball hitting the gutter and heading for oblivion.

The sandwich board guy is still standing over him, mouth open, as if trying to rediscover his train of thought. Outside, the constable reaches for his radio. Sami stands, swings the rucksack over his shoulder and heads for the kitchen.

Lucy's father is standing at the doorway. He says something in Chinese and holds up a meat cleaver like some mad Ninja warrior. Sami pulls out the gun. The cleaver clatters to the tiles. Hands come together. He bows apologetically.

Sami bursts out the side door of the kitchen into Horse and Dolphin Yard. Right is a dead end. Left takes him back to Macclesfield Street where the bobby is waiting. He has no choice.

Suddenly, a police car pulls up, blocking his only exit. Sami tries the nearest door. Locked. Looks for a fire escape. Nothing.

The kitchen door is still open. He throws himself inside. Slams the door. Bolts it shut. Topples a metal shelf. Braces it across the doorframe.

Lucy and her father are staring at him.

'What's upstairs?'

'Our flat,' says Lucy.

'Anyone else home?'

She shakes her head.

'Is there another way out?'

'No.'

'You got a phone?'

She points behind the counter, but doesn't take her eyes off Sami's hand. He's still holding the gun.

'I want you to lock the front door. Can you do that for me?'

Lucy nods.

'Are you going to hurt us?'

'No.'

Sami walks into the main restaurant. Nobody has moved. It's as if they've been zapped by some sort of freeze-ray like you see in cartoons and old episodes of *Star Trek*.

Lucy's mother is at the cash register.

'I need to make a phone call,' Sami tells her. She says something back to him in Chinese.

'My mother doesn't speak English,' explains Lucy. 'She wants you to pay for the call.'

Sami roots for change in his pockets and finds a handful of coins. They spin and rattle on the counter top.

He calls Tony Murphy. Tries to speak. The words are like barbed wire in his throat.

'There's a problem.'

'I told you not to call me again.'

'The police think I have a bomb.'

'How did they get that idea?'

'I might have mentioned it.'

'You must be the world's biggest moron.'

'You got to get me out of here.'

'And how do you suggest I do that, son?'

'You must have contacts.'

'Sure. I'll call the good fairy. She owes me a wish.'

Sami doesn't appreciate the sarcasm. 'You can't leave me here. I still have the shooter.'

Murphy curses. 'I told you to get rid of it.'

'Must have slipped my mind.'

'Listen, you muggy toerag, don't fuck with me. Don't

you *ever* fuck with me.' He's screaming down the phone. 'Destroy the gun. Get rid of it. You hearing me?'

Sami doesn't answer. He's too busy watching events outside. People are hurrying along the street, looking over their shoulders. They're leaving shops, restaurants and the supermarket. Mr Wu's Noodle Bar, the Golden Gate Cake shop, the Pagoda restaurant . . . Police are evacuating the area. Sealing it off.

Tony Murphy is still yelling down the line. 'You get pulled, you keep your mouth shut. Understand? You mention my name and you're dead. Your sister is dead. Your entire family are dead. Am I making myself clear?'

'You got to help me,' pleads Sami.

'I am helping you, son. I'm telling you the truth. Don't call me again. Forget this number. Forget you ever met me.'

'What about Nadia?'

'Yeah. Exactly. You think about your sister.'

Sami tries to protest but the line is silent. He's talking to dead air.

27

Commander Bob Piper surveys the empty streets and the abandoned shops and offices. The perimeter has been secured and civilians evacuated. Two cordons. Concentric circles. It's textbook stuff.

The only people allowed through the outer ring are police and emergency services. The inner ring is for the counter-terrorist squad, CO19 (Specialist Firearms Command) and the bomb squad. Now the only civilians within the cordon are the hostages and the hostage taker.

Piper hates sieges. In the old days they were easy. You gave the guy a few hours to cool down (or sober up) and then issued a final warning. If he didn't surrender you went in. Breaking down doors. Firing teargas. Shooting the bad guys. Restoring order.

But ever since the Jean de Menezes debacle at Stockwell Tube, procedures have been changed. Not so much procedures as public sentiment. Two firearms officers put seven bullets into the head of a Brazilian electrician they mistook for a suicide bomber. Who knew that people would take it so badly? Turned out that shoot to kill is only acceptable if you smoke the right suspect.

There were public inquiries, internal reviews, an inquest and calls for the Commissioner's head on a spike. De Menezes became a poster boy for the civil liberties whingers and bleeding hearts who delight in portraying law enforcement agencies as totalitarian storm troopers.

After the war on terror and the war on drugs there should be a war on irritating people, thinks Piper, on the Marxists, the moaners and the greenies.

Last year a siege in North London went six days. Everyone praised the police for their patience and tolerance – except for local residents, unable to sleep in their own beds or get a change of clothes.

This one can't go on for six days. Tomorrow morning a million people are going to be catching trains and buses into Central London. What then? Chaos.

Piper glances at a TV monitor. The front of the Red Emperor is bathed in light that reflects off the silver and gold letters painted above the main window.

A dozen firearms officers are positioned on the rooftops around the restaurant. Sharpshooters. Trained professionals. One clear shot and they can all go home. In the meantime Piper is supposed to negotiate. Confer. Reach a deal.

That's his dilemma. Piper is a conservative and a believer in law and order, but not in lawyers or judges or in a judicial system which has too many flaws; too many gaps for criminals to slip through.

Piper is also a realist, who has accepted the fact that in all probability his decisions will cause irreparable harm to innocent individuals. That's the nature of policing. No matter how much training you do or how sharp your skills or how modern your armoury, sometimes the most efficient weapon is a broad axe.

The Commissioner has called a media conference. He wants Piper by his side. He will doubtless express full faith in his Commander, thereby ensuring that if the operation goes south, he can blame someone else for the debacle.

28

Tony Murphy is being 'schmeissed'. A giant-sized loofah slaps against his naked body, smearing soap over his large expanse of skin while geysers of steam billowing from pipes condenses on the marble walls and ceiling.

He over-imbibed at the garden party and now he's sweating out the toxins in a Russian steam room at Porchester Spa, an art deco building on Queensway.

The giant loofah smears across his shoulders and down his back. Peter, his masseur, offers him a cold towel.

Normally being 'schmeissed' relaxes Murphy – refreshes the parts other saunas don't reach. Not today. Sami Macbeth is on his mind.

Leaving the steam room, he takes a breathtaking dip in the plunge pool, shrinking his testicles to marbles. Peter is waiting for him at the slab. Lying face down, Murphy closes his eyes and feels the perspiration prickling on his flesh again as strong fingers go to work, breaking down knots of tension in his shoulders and neck.

Peter's hands leave his skin. Maybe he's getting more oil. The door opens. Cool air brushes his flesh.

A moment later comes a different sensation. Murphy rears up, roaring, naked as the day as he was born, only bigger, fatter and whiter. A scalding hot towel drops from his back, leaving an angry red burn.

'Hello, fat man, how's the restaurant business. You look like you've been eating all the fookin' profits.'

Murphy is looking at a familiar face in unfamiliar surroundings – Jimmy Ferris, better known as Ferret.

Irish, Catholic and Scouse, Jimmy has a chip on both shoulders and a nest of angry bees buzzing in his head. Rumour has it he once trained to be a priest. He spent three years in a seminary: up before dawn, mass every morning, vows of silence. Then one day he had a religious epiphany in reverse. He stopped believing in God. This had nothing to do with atheism or humanism or moral relativism. Ferret still believed in a higher divine, supernatural power but it wasn't Jesus or Mohammed or Buddha. The power lay within him. Behold, a nihilist was born.

Ferret approached his new career with the same single-minded fervour that he once gave to God and the Catholic Church. He became an IRA fixer. Nobody ever discovered the exact role he played in the organisation, but his phone number kept appearing on the call sheets whenever they picked up a terror suspect.

Murphy wraps a blue gingham towel around his body,

tucking it under his armpits. Ferret is also wearing a towel, but his body is lean and sinewy, covered in tattoos. He has a gold crown on one of his front teeth, making him appear even more rat-like.

'I always wondered if fat men are fat all over, you know, but you must have trouble finding that thing to piss. Now fat chicks are different. Everyone knows they got tight pussies.'

'What are you doing here, Jimmy?' asks Murphy.

'I've come to check on my supply chain. I hear from our buyer that one of the samples I sent him didn't arrive.'

'There's been a delay.'

'Nobody told me about any fookin' delay.'

'Unforseen circumstances.'

'Do I look like a fookin' eejit, Murphy? You had one fookin' job. You had to take the fookin' guns, retool the fookin' barrels and transport the fookin' things. Now I have buyers questioning my fookin' ability to deliver on my promises.' Ferret brings a whole new meaning to expletive-laden conversation. 'Why was the consignment short?'

'I kept one of the guns.'

'Why?'

'I took a liking to it.'

'That wasn't the fookin' deal. The fookin' guns are supposed to be in fookin' Africa.'

Murphy gets defensive. 'Don't try to heavy me, Jimmy. I was doing you a favour.'

'No,' says Ferret shaking his head. 'You were *repaying* a favour. That's a very fookin' different thing. You owe fookin' people and those fookin' people owe me. That's how the fookin' system works.'

Murphy's throat has gone dry. He can't tell him about Ray Jnr taking the Beretta and getting arrested, or Sami Macbeth stealing it back. Macbeth should have destroyed it by now. What if he hasn't? It doesn't bear thinking about.

Ferret wets one end of a towel and twirls it into a cord, flicking it like a whip. It snaps against Murphy's thigh and he dances away. Ferret moves him around the marble slab, laughing. Then he tosses the towel into the plunge pool and pushes through the misted doors to the changing rooms.

Murphy is panting and pink, but not because of the steam. He gets himself a drink of water from a fountain and spills some of it down his chest.

Maybe it's time to walk away, he thinks. Sail into the sunset or at least fly there first class. Bermuda is nice this time of year. The condo is waiting. But first he has to do something about Sami Macbeth.

29

It should be getting dark outside, but the colour of the light is unnatural. Spotlights are bathing the cobblestones in a brightness that makes them look like the centre of a stage. We're in the right place for drama – the West End. This one is unfolding in three acts.

The front door of the Red Emperor is barricaded with tables turned on their sides and stacked on top of each other. The kitchen door is also sealed and Sami has locked everyone in the storeroom where they're sitting on sacks of rice and cans of cooking oil.

Sami takes the semi-automatic from the plastic evidence bag. Weighs it in his hand. Marvels at the raw power it seems to hold. He likes the way it fits into his hand and the delicate lines his fingertips leave when he strokes the freshly oiled metal.

Taking out the ammunition clip, he counts eighteen slug-like bullets. Hollow points. The magazine takes twenty. Two bullets are missing. Dessie said Ray Garza's boy fired on two rozzers when they tried to arrest him.

A chopper sounds overhead. The whump, whump of the blades seems to shake the air. Sami heads upstairs. Walks through the flat. It has a small kitchen, a bathroom, two bedrooms and a lounge.

Lucy's room has a desk tucked under the window and books piled on either side of her chair. She's studying business or management. Her handwriting is neat and precise.

From the third floor window he can see more police cars and ambulances, parked in Wardour Street. A truck is unloading barricades, lifting them with a portable crane and dropping them across the road. Police in black body armour are crouching behind vehicles.

Sami opens a window. Leans out. He's looking for external stairs or a fire escape. Nothing. The uppermost window leads to a small flat roof overlooking Horse and Dolphin Yard. It's about fourteen foot across to another flat roof on the far side. Even with a run-up he'd struggle to make a jump like that. And even if he could get to the other side, where would he go?

A dark shadow moves at the very edge of his vision. He turns. Someone is watching him. They're crouched behind a brick wall on the opposite side of the yard. A policeman? A sharpshooter?

Fuck. Shit. Fuck.

Sami pulls back from the window and presses his body against the wall, fear sucking at his chest. Tugging a cord he lowers the blind and turns off the lamp on Lucy's desk. Staying low, he moves through the flat, locking windows. Lowering blinds. In darkness, he searches the drawers and cupboards for anything that might be useful – masking tape, a ski mask, scissors, pliers and a pocket knife.

He can hear someone beating on the storeroom door downstairs. Sami takes the shooter from the waistband of his jeans. Unlocks the door.

'It's about fucking time,' says the van driver. 'There ain't enough air. We're suffocating in here.'

'There's plenty of air.'

'And the place is filthy.'

'What are you, the food inspector?'

Lucy protests. 'It's not dirty. I clean it every week.'

Lucy's mother and father are sitting on rice sacks, arm in arm. The girl in the wheelchair and her mother are at the centre of the storeroom. The wheelchair is barely wide enough for the space. Her mother is soft spoken. Modestly dressed.

'Excuse me, sir. It's very dark in here and I get quite claustrophobic.'

'You can come out now,' says Sami. 'Stay away from the windows.' He directs them to sit at tables closest to the kitchen. The van driver sits alone, tilting back his chair and propping his feet on the wall.

Lucy is translating Sami's instructions to her parents, who nod at Sami gratefully. Asians are so polite, he thinks.

204

'Are you still hungry?' Lucy asks him.

'Pardon?'

'You ordered food. Do you still want it?'

'I can pay,' says Sami, peeling a fifty-pound note from the bundle in the rucksack.

'Is it stolen money?' she asks.

'Would it matter?'

Lucy folds the note three times and puts it into a jar above the sink next to a picture of her grandparents in a formal pose dressed in their finest clothes.

Sami watches her prepare, a knife blade blurring with speed as she dices celery, bamboo shoots and broccoli. She heats a wok and the kitchen fills with the hissing of vegetables hitting hot oil.

'Why are you doing this?' she asks.

Sami can't answer her.

'Do you really have a bomb?'

Her eyes look incredibly wise yet she doesn't look older than fourteen.

'Why?' Lucy asks.

'Pardon?'

'Why do you have a bomb?'

It's an obvious question. Sami doesn't have an answer.

'What are you fighting for? What are you protesting against? What do you hate – Western imperialism, decadent bourgeois attitudes? Do you want independence or freedom? Are you an anarchist? Has Britain betrayed the Arab world?'

Sami just wants her to shut up.

'What do you hate about us?' asks Lucy.

'I don't know who "us" is.'

'Western civilisation,' says Lucy. 'Do you know what Gandhi said when he was asked about Western civilisation? He said he thought it was a good idea.'

'He was a lot cleverer than me,' replies Sami.

'I don't think you do have a bomb.' She makes him sound like a failure.

'I have a gun,' he says defensively.

A mobile phone is ringing on the counter beside the cash register. Lucy's phone. She stares at it as though expecting it to do something else, like answer itself.

Lucy picks it up. Presses green. Listens. Hands the phone to Sami.

A deep resonant male voice booms down the line: 'This is London News Radio. Am I speaking to a terrorist?'

Sami doesn't answer.

'Are you a hostage?'

'No.'

'Can you talk? Are you being held at gunpoint?'

'Sorry, who are you?'

'London News Radio.'

'Who did you want to speak to?'

'A terrorist or a hostage.'

Sami looks around the restaurant.

'I'm not a terrorist.'

'So what do you call yourself – a freedom fighter, a

martyr, an insurgent? What group do you represent? Are you affiliated with Osama Bin Laden? We're live to air. Do you have a message for the British people?'

'No.'

'The police are saying you might be Algerian or Moroccan.'

'I was born in Glasgow.'

'But you're Moslem, right?'

'No.'

'Can you explain why you're doing this?'

'Doing what?'

'Holding people hostage. Why didn't you detonate your bomb?'

'Pardon?'

'Your colleague blew himself up. Were you meant to die together?'

He's talking about Dessie.

'Have you harmed any of the hostages? How many are there? What are your demands?'

Sami hangs up. Looks at Lucy, who shrugs.

The van driver has turned on the TV. A policeman is being interviewed. Top brass. Chin out, shoulders back, he's facing a firing squad of cameras and microphones.

'This was a brutal, callous and horrifying act,' he says. 'One of the worst atrocities I have witnessed in my twenty-three years as a police officer . . .'

Sounding more righteous by the sentence, he bristles with intent and stresses his determination to bring the perpetrators to justice . . . no stone unturned . . . all available resources brought to bear . . . blah, blah, blah.

Reporters are shouting questions. They want to know about the second bomber, 'the one who ran away'.

The policeman avoids answering the question. Tries to move on. The reporters won't let him go.

'Why have police evacuated parts of Soho?'

'For operational reasons.'

'Is it true you've cornered a suicide bomber?'

'We hope to arrest a suspect shortly.'

'Does the suspect have a bomb?'

'We have no intelligence to confirm the existence of more devices.'

'Or rule it out?'

'By their very nature people callous enough to kill innocent civilians are hard to stop, but our services and police are doing a heroic job.'

'Is the suspect holding hostages?'

'No comment.'

'Have you made contact with him? What are his demands?'

Sami blinks at the screen. His stomach spasms like he's going to be sick. The brass is asking for public patience and co-operation. Central London will be locked down for a while longer.

The media conference ends. Next they interview the cabbie that kicked Sami out of his cab. He's talking about how he came face to face with the devil.

'He had this crazed look in his eyes, like he was obsessed, you know, and I thought I could hear the bag ticking. He could have blown me up but I kept my cool, know what I'm sayin'? I saved myself and other people.'

Hold the phones, thinks Sami. Get this guy an agent and put him on Oprah.

Next comes the woman from the Crooked Surgeon who let Sami use the phone.

'He had these cold blue piercing eyes. They were looking right through me. It was like he was undressing me, you know, like he wanted to do things to me, obscene things. Clearly he has a very twisted misogynistic view of Western women.'

Everyone is getting their fifteen minutes of fame, thinks Sami, except in the new digital age fifteen minutes is condensed into a sound-bite and should come with an extra large coke and fries.

They're calling it a siege. Nobody ever gets away from a siege. Look what happened at Waco and that school in Russia where all those kids died.

Sami lets his forehead drop onto his forearms and closes his eyes, listening to his heart thudding and smelling sweat rising from his armpits. Even if he destroys the shooter and flushes the drugs, he's guilty of tampering with evidence, perverting the course of justice, breaking and entering, blowing up a train and holding people hostage.

How many years do you get for robbing the Old Bailey

209

or for taking hostages in a restaurant? Fifteen years? Twenty? They're calling him a terrorist. It'll be high security, category A, Parkhurst or Belmarsh.

Twenty years. That's seven thousand and something days. Nadia won't be waiting when he gets out. Neither will Kate Tierney. She'll be long gone, twice married with three kids and thunderous thighs.

They say you only think about escaping for the first five years. After ten you stop thinking about women and by fifteen you're looking forward to a hot cocoa and lights out at ten.

Maybe they won't even bother arresting him. They'll shoot him Butch and Sundance style the moment he sets foot outside. Exclamate him. Full stop. End of story.

30

On the day Nadia started primary school Sami was supposed to walk her to the school gates and hold her hand when she crossed the road. He got as far as the skateboard park where a mate of his was trying a fifty-fifty grind on a handrail. Sami told Nadia to wait for him because he wanted a turn.

She waited for a while but then grew tired of watching the skateboarders. She saw a girl wearing the same school uniform and thought about following her across the road. The lights changed as she stepped out. Tyres screeched. The car couldn't stop. Nadia fell under the front wheels.

Sami saw her lying on the road. He started running; calling for help. Then he kept running, convinced that he'd killed her. Sure she was dead. He was to blame.

Nadia wasn't dead. The nearside tyre had run over one of her school shoes, which was so stiff and new that it didn't give way. It tore all the ligaments in her left foot and she spent two months in a cast.

Sami took his punishment like a man. His skateboard was broken into pieces.

Why does he remember that now, he wonders. Staring at the window, he tries to force Nadia to appear in front of him. He has tried to do it for three days but it hasn't worked.

Outside the restaurant it's gone quiet. Nothing seems to be moving except the Chinese lanterns rocking in the breeze. When Sami presses his left cheek against the glass and looks sideways he can make out the barricades blocking Shaftesbury Avenue. Pressing his opposite cheek to the window, he can see the twin stone dragons outside the Exchange Bar and the fruit stand at the Lucky House Mini Market. Boxes of apples, oranges and bananas are neatly stacked with prices written in coloured markers on white squares of cardboard. The doors are closed. The windows are dark.

'Why are you doing this to us?' demands a voice behind him.

Sami turns. The girl in the wheelchair has broad shoulders and strong arms. Her face might be pretty if her eyes weren't so narrow and hard. Anger seems to be trapped inside her, filling her like a reservoir.

'Doing what?'

'Keeping us prisoner.'

Sami can't answer her.

'When are you going to let us go?'

'Soon.'

'I have to be home.'

'Why?'

The question is so unexpected that she doesn't have an answer.

'I have things to do. I have a life.'

'What's your name?' Sami asks.

Her hands leave her wheels and are pressed into her lap.

'Persephone.'

'How long you been in a wheelchair?'

'Since I was nine.'

'What happened?'

'I got an infection.'

Sami can't think of any more questions, but his silence infuriates her.

'Is that all you got?'

'Pardon?'

'The only question you got? When you look at me is that all you see – a wheelchair? A cripple?'

'No.'

'You didn't ask where I live or what I do. You're not interested in my opinions or my pastimes; what music I like, my favourite films, what I'm reading, it's just the wheelchair. Well let me tell you: I drive a car. I go to the gym four nights a week. I have a boyfriend. I'm a dyna-mite fuck. Want to know more?'

Not really, thinks Sami. 'I'm sorry if I offended you.'

'You're too transparent to offend me,' she says, rocking

back in her chair, raising the small front wheels and spinning away from him.

Now there is a girl with serious issues, thinks Sami, as he watches her depart. It's not just her anger or her bitterness that creates a force field around her. It's as though she uses her disability to selectively embarrass people or socially bludgeon them.

The van driver is still leaning against the wall with his eyes closed.

'You don't look like a Paki or an Arab,' he says.

Sami doesn't answer.

'I suppose you figure you're going to blow a few people up and go straight to heaven; get to sleep with the vestal virgins. How do you Moslems find enough virgins to go round? Maybe they'll run out and you'll end up shagging camels instead.'

Sami's molars are clenched. Hurting.

'I suppose you think 9/11 was a triumph,' continues the van driver. 'But you dumb bastards just made the West stronger. You shoved a pointy stick into the biggest bloody wasp's nest in history and now the Yanks are gonna eat you for breakfast and shit you out before lunch like you're extra-strength All-Bran.'

Sami tells him to shut up. He's not listening.

'Look what happened in Iraq. Saddam bragged that the Republican Guard would lay waste to the infidels. He said they were gonna stain the sand red with American blood. Bollocks! They folded. They fled like frightened rabbits.

214

'Now you got insurgents instead of soldiers. Proper cowards. They bomb schools and mosques. They dress up as women. Booby-trap cripples and retards. Run away. If Gordon Brown had any balls he'd kick every last sand nigger out of this country.'

Sami spins around and kicks at the rear legs of the driver's chair, which are taking his weight. Gravity does the rest. He goes down, landing hard on his back. Winded. Sucking in air.

'I said shut the fuck up,' mutters Sami, pressing the barrel of the shooter into the driver's forehead. Leaving a mark. He pulls away suddenly. Shaking. Frightened of how much he wants to pull the trigger.

Dragging himself up, Sami slumps in a chair, arms hanging between his knees, the gun loose in his fingers. A hand brushes his shoulder. Persephone's mother has crossed the restaurant. She's one of those women who seem to have been beaten down by life, worn smooth like a pebble in a fast moving stream.

'Do you have a headache? I have some paracetamol in my handbag.'

'Thank you, but I'm OK.'

She lowers herself, perching on the edge of a chair, hands clasped in her lap. Enclosed. Bird-like.

'You'll have to forgive Persephone. She can be quite . . . acid-tongued. You see she's very independent and strong-willed. People sometimes mistake it for rudeness.'

'She has her reasons.'

'I used to think it was the accident, but she was always rather demanding.'

'The accident?'

'My husband was driving, God rest his soul. Persephone was thrown out of the car. I was pinned inside.' She pulls back her fringe and Sami sees the scar running across the top of her scalp, just below her hairline.

'When was it?'

'Six years ago.'

'Persephone said it was an infection.'

'She doesn't like talking about what happened. People always want details.'

Her voice drops. She glances behind her.

'I was just wondering . . . hoping really . . . that you might consider letting Persephone go – because of her disability. She wouldn't say bad things about you. You've treated us very well.'

The van driver interrupts.

'You can't let one of us go and not the others. That's fucking discrimination.'

'She's in a wheelchair,' says her mother.

'So what? We give her ramps. We build her lifts. She gets a special fucking pension. It's a rip-off.'

They're shouting at each other.

Sami tells them to be quiet.

Persephone joins the argument. 'I don't want any favours.'

'I bet that's what you say when the Government gives you hand-outs,' says the driver.

'You're an arsehole.'

'And you're in a wheelchair.'

Sami snaps and drives his fist into the driver's stomach. He follows up, hooking him just below the right eye with the butt of the semi-automatic, knocking him across a table.

'I told you to shut up,' he yells, waving the gun like he's conducting an orchestra. Sami balls up a serviette and shoves it in the driver's mouth, sealing it with a length of masking tape ripped from a spool.

'You don't know me,' he says, pressing his face close, squeezing the words out through his teeth. 'I'm not a Moslem and I'm not a terrorist. I'm as British as you are but arseholes like you make me wonder if I should be proud of that.'

The driver's eyes are brimming. Sami has seen guys like him before – fearless on his own turf but a coward in a confrontation.

Rolling him to one side then the other, he pulls back his arms and tapes his wrists together, behind his back. Then he pulls him up onto a chair and loops tape over the curved wooden backrest.

Nobody in the restaurant has spoken. Sami puts the gun away. Wipes his hands.

'Who wants a drink? I'm thirsty.'

31

Bones McGee is considering his position and calculating the odds. Maybe he could cut a deal with vice and roll on Tony Murphy. He could cop a plea to something minor, blame his lack of judgement on work stress, which allowed him to be compromised by a gangster.

He could wear a wire. Set Murphy up. Seek redemption. His police career would be over, of course, but he'd stay out of prison. A man with his background should avoid jail at all costs: a detective, a veteran of the serious crime squad. Dozens of his former collars would be waiting for him inside and they wouldn't be baking cakes and bringing cell-warming presents.

Tony Murphy would turn on Bones like a ballerina in a jewellery box, but that still doesn't mean Bones should do the same. Murphy has a family tree like a parasitic vine. Lop off one branch and a dozen more come looking to strangle you.

And what about Ray Garza? A person couldn't travel far enough or dig a hole deep enough to hide from

Garza. The guy has contacts in the security services, the Home Office and the Met. He plays golf with the Assistant Commissioner for fuck's sake.

None of the options are panning out for Bones. Everything depends on some kid who's holed up in a restaurant in Chinatown. An amateur. A fish. He's probably going to sing like Fat Pav the moment they prise him out of that restaurant. Not the dead Fat Pav but the one who turned 'Nessun Dorma' into an anthem and made a white hankie into a fashion accessory.

Best for all concerned if the kid doesn't make it out alive. Best if he blows himself up. Best if someone puts a bullet in his head.

Leaving his office, Bones steps outside and lets a cold breeze slap him in the face. The sun is a dying orange smudge above the rooftops and traffic is moving again.

He catches a cab to Kings Cross, keeping his head turned to the window so the driver doesn't see his face. Twenty minutes later he catches a second cab back to Piccadilly Circus and takes the stairs to the Underground.

The station is closed, but shops on the concourse have reopened and people are milling around chalk board signs announcing the line closures.

Bones has changed his clothes. He's swapped his wool and cashmere jacket for a vomit-stained overcoat and a woollen hat that belonged to a tramp at Kings Cross. It wasn't a straight swap. The tramp wanted a tenner to close the deal.

A dozen payphones are lined up along one wall. A phone is free. Bones punches in the number for the counter-terrorism hotline. Muffles his voice. Tries to put on a Middle Eastern accent but sounds more like the char wallah in *It Ain't Half Hot Mum*.

'Today is just the beginning,' he says, 'a small illustration of what we can do. Next time the Al Qaeda Martyrs Brigade will kill thousands. We will stain the streets of London with the blood of infidels, the Jews and the Jew lovers, the true terrorists. Praise Allah or prepare to die. We will not negotiate. We will not surrender.'

Bones hangs up. Wipes his fingerprints from the phone. Pulls the woollen hat low over his eyes and exits the station. He ducks into a narrow lane and puts the overcoat and hat in a plastic shopping bag. Later, he'll toss them into a clothing bin in Bayswater. Within a fortnight they'll be on sale in Romania or Albania. Recycling is a wonderful thing.

32

Lucy's mobile rattles on the table. Sami picks it up and listens. A hostage negotiator has found the number. He has one of those matey, avuncular voices that makes him sound like he wants to take Sami under his wing and teach him the ways of the world.

'My name is Bob, what's yours?'

'Is that important?' asks Sami.

'It makes it easier to communicate.'

'We're doing pretty well so far.'

'Just give me a name.'

'David Beckham.'

'A proper name.'

'I'm sure David Beckham thinks it's a proper name.'

'I don't think you're in a position to be glib,' says the negotiator, who seems to lose his place on the page for a moment. 'Can you tell me how many hostages you're holding?'

Hostages? Sami hadn't really thought of them as being hostages.

'They have families,' says Bob. 'I'd like to be able to reassure them that everything is okay.'

Sami can see he has a point. 'There are six of us counting me,' he says.

'Are any of them injured?'

'They're fine.'

'Why are you doing this?'

'Doing what?'

'Holding people hostage?'

Sami doesn't know the answer. It just sort of happened. It's not what the negotiator expects.

'Would you consider giving yourself up?'

'Would you consider letting me go?'

'I can't do that.'

'Well, it looks like a stand-off,' says Sami.

'Listen, I don't know your name, but my job is to make sure that nobody gets hurt and that includes you. I'd be lying if I said I wasn't nervous. There are people out here who aren't very patient.'

'Tell them patience is a virtue.'

'The people you are holding have families and jobs and friends. They've done nothing wrong. I promise you, you have my word, if you let them go, if you walk out of there, hands in the air, unarmed, I'll guarantee your safety. Nobody has to get hurt.'

'And I'll live happily ever after.'

'I'm giving you a chance. We can do this the easy way or—'

'The hard way,' says Sami, finishing the sentence for him.

'I'm just saying you'll make things easier for yourself in the long run.'

Bob is beginning to irritate Sami. He's treating him like an amateur or some wet-behind-the-ears wannabe. Sami isn't a terrorist at all but if he were going to be one, he'd be bloody good at it.

'Maybe we could send in some food,' suggests Bob. 'Are you hungry?'

Sami glances at the stack of takeaway menus on the counter, wondering what sort of IQ a person needs to get a job as a hostage negotiator.

'I'm in a restaurant, Bob. I could send something out if you're feeling peckish.'

'I thought you might want something else . . . other than Chinese.'

'Like what?'

'Pizza. Indian.'

'Chinese is fine.'

Next Bob suggests he send in a two-way radio so they can talk whenever they want.

'Why can't we keep talking on the phone?'

'Two-ways are better. I could send someone in with one.'

'I don't think that's a good idea.'

Sami hears a low rumble from outside. Crouching behind an upturned table, he peers through the window and sees a bulldozer manoeuvre through the gates of Gerrard Street and swing to face the doors of the restaurant. The bucket is raised, shielding the driver.

Sami is still holding the mobile.

'What's happening out there, Bob?'

'Nothing.'

'Are you pissing on my Wheaties, Bob?'

'I don't know what you mean.'

Sami kicks a chair aside and pulls a ski mask over his face. Then he forces the van driver to his feet and opens the front door, using him as a shield. Two steps. He's on the pavement, pressing the semi-automatic to the back of the driver's head.

'You see me, Bob?' he shouts. 'You get that bulldozer out of here or I shoot someone, you understand? Pull a stunt like that again and I'll turn this place into a crater.'

Sami walks backwards through the door, pulling the driver with him. Within a minute the bulldozer has started moving, spinning on wide metal treads and withdrawing.

The van driver's knees buckle. He might have pissed his pants. Sami helps him to a chair.

Bob is still on the phone. 'That wasn't necessary.' He sounds like a schoolmaster.

'Shut up, Bob.' Sami hangs up.

A dripping tap in the kitchen sounds like a clock ticking. Nobody in the restaurant has said anything. Lucy's parents are holding hands. They could be praying. They might be planning their escape.

Persephone is drawing at a table as if trying to ignore what's happening. She has a portfolio in a zip-up folder. Sami glances over her shoulder and sees an image of a half-woman and half-bird, with a hooded beak and a naked body.

'Can I look at some more?' he asks.

She nods.

Sami leafs through the portfolio. Mostly the images are of dark angels and goddesses, who are semi-naked with powerful bodies and demonic eyes. There's nothing pornographic about their nudity.

Persephone tells him her idea for a fantasy comic: a girl in a wheelchair who turns into a crime fighter, a half mythical creature who can't be killed. The idea embarrasses her a little, but she doesn't seem so angry any more. If anything, Sami senses she might be coming on to him. Maybe she's one of those women who get turned on by outlaws and rebels. Kate Tierney is a bit like that, but Sami would forgive Kate anything.

'I need to go to the toilet,' Persephone tells him.

There is no disabled bathroom and her wheelchair won't fit in the cubicle.

'I can do it myself. I just need someone to take me to the door.'

'What then?'

'I crawl.'

'I can't let you crawl. I'll lift you.'

'I don't want you there.'

'I won't stay.'

Sami expects her to say no, but Persephone accepts. He tucks the shooter into the back of his jeans and slips one arm behind her back and another beneath her knees. She doesn't weigh much.

She rests her head against his chest. It's a different girl, he thinks.

The toilets are beside the kitchen. There are two cubicles and a small washroom in between with a basin and mirror.

Sami nudges the washroom door with his hip. Slides sideways, carrying Persephone with her feet first. Making sure he doesn't bump her head.

'You're good at this,' she says. 'I have so many bruises.'

He doesn't feel her hand on his back. She snatches the gun from his waistband and holds it under his chin with both hands. Her eyes are wide.

He pauses. 'Do you still want to go?'

'No. Take me back.'

'I could drop you here.'

'I could shoot you in the head.'

'You won't shoot me.'

'Try me.'

Sami squeezes his eyes shut. 'Go on, then. Do it. Shoot me.'

Her finger closes on the trigger.

'Let everyone go and I'll let you stay here.'

'I can't do that.'

Consternation clouds her eyes. 'Do you want to die?'

'No.'

'I will shoot.'

'No you won't.'

Sami takes his arm from under her knees, letting her legs drape but holding her against him with his face close to hers. The gun is still pressed beneath his chin. He reaches up and closes his fingers around hers, pointing the barrel away from his face and then takes the gun from her hand. He can feel her heart fluttering against his chest, her warm breath against his neck.

She grows soft in his arms. Deflating. He carries her back to her chair.

'For future reference,' he says. 'This switch here is the safety. The gun won't fire unless you take it off.'

33

Ruiz is in a pub on Fleet Street, one of those dark bolt-holes panelled in wood, with leather benches that are scuffed and nicked with age. Clocks don't matter in a place like this. It's a location for serious drinking and romantic meetings and for people who want to know what it feels like to be living back in a cave.

He spent the afternoon ringing hospitals and drug rehab centres, hoping he might find Nadia Macbeth. Fruitless. Thankless. Now a bomb has gone off on the Underground and put things back into perspective.

The barman has a bullet-shaped head, polished until it catches light like the bottles suspended above the bar. He glances up at a TV, which is tuned to the siege in Soho. A message is being broadcast. People are being told to 'Go in, Stay in and Tune in'. Nobody in the bar is listening to the warning except the barman.

'Makes you want to kill a raghead, don't it,' he says.

'Not really,' answers Ruiz, who takes his Guinness and finds a table as far away as possible.

He was supposed to take Darcy for a curry tonight but it's going to take him hours to get home. Most Sundays they go to Brick Lane and she orders a proper thali and a mango lassi.

It's the only time Darcy seems to eat a proper meal, thinks Ruiz, who likes watching her spoon the dhal, pickles and curry sauces onto her rice and fashion it into balls with her fingers before scooping them into her mouth.

A woman shrieks with laughter on the far side of the bar. Ruiz raises his eyes reluctantly and wonders what anyone could find to laugh about on such a day.

What's he doing here? He's not getting paid. He's not on a promise. Miranda isn't suddenly going to invite him into her bed as a thank you if he finds Nadia Macbeth. Although he wouldn't admit it to Miranda, a part of him is quite pleased to be working on a case again. Retirement has never sat particularly well with him, despite his dislike for modern policing and most of the people who populate the Metropolitan Police.

Ruiz doesn't need a reason to get out of bed every morning and he doesn't need to be surrounded by people, not like some who are never certain of exactly who they are until they see themselves reflected in the eyes of others.

His mind is dragged back to Nadia Macbeth. In the past two days she and her brother – two people he knows only from a photograph – have snagged his thoughts and haunted his waking hours. They remind him of a vine that grows in the jungles of Belize that the locals call 'the one way tree'. The tendrils have barbed hooks that are almost invisible until you stumble into them. Then it's too late. You can't go back without tearing your skin to pieces. The only way out is to go forward, deeper into the vines.

A police siren passes outside, growing louder and then softer. Ten or twenty years ago a police siren could increase Ruiz's heart rate and set adrenalin coursing through his system. Not any more. The behaviour of stupid, violent people no longer interests him. Their motives are not his concern. The behaviour of clever, driven, dangerous people is a different story. People like Ray Garza and Tony Murphy.

Just before the terrorist bombings in London on July 7, 2005, a CCTV camera picked up images of a dark-haired man in a light blue shirt, carrying a rucksack. He was filmed entering a pharmacy in Kings Cross where he bought indigestion pills and nail-clippers. Less than fifty minutes later he detonated a bomb that killed twenty-three people and injured more than a hundred.

That's the sort of fact that snags in Ruiz's mind, point-less perhaps, but captivating. When they found the bomber's body parts spread across the carriage, did they come across a finger? Was the nail neatly trimmed?

He calls Fiona Taylor and asks her for another favour – a background check on a Rastafarian junkie and dealer called Puffa.

'You really know how to pick your times,' she tells him. 'We have a live operation in Soho.'

'I can see that,' says Ruiz, glancing at the TV. 'There's no hurry.'

Fiona promises to get back to him. In the meantime Ruiz returns to his Guinness, keeping one eye on the TV screen.

They're broadcasting CCTV footage of a suspect seen running from Oxford Circus Underground. The first part of the video is grainy and blurred. Side-on. A second camera picks up the man as he crosses the street. He stops at a street corner. Looks both ways. Adjusts a rucksack on his back.

The image freezes and zooms in on the suspect's face. There's something familiar about him. Ruiz yells at the barman to turn up the volume. He can't find the remote. He searches. Finds the unit. Amplifies the sound.

Half the story is enough. It's a word association game: siege . . . terrorist . . . hostages . . . Soho.

Another image flashes on screen – a photograph of Sami Macbeth, with long hair, a Nirvana T-shirt and skinny-leg jeans. He's pouting at the camera, going for the angry don't-fuck-with-me look, as though he's posing for publicity pictures instead of a police mug shot.

Ruiz swallows his beer and walks out onto Fleet Street, turns right and strolls past the double-decker buses and black cabs.

Sami Macbeth has been out of jail for fifty-six hours and in that time he has turned himself into a human headline. The kid has a talent for trouble.

34

The street is a no go area. Paper coffee cups and wrappers spin across the pavement, getting trapped against lamp-posts and the tyres of chained bicycles.

Sami tells Lucy to watch the front window. 'Tell me what you can see?'

'Nothing.'

'There must be something.'

'Which part of nothing would you like me to describe?'

A breaking news banner flashes on TV: SOHO SIEGE.

The streets have been cordoned off. Police in black body armour are spilling from buses and taking up positions, as though ready to fight a small war.

'Eyewitnesses say a man claiming to have a bomb took over a restaurant in Chinatown at two o'clock this afternoon. We believe that hostage negotiators have made contact with the hostage taker but as yet his demands are unknown . . .'

A photograph of Sami flashes onto the screen. His police mugshot. He had longer hair, fewer lines and not a care in the world because he knew it was all a misunderstanding and the jewels in Andy Palmer's van had nothing to do with him. He was innocent. The truth would out.

Only it didn't. Sami took the fall. He didn't fall under the wheels of a truck like Andy Palmer. He fell onto the wrong side of the tracks. He fell through the cracks. He fell out of favour.

'. . . The suspect's name is Sami Robert Macbeth, born in Glasgow, raised in south London, to an Algerian mother and a Scottish father. Macbeth was released from prison only days ago having served less than three years for possession of stolen goods. Counter-terrorism experts believe he converted to Islam in prison, influenced by the gangs . . .'

Gangs? Radical Islam? The only prayers Sami said in prison were directed to the parole board.

'An organisation calling itself the Al Qaeda Martyrs Brigade has claimed responsibility for the bombings. It is likely to be one of the loose splinter groups that have flourished since the War on Terror began, with only tenuous links to Al Qaeda, but funded through Middle Eastern banks and sympathisers . . .'

Sami shakes his head in disbelief. Who are these experts?

'Counter-terrorism authorities are also speculating on why the suspect failed to detonate his device. Some believe the device may have misfired or he could have had second thoughts about committing suicide.'

So not only am I an Islamic extremist, I'm also a coward, thinks Sami. How much worse can it get. They know his name. They have his photograph. What hope has he got of finding Nadia now or leading a normal life?

Some time soon they're going to make a decision and 'neutralise the threat'. They'll use SWAT teams or maybe even the SAS, who'll swing from the roof and crash through the doors. Teargas. Flash bangs. Explosions. They'll come in wearing body armour with enough fire-power to blow him into next year.

Sami's mind is fraying, his body aching, his batteries on empty. Whichever way he looks at the situation, he's screwed. If he walks out the front door they're going to kill him or put him away for twenty years in a high secu-rity wing. He blew up a strong room. Stole evidence. They'll blame him for what happened to the train. How many people are dead?

Sami can already smell the boiled cabbage and septic stench of the showers; and feel the scum-coloured water back up around his ankles. The prison sisters will wel-come him with open arms this time. They'll kick his legs apart. Brace him against the wall. Take turns. Nothing is going to protect him if he goes inside again. He'll be a skidmark on the bowl.

If he tells the truth, Murphy will kill Nadia. If he keeps schtum he might survive for a few months inside until Murphy takes out extra insurance and has him killed. It won't matter how long he stays in solitary, eventually he'll be on his own. That's when someone will lift him over a third-floor railing or jam a homemade knife under his ribs.

Sami lowers his eyes and stares at his hands, tightening them into fists, kneading his thumbs against his forefingers. Then he pushes them beneath his thighs to stop them shaking.

The phone rattles on the table.

'Hello, Sami.' It's Bob. 'I know your name now. We don't have to pretend any more.'

'I haven't been pretending.'

'I know but there won't be any mix-ups or confusion. We can have a better dialogue.'

Bob makes it sound like they're on a corporate training weekend.

There is another long pause. Sami considers hanging up, but Bob jumps in with a question.

'Where are you from, Sami?'

'You know where I'm from.'

'You've had a tough few years. Prison and now this . . .'

No shit, thinks Sami, as Bob continues, getting dangerously close to commiserating. He's sounding so affable at any moment he's going invite Sami out for a pint and a kebab.

'You got a family?'

'A sister.'

'What's her name?'

'Nadia.'

'Where is she now?'

That's a good question, thinks Sami. Maybe the police can find her. He could make it a demand.

'I don't know where she is.'

'You lost touch.'

'You could say that.'

Bob Piper covers the mouthpiece. 'Find his sister. We need to talk to her.' He's back with Sami again. 'Tell me what you want and I'll try to help.'

'I want a miracle.'

'I don't do miracles.'

'I want to be somewhere else.'

Sami presses the red button. Ends the call. He's squatting in the corner of the restaurant, his arms crossed over his knees, his chin resting on his arms. The others are watching, waiting for him to do something.

Persephone has packed away her drawings. Her mother is clutching a set of wooden rosary beads, worn smooth by her fingers. Lucy's eyes flit from her parents and back to Sami, somehow concentrating on both.

Sami's guts are churning. When he gets scared it goes straight to his bowels. He's shaking. Strung out. Devoid of hope. Something has broken inside him and he can't go on.

Slowly opening his fists, he touches his face with his fingers. He needs a shave. A shower.

That's when it happens. An idea clicks into place. It's huge. It's risky. It's something he can only fuck up once.

He picks up the mobile.

'Bob, I want the van.'

The negotiator is taken by surprise.

'What van?'

'The one parked outside, next to the restaurant – the white Mercedes.'

'What about the hostages?'

'I'm taking them with me.'

'I can't let you do that.'

'Don't disappoint me, Bob.'

'I mean it, Sami. I can't let you take them.'

'Yes you can. You don't want blood on your hands.'

Bob is asking Sami to stay calm, but that's the thing – he's already calm. This is a calmness he hasn't experienced before.

'Listen to me. You're not taking the van and you're not leaving with the hostages.'

'No, you listen, Bob. You're a negotiator, am I right?'

'Yes.'

'Well how come this isn't a negotiation? In a proper negotiation you'd give me something and I'd give you something in return. We'd barter. We'd agree. So far you don't seem to understand the rules.'

Bob gets annoyed. 'I've been very reasonable.'

'So far you've told me if I give myself up you won't shoot me. That's a threat, not an offer. The way I see it, I'm either going to die today or rot in prison. That's not much of a choice, is it?'

Bob doesn't say anything for a moment.

'I might be able to arrange the van. I need some time.'

'Oh, come on, Bob. The humble servant routine is wearing thin. I saw you on TV. You're in charge. You're the main man.'

'I can't let you leave with the hostages.'

'That's something we can negotiate about. Each time you do something nice for me, Bob, I'll let one of the hostages go.'

'Just one?'

'Maths wasn't your strongest subject, was it Bob?'

35

Bones McGee is pacing his office, stopping occasionally to glance at the TV. The situation isn't improving. He calls Murphy.

'That little problem we discussed earlier – it hasn't gone away.'

Murphy doesn't say a word.

'We got a kid holed up in a restaurant who says he has a bomb. He looks remarkably like the same kid we caught on a CCTV outside the Old Bailey.'

Still there's no reply.

'Are you listening to me, Tony? This kid could tear the arse out of everything.'

'He knows to keep his mouth shut.'

'I appreciate you showing faith in the boy but if he sings we all go down.'

'He won't say a word. I got leverage.'

'Yeah, well I'm pulling the plug, Tony. I'm out. I'm walking away.'

'It doesn't work that way, Bones.'

'Yeah it does. You don't call me. I don't call you. It's that simple.'

'Don't tell me what's simple. I'm not some shit-for-brains Mick just off the ferry at Holyhead. Maybe you think you can play both sides of the fence and get your rozzer mates round my joint knocking on my door with a battering ram, carrying a warrant signed by whats-his-face, the Lord Chancellor.

'Well, don't go getting any ideas. You're not Frank fucking Serpico. You mess with me and I'll start a war with your body parts. I'll cut them off one at a time. I'll dig a hole and bury you so deep not even your arse-sniffing mates in the dog squad will ever find you. You hear what I'm saying, Bones? That's the blood, the guts and the feathers of it. The whole story.'

Silence.

'Are you reading me, you arsehole?'

'Yeah.'

Tony Murphy slams down the phone and grimaces. His ulcer is playing up. What with his gout, high blood pressure and haemorrhoids, he should have bought shares in Boots.

Bones is getting nervous. He has no idea how nervous he should be. If Old Bill gets hold of that shooter Macbeth is carrying, he can forget about his Ibiza apartment and his well-funded retirement.

They're going to test the gun, match the bullet and

then the shit is gonna hit the proverbial. MI5, MI6, Special Branch, SOCA, the CIA and the Mormon Tabernacle Choir, for all Murphy knows, will come looking for them. And they're the good guys, as opposed to Jimmy Ferris and his mates who won't bother with warrants and due process and the Police and Criminal Evidence Act.

Instead Jimmy will take them out onto a deserted beach and put a bullet in their heads. One shot. No tears.

Murphy has always regarded himself as a thinker. Someone interested in exit strategies and contingencies, which are things most villains forget. They plan for an operation going right and ignore the possibilities of fuck-ups or bad luck. These same villains will gladly accept happy accidents as being a bonus but spend a dozen years in prison whinging about how they got screwed by an unfortunate happenstance.

Murphy glances out the patio doors into his garden. The marquee has been packed up and trucked away. A catering van is being loaded with the last of the tables.

Whatever happens he has to distance himself from what happened today, from the robbery, the bombing, from Sami Macbeth. His alibi is secure. A hundred people can vouch for his whereabouts.

How long before they identify Dessie's body? Then they'll come asking questions because everybody knows the Dobermann worked for him. The answer is to distance himself from his old mucker. He could spread a rumour that he and Dessie had fallen out. Tell people Dessie had been skimming the till.

Nobody who knew Dessie is going to seriously believe something like that, but Plod might suck on the worm if Murphy baited the hook the right way.

Suddenly, he sees a new possibility. Sooner or later the rozzers are going to link the Old Bailey job with the bombing. And when they realise what's missing from the evidence room, they'll think Ray Garza hired someone to get his son acquitted. Enter Dessie Fraser, more useful dead than alive.

Sami Macbeth is the only problem. The kid could screw up a one-car funeral.

A decision works its way into Murphy's eyes and he lets out a deep breath through his nose. Stubbing out his cigar, he carries his Scotch through the patio doors and across the lawn. Gabriel is jacketless, sleeves rolled up, polishing the Jag.

'We're taking a drive.'

'Where to, boss?'

'If you knew that you'd be as clever as me.'

36

Bob Piper is sitting in a mobile control room, a Winnebago parked in Wardour Street opposite an Angus Steak House. Spread across a table, weighted down with coffee mugs, are building plans for the Red Emperor restaurant and adjoining buildings, along with satellite images of the surrounding streets. The clarity is remarkable showing individual trees, vehicles and TV aerials.

A few years back a woman in the Netherlands spent an afternoon sunbathing topless on her secluded rooftop patio and then discovered images of herself, near-naked, posted all over the internet because a Google satellite 300 miles above the earth captured the moment.

Piper is studying the satellite images with the head of SO19, the specialist firearms command, and a major who heads the army bomb disposal unit.

Thermal imaging cameras trained on the restaurant show six people inside. Each appears as a white shadow on a dark background. Individuals have been given code-names based on his or her location. Sami Macbeth is

Target Alpha. Right now he's located near the connecting door to the kitchen. Four hostages are located in the body of the dining area, well away from the front windows. One hostage is in the storeroom, a troublemaker perhaps, separated from the others.

Listening devices will be in place within twenty minutes. Technicians are slowly drilling through the walls from the adjoining cake shop threading microphones into position.

Piper tilts back his swivel chair and stretches his arms above his head, making his shirt pull tightly across his chest.

What is Macbeth hoping to achieve? If he does have a bomb, why hasn't he detonated it? Maybe he's bluffing. Maybe the bomb failed to go off or he bottled out.

Now he wants to take a van. It won't happen. Piper can't let a possible suicide bomber go on a joyride through the West End with hostages. No chase scenes. No slapstick.

Piper has to stall him. Make excuses. Give in to the small demands. Sound reasonable.

Normally, the longer the siege goes on, the better it is. Not this time. In the next twelve hours a decision has to be made, Piper's decision. They have to find a way of isolating Macbeth from the others. Then they could detonate a water bomb against the joint wall and blow a man-sized hole into the Red Emperor. One team could go through the front door, another through the hole.

They could reach the hostages in fifteen seconds, all except the one in the storeroom.

The biggest question mark concerns the possibility of booby-traps. If Macbeth does have a bomb, he could have rigged it to explode if there is any attempt to free the hostages. The explosive used in the Tube bombing was TATP, homemade and volatile. Any percussion blast from a water bomb could trigger a chain reaction.

The hotline is ringing. It's the Commissioner. Piper makes eye contact with his senior men, who watch and listen.

'With all due respect, sir, we don't need the SAS.'

Piper sucks in his cheeks. His mouth has gone small.

'Yes, sir.'

'No, sir.'

'My full co-operation, sir.'

Fucking SAS! So what if they abseil off rooftops and swing through windows? They're glory hounds. Headline hunters. They're like piranhas – they only attack when they smell blood in the water.

This is all because of de Menezes, thinks Piper. One dead Brazilian and the Commissioner heads for the tall grass.

The others are waiting for instructions.

'How do you want to proceed, sir?'

'We let him have the van.'

37

Sami feels like it's the first day of his life and not the last one. It's a fluttering deep in his diaphragm, a feverish excitement mixed with fear. He's pacing the dining room, trying to picture what he has to do.

They think he's a terrorist. They're frightened of him. He's frightened of them. He has to use these facts rather than run away from them.

Lucy moves across the restaurant, her footsteps so small and light they barely make a sound.

'Did you really blow up that train?'

'No.'

'But you *are* a terrorist?'

Sami shakes his head.

Lucy looks at him incredulously. She wants an explanation.

Sami shrugs. 'I was in the wrong place at the wrong time with the wrong people.'

'Today?'

'Today . . . three years ago . . . it's the story of my life.'

Lucy waits for more. Sami struggles to explain.

'Have you ever been blamed for something you didn't do and no matter how many times you deny it, nobody will believe you?'

Lucy nods. 'I had a teacher who said I plagiarised an essay. She failed me. I tried to argue with her, but she wouldn't look at the paper again.'

Sami can see how this might be upsetting. 'How long ago did it happen?'

'Four years.'

'That was unfair, but if you look back and be brutally honest, maybe there were times when you got away with stuff. You either didn't get caught or maybe someone else got the blame for something you did.'

'What are you trying to say?'

'I'm saying that for years I've been waiting for things to rebalance, to even up. I'm just plain unlucky.'

'You're making excuses.'

'Think so? I've been over it a lot of times, a lot of nights. I spent nearly three years inside, staring at the walls of a prison cell, thinking maybe there was something I did wrong that I can't remember – some fuck-up or careless mistake like selling a dodgy car or not dipping my headlights at night. Did I kill someone accidentally? Is someone like Persephone riding around in a wheelchair or missing a father because of something I did. Because if there's not – if I've done nothing to deserve this life; if I'm getting kicked from Camden to Christmas for no fucking reason, I'd become a very bitter bastard. Unforgiving. I might even want to kill someone or to kill myself.'

Lucy raises her chin slightly and narrows her eyes. 'You don't punish innocent people just because you're unlucky. Sounds like you're trying to correct yesterday's mistakes. It can't be done. Mark them off. Make a new start.'

'You're a pretty smart cookie for someone your age.'

'I'm twenty-one.'

'You look younger.'

Her hair is cut short and trimmed across her neck in a straight line. Sami wants to reach out and touch it. Lucy moves first, taking his hand. Squeezing it.

'They're going to kill you.'

'I'll be all right.'

'They'll shoot first and do the numbers later.'

'You watch too many films.'

'You could negotiate – give yourself up to someone famous.'

'Like who?'

'Glenda Jackson.'

Sami laughs. 'They'd shoot both of us.'

'You don't have to die.'

Sami looks into her eyes and away. Then he opens his palm as though releasing an invisible bird and watches it flutter away.

38

It takes Ruiz twenty minutes to get from Fleet Street to Covent Garden. He walks with a limping gait, straightening his left leg and swinging his right leg through. If he concentrates really hard he can almost walk normally, but why bother? The limp doesn't embarrass him or make him feel self-conscious.

His mobile vibrates in his pocket.

'Have you seen the news?' asks Miranda. 'They're saying Sami Macbeth has a bomb.'

'I know.'

'Should I do something?'

'Nothing you can do.'

'Something must have happened. I talked to him. He was adamant about not going back inside.'

'Sit tight. I'm here now.'

Chinatown is sealed off, wrapped up in police tape and barricaded with concrete blocks that can thwart a vehicle packed with explosives. Police are guarding the perimeter, keeping sightseers and onlookers at bay.

TV crews have set up cameras on top of broadcast vans and telephoto lenses point from the windows of upstairs flats. Reporters are complaining about being kept so far away from the siege. They want access. Footage. Drama.

Ruiz pushes his way through.

'I need to see the boss,' he says to a senior sergeant.

'Who are you?'

'Vincent Ruiz. I'm a former DI.'

'You picked a bad time, sir.'

'I got some information.'

The sergeant ducks under the police tape and talks into his shoulder blade, pressing the button on a radio. He nods. Nods again. He motions Ruiz to follow him.

They walk along Shaftesbury Avenue and pass through a second checkpoint. A mobile control room has been parked in Wardour Street. Commander Bob Piper is bent at the waist, studying a TV screen. He straightens, turns, taking a moment to study Ruiz over the top of a coffee cup.

The introductions are short. He's a busy man, under pressure, and he isn't going to invite Ruiz to sit down or offer him a coffee.

'The guy inside is called Sami Macbeth?'

'Tell me something I don't know.'

'He was released on parole three days ago. Now he's looking for his sister.'

'How do you know that?'

'He called me. He wanted my help.'

'You know anything about a bomb?'

Ruiz shakes his head. He tells Piper about the drug den in Whitechapel and Sami's meeting with Tony Murphy. Piper isn't taking notes. He's not interested in what happened yesterday or the day before.

'Where would Macbeth get a bomb?'

'I don't know. Maybe he's bluffing.'

'Tell that to the people on that train.'

'My ex-wife is Macbeth's parole officer. She says he wants to go straight. Maybe he's caught up in something and can't get out.'

'And your ex-wife is a good judge of character, is she?'

He's being sarcastic. Ruiz doesn't bite.

Piper is getting tired of the conversation. 'No offence, Mr Ruiz, but I can't rely on your ex-wife's intuition. I have CCTV footage of this guy running from the scene of a bombing. I have his admissions. I have a call from an Al Qaeda splinter group claiming responsibility. And I have five hostages inside with families and friends and the rest of their lives to live.'

'Let me talk to him.'

'Go home, Mr Ruiz. It's not your concern.'

Ruiz is a civilian now. That's why Piper is calling him 'mister'. He's letting him know that he has no authority any more.

Piper signals a DC. 'Escort this gentleman back to the perimeter.'

The phone is ringing. The Commander picks it up. Ruiz can only hear one side of the conversation.

'You can have the van . . . one hostage . . . give me time to clear the roads.'

39

Bones McGee is dressed in dark clothes, carrying a black zip-up holdall, which looks as though it might contain his gym gear. Instead it holds a Blaser R93 single shot, straight pull, bolt action rifle, with a ten shot magazine packed with soft nosed 308s.

It's a sniper's rifle with a vibration absorbing aluminium stock and a two-stage trigger. The 600mm barrel is made of thermally distressed, fluted steel. It's black. It's beautiful. It can blow a big fucking hole in things.

Bones has been five times full bore rifle champion in the Met's annual shoot-off. It would have been six times if the organisers hadn't allowed a ring-in from the FBI to enter. He was so full of Beta Blockers he rattled. Said he had a heart condition. Bullshit.

He reaches the police cordon and flips open his badge. Makes a joke. Keeps walking. The Shaftesbury Hotel has been evacuated and the foyer is forlornly empty. He presses the intercom. A security guard answers. 'The place been searched?' asks Bones.

'It's empty. Everybody's cleared out.'

'I'm here to make sure. Open up.'

The guard appears, studies his badge and unlocks the door. Bones asks about rooms overlooking Shaftesbury Avenue.

'You want to see one?'

'I want to use one.'

The guard shows him a floor plan on the computer. 'How's it going out there?' he asks.

'We'll get the guy.'

Bones takes the lift to the fourth floor and follows a corridor, counting down the room numbers. He swipes an entry card and a green light blinks.

Tossing the holdall onto the bed, he stands at the window and gently parts the curtains by an inch. The Winnebago below him must be the control room. Raising his gaze, he has a view down Macclesfield Street to the heart of Chinatown.

The Red Emperor restaurant is bathed in light, which reflects off the gold lettering above the awning. The street outside is empty except for a white van parked in the adjacent lane.

Bones takes a set of binoculars from the bag and puts an ear jack into the shell of his ear so he can hear the police chatter. Scanning the skyline, he can pick out a handful of dark shadows lying prone on the rooftops or crouching behind walls and chimney pots.

The poor bastards must be freezing, lying in the open

with one eye glued to the scope and a finger curled inside the trigger guard. It's only going to take a shot over their heads and they'll all hit their triggers.

He unzips the holdall from stem to stern and assembles the rifle, something he can do in the dark or blindfolded. Running his forefinger along the barrel, he dips his head so he can sniff the metal and gun oil. Then he clips the barrel onto a bipod and aims it through the window, which is open a crack.

Tucking the stock against his shoulder, he lowers his cheek to brush against the smooth aluminium. Slowly the front of the restaurant swims into focus in the telescopic sight. He adjusts it, making sure the magnified image is sharp within the cross hairs.

One shot to the head will cut Macbeth's kite string. The soft nose bullet will core a plug out of his head and shut down his brain and nervous system. He'll be dead before he hears the shot, before he hits the ground, before he takes another breath.

Bones opens the mini-bar and chooses a soft drink and a can of macadamias. He sits in an armchair, propping his feet on the windowsill. When he finishes the drink, he puts the cans in a plastic bag tied to his waist. He doesn't want to leave any telltale clues behind, which is why he's wearing latex gloves on his hands and a hairnet beneath his cap. He'll burn his clothes afterwards and bury the boots. The rifle will join the fishes.

He's getting too old for this, but he's worked too hard to surrender it all now. One shot is all he wants. With Macbeth out of the way he can ride the storm of questions. Take early retirement. Buy himself a boat.

40

Sami has to choose a hostage. He could ask for a volunteer but that's shirking his responsibilities. None of the people in the restaurant deserve to be involved but Sami can't change what's happened or turn back the clock.

He goes to the storeroom to check on the driver, who is sitting on rice sacks with his legs stretched out like he's trying to sleep.

'Hold your head still,' says Sami, gripping a corner of the masking tape between his thumb and forefinger and ripping it off suddenly.

The driver curses in pain and gingerly touches his lips as if surveying the damage. His wrists are still bound. Meanwhile, Sami squats on his haunches near the door.

'What are you looking at me like that for?' asks the driver.

Sami smiles apologetically. 'You ever been inside?'

'No.'

'You ever done something you regret?'

'What is this – twenty questions?'

'Something really bad.'

The driver shrugs.

'You got a family?'

'My mum and dad.'

'A girlfriend?'

'You're a weird prick.'

Sami is silent for a moment. 'Those things you said to me earlier, my father used to talk to me like that. Treat me like shit. Maybe he felt threatened. Maybe he was just an arsehole.'

'Listen, pal, I'm sorry if I offended you. Family values didn't make a big splash where I came from either.'

'I'm not a terrorist.'

'Whatever.'

'I want you to understand that.'

'It's understood.'

Sami rises from his haunches and closes the storeroom door. Lucy is waiting for him outside.

'Are you going out there?'

'I can't stay in here. I'm getting sick of Chinese food.'

'They're going to kill you.'

'I'll be fine. I need you to come. They won't shoot me if I have you.'

Lucy searches Sami's eyes. 'I don't want to.'

'I know.'

'My mother and father?'

'They'll be safe. I'm leaving them behind.'

'Promise me.'

'My promises aren't really legal tender any more.'

Her voice hardens. 'Promise me.'

'OK.'

Sami begins by taping Lucy's hands behind her back and strapping bags of flour around her waist.

'This doesn't look much like a bomb,' she says.

'Do you know what a bomb looks like?'

'I've seen them on TV.'

'I'm going to put this hood over your head.'

'Why?'

'It's a pillowcase. It's clean. It came from your bed.'

'You've been in my bedroom?'

'It's the only thing I took.'

'I'm scared. Don't make me do this.'

'You'll be fine. It's going to be over soon.'

'Where are you going to take me?'

'I don't think you'll have to go anywhere.'

Sami tears tape from the spool.

'What are you doing now?' she asks.

'I'm taping the barrel of the gun to your head.'

'Why?'

'So they know I'm serious.'

'Does that mean you'll shoot me?'

'If anyone shoots, it won't be me.'

'But if you do . . .'

'I won't.'

Sami calls the negotiator.

'My watch has stopped Bob. Time's up.'

'I'm working as fast as I can.'

'You're trying to delay me. I'm coming out in ten minutes. And listen to me, Bob. I don't want to see a police car, or a van, or a helicopter, or a bike. And I don't want any of your men-in-black taking me out JFK style with a bullet from the grassy fucking knoll. Any sign of Old Bill and she dies. I've got a bomb strapped to her waist that will cut her in two if you try to take me down.'

'You don't need her.'

'Sure I do.'

'What about the others?'

'I'm leaving the rest behind. And I know what you're thinking, Bob. You think I won't risk blowing myself up because I bottled it the first time. Well let me tell you something for nothing. I don't give a shit any more. I'm not a terrorist. Never have been. To me an intifada sounds like an all-you-can eat Mexican meal. So this has nothing to do with religion or politics. I'm a musician, for fuck's sake. I play guitar. My name is Sami Macbeth and I've had a shitty day.'

'I hear you,' says Bob. 'I know you don't want to hurt anyone. Give it up. Surrender to me.'

'I've still got a shot.'

'You'll never get away.'

'Sure I will. I just opened a fortune cookie. It said I'm going to lead a long and fruitful life.'

41

Ruiz drops back beside the bomb squad truck where blast barricades fan out from the chassis, forming a protective shield around the vehicle. A robot with a mechanical arm is poised at the top of a metal ramp.

Elsewhere Wardour Street is strangely empty. Mesh screens are pulled down over shop windows, which are criss-crossed with blast tape. It's like a scene from *Day of the Triffids* or one of those end-of-the-world films where Will Smith or Clive Owen get to be heroes.

The Red Emperor is less than a hundred yards south, partly obscured by the red, gold and black painted gates of Chinatown.

A police radio hacks out static as if clearing its throat. Bob Piper is instructing all units to be in position.

'Target Alpha is coming out. He's taking a hostage.'

The restaurant door opens a crack. A small figure with a pillowcase covering her head and shoulders comes first. Her hands are bound behind her back and her feet are hobbled like a geisha in training. She stumbles down the lone step.

Macbeth is behind her, dressed in a blue boiler suit and a ski mask. He's a foot taller and has to crouch to shield his body behind her. The barrel of a gun is pressed to the back of her head.

Bob Piper is watching the same scene on a closed circuit TV with adrenalin singing in his veins. Macbeth has stepped onto the pavement. His hostage is probably the daughter, Lucy, the smallest and easiest to handle.

Piper hears a voice in his earpiece.

'*Sierra one – I have visual contact. A head shot . . .*'

'Does the hostage have anything around her waist?'

'*Affirmative.*'

Piper studies the screen. Macbeth's right hand is holding the gun, but his left is behind Lucy. He could be holding her belt or a pressure trigger.

'*Sierra two – I have visual contact. I can take down target.*'

'Is Macbeth holding anything in his left hand?'

'*It's behind the hostage, sir.*'

They're nearing the van. Edging sideways. Macbeth is jumpy. Nervous. Every time he jerks his right arm, Lucy's head moves. The barrel of the gun must be taped to her head. He's making sure he doesn't miss.

Macbeth will likely want Lucy to drive. He'll have to undo her hands and feet and take off her hood. He also has to open the van door, which will mean taking one hand off the gun or the detonator. That's the moment.

'Sierra units: look for the target's left hand. If he takes it away from the hostage, neutralise him with all necessary force.'

They have reached the van. Macbeth stops suddenly and seems to be shaking his head. He drops to his knees dragging Lucy with him because the gun is taped to her head. Kneeling on the pavement, he begins yanking his right arm, jerking Lucy's head from side to side like she's a ventriloquist's dummy.

It could be an epileptic fit or some sort of seizure. Maybe he's trying to surrender.

Piper is out of his chair. He leaps from the steps of the Winnebago, landing on heavy boots, and charges towards the restaurant.

'Hold fire. Hold fire,' he bellows, almost crushing a two-way radio in his fist.

Macbeth is still on his knees. Lucy is trying to pull herself free.

'It's over, Sami,' yells Piper. 'Let her go and put your hands in the air.'

Macbeth shakes his head and tries to regain his feet. He's a stubborn bastard.

Pffft! Pffft! Two rounds zoom over Piper's head and there is a hollow *throp* like a watermelon being dropped from a window. Blood sprays across the side of the van and the top of Macbeth's head seems smaller. Half the ski mask has disappeared. He topples sideways, taking Lucy with him. Her body lands across his chest and her legs kick helplessly at the air.

Piper stops dead, holding his breath. Nothing happens. There is no explosion.

'Move! Move! Move!' he yells into the radio. SWAT teams sprint past him, bursting through the doors of the restaurant.

Piper lurches forward towards Lucy. She's hysterical, twisting and squirming on the ground, trying to get away. He tells her to stay calm, worried about the gun, which is still taped to her neck. The barrel is encased in masking tape, which is wrapped around Macbeth's fist. Why would he tape his hand to the gun?

Piper pulls the pillowcase from Lucy's head. Her eyes are wide. She's terrified. The tape is looped around her neck and across her mouth.

'You're safe. It's over. Try not to move.'

A pair of scissors is found. He reaches under the corner of the tape, carefully snipping it away. 'Just lie still until the paramedics take a look at you.'

Lucy isn't listening. She fights to get up. Her clothes are covered in blood and brain and a dark stain has leaked along a crack in the pavement and soaked the knees of her jeans.

'My parents,' she blurts out.

Piper looks up. The hostages are being shepherded out of the restaurant. Lucy's mother and father are clutching each other. Piper lifts Lucy easily and she runs to her parents, hugging them. They huddle together on the footpath with their heads bowed.

A sense of relief floods through Piper. He told his men to hold fire. He told them not to take the shot, but things have worked out OK. Minimal damage, minimal disruption, minimal loss of life; he might even get a commendation.

A voice interrupts this thought.

'You shot the wrong guy.'

Vincent Ruiz is looking down at the body.

'We got the bastard holding the gun.'

'He's not holding a gun.'

Piper follows his gaze. He wants to tell him it's bullshit but a buzz-saw blade of uncertainly is already spinning in his chest. Reaching out he begins to unravel the blood-soaked tape, fighting the dead weight of Macbeth's arms. He peels off the tape, loop by loop, until it lies curled at his feet like the shed skin of a snake.

Even before he finishes, he knows the truth. It's not a sawn off shotgun or a semi-automatic. It's a sealant gun used for fixing leaks around windows and shower screens.

Ignoring the brain matter, Piper peels the ski mask over the dead man's chin and taped mouth.

Why would he tape his own mouth shut?

He uncovers the nostrils and the remaining eye, which is locked open in a vacuous star as though some terrible revelation had been whispered into the dead man's ear just as a bullet tore through his brain.

A voice shouts from the door of the restaurant. 'Hey, boss, we got four hostages inside. Where's the other one?'

Piper rocks back on his heels, unable to focus, staring at the blood on his hands. Right now it feels as though someone has pulled a pin and dropped a grenade down his throat. The loud dull thud is his heart exploding.

42

Perched on the crest of the rooftop, holding onto a chimneypot, Sami Macbeth watches the scene below with a weird sense that he's having an out of body experience except it's not his body lying on the pavement.

The bastards shot me, he thinks. I was on my knees, trying to surrender and they blew my head off.

To be more precise they blew the van driver's head off, but they thought he was Sami so it's almost the same as being shot except Sami isn't the one who's dead.

And even if the van driver was a complete wanker, which he was, he didn't deserve to take one in the canister and have his brains decorating the pavement.

Up until this point, Sami's plan had been perfect. To begin with he made the jump, which was never a certainty. He had climbed out of Lucy's window and scaled the drainpipe onto a narrow bitumen terrace three storeys above Horse and Dolphin Yard. Below him lay a yawning gap. He told himself it was only fourteen feet, but it looked further. It always does when you're three storeys above the ground.

Sami waited until he heard the yelling, when he knew everyone's attention was focused on the front door of the restaurant. Then he took a deep breath, made a sign of the cross, and hurled his body across the gap, his arms wheeling like propellers.

For an age he thought he was going to make it easily because he seemed to be going up, instead of down. And then he realised he might not make it at all. He was falling short.

He reached out as he crashed into the wall, hooking his right arm around the bracket of a satellite dish. His hip and shoulder crashed into the bricks and air punched from his lungs. Somehow he managed to cling on through the pain until his head cleared and his chest filled. He scrambled up onto the tiled roof, avoiding the flimsy gutter.

That's when Sami looked back and saw the van driver lying on the pavement. A black stain leaked from beneath his head and his right arm seemed to be reaching out, pointing to a real target, the one the rozzers *should* have shot.

Dragging his eyes away, Sami tries to think straight. They're going to blame him for this as well. Another death. Add it to the list.

Forcing himself to move, he heads across the rooftops, keeping to the shadows and trying to avoid creating silhouettes against the sky. He walks on the brickwork and steps around the skylights so he doesn't drop in on some spotty Herbert and his missus.

A chopper suddenly sweeps overhead. Sami dives onto his stomach behind a trio of chimney pots. A searchlight turns the rooftop into a brightly lit stage. The chopper seems to hover for a moment and then swings away.

Sami keeps moving. Not looking back. He crosses another half dozen roofs and comes to the next corner, where he shimmies down a drainpipe, hand over hand, jumping the final six feet. The semi-automatic is tucked into the waistband of his jeans, nestled against his back. He heads towards Charing Cross Road and into Long Acre, looking for a park. Parks have trees and shrubs. Parks have hiding places. Parks are good news.

That's when he remembers Kate Tierney. Blonde. Sexy. Darling Kate. Why sleep in a park when he could stay at the Savoy?

43

Bones disassembles his rifle and packs it away, wrapping each component into squares of cloth. He vacuums the carpet with a mini-vac, wipes surfaces clean and washes gun residue from his hands. Satisfied, he takes the lift downstairs and finds the security guard at a console with a dozen TV screens showing footage from cameras inside and outside the hotel.

'I heard shooting,' says the guard.

'We got him.'

'Good for you.'

'I'm going to need your security footage.'

'Which cameras?'

'All of them.'

Bones takes the DVDs from the machines and slides them into the holdall.

'Will I get those back?' asks the guard.

'In due course.'

He swings the bag over his shoulder and waits for the front door to unlock. Outside, he turns right and follows

Shaftesbury Avenue towards Piccadilly Circus. The police cordon is stopping people getting in, not out of the area.

As he passes the Trocadero, he doesn't notice a short, thick-necked man with a shaved head, who is standing in a doorway, watching the police cars pass. Sinbad has both hands cupped around the phone, which looks like a child's toy against his ear.

'Mission accomplished,' Sinbad whispers, 'the kid's no longer a problem.'

Tony Murphy sounds relieved. 'How did you do it?'

'Not me. I couldn't get within a mile of the joint. Must have been the rozzers.'

'Chalk one up for Old Bill.'

'One of 'em must of learned to shoot straight.'

Bones takes a bus from Piccadilly as far as Hyde Park Corner and then walks north to Marble Arch. Then he hails a cab along the Edgware Road as far as Maida Vale and drops the barrel of the rifle into the Grand Union Canal. Other pieces will be disposed of separately, bagged, buried or melted down.

A shame, but you can't be too careful in this day and age. Guns tell stories.

44

The fire door opens. Kate grabs Sami's jacket and throws him against the wall, pressing her body against his like she's trying to flatten her curves. Her tongue traces across his lips.

She pulls back, holds him at arm's length. 'They're saying you're dead . . . on the news . . . you were shot.'

'Someone else.'

'What about the bomb?'

'I never had a bomb. It's a misunderstanding.'

'So you're not a terrorist.'

'No.'

'And you're not hurt?'

'No.'

She slaps him hard across the face. 'That's for scaring the crap out of me.'

Sami holds his cheek. Kate tugs down her blouse which has ridden up and straightens her skirt. 'You can't stay here. I think you're sweet, Sami, but I need this job and I could get into a lot of trouble if someone finds you.'

'Put me in a broom cupboard, a storeroom. I won't tell anyone.'

'You don't understand.'

Sami begs. 'The police are looking for me. I have to find Nadia.'

'How did this happen?'

'It's a long story. Nadia's in trouble.'

Kate reaches out and touches Sami's cheek. 'She's not the one in trouble.'

Sami kisses her fingers.

'If you weren't so adorable . . .' Kate doesn't finish the statement. Instead, she takes him upstairs in her service lift; checks the passageway; opens a suite, closes the curtains.

'I'll register you as a guest on the computer. Housekeeping won't clean the room until midday. Don't answer the door if anyone knocks. Don't touch the phone. I'll try to come back later, but it might be difficult. I'm working a double shift. Please be careful. I'm trusting you.'

Kate kisses him on the lips; wrinkles her nose at his smell. She gently closes the door behind her.

Sami doesn't take a shower. He doesn't have the energy. Instead he collapses on the bed and listens to his heart pounding. How many people died today? They're going to blame him.

He has to sleep. Sleep is good. Sleep will stop him turning paranoid. Right now his head is his own worst enemy. This isn't about thinking straight; it's about thinking around corners.

45

A dozen firearms officers are assembled at Scotland Yard, still wearing dark overalls and bootblack on their faces. Rifles and ammunition are lined up on a table like they're preparing to invade a small African country.

Commander Bob Piper paces back and forth, trying to stop himself from exploding in anger. He wants an explanation. He wants to know which one of these men disobeyed his direct orders and pulled the trigger.

The officers look at each other, waiting for someone else to own up. Nobody does.

Piper's blood pressure is topping out. 'What is this, primary school? I want the officer who discharged his firearm to step forward and explain his actions.'

Still nobody moves.

Piper picks up the nearest rifle, unclips the magazine and begins counting the shells. Slamming it down on the table, he picks up the next one.

'You think I'm some shit-for-brains moron who earned this rank by sniffing arse-cracks? That man you shot today was a decent hard-working delivery driver from Essex who lived with his mother and father and had a dog called Bitzy. I told you to hold fire. Is there anyone in this room who did not hear my command?'

He looks from face to face.

'Are you smiling at me, son?'

'No, sir.'

'You look like you're smiling.'

'I'm nervous, sir.'

'Well, I'll give you something to be nervous about. Do you know what happens when police shoot innocent people? There are inquiries, internal ones and public ones and political ones. Police officers get suspended, careers get ruined, bosses get blamed and newspaper columnists have a field day calling us Keystone Cops who can't be trusted to carry firearms.'

Piper is breathing hard through his nostrils. The last of the weapons has been checked. He turns to his second in charge.

'Have any of these weapons been switched or tampered with?'

'No, sir, they were collected at the scene.'

For a fleeting moment he feels a sense of relief but just as quickly his eyes frame a question. If none of his firearms officers discharged their weapons, who shot the van driver?

Piper looks at his watch. It has just gone 2.00 a.m. The Commissioner wants a report on his desk by seven. What is Piper going to tell him? A security operation that cost a million pounds and shut down the West End for eight hours has resulted in a missing terrorist (who may or may not have a bomb) and a murdered hostage shot by some person or persons unknown.

Then there's the other problem. Radio stations are reporting that the terror suspect was shot dead by police. Sooner or later they're going to discover it was a hostage. If Piper denies police involvement in the shooting they'll call it a cover up and put a blowtorch to his balls. The truth is equally uncomfortable. In the middle of a massive security operation involving a hundred of Scotland Yard's finest, a sniper infiltrated a police cordon and shot a suspected terrorist who turned out to be a delivery driver who stopped off at the restaurant for lunch.

Oh, yeah, they'll just love that.

It's going to be a long day.

46

Sami opens the curtains and examines the morning. The sun is shining, joggers are jogging and the Thames is flowing, sluggish and brown. He watches a lone rower skim across the surface like a water beetle, sliding beneath a bridge. How can a day look so normal?

First he showers and shaves. Then he turns on the TV and watches a media conference at Scotland Yard. A senior policeman is answering questions. The voice is unmistakeable. It's the negotiator.

Bob doesn't sound so confident any more. His eyes are bloodshot and the collar of his shirt is bent upwards at one side. Reaching for a glass of water, he doesn't get a chance to drink. The questions are coming too quickly, shouted by reporters who are up, out of their seats, refusing to sit down.

'I want to reiterate that police firearms officers did not discharge their weapons. A homicide investigation has been launched and we are confident . . .'

'How did a gunman get through the cordon?'

'We're not sure at this—'

'How did he get away?'

'We'll know more when—'

'So the terrorist and the gunman both escaped? Could they be the same person?'

Bob doesn't understand the question.

'Could Macbeth have shot the hostage?'

'Nothing has been ruled out.'

'How did he escape?'

Bob rubs his mouth with the flat of his hand. The microphones pick up the sandpaper-like scratching of his unshaven chin. 'We believe he may have had help of some sort.'

'Are you saying he may have had an accomplice?'

'We haven't ruled it out. We are interested in knowing why Macbeth chose this particular restaurant. Was it planned? Had he arranged to meet someone?'

'Could the victim have been his accomplice?'

Bob blinks at the cameras.

'I couldn't possibly comment at this stage.'

Oh, that's clever, thinks Sami. Shoot the wrong guy and then deflect the blame. Drop an inference, a vague suggestion: we didn't get the right geezer but we got a bad 'un anyway.

Bob is trying to ward off more questions. 'I want you to understand that we're dealing with a very clever, well-trained terrorist operative, perhaps the most dangerous criminal I've come across in twenty years of service. He is utterly ruthless and hell-bent on causing maximum destruction and loss of life.'

A reporter interrupts the speech.

'One of the hostages, Lucy Ho Fook, says she doesn't think he's a terrorist and that he didn't have a bomb.'

Bob's composure is shaken. He stares at the reporter, his mouth locked in a fixed grimace. An aide steps close and whispers in his ear. Bob's mouth moves again.

'Stockholm Syndrome – it's a well-documented phenomenon.'

Sami stares at the TV screen, not knowing whether to laugh or cry. Any moment now they're going to blame him for global warming and Diana's death in the tunnel.

He turns off the TV and stares at the blank screen. Bob said the police didn't shoot the van driver. Surely he must have been lying – covering his arse.

Sami takes out the Beretta and lays it on the bed. It's a monster, a hand cannon, oiled and gleaming. He flicks a switch, the magazine drops into his hands. Eighteen plump bullets fill the clip. Two are missing.

Sami can understand how a person might appreciate the engineering of a weapon like this, but guns aren't something you get sentimental about. Yet this one means something to Murphy. It's the only thing he cared about when Sami called him – not Dessie or the explosion on the Tube, just the gun. He wanted it destroyed.

Sami repacks the magazine and turns the shooter in his hands, looking for a serial number. There isn't one. It's been filed off. The semi-automatic must have a history. Maybe it was used in another crime – something Ray Garza or Tony Murphy don't want known.

Murphy wanted the gun destroyed, which means that Sami has leverage. He turns on Lucy's mobile and makes a call.

'Who's this?'

'Sami Macbeth.'

There is a long pause. Sami wonders if this is what they mean by a pregnant pause: pregnant with possibilities, pregnant with import, fucked-up pregnant?

Tony Murphy finally answers. 'You're supposed to be dead, son, said so on the news.'

'Not me. I'm bullet-proof and bombproof.'

'That you are.'

'You sound disappointed to hear from me.'

'Not at all, son, I'm pleased as punch. It's not every day I get to talk to someone who's dead. My ex-wife comes close. If you don't mind me asking, how did you get out of that restaurant?'

'I took a rooftop stroll.'

'Very impressive.'

'Like you said, Mr Murphy, I have a talent. How's Nadia?'

'She's a bit under the weather today.'

'You better be looking after her.'

'She'll be right as rain when I tell her the good news.'

'I have the package you wanted.'

'A package?'

'We had a deal.'

'I don't make deals with wanted terrorists.'

'Right then, I'll be off. I'll offer the semi-automatic to the cops instead. Tell them the whole story.'

'I'll give Ray Garza the good news.'

Sami's heart flip flops in his chest. 'What's Garza got to do with it?'

'Everything, you cocky little gobshite,' says Murphy, spitting down the phone. 'You think you know the whole story. You don't know a fucking thing. You're wasting your time trying to threaten me, son. Nobody died and made you king of the castle.'

'I just want my sister. I'll swap her for the gun.'

'What makes you think I want it back?'

'You don't. You want it destroyed.'

Murphy doesn't answer. Sami's hunch was right.

'I'll be in touch, Mr Murphy.'

He hangs up. His hands are shaking.

He hears an entry card being skimmed. The door opens. Sami slides the semi-automatic under the pillow and pretends to be asleep. Kate Tierney tiptoes around the bed and wakes him with a kiss.

She notices the gun peeking out from under the pillow.

'Can I hold it? Please. I've never held a gun.'

'It isn't a toy.'

'I know.'

Sami lets her.

281

'Where is the safety catch?'

'There.'

She flicks the switch; points the gun at his head. 'I could call the police right now and have you arrested. I'd sell my story to the *News of the World* for fifty grand: "My night with the Tube bomber".'

'I didn't bomb the Tube.'

'They're not going to care. I'll say you had your evil way with me at gunpoint, six times.'

'Nobody's going to believe that.'

'Four times then.'

Sami reaches out to retrieve the gun. Kate knocks his hand away.

'You think I'm joking? I'm serious.'

For a fleeting moment the mad light in her eyes almost convinces him. Then she laughs and points the barrel of the Beretta at the knot on his bathrobe.

'I'll drop mine if you drop yours. I'm horny.'

47

Monday morning. Ruiz walks along a metal landing with prison cells along one side and a two-storey drop on the other. Every thirty yards a warder unlocks a heavy metal gate. Ruiz steps through, continues walking. Hand mirrors extend from hatches as he passes; disembodied eyes, watching him.

He climbs another set of metal stairs. Nets are strung between the railings to discourage heavy objects such as bodies being thrown from above.

This is the isolation wing where the sex offenders, ponces, prison snitches and the incorrigibly violent are separated from the general prison population.

The interview room has bare walls, three folding chairs and a scarred wooden table bolted to the floor. One of the chairs is already taken. Derek Raynor looks like an Irish navvy with a crop of ginger hair and a long beard reaching down his chest. His top lip is shaved, which makes the beard look like a ginger hammock slung between his ears.

'I'd like to be alone with him,' says Ruiz. 'You can take off the cuffs.'

The older guard shrugs and unshackles the prisoner.

Raynor has made violence his vocation. Banged up at sixteen on a burglary conviction, he was sent to juvenile detention where he attacked a youth-worker, crushing his thorax and cracking open his skull. It was the first of three murders committed in prison. Now he's never getting out.

'Hello, Derek.'

'My name is Abdul Mohammad.'

'Is that right? How is Allah these days? He's getting a higher profile.'

'Are you mocking the Prophet, Mr Ruiz?'

'Me? No. I've seen what happens to people who mock the Prophet. Writers. Cartoonists. Women. Allah isn't famous for his sense of humour.'

Ruiz pulls up a chair opposite, rests his elbows on the table. He fixes Raynor with an ambivalent stare.

'Tell me something, Derek. Does Allah think a murdering scumbag like you turning religious is taking the piss?'

Raynor doesn't respond immediately. Behind the reinforced glass, Ruiz can see the screws at a table. One of them is doing a crossword, while the other is drinking coffee.

'I wasn't a violent man when I entered prison,' says Raynor, his eyes flat and dry. 'The system took a troubled teenage boy and turned him into a monster. Allah has forgiven me and he's taught me to forgive.'

'Who have you forgiven?'

'All those who have wronged me.'

'The youth worker you killed had a widow. I'll be sure to tell her that you've forgiven her husband.'

Raynor stares hard at Ruiz. Small dark flecks are floating in his irises like dead flies caught in amber.

Ruiz changes the subject. 'Ever had anything to do with a con called Sami Macbeth?'

Raynor shakes his head.

'You don't remember him coming to any prayer meetings or asking about joining the Brotherhood?'

'The truth grows in men's souls. I can't see inside all of them.'

'Is that so? Tell me, Derek, how far would you go for the faith? Would you blow up a train?'

Raynor smiles benignly. 'I'd tear down the world so God could rebuild it again in six days.'

'I thought that was the Bible.'

'Read the Koran sometime.'

Ruiz leans across the table, keeping his palms flat on the scarred wood. 'I don't have a problem with you finding God, Derek, and I don't even have an issue with you playing the downtrodden religious martyr, I just want to know if Macbeth mixed with the brothers while he was inside.'

'Not that I can remember. What's he done?'

'The police say he's an Islamic terrorist.'

Raynor smiles to himself. 'Like I said, I can't look into a man's soul.'

The assistant governor turns sideways on a swivel chair, blinking at Ruiz from behind rimless glasses that seem to make his eyes float an inch from his face.

On the windowsill behind him there are dozens of small origami birds, flowers and animals, a white menagerie seemingly frozen in a blizzard.

Ruiz takes a seat. The assistant governor is folding a piece of paper into some sort of antelope, hardly bothering to look at his fingers.

'You released a parolee on Thursday. Sami Macbeth. Name mean anything?'

'Not since yesterday when I turned on the box.'

'They say he's a terrorist.'

'Human beings do bad things sometimes.'

'You normally keep track on the Islamists?'

'Where possible.'

'Did Macbeth ever attend a meeting or ask for a copy of the Koran or a prayer mat?'

'Nope.'

'Didn't mingle with the Brotherhood?'

'Kept pretty much to himself.'

'He ever kick off about anything?'

'Nope.'

'He get hassled by any of the prison sisters?'

286

'Didn't complain.'

So we got a fresh fish, mid-twenties, good-looking and nobody touches him in nearly three years. All of which means he either had a benefactor or a reputation that kept him safe.

'What did you hear about the Hampstead jewellery job?'

'I heard Macbeth did it.'

'He only got done for possession.'

'Everyone knew he did it.'

'Why?'

'He played up to it.'

That's not an argument, thinks Ruiz, as he pops a boiled sweet into his mouth. He offers one to the assistant governor, who shakes his head and pats his waistline.

The lolly rattles against Ruiz's teeth. 'Did Macbeth have any regular visitors?'

'His sister.'

'Anybody else?'

The assistant governor swings in his chair; opens a filing cabinet; licks his thumb; pulls out a file. The cover sheet is a history. The second sheet is a log.

'Nobody visited him more than twice.'

'What about letters?'

He raises an eyebrow. 'We're on dangerous ground here, Mr Ruiz. Normally I'd want to see a warrant.'

'Or we could save time and I could look over your shoulder.'

The assistant governor blinks his magnified eyes and rolls back on his chair.

'Have you seen the view from this side of the desk?'

48

The morning papers are tucked under Sami's door. His face is on every front page.

TUBE BOMBER SLAIN, declares the *Sun* while *The Times* gives him the benefit of the doubt and calls him a 'Terror Suspect'.

Being reported dead is an odd feeling. It's like imagining your own funeral and trying to picture those who might turn up. Sami's friends and old workmates have been contacted by reporters. Nothing positive emerges from the quotes, most of which seem to suggest that Sami's fall from grace was always on the cards.

Kate zips up her skirt. 'You can't stay. They're going to be cleaning the rooms.'

Sami knows she's right, but the streets will be crawling with police and they're all looking for him.

'You need a disguise,' says Kate.

'Like what?'

'Leave it to me.'

She disappears for ten minutes and comes back with

a set of scissors and a bottle of hair dye. Sami sits on a chair in the bathroom while Kate trims his hair, giving him a fringe. Then he leans over the sink and she applies the hair dye.

Kate talks a lot when she's nervous. It's a constant, stream of thought monologue about her job and her family and how she wants to tell her friends about Sami, but she can't because nobody can know and they probably wouldn't believe her anyway.

This whole fugitive business seems to excite her as though she imagines herself to be Bonnie to Sami's Clyde or she's Patricia Arquette and he's Christian Slater in *True Romance*.

'What do you think?'

Sami looks in the mirror. 'I look like the sixth Beatle.'

'I think black hair suits you. Now you need some new clothes.'

She takes him to a storeroom on the floor below. His hair is damp and leaving dark stains on the towel around his neck.

She unlocks the door. There are clothes racks, boxes and suitcases. Kate pulls a charcoal grey pinstriped suit from a hanger. 'These are clothes that guests have left behind,' she explains, as she finds Sami a business shirt and holds up half a dozen ties until she's satisfied.

'You can't carry that rucksack around.'

She moves boxes and pulls an attaché case from the back of the storeroom, blowing dust off the handle.

'The ensemble is complete.'

'I look like a prat.'

'You look kinda cute.'

'If you're into stockbrokers.'

'Only if they're naughty.'

It's almost midday. Sami dumps his old clothes in the rubbish-chute while Kate checks him out of the room. He ponders what to do with the semi-automatic, the drugs and the money. He doesn't want to get caught with them.

Looking around the room he spies the air-conditioning vent. Everyone always hides shit in the air-conditioning vent, he thinks, but maybe there's a reason for that. He pulls off the panel and pushes the bags of cocaine, the money and the gun inside, before replacing the panel again.

Kate knocks on the door.

'Are you ready?'

'I guess so.'

She presses a piece of paper into his hand. It's her address in Barnes. 'Don't answer the phone. Don't read my emails. Don't look at the mess.'

'When will you be home?'

'Soon.'

She kisses him on the lips. The kiss might not mean much in itself, but when she touches his cheek with her fingertip it's as though she doesn't want to let him go. Sami feels his heart turn to porridge.

The lift carries him down and the doors open. Sami walks across the hotel foyer, trying to look like he's a businessman on his way to an important meeting in the city.

'Can I get you a cab, sir?'

Sami nods.

The doorman whistles.

A black cab pulls up.

Sami slips the doorman a fiver and slides into the back seat. He used to think that suits were like straitjackets but this one feels good, expensive, well-cut. Maybe clothes do maketh the man.

49

Vincent Ruiz steps outside the inner door of Wormwood Scrubs and discovers the weather has turned. Dark clouds are tumbling across the sky and rain threatens.

He glances at the name and address in his battered notebook:

Kate Tierney
58 Brook Gardens
Barnes

It's a long shot but Sami Macbeth doesn't have many friends left. Right now he's probably gone to ground but he can't stay hidden forever. He's going to need help.

Ruiz ponders what happened last night. A hundred coppers were outside the restaurant, two helicopters hovered above it and a small army of reporters were camped less than a block away. Police searched every cupboard, every corner, every crawlspace, yet somehow Macbeth managed to slip away. He wasn't in the restaurant. He wasn't in the building. He wasn't on the rooftop. The kid is fucking Houdini.

Bob Piper is claiming police didn't shoot the van driver, which is too outrageous a declaration to be a lie. Which means someone else wanted Macbeth dead and wanted it badly enough to risk taking a shot over the heads of a dozen firearms officers.

This has nothing to do with terrorism. The notion is ridiculous. Macbeth was an unlikely jewel thief and an even less likely extremist.

Reaching his car, Ruiz slides behind the wheel and calls Fiona Taylor.

'Can you talk?'

'I have a meeting in five minutes.' She sounds amused. 'Your name came up in the morning briefing.'

'How so?'

'Bob Piper wants you investigated.'

'What did I do?'

'He says you've been in contact with Sami Macbeth.'

'The kid called me once. He's looking for his sister.'

'So you said. You might be getting a visit.'

'Thanks for the heads-up. Listen, I'm interested in the bombing at the Old Bailey. What was the target?'

'They blew up the evidence room.'

'Anything taken?'

'Eight kilos of cocaine. Cash. A semi-automatic pistol.'

'How much cash?'

'Just shy of fifty thousand pounds.'

Ruiz considers the haul. It's not big enough to warrant the risk.

'Islamic terrorists don't normally steal drugs.'

'We got a call from an Al Qaeda splinter group claiming responsibility.'

'How many other groups claimed it?'

'Six at last count.'

That's the thing about would-be bombers and terror groups: hoax callers outnumber genuine ones and without a code word there's no way of confirming their claims.

Ruiz asks about the shooter.

Fiona Taylor reads off the manifest: 'A Beretta 93R machine pistol with a twenty round magazine and eighteen bullets in the clip.'

'What was it doing in the strong room?'

'It's evidence in an attempted murder case. The perp fired a shot at police.'

'Ray Garza's kid.'

'How did you know?'

'Lucky guess.'

Ruiz is trying to get his head around the coincidences. Ray Jnr turned up at Murphy's garden party. The two must know each other. Maybe Ray Garza organised the robbery to get the boy off, although it's not Garza's style. He'd rather blackmail a judge or bribe a jury than rely on something as clumsy and outdated as blowing up a strong room.

'What did ballistics say about the shooter?'

'They haven't tested it. Some sort of paperwork problem. It should have gone straight to the lab.'

'What about the slug or a shell casing?'

'Unrecovered.'

Ruiz ponders this. 'Without the cocaine and the shooter what happens to the case against Ray Jnr?'

Fiona Taylor catches the inference in his question. 'I hope you're not suggesting that Ray Garza is behind this . . .'

'I'm just trying to make sense of it,' he replies unconvincingly. 'Were there any witnesses?'

'Dozens of them, but most of them were Garza's mates. Things turned ugly when the police tried to arrest him. The officers had to call for back-up. They couldn't secure the crime scene.'

Fiona has to go. 'Hey, one more thing, but you didn't hear it from me: we just ID'd the dead guy on the Tube. His name was Dessie Fraser, a long time associate of Tony Murphy. You know him?'

'By reputation,' says Ruiz. 'He liked writing his signature with a baseball bat.'

'According to Murphy they had a falling out a few weeks back and Dessie went to work for someone else.'

'Did he say who?'

'Ray Garza.'

50

Sami bounces on Kate's bed, checking out her mattress. It's a nice place, a bit too girly and her flat-screen TV is on the small side but at least she hasn't got stuffed toys on her bed.

Half of Kate's clothes are strewn over the dresser and an armchair while make-up and cosmetics fill every inch of the bathroom shelf and the edges of the sink. How many types of moisturiser does a woman need?

Sami looks in the kitchen. You can tell a lot about a girl from the contents of her fridge. Is she a manic dieter, a binge eater, a gourmet cook or a take-out junkie? Kate's fridge has bread, milk, an avocado, a bar of dark chocolate and half a dozen jars of Indian chutneys and pickles. Her freezer has a bottle of vodka and a packet of frozen yoghurt Popsicles. Sami could fall for a girl like this.

He makes himself a coffee and puts his feet up. Ponders how long he should let Murphy stew before calling him again. He also tries to get his head around the shooting.

What if Bob was telling the truth and the police didn't shoot the van driver? Someone else must have been there; someone who wanted Sami dead.

Tony Murphy has the wherewithal to hire a dozen hitmen – he probably has them on speed dial – but it takes more balls than a bingo caller to carry out a hit during a police siege.

The buzzer sounds. Someone is at the door downstairs. Sami presses the intercom.

'Hello?'

Nobody answers. He asks again.

A male voice replies. 'You got a package.'

'Who's it for?'

'Kate Tierney.'

'What is it?'

'Listen, mate, I just deliver 'em, I don't look inside 'em.'

'Just leave it on the steps.'

'Can't do that, someone's gotta sign.'

'Hold on.'

Sami walks to the window of the lounge and opens the curtains. He can't see a delivery van. Smells like fish.

He goes to the window in the kitchen, which overlooks the rear garden. The ground floor has an extension – a flat roof about ten feet below the window. He could lower himself down and then jump onto the grass.

A part of him thinks he's being paranoid. Another part of him says to trust nobody.

Sami returns to the intercom. 'Give me a minute, I got to get a shirt on.'

He goes back to the kitchen window. Slides it upwards. Climbs over the sink and sits on the ledge. Spinning round, he lowers himself down until hanging by his fingertips. He drops the final four feet and crosses the flat roof at a run before leaping onto the lawn.

There's a Wendy house at the back fence, closed up for the winter. A paddling pool has been stuffed inside. That's when Sami realises he isn't alone in the yard. He tries to turn but someone crash-tackles him low and a second man goes high, forcing his face into the turf. His hands are pulled behind his back and bound together with a plastic cable-tie. Tape covers his mouth. A hood slips over his head.

Sami is dragged to his knees. His head is wrenched back.

'Can you hear me, Mr Macbeth?'

Sami nods.

'Stay calm and you won't get hurt. Someone important wants a word with you.'

Sami mumbles into the gag and then shouts as he feels his sleeve forced up and a needle slide into his arm. His mind swims and he swallows the darkness.

51

Ruiz stands outside the address in Barnes, listening to a South West train rattle towards Clapham Junction. The main door is open. He climbs the stairs.

Kate Tierney's flat is on the first floor. One of the timber panels on the door has been kicked out and lies splintered on the floor. The door is open. He steps inside.

Kate Tierney is sitting on a low table at the centre of the lounge, amid the broken pieces of her life. A TV without a screen, a glass coffee table without glass, radiators ripped from walls, wallpaper in ragged strips, carpet and underlay peeled back, a mantelpiece torn from the fireplace, a sofa disembowelled . . .

Water is spilling from the bathroom where the cistern has been torn from a porcelain plinth and dumped in the bathtub. Tiles are smashed. Shards of broken crockery and glass are scattered on the floor.

Kate looks up at Ruiz. Her cheekbones are shining. She's dressed in a black skirt, dark tights and a loose white blouse. Honey-coloured hair is plaited in a French braid down her back.

'Have you called the police?' he asks.

'No.'

'Did they hurt you?'

She shakes her head. Her eyes swim with the knowledge that her life contains elements of loss and betrayal.

'Where's Sami?'

'He's not here. I just got home.'

Ruiz punches a number on his mobile. Calls it in.

'Who are you?' she asks.

'I'm a friend of Sami's.'

Kate blows her nose. Wipes it once, twice, three times. Bunches the soggy tissue in her fist.

'Will they send me to prison for helping him? I know I should have called the police.'

'If I were you, I'd leave Sami out of this. You were robbed. Keep it simple.'

She nods.

'Do you know who did this?'

She shakes her head. 'It wasn't Sami.'

'I know.'

'When did you last see him?'

'This morning.'

'He spent last night with you?'

She lowers her eyes to the Oriental rug, which has been sliced open. 'Don't tell my work. I'll lose my job.'

Water is leaking slowly across the floor. Ruiz finds the stopcock in the bathroom and turns it off.

'Did anyone else know Sami was here?'

Kate shakes her head.

'You didn't tell anyone – a girlfriend or a friend?'

'No.'

Kate takes a cigarette from a packet lying on the floor beside a broken drawer with no base. Her hand is shaking as she tries to flick the flywheel on the lighter. Ruiz does it for her. She holds the cigarette in her clenched fingers, making no attempt to smoke it. Water has reached her shoes.

Ruiz takes it from her. Sits close.

'Listen, Kate, I think you realise how much trouble Sami is in. People are looking for him – not just the police. People who want to hurt him. Did Sami tell you anything?'

'Someone has his sister. Sami is trying to get her back.'

'Did he mention any names?'

'He called someone this morning. I can't remember his name.'

'Was it Tony Murphy?'

'That's him. Sami wanted to arrange a meeting.'

'Why?'

'I don't know.'

Ruiz glances around the flat. 'Does Sami have something Murphy might want?'

'He had a gun.'

'What sort of gun?'

'A black one.'

It must be the Beretta from the Old Bailey strongroom, Ray Jnr's gun.

A police car has pulled up outside. Ruiz gives Kate his card.

'If Sami calls I want you to give him this number. I can't promise him anything, but if he tells me why he's doing this, maybe I can help.'

She takes the card in her hand, presses a soggy tissue against it.

'How are you going to help him?'

'I think Sami is caught up in something that is bigger than he is. He's trying to get out but he just keeps getting in deeper.'

The intercom sounds. Ruiz passes two constables on the stairs. Outside, he watches as another train rattles past towards Clapham Junction. Fallen leaves dance in its wake and a grey squirrel dashes up the nearest tree where it freezes, pretending to be a statue.

This all comes back to the gun, thinks Ruiz. Murphy wanted it stolen, but why? He could be working for Ray Garza or trying to blackmail him or maybe they're locked in some sort of turf war.

Murphy was jacking cars to order when still in his teens, stealing off the streets of Dublin, Manchester and London, shipping them to Eastern Europe and North Africa. Garza was in a similar business, moving looted vehicles out of Iraq and Kuwait after the first Gulf War. Maybe they used the same distribution network or bribed the same customs officers and border guards.

That's where the similarity ends. Wealthy and well-connected, Garza has turned himself into an establishment figure, while Murphy will always be a gangster no matter how many garden parties he throws.

In the meantime, Sami Macbeth has disappeared again – abducted violently and perhaps permanently. Maybe his luck finally ran out, thinks Ruiz, although he isn't convinced. The kid is like Lazarus with a triple heart bypass.

52

Sami wakes in a bed almost as soft as the one at the Savoy. The curtains are open. Light spills across the bed-spread, lighting up dust-motes that float just out of his reach.

Sami looks down. He's naked beneath a blue bathrobe cinched at his waist. Someone has taken his clothes. Getting out of bed, he opens a wardrobe and finds a selection of jeans with a 32-inch waist, along with cotton sweaters in different colours and an oilskin jacket with a fleece lining. Six shoeboxes are stacked on the floor containing Nike trainers, Italian loafers and Oxford brogues – all in Sami's size.

Spooky. He tries not to think about it.

After getting dressed, he goes to the window and opens the curtains. Figures he must be at some sort of country house. The crushed marble driveway circles a fountain and follows a line of oak trees to a stone bridge. In the near distance he can see hedgerows, fields and the outline of farm buildings.

Double doors open onto the balcony. Sami tries the handle. It opens. He steps outside. A movement catches his eye and he notices a woman riding a horse over jumps with painted poles resting between drums. She's wearing jodhpurs, a short red jacket and riding hat. Her blonde hair bounces on her back as her buttocks rise and fall in the saddle.

There is a knock on the door behind him. A maid enters. Her skin is so black it almost has a purple sheen.

'Mr Garza wants you to join him in the library for afternoon tea.'

Sami feels his scrotum tighten as his balls crawl upwards into his body, looking for somewhere safe to hide.

As he laces up his trainers, he tries to think it through. If Ray Garza had wanted him dead, he'd be dead. Now people have seen him – the maid at least. She's a witness. And surely Garza wouldn't give him a choice of clothes if he was going to mess them up with bullet holes.

Murphy must have called him and said Sami was being difficult about handing over the shooter and the drugs. That's all right, thinks Sami. He just has to hold his ground. Insist on getting Nadia. There's no option.

Opening the bedroom door, he stands on a landing and looks down a marble staircase that is like something from *Gone With the Wind* before the fire. A chandelier the size of a Mini Cooper hangs above the entrance hall.

Sami's trainers squeak as he walks. He should have chosen the loafers.

A different maid is polishing the foyer with a machine. 'I'm looking for the library,' says Sami.

She points along a corridor and tells him to keep going as far as the ballroom and then turn right. After that it's the fourth door, just past the billiard room and home theatre.

Sami stops outside the door. Knocks. Waits. Enters. Nobody seems to be around, but a silver coffee pot is sitting on a tray with cups, saucers and paraphernalia.

The room is lined with bookshelves that stretch to the ceiling. The upper ones are reachable via a staircase leading to a walkway that skirts three walls and is draped with heraldic flags and pendants.

Ray Garza emerges from the patio outside, talking on a mobile phone and motioning Sami to take a seat. Garza must be about fifty, but looks good for his age. Tanned. Fit. Dressed in casual trousers, Gucci loafers and a cashmere sweater, he has the relaxed air of someone who knows the value of money because he has a mountain of it.

He ends the call, looks at Sami, smiles. Teenage acne scars have cratered his cheeks and removed any chance of him being handsome.

'Are you interested in politics, Mr Macbeth?'

'No, sir.'

'Neither was I at your age. I didn't read the newspapers,

didn't vote, didn't care what bastards were in power.' Garza's eyes glitter. 'Now I make it my business. Politics is like a microcosm. So is business. Every element is linked, just like in nature.'

Sami has no idea what he's talking about.

'If this is about what I said to Mr Murphy . . .'

Garza raises a hand to dismiss the interruption. His voice is proper and clipped, but Garza didn't go to private school. He grew up in a Bristol tenement, the son of a meat packer at the city abattoir.

'Do you know anything about hyenas, Mr Macbeth?'

Sami wonders if it's a trick question. 'They laugh.'

'Actually, they make a whooping sound, which can't really be mistaken for a laugh. Hyenas have the strongest jaws in the world of mammals. They also have a pseudo penis, which means you can't tell which one is the male or the female when they're born.'

'You know a lot about hyenas, Mr Garza,' says Sami, unable to think of anything else to say.

'I used to have a private zoo until the council closed it down. I had to sell off my animals because the animal liberationists spent six months camped at my front gate. They poisoned my trout lake – I guess they don't care so much about fish – they scared away my feed suppliers and firebombed my vet's car. They didn't seem to appreciate the breeding programme we were running. Some people make it hard for you to do the right thing.'

'I'm sorry.'

'Why are you sorry? It wasn't your fault. Don't ever say sorry for something you didn't do.'

'Yes, sir.'

'Do you know who I am?'

'You're a friend of Tony Murphy's.'

Garza roars with laughter. He rocks back on the Chesterfield sofa, unable to stop himself, wiping tears from his eyes.

'He told you that?'

'Not exactly,' says Sami. 'I just assumed.'

Garza has stopped laughing. It's amazing how quickly his eyes fill with violent intent. 'Why did Tony Murphy ask you to rob an evidence room at the Old Bailey?'

'Mr Murphy didn't give me a reason.'

'But you did it anyway?'

Sami can tell that he's misread the situation and there's no point in lying. He tells Garza everything, recounting what Murphy said to him at the restaurant and at the dog track. He tells him about Nadia and the drug den and Dessie blowing himself up.

'When I saw the evidence bags and your boy's name I just assumed Murphy was doing the job for you.'

Garza's turns his face to the glass doors. Light catches in the pockmarks on his cheeks and they look even more like lunar craters.

'You remember the two gentlemen who brought you here?'

'Yes, sir.'

'If I'd wanted someone to break into an evidence room and take exhibits, they could have done it in twenty minutes and left none of the fucking mess you did.'

'So you didn't want the stuff stolen?'

'Not by you, son.'

Sami feels his insides betray him. He reaches for a coffee cup but his hand is shaking too much.

'If I'm to believe you, Mr Macbeth, I owe you an apology,' says Garza. 'You've been had over by Mr Murphy. Consider it a learning experience.'

'I swear, I had no idea,' says Sami.

Garza motions him to lean closer. 'That still leaves one question. Why did Murphy want you to take the stuff? My lad got himself into trouble. I'll get him a good lawyer – the best – and I'll fund his defence, but if he goes down so be it. Might be what he needs.'

'You don't really mean that,' says Sami.

'Don't I?'

'I've been inside. Prison doesn't teach you any lessons.'

'Do you want to go back inside, Mr Macbeth?'

'No, sir.'

'Sounds like you learned something.'

Garza invites Sami to take a walk with him. Maybe this is where they go into the garden and he hands Sami a shovel to dig his own grave. They walk past the stable block and down a long path between empty enclosures. There are signs still attached to some of the gates. One of them reads: *Saltwater Crocodiles* (Crocodylus porosus).

Inside is a brackish pool, surrounded by rocks and weeds.

'The interesting thing about a saltwater croc is the teeth,' explains Garza. 'They're not razor sharp so they can cut. Instead they're like pegs. That's why a croc rolls its victim over and over, ripping the flesh. The death roll. Sometimes they'll take the carcass underwater and tuck it under a log or a ledge for a few weeks, waiting for the body to go soft before they eat it.'

Sami peers into the murky pool. 'And you're sure this one's gone?'

'Went to Whipsnade.'

Garza opens an inner gate and they walk across a large grass enclosure.

'What exactly did you take from the evidence room?'

'Drugs and a gun.' Sami doesn't mention the cash.

'Where are they now?'

'I have them.'

'Where?'

'In a safe place.'

'Are you purposely being obtuse, Mr Macbeth?'

'No, sir, I don't know what obtuse means. Murphy still has my sister. He wants the gun badly.'

'Why?'

'I don't know. It's all he seems to care about. He wants me to destroy it.'

They reach another enclosure. The sign says, *African Wild Dogs* (Lycaon pictus*).

'It means painted wolf,' explains Garza. 'People some-times mistake them for domestic dogs gone wild.'

'They *look* like dogs,' says Sami.

Garza points to a photograph on the sign. 'They have round bat-like ears and only four toes. Domestic dogs have five. African Wild Dogs are more efficient as killers than lions or leopards or cheetahs. They hunt together, taking turns, chasing down a buffalo or wildebeest and ripping it apart as it runs, eating it alive.

'That's what Tony Murphy is doing to me, tearing chunks of flesh, spreading rumours that I'm behind the robbery. I've had two Members of Parliament cancel appointments in the past twenty-four hours and an old friend from the Lords rang and told me not to bother coming hunting.'

It's just a few knobs, thinks Sami, but doesn't say it out loud.

'Why would Murphy do that?'

Garza's eyes are flat and expressionless. 'Good question, Mr Macbeth. Good question.'

The woman Sami saw riding earlier is talking to a group of gardeners near a cluster of greenhouses. She raises a hand and shades her eyes from the winter sun and for a moment Sami thinks she might wave. Instead she turns away and continues her conversation.

'My wife,' explains Garza. 'She comes from a respectable family; old money. They were so fucking poor when I met her, I had to bail them out and buy this place to keep it from the taxman.

'My wife says I'm cold. She can talk. That's her over there – the ice queen. Five years ago she got busted by the police for giving her personal trainer a blowjob in a car park. The newspapers got hold of the story.

'I squared the indecency charges and I got the newspaper to drop the story. I didn't divorce her. She thought I was going to forgive her. She thought I needed her name to be respectable. That shows how little she knows me. When she came home from her next exercise class, she discovered two twenty-year-old hookers in the hot tub. I told her to get us all a drink.'

Garza gazes at the trees proudly as though he planted them himself.

'I told her if she wanted to stay, she could stay, but if she ever screwed around again, I'd make sure she got nothing, not a pot to piss in. I had all the evidence I needed – substance abuse, alcoholism, psychiatric reports. She'd be lucky to see our son once a fortnight with supervision. People don't screw me twice, Mr Macbeth, do you understand?'

'Yes, sir.'

'I want you to phone Tony Murphy. Organise a meeting. Give him the shooter. Get your sister.'

'Then what?'

'Duck.'

Sami takes a moment to digest the implications.

313

Garza's lips curl upwards into a smile. 'I'm joking, Mr Macbeth. Get your sister. Make sure she's safe.'

Sami tries to enjoy the joke but can't tell if a smile ever reaches his face.

53

Murphy picks up on the second ring.

'It's me,' says Sami, clearing his throat. 'We meet tonight at midnight. Putney Bridge.'

'Where on Putney Bridge?'

'In the middle.'

'You're going to hand me a shooter in the middle of Putney Bridge? Why not take an ad in *The Times*?'

'This way I'll know you're alone. Bring Nadia. Nobody else.'

'And the rozzers will be waiting either end?'

'Only if they follow you.'

'You're a cocky little shite.'

'And you're a fat windbag, Mr Murphy. Now we've cleared that much up, we can both get down to business. Tonight. Midnight. Don't be late.'

The call ends and Murphy drums his fingers on the desk. It could be a trap. Macbeth might already be in police custody. No, Bones would have called him if that had happened. The situation can still be retrieved.

Murphy lights a cigar and tilts his face to blow smoke towards the ceiling. His fingers touch the sides of a whisky glass. The exit strategy is almost in place. It just needs one final piece for the whole jigsaw to land on Ray Garza's head. The trick is not to panic. It's all comedy. He could be dead right or dead depending on the outcome.

Murphy picks up his phone and calls Ray Jnr.

'My boy, my boy,' he says, sounding like a Jewish grandfather. 'It's been too long . . . no hard feelings . . . I got a new batch of girls in. There's one in particular I want you to try. She's sweet as a peach. Come on over.'

54

The front door opens before Ruiz can raise a knuckle. Frank Dibbs must have been watching him open the gate and walk up the path.

'It's about time,' he says, looking irritated.

'Time for what?'

'I've left dozens of phone messages . . . and I've written letters.'

Mr Dibbs is shaped like a sea elephant and is wearing a tartan sweater knitted with love but very little skill.

'Have you brought your noise thingumajig?'

'You seem to have me confused with someone else.'

'You're from the council aren't you? I said to Margaret, "This will be the noise officer from the council." Didn't I, Margaret?'

Margaret must be the woman standing behind him in the hallway wearing a dressing gown and protective glasses. Maybe it's a form of foreplay.

A burst of laughter emanates from the Anglesea Arms

across the road. Three young guys stumble out, shouting to the mates they've left behind.

Mr Dibbs can't hide his disgust. 'You hear that? Every night we have to put up with fights, vomit, drunkenness, broken bottles. Last week we had a shooting.'

'That's what I'm here to talk about,' says Ruiz, pleased to change the subject.

Mr Dibbs doesn't seem disappointed. The shooting is his next favourite subject. He describes it in graphic detail, rising to great levels of personal umbrage, pointing out where the participants were standing.

Mr Dibbs was upstairs when the fight broke out. He looked out of his bedroom window and saw two policemen arguing with a driver of a Porsche parked on the footpath outside the Anglesea Arms.

'The police had opened the boot and one of them lifted out the spare tyre. That's when this young bloke went mad, screaming at them and claiming he was being set up. One of the officers began using his radio and the next thing I saw was the gun.'

'Who had the gun?'

'The young bloke. He was waving it about, yelling at them. I had to duck.'

'Why?'

'Why what?'

'Why did you have to duck?'

'Because of the bullet.'

Mr Dibbs has managed to omit this detail from his account. Ruiz takes him back over it again.

'You saw the flash.'

He nods. 'The bullet hit the house. That's why I ducked.'

'The second sound must have been close.'

'Right below me.'

Ruiz retraces his steps and stands in front of the Dibbs' house. He studies the lilac painted brick façade, scanning the unbroken horizontal lines of mortar beneath the paint.

'Are you sure he was standing over there?'

'Absolutely.'

Ruiz moves back and forth across Wingate Road, searching the asphalt and gutters. Ray Jnr had a Beretta 93R machine pistol set on single shot rather than rapid fire. The shell casing would have been ejected from the breech – but where did it go?

Lying flat on his stomach, Ruiz looks under the parked cars. The nearest drain is eight yards away, covered by a square metal grate. He crawls beneath the chassis of a car and peers between the bars.

'Have you got a torch inside, Mr Dibbs?'

'Of course, we're always prepared.' He doesn't move.

'Perhaps I could borrow it.'

'Oh, right, yes.'

Still lying on his stomach, Ruiz watches tartan trousers with matching slippers disappear into the house and re-emerge a few minutes later. Mr Dibbs hands him a torch. Ruiz nudges it between the bars and tries to peer into the blackness of the drain, which smells of sump oil and dog turds.

Four feet below him, wedged between a flattened hubcap and a broken umbrella, he spies the brass 9mm shell casing.

Ruiz slithers out and fetches a tyre lever from the boot of his Merc. He jams the tapered end beneath the edge of the grate and prises it upwards, far enough to hook his fingers underneath and prop it open.

Leaning head first into the drain, he slips the end of a ballpoint pen into the hollow case and drops it into a Ziploc bag. He's been carrying that bag around for three years, ever since he retired and even before then. Old habits die hardest.

55

Ray Jnr looks at himself in the mirror and sneers, doing his best De Niro impersonation.

'You talking to me?'

'You *talking* to me?'

'You talking to *me*?'

He looks over his shoulder. 'Then who the hell else are you talking to? I'm the only one here.'

He spins and draws his hand from his pocket, finger pointing and thumb cocked, like he's holding a gun.

'Don't mess with me, fucker.'

His eyes are twinkling. He adjusts his hair, teasing it into spikes.

For the past five days Ray Jnr has been dining out on the story of doing time in the 'Big House'. It's like he's been 'made' now. He's a proper wise guy.

There's still the issue of the attempted murder and drugs charges, but his old man will sort that out. He'll huff and puff and call Ray a fuck-up and say, 'not this time, junior', but he'll come through. He always does. Blood is thicker than mud.

Ray Jnr is at Tony Murphy's club in Bayswater, where the girls all look like wannabe models or page-three girls with big hair and bigger racks. It's one of those discreet establishments where a limo picks you up and drops you home and they provide a receipt at the end of the night, which any self-respecting accountant would put straight into a pile labelled 'business expenses'.

Not one of those clubs full of rich old codgers fixated on shagging nanny or being spanked by matron. The place is full of talent – real talent – a classy international smörgåsbord of pussy, fresh off the plane from Prague or the boat from Beijing.

Ray Jnr wouldn't mind a stake in a place like this – he should suggest it to Murphy. Free food, complimentary drinks, discretion guaranteed. So what if some of the girls are coked up, there's never a shortage. They all want to come to London and they don't mind paying the fare.

Tonight is one of Murphy's special parties. Select guests only. A new batch of girls has arrived at the club and Ray Jnr gets to sample the merchandise before it gets bruised. He might even break a girl in; some of them are so naive they're as good as virgins.

Ray Jnr peels back his lips, rubs the charlie off his teeth and takes one final look in the mirror. It's party time.

Murphy watches him leave the bathroom. The CCTV camera covers the hallway and beams images directly to

Murphy's office on the topmost floor of the large Georgian terrace, overlooking a community garden.

Secret cameras are also hidden in each of the eight bedrooms and above the spa. The footage isn't high definition or porn industry quality, but it doesn't have to be. Insurance, you see. Everyone should have insurance. Not your poxy, thirty-quid-a-month life-cover in case you drop off your perch, or income protection in case you damage your wanking hand. Real insurance. Murphy's homemade DVDs are protection against accidents and mistakes and criminal investigations. Hopefully, he'll never need to show them to a wider audience, which is probably a good thing when you see the wobble on that judge's arse as he bangs a girl dressed up like Dorothy in *The Wizard of Oz*. She'd click her heels together and think of home if she could get her legs around his arse.

Murphy puts a phone call in to Bones.

'How's it hanging, partner?'

'I told you not to call me.'

'And I told you that your sorry arse belongs to me, Bones, and you'll do as I say,' Murphy chuckles. 'Are you grinding your teeth, Bones? It's a terrible habit. My wife does it.'

'I can't think why,' says Bones.

'That's more like it. You're getting your sense of humour back.'

Murphy hears static on the line. 'Are you recording this conversation, Bones?'

'No, are you?'

'Maybe we should talk about something else,' suggests Murphy, slipping into football speak. 'Did you see the game at the weekend? That player who should have been axed is still running around. He called me today.'

'What did he want?'

'He's setting up a meeting. Wants to trade.'

'Are you going to say yes?'

'I want to know if he's talking to any other parties, know what I'm saying? Is he playing for the Blues?'

'I've heard nothing, Tony.'

'Maybe you should make a few inquiries. The lad might even have an agent. He's one of yours. A guy called Ruiz.'

'Vincent Ruiz?'

'You know him?'

'Yeah, he's retired.'

'Well, he's not playing golf. He came to see me yesterday.'

'Why?'

'Good question, Bones, find me a good answer. Your manager fucked it up last night. He took off the wrong player. Should have benched the kid permanently. There's another game tonight – a testimonial. The kid is playing his last game.'

'You need any help?'

'I've got it covered this time.'

*

Murphy leans back in his chair and peruses the CCTV monitors. Ray Jnr is stripped to the waist, propped up in bed, watching Nadia Macbeth dance. Dressed in a short black negligee and high heel shoes, her breasts stand out stiffly against the opaque fabric.

Ray Jnr looks a lot like his old man did at the same age, but their taste in women is different. Ray Snr liked them young and demure, the girl-next-door types who looked too old for Sunday school and too young to fuck. Ray Jnr prefers them horny and coked up, wearing lingerie or leather.

Back in the old days, Ray's father used to rely on Murphy to find him girls. 'Just something for the weekend,' he'd say when he organised his diary. Murphy would have the girls delivered in a limo to the hotel, telling them that Garza was a big-shot modelling agent.

Ray Snr was a real coke-hound back then. Like father like son.

Then one night some girl laughed at Ray when he was trying to seduce her and he lost it completely. Raped her. Chewed open her cheek. She topped herself before the trial. Ray dodged a bullet and he swore off drugs completely. He married, concentrated on business, made a fortune.

On screen Ray Jnr has just looped his belt around Nadia's forearm, pulling it tight. A lighted candle and spoon are on the nightstand beside them. The flame dances in Nadia's eyes.

Ray mounts the needle in her vein. Presses the plunger. Nadia sighs and tilts her head back, her mouth open and jaw slack. He pulls the syringe free and puts his hand behind her neck, pulling her towards his lap.

'Come on, baby, now look after me.'

Murphy opens the door and interrupts. Nadia raises her head. Wipes her mouth. The revulsion on her face might never leave her.

Ray Jnr is reclining on the bed, one arm casually behind his head, a joint hovering over the ashtray balanced on his stomach.

Murphy tells Nadia to go next door. Ray Jnr watches her leave.

'You were right about that one.'

'I told you not to inject her.'

'She wanted it.'

'And now she'll want it again in a few hours.'

Ray Jnr draws on the joint, taking a long deep hit. The edges of the paper glow bright red.

'We have business to discuss,' says Murphy. 'I want you *compos mentis.*'

'What's that mean?'

'Of sound mind.'

Ray tries to blow smoke rings. 'I thought it was the name of a band.'

Murphy goes to the bar in the corner and pours himself a Scotch adding a splash of soda from an old-fashioned soda stream. Then he eases back on a sofa that's so big it must have come through the windows.

'The semi-automatic you took from me – the Beretta – it was stolen from a police evidence room yesterday morning, along with the cocaine you were carrying.'

'Allegedly,' says Ray, who is suddenly paying attention. It takes him a few moments to digest the information. A smile creases his face. Goes away. Comes back again. It's like he's responding to some internal dialogue.

'Without the shooter or the drugs, I'm a free man. They'll have to drop the charges.'

'Not so fast, son,' says Murphy. 'Getting away isn't always that easy.'

'Why?'

'You see, the thief who stole this stuff is trying to blackmail your old man. He wants half a million quid or he's going to give the gun and the cocaine to Old Bill and say that *you* put him up to the robbery.'

'Did I fuck!'

'Exactly, but what are the police going to think?'

Ray Jnr stands, slips his belt through the loops, buckles it up.

'Who is this geezer, Tony, do I know him?'

'Sami Macbeth. He's an ex-con.'

Ray Jnr shakes his head. 'And he thinks he can turn me over? He's dreaming.'

'Yeah, but I'm worried,' says Murphy. 'The police already think your old man organised the robbery. They got a team of detectives working on the case. Unless we stop Macbeth, he could send us all to prison.'

'How so?'

Murphy leans forward. Elbows on knees. Scotch close to his lips.

'I should tell you something about that shooter you took from me. It has a history. Nine years ago it was used to kill a journalist in Belfast. The crime was never solved. Don't look at me like that, son, I didn't pull the trigger. Do you need a clue? Think three letters, Paddies in ski masks.'

Ray Jnr is pacing the floor, puffing air through his nostrils. 'The IRA.'

'Just so.'

'But I thought they were old news.'

'Act your fucking age, son. You think the Provos are going to take up knitting just because Gerry Adams and Martin McGuinness get plush offices at Stormont?'

Ray Jnr still can't grasp the issue. Murphy slows down and gives him a history lesson about the Northern Ireland Peace Accord and how Sinn Fein, the IRA's political wing, got a seat at the table because the Provos renounced violence and agreed to decommission weapons.

'You know what decommissioning means, son? It means out of commission. Off limits. Put beyond use. They chose a Canadian general to oversee the operation. A thousand rifles, three tonnes of Semtex, twenty-five surface-to-air missiles, flame throwers, rocket-propelled grenade launchers – you wouldn't believe the shit they decommissioned.'

'What's it got to do with me?' asks Ray.

'Now what do you think would happen if one of these weapons were to turn up somewhere?'

Ray Jnr has stopped pacing. The penny drops from the fortieth floor and lands on his head.

'The shooter you took from me was supposed to get a new barrel and a new firing pin before it was recycled, but that didn't happen. If the police discover where it came from, it's not just your sorry arse in the fire. The entire peace process goes up in flames. Are you getting this, Ray?'

'It's political.'

'Fucking right it's political. And it's going to get personal in a screaming hurry. Governments, political parties, Special Branch, MI6, Criminal Intelligence, SO11 – every one of them will do whatever it takes to save the peace process.'

Ray flinches. 'Why is it my fault? It's your gun.'

Murphy swings from the waist, holding the heavy Scotch glass wrapped in a hand towel. It strikes Ray Jnr flush on the jaw, sending him sprawling across the bed. The glass shatters and a piece is sticking out of Ray Jnr's cheek.

'What'd you do that for?' whines Ray, holding his cheek.

Murphy is standing over him. 'Listen, you muggy prick, you stole that gun from me. Now you're going to get it back. You're going to meet Macbeth tonight and you're going to get the shooter.'

Ray is holding his face. 'Why is he going to give it to me?'

'Because I have his sister.'

'What are you talking about?'

'Macbeth's sister – you were massaging her tonsils.'

'No shit!'

'I shit you not. I've arranged a meeting. You get the stuff. He gets the girl. Then you cut his kite string.'

'You mean I got to kill him?'

'I'm talking about saving your sorry arse and keeping Daddy out of jail.'

Murphy wets the towel and hands it to Ray, who pinches the shard of glass between his fingers and pulls it from his cheek. He holds the towel against his face. Murphy sits on the edge of the bed and turns on his avuncular charm, explaining how he's doing him a favour, contributing to his emotional development and familial ties.

'You're a fuck-up, Ray. Always have been. Well, now's your chance to make amends. You can do something for your old man. Earn his respect. Make him proud. And it's going to make you a name. You want to be a player, son. You want to be a wise guy. You have to be prepared to pull the trigger.'

Ray puffs out his chest. The idea is growing on him.

'I'll have you covered, son. I'm not going to leave you out there on your own. Your old man would never forgive me.'

'What about the girl?'

'What about her?'

'She'll be a witness.'

'You seem handy with the brown, Ray. Give her a little extra juice. Send her on a long trip. One way only. It's what every junkie wants.'

56

Ruiz is sitting on a park bench overlooking the river, watching the sun setting behind a bank of puce-coloured clouds that have brought storms all afternoon.

The air is criss-crossed with birds and, standing in the mud on the shoreline, a large white seabird seems more like a statue than it does a live creature.

Normally Ruiz has a beer at this time of day but he doesn't feel much like drinking or fishing or conversation. Today had not enriched or improved his views on human nature.

He hears his name being called. Darcy is standing at the door of the house, holding the phone.

'Take a message,' he shouts.

'She says it's important.'

Ruiz rubs the heels of his hand into his eyes until bright lights explode behind his eyelids. The colours float and fade as the world comes back into focus.

He limps across the road and takes the phone from Darcy. Fiona Taylor is calling from the Yard.

'How you doing, big man?'

'Been better.'

'The shell casing you sent over – the ballistics boys are looking at it now.'

'Good.'

She hesitates.

'You didn't call me just to tell me that,' says Ruiz.

'We have a problem.'

'What's that?'

'Your fingerprints were found in a flat at Abbey Road – Toby Streak's place. The neighbours say you kicked open the door, forced your way inside, made threats.'

'Has Streak lodged a complaint?'

'No.'

'Then what's the problem?'

'They found his body this morning. It was floating in a flooded grease pit at a garage in Finchley.'

Ruiz can feel a constriction in his throat, but strangely no other emotion. Normally he can find something to regret about any death, but Toby Streak was a skid-mark on the world and if someone laundered his sheets they were performing a public service.

Fiona is still talking. 'Someone beat him to death, Vincent. They broke every rib, both his hands and his kneecaps. Homicide and Serious Crime want to talk to you. They want to know what you were doing in Streak's flat. And they want to know why I looked up his address on the computer.'

Ruiz starts to apologise. Fiona cuts him short.

'Don't sweat it, big man – if arseholes could fly, this place would be an airport. Just don't ask me for any more favours for a while.'

Ruiz feels an odd sense of loss and disappointment. Not for himself. Fiona faces being hauled over the coals, disciplined and maybe even suspended. A letter would go on her file and stay there for ever. They could use it against her when she sought her next promotion.

'Who's the investigating officer?' asks Ruiz.

'DCI Baxter.'

'I didn't know Baxter had made Chief Inspector.'

'Some turds are floaters.'

Ruiz puts the phone back in the cradle and ponders the fate of Toby Streak. Unconsciously, he shivers as though he's left the front door open and the river chill has leaked inside. But this is a different sort of cold; an icy foreboding that penetrates his bones and wakes the little man sleeping at the bottom of his soul.

An hour later he signs his name in the visitor's book at Westminster Morgue and waits for a pathologist to collect him from the waiting room.

They've redecorated since he was here last but the interior design never changes. The aluminium and stainless steel has a minimalist feel and fluorescent lights reflect off every smooth surface. The troughs and drains are running with clear water and the only sound he can hear is the hum of the air conditioning.

The pathologist is wearing a white coat and has eczema on his hands. It's an allergic reaction to latex gloves, he explains, calling it an occupational hazard. Cutting open bodies is an occupational hazard, thinks Ruiz. A skin rash is a skin rash.

Phil Baxter pushes through the swing doors with an urgency that is designed to impress. He's a busy man. Don't stand in his way. Ruiz remembers Baxter as a young DC working the drug squad back in the days when good crack was conversation rather than a Class-A narcotic. Now he's a Detective Chief Inspector – a higher rank than Ruiz ever managed.

Baxter has put on weight, cut his hair shorter, but his wardrobe is the same – the black brogues, dark slacks and a sports jacket.

He offers his hand. Ruiz shakes it. The DCI grips it tightly and turns it over, examining Ruiz's knuckles. He lets him go.

'Sorry to drag you away from your hot cocoa.'

'Get to it, Phil, you're wasting my time.'

The pathologist examines the paperwork and pulls open a stainless steel drawer. The sound is like someone exhaling.

Toby Streak isn't pretty any more. Most of his teeth are broken and his right eye socket no longer has an eye.

Baxter studies Ruiz's face instead of the cadaver. Ruiz

tries not to react, but the sheer ferocity of the attack leaves a mark on his lips and in the corners of his eyes.

'Would you like to know how your friend here died?' asks Baxter.

'He wasn't my friend.'

'You were in his flat.'

'He had information I needed.'

'You beat it out of him.'

'He tripped as I came through the door.'

The pathologist is watching this exchange as though viewing a tennis match, turning back and forth as sentences are volleyed. Baxter interrupts the exchange.

'Tell us how Toby Streak met his maker.'

The pathologist picks up the autopsy report.

'Initially, it seemed as though he died when a rib punctured his heart but he was already on the way. A brain haemorrhage caused by multiple blows to the head.

'We believe they used a tyre iron or a metal bar of some sort. Both his hands and his kneecaps were broken early in the assault. They were held against a hard surface and smashed . . .'

Baxter interrupts to paraphrase. 'He went every round. They propped him up and kept hitting him. See the marks on his neck. Someone held him by the throat to stop him sliding down a wall. He had brick dust in his hair.'

Ruiz has heard enough. He pushes open the door and walks back down the long neon-lit corridor, past the autopsy suites and the dirty body room. Baxter has to jog to catch up and demands that he stop.

Ruiz spins to face him. 'You think I'm good for this? You think I broke that boy's bones in there; that I ripped out his eye, you really believe that?'

Baxter is stunned by the ferocity of Ruiz's anger.

'I think you spent too long in the job, Vincent, mixing with these people, believing they were just like us but without the same advantages or upbringing. Only you're wrong. People don't choose the world they're born into, but some escape it and some embrace it and some get buried by it. I think you know who killed Toby Streak. Maybe you even tried to warn him.'

'I was looking for a girl.'

'Oh, that's right, the sister of a terrorist.'

'Sami Macbeth is no more a terrorist than I am.'

'Is that an admission?'

'Fuck off!'

Ruiz walks down the concrete ramp and across the loading dock. It has started to rain. Exploding raindrops have misted around the security lights and turned the street outside into a neon-coloured pool.

Ruiz stands on the corner looking for a cab. Three of them pass, already occupied. Water leaks beneath the collar of his overcoat, but he's too angry to care. He's working through the details of Toby Streak's last hours like it's a Twelve-Step Programme inside his head.

A police car pulls up. Through the windshield and

beating wipers he sees Phil Baxter in the back seat. He leans over and opens the passenger door.

'I don't need a lift home,' says Ruiz.

'Oh, we're not going home,' replies Baxter.

57

Sami's suit has been dry-cleaned and his shirt pressed. He brushes his teeth, rinses his mouth and spits into the sink. His gums are bleeding. A prison diet. Stress.

Two large black Landcruisers with tinted windows are waiting downstairs. Engines idling. Occupants unknown. There is a knock on the door. It's time.

Ray Garza is standing in the foyer. Sami counts six men, dressed in black. One of them has a hand like a withered claw with the fingers compressed together and curled inward towards his wrist. He has to raise his fist above his eyes to take a cigarette from his mouth.

Car doors open. Close. Seat belts, please. The convoy moves off into a night made darker in the countryside, lit periodically by streaks of lightning that tremble in the clouds.

Sami is in the back seat of the first Landcruiser, sitting next to 'The Claw'. The driver is wearing leather gloves and dark glasses, but his most notable apparel is a shoulder holster with a machine pistol. They're going to start a war, thinks Sami.

The car doors aren't locked. Perhaps he could shove the door open and roll out. He'd bounce along the road. He might even survive. What then?

No, this has to end now. Garza had been right about that much. The rest of his spiel was a self-pitying whine about his unfaithful wife and ungrateful son, as he tried to unload his moral guilt on others, but it didn't take long for his ego to reassert itself and he became the same man. Not just the same man – worse because he was angry.

Sami had witnessed Garza's moment of weakness and become his confessor, which then made him an embarrassment. That's why Garza hadn't spoken another word to him since. Sami was persona non grata, surplus to requirements, a waste of space.

Fuck him. Murphy and Garza could kill each other a dozen times over for all Sami cared. He just wants to get Nadia and to get away; to clean her up and say he's sorry. After that he'll tell the police everything. He'll give himself up and throw himself on the mercy of the court. Unmerciful as it is.

Then his imagination really goes into overdrive. He starts fantasising about arresting Garza and Murphy and bringing down their operations. He can see the headlines spinning into focus: TERROR SUSPECT PARDONED and WANTED MAN TURNS HERO. Next he's meeting the Prime Minister at Downing Street and watching him weep with gratitude. He gets a book deal, Guy Ritchie directs the movie and Sami walks Kate Tierney up the red carpet while she's wearing one of those backless evening dresses that have the paparazzi shouldering each other out of the way and screaming her name. Charlie Cox plays Sami and Sienna Miller plays Kate. (As long as they don't get Jude Law – any guy who's engaged to Sienna Miller and gets caught shagging the nanny is a complete tosser.) All of this is flashing through Sami's head like a badly cut rap video.

Meanwhile, the Landcruisers have crossed the Thames and are heading along Cheyne Walk and the Embankment. Five minutes later they pull up outside the Savoy. The door opens. Sami steps out and the coolness of the air makes him realise he's been sweating.

The hotel doorman ushers Sami inside. He crosses the foyer. The Claw is smelling distance behind him. The knot in Sami's bowels won't go away.

They enter the lift. Sami presses 9. He glances at his minder and gets nothing back. The geezer has ice in his veins and a tumour the size of a football up his arse.

It's not until they reach the corridor that Sami considers how he's going to get in the suite. They're outside the door. He doesn't have an entry card.

'I gave the key back to reception,' explains Sami. 'Should I knock?'

The Claw stares at him blankly. Maybe Sami should ask him one on sport.

Sami knocks. Nobody answers. A black housekeeper is further down the corridor. Shaped like a duck in a blue uniform, she gives Sami a flat stare as he explains that he's locked himself out of his room. She takes a key card from her apron pocket. Slides it into the slot. The door clicks open.

'Thank you, very much,' says Sami. 'Have a nice day.'

She's already waddling away.

The Claw is already inside, searching the room. Making sure Sami hasn't planned an ambush. He's a professional, special forces most likely, who dares wins, trained by Her Majesty and let loose on society.

Sami takes a chair from the desk and sets it down near the wall. Steps up. Unclips the air-conditioning vent and reaches inside. The Beretta is wrapped tightly in a hand-towel. He leaves the bags of cocaine and banknotes.

Sami tucks the semi-automatic into his belt, nestling against the small of his back. He checks his reflection in the mirror to make sure the bulge doesn't show.

They take the lift back down to the foyer, not saying a word. Sami wants to ask The Claw about his hand. How did it happen? Was he wounded in Crap-istan? Did they torture him with a deep fat fryer?

The lift doors slide open. Kate is standing at the reception desk, talking on a phone. She's dressed in her usual work clothes, looking every inch the hostess and hotel manager. Sami knows that body. He knows the colour of her underwear, the hollow between elastic and thigh, the small butterfly tattoo on her left ankle. He can smell her Pantene-scented hair. He can hear the mewling sound she makes when she's nearing nirvana. Please don't look up, he prays.

Kate puts down the phone. Her eyes latch on to his. She's confused. Angry. She wants to walk towards him but Sami's stare makes her hesitate. She looks past him at the minder. Sami steps through the turning door, crosses the footpath, doesn't look back.

Kate's hands are shaking. She opens her handbag and rummages through it, looking for Ruiz's business card. She can't find it. Shit. Shit. Shit.

Upending the bag, she spills the contents onto the counter – lipstick, car keys, breath mints, tissues, a compact . . .

'Are you OK?' asks her colleague.

'Get the number of that car.'

'Which car?'

'The one that's leaving now.'

Kate finds the card and scoops her belongings into her handbag. 'I have to go.'

'Where?'

'Tell Magna I'm not feeling well.'

She runs for the door, stumbling as her left heel slips on the polished marble. The four-wheel drive carrying Sami has stopped at traffic lights in Savoy Lane, fifty yards away.

'Follow that car,' Kate tells a cab driver, as she opens the car door. The driver looks at her through the glass partition, thinking it's a wind-up.

'Are you going to take me or do I get another cab?'

'No problem, love.'

She punches Ruiz's number into her mobile. He's not answering. She sends a text, using both thumbs to punch the letters.

Sami at Savoy 2nite. Fubar. Following him now. Call ASAP.

58

It's almost stopped raining. The police car splashes through puddles and Ruiz watches headlights flaring on the wet windows. Even in darkness he can recognise the location. He's been here before.

Crime scene tape bulges in the breeze as it twirls from posts on either side of a lane. A group of black teenagers are watching from a pizza place across the road, acting like they own the neighbourhood and resent any trespassers.

Ruiz gets out of the car, ducks under the tape. He can smell curry cooking. A fat woman in a pink sari is watching from a balcony. She shields her face with a veil and turns away from his eyes.

They are a few blocks from the river. The last time Ruiz was here he entered on the other side of the building. The place used to be a furniture factory, according to Baxter, until it was turned into council flats and then sold off to a developer who had plans to bulldoze the place and erect luxury flats. He ran into liquidity problems –

namely, water in the lungs. They found him floating in the river near the Thames Barrier.

Thirty yards ahead a bright pool of light has bleached the cobblestones and thrown warped shadows against the brick walls. A car is parked at the centre of the light – a Fiat Panda. As they get closer, Ruiz notices the car has no roof. Closer still he realises that the roof has been pressed in by the weight of an object falling from above.

Beside it now, the object has become a body – a Rastafarian with beaded hair, who has hit the car with such force it has turned it into a bathtub full of blood. Most people travel a good distance and take a lifetime to reach hell. Puffa managed it in seventy feet and less than five seconds.

Baxter's second in command is a Detective Sergeant Frome. Pale, tall, blade-faced, he looks like an undertaker touting for business. Tonight he's been lucky.

'Victim's name is Dwight Powell. Called himself Puffa. Two witnesses say he took a hit of Ice, climbed onto the roof and did a swan dive from the fifth floor,' he tells Baxter.

'Anyone else on the roof with him?'

'That's the only thing they agree upon – perhaps a little too strenuously.'

Ruiz glances up to the roof and back to the car. Twenty feet separate the nearside tyres from the edge of the building.

'Either Puffa was the lovechild of Bob Beaman or someone threw him,' he says.

'Bob who?' asks Frome.

'Mexico. 1968. The Olympics. Beaman set a world record for the long jump and it was twenty-three years before anybody broke it. They called it the greatest leap in history.'

'Before my time,' says Frome dismissively.

'So were the dinosaurs but it doesn't stop people digging them up. Can I talk to the witnesses?'

'You're here to answer questions, not ask them,' replies Baxter.

'You want to blame me for this as well?'

'Two men are dead. You visited both of them on Saturday. Witnesses claim you assaulted and threatened them. I'd say that makes you a suspect. And you might want to tell me why Crim Intel put your car at Tony Murphy's house yesterday; a known villain.'

Ruiz can feel his mobile vibrating and tries to ignore it.

'The problem with you, Baxter, is that you're like the blind man who touches the elephant's trunk and thinks he's holding a snake.'

'And you're the elephant.'

'I'm the big swinging dick.'

Ruiz's mobile has stopped shaking. It beeps instead. Kate Tierney has sent him a text message.

'What does "fubar" mean?' he asks Baxter.

'Fucked up beyond all recognition.'

59

Tony Murphy lifts his face to the sky, feeling the light drizzle cling to his eyelashes. Lately his life seems to be unravelling but tonight he gets it back on track. They say boredom is the brother of misery but after the past few weeks he'd settle for a boring life rather than a dangerous one.

He checks his watch – it's half eleven – and presses speed dial on his mobile.

'You heard anything, Bones?'

'Nothing.'

'No radio chatter?'

'None.'

'Any mention of Putney Bridge?'

'Is that where it's going down?'

'At midnight,' says Murphy.

'What about the kid?'

'He'll be joining his ancestors.'

Murphy ends the call and tucks the phone into his pocket.

Ray Jnr is sitting in a car with Nadia. Shadows like rivulets are running down his face. His hands are shaking. He needs another line to settle his nerves.

'You ought to stop snorting that stuff,' say Murphy.

'And you ought to go jogging.'

The windows are fogged with humidity. One of them is cracked a little to let out Sinbad's cigarette smoke.

'Let's do it,' says Murphy.

'Give it a minute,' replies Ray Jnr, 'it hasn't stopped raining.'

He looks nervous, skittish, like a child waiting for a party to begin. Nadia is beside him, sitting on her hands. Her heart-shaped face is pale, devoid of make-up. Her light cotton dress and sweater cling to her like a second skin. The past week has been a nightmarish blur of drugs, paranoia and revulsion. Now she's going home, according to Murphy. Sami is coming to get her.

She takes a cigarette from a packet on her lap; needs both hands to light it. Blinks smoke from her elongated eyes. Oily coils of her hair hang down across her cheeks as inner demons work their magic on her. Desire. Obsession. Addiction.

A bolt of lightning leaps across the western sky. The rain has eased.

'It's time,' says Murphy.

60

Sami has been waiting on the bridge for fifteen minutes, smelling the brine and feeling the cold dampness blowing off the water. A solitary boat is visible, tethered to a pylon near the boat ramp.

The traffic has thinned out. It's mainly cabs and minicabs and people coming home late. Light seems to evaporate from the surface of the asphalt as each vehicle passes.

Ray Garza and his men must be somewhere nearby, although he can't see any of them.

The number 22 bus from Piccadilly Circus to Putney Common pulls onto the north side of the bridge and pauses at a bus shelter. A passenger gets off. The double-decker pulls away. The figure disappears down stone steps on the east side of the bridge.

The bus has almost rumbled past Sami before he notices two people alone on the brightly lit upper deck. One of them is Nadia. She's sitting near the front, staring straight ahead. A man is directly behind her, head down, face hidden.

A massive flood of relief washes through Sami. Nadia's alive. She's only yards away. He yells and starts running, trying to get her attention but the bus is pulling further away, turning right into Lower Richmond Road.

There's a bus stop around the corner. There's nobody waiting. The driver carries on.

Sami cuts across the road, dodges a car and tears along the footpath past mansion blocks, a row of shops, terraces, a petrol station . . . It must be a trick; a trap. Murphy's doing. Sami's mind is telling him this but his legs are still moving; sprinting after the bus as it veers away from the river.

He's a hundred yards behind and can't see if Nadia is still on board. The Beretta is coming loose from his belt. He reaches back to stop it falling.

Brake lights flare. The bus is stopping. Somebody steps off. It's not Nadia. Still sixty yards away Sami screams at the bus to stop but the driver can't hear him. The doors are closing. Gears engage.

The disembarked passenger throws himself against a wall, holding his briefcase like a shield.

'Where does that bus go?' yells Sami, spinning to confront him.

'Putney Common.'

'How far is that?'

'About two stops.'

The double-decker is disappearing again. Sami

sprints after it, trying to keep the bus in sight. The shops and restaurants are closed and shuttered but he can still smell the hot oil and the rubbish bins out back. Bill posters have plastered the lamp posts and the windows of empty shops.

The bus is three hundred yards ahead, indicating left. It's turning. Sami is growing tired. His shoes weren't meant for running. The row of terraces ends suddenly but the road continues across the common, swallowed by darkness. It's as though a section of the city has collapsed into a black hole leaving only the streetlights behind.

Sami turns the corner. The double-decker has stopped. He can see the driver climbing out from behind the wheel. The bus doors are open. Sami swings inside, ignoring his protests. He runs through the lower deck; climbs the stairs; searches in vain. Nadia's not there.

'Did you see a girl? Where did she get off?'

The driver is a big guy, gut over his belt.

'She's gone.'

'Where did she go?'

He points across the road towards the common. 'They headed that way.'

Sami scans the darkness, the street, the muddy paths, the deeper shadows. Then he spies something moving a hundred yards away, barely visible against the dark walls of a building rising high above the treetops silhouetted against the faint glow of the sky.

'What's that place?' he asks.

'The old Putney Hospital.'

'Why is it dark?'

'They closed it down years ago,' says the driver. 'They can't decide what to do with it.'

He mentions something about making movies there, but Sami is already crossing the road. Slipping the Beretta from his belt, he unclips the safety. Holds it in both hands. He's not thinking any more. Logic, reason, common sense were abandoned back on the bridge when he chose to ignore his own instructions and let Tony Murphy dictate events.

A metal boom gate is padlocked in place across the entrance to the car park and weeds sprout from broken asphalt in the ambulance bays. Odd things are scattered through the weeds. Junk mostly, broken furniture, old appliances, a plastic jerry can collecting rainwater.

The red brick hospital is four storeys high and could fill a city block, but appears out of place on the edge of the common, surrounded by heath and parkland. The doors are sealed with sheets of metal and wood, bolted in place, and guarded by steel mesh fences. The lower windows are also covered, but the upper windows have been left unprotected and many have been punctured with rocks. Knotted and filthy curtains billow from inside.

Security lights are attached to the outer walls, illuminating yellow warning signs:

DANGER
Private Property
KEEP OUT
This site contains serious hazards.
All valuables have been removed.

Sami pauses and for a moment catches a glint of something revealed, a shadow in front of him, which disappears in a patter of raindrops. He listens. Nothing. Glancing up at a window on the first floor, he notices a torch beam flash across the broken glass and disappear.

A metal gate lies open ten yards to his right. A sign on the wall says *Accident & Emergency: All Enquiries to Reception*.

Sami forces open an iron sheet, which is curling at one corner. Nails rip from the rotting frame. He pulls a trailing vine from his ankles and steps inside, smelling the mould and faeces.

His eyes adjust to the dark. He wants to stand still. He wants to move.

Pushing open a second door he emerges into a wide corridor. Low wattage security lights are evenly spaced along the walls, providing just enough light to see as far as a central staircase. Ceiling panels lie broken or missing with wires hanging through them and pools of water have dried and left stains on the grey linoleum floor.

There are doors along either side of the corridor and lighter squares of paintwork where paintings once hung on the walls. Discarded metal trolleys lie abandoned and covered in dust.

Sami scans the scene; listens to the drip of brown water into a sink.

A sign opposite the nursing station gives directions to the various wards. Occupational Therapy and the Rehabilitation Units are on the second floor.

Sami reaches the stairs, which are in darkness. He has to feel his way upwards, one step at a time. On the first floor is another corridor with doors down either side. The X-ray department is ahead; a strip of light leaks from beneath the door. A sign says, *Danger: Radiation*.

He pushes it open, every muscle tense. Nadia is sitting on a metal chair with her hands beneath her thighs, her red eyes like wounds. The robot-like arms of the X-ray equipment seem to be imprisoning her as part of some fearful experiment.

Her eyes meet his; pleading, fearful.

Sami does everything wrong. He steps towards her. Something moves to his left. He gets the Beretta halfway to horizontal before an object smashes hard against his arm sending the gun skittering across the floor.

In his mind's eye, he twists and swings his left fist, fighting for his life, but he doesn't have the opportunity. A second blow strikes him high across the chest and ribs break with a crack. His knees collapse. Nadia sobs.

Lying face down, Sami turns his cheek and sees someone standing next to Nadia. Wrapping her hair in his fist.

Jerking her head. Telling her to be quiet. It's a face he recognises, but not the person he expects.

It's the kid from the cell next door on Sami's last night in prison. The one who couldn't stop talking; the one who blathered and big-noted himself saying his old man was going to post bail for him and how he'd be eating dinner at the Ivy by the next night.

He's looping a belt around Nadia's forearm. Pulling it tight. He taps the end of the needle and pinches skin on her forearm, looking for a vein.

'Don't do it,' groans Sami, through clenched teeth. 'You remember me.'

Ray Jnr pauses. Recognition comes with a twisted smile as though they're sharing a joke.

'Well, fuck me!' He raises a revolver and scratches an itch on his cheek. 'What are you doing here?'

Sami glances at Nadia whose face tells a story of confusion.

'I'm here to get my sister.'

Ray Jnr jerks Nadia's head back; looks at her face and then back at Sami. He can't see the family resemblance.

'Are you sure you got the right girl?'

Sami nods, sucking in a breath.

Nadia looks at the needle almost lovingly. Her cheeks are hollow and her eyes look huge. Sweating and trembling through withdrawal, she wants another hit.

'Well, this is a turn up for the books,' says Ray Jnr,

pulling up a chair and straddling it backwards. 'Why are you trying to blackmail my father?'

'I'm not. He sent me here.'

Ray gives one of those prissy little laughs like there's nobody in the world who's going to believe a story like that.

'It's true. He's outside somewhere.'

'You're trying to get money out of him.'

Sami shakes his head and drags his body up. Every breath lights a fire in his chest. He closes his eyes and tries to do a re-cut on what's happened. Imagines a different outcome where he's not in pain, not in trouble, not going to die. Opening them again, he seeks out Nadia.

'How are you, Princess? I've been looking for you everywhere.'

Her mouth opens. She can't find any words. Instead she falls to her knees and wraps her arms around him. Sami can feel the furnace heat of her cheeks, the dampness of her hands. Her pupils are like pinpricks.

'I missed you,' she whispers.

'I'm here now.'

Ray Jnr is spinning the pistol around his finger. 'Why did you steal the shooter?'

'Murphy told me to do it. He had Nadia.'

'Why would he do that?'

'He needed the gun back.'

Ray Jnr blinks slowly. His thin lips seem rouged against the paleness of his face. He begins to speak in soft insinuating tones.

'You remember that night in prison? You let me talk. I didn't want to close my eyes. I wasn't scared.'

'I know.'

'You think I was scared?'

'No.'

'I've never done this before, but I'm ready, you know.'

'Ready for what?'

'I've made some mistakes but this is going to fix them. I'm going to clean up my act. I'm not going to prison. Not without the gun or the drugs.'

'We won't say anything,' says Sami.

Ray straightens his arm, aiming the pistol at Sami's head. 'Don't fucking interrupt me. Let me give you a news flash, mate, your sister is a junkie, you're a loser and I'm the shit who has to kill you both.'

'You don't have to kill us.'

'What else do you expect me to do?'

'Let us go. I had a deal with Murphy – the gun for my sister.'

Ray Jnr laughs. Still aiming the pistol at Sami, he collects the Beretta from the floor and tucks it into his belt. Then he folds an old blanket around his own pistol, holding both ends together with his left hand to muffle the sound. Ray Jnr places the pistol to Sami's head. Nadia's mouth opens to scream. Ray Jnr hesitates, lowers the pistol. Raises it again. Walks to the window. Turns.

Sami doesn't hear what he's saying. He's too busy looking down the barrel of the gun. It's huge. Gaping.

Sami closes his eyes. The hammer falls. An explosion detonates within his head.

'Don't do it. Please,' he hears himself say, but maybe the words don't come out.

61

Bones McGee has been lying prone in bushes on the eastern side of the hospital for twenty minutes, not far from where Sami Macbeth disappeared inside.

He couldn't get a clean shot on the bridge and followed Macbeth for more than a mile after the kid took off. Now he's cornered in the hospital and has to come out sooner or later.

The breeze dislodges droplets from the branches, pattering on Bones' oilskin jacket. The ground is wet, but the trees and undergrowth offer him plenty of cover. He has a different rifle tonight, his favourite – the L96 – the British Army's sniper rifle of choice.

This time Macbeth isn't getting away. And Tony Murphy's name is also pencilled on the dance card. Murphy has blackmailed Bones for the last time. No more jumping through hoops. No more belittling calls. Two clean shots and the fat lady can sing a requiem.

Murphy said he was meeting Macbeth to do the exchange. They're probably inside now. Murphy will have brought some muscle – dumb-as-dogshit ex-cons bulked up in prison weight rooms – but they won't see Bones until it's too late.

Right now he's feeling pretty relaxed, but the old excitement is growing. It's almost no challenge to take someone down from this range, but this isn't a contest, he tells himself, still smarting over yesterday when he took out the wrong target. The image of the dead van driver has been playing on his mind. He has to squeeze his eyes shut, willing the picture to change.

Opening them again, he sees a flash of torchlight cross a window and a silhouette against a broken pane. Someone is waving a gun around, either Murphy or Macbeth. One shot to the neck and they feel nothing again.

Bones tugs the hood of his rain jacket further over his head to block out any distractions. He gathers up the rifle, lowers the bipod, and tucks the high impact plastic stock against his shoulder. His bottom lip brushes the smoothness of the stock as though lingering over a kiss.

He exhales slowly, holds his breath. Smoothly tightens his finger in the trigger guard.

62

A cab drops Ruiz on the northern approach to Putney Bridge. He hangs back for a few minutes, surveying the scene, looking for anything untoward or out of place. Then he sets off along the footpath looking for Kate Tierney.

He calls her mobile.

'I've lost Sami,' she says, urgently. 'He was on the bridge and then he started running. It was like he was chasing someone.'

'Where are you now?'

'I don't know the name of the road. You have to cross the bridge and turn right.'

'Lower Richmond Road.'

'Maybe.'

Ruiz follows her directions and finds her waiting outside a service station, her hands deep in her coat pockets and wet hair plastered to her forehead.

'Are you OK?'

She nods, bracing her shoulders against the cold. Her

high heels make clicking sounds on the concrete. She describes Sami's sudden appearance at the Savoy. He was with someone; a man in black, who kept his left hand in his pocket.

'How did Sami look?'

'Scared. Trapped.'

'He didn't say anything?'

Kate shakes her head.

'Why would Sami come back to the hotel?'

'I don't know.' She glances along the road in the direction that he disappeared. 'What was he running from?'

Ruiz wants to answer her, but his mind is churning in a kind of underwater panic like a fish caught in a net. Puffa and Toby Streak are dead. Somebody is cleaning up, removing witnesses, tying up loose ends. Sami and his sister could well be next.

Murphy or Garza – it doesn't matter any more. When Ruiz was married to Miranda, she used to argue that the workings of the world were all connected and everything happened for a reason.

Ruiz would try to reason with her, talking himself into a spluttering, head-shaking tirade of frustration, but Miranda wouldn't concede an inch or lose her temper or change her mood. She lived in Laura Ashley-land, he told her, while never admitting that he wanted to live there too. Her world was nicer; gentler. And the sex could still be dirty.

His phone vibrates in a pocket full of coins.

DI Fiona Taylor has her hand cupped over the mouthpiece, trying not to be overheard. Ruiz is listening to her distractedly. Ballistics has tested the shell casing and the computer threw up a match.

'It set off some sort of internal alarm at Vauxhall Cross.' She's talking about MI6. 'Two carloads of spooks arrived at the lab and seized the shell casing. Now they're here. They want to talk to you.'

'Why is MI6 interested?'

'The shell matches one used to murder a journalist in Belfast nine years ago.'

'The same gun?'

'The weapon was supposed to be decommissioned eighteen months ago by the IRA. The destruction was independently verified. The witnesses are beyond reproach.'

'How then . . . ?'

'Exactly.'

'Are they listening to this call?'

'They are.'

'Tell them they can wipe their feet on me tomorrow.'

Ruiz is about to hang up when in the distance beyond the houses there is a bright flash in the darkness of Putney Common, too low for lightning. The sound of a shot reaches him a fraction of a second later. He's already moving.

'What was that?' asks Fiona Taylor, still on the phone.

A second flash lights up the darkness.

'Shots fired,' says Ruiz. 'Lower Richmond Road – near the Common, I need back-up.'

In the same breath he turns and yells to Kate. 'You stay here. Don't move. The police are coming.'

63

The hole in Ray Jnr's throat is no bigger than a cigarette burn, but the matching one at the back of his skull is the size of a fist. His shirt is soaked with blood, which leaks across the linoleum in a black pool that has reached the toe of Sami's left shoe.

Ray had hesitated, trying to decide if he was going to shoot Sami. Then he lowered the gun and started talking again, saying that Sami should get Nadia out and he'd try to square it with Murphy. Arrange a deal. Do his best. He was in mid-sentence, looking out the window when the high velocity bullet took out his throat.

Sami crouches next to the body, feeling for a pulse. Ray's mouth relaxes and his tongue peeks out as though he wants to say something.

Nadia is still sitting on the chair. One hand is clamped across her mouth as though trying to muffle a scream. The other kneads the front of her dress into a ball in her fist. Her body seems to spasm.

Sami scampers to the window, peers out a corner of

the watery glass. A bullet punches into the frame beside his head. He pulls away. Stays low. Crawls to the body and pulls the semi-automatic from Ray's belt. He and Nadia crouch together, breathing the same air.

'Are you hurt?' he asks.

She shakes her head.

'Can you walk?'

She nods.

'We have to get out of here.'

'I'm sorry.'

'You got nothing to be sorry about.'

She pulls at his arm, wanting him to listen. 'They did things to me.'

'I know. It's not important any more.'

Sami doesn't want to listen. He wants to pretend it never happened.

Nadia pulls away from him and crawls across the linoleum towards Ray Jnr. Kneeling beside his body, she needs both hands to lift his head and smash it on the floor. Over and over.

Sami has to unhook her fingers and hold her arms down. He can smell her snot and tears. Feel her heart beating.

'He raped me,' Nadia sobs.

Her eyes shine with tears. Sami can feel his own tears coming – the ones he didn't shed for his mother or father. In his mind he can see Ray Jnr with his pants down, between Nadia's thighs, pounding her flesh, ignoring her pain.

'It's over now,' he says. 'We have to get out of here.'

'Can you make it go away?' she asks, trembling. Flecks of charcoal seem to float in the brown of her eyes.

'No,' says Sami, his heart breaking.

Ignoring his broken ribs, Sami crushes himself against her, feeling her heart beating. It is like a clock counting the seconds for both of them.

Someone is coming along the corridor. Sami holds his finger to his lips. He motions Nadia to hide. Crouching in the shadows behind the door, he waits for it to swing open. He sees forearms and a rifle before launching his shoulder against the wood, smashing it closed. Grabbing a plank of wood, he swings it hard across the fallen figure. Sends him down, legs quivering, a strip of wood embedded in his spine with rusty nails.

Sami takes Nadia's hand and they zigzag along the main corridor to the central staircase. Descend. As he reaches the ground floor, something makes him stop.

The main entrance is to the right. Two, three, four men are moving along the passage, spreading out, sheltering in doorways. Keeping each other covered.

Shotgun pellets spray the brickwork near Sami's right arm. He hears another shell ratchet into the chamber.

A second bullet from a different angle slams into the hospital sign above Nadia's head, punctuating the name of the specialist oncologist. Suddenly gunfire is coming in bursts and rounds, dancing off the walls and floor. Murphy's men and Garza's men are shooting at each other from opposite ends of the corridor.

Sami climbs the stairs, retracing his steps, urging Nadia on. He has to wrap his arm around her waist to stop her falling. Sulphur and cordite float upwards through the stairwell. She stops. Vomits.

Maybe Sami could outrun them without Nadia, but he's not losing her again. One way or another, they're getting out of here. Heading along a different corridor, he passes the occupational therapy rooms. Opening doors, he goes to the windows, looking for a way out. Smashing glass and running the Beretta around the jagged edges, he leans out looking for a fire escape or some other way down.

Sami stops. Listens.

'What is it?' she asks.

'Nothing.'

'Tell me.'

'There's someone coming.'

'That's what I thought.'

'We can't outrun them.'

'We have to go.'

'Can't we hide here?'

'They'll find us.'

'You go,' says Nadia, leaning against a wall. Her legs are giving way.

'Not without you.'

Back in the corridor, they pass through swinging doors and Sami shoves a plank of wood between the handles to buy them more time.

There is some sort of gas or fuel tank lying on the floor. He pushes it against the door and they keep running.

A bullet gouges a white streak across the top of the wall above his head. Someone is firing through the barricaded door and trying to shoulder it open. The hinges give way. Sami pushes Nadia ahead of him. He turns, pivoting onto one knee, resting one buttock on his heel and holding the Beretta with both hands. He aims at the tank and squeezes the trigger. In a matter of seconds he empties the clip in a deafening roar. His hands are numb from the recoil.

The explosion is a burst of white blue flames that billows outwards as if the air itself were on fire. Men are screaming. One of them staggers through the flames, silhouetted against the fireball. His clothes are smoking. He sways from side to side, drops to one knee, falls.

Sami keeps trying doors, looking for an exit. They're locked in. Trapped. Turning left, he runs the length of another corridor, pulling Nadia with him. They reach a new flight of stairs. The gunfire is becoming more sporadic downstairs.

Sami has no plan. He isn't headed for a particular exit or gate. He's only running.

A large window fills with a flash of lightning and goes dark again. Sami looks down. The ground is clear. Beyond he can see open ground and trees with headlights winking between them. If he could get there, he could flag down a car. Get Nadia to hospital.

She has slumped on the stairs, resting her head against the handrail.

Sami gathers a mattress in both his arms.

'Come on, we're going to jump.'

'I can't, Sami, I'm sorry.'

'Yes, you can.'

'No.'

Sami screams at her, 'Listen, Princess, suck it in. I know they did terrible things. I know you're hurting. But we're not giving up.' He does a fireman's lift, hoisting her over his shoulder, ignoring the pain in his chest.

Holding the mattress in both arms he runs at the window, breaking glass. Falling. They land together and roll from the mattress onto their backs on muddy turf. Winded. Disorientated.

There's no time to take an inventory. Sami grabs Nadia again and drags her into thorn bushes. Turning, he catches a glimpse of someone watching from the broken window. They'll have to come down the stairs and find a door.

Nadia's body has gone limp. A flash of lightning reveals blood on her lips and beyond her a wire fence and a gate.

64

Ruiz climbs the stairs two at a time, kicking bottles and debris aside. The gunfire has stopped but he can hear shouts from distant corners of the hospital.

There were two bodies downstairs, one near the main entrance and a second further along the corridor. Both were dressed in black. Armed. He took a pistol from one of them, who was in no position to argue.

Ruiz pauses. Listens. The sound of a soft groan punctuates a roll of thunder. He moves to the left. The X-ray room has warning signs about radiation and unauthorised entry. The double doors are splintered and smeared with blood.

He raises his foot and pushes it open. A body lies in a dark pool that looks like sump oil and smells like death. Ray Jnr; shot through the neck by a high velocity round; dead where he fell.

Ruiz scans the room and notices a smeared trail of blood that disappears behind a partition used to protect radiologists from exposure during X-rays.

A rasping breath comes from the other side; someone in pain, trying not to make a sound. Moving to his right, Ruiz uses the robotic arms of the machine as cover, he crouches and peers around the bed-sized plinth beneath the X-ray camera.

Bones McGee lifts his head from the rifle, which is aiming at the other side of the partition. A question forms in his eyes.

'I see you're still trying to make the Olympic shooting team, Bones. You're a little early. Opening Ceremony isn't until 2012.'

Ruiz quickly catalogues the scene. Bones has a high velocity rifle. He also has a shattered piece of wood that appears to be stuck to his spine. Looking at the trail of blood, he must have dragged himself this far.

'So how are things going?' he asks.

'I can't feel them,' says Bones, looking at his legs, which flop at odd angles.

'You want me to call an ambulance?'

Bones shakes his head. 'You should have stayed out of this, Ruiz.'

'I'm not the one who's paralysed.'

Bones rests the rifle on his lap and brushes a non-existent fringe from his eyes. His finger is still on the trigger.

'Where's Sami Macbeth?'

'That's him over there,' says Bones.

'No it's not.'

Bones doesn't answer. Ruiz fills the silence.

'I figured there had to be someone on the inside. Tony Murphy needed floor plans of the Old Bailey and knowledge of the camera system. And someone had to sabotage the lift and set up a cover story to get them inside. You're the man, Bones. That's why you're here. And Murphy must be paying your rent rather than Ray Garza.' He motions to the body on the floor. 'If you were working for Garza you wouldn't have shot his boy.'

Bones seems to gag and swallow hard. His eyes are plaintive like a supplicant's.

'I'm sort of fucked,' he mumbles.

'You are.'

'You going to arrest me?'

'I am.'

'Are you armed?'

Ruiz raises the pistol.

Bones leans his head back against the wall and gazes out the window as if looking into the future and finding nothing to look forward to. In his next breath he swings the rifle across his body taking aim. The pistol jerks in Ruiz's hands. The recoil snaps his wrists in the air.

Bones looks down at the hole in his chest as if grading Ruiz on his marksmanship and giving him a C for effort. Then he slides sideways down the wall, resting his rifle gently beside his head.

65

Sami covers the first few hundred yards across open ground heading for a line of trees that is etched darker against the low clouds. For half that distance Nadia hadn't seemed so heavy, but now he's labouring. Slowing down.

Sweat dims Sami's vision and his mind is whirling like a broken fan belt in a runaway engine. Something slips through the grass ahead of him and disappears. It could be an animal. Something feral. He changes direction. The ground pitches forward. He notices a trail of silver water, a small stream surrounded by rotting trees and fallen logs. Everything seems scaled up and reeks of mould and decay.

The rain is heavier, drowning out other sounds. He has no weapon. The clip was empty. He threw the Beretta away.

Ahead he sees a chain-link fence topped with barbed wire. A building site. Turf has been peeled back and the topsoil scraped away by heavy machinery, bulldozers and earthmovers. Massive drainage pipes are stacked along the fence and silver pools of water indicate where boring machines have punched vertical holes deep into the earth.

He notices a gap beneath the fence where a ditch has been dug to let water drain away. He drops to his knees, lowering Nadia to the ground. Jumping into the ditch, he lifts her onto his back, screaming at the pain in his chest. Mud clutches at his shoes as he wades through knee-deep water, ducking beneath the fence. He falls. Gets to his feet. They give way again.

Dragging himself up the bank, he doesn't have the strength to lift Nadia. Sitting on the ground, digging his shoes into the earth, he leans back and pulls. It feels like someone has taken a branding iron to his heart.

Suddenly, a forearm drops past Sami's eyes and tightens across his throat, closing his windpipe. He can smell wet clothes and hear a rasping breath. Kicking his legs, he tries to twist free. One hand rises to his neck. The other loses grip on Nadia, who slides sideways into the ditch and comes to rest with her head just above the waterline.

Sami is being lifted and turned, held still. Tony Murphy swings a fist into his stomach. Hits him again. Gets into a rhythm.

The fat man is breathing hard. Saliva bubbles in his mouth.

'Where is the gun?'

Sinbad loosens his forearm so that Sami can speak.

'I dropped it.'

'Like fuck you did.'

'Back there – at the hospital.'

'Where?'

Sami struggles to remember.

'It was before I jumped out the window.'

He wants to reach Nadia. She's slipping further down the bank, her face almost touching the water. 'Please let me help her.'

Murphy glances back towards the hospital.

'Who did you bring?'

'Ray Garza.'

Murphy pulls a gun from a shoulder holster. Points it towards Nadia's body.

'She's done nothing wrong,' screams Sami.

'You'll watch her die and then I'll kill you.'

He walks to the edge of the ditch and lowers his foot, pushing her head beneath the surface.

Sami hurls himself towards the ditch, but Sinbad wraps a forearm around his throat again. Sami kicks his legs and twists, trying to claw his fingers beneath the crushing pressure squeezing his windpipe.

Trembling with waves of nausea and shock, he's losing consciousness. So this is how death comes. It's not a disease that takes him in sleep when he's an old man and it's not the monster that stalked his childhood dreams. Instead, in those few seconds, he glimpses the damp blackness of puddles and smells the stench of decay.

From somewhere far away he hears a hollow *popping* sound and Sinbad's head slams against his own. The forearm loosens around his throat. Sinbad collapses forward like a slaughtered beast, his brains in Sami's hair.

Murphy rears backwards in surprise and seems to hover on the edge of a flooded hole, swinging his arms in small circles, trying to regain his balance. His toes rise. The fight is lost. Gravity takes over, sending him backwards into the hole.

Murphy surfaces and claws at the muddy sides looking for a foothold or a handhold, but earth crumbles in his hands. He swallows water, coughs and takes another mouthful. The hole is too narrow for him to kick his legs and stay above the surface.

Sami reaches Nadia and rolls her over. She's alive. Conscious. He drags her out of the ditch and hears Murphy calling for help. His head looks like a sculptured clay bust, slick and shining, rearing up from the water with his mouth open, then disappearing again.

His eyes and ears are full of mud. He can't see or hear. And his hands keep reaching up, as though trying to breathe through his fingertips.

Sami doesn't stop to think. A moment ago he wanted Murphy dead. Wanted to do it close up. Would have pulled the trigger himself. Emptied an entire magazine into him. But now he crawls to the edge of the hole and grabs one of Murphy's flailing hands. The clay is so slippery and Murphy so heavy, he can't pull him out. He hunts around for something else. A plank. Drags it across the flooded hole.

Murphy reaches up and hooks his fingers over either side. He can hold his head above the water. Breathe.

'Step away,' says a voice. Sami turns slowly. Ray Garza has a gun in his outstretched hand.

'He'll drown.'

'Let him.'

Sirens are coming. The sound cuts through the rain and crosses the common.

Ray Garza walks to the edge of the flooded hole and steps onto the plank. His shoes are next to Murphy's fingers, which are struggling to get purchase on the wood.

'Hello, Murphy. I was going to dig a hole and bury you but you found one all by yourself.'

Garza raises the toe of his muddy shoe and pivots on his heel, lowering it again on Murphy's fingers. The fat man's face contorts in pain. One hand collapses from the plank.

'Do you think I'm a cunt, Murphy? Do you? Do you think I'm going to let some dumb-as-fuck Mick tear down everything I've built?'

'You got it wrong, Ray. This has nothing to do with you.'

'It has everything to do with me.'

The sirens are getting closer. Garza raises his other shoe and lowers it on Murphy's fingers.

'Just tell me why you did it.'

379

'It was a mistake. Your boy fucked up. He took something that didn't belong . . .'

Murphy fingers slide off the plank and he disappears beneath the muddy surface, rearing up again a few moments later, more mud than flesh.

Another figure emerges from the darkness. Sami doesn't recognise him, but he's holding a pistol on Garza and looks like he knows how to use it. For a long while nothing changes. The stranger doesn't move. Garza doesn't move. Nobody acknowledges anyone.

Then the stranger says, 'It's over, Ray. Drop the gun.'

Garza turns slowly. Lowers his gun. 'I'm here making a citizen's arrest, what's your excuse?'

'Unfinished business.' Ruiz glances at Sami. 'Are you OK?'

Sami nods.

'How about your sister?'

He nods again. 'Who are you?'

'I'm the ex-husband of your parole officer.'

Sami tries to make the connection. It takes a while. Eventually he remembers leaving a message for an ex-detective called Vincent Ruiz.

'Sorry it took me so long.'

'That's OK,' says Sami. 'How did you find me?'

'Girl called Kate Tierney. You might want to do something nice for her. Buy her flowers. Take her to dinner. Girls like stuff like that.'

66

The wind has risen, shunting the clouds away. Now the moon emerges, shining onto puddles and creating thousands of silver lights on the common.

Police cars have surrounded the old hospital, which doesn't seem abandoned any more. It was sleeping and now it's come back to life with paramedics working in the corridors and bodies being wheeled from within.

Nadia is sitting inside an ambulance with a blanket around her shoulders and an oxygen mask over her face. Sami is wearing handcuffs and is under guard, but they've let him sit with his sister. His ribs are broken. He'll need X-rays; painkillers. The adrenalin has stopped coursing through his system and exhaustion takes over. He closes his eyes.

Torches move across the common. Tony Murphy is being carried on a stretcher. It takes six men. Mud has been washed from his eyes and mouth, but his clothes make him look like a terracotta statue dug up from a swamp.

Ruiz watches two detectives climb into the back of an ambulance on either side of Murphy. Then he notices Ray Garza, arguing with Fiona Taylor and demanding to see his lawyer. Garza claims he was trying to apprehend the gang that robbed the Old Bailey and to stop Murphy framing him.

'Listen, sweetheart, you should be thanking me instead of treating me like a criminal,' he says. 'Maybe I should talk to one of your superiors.'

Fiona Taylor doesn't let her anger show but she'll find a way of taking it out on Garza.

Another body is being brought out on a trolley, wheels rattling over the broken asphalt. Fiona Taylor tells the paramedics to stop. She summons Garza over.

'Would you like to make a formal identification now or do it at the morgue?'

'What do you mean?'

Fiona unbuckles one of the straps and peels back the corner of the sheet, revealing a face; a young man, serene given the circumstances. He might even be sleeping except for the blueness around his lips and the small hole in his neck at his larynx.

Ray Garza's face says everything. Murphy sent a boy to do a man's job – *Garza's* boy; his wayward son; his only child.

Reaching out, he touches Ray Jnr, brushing the fringe from his eyes, letting his fingertips drift lower to his lips, willing him to breathe. Garza's eyes fold for just a moment before he throws back his head and howls. Devastated. Inconsolable.

Ruiz watches without any sense of triumph or satisfaction. For twenty-two years he has wanted to see Garza pay for what he did to Jane Lanfranchi, to see a cell door welded shut behind him. But revenge is a poisonous emotion. Jane Lanfranchi's parents lost a beautiful daughter. Ray Garza lost a good-for-nothing son. That doesn't make it even. It doesn't make it ironic. It certainly doesn't make it right.

Four Months Later

Sami Macbeth is back at the Old Bailey. Third time lucky. His trial begins today and the courtroom is so full they've had to close the doors and limit public access.

Emerging from the underground cells, flanked by guards, Sami feels like he's sneaking into the place when everyone else has had to queue for a seat.

He looks around the courtroom. Nadia is sitting in the front row of the public gallery. Kate Tierney is next to her. Holding hands. Keeping their fingers crossed.

Sami has everything crossed. He's not particularly religious but he prayed this morning. It was easier than he thought, like having a one-sided conversation with someone in a coma.

Sami turns. Waves. They wave back. A few other friends are also in the gallery, including some of his mates who made quick readies selling stories about Sami to the tabloids. Their looks seem to say, 'No hard feelings, mate, I was misquoted.'

Vincent Ruiz is sitting next to ex-wife Miranda, Sami's

parole officer, who looks like she's only wearing black until they invent a darker colour.

Ruiz arranged for Sami to get a decent solicitor this time, although Eddie Barrett doesn't look much like a lawyer. He has a bulldog walk and growls at people like he needs distemper shots. Sami hasn't met his silk, but Eddie has faith in the guy.

The prosecutor is a woman, who has short hair and a tailored black suit. She's going for the androgynous look that turns professional women into lovely mysteries.

Everyone rises. The judge is coming – a crusty old fart, who puts a cushion on his seat. Settles down. Reads a long letter, which might be from his mother or could be important.

He takes off his glasses. Raises his eyes.

'Am I to understand, Mrs Lascelle, that the Crown Prosecution Service has sought advice from the Attorney General and decided to alter its position on this matter?'

'Yes, your honour.'

The judge looks at Sami's QC. 'And you're satisfied with the case to proceed on this basis, Mr Gallagher?'

'Yes, your honour.'

'Has your client been made aware of the situation?'

'I haven't had an opportunity to consult with him. Perhaps I could take a few moments . . .'

'By all means.'

The judge puts his glasses back on and returns to his mum's letter. Sami's QC sweeps his black robes behind him and leaves the bar table to talk to his client. His horsehair wig seems too small for his head, or maybe his brain is too big.

In a low rumbling whisper he begins telling Sami that he no longer has to enter a plea as the charges will 'lay on file' for the foreseeable future.

From this point in the briefing Sami becomes fixated on the idea of entering a plea and becomes completely lost.

Eddie Barrett joins them. 'Trust me, kid, do as he says.'

'I did that last time.'

'This is a better deal.'

Mr Gallagher goes back to the bar. The judge folds the letter and puts it in a file. Then he begins writing notes. For the next twenty minutes the courtroom has to watch him scribbling, with nobody saying anything above a whisper.

Finally, he's ready. He blinks through his glasses at Sami, addressing him directly.

'Let me say this, Mr Macbeth. I spent last night reading the details of this case and I can only conclude that you are, without question, one of the unluckiest people to ever set foot in my courtroom. You also appear to have the unfortunate ability to turn a desperate situation into a hopeless one. Does that seem a fair thing to say?'

'Yes, your honour.'

'Armed robbery, manslaughter, grievous bodily harm, abduction, firearms charges, possession of explosives, trespassing, criminal damage . . . I could go on, but there doesn't appear much point given I've been asked to let these matters lay on file until some later, indeterminate date.

'Conceivably the Crown Prosecution Service has thought long and hard about how to proceed in this matter and has chosen to seek your co-operation in other matters before these courts.

'Based upon the recommendations of the CPS and the Attorney General and given the ordeal that you and your sister have endured, I struggle to see how society would benefit from your further incarceration.'

He bangs a polished wooden thingummy on his desk and tells the clerk of the court to dismiss prospective jurors or reassign them to a different jury pool.

Sami raises his hand as though he's still at school.

The judge pauses and looks at him quizzically.

'You have a question, Mr Macbeth?'

'Yes, your honour, I just wondered or hoped, really, that you could explain to me what just happened?'

'There will be no trial today. You're free to go.'

'Free?'

'The allegations against you, Mr Macbeth, have been set aside. They may one day be resurrected but that depends on your co-operation. What you *know*, Mr Macbeth, has become more important than what you've done.'

The judge is gathering his papers to leave.

Sami is dumbstruck. 'Thank you,' he whispers.

His voice carries to the bench. The judge stops and turns.

'Good luck, Mr Macbeth. It may well be that your sole purpose in life is to serve as a warning to others. That's for the future to decide.'

Terminal Four at Heathrow Airport is like a third world outpost with families of refugees taking up corners of the lounge and backpackers sprawled out on hard plastic chairs that will outlive civilisation.

Vincent Ruiz has been allowed airside, along with Miranda. They're watching Sami and Nadia stock up on suntan lotion and travel guides. According to the witness protection guidelines their destination is supposed to be a secret but Sami is wearing a *Save the Whales – Harpoon a Jap* T-shirt promoting Greenpeace in Australia.

'So you're ready,' says Ruiz.

'We're ready.'

Nadia is showing Miranda her purchases. Sami looks up at the departures board.

'Guess we'd better go.'

'I guess so.'

'We'll be back for the trial.'

'You will.'

'Do you think Murphy and Garza will go to prison?'

'That's not your problem. You swear on oath. You tell the truth. You walk away.'

391

'Just like that.'

'Just like that.'

'And what happens then?'

'The rest of your lives.'

Sami nods. Ruiz wants to say stuff like 'stay in touch' and 'don't be a stranger' but none of that's going to be possible. From now on Sami and Nadia will always be someone different. Someone new.

Miranda gives Sami a hug.

'Looks like I'll never be a rock god.'

'You can still have a band. Just don't get too famous.'

'I could wear make-up.'

'Too seventies.'

The goodbyes are said. The hugs are given. Sami and Nadia disappear through the gate into an aeroplane that's so huge it takes a leap of faith to imagine it could sail through the air.

The psychologist, Joe O'Loughlin, once told Ruiz about one of his patients, a commercial pilot, who believed that God picked up each plane on take-off and set it down again on landing. There was nothing that said the guy couldn't fly. He's probably still working.

Ruiz and Miranda walk back through the terminal and step outside.

'You want to come to Paris with me?' he asks.

'Why?'

'Because I've bought the tickets and I don't know if Eurostar will give me a refund?'

'You want my body?'

'Not as a temple – I want it as an adventure play-ground.'

Miranda laughs. 'You haven't changed.'

Ruiz looks aghast. 'You mean after all the work I've done on myself, trying to shed my bad habits and personality traits . . . and I'm still the same.'

She sighs and tucks her arm through his. 'When do we leave?'

'Saturday.'

'I choose the hotel. You pay the bill.'

He sighs happily. 'It was ever thus.'